D0119953

Hackney, That Rose-Red Empire

By the Same Author

FICTION
White Chappell, Scarlet Tracings
Downriver
Radon Daughters
Slow Chocolate Autopsy *(with Dave McKean)*
Landor's Tower
White Goods
Dining on Stones

DOCUMENTARY
The Kodak Mantra Diaries
Lights Out for the Territory
Liquid City *(with Marc Atkins)*
Rodinsky's Room *(with Rachel Lichtenstein)*
Crash *(on Cronenberg/Ballard film)*
Dark-Lanthorns
Sorry Meniscus
London Orbital: A Walk around the M25
The Verbals *(interview with Kevin Jackson)*
Edge of the Orison
London: City of Disappearances *(editor)*

POETRY
Back Garden Poems
Muscat's Würm
The Birth Rug
Lud Heat
Suicide Bridge
Flesh Eggs & Scalp Metal: Selected Poems
Jack Elam's Other Eye
Penguin Modern Poets 10
The Ebbing of the Kraft
Conductors of Chaos *(editor)*
Saddling the Rabbit
The Firewall: Selected Poems
Buried at Sea

Hackney, That Rose-Red Empire

A Confidential Report

IAIN SINCLAIR

With original prints and drawings by
OONA GRIMES

HAMISH HAMILTON
an imprint of
PENGUIN BOOKS

HAMISH HAMILTON

Published by the Penguin Group
Penguin Books Ltd, 80 Strand, London WC2R 0RL, England
Penguin Group (USA) Inc., 375 Hudson Street, New York, New York 10014, USA
Penguin Group (Canada), 90 Eglinton Avenue East, Suite 700, Toronto, Ontario,
Canada M4P 2Y3 (a division of Pearson Penguin Canada Inc.)
Penguin Ireland, 25 St Stephen's Green, Dublin 2, Ireland (a division of Penguin Books Ltd)
Penguin Group (Australia), 250 Camberwell Road, Camberwell, Victoria 3124, Australia
(a division of Pearson Australia Group Pty Ltd)
Penguin Books India Pvt Ltd, 11 Community Centre, Panchsheel Park,
New Delhi – 110 017, India
Penguin Group (NZ), 67 Apollo Drive, Rosedale, North Shore 0632, New Zealand
(a division of Pearson New Zealand Ltd)
Penguin Books (South Africa) (Pty) Ltd, 24 Sturdee Avenue, Rosebank, Johannesburg 2196, South Africa
Penguin Books Ltd, Registered Offices: 80 Strand, London WC2R 0RL, England

www.penguin.com

First published 2009
1

Copyright © Iain Sinclair, 2009
Prints and drawings copyright © Oona Grimes, 2009
The Acknowledgements on pp. 579–81 constitute an extension of this copyright page

The moral right of the author has been asserted

Set in 12/14.75 pt Monotype Dante
Typeset by Palimpsest Book Production Limited, Grangemouth, Stirlingshire
Printed in England by Clays Ltd, St Ives plc

A CIP catalogue record for this book is available from the British Library

HARDBACK
ISBN: 978-0-241-14216-5
TRADE PAPERBACK
ISBN: 978-0-241-14217-2

www.greenpenguin.co.uk

Mixed Sources
Product group from well-managed
forests and other controlled sources
www.fsc.org Cert no. SA-COC-1592
© 1996 Forest Stewardship Council
FSC

Penguin Books is committed to a sustainable future
for our business, our readers and our planet.
The book in your hands is made from paper
certified by the Forest Stewardship Council.

i.m. Bill Griffiths, Ian Breakwell, Paul Burwell

Contents

Contents

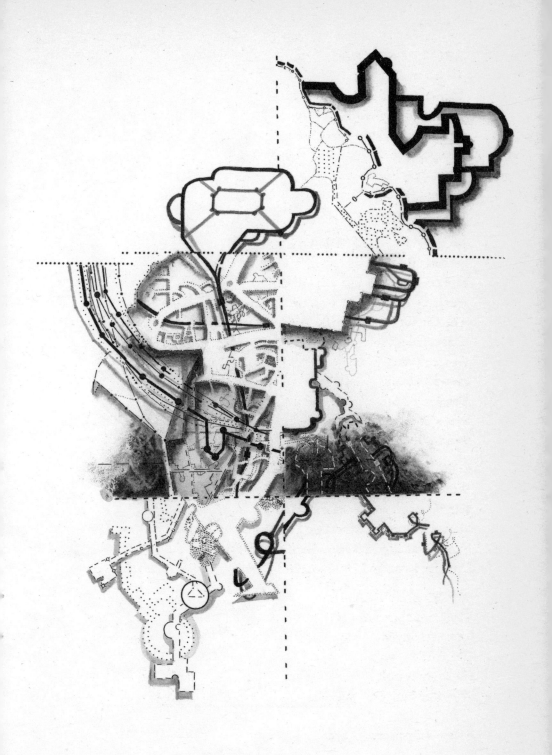

THE CYCLE

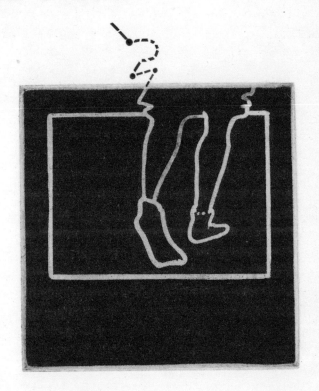

Geography is destiny.

– James Ellroy

London Fields

We are the rubbish, outmoded and unrequired. Dumped on wet pavings and left there for weeks, in the expectation of becoming art objects, a baleful warning. Nobody pays me to do this. It is my own choice, to identify with detritus in a place that has declared war on unconvinced recyclers while erecting expensive memorials to the absence of memory. This is a borough that has dedicated itself to obliterating the meaning of shame.

I am coming west off the avenue, under a canopy of London plane trees old enough to appear in sepia postcards: coming home, at the end of an afternoon walk. Councils of sleek crows. Magpies imitating road drills. It's a habit I can't break, the habit of Hackney: writing and walking, thirty years in one house. Thirty years of misreading the signs, making fictions: with a bounce in the step, cartilage audibly complaining, like the electric coffee-grinder our children remember. And we have forgotten. Five miles of canal bank, Victoria Park, heights of Homerton; running over the day's work, half-noticing revisions in the fabric of things. But returning always, as light fails, to the same kitchen, a meal in preparation. The undervalued dispensation of domestic life.

Lines of trees outrank us, their bulk is astonishing. Skins encrusted with witness: patches of green over grey, over fleshy orange. Scars, carcinogenic lumps. Hawser roots suck at dirt. The avenues have been set, as we discover from old maps, in strict patterns, an arcane geometry. Aisles of grappling Neo-Romantic branches. A blood meadow: London Fields. Public ground for the fattening of herds and flocks, Norfolk geese, before they are driven, by very particular routes, to Smithfield slaughter. Chartered markets service drovers, incomers. They exist to peddle plunder and to fleece the unwary.

I've grown quite fond, lately, of that sculpture, a civic intervention, at the south-east corner of the Fields, near the drinkers' table;
across from Sheep Lane and Beck Road, where the official-unofficial
artists live. The professional alcoholics, out at first light, string dogs
and blue bags, act as courtiers to a lifeless Pearly King and Queen;
who sit, silent witnesses to so much agitation and hallucinatory
folly. Crowned with bowler hats, eyes made red, they offer dishes
of fruit from generous laps. A frozen tide encloses them, sea-
pebbles, pebbledash. Mosaic altars have been decorated by
schoolkids: lobsters, flying fish, crabs. In beds of lavender. Buddhas
of the city, the statues survive, untargeted by fundamentalists,
iconoclasts. The oracular indifference of this rounded couple is a
virtue. They are assembled from chips and splinters of bright tile:
reconstituted damage. The ruins of demolished terraces, which
once ran to the edge of the Fields, have formed themselves into
twinned, male and female, votive presences. They are authentically
regal, divinely righteous, impervious to bribes or flattery. And they
have adapted, graciously, to where they are, among rippling
concrete dunes, troughs of hardy perennials, a backdrop of public
housing. A small flock of grey sheep attend them, backs mossy
with velvet. The whole tableau, its origins obscure, is being quietly
absorbed into nature: 'economic migrants from an Antoni Gaudí
theme park'. As a visiting, over-bright student said to me.

Going west, I dodge through the stutter of evening traffic and
into Shrubland Road, at the point where it splits off into Albion
Drive. A French culture pundit, digital camera in hand, tracking
across from the nearest Underground station – which is not so
near – was excited by the faded sign hanging outside the doomed
public house, the Havelock. Plenty of Hackney old-timers, I
discover as I conduct interviews for this book, navigate their
memory-terrain by way of pubs. *Do you remember?* Being on first-
name terms with the vampire landlady? Crowblack fright wig,
purple talons, heavy gold manacles on thin wrist. Villainies of
yesteryear: smoked ghosts propping up afternoon bars, sentimental
about dead gangsters, shoplifting grannies. Holloway Nan. Shirley

Pitts. Or revived literary societies in back rooms? Politics, conspiracies, pool. The Havelock is an anachronism. The coalfire fug, dirty
glasses and recidivist linoleum. These old brown boozers are
London fictions in embryo, waiting for the right ventriloquist:
Patrick Hamilton, Derek Raymond, T. S. Eliot. Listening is also
writing. First the pubs, then the petrol stations: they are declared
redundant.

Havelock, the face on the board, is now insulted by accidental
tower blocks, an opportunistic sprawl of human storage facilities.
By new natives, Catholics, Muslims. In life, he was a Bible-beating
Baptist. 'Deeply religious, a stern disciplinarian,' so they say. A
baronet, India hand. Afghan campaign of 1839–40. The first Punjab
War. He commanded a division in the Persian expedition of 1856–7.
Before dying of dysentery. Which might offer a clue as to the origin
of the pub sign that fascinates the Frenchman – who shows me his
digital capture, demanding an explanation.

There are two Havelocks: on one side a white man in dress
uniform, braids and buckles; and on the other, a black version of
the same, the negative of the original print. This is like some
anticolonial voodoo icon out of Haiti. That's what the Frenchman
thinks. Havelock, the unbending officer of empire, revenger of
Afghan outrages, blacks up to confront Hackney's shanty-town
sprawl. Bowels excavated, he is white as a worm. Erased from
history. A man forgotten. And a pub that is about to become a
minor property speculation: aspirational flats with slender, bicycle-
decorated balconies and an ecologically approved deficiency in
parking space.

There is no sense of regeneration here. Thank god. Not yet.
Business as usual. Cornershop steel-shuttered like Belfast and bristling with handwritten warnings to schoolkids. Hooded chemical
brokers start young. And finish young too, many of them. But
with old faces, fixed, incapable of registering surprise. Urban planners have tossed off a traffic-calming zone, a low brick enclosure
where citizens can shoot the breeze, coming together, informally,
to debate the issues of the day. A tub of mud functions as repository

for bright cans and yellow cartons with mouths agape like rat traps modelled in soft cheese. There is a buzz about this end of Shrubland Road, the mid-Victorian real-estate speculation by a relative of Cecil Rhodes. Terraces knocked up fast to the design of a man called Catling. The local authorities, back then, waived planning permissions, amputated portions of common land, the fringe of London Fields, and covered the ground with reefs of private housing. Albion does *drive*. The suburban pretension of that title is fully justified. A through-route fairground ride of humps and potholes that allows the statutory authorities to have it both ways: a cash cow of parking fines, road taxes, congestion charges *and* a method of crippling motor vehicles by neglect of the surfaces on which they are forced to operate.

Taking the right fork, into Albion Drive, brings me under the scratchy abundance of a fig tree that overhangs the pavement, heavy with sour-green grenades, polyps, empurpled fruit testicles. As twilight footsteps pad closer, ever closer, I suck the nectars, relishing pointless fecundity. In Hackney, we walk in a constant audition of sound, safe in the membrane of previous experience: the bad thing has not happened. Not yet, never. We are still here, still around; we must have made the right decision, crossed the road at the optimum time, avoided eye contact, jumped back from the kerb before the siren-screaming cop car rocketed over the humpbacked bridge. Motorcyclists slow significantly, sizing up our bags, checking on mobile-phone activity. Cycle bandits, out of nowhere, are at our shoulder. They nudge. Blade carving through straps. This is nothing, a toll on the privilege of living here; a community charge that sometimes, infrequently, steps over the mark: death. No longer a name on the electoral register, a statistic.

Preoccupied, contained in the dream of place, my harmless excursion, one walk fading into the footprints of the last, ruptures. With the breeze of the savage downward stroke, I swerve just enough to deflect the main force of the blow. Pain is nothing: a caressing slice into the skin of a balding cranium, no cerebellum-denting impact. It's a paper cut. Nothing, nothing at the time. A shock, when it happens on safe ground. And at the precise point, Anna later remarks, where paving slabs give way to tarmac, lumpy porridge from an Irish cauldron. Broader avenues, like our immediate neighbour, Middleton Road, domicile of various Hackney councillors, are paved throughout.

I have been stabbed in the head, that's all. No ice pick, a kiss. Late afternoon, late autumn. Creatures of the shadows ducking under the radar. My reaction is immediate, instinctive, foolish. I grab for the youth. I think, strange as it seems, that he has stubbed out a light bulb on my naked skull. *Lights out.* A necessary warning against meditating on pub signs, statuary, cattle trails. My assailant is a justified critic. A guerrilla editor. He's away, between cars: into the Fields Estate, a warren. Anaemic brickwork with stains of yellow dribble from overflow pipes. Replacement windows that need to be replaced. A blue door. And in this portal, blocking access, the darkness into which my attacker has vanished, I come up against an awkward interference of ASBOs, all shapes and sizes, colours and ages. Unrepentant whites. Pre-Dagenham. A last hurrah for petty, malicious, lumpen aggravation. But there's no future in it, indiscriminate violence. Cash crime. They need a business plan, a sponsor. They have not yet been branded by the council as a 'negative youth affiliation'. Nobody puts them on television without a cellophane carpet of flowers, crucified teddy bears and handwritten poems.

It's my own fault, for being visible in my difference, and too ancient to be moving through this place at this hour. My history is all used up. No point, this rush of blood, in grabbing anyone, dishing out unwarranted retribution. Rage is a stupid affliction. A man, a couple of years short of sixty, reverting to jungle-law slapstick. Idiotic. Insane. Unless it becomes part of a book.

In the bath, when I washed off the dry blood, I found a delicate residue of eggshell. Some of the shards had to be picked out of the wound with tweezers. The boy, my assailant, had a very unusual method of preparing an omelette. A sharp tap would have done; my skull, weathered by long exposure to Hackney's microclimate, is hard as a cycle helmet. But I assembled enough of the tiny pieces to establish that the weapon was not organic. No straw-nested bullet from a farmers' market. The viscous slime that ran down my collar wasn't brain matter, just past-its-sell-by yolk.

Next day I uncovered the background of this apparently meaningless event. The gang were car-jackers who pelted vehicles, while they made their rat runs down Albion Drive, with eggs. Windscreens were smeared as drivers slowed for the first in the chain of sleeping policemen. Motorists would be tempted to give chase, while a quick-handed lad, at the blind side, reached inside to snatch the radio, mobile phone or disability disc. It was my bad luck to chance along at the end of a flat day. These scams have a limited life. It's pretty tough being a villain in Hackney. There's too much competition. But the lightbulb moment of the egg on the head was valuable. I knew then, blood and soap and albumen, that it was time to start thinking about the territory where my life had formed and unravelled. It wouldn't be around much longer.

And one more thing: as I lifted my head, after the blow, I noticed an owl fluffing out its feathers in the cracked window of a derelict house that nobody had any good reason, as yet, to demolish.

This Property

April 2007. You have to start somewhere.

Anna.

In bed. Launching into *Winter in Madrid* by C. J. Sansom. She says she hates it when books open with dates, because you have to remember them, remember where you are. The place, the period. I'm reading Stewart Home, *Memphis Underground*. It's one of those slender Jiffy-bag paperbacks that contain much more than their physical dimensions seem to promise. I recognize a few of the riffs, about Arthur Machen, mystical geometries, pathways out of London. I think I wrote them, but I can't be sure. In Home everything spirals back on itself in a pathological accounting of bands, books, names, streets. An obsessive reworking of episodes at which I was present, but which I failed to copyright. And even if I did write it, who cares, as the manic Home slashes, grabs, mugs his way through the canon. He has grasped the key mode of contemporary art, theft. Repetition. Keep on saying it until somebody pays you some attention. Only the familiar is familiar.

I have been working on a Hackney book for a while now, heaping up insane quantities of material, logging interviews without number: forty years. And I haven't achieved the starting point, that impossible first sentence. The guiding principle was a quote from William Blake: 'Tho' obscured, this is the form of the Angelic land.'

The first words of Home's novel. I should have stopped there.

One afternoon Stewart shocked me by arriving on my doorstep without his bicycle. He had come to record his memories of crack houses, squats, co-operatives. He had recently lost an excellent perch on the Golden Lane Estate in the Barbican. Hackney, we agreed, is property. That is all it's about, mortgages, debt-management. The cost of being where you are. Home's entire catalogue, when you come down to it, dozens of frantic compositions made in the teeth of the storm, concerns eviction. Mess up with current woman, on your bike. A borrowed couch, a floor, whisky talk: new novel (new debts). He circles the sprawling borough, its hot nuclear core. But Hackney is an old suburb, a refuge – which is precisely what Home is fleeing: the idea of suburbia as exile, divorce from the action. A hide of surrogate or actual parents.

In this new book, new today, 25 April 2007, Home has pasted the property interview he gave me into his published text – before I've even had time to transcribe it. He sweeps across the geography of London, on foot, bicycle abandoned as part of the Golden Lane eviction; speeding from publisher to independent film-maker, patron to website interview, Hoxton to Shoreditch, Brick Lane.

'Mare Street had changed. It had become trendy since I'd first started visiting it regularly as a callow youth of sixteen for various parties against racism,' he said.

The Mare Street riff is a standard in Hackney reportage. Dr David Widgery, on the bus, heading south towards his Limehouse practice: mass-observing, listening, transcribing. 'Rain pelting down. The road at a standstill through sheer weight of traffic; ill-tempered cars, double-banked buses and grinding HGVs. People dart dangerously between vehicles, building workers jack-in-a-box out of Transits, mothers weave buggies between revving Cortinas. The terracotta muse high above the roof of the Hackney Empire waves people to work.' Social realism works through an accumulation of gritty detail, the drumbeat of fast-moving lists.

The forgotten post-war novelist, Roland Camberton, published *Rain on the Pavements* – with a high-angle Mare Street long shot by John Minton on its dustwrapper – in 1951. Before vanishing and never being heard from again. But these were engaged and passionate writers, absorbed in the crowd; Widgery's jazzy, Beat-inflected prose, Camberton's mocking humour. John Minton's trade unionists march onward with their unreadable banner, protesting against impossibly yellow weather.

Home has no time for local picaresque, scene setting, he has an appointment to keep at the Homerton Hospital. A man in a coma: Mick Cohen, underground film-maker. There are a lot of those in Hackney, no shortage of Cohens. The Spitalfields interview was for a film about gentrification. The woman with whom Stewart shares hummus salad in pitta bread has just returned from an arts conference where a lot of people had been talking about how rising property prices were making it impossible for them to pursue their cultural practice in London.

I have years of interviews with Hackney dwellers, one tape leading to another, story within a story, and they're all, these talkers, self-confessed artists. Even the doctors, surgeons, barbers, bus drivers: they have their hobbies, collections of Matchbox Toys from the Lesney Factory on the edge of the marshes, gigs at the Royal College of Art. The would-be-writers, future painters, uncommissioned film-makers are the worst; they want to rehearse their proposals, to record hours of anecdotes from books that will never be completed. Or started. Unless I can be persuaded to promote them, talk them up, send them to eager publishers.

The archive itself is now a property. Images are property. History isn't the province of memory-men, it belongs to speculators, anal retentives smart enough not to throw away their rubbish. Rubbish and property: twinned themes. Eco defaulters, those who refuse to compost, are the latest criminals. If you don't separate your tea bags from your plastic mineral-water bottles, you'll be prosecuted, fined, evicted. Early-morning streets are dressed with every shade of bucket and bin, stacked with nearly new white goods, vacuum cleaners, CDs in cellophane, computers, lavatory bowls that nobody wants. This is not property, this is the antimatter of a virtual world subject to hourly revision. The flotsam and tidewrack of cyberspace. Scavengers have abandoned the skips of our neat inner-city villages, the steady gaze of the energy police, for the deregulated wastelands of the emerging Olympic Park. They're all out there, with bicycles, handcarts, vans, with pliers, bolt-cutters and knives, asset-stripping ruins, peeling electricity cables, getting the price of a drink together. So that they can settle on a companionable bench, with a view of water, to smoke and chug in ruminative silence. Absorbed in the landscape they occupy, pilgrims and sadhus of the immediate. The ordinary. The last self-funding, self-motivating human machines in the borough. Lost ones on their first days to heaven.

Hackney, I decided, would be a story of money and cars. Two subjects about which I knew absolutely nothing. A great beginning. I had a title, *Black Teeth*, and a plan: unity of time and place, one weekend fending off a debt crisis against threats of bailiffs and summary violence. But that was too mundane, too close to fiction.

'Lit-fic's a dead duck,' my editor said. 'Carry on with the same book but pepper it with real names, actual locations. The London heritage stuff still plays. We'll squeeze you into the travel sections.'

So what about *Life and Debt on the Eastern Front*? Too Russian. *The Empire of Hackney: Its Fallen Rise*. Too cleverdick. Nobody reads Gibbon. The title will look after itself, concentrate on that first line. First chapter. First section. Like building an upside-down pyramid, it all starts with a single brick.

'I want to combine popular story telling, poetics and critique. I am Death. I am Undead. I stopped living. Ad nauseam.'

That's how Stewart Home finishes.

Down from Highgate thro' Hackney

Stepping out, the spread of the town enhanced by failing vision, the novelty of a remote white-ribbed King's Cross development: Highgate. The lengthy down escalator of the hill, its refracted wealth. Walk it and you are part of it: private schools for private money, Whittington's black cat, Andrew Marvell's hole in the wall. Anna, in her dreams, would live here. Up above the swamp. On summer heights where our lost Hackney Brook once rose.

Remember those Saturdays? The period when Anna was pictured in a coffee-table book, *Flea Markets in Europe*; long hair pinned back, collar up, blue coat with military epaulettes from a pine-stripping place on Balls Pond Road? She was presiding over my Camden Passage stall. A flat table of used books. Striking young woman, young mother, catching the photographer's eye. No easy thing, stolen images in street markets. *Sawdust Caesar*: a book about Mussolini. A biography of Jan Christiaan Smuts. Remnants of my father's library? Was he already dead? Or had I bought, for resale, titles I recognized from my childhood? While Anna took her day in the market, I came with the children to Waterlow Park. Squirrels, then a novelty, ran up my legs to perch on my shoulders before leaping away downhill to invade the rest of London. Karl Marx: I marched the children over to see the great hieratic head, the black paperweight holding down so many tracts. A plot in Highgate Cemetery was the only way fortunate Hackney writers, with good connections, were ever going to migrate up here.

I had located, on Highgate Hill, a furniture shop heaped with German literature; an obviously Jewish collection, pristine in dust-wrappers. Kafka. Canetti. Hermann Broch. Alfred Döblin's *Berlin Alexanderplatz*. The difficulty being that the shop, by next week, might be gone. Time was pressing, Anna to be collected, car loaded,

cherry bakewell treats bought at a corner shop on the way home
to Hackney. I scanned the books, fast, leaving four-year-old William
in the car with his older sister. At least he didn't drive it away. He
set the windscreen-wipers going, scraping cones of smear, so that
they couldn't be stopped. As our agitated family party juddered
back down to Islington. Market traders with a capital fund of about
fifty pounds. But without debts or mortgages. In the city, in our
own house. Metal steps descending to a cat-napping, Henri
Rousseau garden of vegetables and cannabis plants.

A slight ache.

Which was becoming more pronounced with every step closer
to Archway. Black suede-type slipper shoes. A special offer that was
not so special. Pain exists to be walked through – *but what if you
can't walk*? One problem was settled for now: the teeth. Nothing
headline generating, by way of cost, light tinkering, a month's
worth of old money. The dentist, tall and Scandinavian, has an
interest in art, London's heritage. It's up there on the wall, Turner
splashes to take your mind off the smoking drill. I find myself
thinking of another Highgate exile with a bad mouth, Samuel
Taylor Coleridge. Who was stalked by a man hired to keep him
away from the apothecary. Arbitrary jump cuts of consciousness
as I sprawl on this plastic-sheathed airline chair and the oral-
mechanic probes for an icicle nerve. Coleridge and Wordsworth.
Family holidays in the west. 'Quantock ridge in smudge of sun.'

I am looking forward to the walk home. A free afternoon. No
meetings, no students, nothing overdue: apart from the Hackney
book. Which is more of a way of life than a serious project. My
children have left home. I can enjoy the liberty of the city: accidental encounters, fresh discoveries. No cash in my pocket, nothing
to tempt me into junkshops or cafés. There is a cheque to pay in,
an insignificant amount but useful. A small credit to reverse the
flow of standing orders, surcharges, council threats. I've carried
the cheque around for a week, on random London diagonals,
without coming across an operative HSBC bank.

When you notice the fact that one step is made after another, you're in trouble. Zephyrs of diesel grit. Drifting bands of batter-waft: frying onions, burgers. But no filling stations, those green-shaded pagodas have gone, not economic. More use as development sites. No HSBC banks either. *Is the cheque still there?* At the last count thirteen payments were outstanding; the chaff of journalism, talks delivered months ago to colleges where the mass of required forms far outweighs the script for the lecture. It takes an afternoon to prepare your material and a week to figure out the online invoice requirements. Calling yourself 'freelance' is a confession of penury. The new universities take the 'free' part too literally. Writers without tenure are public beggars.

Plenty of money-transfer activity on Holloway Road. They'll take your cash and send it on holiday, anywhere in the globe. Hole-in-the-wall fiscal launderettes. Sirens and shakedowns. Collisions. Power walkers sweep past as I make the error of looking at things, recalling previous incidents, journeys.

By Highbury Corner, the pain has progressed from ankle to calf. Air thickens and early pollen makes my eyes water. Tomorrow will clear or confirm this condition: as a problem. Mouth fixed, leg shot. Walter Sickert ran a painting school on Highbury Place. Write that down, it might be useful. Blue plaques are the Islington equivalent of Hackney's Sky satellite dishes.

With my leg gone, I had no choice but to excavate my bicycle. When I worked as a labourer, packing cigars in Clerkenwell, I cycled. The bike cost £6 in Kingsland Waste Market. I wobbled around the notorious Old Street roundabout without damage. I cycled down Homerton High Street, past the Lesney Matchbox Toys Factory, on to the Marshes, when I had the task of painting white lines for the football pitches. At an era when the canal path was overgrown and forbidden, I peddled to Limehouse, through Victoria Park, down Grove Road and Burdett Road, to work as a gardener. The sharp-saddled bicycle was a collaborator in any reading of the city. Territory crossed and crisscrossed: burial grounds and back rivers explored.

It was too late in life to mount up again; a terrible reversion, the penultimate stage before the electrified buggy, the golf cart of the incapacitated, waiting for a ramp to descend from the special-needs bus. Both tyres were flat, the gears didn't work: the yellow wreck supported me like a Limerick drunk as I hobbled towards Mare Street, London Fields Cycles. In the old days, the never-were days, you could take in a bike smarting from its latest catastrophe: no problem, small cash transaction, straight back on the road. Now it's like seeing an overworked oncologist, you make an appointment. This is a borough where cycling is close to compulsory; yellow-tabard squads set up checkpoints on London Fields or by the canal gate at Cat and Mutton Bridge. To harass and advise. To offer nutty cakes and green apples. To share your sorrow at the absence of a working bell.

Ting ting.

Best practice. Fit for purpose. Take home a leaflet.

Cyclists should slow down, ring with **Two Tings** and let other users through the bridge before continuing. Never pass a pedestrian or another cyclist underneath a bridge. The waterways and towpaths have many historic structures and important wildlife habitats. The Regent's Canal has been designated a Site of Metropolitan Importance.

There is a three-month waiting list before you can book your bike in for a check-up. The cycle health service is in crisis. And don't imagine you can breeze into the surgery one afternoon with anything as trivial as a buckled wheel. They have a rigid system: the first five patients, chosen from an orderly queue, out on the street, will be admitted at 8 a.m. To receive a ticket and to wait while basic treatment is given. No point in hanging about checking the alternatives, new bikes kick in at around £250 for a basic model. They have cycling maps, but not of this area. They have an array of gaudy-tough helmets like laminated skulls. They have everything in fluorescent yellows and greens, psychotropic decay, vampire mouth scarlet, fairground gothic.

I arrive, second in line, at half-seven. I have to get away sharpish, Renchi is dropping in at Albion Drive for a cup of fruit tea. Renchi Bicknell of Glastonbury, with Vanessa, his wife and partner in a B&B operation. There is a significance about the times when Renchi manifests in the city. We walked the acoustic footprints of the M25; he, coming from outside the motorway, to meet me, pushing out from the centre. Whatever emerged from those excursions was a proof of difference, a sympathetic dialogue between separated worlds. It was Renchi who brought me here in the first place: 1968. A communal house in De Beauvoir Road. His sisters had already staked out parts of Islington and this raid, across Southgate Road, a boundary, was a demonstration of the way inherited capital flows east. Six of us in an area that was unknown, coming together after Dublin, from West and North London. I was the only one who had lived, twice, south of the river. Now here was Renchi, returned, prompting me to get this bicycle surgery done as quickly as possible.

Southgate Road: 1907. The year of Joseph Conrad's *The Secret Agent*. Special Branch liaising with the Tsar's secret police. Watchmen at Liverpool Street Station waiting for the Harwich train. The Georgian bandit, Soso Djugashvili, also known as Joseph Stalin, was expected for the Fifth Congress of the Russian Social-Democratic Workers Party. To be held at the Revd Swann's Brotherhood Church, Southgate Road. Lenin. Trotsky.

Stalin and Maksim Litvinov kipped in Fieldgate Street, Whitechapel, in Jack London's 'Monster Doss House'. The twin towers of Tower House. Eileen, in the pub next door (once a synagogue, now an upmarket curry franchise), opened a biscuit tin and showed me the nicotine-yellow, friable cuttings. Subversives. Agitators. Political exiles. They slip across the border. Then as now.

2007: public conveniences, generously provided in the civic confidence of the imperialist era, are being restored. *Ting ting.* The Gents in Stamford Hill, so locals report, is occupied, nightly, by Polish builders.

RUSSIAN REVOLUTIONISTS AFRAID OF THE CAMERA.

Block headline. *Daily Mirror*, 1907. Southgate Road. Procession of men in bourgeois-workers' funeral outfits, umbrellas, removed bowlers disguising beards. Iron railings. Lumpy ecclesiastical bricks. Churches like prisons. Journalists are spooks, double agents, narks. Pigment is metaphor: blood red. *Not til the red fog rises.* Afraid of the camera's cyclopean eye, as they walk heads bowed towards it. Fifth Congress. Third World. *The Sign of Four.*

Astrid Proll, driver for the Red Army Faction, that counter-cultural eruption of the late 1960s, on the run, escaping from the suicide fate of her colleagues in Stammheim's futurist prison, was somewhere in London. Half-forgotten: not by the watchers, the bill posters, the graffiti polemicists.

FREE ASTRID PROLL. Underneath the Westway. Noticed by a German cameraman, Martin Schäfer, Wim Wenders associate, working on Chris Petit's English road film, *Radio On*. Proll is a presence, an absence around which a number of contradictory myths accumulate. She was arrested, while training young black offenders as motor mechanics, in a West Hampstead garage. She had marched into the local cop shop to register a protest on behalf of one of her charges. Celebrity mug shot. Lightbulb of recognition. After Paddington Green, then HMP Brixton, a return to Germany. On her release, Proll trained in film, Hamburg. She published her Paris snapshots, Baader-Meinhof on holiday. Cafés, mirrors. Ricard ashtrays. She edited a scrapbook of archival friezes, late history. And introduced it as: 'pictures of dead people'. The key sentence jumps out: *We were afraid of photographs.*

Hackney is this: cameras and bicycles. On thin balconies of recent flats. Chained to fences. In the windows of council front-operations, TfL promotions. Sponsorship of bicycles and cameras. The folded maps in the London Fields cycle shop, highlighting cycle paths, are free: propaganda. They demonstrate how territory can be invaded by any determined special-interest group and how all maps are political, they are about *not* telling. Giving users just enough rope to hang themselves. *Ting ting.*

There's a man, number eight in the queue, with a young child, a girl, in his arms – and they're telling him he'll have to go away, try again tomorrow. Which he simply cannot understand. 'Well,' he says, 'well well, but . . . can I leave the machine?'

'Sorry. First five, every morning, that's it.'

There is a notice in the window: 'Eight O Clock Drop. We will only do punctures, cables and brake blocks. One item per customer. We will be operating a "no leave" policy.' *Ting.*

'I had to get over here, before work, bring my daughter, from Kentish Town, before nursery. It's a difficult drive.'

They're sympathetic, the fit young mechanics, the women in dungarees, but there is nothing they can do. There has to be a system or it would be chaos, punctures leaking, wrecks everywhere like a Shoreditch art installation. Please help yourself to a complimentary plan of Canary Wharf. *Unlock the history of London's river. English Partnerships at Greenwich Peninsula. Investing in the 21st Century.*

'If you can't find the map you want, there's a website. You can order from there.'

I'm lucky, my puncture will be treated immediately. I have half an hour to kill in the council zone, the official centre of governance for Hackney. If I can't walk, I can limp and learn. Street frontage, south of the Town Hall, is non-commercial, wide-windowed: walk-through fast food (access to library), HSBC bank, cycle surgery, and various job-seeking arcades with machines that print out employment possibilities, on a daily basis. You have to shop for a parking space, purchasing books of tickets like a raffle or a lottery scratchcard. All the paperwork aspires to the condition of an environment-improving gamble, an investment, blank cheque in the future. Colour-coded hard plastic chairs. Near-artworks, digital images, that key up the best of the borough. Calendar illustrations of Hackney Marshes, Springfield Park, London Fields. Urban pastoral. The green lungs that kept the lowlife fit for smoking, their sixty-a-day habits. And here too, in case your experience of the real thing is overwhelming, is a large colour print of the Hackney Empire: the sheer cliff of that much loved, much restored old music hall. The rose-red endstop of the Town Hall precinct. With its vast lettering: HACKNEY EMPIRE. An East German memory-prompt banished to a sculpture park after the Wall came down: present and loud and stripped of meaning.

The council are going to splash out – credit rich at last, slush funds kicking in – on new premises in keeping with their burnished status. That's what regeneration is really about, fancier council offices. But the white block, sharp-angled 1934 Town Hall, with its balcony and flags, is a civic boast of some substance. You could do a Mussolini, an Oswald Mosley, up there, stiff left arm resting on parapet. Broad steps – seven, then five more – separate the building and its secure entrance from the street. An impression amplified by the formal garden, behind the lively bus stop. The war memorial has been restored. There are palm trees. Sometimes a high police horse tosses its head in front of the south wall of the theatre.

Active council functionaries come and go, they meet and greet, gabbling into mouthpieces and cellphones. Today they are, for the most part, black. It's impertinent and probably illegal to remark on the fact. Or to notice, with anything more than vulgar curiosity, a register of social change: that by afternoon all the voices along the Regent's Canal between Queensbridge Road and Victoria Park are Russian, French, Italian, German. I've seen Poles so drunk they are making cocktails from the dregs of bottles left in bins that haven't been emptied for weeks. You can't say this. Or even think it, although I do: there is something stirring about a white building under black occupation. Like the presidential palace of an African state that has been destroyed by waves of colonialism; first plunder, then conspicuous charity. But this monoculturalism is an illusion,

Hasidic men pass down the marble hall to register births. There are numerous traces, among council clients, of old Jewish Hackney. Of all Hackneys. Including the false memory of a photograph I took, 35mm black and white, of Renchi Bicknell in a pinstripe suit, white socks, bounding across these steps: to be married for the first time. 1969? A ceremony I must have witnessed. I do remember the conclusion of the day, driving to Cambridge, warm afternoon, my cheap fawn suit. Like a terrible anticipatory homage to Ken Livingstone.

I cycle home across London Fields, sticking to the allocated green track (until it vanishes). I bump into a neighbour who throws me by asking, with some hesitation, if I could supply her with a poem about the future. She is doing the post round. It's that hour of the day: when householders redistribute wrongly delivered packages. If correspondence arrives in the right street, or within half a mile of it, temporary postmen reckon the job's done. It seems discourteous to point out minor errors. The situation has improved of late. I haven't noticed any grey sacks floating in the canal or found bundles of opened envelopes behind our hedge. Some of the posties stick with this miserable round for at least a fortnight.

I comb through notebooks, things published and unpublished, but I can't find a single poem that touches on the future. Everything is resolutely nudged by the now, under the drag of an invented past. I'm sorry, Harriet, I have no idea what the future holds. Or what it is. The architect Erich Mendelsohn, who was responsible for the De La Warr Pavilion in Bexhill-on-Sea, said: 'Only he who cannot forget has no free mind.' In Berlin they labour to exorcize the past. In Hackney we must train ourselves to exorcize the future.

PARK BARBERS

Memory is built to last.

– J. H. Prynne

Gore Road

It's not just the red cranes looming over the towpath, or the acknowledgement that feeling good, walking again, events must very soon take a turn for the worse. Shadows have shadows. Static water is opaque and unreadable. Seeing what's wrong is not much of a stimulus to start work. I want some inkling of the virtues of this place and of our lives in it. I want what I don't know: the names of animals, trees, plants, stones. A method for disappearing, absolutely, into the tapestry.

Forty years and I have learnt nothing, nothing useful, about the people, factories, politics and personalities of Hackney. The name has declined to a brand identity. A chart-topper: worst services, best crime, dump of dumps. A map that is a boast on a public signboard, a borough outline like a parody of England. My ignorance of the area in which I have made my life, watched my children grow up, is shameful. I've walked over much of it, on a daily basis, taken thousands of photographs, kept an 8mm film diary for seven years: what does it amount to? Strategies for avoiding engagement, elective amnesia, dream-paths that keep me submerged in the dream.

I'm at the age when the friends who came here with me, in the 1960s, have gone, moved out. The provinces or the cemetery. And the next wave after them: schools, children, the pressure of the streets. Writers who can no longer afford to write, not here. And the ones who took their real-estate profits and slid sideways into Islington or Clerkenwell. Human contact with fellow spirits becomes a matter of telephone conversations. Rachel Lichtenstein, with whom I collaborated on a book about David Rodinsky, the Princelet Street hermit, had relocated to Leigh-on-Sea: down the line from Fenchurch Street, back to her childhood territory in

Southend. She was assembling an oral history of Brick Lane. I admired her tenacity, the sympathy she brought to the interviews she conducted, her talent as a curator of memory-spaces and people prepared to talk about them. There would be technical difficulties, for sure, fights over intellectual property, confessees who reneged on their confessions, but Rachel always managed to present her subjects in the best possible light. I couldn't go that far. I was too fond of flaws, eccentricity. Characters who subverted any role assigned to them. Fictional projections who grew real flesh.

'You should start your Hackney book with Uncle Sid,' Rachel told me. 'Before it's too late.' A cousin of her father, Sidney Kirsh lived in Gore Road, Victoria Park. Hackney, strapped for cash, had handed over the park, in its entirety, to Tower Hamlets. In years past, the days of Sid's pomp, there was an imaginary border running through the grass. You could find marker stones if you looked for them. Sid's Victoria Park was a staging post on the northwest passage out of the Whitechapel ghetto. 'He's a storyteller,' Rachel said. 'He's eighty-seven now, but he remembers everything.'

For me, this was a detective story. I knew where the body of our poor borough was lying and who had killed it, but I didn't know why. The previous history of the corpse was a blank. Conflicting versions of the same episodes would have to be investigated. I thought of an Orson Welles film I'd seen, years ago: *Mr Arkadin* (aka *Confidential Report*). A ludicrously bearded and putty-nosed tycoon hires a burnt-out hack to investigate his past. Witnesses, having related their part of the story, are bumped off. My interviews, however tactfully pitched, were still interrogations: to discover the rules of engagement. You start with lies, evasions, and you uncover a shape. For months, taking on anything and everything to fund my research, I gathered Hackney books, chased references, collected news cuttings, ran old films, hounded suspects. Like Arkadin I wanted to know who I was and where I had been hiding. And then what? *Confidential Report* opens with an empty plane approaching Madrid.

Rachel circled Jewish Whitechapel, soliciting resolution – and finding it. Once I walked through that first door, I was lost. The process could go on for ever. Hackney had no beginning, no end, its boundaries were strategic; they expanded or contracted in accordance with the political whims of the moment. But there was something, a trace element, that was specific: a word, a broken sentence, an unnoticed detail in a dull painting hanging in an unvisited municipal gallery. And Sidney Kirsh, my hunch told me, owned a part of it. Alive in Victoria Park, in all worlds, at this time. Our time, today: 12 January 2006.

I've been here before, these close rooms, in other parts of London. In Golders Green, Fortune Green, Hampstead Garden Suburb: when I worked as a gardener, grass-cutter, ripper out of weeds (and shrubs), for a pound an hour, once a week. I'd been in North London, servicing the narrow strips on either side of a concrete path, for a man who said he wrote historical novels, under a selection of aliases, uncommissioned radio scripts. Breath ripe with afternoon sherry. He tried to make up a pound from milk coppers and woolly sixpences, the lint of deep-pocket cardigans. Objects had accumulated over the years of neglect and solitude. He snorted the plastic seats of indented chairs for testosterone contrails of the young actors, hopeful of preferment, who no longer called. Windows wouldn't open and sweat-bandage curtains moved with his rasped breathing like an anticipation of the future oxygen tent. Even the books this man showed me, he may indeed have written them, had laminated skins stuck to the dustwrappers. They looked as if they had been gathered up from the closing sale in a public library. I had to stand there, paw out, listening to these legends of the city, before he would release the hot trickle of coins. The cliffhanger autobiography, what happened with Maclaren-Ross that night in the Turkish baths at Russell Square, would keep until next time, next year. No point in my returning in the winter. Nothing grew.

When I got home, exhausted, Anna had to admit that the

contractions were coming quite strongly, she'd gone into labour. A busy night ahead, midwife rushing to the wrong Albion, Albion Road in Stoke Newington. The ambulance that should have taken us to Bart's arrived in time to ask if the crew, since they didn't have anything better to do, could witness the birth. 'Fuck off,' Anna screamed. 'Now!' The disappointed youth backing away from the door, upstairs to our small kitchen, to join the others. Boil water. Now I understood what that meant in the old Westerns. Endless cups of tea. William was delivered at home, on film, in the early hours. A great thing, a gift. And a further initiation into the mysteries of place. The uncollected afterbirth was buried in the garden.

Sidney Kirsh is a pre-war London size, his head reaching somewhere about the middle of my chest. He's bright-eyed, alert. He answers the door in trailing tartan dressing-gown and slippers. The ground-floor flat, operated by Crown Properties, has a gauzy, cataract view of a triangle of garden. Beyond that, on the street, the borough architects have come up with a pedestrian obstacle, a burial mound with a sloping lid of sea pebbles. In summer, white roses break through the leaves of a solitary ash tree. Mr Kirsh's vestigial lawn is a quilt of undisturbed leaves. Getting my measure, on the instant, he asks if I'd like to take on some basic remedial work out there: raking, scything, sweeping. He had a boy, once, but he proved unreliable. Then a friend, a young man from the Philippines, gave it a shot. 'I had to watch him all the time,' Sid said. 'I could give you a list as long as your arm of the things that disappeared out of that garden.'

I have never fancied gardening in Hackney, not since my vegetable patch was invaded by squirrels and foxes. Renchi Bicknell, who worked in Victoria Park when I was in Limehouse, did private contracts in this locality. He put an advert in the *Hackney Gazette*. All the takers lived in Sharon Gardens, a transported fragment of Golders Green; a self-declared suburb, one street. Villas. Semis. Bowed fronts, leaded windows. Portholes with stained glass.

Garden patches to be kept as neat as front rooms, lounges. Renchi didn't take to it, the fuss. Manoeuvring an electric mower, in a tangle of cable, around Sunday-smart motor vehicles.

The furniture in Sidney's warm cabin is substantial, every armchair a presence as solid as Gladstone. The walls are dressed with family photographs and paintings. The paintings are stories. I'm waiting for Mr Kirsh to wiggle his ears. Rachel says that when she lived around the corner, her two boys were mesmerized as Sid performed his party trick.

I've never had much use for pocket-recorders. They don't work, for me or on me. And if I glance away from Sid's face, those burning eyes, even for a moment, he stops talking. 'I've gone on too long. You've got things to do. You're a busy man.'

I grew up in the East End, I didn't grow up in Hackney. I came to this area at fourteen, fifteen. If you walk down Gore Road to the Crown Office and look back to the corner, that's where I lived. The main road, Victoria Park Road. Twelve rooms. I finished up living in them all on my own. The rest of the family? Some died, some married.

I've stayed in Hackney all my life, except during the war. I was six and a half years away in the army. They started bombing here and my parents moved to Hinckley in Leicestershire. We took over an estate. When the war was virtually over, I told my father I was coming back to London. He said, 'Son, if you go, don't get the old house, get the one next door. It has got an additional building on the side, we'll have more room.'

I went to the agent. He said, 'With pleasure, Mr Kirsh.' We moved next door. My father had the first floor with kitchen. My brother had the second floor with his wife. I had the top floor with my wife. And down in the basement, we eventually got my grandmother and grandfather. After a few years my brother moved away.

What happened is that I was working with a friend of mine, I'd known him for many years, and he said, 'Come and help us at weekends.' I said, 'Right.' It suited me. I was playing table tennis most of the time. See them, over there, the cups? See how many I've won? I got paid a couple of times. I had a proposition to play for a firm of furriers, they were determined to win the league.

This feller I was working with, he says, 'I've been offered a shop. I don't fancy it down there, too Irish.' I said, 'All right, I'll go down and have a look.' And my goodness, at lunchtime, they were queuing up at the door. I thought, this is good enough for me. I spoke to the young chap. I said, 'Who's the boss here?' He said, 'He's outside feeding the rabbits.' George was his name. He said, 'What you want?' I said, 'I've heard this shop is for sale, what d'you reckon?' He said, 'Are you a communist?' I said, 'Yes.' He said, 'You can have it.' 'What about a lease?' He said, 'Write up a lease and I'll sign it.' Which I did. I had three, four men working all the time.

Poplar was wonderful. I learnt to paint there – as you can see on the walls. But I had to think about taking on the business, I can tell you. When I went down there, they said, 'They don't like Jews here.' Rubbish! They were an educated bunch, the dockers. I did a painting. The feller in the barber's chair says, 'I paint.' I got into trouble fixing my background. This bloke told me what to do. In three months the shop looked like an art gallery. They were all bringing paintings in. I've got some of them here. The dockers were a great bunch. And the men from the factories, Tate & Lyle.

Before I got into that business, barbering, I was in plastics. I wasn't really a communist. In the East End we voted in a communist member of parliament. I lost my faith in communism during the war. One minute they were saying, 'Don't fight a capitalist war, stop fighting against Hitler.' And then, as soon as Russia comes in, they say, 'Why haven't you opened up a second front?'

One afternoon a chap, a tubby chap, came into my shop. He said, 'I understand you deal in purses?' I said, 'Yeah.' He said, 'I've got a sample here if you want some.' I took him out the back and showed him that I was the one who made them. I made the purses he was trying to flog. He said, 'You've got a barber shop here, I'm a barber.' I said, 'Do you want a job?' He said, 'Yeah.' I took him on. He was a bit of a gambler, we finished up opening one of the first betting shops in Poplar.

Poplar was different, you understand? My barber shop, anything could *happen. The Canadian seamen pulled a strike on their ship in the docks, the Beaverbrook. They couldn't strike in their own country, because they'd send the thugs in to beat them up, and then blacklegs would do the work. The headquarters of the strike was the barber shop. They were good customers.*

The habit with the dockers was to come in the morning and be appointed to a ship. The manager would say, 'The Beaverbrook.' 'Can't. It's blacked.' Eventually the whole docks were on strike, they wouldn't work that ship. The strike lasted six weeks. London was virtually on its knees.

This would have been about '48, '49. The Daily Mirror *had a headline:* STRIKE ORGANIZED FROM BARBER SHOP. *The seamen weren't communists, they really had a grievance. I had a telephone bill a mile high. I was in that barber shop until '66, '67.*

This was fascinating, it was exactly what I expected. If I could have persuaded the bricks to speak, the bagel shop, the small Jewish burial ground on Lauriston Road, the traces of human fat in curls of hair swept from the floor of the barber shop, this is what they would have said. Houses expand and contract around families eager to acquire new bloodstock, before they reconfigure and move on.

Mr Kirsh has Rachel's gift for making the best of what has happened, seeing autobiography as a Dickensian novel, arbitrary but inevitable. Dressed by coincidence. Harsh with sentiment. Table tennis, I had forgotten, was a very Jewish game, played in industrial premises between competitive firms and clubs.

Sid's story, once I had reassured myself that the recorder was picking up this light voice, sailed on through fading newsreels of courtship and war. Human dramas that informed the room in which we were sitting, with the clutter of photographs and trophies.

I had a job, just before the war broke out, down in Cadogan Terrace. Know it? Bottom end of Victoria Park, before you get to Hackney Wick.

That's how I met my wife. Coming down King Edward's Road, I heard a sound as I walked past one of those buildings: plip-plop plip-plop. Table tennis. I was quite young at the time and hadn't taken up the game seriously. They were really playing, playing the table, when all I was doing was patting a ball across the net. When I went down to the club, there was a girl, a young lady, standing talking to a lot of other onlookers. I looked at her and she looked at me. Next thing, I went to a wedding. And there she was, a guest at another wedding that was happening in front of ours. The place was crowded. I got a seat and she was sitting there opposite me. We smiled at each other. And she went out and that was that.

I got this job in Cadogan Terrace in a barber shop and the barber had four daughters. One was married, three of them were not married. Their ages ranged from about thirteen to nineteen. It was a Ladies and Gents operation, men and women.

One day I finished a customer in the Ladies and walked into the Gents and the oldest daughter, with a friend, came in through the door. The friend was her, the girl from the wedding. This time I spoke to her. Courted her for quite a while, then war broke out. She wrote to me every day. My kitbag was full. Every time I moved on, I had to throw the letters away. I had nowhere to put my clothes.

I stopped getting letters. My parents informed me that where she lived, this girl, it had been bombed flat. We lost touch with each other. I was asked to go down to London by my commanding officer, to pick up some things for him. I was in Aldgate when the bombing started. It didn't affect me. I never thought I was part of the war. It was like watching a film. The bombs were falling but I knew they were not for me.

As I walked along, I saw a woman in a doorway, crying her eyes out, screaming. I said, 'What's up?' She said, 'I'm frightened, I'm frightened.' I said, 'Why don't you go down the air-raid shelter?' I stood with her for a while, until the sirens went. She thanked me and walked away.

After I left her, I went down into the tube – it may have been Aldgate – to get a train. The girl from Cadogan Terrace, the one I lost touch with, was on the platform with her parents, stretched out. They'd been bombed and hadn't got another place yet. I spoke to her and told her she'd better

come up to Hinckley to stay with my mother. She came up and we even-
tually got married.

He doesn't show it, the aftermath of recent invasive surgery, the excavating of painful memories, but Mr Kirsh must be using up his strength. The war years were the highlight of so many lives. The aftermath, the social history of this part of London, was a slow decline. Even in 1969, when I began digging my front garden in Albion Drive, I uncovered pieces of rusted shrapnel, fins of some kind of bomb, along with the stones and bones of generations. Mr Kirsh felt an obligation to tie up loose ends, to carry his narra-tive forward to the point where it would dissolve into the view of the small garden beyond his milky window.

The barber shop wasn't there any more. The council made a compulsory purchase. The docks were closing down. I wasn't too unhappy about it. I thought I'd get a nice sum of money, but I didn't. The brickwork was appalling. I had done up the inside beautifully, the glass, windows, everything. The outside wasn't so smart. I remember on one occasion I had to put a nail in the wall and the brick went right through. When the council came to see my premises, they said, 'We're giving you nothing for the building. We'll give you something for the rest of your lease.'

Time went by, my wife died. My children got married. I was stuck in a twelve-room house on my own, Victoria Park Road. It was a Crown Property. The caretaker of this place where I am now said, 'Come down and have a look.' He showed me this one. I've been here ever since. That's virtually the end of my story.

The wife used Victoria Park more than I did. I never knew anybody around here. It was a predominantly Jewish area, especially Gore Road. The Lauriston Road shops were Jewish, mainly delicatessens, wet fish. It was a thriving area.

If I had to shop, I'd tend to go down the East End, Mile End Waste, Cannon Street Road, stalls all the way. When my father, years ago, told me we were leaving the East End for Hackney, I was really upset. I felt we were going miles away. I wasn't, when I was a young man, much of a synagogue-goer. When I was a little boy, my father took me to a synagogue in Jubilee Street.

When we moved up here I went to a synagogue in Brenthouse Road, off Mare Street. My father went to Ainsworth Road. It's called Skipworth Road now. He belonged to a different part of the religion. I went to my synagogue with my brother on high days and holidays.

We've got a Jewish cemetery up here, Lauriston Road. There's two or three of them around the East End. I've got a plot, out by Epping Forest. I buried the wife there. And I bought the plot next to it. If I could get building permission I'd be a rich man. I paid £25 for that plot.

The synagogue that I belong to now, it's huge and beautiful. My religious beliefs are beyond belief. But it's my tribe and I support them. There are only about fifteen or twenty of us left, mostly women. They've all moved away. There are very few Jewish people in Hackney. There used to be four customers for the Jewish Chronicle in our paper shop. Now there is only me.

There's a little house by the burial ground in Lauriston Road, there was a woman there. She could tell you something about Hackney. She was there, with her parents and grandparents, it was all fields. She died. Now they're thinking of closing down the synagogue. They're wasting their money.

Shadows from the five trees in Sid's garden play on the net curtains. As the small room darkens, I feel the heat of that voice as it is squeezed and compressed into my silver box, the pocket-recorder. Anecdotes become fictions, playlets: table tennis, chess, dancing. Mr and Mrs Kirsh went to clubs in the West End, they loved to tango. Hotels were hired. 'A nice sociable crowd,' Sid said. 'We dined out. We used to go on boat trips, things like that.'

Victoria Park, always at the edge of vision, was as good as the English Channel. Who needs Bournemouth when there are benches on which to enjoy filtered sunlight? Rose gardens. Enclosed meadows. Like so many barbers of the 1930s and 1940s, Mr Kirsh exploited the only hour of the day available to him, to step out into the park. Early mist on the water, a pink sky lightening over the trees. A time that was his own.

The park has changed. They used to have a penny ride on a motorboat, round that lake. There was a pagoda on one of the islands. I used to get up, before work, and take a skiff out. It was a special price, early. A single rowing boat. I used to enjoy doing that.

We used to go up to that big monument and have a drink. You can't do that any more. It was my walk. I went up about a month ago, all fenced off. No fountain, no water. And what about the swimming pool, the lido? I used that quite a lot when I was a young man. I don't know where my middle-age has gone. I was a young man up to a couple of months ago.

Charlotte Street

There had been some loose talk about Jean-Luc Godard in Hackney. Montague Road, they said. Another Jewish enclave, near Ridley Road Market. And way back in the 1960s: historic time, archive time. Budget programming. The TV people, the last of the cultural salvage men, were maundering on about a pre-Olympic Hackney night for BBC2 (or: 3, 4, 5, 6). Griff Rhys-Jones. Barbara Windsor as Marie Lloyd. Rappers and snappers. Pete Doherty, obviously. Genesis P-Orridge and Cosey Fanni Tutti in their Beck Road bunker. Rock against Racism in Victoria Park. The Angry Brigade. David Cronenberg, who had finished shooting his fantasy about Russian Mafia torture freaks infiltrating the most attractively grungy corners of Broadway Market, was now scouting locations for a revamp of Martin Amis's *London Fields*. The point being that Hackney was the new Notting Hill: the stolen name on the map, the drovers' patch, could be returned to its place of origin, rescued from its outing up west.

They called in two directors who wouldn't get the gig, steady-hands of yesteryear with substantial but cryogenic back catalogues: Chris Petit and Paul Tickell. Nobody did exhaustion, world-weariness (justified), better than this pair; competitive and centimetre-calibrated degrees of stubble. They dressed down in classic leather coats, Stasi tailoring. The coats never came off. They didn't want to look as if they were staying, that degree of commitment to restaurant or bar might be interpreted as a full-blooded endorsement. Wardrobes were near quotations of obscure but significant films. They spent hours on Jesuitical buzzcuts and hair-memories that could be exhibited in public without embarrassment. And they knew how to listen, these men. While appearing to stare out of the window. They relished crafted soundtracks, nameless bands, doctored retrievals.

The menu, in this high-end, Charlotte Street Indian restaurant (in which no Indian ever set foot), would be treated like a first draft script: sent back unopened, worked with despite serious reservations. Opening your mouth at a table of more than two people was a doomed enterprise. Petit, given the choice, would dine alone, beer and bone marrow, with L-F. Céline's *London Bridge* for company.

The game was up, but last lunches, dark olives and warm bread in baskets, might run on, unchallenged by accountants, for a few more years. Nothing was going to be commissioned or even discussed. Our man, Neil Murger, would be the last to arrive, as I would be the first, pecking order in reverse. Murger was old school, semaphoring for house red before he sat down, French-blue shirt coming loose; happier to talk than to listen. He was too thirsty, too well settled into his body mass, to flitter between channels, jockeying for preferment. The veteran producer, it struck me, was strategically deaf in one ear (which one depended on where he was sitting). The fact that nobody expected anything from anybody else, no auditions, no tantrums, rescued what might otherwise have been a funereal occasion: a wake for slippery names extracted from a foreclosed memory-bank. I was there – *why was I there?* – for no good reason, beyond the boast that I'd begun, of late, to assemble a comprehensive filmography of Hackney. Not a lot of television researchers knew, or cared, that Carol Reed's *Odd Man Out*, with James Mason as an IRA gunman on the run through an expressionist Belfast, was shot in Haggerston Park, E2. The history of this public garden, when it belonged to the Imperial Gas, Light and Coke Company, had been set aside, as we paid our respects to the gate from which Mason staged his dying walk into the snow. The misappropriation of Gas Company funds, the falsifying of stock accounts, the illegal payments to council officials, way back in the 1820s, had no bearing on current urban politics.

The Kray associate, Tony Lambrianou, who grew up in the nearby flats, Belford Court, and who got his start nicking coal and coke from this site, loved Carol Reed. The little Wolf Mankowitz fairy tale, *A Kid for Two Farthings*, which Reed shot, a mile or so down the road, in and around Brick Lane, was a favourite topic for Lambrianou and his chums, when they met in the Belgrave Arms. Or the Black Bull on Livermere Road. Where Tony sorted out business with Jack McVitie.

'Diana Dors? Remember her, Jack? Lovely woman. A real English rose in a mink bikini. And that kiddie, the little girl, passing over? The unicorn? Incredible, incredible. Brought tears to my eyes. Just incredible.'

Jack groaned and washed down another handful of pills with a brandy chaser. Before trousering a fat envelope from the landlord, Scotch Pat.

The Gainsborough Studios, along the Regent's Canal, on the edge of Islington, documentarists registered that one: Hitchcock. A local author, under the alias of Sebastian Bell, self-published a novel in which he tried to prove that Hitch filmed the opening music-hall sequence of *The 39 Steps* in the Hackney Empire (instead of the studio). Bell has a wish-fulfilment cameo of the portly director, on a Mare Street bus, lining up a scene that never happened – but which is happening now because this writer has introduced it into the borough's subterranean mythology.

'We're clearly meant to understand,' Bell says, 'we're in a rough old place. Strange though – what would Hannay be doing in Hackney? How would a visitor to London from Canada end up in Hackney? Hackney, after all, is one of London's twilight zones, neither fish nor fowl. It's not North London, neither is it the East. It's by no means easy to get to. It has no tube, is poorly served by buses and its railway stations are on lines that link only to the hubs of other twilight zones.'

A second bottle appears, a third; our starters are imminent. Nobody can remember what they ordered. Did we order? Or do the waiters, after a fixed interval of time, eavesdropping on overlapping monologues, the dry crunch of poppadoms, fine linen smeared with gobs of chutney, choose for us?

None of the film-makers have heard of Bell, his book, or his theories about Hitchcock. They only thing this trio have in common is that they appear in Stewart Home's *Memphis Underground*. Petit and Tickell under their own names and Murger under a flag of convenience. Tickell has been floating Home projects for years without much success. Petit shot Home in an aluminium suit so electrostatic that it threw his camera into convulsions. He rather liked the effect: epileptic strobe. The suit gets its own chapter in Home's novel. Perched on a flyover, beyond the Blackwall Tunnel, on the morning after Diana's fatal crash in the Paris underpass, Stewart was a skinhead turkey basted in Bacofoil, spouting conspiracy theories in a tight-throated amphetamine whine.

Hitchcock in Hackney? The yawning indifference of my audience flatly contradicted Bell's assertion. 'The fact that Robert Donat, Hitchcock and the crew were once right here in Hackney is not without interest.' You could tell when Murger switched off: he forked in a blind mouthful. And action-painted with a husk of bread.

But my Godard anecdote stood up. Mainly because nobody had seen the film. If you fancy building a mystique, bury your archive. Announce that you have only six months to live and let the critics, serial sentimentalists, do the work for you. This Godard thing was called *British Sounds*. The assembly line at Cowley. A union meeting in Dagenham. Leftist students at Essex University. And a nude descending a Montague Road staircase. Colchester, Cambridge, Hackney: the covert 1960s triangulation. Especially that part of Hackney around Cecilia Road and Shacklewell Lane. Sad bedsits of Graham Road. Amhurst Road: a study in amnesia. Oversize houses, divided into multi-occupied flats, creep towards Stoke Newington. The area, as it lost its Jewish identity, was caught by Alexander Baron in his novel *The Lowlife*. Anarchists, poets, self-publishers: they went to ground. Cultivating pubs, plotting, picking up benefits.

Godard wanted the feminist, leftist writer, Sheila Rowbotham, to deliver a reading from a *Black Dwarf* polemic, while walking naked up and down the stairs. Rowbotham was having none of it, the walking part. A model was brought in. Or so I heard. The film, commissioned by London Weekend Television, never broadcast and rarely seen, proved elusive. I knew a woman who had witnessed it, in her student days, at MIT, the high-flying Massachusetts Institute of Technology. Or it might have been Harvard. Godard announced to this gathering of the future elite, technocrats, think-tank philosophers, that they should consider themselves co-directors of the documentary they were about to see. Films were never more than provocations of discussion, fuses for direct action. The questions after the screening, respectful at first, probed the director's use of sound, the complexity of the mix. The din, the postgraduates had to admit, was impenetrable. Godard, affronted by this impertinence, stormed out, cursing, horse-snorting yellow smoke.

Murger, dismissing the waiter who was swooping on his unguarded plate, picked up the Rowbotham reference. He had worked with her; before television became a branding exercise, the promotional apparatus for puffing other promotions, conferring celebrity on those who are capable of burnishing product. Media only recognizes those who appear on the media.

'Couldn't catch a word she uttered,' he said. 'Like trying to hear snowflakes fall. Godard should have got the model to read the tract and Sheila to do the walking. Handsome chick.'

Older than my fellow lunchers, I was nostalgic for the era of challenging documentation associated with film-makers like Marc Karlin. Karlin had been permitted, as a sort of elegy for a vanishing era, to shoot portraits of Rowbotham and the Limehouse GP, David Widgery. You witnessed them, alive, moving across a London landscape, involved with how the city works (or doesn't). Widgery hauls himself through cold-water tenements, threatened hospitals. He talks sympathetically to gaunt, dying men, as they enjoy a cigarette on their way down the ramp to the outpatients' clinic.

'Do you drink alcohol?'

'No, never.'

'Wise man. Much wiser than me. We're getting older. How little time we have on the planet.'

The limping doctor is in dialogue with the invisibles, unregistered or unlanguaged immigrants hanging on, by a thread; cave dwellers in pre-privatized tower blocks. And with his own demons too. Dark spirits of place. Wounds of capital. The urge to write, perform, sublimate in speech: as he soothes and reassures confused patients or argues with bureaucrats. The camera enjoys his madness, the energy. The sharp bones and creases of his skull.

'We've got three generations in the one bed,' says a proud Irish mother. 'All in work.'

The Vietnamese wife, waiting for a husband who does not return, looks downriver at new lights. And, through an interpreter, admits that she is too scared to go out. Perhaps he went to another building? They are all the same.

Mr Joseph Murphy slept in the toilets, when they were open, in Ridley Road Market.

'The police took me in a couple of times. I would never lie to you, doctor. It was only the cider, special brew. They told me to touch my nose. They've ruined the country, the Tories.'

'What colour is your phlegm?'

From the top of his bus, heading south down Mare Street, the bravura opening of *Some Lives! A GP's East End*, Widgery might have registered them, the wealthier incomers, Sebastian Bell's transatlantic tourists. I had a rational explanation for the presence of Canadians in Hackney. They were lost, definitively. They turned to me, when I was walking, in the cocoon, as they shuddered from taxis, clutching maps all-ways-up, cologne-saturated against the bite of post-industrial air. 'Excuse me, sir, we've gotten ourselves a little confused. Could you direct us to the Burberry franchise?'

Canadians, Japanese: so white, so pale. So fresh. They are after factory prices, discounts. A shield against radiation, dirty bombs. Germ-repelling prophylactic wraps of 1940s film noir. Coats styled from the trenches for ghosts who would never return from France. And now endorsed by Kate Moss, an honorary Hackney bride, guesting at the Empire with Pete Doherty. Regular lock-in drinker, indoor smoker, at the Dolphin on Mare Street. An image too wise to open her mouth.

After Burberry-questing Canadians, blatant as CIA stringers in Berlin, had been nudged east into wastelands of defunct civic buildings, fenced properties waiting on development packages, where they hoped to exchange current rainwear for newer versions of the same at bargain prices, I saw a man spill out of a Vietnamese restaurant on the corner of Ellingfort Road. He sprinted, jacketless, white-shirted, into the maelstrom of traffic; believing that, in his suicidal dive, he would become invisible. I lost him behind a bus which was nudging out into an unbroken line of cars, white vans and lane-weaving motorcycle messengers. The runner disappeared, but I heard the horns, the screech of brakes, a metal-on-metal shunt. Nothing out of the ordinary. The soothing muzak of managed rage: horn choruses, sirens.

The window of the restaurant in which I caught my own reflection, a camera-cyclops, was dressed with photocopied recommendations, neon part-words, paper lanterns and a written account, in two languages, of a recent murder – which seemed to be, ahead the event, a short fiction based on the drama I was now witnessing.

On Thursday 17th August 2006 at about 4.10pm, Minh Thanh Nguyen was attacked in Mare Street, Hackney, E9, by a group of men. He suffered stab wounds and died of his injuries shortly afterwards. A silver Audi and another blue or dark green car was seen to leave the area at speed.

In his pink-on-red autopsy passport, Minh Thanh Nguyen seems very young. And grateful to be where he is, welcoming the camera's intrusion. He has prominent ears and a broad smile. With lipstick traces. A face so simple in its design that it might have been sketched on the back of a thumb.

Explosive laughter is cancelled as the restaurant door closes. A large woman, at a table of partying town-hall bureaucrats, jackets off, shudders and shakes, opening her throat in a now silent roar. The Vietnamese boy, lying in the street, is a waiter who didn't want to wait. Slow-burning resentment reached a critical state. The men who jumped from the Audi could have been helping him, staunching the blood on his white shirt, or puncturing flesh, kneeling on his chest to rip out his heart with their bare hands. It was impossible, at this angle, to tell. But they did, as the official account foretold, drive off at speed. The dying man managed to crawl a few yards, and then he huddled into a ball: watched by other men in white shirts from the doorway of the restaurant. You could smell fish, snails in garlic, and various acrid, permitted smokes.

Not here, not in Charlotte Street. Where, in fit-for-purpose times, restaurants empty by two o'clock. We're alone and loud. Murger doesn't have the concentration to follow my rambling anecdotes. There will be no film, no Hackney night. No book. The lunch has outlived its occasion. Old lags meet to keep the rituals alive, simply that. We approve the release of tension that comes when there is nothing to pitch, no patronage to dispense. We proselytize new diets, exercise regimes, mortality postponed for an hour. Mineral water is ordered with a flourish but untouched.

The unexpected bonus for me comes with Murger's own tale: that's why he's picking up the bill. He has nothing to offer by way of employment, it's the other way round; he wants his Hackney testament to be taken down. He wants to become part of the apparatus of research for a book that will never be written. Reality, for Murger, was lodged somewhere close to Lauriston Road and Victoria Park. Deep memories, as mapped and validated as those of Sidney Kirsh, were Irish and Catholic. The producer talked of his childhood, schooling; of serving at mass, beating the bounds of the parish. Catholics and Jews lived side by side, contiguous biographies with few points of contact or difference. Comfortable migrants who did not notice the existence of any person outside their immediate tribe.

If you searched now for Catholic traces, they were still active:

the hospice for which Murger collected coins. You saw the white Madonna, posed on a balcony like a debt collector, as you advanced down Beck Road. St John the Baptist had a sloping roof of wave-pattern tiles above dirty red brick, gold spikes on black railings. Cardinal Pole, a substantial enclosed property, backing on to Well Street Common, enjoyed an ambiguous reputation, academic achievement with rumours of bullying among the pupils. High walls around a turreted building that looked like a Victorian public school. Children would be marked by these establishments, their rituals, for the rest of their lives. There were more Hackneys, stepping off my usual paths, than I could ever know.

Tickell had attended a seminary; he was an inquisitor distracted from his vocation by the sirens of punk, seductive noises outside the cloister. Chris Petit, up in the Yorkshire wilds, had been schooled with Antony Gormley, Julian Fellowes and other high-Catholic aristos, spooks, priest dodgers. I was the only Protestant, Welsh Methodist, at this heretical second- or third-generation Irish table. I was badly out of key with the times, the counter-reformation of Tony and Cherie Blair, when private devotions became public property and strange beliefs can justify political adventurism and foreign wars. The film-makers, having broken free of dogma, had only special forms of abstinence to offer, by way of heritage: drink taken, swiftly, thirstily, as they came out of a lasciviously prolonged Lenten denial. Cool beer before the conviviality of wine. Sin postponed is so much sweeter.

I couldn't be certain, searching the Lauriston Road area for relics of Murger's Irish past, what status that church, St John of Jerusalem, enjoyed. Its sharp green spike, noticed through the trees of Victoria Park, had drawn me on. Opening times were eccentric and irregular. Parish Mass was at 10 a.m. every Sunday. The tympanum above the porch published a chopped legend: DO NOT BE AFRAID. Jesus walked across the waves. His left hand was missing, a sacrifice. He gestured with an empty sleeve.

Lauriston Road

I have never worked with a researcher. And I never will. I couldn't afford it. And anyway my research is the book. With optional feints and flourishes. I'd be happy to hire a pro to take care of the daily grind, the writing, but I want to hang on to the business of gathering material, that's the fun part. I'm useless at libraries, prejudiced against Google-slurry, but eager to carry home junk from the road: pamphlets, snapshots, conversations with hangers about, dog walkers. The story is accidental. It tells itself – if we don't mangle that complex elegance through faulty memory.

Those were my beliefs until an insinuating character sidled up to me, after a reading with a celebrated London author, and said: 'I write his stuff. And I could do it for you.' The novelist, a selfless craftsman, was far too busy with his media commitments to drudge through reference books, trade directories, letters, manuscripts: he did the style. The concept. The marketing. While his oppo, for a decent bung, tramped the hard miles, filing detailed reports from internet cafés. Conducting interviews. Getting hassled by security.

It was time for me to join the real world. I picked up the phone to call the man that Chris Petit, with some reluctance, had recommended. 'He's not bad – if you know how to handle him.' Writers, exchanging these tips, are pretty much announcing their retirement. It's like handing on a mistress. You have to recognize that most of the material on display in the windows of the book chains has been put through an assembly line more effective than Dagenham. Author portraits are as fraudulent as those brief biographies. The unnamed are the ones who are doing the work, out there, embedded in a fiction that is not of their making.

Petit's former researcher, a person called Kaporal, was part-Breton, part-Pole, mostly South London. Herne Hill. He was reputed to work fast; in and out of America, when they let him, hire car and Holiday Inn. Driving alone, sweating profusely: chasing rumours. Badlands, motowns. He maintained contact with a network of other 'risk assessment' technicians, who fronted as television journalists, reporting on earthquakes in Ankara, plague in Quezon City, unusual cellphone traffic out of Frankfurt. Conspiracy was a given: you learn to knit with electricity, prints of prints, to arrive at Xerox truth. Nothingness. White noise. The sludge at the bottom of the virtual world is always the same: child pornography, weapon fetishism, debased forms of the occult. Inland empires in which the midnight sun, like a prison bulb, can never be shut off.

Kaporal was a bounty hunter, trading dubious information, toying with a rosary of plastic skulls, which had been looped through complimentary keyrings from middle-European Turkish restaurants.

'It's a thousand a week,' he said. 'I can give you the bones of Hackney in seven days. Land deals: Russians, Saudis. The City guy in Broadway Market, Dr Whatever . . . sounds like Rotten. And the child abuse thing, Trottergate. Voodoo cults. Trade in body parts. Bush meat in Ridley Road. Deaths in custody. The assassination of Harry Stanley. Cashmoney OK? In advance.'

The man was a virtuoso of the keyboard. Through a steady glugging of coffee, I could hear the keys rattle, sharp pings of the incoming messages: Kaporal talked through a blizzard of mal-information, warped statistics. The sewage of hyperspace. My only problem was his fee. The researcher would begin as soon as he was paid, a coin-in-the-slot monkey. Who was on the point of flying off to some forest in Finland, taking a cargo boat to Hamburg. There was never a shortfall of risks to be assessed.

It took me three months, not the work, the promises, but actually getting my hands on the cheques. I accepted any commission that related to Hackney: barber shops for a style magazine, off-message Olympic soothsaying, radio punditry from the Lower Lea Valley. I knocked out whither-London rhetoric for plausible Irish architects in the pay of American museums. I marched late-rising, yawning students down canals, across parks, through allotments. I peddled notebooks. I flogged boxes of manuscripts, letters from the dead, the druggy ephemera of countercultural exiles.

The institutions were the worst, invoices never went to the right place. Curators who had issued the original invitation moved sideways, Tate to National Portrait Gallery, Hayward to Tate again, before you could get past the answer machine. Reliable payers, once the piece made it into print, sat on reviews for nine months, a year. Meanwhile, bills spiralled, council-tax demands doubled, utilities were competitive. Storage, if you tried to hang on to an archive from which to work, cost more than Rachman paid for a terrace of houses in Notting Hill back in the 1950s. Storage is the growth industry, twinned with the cult of minimalist lifestyles; empty apartments kept empty, as a long-term investment. Entire blocks, Kaporal assured me, were being bought, in advance, by West Ham footballers as a hedge against the annual threat of relegation. Money has its own architecture. Money of a kind that Kaporal refused to recognize. He liked getting his large hands dirty, pressing juice from greasy coins. He could read the curve of the future in the temperature of human touch.

On his way to a private screening in Wilkes Street, Spitalfields, the elusive researcher agreed to drop in at the Royal Inn on the Park, Lauriston Road, with a bag of files, material he could forget as soon as my brown envelope was in his pocket. The pub was another grand Hackney facelift: white and flower-decked. But this was still the bar where 'Big Jim' Moody, a South Londoner on the run, was blown away by an unknown assailant. I decided to take the opportunity, walking in that direction, closing in on Kaporal, to interview Rachel Lichtenstein. Respectful of earlier waves of Jewish migration, a blue plaque on Old Ford Road for the ghetto novelist Israel Zangwill, Rachel tried to find a family home in the Lauriston area, in Victoria Park Village; and before that in a new estate on a slope beneath the gloomy Hackney Hospital, at the edge of the Wick.

Chasing Brick Lane witnesses for her current work in progress, Rachel was back in town. It was no longer viable to live, with her husband and two young sons, in Hackney. She commuted, stayed with friends, took the train to Leigh-on-Sea; a new beginning in the area where she had grown up. Those huge skies over the widening Thames Estuary. A setting in which legends of London, remembrances of a Polish or Russian heritage, could find their necessary form.

Rachel, who had been carrying out a project, that morning, with the children in Lauriston School, was waiting for me in Frock's, a bar-bistro that had recently changed hands. This was where my son William got his first job: just before his fourteenth birthday. Nothing like keeping up old traditions, we thought; child labour, kitchen slavery. He learnt to cook buttery scrambled eggs, to wash dishes, serve at table. And he was rewarded with trips to France. The pupils in Lauriston School were assembling a book. 'It's astonishing,' Rachel said, 'they speak fifty different languages.'

In November 1948, Oswald Mosley, founder of the Union Movement, made a speech at Lauriston School to five hundred supporters, mainly women and young girls. His theme, he announced, would be 'the development of the Party's new policy of union with the peoples of Europe against the threat of devastation from Oriental forces, and to Britain's recovery by exploiting the wealth of Africa'.

During the war, prisoners from Victoria Park, undergoing a denazification programme, were allowed out in the evening to attend meetings at the popular fascist pitch in Gore Road; where the burning of synagogues was advocated. Harry Hynd, MP for Hackney Central, offered to stand guard in Brenthouse Road.

4 May 2006. With long, lightened or sunbleached hair, and wearing spectacles (the cost of hours at the computer) that gave her an air of authority to go with her position as householder, archivist, Rachel relished the buzz of being back in town. It was hard, she said, to juggle the pleasures and duties of domesticity with the hunger to spend hours digging out stories, recording the

voices of those who were fading into whispers, or were timid of the instrument placed in front of them on the table.

We moved to Hackney Wick because it was the only place we could afford that seemed big enough for an expanding family. I wanted to be in East London. We bought this house before it was even built. A brand-new estate. Quite big houses, up on this hill. The estate looked very green in the brochure. We moved in and, very quickly, it went wrong. I absolutely hated it. I felt like we were stuck on a remote island, surrounded by darkness. It was a rough area. The Hackney Wick station was terrifying. People were always getting stabbed and raped. There were no shops.

Within a couple of months of moving in, we put the property back on the market. I couldn't stand it. It wasn't part of anything. You didn't want to walk around there. All of my neighbours were broken into, trashed. I was pregnant with Daniel. I was at home, hot and pregnant, listening to the sound of doors being kicked in all around me. I remember hearing this burglary happening next door and being too scared to do anything about it, all this crashing and banging and breaking glass.

I liked the idea of socially mixed housing. It was half housing association and half private, but it didn't work. The estate wasn't maintained. It was all nice little gardens when we started, but the rubbish bins weren't emptied. The litter! You'd open the front door on this wasteland, rubbish blowing around your ankles.

Some very scary people moved in and I wanted to get us out as quickly as possible. Right behind the estate was a drug-treatment hospital, right at the back of our garden. When we moved in the garden was lovely and we had some really good neighbours. Very soon it collapsed, became impossible, frightening. Uninhabitable actually. It was a prison island in the end, locked in by motorways and crumbling hospitals, stalked by disturbed people. Who would have thought of planting human beings in such a place?

We moved as soon as we could arrange it to a strange house near Victoria Park. I always seem to live alongside Jewish cemeteries or bombsites. This place had been bombed. It was a Victorian street that had been flattened and where mews houses had been built, originally as studios. I chose it because I felt threatened in Hackney Wick, our property was exposed at front and back. The new house was a kind of cave, with no windows at the rear. It was big. The estate agent described it as 'lofty'. It wasn't. It was a cavern.

The other people around us were young and trendy. They were internet designers, fashion folk. I wanted to be near the park. I wanted to be near the school. The house became too small for us very quickly. We lived in Victoria Park for ten years, the park was part of our lives. We were always in the children's play area and the One O'clock Club. You'd meet people in the park, there was a sense of community. Obviously, my family had lived in this area before, Uncle Sid – Sidney Kirsh – was around the corner in Gore Road. I felt connected to that little piece of ground.

I found Lauriston Road, with all the cafés and shops, difficult – particularly when David started going to school. I enjoy chatting with all sorts of people, I cross barriers very easily. There was a real divide between the very middle-class, just-moved-into-Hackney, tons-of-money parents, who would clique together, and the young families who had lived here all their lives. That street was a weird mix of posh little restaurants, bistros, boutiques, delicatessens and all this other regular stuff that was going on. I felt a lot of people were there because they felt Hackney was a bit edgy and cool. Actually it was a middle-class enclave in which we couldn't afford to live. That was one of the reasons why we were forced out. I also found the crime in the immediate area very alarming.

When Daniel was a baby we had a nanny. She was coming back to the house one day with the children. David must have been two and a half. They approached the front door. I was upstairs, transcribing Whitechapel interviews, with my headphones on. I didn't hear them. The nanny opened the door, David went inside. She stepped back to get her stuff from the buggy. Somebody came up from behind and attacked her. David shut the door in her face. This tiny little boy! She was mugged on the doorstep, viciously, pushed over. She was screaming so loudly that I heard her and came down. It was crazy. David at two and a half . . . I was really cross with him. But he was protecting his baby brother.

We had this neighbour, right opposite, a big boxer, a black guy with *dreadlocks. I told him about it. He said, 'If I'd fucking seen him, I'd have chopped his arms off with my Samurai sword.'*

I felt the darkness closing in. It was leaking into my home. Walking the kids to school, you'd be going past all those blue-and-yellow tin signs advertising the most recent outrages, assaults, rapes, hit-and-run drivers. When that girl, the artist, was murdered in the park, it really did something to me. We were already thinking of leaving. We were struggling financially. The killing of Margaret Muller stopped the park being a sacred space. I couldn't let the kids run free any more. I was nervous of the trees, the wide-open spaces I once loved. It was such a horrible incident. She was a young painter, about the same age as me. It was devastating.

There were several entrances to the Royal Inn on the Park, as 'Big Jim' Moody discovered: four shots in the chest, point-blank range, from a Webley .38. Sudden silence. Burnt air. Before the sirens, which were sounding now, a chorus Hackney dwellers accept as confirmation that they are in the right place, back home. If they send for the red chopper, from the roof of the Royal Whitechapel Hospital, you know you're in bother. Nothing more than a nick from a blade, a cleaver embedded in the skull, and you can walk to the Homerton like a proper man. Hop a 236, if you're lucky. A lovely ride, monitor screen in colour, carries you right to the door.

I had no idea what Kaporal looked like.

'Used,' Petit said. 'In the way Americans describe old books. Leathery. Black T-shirt if he's out for the evening. Bulky, but not wobbling fat. Eats on the hoof with his fingers. Could be ex-job.'

There was such a man, at the bar, sandwich in hand, waiting on my nod before he ordered his pint. Grinning: like the shock therapy was beginning to wear off. No bags, no box files. No socks.

'I hit the Victory in Vyner Street on my way over,' he said. 'Major crim hangout. Quiet drink with an informant, bowl of crisps, pickled egg, saveloy. Motor pulls up, two heavies get out. The little bloke is carrying a rolled-up newspaper at a very strange angle. *Hackney Gazette*. I picked it up when they left. WEBSITE LINK TO TERROR. CALL FOR INVESTIGATION INTO EVANGELIST GANG. TV STAR BITES HOMELESS MAN.

'This guy, the dwarf with one arm, is lifted into the air by his mate. He pulls a machete out of the paper and brings it down, hard, on the head of the man on the stool next to me. Landlord grabs ice cubes for the wound and refuses to send for an ambulance. It's his ear, chopped clean off. Bloody cubes roll across the floor and are licked by the pub dog. Who sniffs the ear, then swallows it – before the geezer can move. We had a good laugh. The guy sat there, watching the racing, holding a bloody towel of ice cubes against his head. The landlord, fair play, gave him a brandy on the house.

'I saved you the newspaper. It's outside in the car, with the rest of the stuff. Everything you need in 211 pages, basic. Make it a Grolsch, thanks.'

Kaporal completed his confidential report into Hackney in six days; on the seventh, he hit the pubs. Those were his methods and they worked. He understood how to get inside the belly of the beast. Say the words 'Hackney Council' and humans freeze; loud but unproven rumours of incompetence and corruption are a given, forests of self-justifying prose in fifty languages, but nothing to be done. We have been bored into submission. And boredom is where Kaporal starts. The truth is out there, if you have the stamina to pursue it: buried deep within documents like the 'A to Z of Hackney Council Services'. A cyberspace wasteland that only idiot savants are prepared to investigate. Boredom as the ultimate firewall of terror.

'I experience a pulse-quickening, physical thrill,' Kaporal said, 'when I submerge myself in lists. Once you break the protective flak down into an alphabet, it comes to life. I've highlighted the promising items for you. I always know when I've plucked the cherry, I have to break off for a wank.'

- Dangerous Structures – see **Planning Service**
- Dead Animals – see **Pest Control**
- Defence Policy – see **CCTV and Emergency Planning Service**
- Deportation – see **Refugees/Asylum Seekers**
- Drug Action Team
- Dumped Rubbish and Abandoned Vehicles
- Empty Properties – see **Council Housing**
- Faith Groups – see **Religion**
- Filming in Hackney – see **Hackney Communications Centre**
- Fraud – see **Audit and Anti-Fraud Division**
- Fraud Hotline (Council Housing)
- Hackney Marshes
- Hackney Mortuary – see **Mortuary**
- HIV Related Brain Impairment – see **Mildmay Hospital**
- Illegal Trading – see **Trading Standards**
- Income Collection and Recovery (Right to Buy)
- Infestation – see **Pest Control**
- Listed Buildings – see **Local History**
- Mice – see **Pest Control**
- Noisy Parties – see **Noise Service**
- Paralympic Games – see **Lower Lea Valley Regeneration**
- Pools – see **Swimming**
- Racial Harassment
- Rats – see **Pest Control**
- School Absence – see **Education Services**
- School Exclusions
- Sewers and Drains
- Sexual Abuse
- Sheltered Housing
- Stray Dogs
- Street Furniture
- Substance Misuse Team
- Table Tennis
- Tourist Information

- Traffic Calming
- Turkey Meat – see **Environmental Health**
- Unfair Dismissals – see **Trade Union**
- War Memorials
- Welfare Food Sales
- Whistleblower Hotline – see **Audit and Anti-Fraud Division**
- Women's Refuge

Squeezing poetry out of lists, that was Kaporal's singular gift. Showing us fear in a handful of dusty files. The man was a late-modern master who had taken the ego out of composition. The world was his forest. His hired car rattled with foil trays, reeked of saturated fats and cigarette smoke; he was late for the next appointment. Coffee and sausage sandwich under the halogen lights of a night football enclosure: listening to gossip, anticipating violence. A cushion of unopened airmail letters in the back pocket of his elasticized jeans. A wife who didn't outlast the honeymoon.

Before I parted from Rachel, who was going up west for lunch with her agent, I asked for news of Sidney Kirsh.

'He's frail, but lively as ever. He won't walk down to the shops now. Not since he was attacked on the street.'

Whenever I passed Mr Kirsh's flat, in my afternoon wanderings, I checked the gauzy curtains for signs of life. Movement. Somebody staring back at me.

Rachel was shod in slope-soled black trainers, which she said were inspired by the stance of barefoot Masai warriors. They had cured her back, put the spring into her Achilles tendons. Removed to the seaside – whelks, prawns, on-shore breezes from the oil refineries of Canvey Island – she had the freedom to write. While the boys were in school. With the garden door open, she heard once again the racket of street traders, unlicensed scholars, Yiddish poets, anarchists, tailors and barbers.

ASYLUM

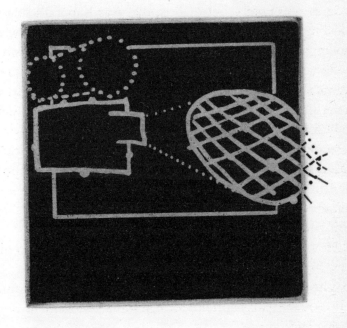

They come here seeking asylum and discover a madhouse.

– Matthew De Abaitua, *The Red Men*

De Beauvoir Road

They are dangerous things, if you look too closely, old photographs. The configuration of a lovingly observed face will change. A death-in-life instant begins to breathe; as your own breath, while you hold the print so tightly in your hands, stops. The shutter snaps its sexual trigger. It is not the vision released by acrid chemicals in a shallow dish that is fixed, it is the prurient attention of the image-thief. No two people witness the same scene.

There is a photograph of Anna, now framed, from the summer of 1968. It stays down on the coast, in a flat where there is room for such things. She is sitting, balanced, at an open window; sunlight behind her, the backlit effect I was going for. Her hair has been reconsidered for her new job as an infant teacher. Trees in full leaf. Fine white cotton blouse, pale green bolero: colour as memory. The print is monochrome. Anna in her early twenties. She smiles. Concentration flickers between the letter or document she is reading and this intrusion: I am a camera-cyclops, overemphasizing the moment. A woman, holding a book, perched on the ledge of an open window: a genre piece. A painterly quotation signalling a new intimacy with the model.

'I was so young,' she says.

Catching me with the photograph, Anna remembers the occasion, what it meant: that she was resting the sheet of paper on a thick and forgotten paperback. An estate agent's list of Hackney properties, the house in Albion Drive. The only one I ever agreed to visit: the place where we would live for the next forty years.

We couldn't manage Golders Green. We'd been away, through the winter, a rented house on the island of Gozo that cost less than a room on Haverstock Hill. We visited the Ionic Cinema on Finchley

Road and I bought an Incredible String Band LP, *The Hangman's Beautiful Daughter*, but it didn't take. The brownness of North London furniture: we were paying guests who had outstayed our welcome. Without this banishment to a land of sugared cakes and crisp European newspapers, the time it took to get anywhere we wanted to be, Anna would not have agreed on the Sunday-afternoon excursion to Hackney. I had been there twice before: once as a film student tracking down a Joseph Losey film, *The Criminal* – by bus, tube and bus again, out of West Norwood; and once on foot along the canal from Camden Town. That walk, with two friends, was the clincher: how London takes its meaning from water, warehouses with broken windows, humming generators, wood yards, muddy paths open to trespass. Waterways were protected from the public, from potential thieves and vandals. We were expelled at Islington, over the hill to pick up the canal as it emerged from the tunnel at Colebrooke Row: now there were green, creeper-draped gardens, narrowboats; the City Road Basin with its startling view of Hawksmoor's white obelisk at St Luke's, Old Street, on the southern horizon.

We reached what I now know was Victoria Park. Far enough. Far enough away from territory I knew, that northern spine: Stockwell, Kennington, Waterloo, Charing Cross, Leicester Square, Tottenham Court Road, Camden Town, Chalk Farm, Belsize Park. Brixton Market, on foot, to the National Film Theatre; to the Everyman, Hampstead, for its Bergman season. Even when we lived in Rudall Crescent and on Haverstock Hill, with the bistros, pub lunches, bookshops, bank where you didn't have to queue, we knew it couldn't last. But the uncharted scale of this East London park, without tourists or celebrated views, was mysterious and alluring. Anna and I came away delirious, appreciating that there was much more to discover. About London. And about ourselves.

Hackney streets had no use for us. We had invaded a zone with no self-consciousness, no conceit. A working place that didn't, in the pinch of the time, work any more. We settled in a pub called the Old Ship, at the side of the dirty pink block of the Hackney Empire, a defunct music hall. There was a sloping, tiled passageway and a dark bar in which to absorb the experiences of the walk. I could disappear into this, I thought, without effort: afternoon drinkers nursing pints, a curtain of smoke to keep the street at a safe distance. Hampstead, Camden Town, The Congress of the Dialectics of Liberation in the Roundhouse, Allen Ginsberg, William Burroughs, a life in documentary films: it drained away. Those things were diary entries written by a stranger.

There are few cars in this part of Hackney, which is scarcely Hackney at all. Incomers resolutely face west: the N1 postcode a proud boast. I'm intrigued and a little alarmed by the notion of occupying an entire house; six people, potentially. Three couples. We'd be stretching it to call ourselves a commune. How it worked was that Renchi had sisters in Islington, contacts, they knew a man, a film-maker, prepared to rent out his property. Renchi decided to sublet to Dublin friends. The meal, on that Sunday, was the first of many.

  We did not, in 1968, have any proper sense of local industries, street garages, betting shops, churches peddling Cliff Richard-franchised Christianity. Or the outstations of R. D. Laing's anti-psychiatry movement: arks of insanity incubating insanity. Or ghosts of great houses with formal gardens. Independent printing presses. Markets. Future marriages, alliances, schisms, children. In the sour dark of a late afternoon in February, a young couple not knowing who they are, or where they are going, find themselves in a very specific place that is suffering from the same amnesiac condition: De Beauvoir Road.

  A square white house in a wide street punctuated by naked and spindly trees. Three steps up to a grey-green door with brass knocker and thin vertical slit for thin vertical letters. Generous front window, its ledge decorated with ironwork curlicues that match the colour of the door. And white pillars, I'd forgotten those: twin Corinthian columns, one on each side of the porch. Moving inside we encounter the coarseness of hessian underfoot. A round white table. White walls. Pine cupboards. I sense already the damage we are going to inflict; but I want it, this new place. The host couple offer us the best bedroom and, spoilt creatures that we are, we accept. I'm excited by disorientation, the life that is not my life: unearned furniture, telephones without coin-slots, a garden. There would be much talk, many disputes, managed silences, at that smooth table.

Years later, out of the blue, I was contacted by a De Beauvoir woman who invited me to talk to a book-discussion group, the Hackney Hardcore. It being a local event, in a weak moment, I accepted.

'Where will this happen?'

I imagined, from the confidence of her tone, that there must have been another revival of the Hackney Literary and Philosophical Society, a hard-drinking leftist cabal who used to gather in an upstairs room of the Prince George in Parkholme Road to listen to scholars like Professor Bill Fishman.

'The Groucho Club,' she said. 'Dean Street. Table booked in the restaurant.'

You couldn't hear yourself think, let alone talk, but it was obvious there were scores to settle. The Hackney Hardcore, being media folk, faces and former faces, were able to make a passable stab at eviscerating my book, its competence, its blatant flaws, without having to actually open it. One of the Clerkenwell architects thought he might skim a few pages of next week's choice, by a man who had a previous connection with his third wife, to provide himself with sufficient ammunition for a character assassination.

New Hackney, De Beauvoir Town: it's an edgy address on the way to somewhere better; part of the classic Blairite trajectory – leading right back to Tony himself, who sat out the early Thatcher years in Mapledene Village, a sanitized ghetto of tax lawyers, helmeted City cyclists and black T-shirt comics with production companies, tucked between Queensbridge Road and London

Fields. Chelsea tractors giving birth to a litter of tiny silver pods who feed, by hose, from the teat of electricity.

In the communal taxi, after the Groucho Club farce, we negotiated the broad avenues where I lodged in '68. I realized that my host for the evening, a lively arts presenter, was also a person very much in the news. She had rescued a stalled career by publishing the definitive account of how to become a cash-starved property millionaire. A platinum-card pauper. London houses, holiday villas in Tuscany and Provence: they accumulate. Impulse buys after a good lunch. Shoes, handbags, war-zone orphans. You know people, you have access to unlimited credit. Relationships founder, extended families extend. New Hackney is a columnist's wet dream, autopilot angst with cycle lanes, but you pay a premium for frontier life. Stonking council tax. Heavy storage and insurance bills. Quarter-light windows smashed every Friday night. Taxi accounts. Black cabs everywhere. Back from town and in again. Media downsizing: old hands marginalized or laid off. Threatened with Salford. Slow payment and non-payment for freelance work. And suddenly you can't afford a bottle of milk. No freebies at the minimart. Credit cards shredded. Or cloned. You are one of them, the faceless others who are stabbed on late-night buses. Self-exiled to Crusoe's island (Stoke Newington): with a potential fortune in bricks and mortar, zilch in the current account.

As we have a whip-round to make up the cab fare, I ask my fellow travellers where they go for a drink, or where they eat in this area. At home in Hackney.

'Are we in Hackney?'

They have heard of Kingsland Road, on the back end of the local news, blue-and-white ribbons, flashing lights, but they've never had reason to visit it. They sleep here, secure inside stucco units of mid-Victorian speculative housing contained within the rectangle made by Downham Road, Southgate Road, Balls Pond Road, Kingsland Road. The last generation of confused incomers to rough it: before the London Fields revival, the second coming of Broadway Market. Belgian beers and pre-famous graffiti.

But in the troubled sleep of De Beauvoir Town, monsters crawl and swim; memory-traces of old Hackney bedlams, the shit and straw of satanic madhouses lurking beyond the walls of the City. Blotting up damage. Incubi and succubi attend the recently impoverished with garlands of nightsweat: final demands, failed commissions, overdue novels. A face that is your face in a mirror that refuses to recognize it. Nakedness as the final disguise. Until that story too can be captured, polished and made tame.

In 1968 we were pioneer colonists, no more enlightened than the Hackney Hardcore, scratching our way through a mess of prejudices and received opinions. We owned nothing, we earned nothing; after four years in Dublin, it was hard to settle to regular work. I was educated to the point of being unemployable. Tom Baker, a gifted carpenter and handyman, had not yet put aside the siren song of the film industry. His credit as co-writer of the Michael Reeves film *Witchfinder General* only prolonged the agony. Scrapbooks of the period reveal a group of the accidentally young in random clothes. We had no experience before this of central heating: polo-neck sweater in brown for Tom, purple shirt for Renchi, probably borrowed somewhere on his travels between Liverpool and London. Short skirts for Anna, Judith, Bridget.

I couldn't think who, if anyone, did the cleaning. Anna remembers getting stuck into the kitchen when I was away with Renchi in Dublin, researching a never-made documentary. Judith, who has a sharp eye for such things, a Jamesian scholar, remarked on this event: displacement activity. Bridget attacked the grease-tray of the cooker, which, it appeared, had never previously been touched. One evening we noticed a tribe of small brown-grey mice running up and down the kitchen curtains. After the usual debates and anthropomorphic handwringing, Anna took care of the poison saucers. An activity which would become a seasonal domestic chore. The meaty-marzipan odour of small rodents rotting behind the skirting boards was a given in Hackney life.

We took it in turns to cook, the women doing more of it than the men: you never knew how many people would pass through or sleep somewhere about the place. Renchi in particular had the habit of scattering invitations to all and sundry, using the offer of a meal as a way of ending an awkward telephone conversation with good grace. There were outpatients and occasional vagrants brought in from the streets. Some of them stayed for months. Sent downstairs in the middle of the night to investigate noises coming from the kitchen, I found an Irishman in a string vest and unlaced boots, nothing else, burning a pan of bacon.

In Dublin, and before that in South London, I ate in cafés. I was a frying-pan cook with a sideline dropping kitchen scraps into packets of processed soup (which I had been known to heat on the stub of a candle). Primitive spaghetti improvisations were also possible. My fish stew was thought to be an acquired taste. It involved a cauldron, hours of simmering, scaly lumps and tentacles chosen for their colour from the soused slabs of Ridley Road Market. I would chuck in herbs as they came to hand (from among the cat-perfumed garden weeds or growing free in the cracks of kitchen tiles). And enliven the bubbling sludge with unpeeled pota-toes, sweating onions, sour wine, HP sauce, soy sauce, a worm of tomato paste. Kill or cure.

Tom was fastidious about his omelettes, the timing, the ingre-dients. They fluffed up, buttery and rich. His standard dish, we never tired of it, was chilli con carne. Budget mince and beans with a hunk of bread. Renchi was an inventive cook, dishes to be eaten as and when they appeared at the table, in no particular order. The inspiration was painterly. His themed green meal found-ered when the jelly pie melted in the oven, slippery gunge leaking through ill-fitting doors to add to the psychedelic revisions of the black-and-white, op-art rubber floor.

The men never did any cleaning, Anna reckoned. But she was wrong. In Gozo, where there was time for such indulgences, I painted a little portrait of her sunbathing, topless, reading *Voices from Women's Liberation*. Liberated from false memory. I turned up a photograph of Tom, white jeans like David Hemmings in *BlowUp*, sweeping one-handed around the sitting room – where Renchi and Judith slept on a sofabed – with a Hoover. And here is Renchi drying dishes at a heaped sink. Oh yes, we did our share. Even if, most of the time, we talked film, floated schemes, played cricket in the garden, and took off for walks up the Lea Valley – while Anna and Judith did the crash course that would give them direct entry to primary-school teaching. The women dressed respectably for their commute while the men lounged around, brewing coffee, smoking and failing to land a single commission. It wasn't enough to live in a successful film-maker's house. The glamour didn't rub off. I remember the feel of the vacuum cleaner bumping over coarse hessian when I manoeuvred it around the grey box of the record player. Frank Zappa: *Cruising with Ruben and the Jets*.

There were discussions about the events of '68, but nobody left for Paris. Direct action never got beyond the screenplay. After a morning scouring South London markets, we read American comics in the park, near Waterloo, waiting to meet Judith and Anna on their lunch break. Tom chews his thumb and frowns over *Army War: Sgt Rock (DC's Startling New Combat Team)*.

I had been in Grosvenor Square with Tom, demonstrating in favour of a study of crowd behaviour, tidal movement, involuntary peristalsis, as much as anything else. The shock of the horses, their size, coming straight at us: the lengths to which the state would go to protect American interests, the embassy with its oversize eagle. I didn't understand how these streets worked but it was clear that we had been boxed in, there was no way out. The violence, if you weren't in the front line, those who attempted a direct assault on the embassy, was spasmodic. Unconnected frames would have to be edited together, much later, to achieve meaning.

Tom was trapped in this demo because he was researching politics for a film that would use the Irish Troubles as a backdrop. The producer, Michael Klinger, who was looking for a new project for Michael Reeves, suggested that they exploit the success of *Bonnie and Clyde* – an inspiration to Germany's Red Army Faction – by finding a suitable plot involving Thompson sub-machine guns and blood-spattered, slow-motion bank raids. Tom suggested Belfast or Dublin in the 1920s.

While we were penned in the gardens of Grosvenor Square, Tom told me a story about Paris. He'd heard it in Rome. This man, a scriptwriter fallen on hard times, decided to kill himself. But first he wanted to enjoy a great meal, premier cru, at a favourite neighbourhood restaurant. He chose his bottle, poured a glass, lit a cigarette. He opted for the steak, the biggest they could provide. This was, he told the *patron*, a special occasion.

'Another film, perhaps? For the Americans?'

'Much better than that. Believe me.'

'My congratulations.'

Prime beef overspilled the white of the plate. The *patron*, satisfied, went back behind the bar: polite conversation with the standing drinkers. The suicide took up the steak, slippery with butter and garlic and, gagging, crammed it down his throat – until the passage of breath was stopped. Tom didn't say if the writer went blue or if he choked on his own vomit.

We had our disagreements about film, but the major area of competition in that De Beauvoir Road house was sickness. Strategic malfunctions. Freak-outs. With mild hay fever brought on by a day's walk to Waltham Abbey, I was the loser: nothing interesting to report by way of symptoms, no doctor's surgery visited in years. Tom did headaches, stomach cramps, career-doubt, money-doubt, cosmic-doubt: the existential horror of taking a decision on choice of socks. Could he risk the pleasure of an overland journey to Nepal? Or would he prefer the ecstasy of denial (cash set aside for a greater expedition in some impossible-to-imagine future)?

Renchi had his fits to trump us both and a history of visions, epiphanies that might provoke his art. On the pine sideboard stood a savage, fold-out Bicknell triptych based on Godard's *Pierrot le fou*: a mash of teeth, eyes, hooked hands, smudged lettering. Taken back to West Cork a few years later, borrowed by an American friend, this strident cartoon was allowed to weather in an outhouse-byre: cracked, mulched, warped with damp. In front of the De

Beauvoir Road painting, on a straw mat, was a Bolex 16mm camera – presumably liberated, by me, from Waltham Forest Technical College.

In the scrapbook images of 1968, the young women are well presented, all of them. Alert, alive and of their period; a time when it was possible to manage style on little money. Bridget, with her long tumble of hair and vestigial skirts, brought villages to an awed paralysis, men and women, when she visited us in Gozo and wobbled across the island on a borrowed bicycle. Judith's hair, cut somewhere fancy, one of those places with two lower-case christian names, was a geometric fringe, reddish; an Anna Karina quote or approving acknowledgement of the actress Macha Méril from Godard's *Une femme mariée*. The eyelashes. The enigmatic flutter. But Judith might disappear under the bedclothes, while Renchi talked on, unconcerned, with the latest trawl of dinner-table vagrants. Bridget could faint on demand or tumble down the stairs. Anna, brought up in a hard school, managed her ailments; they were not to be discussed – up to the point of a complete breakdown when confronted by the feral energies of her first infant class. The way they jumped out of the window when she came into the room, or carried on with their mayhem, treating her as a temporary nuisance from another world.

Thinking back to the early days in Hackney schools, Judith recalled, with astonishment, how they had been allowed to take two little black boys, Albert and Canute, to the cinema to see a Morecambe and Wise romp, then home to the De Beauvoir Road madhouse for high tea.

The laurels for sickness drama went to Renchi, very soon after our arrival, when an agonizing attack, carpet-chewing pain, far beyond his commonplace petit mal seizures, had me rushing him around the corner to Kingsland Road's Metropolitan Hospital (now a secure nest of workshops, offices and funded hobbyists). Acute appendicitis, the knife. They gave me a black plastic bag to carry his clothes home.

'Sorry. That's all that's left,' I said to Judith, in a clunking reflex of ill-judged humour. She screamed and ran upstairs.

The small, tightly sprung, close-bearded nurse who presented me with the bag, I wouldn't forget. He was smoking a large spliff and was dressed in the nicotine-brown overall of a storeman. Dirty plimsolls without socks. And jeans that looked as if they'd been borrowed from a very slight woman. They were kept barely decent by premature-punk safety pins.

This character saw me trying to read the title of the book wedged into his pocket and he pulled it out. *The Function of the Orgasm* by Wilhelm Reich. A Panther Book in a light blue cover.

'Your mate should make it, cut and chuck,' the man said. 'Not one of mine. I do the stiffs. Down below. Come round any night. Ian. Ian Askead. We get plenty of fresh meat, especially weekends.'

Askead was one of those figures who turn up in the tabloids, arrested for impersonating a surgeon, carrying out intricate procedures, quite successfully, good kill rate, for five years. There were more London hospitals in those days; walk in, take your chance, quacks free to run their private kingdoms, body-snatchers on the loose, casual employment for urban terrorists. If he had possessed a business card, it would have read: The Accused.

He had a wolf's smile. 'The energy source of the neurosis,' he quoted from Reich, 'lies in the differential between accumulation and discharge of sexual energy.'

He liked the way I filmed Renchi's pain-pinched face. And then the night street from the high window.

'Come down to the morgue,' he said. 'For a cup of tea. I have a notion that you could channel the dead by way of long-exposure prints. Postmortem portraits absorb subject and photographer into a composite other. Or so I'd like you to prove.'

WASTE

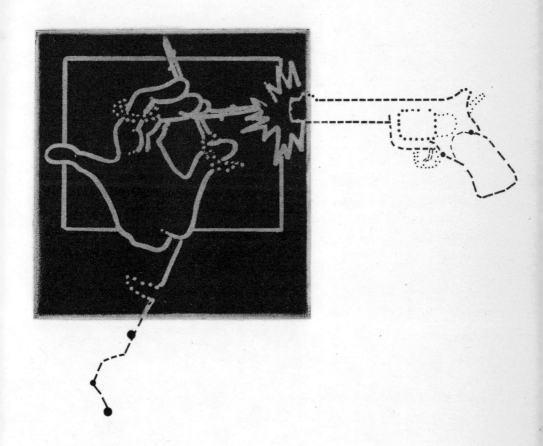

His landscape would *always* be Hackney or Dalston . . . he would *always*, on hot, passionate summer afternoons, be kicking his way through discarded cabbage-leaves in London markets.

– Roland Camberton, *Rain on the Pavements*

Rain on the Pavements (and Hair)

I kept returning to Roland Camberton and that provocative 1951 Hackney novel, *Rain on the Pavements*. Provocative but unopened. I re-read the lightly fictionalized account of a young Jewish writer's childhood and education, the discovery of another London beyond the memory-ground that would continue to haunt him. After making a collection of useful extracts, I put the book aside. It was now an object: to be touched, handled, as proof that such a work was possible. Autobiography. Humour. Topography. Resolution. Zany characters who never outstay their welcome.

John Minton's cover illustration is not quite Mare Street. He sketches a domed building that is neither the Central Library nor the old Hackney Empire. A yellow cloud leaks a shower that falls everywhere – except on the pavements; where children play with hoops and marchers make their non-specific protest. No point of vantage offers that precise view: not the roof of the Town Hall, nor St Augustine's Tower. Minton, a drinking companion of Camberton from Soho, has levitated over an idealized Hackney: six years before his suicide. And before the unexplained disappearance of Camberton. Who never published another book.

I took a paragraph from *Rain on the Pavements* as my statement of intent. The book was in code. Secret instructions laid down for future investigators. Camberton was like Akim Tamiroff in Godard's *Alphaville*: a heroic but embattled survivor from an earlier culture, hiding out, unshaven, his final report decaying in the orange box of some obscure street dealer. Stalls where urban poetry shares space with pulp and porn.

'It was necessary,' Camberton wrote, 'to know every alley, every cul-de-sac, every arch, every passageway; every school, every hospital, every church, every synagogue; every police station, every post office, every labour exchange, every lavatory; every curious shop name, every kids' gang, every hiding-place, every muttering old man or woman whose appearance alone was enough to terrify them. In fact everything; and having got to know everything, they had to hold this information firmly, to keep abreast of change, to locate the new positions of beggars, newsboys, hawkers, street shows, gypsies, political meetings.'

Tamiroff was an associate of Orson Welles; he has a wig-juggling cameo as border-town pimp with bootlace tie in *Touch of Evil*. A pre-Hackney alien, Akim could do Mexican, Turkish, Russian on demand. But this was a dead end. Who could imagine Welles on Camberton's Mare Street? Close the file. Having given up his memories to the researcher in *Confidential Report*, Tamiroff dies.

I would begin my quest, learning about every stone, every small business, by walking north up Kingsland Road and logging barber shops. Barbers were the best indicators of minuscule shifts in the culture. Immigrants could always beg or borrow a pair of scissors, a chair, a broom. A cut-throat razor. They could aspire to pomade, rubber goods for the weekend. A fancy mirror. A flag. An inscribed portrait of a nightclub singer. A landscape of the old country with mountains and sea.

Barber shops were clubs for the unclubbable, for deviants, professional gamblers, musicians for hire, hustlers and silkshirt mobsters who would not be accepted for membership anywhere else. The reinvented, the tellers of tales. A morning refuge for pimps, nightworkers who had to find new ways to fumigate dirty money. Barbers were dumb recipients of all the city's secrets. Once qualified, apprenticeship served under a harsh regime, they could move easily between countries. The only language required was the warm towel, the deft flick across the chair, mimed subservience. Barbering was a Yiddish trade. Old working men, like sheep, grew their hair for winter warmth and were shorn for summer. Barbers were unofficial ambassadors, running linoleum-floored embassies, making fellow villagers welcome: synagogues for the secular.

What I sensed on Kingsland Road was that barber shops represented singular attempts to make a living, own property, build up
funds with which to return home in glory. The betting shops that
shadowed them – and often took them over – belonged to companies, combines. The council, naturally, were more sympathetic
to slot-machines, horse-race monitors. Politics is for gamblers. The
illegitimate enterprises of a previous era become the new orthodoxy.

'A gambler's day goes pleasantly enough. He gets up late ... His
first call is at the barber's, where a long session is as much devoted
to business – discussing the afternoon's race-cards with the boys,
telling them how he got on last night and hearing their stories – as
to the pleasure of lying under hot towels.'

Life is truly golden when you don't have to do your own shaving.
You are one of the elect. Alexander Baron's 1963 Hackney novel,
The Lowlife, catches it beautifully, the society of the post-war barber
shop: the intimacy of strangers, professionally soothing chat (no
politics), perfumed air (coconut oil, pine tar). Click of the scissors.
Peer-group banter. An improved self-portrait emerging from the
mirror above the washbasin. A confirmation of status.

In working-class districts of Hackney, like Shacklewell Lane,
regulars had their own numbered shaving mugs. Lew Lessen, the
man in the blue overall, served a long apprenticeship with punishing
hours, 8 a.m. to 8 p.m. – before he was let loose on paying
customers. He practised shaving by lathering a beer bottle and
working the razor until there was no clink. Shaving came cheaper
than a trim, but was often a harder task. On Friday nights and
Saturday mornings, labourers brought in their sandpaper chins,
their barbed-wire stubble, for the full treatment. Good barbers, as
a mark of respect, were balder than their clients.

If you had time to put in two hours at the hairdresser, you were
in the life. You advertised your non-labouring status: as gambler,
gigolo, showbiz hoofer, promoter of rackety schemes. The Look
was hard-edged, Italianate: Ray Danton, George Raft. Aerodynamic

barnet, close-fitting suit. It aped America, Chicago massacres in stylish swivel chairs. The rogues' gallery of male models exhibited in barber-shop windows didn't change for generations.

I lived in Hackney for twenty-five years before I had my first paid-for haircut – by then, it was too late; the gesture was elegiac. Saint's Barbers in Cambridge Heath Road was Greek Cypriot, efficient, a little melancholy. Slow chat if you insist on it. Another customer, Tony Lambrianou, was horrified by a bookdealer's skinhead crop. Such barbarism is associated, in folk memory, with military buzzcuts, electric-chair rehearsals, mortuary make-overs.

When I set out to explore the local shift from old Jewish to Turkish, Turkish Cypriot, West Indian, African, Vietnamese, I couldn't reach the first shop on my list. Middleton Road was closed with blue-and-white ribbons. A hand-drawn cardboard rectangle announced: BARBER SHOP. This was an active black enterprise, operating in the gap between cultivated privacy and the twitch of justified paranoia. The scene would very soon be decorated by one of those bright tin panels that act as advertisements for crime: FIREARMS INCIDENT. A car. A gun. A barber shop. The synopsis for a straight-to-video movie.

Kingsland Road barber shops in-fill the gaps between fast-food joints, upstairs solicitors specializing in debt or deportation resistance, internet cafés and nail parlours that double as money-transfer operations. Narrow Turkish outfits combine a busy card school with occasional interruptions of male hairdressing. Avant Garde is aspirational, grey lettering on black – but Aladin is less intimidating. I get a decent trim for £7. All done in less than ten minutes. The barber has been in business for fifteen years and like so many in the game he lives outside the borough. I'm the only paying customer.

'A bad road, this one,' he says, 'Tottenham to Shoreditch. Always trouble.'

Fellow countrymen drift in and out, ignoring me, nodding to the barber, exchanging a few remarks.

Darwood Grace, a Hackney-born-and-bred actor and rap poet, when I question him about the shops where I'm never going to be welcome, refutes the notion that barbers are in any way connected with drugs. 'They do so well, they don't need it.'

Africans favour Faze 2, the Ghanaian 'coiffeur' on the west side of Kingsland Road. West Indians use the cluster of shops on the east side, near Dalston Junction. There is always one star cutter. It used to be Ike at Hibiscus. Celebrities look in, the boxer Audley Harrison was a regular. Ordinary customers might have to wait, uncomplaining, for two or three hours. Barbers rent their chairs. They are performers with a following from all over town. The atmosphere is sociable, gossipy. There is always music. The Turkish shops prefer large television sets, often two of them: piped serials from the home country with muted analgesic dross for locals.

Darwood goes to Tony, next to the Chinese takeaway. He's into short-back-and-sides, but *measured*, millimetre accurate. Young black men never shave at home. They're customized with clippers, not razor. The Look is subject to constant revision. White youths, shifting allegiance, might try Pamukkale on Balls Pond Road. They order by numbers: 'Six on top, 2 at the sides.' Zero being skin, pure. Barbers are both mechanics and artists. Ike, so Darwood recalls, won a hairdressing competition by carving a portrait of Malcolm X into the back of the model's head, twinned with a map of Africa.

I could drift on, north, beyond Ridley Road Market: mosques, Turkish restaurants, grander hairdressers with names like Golden Scissors and Pasha's Barbers; bigger televisions, faux-marble basins. I pause at a window that looks, superficially, like one of those exhibitions of fancy boys. But the temperature has altered and the hair is all wrong: unshaped, natural. These are Kurdish freedom fighters, the war dead. From the war that never ends.

'Young people,' Darwood tells me, 'are not interested in politics. Muslims, white: they don't want to know. Hair is more important.'

This Kurdish shop, the political window, is a step too far; the end of my barber-shop promenade and the beginning of something else. Less strolling, more staring.

Patrick Rain, our school-keeper, had a pristine leisure outfit for every hour of the day. He rose early, around 4.30 a.m., and missed nothing. I was never quite sure if his earpiece was a hearing aid or a link to some secret-police facility. He was the accepted authority on murders in the night, drug arrests, body bags, turf wars. He reckoned – 'Iain, I can tell you this much' – that the barber shop on Middleton Road was owned by a Nigerian woman and that it divided into separate salons for men and women. The shooting occurred in the male part of the enterprise. I noticed that after the handwritten card vanished from the window, the business was retitled. The first 'F' was in a different font, it disappeared, leaving you with a concern called Lawless Finish.

'Si-reens,' Patrick said. 'All night long. Si-reens and helicopters. It's not worth going to bed.'

It was impossible to photograph the windows of Kingsland Road barber shops. I tried, at all hours, but never managed to escape the lurkers and loiterers, hoodies with phones clamped to their chins like electric razors. Loud whisperers on pavement bicycles. The ones who patrol the newsagent, spotting scratchcard winners, undercutting cigarette prices with contraband bundles.

Barbers in doorways. Cameras alert them, offend them. Cameras gather evidence. They disturb the climate of managed paranoia. They stop time: that great river in which nothing is more significant than anything else. Single images are pinned to the wall of the incident room in the Stoke Newington police station. Single images, arranged and rearranged, create a narrative, solicit a conclusion: guilty.

From a safe distance – it was getting dark – I risked a shot of the barber shop where the shooting had taken place. The flash gave me away. Like a flare over no man's land. Photographing yellow-and-blue tin notices is easy. Text doesn't interest the custodians of property. My murder album was growing.

ON WED 29TH NOV 06 AT ABOUT 2.45PM A FIREARMS INCIDENT
TOOK PLACE IN MIDDLETON ROAD NEAR TO THE JUNCTION
WITH KINGSLAND ROAD. DID YOU SEE OR HEAR ANYTHING?
PLEASE CALL US.

What did I see? Blue-and-white ribbon. Building work on a bridge
that once took a railway down to Liverpool Street, then didn't,
and will again: a Transport for London promise. A goad to developers stretching the City beyond Shoreditch, shoehorning
developments into unlikely lacunae, closing roads. I see scaffolding,
boarded-up shops, enterprises that have run out of enterprise. I
see street muggers, relatively harmless, and corporate muggers
who will gut, fillet and repackage the entire strip of the Great
North Road. I see the pole with its camera-eye turning Hackney
into a real-time movie. Bleeding the excitement out of crime.

They pile into a car, four-handed, and cut across my path, with
a screech of brakes, before I've reached Mayfield Road and the
turn into Albion Square. Loose leather coats with deep pockets.
'What you doing, man?'

I've been through dozens of these routines with City snatch
squads and security vigilantes on edge-land estates, but never with
a mob of militant barbers. I offer the usual flannel; the consequences, if I fail to convince them, might be extreme. I have a
doctorate in affable vagueness. A crazy old coot guilty of possessing
something as antiquated as a 35mm analogue camera. A version,
then, of the truth: 'I'm interested in shopfronts.'

In Broadway Market, on a stall specializing in expensive books by
photographers, I came across *Hackney Wick*, a portfolio by Stephen
Gill. There were numerous points of interest: the book was self-
published, independent in spirit, quirkily topographical and it
provided an excellent representation of something that was no
longer there. Gill had picked up a Coronet camera for 50p at the
Hackney Wick boot fair, and he used it, soft at the edges, to
celebrate the last rites of the Sunday market that took place at the

former dog track. But, most provoking of all, these were the photographs I would have taken if I had Gill's expertise, his touch, his determination to be there, day after day: until the pile of random images made sense. By becoming a book, a collection.

We made contact. I visited Gill's Bethnal Green studio and admired his collection of books by other photographers, his respect for memory and archive. Beyond the window, I could see the trains that Gill would jump on, at whim, for estuarine excursions, potential projects, records of sleepers, paperback readers, or those who simply acted the part by staring out at damp fields.

Stephen agreed to be interviewed for my Hackney book. He had grown up in Bristol and had come to London to work, as a dark-room assistant, telephone answerer, courier of prints in taxis, at the prestigious Magnum Agency. Now he lived in Darnley Road, off Mare Street, and he cycled out, most mornings, along the River Lea and around the future Olympic Park. He liked my notion of walking a triangle – Kingsland Road, Mare Street, Hackney Road – making shots of barber shops. It suited his conceptual method of expressing his love for the borough. But he had serious reservations about my unspoken suggestion that barbers could in any way be connected with illegal activity.

'A bad stereotype,' he said.

There shouldn't be any difficulty, Gill insisted, about ingratiating himself with the barbers, to the point where they would allow him to make a promotional record of their premises.

'I would be slightly worried,' Stephen emailed me, 'if your text, based on our walk, did suggest that some barbers are linked to drug dealing, as I simply don't think it is possible to say any more what kind of business is running from drug money. Many are just trying to keep their heads above the water. Hackney gets so much stick and of course we should present the truth as we see it, but I would also love to help Hackney get back on its feet. I am sure many businesses do have some goings on with drugs, but one is just as likely to find carpet sellers, TV repair, pizza delivery, newsagents etc who have dodgy things going on. I felt I should just mention my feelings on those issues really as I so often hear people say things like "oh look at that guy in his nice car, he must be a pimp or drug dealer" and it annoys me so much.'

Our walk begins with corrugated-roller security screens. There are no windows on view. Black barbers don't open before midday. Gill, without bicycle, is removed by a few degrees from his natural rhythm. A soft-spoken, sharp-eyed man. But no easy touch. He has managed his career very successfully, by working long hours and sticking with assignments of his own devising. *Hackney Wick*, so he tells me, is to be found on eBay at £400. There is a new project afoot that will keep a record of the Lower Lea Valley, up to the moment when the skeleton of the first Olympic building appears. *Archaeology in Reverse*, he calls it. 'You learn to think in images. And in the strategic arrangement of images. Language is imprecise. It muddies the water.'

Low on the fence at the corner of Middleton Road, Stephen notices a remnant of the blue-and-white incident tape – which I photograph and he spurns. He might do something, I suggest, with the collection of metal shutters: in silver, blue, perforated like Aertex. Barbers and nail boutiques: these are nocturnal operations.

When Gill returned to make contact with the shop owners, it wasn't entirely the smooth passage he anticipated. I chatted to Mr Aladin, after the photographer's visit, and he laughed. 'No way, no way.' The privacy of the card-players in the back room was inviolate. The barbers have all the portraits they need: catalogue models who look like dummies dressed with human hair, lard sculptures. Glamour portfolios play against the grid of Kurdish martyrs in the shop window, further up Kingsland Road: men with scarlet head-bands and yellow stars, moustaches, beards. The men frown, the women smile: just faintly, a reflex curl of the lip contradicted by dark-rimmed eyes. KAHRAMANLAR OLMEZ HALK HALK YENILMEZ! STOP THE DEATHS.

Conversation, yes, the barbers do conversation. Rubber plants. Motorbikes inside the shop. Eagles for Istanbul football teams. But leave the camera at home, please. Stephen sniffles, it is the season of pollen allergies. He leads me into fascinating caverns at Dalston Junction where they sell wigs, hair-straightening chemicals, extensions, gels. So much life, so much competition: the photographer is welcome in shops that are storerooms.

There are no surprises after the rebranded Gillett Square, a major council enterprise: East Berlin with official art and block-buildings that take their look from customized Portakabins. Alongside the terracotta slab of the Dalston Culture House you will find a series of slate-grey booths that should be selling tickets to concerts by tribute bands. One of them does hair: CHICAGO BARBERS (WE SELL ITALIAN SHOES, PERFUMES & SUITS). ADULTS £6, CHILDREN £4. Not one solitary person, dog walker, blue-bag vagrant, passes through this square. The architecture is against it, Kingsland Road takes the flow, the buzz. Strategic cameras transmit an empty set into a covert editing suite where low-paid voyeurs lose their days (and nights) watching nothing happen, very slowly. Having purged the square of its natural clients, the street drinkers, the sponsors are left with a loud absence that can be recorded in real-time but not photographed. A 'Mediterranean-style square with a drinking ban' is the boast on promotional sheets pushed through our letter boxes. An absurdity that will make no sense until global warming rolls a warm sea down the course of the old Hackney Brook.

The following weekend, without my interference, Gill repeats our walk. He gets no further, coming north from Shoreditch, than the Whiston Road turn, where he encounters a family party. Dressed in dark clothes. Two sets of grandparents, he reports. With grieving parents, young children. About twelve persons carrying flowers. Which they weave through a fence, before attaching a number of cards and drawings. And they are wailing. Yes, *wailing*.

There is no question of lifting his camera, though Gill does have a fancy for covering funerals. The formal qualities appeal to him. The rituals. The stoic comedy of dispersal. This event is not a funeral, it is a return to the scene of a very recent death.

A young man of seventeen, on his bicycle, going left at the lights, was crushed under the high wheels of a preoccupied heavy-goods vehicle with no inkling of his existence. He was extinguished in an instant. For a few weeks the drama will be memorialized by a curtain of wilting, drooping flowers. The bones of the story can be found, inscribed on blue-and-yellow tin. With a request for further information. Cellophane chokes the trapped flower heads: the noise of colour against the momentum of the busy road. A deadly double act has been introduced into the borough: eco-inspired cyclists and relentless convoys of lorries, heading east, to service the deadlines of the Olympic Park. They don't see each other. They don't belong in the same dream.

Middleton Road

Middleton Road wasn't always Middleton Road; the eastern segment, between Queensbridge Road and London Fields, was once Albert Road. It's broader than Albion Drive, the parallel southern neighbour, and better served: Hackney councillors have taken up residence. The western strip, a humped rat run between Queensbridge Road and Kingsland Road, remains something of a front line: a random demographic sample trapped between the fiercely perpetuated oasis of Albion Square and the flagship disaster of the Holly Street Estate. If there is a fashionable way of getting urban planning wrong, Holly Street has tried it: tight Victorian terraces demolished for tower blocks (leaking, crumbling, populated by jumpers), which were themselves demolished to make way for low-level H-blocks: based, presumably, on HM Prison Maze at Long Kesh. Holding camps for social engineering. And visited, so he boasts, by the preacher/politician Tony Blair, at the start of a glittering career of photo opportunities. Those early Hackney days are unrecorded, but Tony has been back many times since, to large it on the front page of the *Hackney Gazette*.

A favourite Blair location is 'The Building Exploratory', a model village on an upper floor of the Queensbridge Primary School. Photographed here – like Lady Thatcher with the maquette of Canary Wharf – Blair rises over a dwarf principality: a blue-suited King Kong, close-shaved, Max Factored. A sweat-slicked moon-face with rictal grin pressed against the tiny windows of a faithfully reproduced miniature of one of the detonated Holly Street towers. They have recordings made by the expelled tenants and toy television sets that flicker in shadowy interiors. There are maps memorializing addresses where bombs fell in the 1940s. Fragments of brick and tile demonstrate succeeding geological eras. Hackney as primal swamp: a huddle of huts beside a broad river. And Hackney the asylum from the city's pestilence, the original garden suburb.

At night, orange lights in these knee-high tower blocks do not go out and the voices of inhabitants are still heard. I think we are all in there, our ghost skins, our disembodied memories. There are even rumours that neighbours no longer seen on the street have taken up residence in the second life of the model Hackney. In troubled sleep, the small protection of this village contained within a secure school building infects our dreams. We are the robotic residue of dramas enacted by eidolons and spectral selves.

Trapped inside my house in a reproduction Albion Drive, I witnessed the latest procession of dignitaries, flag-bedecked mayoral limousines, come to pay homage to this prime facility, London as a teaching aid. There were helicopters overhead and motorbike outriders for the prime minister: his flashing smile, his wave. The way he bounds up the stairs, promoting his late-youthful energy. Fit for purpose. Sprinting down corridors where pupils are forbidden to run.

Forgotten friends from our early days tell their tales, make their complaints heard from within the plywood depths of a shrunken Middleton Road. The special-needs teacher assaulted with a pig's head who spent the next thirty years, buried in legal documents, fighting her own case for compensation. And her husband, the council building foreman, asked to smash up new kitchen equipment, who stumbled on a web of scams, pay-offs, kickbacks – and was offered the choice of immediate retirement on health grounds, a full pension. Or something worse. That which can be imagined is what happens.

I witnessed an altercation between a policeman and a policewoman, safe in their car, and a black youth, walking down the middle of Albion Drive. How it escalated, this battle for respect. The apology the youth demanded for what he perceived as racial abuse.

'Why you cuss me, man?'

The way the police defend their status, as motorists, right up to the point where they are forced to exit the vehicle: physical confrontation, rolling on the ground. Cuffs, restraint. No winners, much hurt.

'I know street law, man. I want to know *your* law. I want to see the book of conduct.'

It floods back. 30 November 1984: the incident when armed robbers tried to hold up the school payroll van. A bungled, sold-out operation. The sorry villains were surrounded, unmanned, handled with extreme prejudice. Whatever daylight they possessed was stomped out of them as they lay, trussed like chickens, on the pavement. When it was over, the plainclothesmen leant against macho motors, chatting and smoking, while they waited for the meat van to remove the living bodies.

I took a few snapshots, made a note for the files. And went back to work, preparing that week's trawl of used books for market. I had a mint copy in dustwrapper, from Kingsland Waste, of *Elephant and Castle*, a London novel by R. C. Hutchinson. But not much hope of selling it. Unless I could find an angle, a way of talking it up. To find the extraordinary in the apparently mundane, that's the gimmick.

After appearing in the *Hackney Gazette*, interviewed in Abney Park Cemetery, poking about, trying unsuccessfully to locate the grave of Edward Calvert (engraver, disciple of William Blake), I received a number of curious communications. One of them, from Ann Jameson, I followed up: immediately. Ann lived in Middleton Road, opposite the newly revised mustard-brick, neo-suburban Holly Street Estate. Pretty much at the spot where the car of angry barbers confronted me, patting their pockets.

Ann wanted to offer testament to her passage through the borough (and life). I was the wrong Iain. She confused me, as I soon discovered, with the man Jonathan Meades described as 'the master topographer'. Ian Nairn. Who was long dead. But in

Hackney that's no disqualification. Walking the perimeter, the dead are always with us, interrupting our meditation, making the invisible audible. Those medical men, Dr Benjamin Clarke and Dr William Robinson, local nineteenth-century historians, were often at my shoulder: especially in Abney Park. Stoke Newington was a bone of contention. Was it part of Hackney? Clarke, a generous man, allowed it a coda in his book, an extra chapter to demonstrate colonization by the land-greed of the borough. He needed the old burial ground as a source of anecdotes. He recalled, for example, the Turkey merchant and governor of the Bank of England, Mr Cook, who died in a Stoke Newington mansion in 1752.

'And by his will ordered that his body should be carried to Morden College; that there it was to be taken out of the coffin, wrapped round with a winding sheet after Eastern fashion, and buried, standing upright in the earth; and the coffin was to be laid by for the use of the first pensioner who might need it.'

What Meades prized in Nairn was 'the feeling of communicable joy at being *employed and paid* to indulge passionate curiosity'. If I was the shadow of Nairn to whom Ann Jameson could make her statement, I was happy to play the part: take tea, sit on the lawn, listen. Her softly spoken voice, rushing then hesitating, giving way to abrupt laughter, weaves through my tape beneath the usual auditory thatch of planes, ambulances, sirens, motorbikes, horns.

The major hook was that Ann Jameson happened to be the daughter of R. C. Hutchinson. A reforgotten London author – whose work I had sold but never read.

Now I'm having a very happy section of my life, because for the first time I'm not only on my own but I've got heaps of money and heaps of time. And I don't have to move or do any of the things that widows have to do. I feel extremely lucky.

I bought the house, with my husband, Don, in '85 and we had it all done up. It was a complete mess, multi-occupied, all the doors smashed. We made the move in November '86. It was just twenty years ago.

I could hardly persuade Don to move here at all. I was moving from a little almshouse, one of the Trinity Green Almshouses in Mile End Road. I'd got a 1695 house. I'd been living there for a few years before we moved to Hackney.

Don had another marriage and lived in posh Essex, Buckhurst Hill. I had to buy this house when he was very ill. I took a chance. I was in a position to do it. Another stroke of luck: when I first went to Trinity Green, I was paying £2 and 10 shillings in old money, as a tenant of the LCC. Then the right to buy came in – 1980 – and I bought for £10,000. The value of my property went up 600 per cent. The rise wouldn't have done me any good if I had to go on living there – as my old neighbour still does.

Not only did Don have his property, I had mine. We had plenty of money to make good this place. We bought it for £62,000. We spent £40,000 refurbishing it. The only bathroom was down in the basement and was used by all the flats.

Holly Street has changed to an amazing degree. I thought they had knocked down all the Victorian houses like this one. I thought they'd been bombed. I was horrified when I found out they'd actually been demolished in order to make these horrible blocks. My brother witnessed them being built or assembled. We did have a couple of burglaries from the Holly Street flats. They'd seen us going out to the car on a Saturday morning. One of them broke down the front door and came in. The police didn't dare to enter Holly Street. That was the end of it.

But Hackney has been wonderful too. Don, instead of calling it the OSP, Other Sodding Place, called it home at last. He couldn't get over the area. He grew up in East Ham. They were taught to think how awful Hackney was.

I love the recent changes. It's very difficult to separate them from my growing confidence, the good luck I've been having. There's been a wonderful change in neighbours. When I first came here, there were three generations living in this house. The middle generation had been born here. They had two adolescent children and a horrid little dog that never got used to us. It stood on its lean-to kennel, yelping, day and night. They moved out eventually and Jack and Gary came. Gary was a builder, he gave us a side wall to our garage. And a roof. We didn't like him particularly as a neighbour. He was very, very odd. He used to have odd ways of celebrating the girls who came to stay with him. He'd sit on his Harley-Davidson bike indoors. He never used it outside. What in fact he used it for, well . . . Ha! We heard, through the wall, everything that went on. The bike, the girls. He put in a lot of lovely German cooking equipment, but never cooked. He would go off to his mother's. Not a happy man really.

When my husband was in hospital for many weeks, before he died, the doctor said, 'Why don't you bring him home? He's only having palliative care.' This was support for something I wouldn't have had the courage to undertake on my own. It meant having a feeding pump, carers coming in. It was much better to have Don at home. Much better than going to see him in the morgue at the hospital, the Homerton.

We had a memorial service in the church, All Saints, just behind where you live. I never set foot in it before. They've got a very friendly vicar, Rose. An awful lot of people knew Don. Far more than I realized. He'd been going around on his electric buggy. He did the shopping for me. Although profoundly deaf, he had relationships with everybody – which I hadn't managed to do. All these people came up, after the service, to say he was a very good friend. We had a hundred people.

Another friend of mine went back to All Saints the other day, for its 150th anniversary. She said there were only blacks.

I'm very rational now. I'm not a Christian at all. I think religion does an awful lot of harm. But my brother Jeremy is a retired vicar. His longest time was in Hackney, at St John the Baptist in Hoxton. They moved into the vicarage, having lived in the south part of Mortimer Road. He's too saintly, my brother. He followed my mother. We were brought up to be very Christian. Going to church every single Sunday. And not only that, but having to teach at Sunday school. It was unspoken devotion.

We didn't see much of my father. Morning and evening, he worked. It took him about three years to write each book. You can come up and see them if you like. Very well crafted, just crafted, that's it. He was interested in style. We have got his seventeen-year-old's schoolboy's diary – which shows that he did have doubts. When he married my mother, Margaret, he didn't dare to be other than very, very devoted. I think he *would have been a better author if he hadn't had all his characters becoming so unnaturally good.*

He gets his background, even for a London novel like Elephant and Castle, from a book. He didn't wander round the streets. He was completely the opposite of you. Nearly all his books are set abroad, it was only Elephant and Castle that is really in England. And it didn't do so well. He got the Daily Telegraph prize for the book he wrote before the war.

It's just chance that I have any connections with London. When I was looking for accommodation, as a single girl, the Mile End Road almshouses happened to become available to people other than social workers. I found out about this and managed to get one on Trinity Green. Otherwise I had no connection with the East End. It does annoy me when journalists talk about Hackney in the national papers and they say that it is in the East End. I wish we had kept to the NE postcode. Our postcode should be NE, North London.

I do use Kingsland Waste Market. I was very surprised by one of the market women. She said, 'Aren't you the one who used to go round with the old man on the scooter?' I liked talking to her. One of the things Don left behind – he was very parsimonious about a lot of things, but not paper, stationery – was about thirty rolls of sticky brown tape. I thought I would give it to the market girl, the first stall I found selling such things. So I came home, got the tapes and took them back to her. She started talking about her difficulty in getting married. I suggested she try the internet. Haha!

I know Norman of course. His stall is a treasure trove. We had him take away some things we'd had for years. I got him to take away Don's latest chair. It was very comfortable, but it wasn't what I like. The authorities take all the wrong decisions over the market – but then you can't expect people who want to be local councillors to be all that bright, can you? I don't really understand why we have local government at all. There are so many different areas within each borough anyway.

The best houses in Albion Square would go for a million now. I feel very, very lucky that we're not right in that space. I wouldn't like to see those people every time I come out. I'd very much rather be a bit outside. I've been a real outsider all my life. You've been an outsider too. I've never seen you at the Square party. I only realized you lived so close at hand when I saw you in the Hackney Gazette.

One of the Albion Square ladies was very supportive at the time of Don's memorial service. I decided to take her to Dalston for lunch, the Shanghai. She'd never been in Dalston before. She's very frightened of the area. She saw my bag was slung a bit carelessly over the back of my chair. She said, 'Be careful with your bag.' She was scared, very scared.

We went inside. Ann Jameson had set herself a task more formidable than my Hackney researches, she was archiving family histories from untold mounds of hard evidence: letters, photographs, internet trawls, her father's books and papers.

She led me upstairs to a workroom. It was organized around her files, the computer. She was a professional when it came to downloading clues. Almost all Hutchinson's novels, in multiple editions, with and without wrappers, had been retrieved from Kingsland Waste Market, from church jumble sales and charity shops. As I blundered around, recording and transcribing Hackney, so Ann Jameson gathered up yellowing memorials to her father.

I was born in Norwich, three of us were born in Norwich, because my father didn't feel he could rely on his writing at the beginning. He got a job with Colman's Mustard. He was an advertising manager. They were recruiting Oxford graduates. We had to stay in Norwich until 1935. Then we moved to Birdlip in Gloucestershire. A house that happened to be going, Kingsholm Cottage.

We were always different somehow. We didn't have neighbours. Then Ray – I call my father 'Ray' now – had to take us to school. He wrote in the Cheltenham library because he had to bring my brother Jeremy home at midday. I came home in the afternoon. My father didn't find that easy.

My mother was very shy, she wanted her family to herself. They were different personalities. They were an Oxford couple. My mother didn't have many friends. In 1938 we moved to Hampshire. My mother wanted Ray to herself. She would cry when she didn't get a letter from him, whenever they were separated. And she would tell him about the crying and the cause of it.

I did determine not to use the word 'mad' when I talked to you, because I've just been reading a book about Virginia Woolf and how she wasn't really mad.

I sometimes wandered into the Holly Street Estate. My husband never would! I liked the adventure, finding new ways through into Dalston Lane. It's so wonderful on my bicycle. I scoot up there, down the road that runs into the back of the Sainsbury's complex. I've got a bike that takes an awful lot in the basket.

Before I leave, Ann presents me with an American first edition of *Elephant and Castle: A Reconstruction*. I won't sell it. The book is far too wrecked for that, on the wrong side of a 'reading' copy. Spine flapping, Boots Lending Library label partly removed. But I will read it, one day, a complex epic (Hutchinson was in thrall to Proust) of 658 pages. A length no reputable publisher would now countenance for a literary novel.

The status of Hutchinson's text hovers between document and fiction. There are real and contrived letters, walk-on cameos by the author. A novel of substance, unpopular with reviewers in its own day, *Elephant and Castle* has been banished to charity shops. And to Ann Jameson's narrow Middleton Road studio. A duplicate city reinvented in a Cheltenham library.

'Events trail shadows larger than themselves,' I read. 'Much that people afterwards said about those days came from springs of imagination almost free from the pollution of fact.'

Kingsland Waste

The Waste lives down to its name, it's a market of markets; intensely local and of diminishing interest to outsiders, fetishized collectors. In the 90s (John Major not Aubrey Beardsley), I would sometimes run into Rachel Whiteread, who lived just beyond the west end of Albion Square, alongside the Duke of Wellington pub. Rising with Hackney, she was soon to outgrow it, moving south to a reconditioned synagogue on the border of Bethnal Green and Spitalfields. Dressed down, bibbed and booted, Rachel would be inspecting, without the predatory eye of the bargain hunter, goods spread across a ramshackle improvisation of stalls and boxes by Norman Palmer. Everyone knew and respected Norman: as the last of the dealers who presented accidents of plunder on a weekly basis. A managed illusion of novelty kept his punters hot. He had an eye for oddities and his prices were always reasonable. In the dirt, near the stall, were a series of storage trays and tea chests, Whiteread auditions, stacked with books that had to be lifted out, item by item: there was no easy way. The market floor became a swamp of rejected volumes. At the end of the day's trading, ahead of the council carts, scavengers advanced, raking over spurned libraries, slippery dunes of paper: refuse is a commodity that is never refused.

Rachel's browsing, her Saturday-morning market walk, was a standard East End reflex for off-duty artists: drift as a stimulus to future projects. Goods were scanned with peripheral vision. The meandering stroll offered relief from studio discipline, the strain of explaining and promoting work that was instinctive and arbitrary. The Kingsland Waste Market was a private view, open to all, a Royal Academy Summer Show of installations, photoworks, wrecked medicine cabinets. It combined the functions of sponsored exhibition and gift shop. There were traditional elements (racks of jeans, tools, budget cosmetics, CDs, DVDs, batteries, sticky tape) and also late-surrealist innovations. A stuffed goat mounted on a lawnmower. A diver's helmet filled with goldfish. A tray of keys gouged from an ancient typewriter. Whiteread was happy to avoid anything that might inspire her art. She was following a routine, a sanctioned route: off duty, in her place. Difficulty was the motif, storms raged around her current commission, the Holocaust Memorial for the Judenplatz in Vienna. A frosty casting of reversed books, a blind library of unwritten texts.

In earlier times, late 1960s, when the Waste heaved and seethed with knock-offs, electrical parts, rusty spanners, the apprentice sculptor Brian Catling made his stately progress, towering over Cockney aboriginals, beachcombing for objects to be pouched against future constructions: machines that were also sets, lethal gifts for godchildren and for the children of patrons who kept him fed. The market was a stream of cargo cult goods in which Catling knew just how to wade.

Kingsland Waste had been long established on these wide pavements; by the 1970s, it was running at more than a hundred stalls, with attendant parasites, fly-pitchers, watch-flashers, inside-the-jacket men with necklaces, gold coins, parrots and pornography. The kind of merchandise we lost soon after our arrival in Albion Drive. A street fund to which, through our first two or three burglaries, we were involuntary contributors. A policeman, sniffing around after the original break-in, muttered sympathetically that it was 'terrible, terrible, absolutely shocking' to see a room left in that state. Not realizing nothing had been touched, this was how I worked. Up to the elbows in books, papers, paints, maps, stones.

When I fished out a bag of unlabelled tapes from one of Norman Palmer's boxes, I found a recording of Basil Bunting reading a selection from the *Cantos* of Ezra Pound and some Wordsworth. A haunting conjunction, the living poet ventriloquized to great effect by the dead. The only way I could actually play the tape – and

I did constantly, wherever I went – was in the car. All my other machines were wrecked or sitting on the pavements of Hackney waiting for a feeble-minded cash buyer. Two weeks into my possession, Bunting was gone. Quarter-light window smashed, Friday-night toll: no car radio to be had, bag of tapes snatched. To find their way back, I assume, to the mounds from which they came. Look on the episode as cultural rental. Premature recycling. But if you should encounter this Bunting cassette on your travels, let me know. I'm in the market.

The Waste begins just beyond the ancient Toll Booth or barrier, that precursor of Ken Livingstone's congestion charge. The Fox pub, a Truman's house, was rebuilt in 1790, at the front of a much older alehouse of the same name. It serviced thirsty drovers arriving in town and travellers setting themselves up for the road out. Rough ground, owned by the Rector of Dalston as part of his glebe, evolved into an open space for political meetings and general trade. Licensed by the present Hackney Council, the market is seen as an encumbrance to the new fundamentalism: discrimination against rubbish, a coloured plastic bin for every form of household waste. *Waste* has become a prohibited term. The original market, left to its own devices, was a self-sustaining ecological system. If anyone would give an object a home, for cash, that item had value – if not, it disappeared into the general mound, the urban moraine, to be picked over at no fee. And afterwards the whole mess was swallowed up by contractors on overtime.

I was struck, at the very end of my dealing days, by the confidence with which Balkan newcomers, dead-baby professionals (doped in the arms of surrogate mothers), invaded this Saturday-market strip. I had to learn how to take photographs from waist level, framing by instinct, no flash. Only the dull click to give you away. Peddlers of contraband cigarettes, dust tubes. Petty thieves: Norman Palmer abhorred them, the way they clustered and mobbed, swept the stalls in long skirts with deep pockets, their identifying features hidden by headscarves. The forests of surveillance cameras were not yet in place. By late afternoon, it was apocalyptic: the anti-ecology, the riposte to every form of correctness. Books flung on the ground. Burst sacks of clothes. Indestructible plastic toys. Smashed fruit. Burgers, chips. Empty video husks. Newspaper with nothing to wrap.

But Norman was always chipper, chatting to appreciative customers. Of late, pressure from the council annoyed him, absurdist rules: that he could trade only in certain pre-defined commodities. One of the other stallholders witnessed his van being craned away, hijacked, seized by the authorities. It was becoming difficult to find somewhere to park within miles of the market; dealers from other parts of town were falling away. End of an era, certainly. Norman agreed to give me an interview. He liked books of local history and, over the years, had supplied me with many odd and entertaining volumes.

29 August 2006. Norman Palmer lives on a hill, above reservoirs, in the Lea Valley. A road in which he can park his van: but already there are encroachments, the city is getting its revenge on the escapees of the 1960s and 1970s, new estates nudge the neat avenues and quiet cul-de-sacs of Chingford. The slopes on which the Kray Twins, Reg's sad wife, the famous mother, are all sleeping. Freighted with floral tributes. Anchored in wreaths.

There is a lush, well-watered garden and a villa of objects, glass cabinets, exotic birds. I feel the contrast with what I have left behind in Albion Drive: a house plunged into darkness, electrics shot, tallow and tar smells seeping from beneath the floorboards, seething clusters of black flies on the window panes of the sitting room. Scratching of swift feet in the eaves, creatures scampering over our heads, behind the walls. A family of foxes in residence beneath the garden shed. Squirrels kicking off the slates.

Norman has a fox too. Before we settle to our talk, he goes outside, crosses the road to leave meat for a shy red beast who emerges, right on cue, from another garden. The fox nods a brief acknowledgement and bloodies his sharp nose as he tears at his nightly tribute.

Returned indoors, I admire the collection of Chinese porcelain, the way the solid furniture and thick carpets baffle sound. Our recording is barely inconvenienced by the shrieking derision of the mynah birds and parrots. There is a carafe of claret and a heavy goblet. I'm so relaxed out here, in this other life, that I fail to activate the first side of the tape, during which Norman explains how he was made redundant by an oil company. He had a job cruising the edge-lands, Essex, Surrey, dormitory towns and newly occupied places, prospecting for petrol stations. A scout in the frontier sense. There was always time, promising site identified, to hit the antique shops. Now of course that occupation has gone into reverse, location hunters are deciding which petrol stations to close down. And the blight has struck the inner city: pre-development wastegrounds behind plywood fences.

With stock in hand, Norman began to trade south of the river in East Street Market – and then in Kingsland Waste. He has been on his Hackney pitch for twenty-five years; first as a regular, then as a casual. A permanent casual. The rental is £25 per stall. His colleague, Harry, takes five, rolls in at four-thirty in the morning and flogs clothes to dealers. The random stuff he spreads across the floor is hoovered up from assorted charities.

Norman has an established clientele: Dan Cruickshank is a regular, muttering enthusiastically, discoursing on this and that. There is a woman from Stoke Newington who writes about dogs. Acquisitive teachers mark up the week's effort. Hoarders, obsessives, ragged fanatics. The Waste stall, Norman reckons, is an unlicensed academy.

He is assisted, now that his old mum has stepped down, by the redoubtable and electively mute Ralph: who accepts cashmoney and does the lifting and dragging. But he knows his stuff, this man, he started in Cheshire Street, with his brother, buying German-language primers, so that he could collect Second War memorabilia. Over the years, Ralph has amassed a valuable holding.

The problem with the Waste, Norman tells me, is that there is no collective voice, no spokesperson to argue their case.

I concentrate on pushing the right buttons. Now the story is told. How the dealing life continues, despite everything.

I do a lot of probate and quite often clear the houses.

I got my knowledge when I was doing the oil-company thing, with Chevron, Standard Oil of California. The sales director used to come out with me, regular, once a month, to see the plans I was working on, the prospects. We used to work until about twelve o'clock, lunchtime. Then he'd say, 'Norman, where are the antique shops?' Mainly Home Counties this was. He would buy clocks. When he went back to Dallas, he had six containers full of antique clocks. And most of those were bought out of his expenses. Whack!

I had an interest in Chinese porcelain at the time. It has become prohibitively expensive now. Going round on behalf of the oil company, I kept my eyes open. When I was eventually made redundant by Chevron, I thought: 'Well, all right, I know what I'll do.'

We've got four children. With four children it's difficult to live. My wife, June, used to go to jumble sales. There was always an interest in what you could pick up.

I was born in Mildmay Road, down from Ridley Road. As a kid I used to go to the Waste. A fantastic area in which to grow up. Mosley preaching on the corner of Shacklewell Lane, outside the synagogue. He used to spout, regular as clockwork, on Shacklewell Lane.

One of my friends at school, Monty Goldman, is always trying to become mayor of Hackney. Little Jewish feller. He'd come to school on a Monday with a black eye from fighting the blackshirts.

I went to school in Parmiter's, up in Bethnal Green. I used to live in Clapton, Stamford Hill. I really do know Hackney. It used to be a marvellous market, the Waste. You could buy anything there. Particularly if you were interested in tools, clocks, watches. Fantastic. There's still a tremendous interest in old tools. I have a couple of dealers who are seriously into antique tools.

I was too young to appreciate Hackney in the war period. I was evacuated to Bath and when that got bombed, we were brought back. My brother is six years older. He remembers how everybody was down the pawnshop. The dodging around, nicking stuff off fruit stalls. I was too young for that. My brother Ken often told tales of tricks and dodges.

Even these days a high percentage of goods are nicked from my stall every week. You've got an influx of people for whom thieving is second nature. They don't think anything of it. Take the Nigerians. On Saturday there was a huge Nigerian, he's got loads of gear in his arms and suddenly the stallholder is saying, 'Oy oy oy, you haven't paid for that.' He's taking absolutely no notice whatsoever. He loads up his car and drives off. Ha!

Then you get the Eastern European gypsies coming down. A woman with a plastic baby in her arms and this great stomach that looks like a pregnancy and is actually a cage with an empty space in it. The real arms of those women go way down here. Ha! I've had that as well.

At one time, this wholesaler was bringing stuff down, cut glass from Poland, cutlery sets, all cheap. He'd say, 'Have a go at these, Norman.' And he'd pile it up and say, 'I'll be back later.' He took away whatever hadn't been sold. But whole sets were vanishing! In front of your eyes. I couldn't understand it. They were disappearing up women's skirts, gypsies. I had to stop doing the sets. When it came to the weighing out, the man from Palmerston Road wasn't interested in where they'd gone. Unbelievable!

It was astonishing the authorities allowed those cigarette sellers to carry on. It was a huge racket. The gypsies were amazing characters. Their attitude was: 'I'm a crook – so what?' It didn't matter how obvious they were, they still managed to operate.

I don't know how a lot of the stalls in the Waste earn money. The gypsies were thieving off people who could least afford it. I think most of the street markets are hanging on by their fingernails. If they move off into boot sales, they're going to take even less money. They built up a very big market at the back of Walthamstow Town Hall. It was along similar lines to Hackney Wick.

With the advent of the council's interest in the market, things changed. Harry used to leave a load of stuff behind when he went home. But the council imposed a restriction. They said, 'If you leave stuff, you'll have a £75 fine.' They were claiming that the market was very, very expensive to run.

Harry still leaves stuff, nothing like he did. I still leave stuff. Most of what I leave is harmless or useful to the right person. At one time a couple of schools came down to take away the books.

It did dawn on the council that this was degrading for the area, scavengers crawling over mountains of rubbish. So they gave Harry an official warning.

It's amazing how he's made a go of it. I've never found anything worthwhile on his stalls. But he takes serious amounts of money. If you took Harry away from the market, you might as well close the place down. But is it worth saving? Unless they can solve access – which they can't – you'll never build the market up again. The people who are left, up the Waste or in Whitechapel, they're not earning a fantastic living.

It's fading away, the market culture. If I was young I'd be concerned. I've got people coming to me that have units or shops in Camden Passage, people who are young enough to have quite a few years ahead of them, and they are seriously worried. They're going to have to move out. They're not doing the business. At one time there were couriers herding Italians and Americans around places like Camden Passage. It doesn't happen now.

Development and regeneration never helps. You can't move across from the Waste to Broadway Market by London Fields. It's not just council regulations, it's space. To operate and generate interest in the junky bits and pieces that I offer, you need space. A lot of space.

When you've got the momentum going, it generates that lovely rush of competition. That's what kills them. The council are saying, 'To provide the space you want to operate, you need a large area, with car parking provided.' That will always be the downfall: car parking, accessibility for the public. If it's not easy for people to get at you, you're in trouble. If the market's big enough, like Brick Lane and Cheshire Street, you don't mind parking a mile away. Having a bit of a stroll. If I couldn't park my van at the back of the stall that would be the finish of it.

I was getting parking tickets when I used to park in Middleton Road. I couldn't park alongside the stall on the Waste. I had to arrive early, unload, park the van somewhere and come back. You have to be able to arrive on site. If you can't do that you're in trouble straight away. That's from the trader's point of view. The public? You need access and no aggravation.

June can't get out of Chingford fast enough. She can see the place changing before her eyes. We've got an estate slapped down around the corner. People are moving away from here in droves. Really. Because of the policies conducted by Waltham Forest Council. They love the idea of integrating the socially deprived. It sounds like a commendable idea, but it doesn't work.

I don't see a need for us to move, to be honest. I can park the van right outside. June, every time she goes down to Morrisons, comes back saying, 'I remember when . . .' She starts counting coloured people at bus stops. That undermines her position a little, I think. It's still a perfectly nice area and I have no problem with it. But it has changed, seriously changed. Let's put it this way, it won't get any better.

Hackney is improving all the time. You can see plenty of money being spent on properties. The borough is coming back to its former self. I've noticed it, driving around. It's nice to see. It's still on the up, the rise. And the further it goes, the more it conditions people – even the ones trying to cause trouble – the better. Troublemakers are stalled by the fact that they're in a nice area. Once they feel a bit of pride about where they live, anything is possible.

The Flycatcher of Graham Road

He stands at the study window, mid-morning no brighter than dawn's dim cataract: Hackney light double-filtered by smeared panes and his thick spectacles (one arm of which is secured with a blob of pink plaster). Arm fishing inside loose flannels, the watcher rakes a pinched scrotum, sniffs his fingers and snatches up a copy of *Marxism Today*. Which he uses, with an angry slash, to dislodge a pair of mating flies from the surgical gauze of the net curtains. Fresh sticky-blue corpses are arranged, with the others, on a chipped and coffee-ringed saucer. Later, when the sorry creature is at the limit of its endurance, the murdered insects will be fed to an axolotl. It is morbidly immobile in its high-sided tank, sprawled flaccid on a gravel beach: a being that the man loathes even more than himself, more than the worst of his private impulses.

He is a prisoner of the city, this journalist, art scribe. He watches, waits: for recognition, reinvention. Neurotically, he scans roof-scapes, the coughing road with its proletarian shufflers. The cell of his book-lined study. The tank with its lizardly captive: a prisoner's prisoner. His wife, an Italian, teaches in a local school which the man finds 'rough and rowdy as they come'. Menzies Tanner is not rough or rowdy; he is damaged, hurt, in thrall to pornography, cranking peephole machines in which grey shadows grind and sweat according to the momentum of suppressed desire. Chewed hangnails. Blistered tongue. Language-runs, word-pellets to be squirted on to the page, never spoken.

Coming out of Cambridge, late-modernism, left-field politics, and beginning to write under the inspiration of John Berger, Tanner was absorbed into Hackney as the cheapest equivalent of Berger's alpine retreat: a necessary distance from which to view the noble peasants of London. Graham Road flows sluggishly between Dalston Lane and Mare Street. There is a building, at the western end, marked with a red cross. He is much too preoccupied to notice buildings, but he notices this one – where he misses the discreet German Hospital, which is set back, under development. Here, Tanner wrote, was a street of substantial villas fallen on hard times, multiple-occupied by legions of the disappeared. Certain addresses carry certain pains; you grow to resemble the bricks that surround you. Tanner intensifies this effect by psychic transference with the reptile in the tank: until the beast becomes his Dorian Gray, his attic portrait. But art writers are also dealers, they fix the market. Pictures and property: use one as collateral against the other. A house in Graham Road against a Leon Kossoff. One of those stunning panoramic spreads produced from Kossoff's Dalston Lane studio, when he gazes down the tracks towards Ridley Road Market and the fleshing sheds.

I used to meet Tanner from time to time, social gatherings at a neighbour's house – and although we didn't really get along, with prejudices on both sides and rivalry at the bookstall on Kingsland Waste, we chatted. He knew some of the Cambridge poets I had recently come across, although such matters, he implied, belonged in a past from which he was extricating himself; as he underwent the lengthy process of Freudian analysis and the not altogether unpleasant task of talking about himself for an hour each week, uninterrupted: the fascinating flaws, treacheries, sufferings. Tanner was employing, at his wife's expense, a paid facilitator, a gentle dominatrix with an impressive collection of degrees. Just as, cash-in-hand, he used sex workers who were, in their own right, part of the mechanics of the city. And of art. Phone-box models for hire. Accepting, but never soliciting, the questionable immortality of oil paint, film and word-showers.

Later, much later, when Tanner was dead, heart attack at a pre-opening champagne launch for the London Eye, I was commissioned to write a piece on a show of Kossoff drawings for the influential magazine the former Graham Road hack owned and edited.

Drifting to the right, remarrying into money and influence, Tanner had become a visible and well-regarded cultural commentator. He escaped to the leafy Oxford suburbs and spoke of Hackney only in terms of Kossoff paintings.

It was an enthusiasm I was happy to share. I asked my neighbour, an art historian and friend of Tanner, if she knew where Kossoff's Dalston Junction paintings, from 1974–5, were to be found. I loved the way thick paint cracked and was scored with white scratches like very old film: these works were utterly estranged from the clarity of the coming digital age. They represented the antithesis of the hyper-real industrial print. Eye-mud applied with a savage trowel. Technical difficulties are lightly worn. There is an absolute respect for subject. Like Tanner in Graham Road, Kossoff stood at his high window: but he saw the world's colour in the centrifugal force of those diminishing railway lines and implied journeys. The Dalston Lane studio was never more than a temporary perch, relished and abandoned: so that it was free to become a provocation to memory, a source of renewal to anonymous others, the audience for such things.

'One of the best paintings,' Harriet said, 'was given to Menzies Tanner. As a gesture of gratitude on Kossoff's part for a sympathetic review. I think it's in Cape Town now, with his widow.'

Tanner published a portrait of Dalston, as seen from his Graham Road window, while he was still under analysis, disillusioned with Marxism and modernism, moving inexorably towards Rome. And posthumous confession: guilty of every vice he no longer practised. The spiritual journey reminded me of Tony Blair: how smoothly the pendulum of conscience coincided with the requirements of a fortunate career. Tanner took care of the baby, with some reluctance, while his wife attended mass. He settled the babbling infant in a buggy, positioned so that she could watch the unmoving axolotl, while he typed up his thoughts on the pains and pleasures of fatherhood. There was a legacy to secure, the apologia of the East London years: *Falling into Eternity*. This paperback original, brought out by an independent press owned by a benevolent

American patron, was a tactfully edited collage of journal entries and revamped reviews: Cambridge, Hackney, Calabria, New York.

'The axolotl reminds me,' Tanner began, 'that recently I have been peering into Samuel Beckett, the murderer of the novel.'

Peering is right. The knuckling of bloodshot eyes. The scratching at scabious skin. Human actions misinterpreted on a distant street. Constructing a laboured fiction out of Tanner's fiction, his fable of lost time, I realized that I was only perpetuating an extreme version of myself: the weak-eyed man at the window, the book-heaped room, the wife taking on the burden of work and child-rearing in support of the folly of authorship. Before Tanner could make his escape to Oxford, he would have to murder not only the novel but also his pale-bellied avatar, the salamander in its milky waterbed. The pet axolotl, armoured, scaled, fed on bloodsucking flies, was the true spirit of Graham Road.

'It died, most conveniently,' Tanner recorded, 'three days before I left for New York. I had come to hate the reptile. The sounds it made filled me with nauseous loathing. I resented having to hunt for flies and woodlice. The creature rejected most of the food I gave it, spitting it out as soon as my back was turned. I despised the futility of its imprisoned life. Coming back from the Saturday market on Kingsland Waste, I noticed it had developed a fungus which had spread from its underbelly right up its gills and throat – and also, in the opposite direction, to the gash of its anus.'

A solipsistic diary entry from *Falling into Eternity* claims to discover, in the sluggish passage of clouds over this part of Hackney, a silent Soviet cinema through which the ghosts of labour history swim: vaporous forms holding up symbols of industry and war. But I cannot convince myself there is anything in Tanner's report on his past life which is not a lie. His wife comes into the room and challenges him about the time he wastes staring out of a window he can't be bothered to clean – and Tanner realizes that the gasworks he has mentioned so often in his journals are the ones on the canal, beyond London Fields. Objects, buildings and people, are oblivious to his introspective meddling with their status. He has invented them, as they suit his purpose. They are simply marks, insect smears, pigeon dirt, trapped in the glass.

'The scene out there,' Tanner admits, 'has no intrinsic reality. It's a painting bungled by amateurs. A Cubist landscape assembled by committee.'

He took no steps, during the lost Dalston years, to establish a connection between the activity of gazing and the terrain mapped on his consciousness by the act of walking through it. The *Falling into Eternity* diary is a retrospective fiction, a spoilt novel. Tanner, despite the Rousseau boasts of bad behaviour, never achieved a paragraph to equal Kossoff's hungry seizure of the view down on the railway and Ridley Road Market. He wasn't greedy enough or generous enough: to let the eye play, freely, to open the heart. To compete with the modest Jewish artist; the day-tripper who travelled east, along the line from Willesden Junction, to a rented room. In the borough where he lived as a child.

This undistinguished street, a transit between one life and another, is a good place for slow incubation, reverie, retreat. Against the harsh truth of what the city will do to those who move too far from civic benevolence: the unseen, the unrecorded. Thomas Holmes in his documentary reportage, *London's Underworld* (published in 1912), tells how Ellen Langes, a blouse-maker of Graham Road, starved to death, at the age of fifty-nine. Out of work, she sold all her household goods – and then, hidden behind curtains of respectability, she went without food, wasting, losing strength; dying unsupported, unnoticed. Until Holmes made the incident a sentence or two in his account of the underbelly of London. Economic recession, a downturn in the garment market, a change of fashion, and it is not only the ghettos of Spitalfields and Aldgate that feel the pinch: in suburban Hackney, in rooms they can no longer afford, skilled workers face starvation. And meanwhile the feverish Joseph Conrad, returned from his nightmare on the Congo, factors a parallel horror in Graham Road's German Hospital. He has brought back, to stimulate and appease memory, journals that seed a fable of insane colonialism. *Heart of Darkness*: Dalston.

When we discuss these Hackney conjunctions in the Charlotte Street restaurant, Neil Murger shocks us by revealing that he can't be doing with Conrad. *Heart of Darkness, The Secret Agent, Victory*: he has never been able to see what all the fuss is about. Long-winded, contrived, laboured in their Flaubertian self-consciousness. Tickell stared at his plate. Petit caught my eye and later remarked that, in his opinion, Murger had never opened a book by Conrad in his life. His judgement was based entirely on film, botched efforts, commissioned documentaries that went hugely overbudget. Horror stories about Nicolas Roeg and Francis Ford Coppola. Nobody could do a thing with *Nostromo*. There's nothing more futile than a 'novelized' movie, the definition of cultural cannibalism. We drank to that, Petit and I having spent the last decade turning old screenplays into graphic novels and back into television. 'Intratextual weave', they call it, the boys from the new universities.

Tanner didn't read Conrad either. He watched television in bed. And seethed, wondering why he wasn't on it. He woke his wife by shouting at the screen. Having arrived in Hackney with his Marxist convictions firmly in place, he lost faith when confronted by the life and behaviour of the urban proletariat: at bus stops, fish stalls, stationers where they sold him the special notebooks he required for the composition of his journals. He could no longer communicate with his former friends. Some of them, through social work, placement in psychiatric safe houses, poetry squats, were making the adjustment. Such writing as they produced was invisible. And unpaid. Tanner wrote for cash: art crit, polemics. Later, as his name became known, restaurants. Norfolk churches. Trees. And cars (he didn't drive). Meanwhile, cadres of Cambridge and Essex poet-militants received an energy transfusion from the realpolitik of Dalston and Stoke Newington.

'They drifted,' Tanner noted with a shudder, 'towards the fringes of the Angry Brigade, Anarchism, and a now forgotten cult of the late 1960s and early 1970s, "Situationism". They thought random letter bombs could revitalize a sluggish historical process.'

Situationism would be back, customized by Stewart Home, rebranded as 'Psychogeography': while Tanner discovered William Morris, Richard Jefferies and the English countryside. Situationism-lite migrated to shops in Hoxton: handmade artists' books, re-mappings, found objects. Impresarios of punk plotted their Xeroxed hustles and scams.

Tanner's doomed axolotl was luckier than Trotsky, it escaped from Mexico City. To die in a Hackney tank. The solitary reptile remained in the larval stage as a sexually mature adult. The fringed head was an Aztec throwback. You could chew on the creature's ribs and spit out fire. Fungus swallowed it. Bags packed, taxi at the door, Tanner dumped the ancient lizard in a shit-crusted toilet bowl. Which failed to flush. He knew, in that instant, where his future lay: foregrounding the porn and downplaying the art. And publishing first in Paris. Translated back into English, wheedling tone of voice disguised, *Falling into Eternity* stayed on the bestseller list long enough to become a TV play. And the launch of Tanner's fortune.

Conrad's Monkey

Joseph Conrad, not yet Conrad, back from the sea, back to the gravy of rented London rooms, the future books that were waiting impatiently for him, brought a companion: an evil-tempered monkey. A marriage of convenience. Mutual loathing. Suspicion of the grey world in which they found themselves. Master mariner (downgraded to second mate) and impulse-buy pet: chained like reluctant lovers. The trim-bearded mandarin, in high collar, is the prisoner of his red-mouthed familiar. Curved eyebrows meet, inverted commas. The mouth is so tight it might as well be stitched.

It sprang, it nipped: a difficulty in the Sailors' Home, a scandal in the boarding house. The monkey, all too soon, vanishes from the story. Biographers lose interest, scholars avert their gaze. There is not much evidence to go on. This was an atypical act for Conrad, that paradigm of early modernism; the alienated and stateless craftsman cursed by the need to shape and reshape complex fictions. To sell himself in an expanding and hungry market. With the awful risk that his efforts might be well received. He would have to produce more words, stories, lies. And in this clumsy tradesman's language, English.

Conrad lost chapters, entire manuscripts, as a matter of principle. He left them in Berlin cafés and was appalled when some alert waiter came running after him with the abandoned bag. He flung drafts, which had given him infinite pains, rheumatic cramps, malarial sweats, fugues of despair, into the fire. The disgusted monkey, a potential fictional device, took off. To become its own author. To haunt the trees in the riverside reaches of London. To found a dynasty. To chatter in the ears of susceptible wanderers.

Drifting through Wapping, copying inscriptions on gravestones removed from their original setting, I heard a commotion of marmosets in Scandrett Street. You could smell the cinnamon in spice warehouses that were being converted into avant-garde galleries and recording studios. The story I was contriving, in the dementia of the Thatcher era, involved monkeys and a fanatical collector of Conrad, hiding out in one of the last council flats, a sturdy veteran of the post-war Labour restoration of bomb-damaged docklands. The momentum of my tale pulled towards suicide, a true episode, one of the first Narrow Street developers attaching himself to an iron hoop and standing in mud, waiting on the tide. What struck me now was the way a walk, brooding on some unwritten chapter, would bring forth messengers from that realm where the undead of fiction coexist with mythical biographies of London writers; with post-historic traces, stones, totemic animals.

Checking the title I typed for this section, I noticed an error: 'Conrad's Money'. Which was no error, but the accidental heart of it: failing investments in South Africa, disputes with his literary agent (Pinker), collapsed banks. Wife and son finding new ways to blow their allowance. Needy relatives, servants, school fees. A gas-guzzling Cadillac. And, above everything, like the British weather, medical bills. Jessie's knee, his gout. Competitive depressions. The anguish. The horror.

Writing, or the state of mind that must be endured ahead of the act, is a form of mediumship: you see what you need to see. Now it was the turn of my Kurtz, the legendary disappearing book-runner, Driffield. Driff had to be a major element in any attempt at retelling the story of Kingsland Waste. I used to sit with him, while he sucked up mugs of coffee, in Arthur's Café (Est. 1935), on the far side of the road, away from the action. They knew him, they tolerated his eccentricities. The Waste, so Driff explained, was worth the cycle ride from Notting Hill, because he could make it part of a loop that carried him north to Stoke Newington and on to god-knows-where: Finsbury Park, Holloway Road, Kentish Town, Camden. The skinhead's requirements were specific: in terms of the books he wanted (golf, suicide, embroidery) or re-fuelling (black coffee, more coffee, wholesale quantities of vegetarian mush, curried or otherwise). But the man was long gone, the fact that he would feature in my next chapter did not produce him. A pity. I discovered, when it was too late, that the red-cheeked cyclist kept a bolthole in Ritson Road. That was why he was happy to drop in on Albion Drive, late into the evening, with fresh purchases.

After years of rehearsed vanishings, from which he would return, refreshed and louder than ever, Driffield achieved the real thing: disappearance. Creditors were closing in, magazines collapsed, all sorts of rumours had the police on his tail. For almost a decade he went to ground. And in this absence, London changed. Contemporary fictions had no room for such caricatures: the ticks, the megaphone monologues, the fancy dress. London was other-wise engaged; putting up barriers on railway stations, private roads, gated estates. You could no longer explore Britain on a platform ticket (bicycle in tow). Secondhand bookshops were being hacked down like the Amazonian rainforest. The internet didn't do coffee and wholemeal biscuits the size of LPs. The age of non-paying first-class train travel was over. And street markets were shallow harbours on the edge of an eBay.

I attempted a nostalgic obituary for the lost cyclist in a book called *London: City of Disappearances*: 'Think of the vanished Driff as Kurtz. The Brando version. Heavier, half-naked, sweating in the dark. Reading by candlelight as his demons gather around him. Ambulances, squad cars. Beams from surveillance helicopters. Some splinter of Polish iron infiltrated his soul.'

That room was Ritson Road, another view from a high window: into the stockade of the decommissioned German Hospital. Ian Askead, when I met him on the Waste, told me that Driff had been seeing one of the nurses. A married lady with a large, hard-drinking surgeon husband. A ex-military man with a Scottish temper and the regimental record for speed of amputation in the field. Although they had vanished, the nurses and doctors, a microclimate of rumour persisted: frantic couplings in cupboards and corridors, interactions between registrar and midwife, anaesthetist and scrubber. Hackney's hospitals, whatever you inflict on them, survive as reservoirs of deep-memory. Flashes of heightened consciousness: nano-visions under the knife, at the point of death. Unexplained lights in frosted windows. Wavering shadows across courtyards where no trees have ever been planted.

And all this time, although I was foolish enough not to recognize it, Driff was on a major quest: for the Northwest Passage. An escape from London. From vengeful husbands and fathers. From nightsweats, debt-processors, taxmen. The private detective who stuck to his trail for three years, Stafford to Stratford East, Galway to Gloucester, had no foul papers to deliver, no summons, no physical retribution. He was carrying, along with his drip-dry shirt, battery-operated toothbrush, Polo mints, a large cheque. Which weighed nothing. £27,348. For Driffield. A share of the estate of a grateful collector, a man for whom Driff combed Kingsland Waste, Maidstone Market, the Westway section of Portobello Road, searching for magic books: conjuring, rope tricks, memoirs of Houdini. Confronted in a Penzance boarding house, the snarling dealer accepted the proffered envelope. He bought his dream ticket for India and left Hackney: for ever.

Driffield vanished and Conrad returned, books and events were arranged around the 150th anniversary of the writer's birth; when, once more, plot lines closed in on the German Hospital in Graham Road. John Stape, in *The Several Lives of Joseph Conrad*, discussed the novelist's slow recovery from the traumas of the Congo, malaria and imperialism. A brief Hackney respite.

'A claim that he became involved with a woman attached to the hospital and even fathered a son by her,' Stape wrote, 'has not withstood investigation.' Driffield as the elective son, the inheritor? I don't think so. Time to get right away, my own northwest passage, Cumbria. We had a family wedding in Sedbergh.

I like the town, the setting, the knowledge that the poet Basil Bunting is buried, on the banks of the River Rawthey, at Brigflatts, a Quaker Meeting House. Plain stones, curved, in a shaded place. 'If you sit in silence,' Bunting said, 'if you empty your head of all things, there is hope that something, no doubt out of the unconscious, will appear.'

A certain something was sucking the life out of this town; it had attempted, since my previous visit, to reposition itself as the 'English Hay', another graveyard of dead libraries. Proper shops, grocers, haberdashers, curry shacks, were being replaced by nicely mannered but neurotic book boutiques. A draggle of fell walkers, sheltering from horizontal rain, taking pride in not buying, had been pitched as a form of regeneration.

Buying a newspaper from the only non-bookshop on the main street, I walked straight into him, his table. Anna was the first to spot the infamous yellow sweater. She took off, at speed, knowing the morning was gone. Driffield, mouth bared in a seizure of thick cappuccino foam, was grunting over a spread of broadsheets, waiting for the shops to open. He'd cycled over from Kendal. And before that Morecambe. He was back on the road, but couldn't cope with the reluctance of dealers to begin the day's trade. Now he dealt in a single author, Burton. I misunderstood him, convinced that he was after Robert, *The Anatomy of Melancholy*: an old favourite from the days when he collected books on suicide. But this was the swashbuckler, Richard, explorer and erotologist; the one whose stone-tent mausoleum I had visited in Mortlake. Driffield had found a battered first edition of *The Lake Regions of Central Africa*, with map, and wanted to pull a switch with a grumpy Sedbergh man who had a clean copy, lacking map. Also in Driff's pouch, how he came by it I don't know, was a letter from Burton's wife, Isabel: the one who burnt his manuscripts and denied him a burial out in the trackless desert wastes.

I accept a large coffee from Driff, he was always generous. And I rush off to Anna's sister's house to borrow a mini-disc recorder.

I might never coincide with the wandering book-runner again. I wanted some evidence of his dealings with Hackney. He was starved of company and eager to talk.

I used to wake up quite often, when I had the room overlooking the German Hospital, at two or three in the morning. I used to go to the bagel shop. I used to have two cream-cheese bagels – with another two which I gave to L, when she woke up. At eight or nine o'clock. I would also get a lovely chocolate muffin. The lady behind the counter in Ridley Road, as soon as she spotted me, started bagging up the bagels. I might also have a slice of apple strudel.

Anyway, one Friday night/Saturday morning, I went there about three o'clock. There used to be all these black kids from the nightclubs, when they'd been thrown out. It was very, very heavy. I could see there were two groups. Everybody milling around and nobody ordering. Nobody wanted to be first. I thought, 'Fuck this for a laugh.' I marched straight up to the counter. I could see the lady was terrified. I said, 'Could I have two cream-cheese bagels and a chocolate muffin?'

When I was handing the notes over the counter, I saw that there was a knife, right across my throat. It looked like a machete! There was another guy on the other side with his blade. They were about to butcher each other. All the people in the place began cheering. They thought I'd done it on purpose. It was short-sightedness. Anything but bravery. I would have run a mile.

My friend's daughter, the girl from Ritson Road, worked in that shop. She couldn't stand it more than two days. Because of the dirt. She said the only way they could keep it clean was by setting cockroaches to wipe out other cockroaches. There were some really strange ladies working there.

It was hideous that market, Ridley Road. And the station, Dalston-Kingsland. There were rats running up the grassy knoll by the platform. I complained to the guy in the ticket office. He said, 'What do you expect me to do about it?' I said, 'I expect you to complain on my behalf.' I got a volley of abuse.

Another morning, setting out for the bagel shop, I saw these rats scurrying into the lock-ups. I couldn't get the council to do anything, so I wrote a letter to the Hackney Gazette. 'Are you aware of the rats in Kingsland Road? I wouldn't complain but the rats own two premises in Ridley Road. Are they paying full council tax? They must be very rich.'

They published the letter. An official came round. They discovered that the premises, which backed on to where we lived, belonged to the council themselves. They couldn't do anything about this plague. One part of the council was not allowed to bring legislation against another. But they did exterminate the rats.

I hated Ridley Road. When I went to the bagel shop, I had to zigzag all the way through the market, avoiding the reek of all those butcher's shops with their hooks of rotting meat. They smelt. They made me ill.

One night I was coming back along Kingsland Road, it was snowing. I think I'd come from the City. The snow stopped. There was a car parked right opposite the Waste. As I got close to it, I could see it was a bloke and a woman, having an altercation. Not only an altercation. By the time I came alongside, he was strangling her.

I didn't know what to do. I knocked on the window and said, 'Can I help you?' The man wouldn't let go of the lady's throat. She said, 'Fuck off, you nosey old cunt.' She was cursing me. It was always a very, very strange area. You never knew when you should interfere.

The odd thing about living in Hackney is that everybody is so entrenched. You've got working-class people for whom all the others are interlopers. You had black people for whom whites were interlopers. You had middle-class people about whom all the others agreed: get rid of them. It was ten different Hackneys, nothing overlapped.

It was a very class-conscious area. I thought Hackney was the poorest borough in Britain. They boasted about it. They were always brandishing the statistics: 'The poorest borough in Britain.' I've been to places a lot poorer. I went once to the outskirts of Hull. It's embarrassing to go into charity shops there. People are buying secondhand knickers that are falling apart. You wouldn't see that in Hackney. That's what I don't understand. It's middle-class people who use the Oxfam shop in Kingsland Road. It's their department store, better than John Lewis.

I ate out all the time. I went out to get my breakfast. I went to a café. I'm putting on weight like mad these days, because I eat at home. I now have a 40-inch waist, 42-inch shoulder, 17-inch collar. This is overweight, technically. I can't afford to eat out.

The street markets are failing. It's always the council. Every time a stall-holder drops out, there are fewer stalls – and they put up the rent. They don't want a market. Kingsland Road is a chartered market. The council can't get rid of it.

You know Dalston Lane? The bit your friend Patrick Wright did his book about? I used to do better there than down the Waste. On the left-hand side, going east, there was a shop that sold basins and sanitary ware. I found wonderful books there. An open-air yard. With another junkshop on the corner. They didn't open very often. Then a mad lady who used to work for the Daily Mirror *tried a bookshop on Sandringham Road. I used to do quite well in there.*

I don't enjoy my urban expeditions now, when I'm on the bike: all those cameras watching me. It never used to happen in Hackney. I was more integrated. I don't see anybody, these days, going round scavenging the streets. I'm only allowed two items a day. I made that rule. I usually find my items on the way to the newsagent in the morning. The poor man, he can't work me out. I buy all these papers. First thing. I look unbelievably scruffy, unshaved. One day I turned up with an enormous Art Deco silver rack under my arm. I give him a wad of cash for newspapers. The dichotomy is too much.

I had my bicycle stolen down there, but never in Hackney.

I have lost seven bikes outside my house. The first day I moved, the bike was locked at the back wheel. It wasn't locked to the railings. Sometimes I forget. Bang! Gone. The last time it was two bikes at once. I now have three locks on each machine. I have a Marin bicycle. The best there is. They come from Marin County. They're built for dealing with the mountains, going up and down. I paid extra for this bike. It doesn't have the Marin name. It looks like a wreck. When I took it to the shop, the guy started to clean it up for me. I said, 'Don't do that. We don't want them to think this is a good bike.' I have another beautiful Marin that I have to keep indoors. A work of art. I hang it on the wall, where the water tank is, look at it when I'm lying in bed and can't sleep. Waiting for the light.

Joseph Conrad, shocked into fatherhood, presented with the yowling Boris, his first son, made this pronouncement: 'He looks like a monkey.' Acknowledging perhaps that his abandoned familiar, the red-faced marmoset, had returned to haunt him: a future man, true son of his father, who would outstrip him in debt. Begging letters. War wounds. Madness. Boris would serve time, after one minor fiscal crisis, in Wormwood Scrubs. A monkey-soul in an English cage.

With the passage of years, the constant, energy-sapping changes of property, Conrad's mask bit harder into thinning flesh. Hugh Walpole, one of the last of the surrogate sons, visiting the great writer in his perch outside Canterbury, found him much as expected: raw-nerved, coughing. 'J. C. much worse – shrivelling up, looks like an old monkey and does nothing all day.'

Jessie, the pillow-wife, munched chocolates in the night, composed a cookbook, and blew up to twenty stone. Barely able to walk, she let the surgeons shave bone, drawing the line only when Sir Robert Jones suggested replacing her kneecap with that of an ape.

Dalston Lane

It's an accident which buildings survive (not as themselves) and which are erased as effectively as the houses of serial killers: Fred West in Gloucester, Reginald Christie in Notting Hill. The police station in Dalston Lane is no longer a police station, although the rind of memory, of deaths in custody, sobbing victims of crime, hangs on, infecting dull red bricks. Cape House Accommodation, it says. 'If someone is not on duty when you arrive please allow approximately fifteen minutes for the guard to finish his patrol of the building.' The public library, never very inviting, remains. A permanent book sale. Reinforced by exclamation points. COLLECT YOUR FREE I ♥ HACKNEY BADGE HERE!!!

Driffield's charity pits have been invited to move on. But the afterburn of that intrepid cultural historian Patrick Wright (too tall for the locality) eddies around the chaotic bus stop: a spectre from St Philip's Road still very much active, years after the host body has left town. Wright's *A Journey through Ruins: The Last Days of London*, published in 1991, is a pertinent account of the microclimate of Dalston Lane, that crookbacked singularity. Even before it went out of print, Wright's book reversed Joyce's boast about *Ulysses*: that an obliterated Dublin could be rebuilt from his words. Patrick's long-breathed elegy, delivered by a man who is functioning on one lung, was a blueprint for destruction. He brought attention down on a place that had done its best to cultivate obscurity, as a necessary camouflage. Once a street is noticed, it's doomed. Endgame squatters, slogans. DALSTON! WHO ASKED U? PROTECTED BY OCCUPATION. Torched terraces. Overlapping, many-coloured tags. Aerosol signatures on silver roll-down shutters. Scrofulous rubble held up by flyers for weekend noise events. THIS WORLD IS RULED BY THOSE WHO LIE.

They said, the ones who make it their business to investigate such things, that there was a direct relationship between properties that applied for conservation status and arson attacks, petrol bombs. Unexplained fires. Moscow methods arrived in town with the first sniff of post-Soviet money. Russian clubs were opening in the unlikeliest places. We no longer had much to offer in the way of oil and utilities, energy resources, but we had heritage to asset-strip: Georgian wrecks proud of their status. Dalston Junction, with the promised railway link, would become an extension of the City. A concrete shelf on which anything could be set. A tabula rasa for the fantasies of urban planners.

Wright had a title for this area: 'The Undemolished World'. A risky metaphor that was immediately stood on its head: retribution under the hard-hatted guise of social regeneration. Or, looked at from another perspective, good old-fashioned railway piracy. Fences. Enclosures. Demolition. Camera poles. Low-paid mercenaries in yellow tabards tagged by their own radios: hardwired to unseen controllers. Exploited (and often illegal) immigrants are the prisoners of what they guard; living symbols of the melancholy of an occupied city. Night-stalkers in empty blocks. Screen-watchers in frontier huts. Catch them at a padlocked gate and they are willing, sometimes, to talk. To offer a glimpse inside the condemned building, before the wrecking crew arrive.

I took a final look at Labyrinth, the blackened husk of a Victorian theatre. Patrick namechecked it, in a former incarnation, as 'the New Four Aces Club (the site of occasional shootings and subject of intense Press speculation about the fabled West Indian Yardies)'. A solitary female squatter shivered on the roof. My companion, a Cambridge geography student researching surveillance systems, talked to the inactive-activists on street-scavenged sofas. The ones who passed out leaflets. They knew that, one night very soon, the shock troops of capital would kick down the doors. Meanwhile, they rolled thin cigarettes and sipped weak tea. And produced petitions, low-concept artworks, grids of digital photographs. They were describing a notable thing from another era, a thing which was no longer there: done deal. While councillors had their wrists gently slapped for malpractice. The casting vote, on the sanctioned vandalism, falling to a man who 'failed to disclose his employment with a government body who had signalled their support for the scheme'.

DEMOLITION MAN: screamed the *Hackney Gazette*. 'Cllr Darren Parker admitted an "error of judgement" by not declaring a personal interest in a proposal to bulldoze one of Hackney's grandest buildings and build a 19-storey high rise.'

The absent-minded Councillor Parker was subsequently cleared of all blame in this unfortunate affair. But Labyrinth was already part of the yellow dust from which the city of spectacle, computer-generated, would climb: imaginary towers alongside a steel ladder, the zip-fastener of the railway linking suburban Dalston to nobody-quite-knows-where. Not Liverpool Street, not now. Peep through the chainlink mesh at acres of inarticulate mud, the residue of all that vibrant life: circus, music hall, cinema, black club, ecstasy barn. An ugly green fence masks naked earth, unseeded by investment, chewed up by earthmovers in anticipation of the first cash crop. London abdicates content in favour of concept. The back story is subverted. The guilty writer energized by these crimes, by rumours. We reminisce about events that never happened: dramas in bagel shops, male-on-female violence in cars, street markets where everything was cheap – and the characters required for the next chapter were sitting alongside displays of single shoes and worn-out scarlet knickers.

I was hunting for Swanny, a half-legendary being, like the Mole Man of Mortimer Road. A doctor, quack, abortionist. Struck off, so they said, removed from the register. Some people confused him with the Revd Swann of the Brotherhood Church. And others with the Dr Swan who dispensed drugs from his surgery at the southern end of Queensbridge Road. A haven for paper-hangers, punters of bent prescriptions, sob-story specialists, junkies with ready cash. Waves of addiction swept across London from Swan's airless flat, which was across the street from the convent with its crucified-Christ alcove, its bells. Veteran nuns, black-bag walkers, stalked the neighbourhood, moving at fabric-burning speed. Up Queensbridge Road and out along the canal towards Victoria Park. Holy crows with shining eyes, bent spines, an unspoken challenge to every slouching wanderer. Faith has its slipstreams.

Swanny, under a pseudonym, collaborated with William Burroughs in researching an article for *The British Journal of Addiction* – which was edited by J. Yerbury Dent, the man who supervised Bill's apomorphine withdrawal-cure. They decided to celebrate publication, the scrupulous account of beating addiction, with a week-long brandy-coke-speed bender in Hove. In the company of two Algerian boys and a young friend of Ronnie Kray's from Stamford Hill. The DHSS hotel where they partied, living off non-existent room service, foil trays and syringes, was an early investment of the south coast property tycoon Nicholas van Hoogstraten. That was the thing about the 1960s, it was just like Hackney: everything collided with everything else. Everybody met everybody. And the liars lived to sell the story. By way of some top-dollar sharkish agent who didn't take prisoners.

Neither the Burroughs connection nor the later association with Alex Trocchi, for whom Swanny stole antiquarian medical tracts from private libraries, was the real hook: not for me. Not now, when every lead had to be traced back to Hackney. Swanny, I discovered, was the probable subject of the last-known fiction of Roland Camberton: a story he published in an underground magazine, shortly after the death of Julian Maclaren-Ross. The piece had been commissioned from a dying man – and Camberton, an old friend and older enemy of Maclaren-Ross, inherited the gig.

I've seen one copy of this mag, in a dealer's collection, which was not yet catalogued or offered for sale. Martin Stone, knowing of my interest in Camberton, let me examine the piece. I was refused permission to transcribe it or to discuss the content in detail. Camberton might have rented out his name to another hack, it often happened. The swashbuckling vigour of his post-war style was still there, but the tone was darker. There was no attempt at narrative structure. You could almost believe that Camberton had been drinking with Burroughs, experimenting with a cut-up technique, splicing in random tape-recordings from the street.

Swanny, in Camberton's fiction, works in the German Hospital. A self-prescribing addict. Ace surgeon. Plucker of forbidden fruit. Hands trembling, he delivers a healthy son, born after an hysterical night's struggle, to an orthodox woman from Stamford Hill. The story is fragmented, with bits of radio, obscene riffs from nursing staff, German/Jewish misunderstandings and eventual grudging respect: before Swanny walks away, in bloody apron, into a new morning.

That was why I accepted an invitation to talk about *London: City of Disappearances* to a group who called themselves the Boas Society. They foregathered, once a month, to set Hackney to rights, to debate allotments, threatened theatres, Broadway Market squats: and to demolish, by way of compensation, several crates of cheap wine. I didn't know if the Boas bit was a Masonic reference or a tribute to Harryboy Boas, the narrator of Alexander Baron's novel, *The Lowlife*. But the Society met in the old German Hospital, which had now been converted into private flats. Their declared intention, so they informed me in a rather terse email, was 'to oppose the Griffin'. The Griffin being the City of London. Its rapacious greed, its sinister network of alliances.

Gaining entry to the hospital building, meeting local activists such as the solicitor Bill Parry-Davies, and the clergyman-author-chairperson, William Taylor, might turn up useful information on Swanny. The nineteenth-century medics Benjamin Clarke and William Robinson walked the bounds of our borough, recording, revising, rescuing history. Their published books and articles, stored in local libraries, contrived a soothing fiction, a past of orchards and great houses, clear streams, farms, windmills, dukes, courtiers, poets. Swanny *was* history, a being who defied documentation: an unresolved challenge. An absence.

The German Hospital, I hoped, would be Hackney's answer to

yage, the hallucinatory weed Burroughs chased through the Amazonian rainforests.

'Yage is a unique narcotic,' he told me, when I interviewed him in Lawrence, Kansas. 'There is always a shift of viewpoint, an extension of consciousness beyond ordinary experience. It is used during initiations as an anaesthetic before painful ordeals. Medicine Men use it to foretell the future, locate lost or stolen objects. Or to name the perpetrator of a crime.'

'What are you working on now?' I asked, as he followed the curve of the winter sun, waiting for his young associate to pour the day's first drink.

'Nothing,' he said, 'but I'm watching the property prices.'

The German Hospital

Records begin with the south-facing gardens of a private house on an estate belonging to Robert Graham. The house becomes an Infant Orphan Asylum. Orphans are plentiful in Hackney. But so are Germans considerate of their fellow countrymen, the ones who sweat among the sugar-boiling vats of Whitechapel. The asylum evolves into a hospital for the German community in London: before they are rounded up, in time of war, exiled to the Isle of Man. Florence Nightingale, so the books tell us, trained here. As a prelude to the butchery of the Crimean campaign, when surgeons' tents were a shambles of unconnected limbs and nursing an adjunct to prostitution. Camp-followers feed and succour brutalized men, stripping corpses.

CHRISTO IN AERGROTIS: a plaque above a stuccoed Tuscan doorway. Christ in Suffering. Human pain and its relief, death.

Hospitals are a recent intervention in the urban landscape; those who could afford it, in the eighteenth and early nineteenth centuries, were treated at home. The lower orders took their chances in the street, with barbers and mountebanks: or were dragged indoors, to spit red on a dirty floor. Benevolence had a brief Victorian vogue, when the punishment of sickness was given over to military discipline. To the strict Lutheran deaconesses of the German Hospital. Their church in Ritson Road, a Gothic Revival spectacle, gargoyles hanging from the steeple like Barbary apes, is now The Faith Tabernacle Church of God: a black messiah. The last pastor, Schönberger, an ardent Nazi, returned home in 1939, leaving behind him a divided flock.

I meant to work up a few notes for my talk to the Boas Society on an ill-advised expedition out of town, a literary festival in

Brittany. But you know how it is, travel. A way of falling under suspicion, of carrying the wrong shape and size of luggage, sharing exhausted air in a glorified cigar tube that is burning up the earth's resources. Removing your belt, exposing your socks. Treadmilling an enervated and overpriced shopping mall. Wired on coffee. The best of St-Malo in summer, in pelting rain, winds that blew away the book tent, was the discovery of a Conrad celebration in a small cinema, tucked against the old walls. St-Malo is a sea town, small yachts tacking recklessly through cross-channel hovercraft, large yachts ready to confront the ocean. Public statuary in tribute to solo voyagers and pirate admirals.

The Conrad lecture stretched my French beyond its capacity, but the rhythms were soothing: like the sea, like waves taking your breath, knocking you down, letting you up again. The bonus was the film *Victory*, the 1995 Mark Peploe version. Not much in itself, but a prompt to search out a copy of the book. Conrad had driven to Canterbury, with Pinker, to view the silent-screen production by Maurice Tourneur. He winced, ground his teeth, but remained enthusiastic, in his own fashion, about the deal with Lasky-Famous Players, which netted him 20,000 dollars. *Nostromo* became *The Silver Treasure* and is now lost. Along with the 1927 attempt at *Romance*. Sunk without a trace. That, Conrad thought, was the great advantage of this new medium. It self-destructed, nothing went up in flames like nitrate stock.

In *Victory*, the balding Swede, Heyst, hides from the shame of human contact on his circular island. As Conrad brooded and fumed in Stanford-le-Hope and a succession of rented and impossible Kentish farmhouses. The Peploe film, its colour, white suits, blue seas, lulled me: carried me away from misgivings about Hackney and the Boas Society. I wondered if Conrad's attitude towards Germans was conditioned by the time he spent, at such a low ebb, in Dalston. In the German Hospital. *Victory* was published in 1915. He was free to vent his prejudices on the person of the bearded hotel-keeper Schomberg (the name chiming, prophetically, with that of the Nazi pastor of the Lutheran church).

It was a patriotic duty to expose the flaws in the Teutonic character; Schomberg is not merely a domestic tyrant, he is a self-appointed lieutenant-of-the-reserve.

Conrad died in 1924. And was buried in Canterbury. The voice, by the end, was not the whole man. The difficulty of bringing out complex sentences was given over to dictation; paragraphs rattled off to a silent typist. Visitors commented on a tired author impersonation by a fading man. A performance piece against the finality of text: where nothing can be altered or excused.

I discovered that Conrad had carried his wife, Jessie, out of England for the first time, for her honeymoon. They took passage to St-Malo. *Marlow.* The sonar echo is the ghost: a place becomes a man. Not the heretic playwright, Christopher Marlowe, stabbed through the eye in Deptford. Further downriver, Gravesend: *Heart of Darkness*. Marlow, the crusty narrator, is thought to be Conrad's alter ego: a familiar spirit, a whispering daemon.

And Jessie's surrogate, Winnie Verloc in *The Secret Agent*, after she has butchered her double-dealing pornographer husband, where is she fleeing? By night train. By boat to St-Malo. A voyage she will not complete, going over the side. Marriage annulled. The short story that emerged from the original Brittany honeymoon is one of Conrad's most savage efforts: 'The Idiots'. A tale of degeneracy and sexual coercion: inspired, as Jessie recalled, by the sight of retarded siblings on the road from Lannion to Ile Grande.

I had expected to be going into the main building of the Graham Road hospital, which had been laid out on the pavilion principle by Thomas Leverton Donaldson and Edward Augustus Grüning. 'Diaper' pattern bricks: diamond shapes threaded into the regular courses. A blend of smooth curves and sharp angles, stepped gables and rounded gables. A place that wore its authority lightly, its manufactured identity as a refuge for respectable German gentlefolk and for Jewish workers from the sugar factories of Whitechapel. But no, I was instructed to take the entrance off Fassett Square.

I looked, first, at how the old hospital had adapted to its new identity: as private flats. Children raced around an ornamental flower bed. The house for the young doctors was conveniently close to that of the nurses. The care with which the design had been carried out lent the present development a certain dignity. There was none of the reflex fakery of cod-Dutch estates along the eastern rim of the Isle of Dogs. Or recent yellow-brick assemblages gifted on Hackney, squares and grids with no purpose beyond social control. And speed of construction.

The once-popular miasma theory, around which the German Hospital had been built, insisted on separation between units. Foul breath from syphilitics must not be allowed into corridors patrolled by Lutheran nurses, deaconesses trained at the Kaiserwerth Institute. Windows were kept open. Floors were scrubbed. A nest of discrete modules protected from the general malaise of Dalston. Nurses in lesser institutions were hired from the streets, unwashed, having limited acquaintance with Teutonic notions of hygiene. They serviced the dying. Young medical men accepted their favours as a rite of passage. Consultants, living away from the hospital, never acknowledged their presence. Sexual congress was part of the equation, pleasant but unimportant.

They told me, the Boas Society people, how informal and delightfully democratic their meetings were. 'Go down Graham Road to the Marie Lloyd blue plaque and turn sharp left.'

But you can't get out of Fassett Square, it's a closed system, end-stopped by the North London Line – unlike its notorious imitator, Albert Square in *EastEnders*. The real Fassett Square houses a community of bookish newcomers prepared to keep the gardens up to the mark, to honour their history (hospital, borough), and to flog bijou residences that retain 'a wealth of charming original features'. For around £695,000. Freehold.

It was the factory, or what I'd always taken for a stranded industrial block to the east of the German Hospital, that's where the Society met: on the flat roof. How had I missed this prime example of 1936 modernism? A Bauhaus-influenced design by Burnet, Tait and Lorne.

'Coffee?' said Alice Oller. Who was waiting for me at the front entrance: cherry-varnish hair and shoes, with period-aspirational geometric earrings and a splotchy black-and-white shift, cut against the bias. 'Would you like to see our flat before you go up?'

Alice lived with her boyfriend, a practising sound-poet/dub-technician, in what had once been the nurses' quarters. Fresh air, light, space: the architect's ideals were in sympathy with the whims and desires of the newcomers, the retro-aesthetic colonists of Dalston. This was a boat building, a landlocked liner: curved metal rails, balustrades, wide decks. The tall windows with their bevelled hinges were original. 'Cantilevered,' the boyfriend said, 'steel frames like Crittall windows.' He pointed out the maternity wing: its sunroom bellied out from the north wall.

Cream corridors broad enough to push two gurneys in opposite directions, a Mondrian grid of window-panel reflections. And every-where, at every turn as you climbed the stairs: views. The warm redbrick of the older hospital blocks, curtains of greenery. The townscape of Hackney kept at a polite distance: a playful backdrop, not a threatening reality.

When we paused to admire circular balconies and sun decks, gardens below, I found myself staring back into the much smaller windows of the Flemish blocks with their scarlet shutters: what memory-traces were imprinted on glass? This model of what a hospital should be, roomy, clean, uncluttered, gave itself up, without a struggle, to development by Anne Currell, our hotshot estate agent and re-imaginer. The one who puts personalized letters through the door.

This letter is not in any way intended to be a pitch for business. Please find a copy of the article as it appeared in last Sunday's *Observer*. No one can second-guess what may happen over the next few months, I suspect there may be a softening of the market due to a combination of unsustainable increases and interest free rises.

There is no doubt that we have seen increases in property prices particularly in selected areas of Hackney which are unrealistic and it is my belief that this rate will not continue.

The *Observer* piece featured Albion Drive residents crowing about their good fortune in living in such a paradise of social democracy and soaring property values. Estate agents were the alchemists of progress. Once, they tracked artists and squatters into the badlands; now the new technocracy (curators, website designers, TV comics gravid with novels) followed them, grateful for the opportunity to get a foothold in something as significant as a former hospital or seductively gothic asylum.

Emerging on to the flat roof, I was dazzled by the verdant spread of Hackney, its railways and churches. One of the Boas people told me how unhappy they had been with the soap opera *EastEnders* when it first appeared. Researchers questioned old-established residents of Fassett Square at great length. And then used the stories, the hurt of their lives, uncredited and without payment. They enjoyed chatting to sympathetic young women, never imagining that half-forgotten intimacies would become the scandal of the nation. Noticing my pocket-recorder (carried in the hope of coming across Swanny, the renegade surgeon), they said that they would be wary now of talking to any writer. Contract first, cash down. Then gossip.

I gave the Boas folk, lounging around the roof deck, a standard riff: how every disappearance clears a space on the map, a hole in the perimeter fence through which the future can be glimpsed. I tried to make the talk relevant, by responding to this place, the hospital. To Conrad in Hackney, when he lodged with William Ward at 6 Dynevor Road, Stoke Newington. And how, recovering from the horrors of the Congo, he discovered that there was as much darkness in shuttered Graham Road rooms where those who were too ill to work starved to death. The world, I concluded, was constructed from two warring but interdependent elements, poetry and politics. A statement designed to provoke the missionary chair-person, William Taylor.

I have to admit to a certain edge, in defence of my position as editor of *City of Disappearances*. All true London books, I believed, were collaborations, anthologies of alternate witness. Taylor, in advance of the meeting, emailed members of the Boas Society, inviting them to question whether 'recovering lost stories of the past has any importance in the light of our current engagement with the Griffin?' His conclusion? 'All this endless narrating and re-narrating is a little bit of a luxury, when there is a job of work to be done.'

My sense of inadequacy was compounded when John, a leading figure from the Manor Garden allotments, came over, drink in hand, to say hello. I felt a complete fraud, pontificating on local history I'd picked up from pamphlets and sepia photographs in pubs, when this man, always smiling, had lived in the area all his life. As a working gardener, he knew every blade of grass: by experience. He had cycled down every street in the borough, fulfilling Roland Camberston's instructions, noticing every shop, every pub, between parties and jobs and family visits: and not as a neurotic cultural duty. John had no idea where Swanny was to be found, though he did introduce me to another doctor, a grave, quietly spoken man with experience of many Hackney hospitals. Dr Peter Bruggen, in his retirement, had developed a fascination for exploring and researching the territory where he had operated for so many years. He had been too busy, in his early life, to notice what lay around him. He said that he would be happy to give me an interview.

Alice's partner leant on the rail, smoking contemplatively, reading the Hackney landscape and speculating on its confusing perspectives: how Mare Street appeared so far away. Clots of green swallowed up tight terraces and sharply angled roofs. The young man knew nothing about Labyrinth, the demolished theatre, but he did know somebody, a friend of Alice, who boasted of being a regular at the height of the rave era. He would give her a call, see if she was in: Anya Gris, the architect. The one who had a show recently at the Pumping House in Wapping. She wanted to meet me. She had an Olympic project to discuss, a way of retaining the Lower Lea Valley as a virtual-world wilderness, by folding estates and stadiums back into the earth before they emerged. Allowing the whole frantic business to happen in the head, as an hallucination of choice, while the actual ground remained inviolate.

'Anya found the tunnels,' the dub-poet said, 'running from Fassett Square to the Junction, connecting to the rail system. Something nuclear, she thinks.'

Not one building Anya designed had been built. Construction was never the point, she provoked debate. No structure that can be commissioned, she asserted, was worth making. The aim of human existence was to do absolutely nothing: gracefully. Any intervention was doomed to make things worse. Architects must learn modesty, how to explain and celebrate what was already there. Adapt, revive, invigorate. Putting in a tender was the simplest way of testing your integrity. If you win, tear up the plans. Start again. Fail better.

She knew Rachel Lichtenstein and shared elements of her background. She had been sufficiently inspired by Rachel's account of the unfortunate David Rodinsky to conceive, in computer-generated form, a dream-hospital; a place of pilgrimage, a structure that wrapped itself around a motorway junction, beneath the hill where the Claybury Asylum once stood. Moving into the German Hospital was as close as she could come to realizing her vision. Those who slept within this wing, she suggested, altered the nature of the building with their fantasies. Especially sexual fantasies. Like Ian Askead, with whom she was acquainted, Anya was a Reichian. All the tenants of this block, she said, were voluntary patients, architects by proxy. They loved and respected the tiled terraces, austere masculine geometries that played against the feminine sweep of handrails, the bent and androgynous rods on which sunblinds could be draped.

Anya's flat opened directly on to the roof terrace, a bicycle was parked outside. She brewed a pot of coffee and I settled myself to record her account of lost weekends at the Labyrinth.

You have to go right back to the 1970s. I couldn't tell you where it was exactly. Near Dalston Lane? I was squatting with a boyfriend in a Victorian terraced house with a big garden. The rooms were painted in rainbow colours. There was no electricity or water. There was a drug dealer on the premises who lived in the bath. There were huge amounts of comings and goings. It was all quite friendly. I had a placement with an architect in West London, Theo Crosby, and was finding it rather hard: the travel. I didn't buy into memorial sculpture and Crosby's notion of the epic. After a couple of months, and the odd disagreement, he let me go.

I didn't get involved with the political element, some of the others were going to meetings in pubs. There were Dutch provos and Germans around, a women's group who gave me a hard time. People went off on marches every weekend. The SWP sold their papers outside the station, up Kingsland Road. It was a really hot summer. We rigged a canopy and a slung a hammock between two willow trees.

The house, basically, was falling down. We used it as a place to sleep. You could hear the trains going from Dalston Junction to Broad Street. It was quite soothing to think of the workaday world carrying on without me. Hackney was still a garden suburb and I felt weirdly at home. I'd grown up in Totteridge. My family were all high achievers. My sister worked in Blair's office, for fuck's sake.

It must have been a few years later that I started going to the Four Aces, a black club. There was a big gap, I was travelling, New Zealand, Crete. Before I came back and finished my training at the Architectural Association. Where I got into a thing with one of the lecturers. As you do.

Jonathan was a big love affair, the first one that really meant something to me. I'd always been anti-drug, I'd never experimented – just grass. He lived in Hoxton. We got a minicab to Dalston. The club started very late. On Friday and Saturday nights, Dalston Junction was transformed. I guess this must have been around 1991. It was the period of the early underground rave scene, before it became mainstream. A word-of-mouth thing. Warehouses around the Junction. You got masses of young people on the street who would queue for hours. They would be standing there, freezing in their club gear. It was a dive. You didn't take a coat or anything you couldn't keep in your hand.

I remember the first time I walked through the door. It used to be an old cinema, a vaulted space. The ruined grandeur was heartbreaking. It was a club with a loose door policy, no searching, no questions asked. It was expensive to get in, £15. Which at that time was a lot of money.

So you walk into a black cavernous space with state-of-the-art laser projectors shooting beams through an atmosphere that is filled with smoke. Lights and mad music. Cranked up, speeded up. Hard house music. There was a code of behaviour which fascinated me. It was like floating into a spooky religious scene. You stood in long lines, looking towards the DJ on the stage. The DJ was god! Everyone is doing this spastic dancing. And pointing. Really crazed and tribal. You don't dance with somebody. You stay in line and face the same way. People in white gloves, Day-Glo stuff, blowing horns. You couldn't stay in there without drugs. Drugs were the whole thing.

I was with a man I was madly in love with. He gave me three ecstasy tablets – which could have killed me. I hallucinated that all these ravers had turned into Stamford Hill Hasids. Crows! It was the funniest thing I've seen in my life, they were davening. Mad prayers to save the city! Huge crazy eyes and mad faces: as if they were in pain. Dancing on hot coals. The most intense pain and pleasure, all at one time. Pure Bedlam!

The effect lasted for ten hours. You would be in there until six in the morning. Dancing non-stop. Part of the code is that it's never sexual. Even though it very much was. There were girls in bras and tiny little outfits and trainers, but you didn't see people snogging. It was friendly, winking and stroking. You'd give each other massages. People would walk around with Sinexes stuck up their noses and they'd offer them to you. To wake you up, give you a jolt. You would be absolutely exhausted. No alcohol was sold, only water. You drank water, gallons of it. It was a ravers' code to look out for people who were about to collapse.

You'd get these great, hairy, tattooed blokes – who in another situation would beat you up – giving you huge sweaty embraces. They took their shirts off. Acres of skin and sweat. It was dripping, drenched. You were packed together, responding physically, emotionally, to the music. We all had our hands in the air. The most fantastic party you can imagine. After it, you'd sleep for two days. You'd meet remarkable people. The rave scene took away all barriers of class and culture.

The thing I loved about Dalston Junction was that you created this spinning, touching, whirling mass of people. It felt as if all the people who were in the street had been sucked into this space and then spilled out again, totally transformed. It was as if that wall painting on Dalston Lane, with the banners and trumpets and faces, had been brought to life by sound! You would find doctors, lawyers, architects, psychiatrists. With local people. You'd end up gabbing away like crazy because you're off your head on drugs. Then a pile of people would head back to your room and you'd sit there talking nonsense for hours. I met fantastic people. You couldn't tell if someone was fourteen or forty. It was paradise. Nothing came close to it. Speak to anyone who went to the Labyrinth at that time and they'd agree. The city became a site of visions and possibilities, wild utopian schemes: gardens to plant, rivers to uncover, schools to rescue, asylums to be thrown open. We saw what lay beneath the stones and the dirt and the anger and the noise and the bad will of all those who refuse to recognize what is lying around them. Hackney is actually heaven!

The reason the club was called the Labyrinth was that it had all these underground spaces. You had the main area, painted with weird cartoon graffiti, and the stage with these speeded-up children's voices and music, and people moving in a slow drowning way because they're off their heads on drugs. You walk downstairs into a cellar and there are different rooms with different music, chill-out spaces. There is also a garden, quite a big garden. People go out there and rest from the dancing. You wander the dark stairways and corridors talking to everybody, to intimate strangers. It was really loved-up. We were hugging. People were falling madly in love and having ultra-intense relationships. Once that scene was over, you never saw them again.

It would go on all night, then they'd open these enormous doors and all this steam and sweat and smoke would pour out. The sun would be coming up and these zombie-looking vampire people would flood away into London. Mad eyes! Naked bodies covered in mud from the garden.

I was thin as a rake. When you take these things you don't eat. You dance until your toenails fall off. It's all about eye contact. You'd dance all night in rows, meet someone, go into a mad frenzy.

While I was spending my weekends submerged in Labyrinth, I was living alone in a cellar in Smithfield. I had walked from Norwich, on the trail of animals brought to London for slaughter. I was totally fixated on what I called blood roads. My life was very extreme. In Norwich Art School, this lecturer, an old guy, had turned me on to masks. I was absorbed in dark stuff. And in the affair with Jonathan. Who was fifteen years older than me. And married. With kids. I was building an environment in that cellar – which I had no right to occupy. I thought I would stay away from the light entirely, until I understood what the subterranean meant. Tunnels, drains, strip-clubs, bearpits. Weekends in Labyrinth were both an extension of my work and a release from it. It was the only time that I have truly experienced daylight. You could go up on to the roof, up the iron stairs, and see the whole of Dalston pulsing. Then you'd go back inside: carrying with you that intense vision of the streets.

There were darker things going on. People were smoking crack. Jonathan got hooked. The scene petered out for me when the relationship finished. It became quite dark. Jonathan had trouble doing his job, he was using heavier drugs. He moved out into a derelict warehouse in Hackney Wick. He said that he could see the world ending from his window, spider-patterns of smashed glass. Balkan wars before they happened. We split up. By then the rave scene was everywhere, it travelled around London on the orbital motorway, out into Essex. The magic was gone.

When we spilled out, back into the streets, all the other clubs were emptying, the black clubs, R & B clubs: all these foxy, dolled-up black women. There wasn't any trouble. Six o'clock in the morning, early 1990s, Dalston Junction: wild. We'd go round to the bagel shop in Ridley Road. Then we'd be hit on by these really dodgy minicab drivers. You'd get into the car completely exhausted with a Turkish man, chain-smoking, playing with his beads. You could barely remember your own address. You didn't care where he was taking you. One morning this guy told me he had to drop off a mate and I was, like: 'Oh sure, right, cool.' The car stopped in an industrial estate, it was in Edmonton, by the river. The engine was still running, they were playing some wild music and smoking. I just kept talking talking and talking. I opened the door and ran away. I remember the name: I was on Angel Road. By the North Circular. I had to get back to Vauxhall.

I found out later that Jonathan had paid them, the Turks. It was madness. Anything could have happened.

In Dalston, it was the building itself that excited me. Labyrinth. The way it survived all those years, the transformations. It taught me so much about how, in architecture, you should never impose but always respond. I tried other places but they didn't do it for me. I was ridiculously in love, not just with a man but with the whole scene, with London, with Hackney. And there was the thing we did. When you swallowed these drugs, it took about half an hour to kick in. You get what they call a rush and suddenly your whole body is – phwwerr!!! – orgasmic. You have to dance. I think they developed ecstasy for the German army in the First War to keep them marching. The drug makes you jittery, you have to move. You hallucinate and you feel warm towards your fellow men. The drugs that have come since, like cocaine, haven't interested me. The laser lighting at Labyrinth was specific to ecstasy. What it would do is connect people to light as it travelled through smoke: like an ambulance entering a bombed city! And these huge smiley faces. You see someone, you make a connection. It's exciting, to have this with a stranger.

What happened next to the Labyrinth Club, at the time jungle music came in, was much darker. A very dark scene. It was horrible music actually, aggressive and dark. And the drugs got darker. I didn't like it at all. People began to look like creatures in a zoo, panic-stricken, dead-eyed, grinding their teeth. I thought then the building was doomed. It was over. For all of us. For Dalston.

Parked at the back of the German Hospital, as an oblique tribute to Joseph Conrad, was a distressed, fashion-accessory Cadillac. In layers of sedimentary brown: red mud with traces of iron. *Brougham d'Elegance* it said on the hood.

Shortly before the First War, Conrad purchased a Cadillac. He was thought to be an unpredictable motorist. He navigated as if at sea: tacking hard into an east wind as he swung the rudder, to lodge his land-schooner, yet again, in a Kentish ditch. After the Hollywood film money, there were chauffeurs.

Walking home, with Anya's Dionysiac tribute to Labyrinth ringing in my ears, I saw a different Hackney. Cars, headlights full beam, are stopped, dos-à-dos, in the middle of the road. While lengthy negotiations are pursued. Hammer music lifts swirls of dust. Dudes, who seem to have the gift of steering by some form of mind control, fire joints while shouting into mobile phones. Chariots of respect, German-engineered, nudge each other aside: don't give the bastards an inch. Scorn for generations of colonial oppression is manifested by a refusal to indicate. Why should you help the Man by telling him where you want to go? Screaming police sirens, demented cicadas of the Hackney night, carve up the territory, always squealing to a halt in time to miss the action. Sirens are a confirmation that crime is safely over the horizon. The faster we travel, the less chance we will arrive: Dalston physics. A special theory of relativity. There was total agreement: the cops would go mob-handed to one part of town, well away from the action, and the malefactors would cluster somewhere else. Collaborative posturing, no loss of face. The weather blanket covering one of the great police horses said: 'Video Equipped'.

Wide pavements are all very well, once you've negotiated the permanent holes, cones, barriers and regiments of recycling bins at which passing motorists hurl their cartons. And miss. Scavengers examine and reject shirts, underpants, tracksuit bottoms. Rats' nests. Fast-food for crows and foxes.

A woman in a black BMW comes off-road, sweeping across me, to bump over the high kerb and wedge herself in a concrete garden. She slumps over the horn, screaming at a dark house. Her headlights illuminate the estate-agent's sign: FELICITY J LORD. HACKNEY

EMPIRE. Orange sky to match the orange shutters on condemned blocks of flats. Empire of insanity. Like the credits for that television toga-buster *Rome*: when ithyphallic graffiti comes to life. A preamble to orgies of blood, rapine and trashed history. The fallen rise. Our darling city.

DOMESTIC EXOTIC

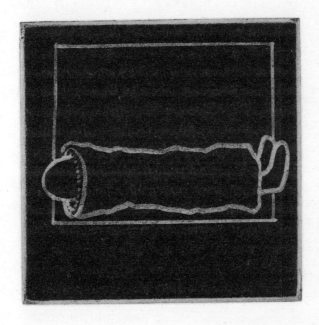

I have told not narrative but ourselves – no narrative but ourselves.

– George Oppen

Albion Drive

The beam of the resurrected 8mm projector, a thing of grinding gears and rubber bands, throws up a title: May 1st 1969. The cone of light, with its washed-out colours, its sentient ghosts, crafts a stained-glass rectangle on to the white wall. Summoned from years of sleep in a grey filing cabinet, Renchi grins once more and gobbles the horizontally presented stalk of a pear. A green cloth disguises the pitted surface of a cheap kitchen table.

'Why didn't we go down the market to find something better?' says the present, hovering, 2007 Anna. Who appears, back then, leaning against the diamond pane of the kitchen door (with its skinny plywood boxing). Yellow tiles. Speckled laminate work surfaces. Everything twice bodged: by the father of the escaping family – nails, trailing wire, original features entombed – and then by us, know-nothing technophobes, handless bunglers with rented power tools.

Life was kitchens and cameras. Anna worked in a school called Thomas Abney in Stamford Hill. I travelled to Walthamstow as a part-time minder of day-release mechanics, white smokers with Mod tendencies, good-natured for the most part, tolerant of the absurdity of a fate that inflicted this interval of cultural busking on their realist existence. With the Rockers, leathery aboriginals, it was more fun: they liked a ruck in the car park. No hard feelings, rite of passage. They came at me mob-handed; one fat, one old-faced midget – and the third, trouble, the only biker with a bike. His sidekicks were unnecessary, a barking chorus. I smashed the juvenile with a film can containing Kurosawa's *Throne of Blood*. They loved the bit where Mifune/Macbeth is punctured by whistling arrows, the rest they could do without. A legitimate nudge, shoulder to shoulder, sent the lardy one tumbling into a municipal flower bed. And then – it was like wrestling a golf bag filled with spanners – I rolled through sharp gravel with the biker, lacerating the Carnaby Street suit I'd bought for Renchi's wedding.

This incident was unfilmed. As was the pair of flouncy scarlet knickers one of the students secreted in the passenger-side door of the old red Mini as something for me to talk my way out of with Anna. The gesture was in keeping with the febrile climate of that institution, the Technical College with its remorseless corridors, numbered offices and cubbyholes, night-strobing light tubes. The hum of bug-burning electricity got into your head, sapping your will to live. A Stalinist bureaucracy meant that any money earned was always months in arrears, minor discrepancies could be found in every pay claim. The monster building was an unmapped citadel of quarrelling and hysterical fiefdoms, weasels jockeying for preferment, endless paperwork, unexplained departures. Twice-exiled communists, New York Jews who left California for Mexico City, found a storeroom and claimed it as their own. They were never seen again. One such McCarthy-persecuted refugee, after talking for hours about Hollywood B-feature hackwork, went crazy – seeing the politics of the college as a reprise of his earlier life. He gifted me his job as film lecturer. Curator of cameras, projectors, film stock. Very little of which had been used during the entire period of his lectureship: he was a purist, an old-style documentary maker; he dispatched a pod of students to remote parts of London – Heathrow, Paddington Station, Tilbury – from which they returned, defeated, with zilch in the can. Too dark, too wet. What they took months to learn was that the expedition, the journey, was the whole experience. That was the Zen of film-making: carry the kit and do nothing. Take coffee in a greasy spoon and keep your ears open. Watch the rain. Pick up discarded newspapers. Never shoot a single frame until you are ready to accept the dictation of the city.

One night, returning a Bolex, borrowed to record a Hackney protest organized by Ian Askead, posters pasted in the windows of empty council properties, I found that my windowless bolthole was occupied: by a senior member of the Liberal Studies department, a very smooth operator who did just enough teaching to line up the talent. And a long-haired, long-legged young woman. Stockinged but skirtless. A language student who was facedown, alongside juggling and bouncing reels of film, on the editing bench. The professional educator was status-secure in a narrow-lapelled metal-grey suit, white poplin shirt, tie loosened: he lifted his left hand in a token salute. There was a distinct clink from his heavy wedding ring as he gripped the bench in climactic spasm. I acknowledged my intrusion and walked away, shoes squeaking, down the aggressive rubber of the mile-long corridor.

We bought a house, the first I ever looked at, strolling east, beyond Kingsland Road, from De Beauvoir Town. Autumn 1968. Cost: £3,500. Two families, parents and kids upstairs, grandparents down, occupied this mid-Victorian terraced property. They ached for escape, to Essex, the forest fringes, Ongar. They had sat out the war, a crack ran through the wall from the vibrations of a V2 rocket on Holly Street (intimations of coming events), and endured the peace; but whatever it was they mistook for the spirit of place was threatened. By a compulsory purchase order. The advance of tower-block triffids. And the invasion of the borough by cultural difference, people from elsewhere.

This was the only time in twenty years when I had more money than was needed: on the day, for the day. Labouring wages came in a small brown envelope and were spent before the next weekend. After the Ginsberg documentary, the carrier bag of readies delivered by the Germans to the hotel in Park Lane, I had about half the sum required to close the deal. I knew nothing about mortgages but didn't like the smack of death in that word: an inherited puritan ethic, buy only what you can pay for in cash. I would have to borrow the shortfall from my father, knowing (as I'm sure he did too) that I would never be able to make good the debt.

It was the best investment either of us ever made. And my life turned on it. My parents, in South Wales, must have owned six or seven properties, three surgeries and houses occupied by the doctors who had been assistants to my grandfather at the time when the National Health Service was introduced. The whole portfolio, sold or disposed of at the worst time, amounted to one newly built cod-Georgian villa for their retirement. This East London ruin, as they must have considered it, would have bought a terrace of those picturesque miners' cottages photographed, in their home town, by Robert Frank in 1953.

I knew I couldn't stay in Walthamstow. That era was finished, along with the interesting and unpredictable students, the freedom to float. It was all paper now: financial targets, research objectives. Issues. Best practice. You keep the same real estate – including a swimming pool which would survive up to the point, forty years later, when the grand Olympic project sucked resources out of the area – but you rebrand: Polytechnic, City Academy, University. You cull the freaks, the wild cards. I was unemployable. A householder, ratepayer, married man: who would have to busk an absence of marketable skills into finagling a living out of a place in which we were strangers who didn't know the rules. Or the language. And where, by occupying a property, we were legitimate class targets. The only job on offer was as a clerk, handing out or refusing unemployment benefits to others.

That photograph of Anna sitting in the window at De Beauvoir Road, reading an estate agent's printout, comes to life. We walk through De Beauvoir Square, those eccentric Dutch houses that now fetch close to a million pounds, past the Metropolitan Hospital, across Kingsland Road, under the railway bridge. To the smell, so specific and ineradicable, of this Albion Drive house: burnt almonds, sour milk, fish stew, orange-pulp bubbling in a saucepan, mice, linoleum wax, work boots, babies. Dead books. Years of lives. The arrangement of bricks, timbers, plaster, over this ground: the meadow, the farm seen in John Rocque's 1745 map of the Parish of Hackney. A survey which reveals: nothing. A welcoming gap beyond rotated crops, worked soil. The pastoral fringes of the original city. The undertow of all our subsequent dreams: love.

When Anna let the Irish builders loose, in the 1980s, they discovered a well or subterranean shrine, a rounded arch of ancient bricks beneath the floor of a potential child's bedroom. They were digging out a drain. Half the house was rubble. When we took possession, we had an outside privy and a tin bathtub hanging from the wall. The history of London was in the stains around its rim. That's why new council flats, in tower blocks, were so popular.

'Roman, for sure, 'tis older than you are, boss,' said the man with a pick, the romantic.

'Cesspit,' said the gaffer. 'Bury the fucker now, Mick. Before the council are on to us.'

I was too preoccupied, detached from the process, the noise, the dust of crumbling walls, the drilling. My father had died, my mother was drifting out of the immediate and back to a sharpened and recovered childhood. She took me, at first, for her husband – and then her father. Anna was in hospital. There were three children to be fed, dressed, taken to school. And I was trying to write, in short bursts, an endless novel called *Downriver*. To my shame, I let the shrine go. 'Carry on, boys.' Before Hackney officials are called in, before the whole dire business grinds to another six-week halt. Red letters on yellow forms. Men with clipboards. The fine grit of brick-dust choking my electric typewriter. The Irish came and went at whim, as the weather broke, or more promising short-term jobs were offered. Our Mithraic cavern was filled with debris, choked in concrete. But we knew it was there.

You wouldn't suspect, watching the 1969 diary films now, that Anna was in crisis. The camera tracks out from the kitchen, on to the stoop, to stare back through the window. A slab of Swiss roll held aloft, a cup of tea; then she curls up to sleep, alongside the cat, on the battered leather sofa – which was respectably battered, inherited sheen. The teaching was too much, too soon: a reception class of forty-two infants who treated new young women as fair game. Most of the kids sprung from the window, and away; others ran around shrieking or lay on the floor in play-dead bundles. Valium, diazepam: for the relief of anxiety, a drowning numbness of waking slumber. The reality of the city pressed too hard on raw nerves. In ways that home movies, with their affectless recitation of breakfast trays, kitchen debates, picnics on the grass, could not reveal.

Strings of soft light flatter our youth, the documented evidence of fictional lives. Down the iron stairs they come, Renchi and Judith, Tom and Bridget, the Velascos (Charlie and Syd) – who were married a month before us and now hold up a novel daughter to delight the recording instrument. I served the spaghetti that would become a staple of family life. They learnt, over the years, to humour my surf-and-turf revisions, tiny adjustments in flavour and intensity.

The hand-held camera, in communal use, circles like a hungry dog. Dappled sunlight. New faces on old ground. The gardens on either side of us are immaculate parlour extensions, every rose accounted for, paths swept, edges trimmed. Our neighbours are venerable, very white, widowed or in partnerships so long established that couples are never apart; on the street, they stop to talk, an excuse to regain breath, as they make the epic 200-yard traverse to the post office behind the flats.

Alongside the box of 8mm films, in the metal cabinet, I found a blue folder with typed notes; intended, I suspect, to be read in parallel with the flow of mute images.

March 19, 1969. The British Constitution class, bored with talk of Ginsberg, R. D. Laing, Black Mountain College, the French Situationists, have asked if they can use the period for revision. I said: 'Sure — but let me check you off on the register, so I get paid.'

I am sitting in a classroom that isn't mine, projector loaded, blinds drawn, radiator full on

(can't be turned off). Loud birdsong. Greenery
behind the window I've finally managed to open.
Drilling from a range of building sites. Train
pulling into Walthamstow Central.

The film this afternoon is <u>David Holzman's Diary</u>.
By Jim McBride. My choice. I don't expect it to go
down well.

Yesterday, feeling lousy, I accompanied Renchi to
a camera shop on Kingsland Road run by a whispering
man with bottled red hair. He wore a zipped-up
golfing jacket. We tried out an antique field-
telephone system, but he wasn't keen to sell. I
wonder what the set-up really is?

Coffee in the corner place, opposite the Dalston
Junction station. The view from the window stayed
with me all day. The coffee had no taste. We
discussed the idea of keeping a film diary of life
in Hackney. I'm nodding but my head's thick with
phlegm, I can't take in what Renchi is saying.

I was so far out of it I spent the afternoon
sprawled on the sofa reading John Betjeman. He was
fond of Albion Square. As was Geoffrey Fletcher,
the <u>London Nobody Knows</u> man. Fletcher did a series
of pen-and-ink sketches of the Square, uncombed
foliage and no cars, in 1965. For the <u>Telegraph</u>.
Before Betjeman, I'd been flicking through Keats and
wondering about the qualities that Tom likes so
much, the London essence.

We'll begin this diary with 'songs' in the style of
Stan Brakhage. Portraits. Places. A taped interview
with the paper-seller from whom Anna buys the
<u>Standard</u> every night on her way home. Constantly
changing f-stops, varied lengths of shot. Cutting in
camera. And we should do something, very soon,

about the <u>Orphans</u> project. A trip to Dublin to catch up with the Dr Strangely Strange group: 'folk, psychedelic, blues and baroque'. Things are fragmenting over there, hippie communards drifting to the West, Cork and Dingle, while others, in Berlin, are becoming politically engaged, getting involved with Rudi Dutschke and student activism.

As predicted, the afternoon class are comprehensively bored by <u>David Holzman</u>. They can't be arsed to wonder if it's a real diary or not. The only spark of interest comes with the fish-eye shots, the girlfriend in bed. Bare breasts.

The art students, later on, were most taken with the opening sequence, the atmosphere of a particular district of New York. Films work best, they reckon, before the narrative kicks in. They want me to get hold of Warhol's <u>Empire</u>. Stoners staring at stone.

What the camera doesn't get, pressing tight against the faces at the kitchen table, is the decision to script, finance, shoot and promote *Orphans*, a documentary about the Dublin bohemians who once lived in a communal flat at 55 Lower Mount Street, but who relocated to Sandymount Strand. Apple, the Beatles offshoot, made noises about encouraging innovative independent production: a dead end. The more urgent quest, under the baleful stare of the three panels of Renchi's *Pierrot le fou* painting, was to make contact with Jean-Luc Godard. The mix in our proposal, backed by photographs from a recent Irish visit and several rolls of trial footage, was irresistible: the hippie spirit, its paradoxes, and the search for a breakaway band member, lumberjack-shirted Angus Airlie – rumoured to be living in Hamburg, associating with the cadre who became the Red Army Faction (known to the tabloids as the Baader-Meinhof Gang).

In November 1969, although we knew nothing about this at the time, Astrid Proll was carrying out her own diary project, a sequence of photographs in a Paris café, urban terrorists on the run: her brother, the cigar-chomping Thorwald, Gudrun Enslin, Andreas Baader, Peter Brosch. They mug for the camera, play with cigarettes. Confident reflections in long mirrors. Leather jackets. Enslin's straight shoulder-length hair. Dark-rimmed eyes. *Bande à part*: the Outsiders. They were aping the Godard movie Tom and I saw in Paris: where the elusive director was not to be found. Proll's reportage, less than a dozen shots, surviving her period in prison, exile, Hamburg, emerged in the early years of the next century as a boxed set, numbered and signed; an 'iconic' work offered for sale through international art brokers.

The *Orphans* script never reached Godard. Or, if it did, he chose not to reply; he was otherwise engaged. While we phoned contacts all over Europe, the man was in Hackney, between the German Hospital and Ridley Road Market, shooting *British Sounds*.

Now, in 2007, cinema is largely a matter of research, DVDs obligingly provided by The Film Shop in Broadway Market. Frozen frames. Publicity stills. Off-balance compositions achieved by predators on Vespa motor-scooters. Flicking aimlessly through the coffee-table album, *Magnum Cinema*, to help conjure up a time when the doings of legendary directors were of moment to our lives, I find David Hemmings sneak-shooting over the green fence in Maryon Park for Antonioni's *BlowUp*. I arrived at the location in Charlton, after a haphazard search, in 1969. The magic of 'Swinging London' had already faded: it was place that mattered, a natural amphitheatre, paths, steps, wind in the leaves; all of it infected for ever by the process of industrial film-making. Product is repackaged, digitally enhanced, cleaned up, reinterpreted for a new generation. The thing itself, the repertory movie, has deconstructed into fragments, all trace of the original narrative removed. Homeless ghosts on well-tended tennis courts. Rough sleepers in the undergrowth. Killings waiting to happen.

On the previous page of *Magnum Cinema*, Godard stands beside a fence of sharpened stakes, a corrugated hutch, adjusting his tie, pincering a cigarette stub, wearing a suit. Tinted glasses for a dark world. At his left shoulder is a personalized postbox: VELASCO. Reminding me of Charlie and Syd: that garden picnic. We didn't see them again for decades. They were busy professionals, educationalists, advisers. Waiting for the culture shift, the Blair years, when the persuasive talkers, flexible conceptualists, would come into their own. Here, I felt, was a parallel relationship, the Islington version of our own Hackney marriage.

Syd was an Israeli, intelligent, dramatic, fighting endless wars in committee rooms: for the better life. Charlie, more laid-back, with a rich chemical history, attendance at Arts Labs and 24-Hour-Technicolor-Dreams, devoted every spare moment of his time to playing, and later witnessing, football. If there was a cup replay in Hull on a wet Wednesday in February, he was there. A Euro qualifier in Iceland? An African Nations match, at which he knew he would be hustled, mugged, and quite possibly left for dead in a sewage stream? Unmissable. As our cracked house acquired its insulation of books and papers, Charlie's office, the spare bedroom, filled with programmes, used tickets scavenged from the terraces, signed portraits of Cliff Jones, the speedy Tottenham winger on whose game he based his own. It was Charlie who drew Blair out of Hackney, demonstrating that it was time to move on. The next step on the property ladder. Better tennis courts. Fewer guns. Restaurants on Upper Street for deal-making dinners at which you did not have to eat.

The Triangle

Jayne Mansfield, *Hollywood Babylon* siren, mammal superstar, Catholic/Satanist porno-pin-up decapitated by guillotine windscreen, in the early hours of the morning of 29 June 1967, on the road between Biloxi and New Orleans, swayed into the low church hall and community centre of All Saints, Haggerston, to declare open a convention of East London budgerigar fanciers. September 1959.

That's about as Fortean weird as it gets: the mechanics of movement, the dietary and cultural improbabilities. Yes, local bad boys, George Raft-fancying Bethnal Green hoodlums, liked to import American photo opportunities, screen and showbiz automata at the end of their tethers; out of favour, on suspension, in hock to the Mafia. Indigent. Tax-busted. Dope-hungry. Punchdrunk basketcase palookas. The mute thrush, Judy Garland. Joe Louis with the wrong kind of shuffle. The monolithic malevolence of Sonny Liston, holes in his dead eyes: as if he were wearing the black pennies before they laid him out in the Palm Mortuary, Las Vegas. Billy Daniels. And Raft himself, trying to remember how he did it, shot the Look across white tables with too many bottles on them. A private wax museum of sleepwalking self-imitators acting out a twilight existence as their own body doubles.

The Kray Twins, so John Pearson, their first biographer, told me, gathered a Spanish court of killer dwarfs, dockers in pink leotards and lesbian nurses who did damage on request around them on Friday nights in the Old Horns. By blood, the Krays were circus folk, entertainers. They loved a good knees-up.

But that was the 1960s, film and performance leaked into the London night like sewage from worn-out Victorian pipes; clubs were theatres where group portraits could be assembled by anonymous journeymen to promote status. Celebrity was tactile: shared Winstons, shared sweat. The perfumed gangster picks up an imaginary tab (the protection he offers, insurance against his own spite). The cinema sheet was porous: violence begins every-where, smiling teeth and lipstick on the glass. No separation between film-script, newspaper report, novelization: posthumous twenty-five-year wet dreams in a solitary cell. The men, the torpedoes, are homosexual, armoured in the brittle varnish of narcissism. The divas, the arm candy, are beards: parodic domes-ticity, confused gender identity; heavy white furs in monsoon, mob-crush temperatures. Everybody wants to touch every body: pinch, lick, taste. Prove. Secure a florid signature on lobby prints or legal documents.

Haggerston was different. Mansfield, an intelligent woman on a global publicity assault, would travel anywhere (including Vietnam) with the same camera-caressing, Michelin-lipped smile; the four-inch heels, transvestite abundance of hair, sheath dress that made walking, limo to church hall, a legerdemain of slithering juggling bodymass, stretched satin and threatened shoulder-straps. Stateside, there would be two ratty chihuahuas, hairless, trembling, clutched over her exposed breasts. And there would be children with exotic names. And complicated dyslexic lives ahead of them. The dogs were safely behind bars, in Heathrow quarantine. The kids were in the Beverly Hills Pink Palace with a favourite minder. New British pets, sentimental gifts from temporary patrons addicted to reflex generosity (in lieu of proper payment), left their stringy turds and wet splats steaming in thick-pile hotel carpets. The ones that were not found, behind preposterous dictator-scale sofas, were the worst: an evil stench of pampered captivity. While Mansfield bathed, publicly, in champagne showers. And auditioned unsuitable, frequently violent lovers.

She came to austere, monochrome England, her Californian studio career pretty much in ruins, to shoot a noir feuilleton cobbled together, phoned-in direction, by Terence Young – a Soho face whose James Bond franchise pension was just around the corner.

In an era when afternoon-drinking clubs offered the permissions of ersatz night, Young associated, on clubbable terms, with Eddie Chapman, safe-blower, triple agent, entrepreneur: a man with a story to sell. The movie encyclopaedist, David Thomson, characterizes the director as a man trading on 'carnal supercharge'. Young lurched, with no visible strain, between military hardware, parachute-regiment propaganda and architectural exposés of mammal goddesses: Mansfield, Anita Ekberg. Or Ursula Andress, emerging from the sea, a militarized Nordic 'Birth of Venus'. Such was the topographical scrutiny Young lavished on Jayne's deftly exposed armature that his little exploitational skinflick should have been titled *Mansfield Park* rather than *Too Hot to Handle*.

Jayne played, in this film as in others, the absence of self; the dim version that conceptualists imposed on her. As if exhibitionism, voluptuous displays of American family values, the body as a deformity of superfluous health and vitality, was the true thing: the residue of a unique human consciousness. When we starved, she was our strawberry milkshake, and from her muscled breasts (not as vast as they appeared, cantilevered from a prominent ribcage) issued forth a gush of stars, sherbet fountains of planetary dust. An innocent era, when Homeric gods and goddesses, brought across the Atlantic by war, might couple, in disguised forms, with the broken mouths and pinched frames of late Europeans. Mansfield, in her bravely borne excesses, was the final manifesto of this mythology: she came to Hackney from the cover of *Life* magazine, out of *Time*, dripping from a surf of sleaze stories, sheet-sniffing voyeurism, eavesdropping technologies. She was an overripe consignment of Marshall Plan aid, a gift-wrapped Trojan horse intended to secure us in the chains of American cultural colonialism.

Mansfield, the steroidal Monroe clone escaped from a Howard Hughes laboratory, is the ultimate magnet for male voyeurism, a splash-Madonna of centrefolds, a fertility-enhancing Venus of Willendorf in an infertile decade. The cast-list of this English film implodes. Everybody sleeps with everybody. *Too Hot to Handle* has an alternate title: *Playgirl after Dark*. In the movie, Mansfield is an exotic dancer – now her main source of income, Las Vegas: market value plummeting, cash managed by the latest predator boyfriend. The last of a long line is a short abrasive Jew called Sam Brody – who, in an earlier incarnation, played a minor role in the Jack Ruby trial. All the threads of conspiracy converge on Dallas: strip-clubs, hairy men in sharkskin suits and Lee Marvin dark glasses, disgruntled Cubans, shopping-mall access to effective death weaponry. Sick politicians who use television like a sunray lamp. Surveillance tapes that nobody has the time to transcribe.

After London, Mansfield returned home – in our wilderness of mirrors – to appear in *The George Raft Story*. In which, ironically, there was no part for George. He was impersonated by Ray Danton, whose slick moves, obediently inky hair and sharp Italianate suits, were an inspiration to the Krays and other emerging local talent who took film magazines along, as prompts, to Woods the tailor in Kingsland Road.

Cinematic memories are not to be trusted. Even the shop in Broadway Market can't supply me with Mansfield's performance in *Too Hot to Handle*. All I have to work with is a smudged front-page photograph from the *Hackney Gazette* (25 September 1959). JAYNE AMONG THE BIRDS. 'Glamorous American film star Jayne Mansfield visited the East London Budgerigar and Foreign Birds Society's show at All Saints Hall, Haggerston. She presented the prizes and had a rapturous reception from crowds of local fans.'

Among these fans, so I learnt thirty years later, walking to the boarded-up and rubbish-strewn precinct known as the 'Triangle', was a Greek Cypriot youth from the neighbouring flats. This seventeen-year-old had left the Queensbridge Road School, which had an enviable reputation, back then, for producing premier league armed robbers, malleable heavyweights and midfield hardmen such as Ron 'Chopper' Harris. Tony Lambrianou had thrown in his job with a bedding company in Hackney Road. 'From that period on,' he told me, 'I started getting into villainy. Properly.' As if villainy were an address. Like Hare Marsh. Or Evering Road. There were expeditions to the Midlands, cars could always be acquired, beds borrowed, bedmates shared; a bit of this and that in Nuneaton, followed by a first experience of prison: Winson Green, Birmingham.

The leonine Lambrianou, sallow of skin, slim tie, three-peak handkerchief peeping from breast pocket, is on his way to a meet. A drink at the Black Bull and over to Hoxton, the Green Man. He has previous at All Saints Hall. Denied access to a function, for being improperly dressed, the juvenile Tony and his brother Chris answered this perceived lack of respect by burning the stage. No danger of that now, the boy's sharp as a razor. Shoes bright as a coffin-carrier.

Mansfield speaks of trying to secure herself an experienced older man, a protector to replace the father who died at the wheel, heart attack, with the child Jayne beside him. 'I loved to sit on Daddy's lap,' she said, knowing what she said. 'And have him hold me, hug me, caress me and kiss me. My mother would often scold us. She said it wasn't ladylike to be sitting on a man's lap. She'd say that I got his trousers wrinkled.' The Carlo Ponti/Sophia Loren relationship was one to which Jayne made constant admiring reference. The secure but open marriage. In reality, she cohabited with short-fuse hustlers, card-sharks, bar boys. A Hungarian muscle-man plucked from Mae West's chorus line. A smooth dancer, around Lambrianou's age, she encountered in a Venezuelan nightclub. Then there was Anton LaVey, the San Francisco Satanist, former circus hand, lion-keeper: the Devil's consul on the West Coast. The one who put a curse on Sam Brody's cars.

It was natural, bottom-wriggling across red leather, clambering out of the black limo on Haggerston Road, between church and church hall, that Jayne expected male attention: the sexless embrace of security, professional attendants to hold back the crowds, clear sightlines for photographers. Invisible arms to catch her coat. Nothing of the sort was available, the East London birdmen were more interested in their caged beauties. A knot of lipless old boys in flat caps. Two or three women hovering, half-curious, encumbered by kids. And the septic Lambrianou: who looked the part, a rub-off Ray Danton with sculpted cheekbones and heavy brows waiting on a Mansfield audition. An XL chauffeur's cap with polished peak. Eye on the main chance, the action.

English weather required a stylish white raincoat (perhaps stitched and finished in Hackney) carried loosely around the shoulders. Mansfield took Marilyn Monroe's 1957 descent at Heathrow as her model: the showgirl's wiggle, a moue of surprised delight at the banked cameras. This newsreel arrival was the best of it (before the sniping silences of a disgruntled husband, the queeny asperity of her stiff-backed director). Mansfield worked hard to duplicate the effect.

Courtier-like, Lambrianou accepted the shrugged and shed coat. And remained where he stood as the thin-ribbed mob followed Jayne inside the church hall. From which point, the only evidence is the photograph in the *Gazette*. An argument in scale and quality of hair: Mansfield is imposed on a monochrome scene, tracked by a dusty shaft of golden light. The hard silver buttons of the old bill, the sharp peaks of their helmets, worn indoors, threaten the bronzed length of her naked back. Other men, creosoted in Brylcreem, take heat from the luxuriant tumble of managed locks. Jayne coos at the cages. And they coo right back. Avian twitter making good the hungry silence of the church-hall crowd: their cheap smoke-breath, the rifling farts of sour excitement.

The Mansfield raincoat, bundled tight, is already on the bar of the Black Bull. A salient part in an anecdote Lambrianou is working up – which will serve him well in the lean years when he comes out of prison after the McVitie trial. Dispirited, in a miasma of pre-cancer melancholy, banished across the river, Tony recounts once again the legend of that afternoon: how he tried to flog the coat to the landlady in the Bull. A red-wigged Medusa whose chin, if she ever became dislodged from her stool, would barely have reached the plateau of the bar. The stolen garment, as the vendor saw at once, would have wrapped her like a lemur in a pearly shroud. Glazed eyes flashed fire, the opportunist thief fled.

Lambrianou considered the canal, almost deciding to let the bundle, now wrapped in newspaper, float away, harmless as an unwanted foetus. Then failing again in the Green Man, even for the price of a drink, he flogged the fragrant memorabilia, the only DNA-enhanced evidence of Mansfield's Hackney visit, to a stall on the market. Where it languished and weathered, to the point where the mac was indistinguishable from the rags and tatters of Hoxton's recently deceased: the stripped corpses of the poor who were still obliged, postmortem, to earn a crust for others.

Some trace of Jayne Mansfield's ill-luck held to the Triangle. The fish shop failed. The butcher. The bread shop. Both greengrocers turned it in: one of them, a very fit Judo enthusiast, died of a heart attack. The post office, scene of so many rucks and rows, numerous episodes of attempted robbery and fraud, was decommissioned. Speculations, optimistically funded by the council, crashed. Wine bars and specialist ethnic cuisines that never made it to a second month. The Black Bull was squatted by German professionals, then pulled down. Memorialized by a set of coloured bins, bottle banks from which many bottles were withdrawn. CCTV cameras were installed. The betting shop enlarged its premises and thrived. The Asian newsagent, obliged to serve care-in-the-community waifs, babble-ranters, single-slipper tobacco-addicts soliciting half a cigarette, pitched his trade towards scratchcards and Lottery scams to tax the most helpless members of society, funding evermore grandiose brownfield follies.

Cars parked mid-road, drums beating, electric windows down. Speeding chauffeurs honked, elbow to horn, mobile phones in both fists. Staved-in headlights, sparking exhausts, wonky fenders: off-the-book motor-trade business, doctored MOT certificates from railway-arch garages. The war-zone geometry of this profane eye-of-grass within a blunt Triangle was the aftermath of Anton LaVey's anathema on cars. Mansfield's manager, Sam Brody, touring the

San Francisco coven, dissed a skull, snuffed a black candle. LaVey told him he'd be dead within a year. Which must have come as a relief from this state of perpetual hospitalization, the breaking of bones every time he got behind the wheel. There were ugly spirits abroad: LaVey, a sometime colleague of underground film-maker Kenneth Anger (who visited London, frequently, in these years), lived for a short time with Marilyn Monroe. Marilyn was to the Detroit automobile industry what Dick Cheney was to Iraq: ruination. The smoothest engines died at her touch. She parked where she could, on pavements, against wounded trees, in hot-pillow motels whose locations she could never remember. Susan Atkins, one of the Charles Manson dune-buggy slaughter battalion, had an early gig, climbing out of a coffin in LaVey's 'Topless Witches' Review'.

'Movie money,' Jayne said, 'you can't keep.'

Much of her fortune had vanished before the flying windscreen decapitated her on the road to New Orleans, that bougainvillea-scented voodoo city waiting for floods. Her second husband, Mickey Hargitay, identified the body, in two parts. Tasteless commentators speculated on whether they'd be able to sew the head back on in time for the funeral.

The fact that the All Saints Church bristled with angels made me suspect the worst, they were carrying excess insurance. The building was around the same age as our house. Its walls were dressed with a crumble of grey boulders, like antique walnut shells stuck in icing sugar. But Anna decided, and joined the congregation a few times to show willing, that our first child, Farne, should be christened. It was that era: Farne was five years old. I wrote to Lindisfarne, where the ceremony would have carried some significance, and was told the thing was impossible. Parishioners only. We had visited Holy Island and the Farne Islands when Anna was so heavily pregnant that it took two men, one pulling, one pushing, to haul her up the ladder from the boat, and to roll her out on the dock. The spirit of place was powerful. Sitting in the ruins of the abbey, I responded, seeing life in moving shadows, monkish presences in blood-brown habits; continuity, permission to name. Daughters of the early 1970s fetched up with Native American weather tags – Rainbow, Sky – or title to one of the sacred islands of our Celtic fringe. But none of this allowed them to be watermarked across their puckered brows on the ground of their elective tribe.

5 March 1978: the event. Brian Catling, present, as godfather. And Judith Bicknell as godmother. When it comes to it, we try to respect the rules of ritual, the community of this church, its tiny congregation. One or two of the old folk have come along, the vicar is in flow. There was close attention to what was happening, no holding aloof, when Catling heard a soft click against the stone. A man called Harry had slumped, coughing out his teeth, which bounced once on the aisle, before Brian swooped with a large red handkerchief. With Renchi's help, he got Harry out to the porch while the vicar carried on with the dipping and marking. News was brought through, in whispers, that this elderly and faithful parishioner had died. The ceremony now became a double-event, memorial tribute and welcome; one valued member of the flock departing and a new soul joining the Christian fellowship.

Not long after this, so it was rumoured, the vicar's wife, mother of numerous children, left the adjoining vicarage to enlist in a Stoke Newington lesbian commune. Our son and our younger daughter were not christened.

Tony Lambrianou, tears in his eyes, remembered how his mother enrolled him, along with his brothers, in the congregation of All Saints Church, as soon as the family moved to Haggerston. Sunday school too. Never missed. Wouldn't dare. Brought up strict. Christian values. Those were the days. No drugs, no litter. You could leave the front door unlatched. Not a spot on his white shirt.

'We used to take round the collecting trays,' Tony said. 'And hold on to them. Believe me, when anything went missing from that church, it was down to me or one of my brothers.'

Stonebridge Estate

The estates south of the Triangle are sealed-off prison islands, benevolently intended, incubating malcontent and mischief – as well as lives of ordinary human getting and being, survivalism, the slow accretion of site-specific memory. This place is their place and the alarm felt by outsiders is not part of the native register. The term 'estate', despite a thorough rinsing in council-speak, consultation notices that appear as harbingers of expulsion (followed by rapid demolition), can't shake free of the mocking echo of the great houses – formal gardens, intimidating gates, lodges, stables, managed orchards – that once occupied the northern fringes of the city. Pastoral Hackney, bucolic Bethnal Green.

Balmes House, a little to the west of here, along the canal, on the border between Hoxton and De Beauvoir Town, was a prime example. Once the home of Sir George Whitmore, Lord Mayor of London and fervent Royalist, it declined to a Hogarthian madhouse in the charge of a man called Warburton (a brutal keeper who married the owner's daughter). Warburton prospered: as his charges, chained and gibbering, lay on straw in their own excrement. Sir George greeted Charles I, returned from a fool's errand in Scotland, at Balmes House; before a triumphant entry, via Hoxton, into London. Warburton put his money into property. Amateur historians speculate that the term 'barmy' (or balmy) derives from Balmes House – from the period after the asylum was torn down, the gardens built over. A time when former inmates wandered parks and green spaces, taking the air, rubbing tender ankles, finding it impossible to relocate themselves outside the structure that once contained them.

Descendants of Warburton's charges can be found, gathered around a fixed table, in London Fields, close by the concrete effigies of the Pearly King and Queen. Dogs at their feet, they breakfast on Special Brew, and argue the world to rights in a lively but contained manner. Their alfresco democracy has real charm. They converge at or before first light. When I pass through the Fields in a winter dawn, we nod to each other. The well-maintained flats on this corner, a council estate from a good period of red brick and solid balconies (now dressed with geraniums), carry a grey plaque: WARBURTON HOUSE. Between Warburton House with its forecourt of expensive motors and Mare Street, you'll find Warburton Road and Warburton Street. Old histories become our story, a map of walking, memory-sparks struck from flashing boots.

Warburton is easy: a chancer, a climber, a man who is quite forgotten but whose name is scattered throughout an indifferent Hackney. Samuel Richardson, father of the English novel, is another case entirely. What has he to do with the borough? Twin estates between Triangle and canal: Haggerston and Stonebridge. Haggerston, the reef of crumbling LCC dreadnoughts, has been named and coded by a Richardson obsessive: the individual blocks have titles like Harlowe, Pamela, Lovelace, Samuel. Now, at the point of demolition, reinvention, orange panels across windows, a local man has made it his business to research the connection. To run Richardson to ground: as a cultural godfather, a reason to justify staying on in this tight enclave, despite the uncivil engineering, the closed roads and footpaths, the dust, the dogs. The raging psychopathology that undermines habits of settled domestic life.

On 22 June 2005, I received a letter from Erol Kagan of Clarissa Street, E8. This in itself was worthy of note: most of my correspondence was redistributed by hand. The official system had collapsed. Many hours were spent in queues, along Emma Street, clutching my docket for a parcel that would never be seen again. The lowest point came when a two-hour pavement snake, followed by an interminable search by a bored and frustrated sorter, delivered an envelope for which I was charged a penalty fee: insufficient postage (no stamp). Tearing the thing open as I stomped home through Haggerston Park, resenting the morning's work lost (the office closes at lunchtime), I discovered a badly printed invitation to a vanity art show, looped digital dredging in the distant wake of W. G. Sebald. The unlanced boil of a nuclear power station overlooking an oatmeal sea.

A letter, safely delivered, was a rare privilege. I celebrated with a cafetière of organic-ethical-Ethiopian coffee.

I have been living in Haggerston all my life – In fact in the same estate, I am now 31 years old! My parents have left home, I am married with two kids yet still live in the same house! I am very upset that most of my childhood memories are being destroyed, Laburnum School and Haggerston Baths in particular but I just cannot leave my beloved Haggerston.

I spend most of my spare time researching and documenting the history of Haggerston. I have accumulated a tremendous wealth of information, articles and historic documents on this subject.

I would be delighted if I could actually meet with you one day to share the information I have gathered and also ask you some questions. There are many parts of my research unanswered including the link between Haggerston and Stonebridge Estate and the novelist Samuel Richardson. I am also keen to meet with older generations that have been living in Haggerston. As currently I appear to be the longest serving member!

I knew Richardson best – sampled but never inhaled – through Henry Fielding's spirited parodies of the epistolary novels that served up rapes and ravishments, but made you wait for them, along with a dose of moralizing retribution. Fielding, a Bow Street magistrate, investigator of legal corruption, a man who proposed the abolition of hanging, was a considerable London figure. But Richardson? Investigation challenged my lazy prejudices. By family, education, trade, this man was the real thing: a 'good apprentice' who rose through his own efforts, a man of property. You could look on Richardson as a kindred spirit of William Blake: without the poetry, the vision. He took up printing: Aldersgate compositor, corrector of the press, self-publisher. He married his master's daughter, learnt to set newspapers, broadsheets, political pamphlets. He got money, status, recognition: a business in the City, a house in the suburbs.

Which suburbs? Hackney was then a village and Haggerston a bare hamlet, a few muddy lanes, a brook. Richardson helped to create a literary form, the novel, that suited his temperament and inclinations. He was as much a Londoner as Peter Ackroyd. And as circumspect in the revelation of the bare facts of his life (which were no affair of literary snoops and mythologizers). Who knows if Ackroyd ever slept in Hackney? In his Dickens biography, doesn't Peter run into his great predecessor on Kingsland Road?

The navigation, Albion Drive to Clarissa Street, gets trickier every year. I have the fantasy, as I push deeper into my Hackney book, that everything and everybody can be found within 440 yards of my house. Of the buried chamber with its brick arch. All the key witnesses are within one lap of the Olympic track. Erol's substantial archive fits the rule. Walking through the low-level flats, the Triangle, the estates, is problematic; social planners have blocked rat runs, sealed doors, put barriers across roads. Cutting out, so they believe, the escape routes of street dealers and balcony gangs. Crack houses have been spectacularly raided – with camera crews in attendance. And the result? Urban drift, melancholy bordering on catatonia. Robotic shufflers. Nervous pedestrians breaking into a slouching half-run, in case the pavement they are using will be discontinued before they reach the Lottery-card dispenser. Stephen Gill tells me that Hackney, with ninety active enterprises, has more betting shops than any other London borough. They are colonizing Mare Street, like a flock of crows, in anticipation of the Olympic bonanza. Gambling has been categorized as a 'financial service', leaving William Hill and his competitors free to take over any redundant bank or failed insurance brokerage: without unnecessary paperwork. Gill is gathering up and photographing an origami of crumpled, chewed and twisted betting slips. He records the name of the nag and the relevant loss, from £2.20 to £500.

A West African patriarch, who has assembled his entire family, wife, two sons, daughter, outside the newsagent, snatches a ticket from the street-machine and presses it to the lips of the youngest boy. 'Bless,' he says. 'Bless our good fortune.' Before he strides imperiously into the narrow shop, pushing aside single-cigarette cadgers, the confused patrons of a complicated and expensive transport system. Tickets to viral torpedoes. Tickets to stalled tunnels. Tickets to tear up before they entitle you to anything. Consoling junk foods. Sugar hits for the single schoolkid allowed in at one time. Salt licks. Papers full of naked bodies, burnt, bombed or plumped up like inflated rubber chickens. The always-missing child, her wide accusing eyes.

23 May 2006: Erol confesses, he is a City man with an office in Mitre Square. His collection is an act of love for a place that is vanishing, every time he steps outside his door. As we talk, the computer pings, apologetically, to alert him to another Haggerston item coming on to the market. He tells me that he picked up a copy of William Robinson's pioneering, two-volume history of Hackney for £64. Mr Kagan has never felt comfortable, or been made welcome, at the Archives Department and Local Studies Library in Downham Road. He works best at home.

The family were gathered around a large television set in a smartly furnished living room. We exchanged greetings, before going through to the adjoining study, the Haggerston store. There is little or no contact with the neighbours, Erol says, they never stay on the estate more than a few months. The garden patch is not much used. He tried growing melons, but the partition fence never felt secure enough to separate his crop from a breeder of pit bulls. And the man's urgent, earth-ripping playmates with their dangling, swaying undercarriages.

I was born here, but I have quite a mixed background: Turkish Cypriot, Sudanese. My parents came over in the 1970s, '73, just before the Cyprus war. My wife Nadia's parents came in the 1960s. They settled in an interesting house in Newington Green, the oldest brick house in the country. Henry VIII's hunting lodge. Nadia was actually born there. Her father sold it for £30,000. Current value? £2 million. Ha! Yeah!

I've been to Cyprus, my parents' old house, but it's not the same feeling. To me, this is home. I could never live anywhere else. I have this need to dig deep, to document what I find.

I grew up, overlooking the canal, in Dunston House. On the ground floor. My parents, as soon as they arrived here, were offered an entire house on Albion Square. They said, 'No no. Too old.' They wanted something new. Ha!

I'd go fishing, across the road, for tiddlers. A terrible place to live. The canal absolutely stank. In summer especially. You would never guess that one day canalside properties would be desirable. I worked, as a young kid, when I was in Laburnum School, on one of those mosaics you see from the canal path, as you go under the Haggerston Road Bridge. It was a good school. We went out on the water, from alongside the wood yard.

Then I moved up to the school opposite where you live. I don't know what it is now. But it's not a school, is it? I went to college and took some A levels. Then did a foundation course in accountancy. I joined a firm as a trainee accountant, before I qualified. That was in Holborn. I moved into systems, accounting systems. I implemented a system for John Lewis. Financial services for the John Lewis Partnership. I started my own company as an independent contractor. In the City. I landed a large contract with a telecom company and began to move around the world. Three years travelling between Geneva, Paris, other parts of Europe. That's when I started getting interested in local history.

When I became successful, I didn't move out to Surrey. I stayed in Haggerston. It's the area, I'm really attached to it. I can't live anywhere else.

My entertaining is all done in the City. I take clients out, lunches, drinks. When I'm here, at home, I spend my time working through my archives, my books. I walk around all the time.

As a kid I used to go for a wash to Haggerston Baths. Now they're closed, locked up. No baths, no laundry, no gym, no swimming. The building looks derelict. They have let it decay. Even from my current perspective, I'm not happy about what's happening. Local people can't afford the area. They're moving out. I was quite upset to see Laburnum School knocked down. One day it was there and the next it wasn't. Quite shocking. I saw a bell tower standing in the rubble. I don't know how it got there – or where it went. It is criminal, knocking down a building like that, an historic building.

I always asked people a question when I was young: 'What was here before?' I was intrigued to know. I've had a successful professional career, travelling all over the place, but it always comes back to a longing for home. That's when you realize: this is home. When I got back from my other life, I was thirsty for research, more knowledge about the ground beneath my feet.

There are people working on Hackney histories, but no one is doing Haggerston. I search eBay constantly. I have alerts that tell me when something on Haggerston has appeared. I haunt old bookshops, ephemera fairs. I collect things and stick them in boxes, shove them away. One day I'll have time to read those books. I have postcards, photographs, maps. Here is a postcard I bought because it was sent to someone in Haggerston. Here is an old map of the parish of Shoreditch. Your house in Albion Drive is just inside the border.

There used to be a station in Haggerston. They closed it down. Now they're going to open it up again. This postcard is of Haggerston Station in 1925. This is the goods depot, between Broad Street and Dalston Junction. That is Shoreditch Station. If you go down Kingsland Road, towards the City, you've got Shoreditch Church on the left. Before that you've got an old girls' school, it used to be a school. Opposite that site is a corner building. That building was once the Shoreditch Station.

It's hard to record all of these places before they knock them down. On Queensbridge Road, when you go over the canal bridge, they're building new QEII luxury apartments. There was once an estate on that site. That's where the old Haggerston Church would have been.

A chap called Lee – Lee Street was named after him – had the land, even before the canal was dug. It was all fields and market gardens. Nursery Road has been brought back, they liked the sound of that one. The oldest road in the area.

The original manor of Haggerston stood where those new flats were built in the 1990s, opposite Laburnum School. Edmond Halley was born around there. His study was actually on the site of those flats. There was uproar from historians and the heritage people when the flats were built. If they'd had time for a dig, they would have found significant archaeological remains, material relating to Halley, the discoverer of the comet.

I've done the research. Halley was born, here in Haggerston, in 1656. He died in 1742. When he was twenty he sailed to St Helena to make astronomical observations. He discussed the law of force under which the planets move in elliptical orbits with Isaac Newton. Our local man! A hero of science! Where is the blue plaque? He published the complete works of Apollonius. After Flamsteed he was appointed Astrologer Royal. His researches – ha! – were as mad as mine: gunnery, ballistics, diving bells, the precise location of Julius Caesar's landing in Britain.

There are legal documents on parchment, relating to Stonebridge House. I haven't gone through them properly. The area where the house stood was later linked to the tobacco industry. There's still so much to find out.

I was looking through the Friends Reunited website for people who lived in this area and I found an old lady who was born and had lived all her life in Samuel House. She's in Essex now. She mentioned that Richardson, the novelist, had his house somewhere around here. All the blocks on the estate are named with Richardson associations: Clarissa House, Samuel House, Richardson Close. It was never clear how these places were named. I'd love to find out.

Another thing, that lamp post. I've often wondered about how it got there, why it survived. Behind All Saints Church, to the right, down Livermere Road. Have you noticed it? It's Georgian or early Victorian. I've never seen another one like it. I wander this area constantly and I often fetch up there, standing beside that lamp post, in the twilight, at the back of the flats. It's very strange to find a thing like that in the middle of an estate.

Queensbridge Road

The comet, Anna suggests, when I tell her about Halley, would have been visible to terrestrial observers at the time when Farne was enrolled in the Comet Nursery, over the canal, in Orsman Road, Hoxton. Was it from Halley and his Haggerston connections that the nursery got its name? For years, first with Farne, then William, we made that short journey, crossing invisible boundaries: territorial transgression. Our metaphorical comet, scratching its belly on the sharp, pencil-point tower of the mosque on Laburnum Street, had come to ground. An electronic call to prayer reverberated over diminished and deserted streets, over the cancelled swimming pool, so fondly recalled by Erol Kagan.

In September 2006, I walked out to see the film-maker Emily Richardson. She lived on Queensbridge Road, at the Hackney Road end: in the Victorian terrace where the notorious Dr Swan once kept his drug-dispensing surgery. Swan had long since departed. The terrace had been improved into small but desirable flats: convenient for Columbia Road's Sunday flower market and the nicely kept Haggerston Park. Emily, commissioned to make a three-screen film, *Transit*, about whatever it is that lies beneath London – memory-sludge, alligators, carcasses of cattle and dogs, mystery religions, crowns, coins, rivers – had also been concerned about what lay within her own body, the child she was carrying. A transitional project at a pivotal point in her life in a city that was remaking itself with ever-increasing velocity. I would improvise remarks on these themes, without seeing the footage (drifts through Ridley Road Market, Waterden Road on the perimeter of the Olympic Park, subterranean Smithfield): before it was projected on three screens, with overlapping sound, among the arches of a former slaughterhouse. In return for my services, Emily would record an account of the birth of her son in the Homerton Hospital. A location, I felt sure, that would recur in my book.

There were times when Queensbridge Road, with its broad pavements, hectic traffic, permanent cones and obstacles, was best avoided. That light-jumping charge of killer vans and sacrificial bicycles that brought you past Ridley Road, Dalston Lane, the fringes of Hackney Downs, to Clapton. Aka: the Crime Scene. Murder Mile. Why so modest? The topography of drive-by assassinations, blue-and-white tape, flowering concrete, was spreading: in an elegant correlation to soaring house prices. To fluctuations on the underground NASDAQ, our chemical-commodities market. Postcode revenge killings by tribal groups with a neurotic attitude to territory: rucksacks filled with disconnected Sat Nav gizmos, the cargo-cult scavenging of urban hunter-gatherers. Ripped-out electronic hardware, until it is traded, is trash. A useless burden. Outdated as soon as it comes into your possession. The confirmation that you are beyond the credit system. Slaves of the consumer spectacle peddling secondhand junk in a plunging market.

'Drugs have become our main problem,' said the *Neighbourhood Watch Newsletter* in June 2005. 'Both because most reported crimes in the area are drug related and because of the influx of crack dealers and users hanging round the streets. Dalston Junction has become a "dispersion zone", so that we are experiencing "spillover", especially on the corner of Middleton Road and Kingsland Road. We have been promised a surveillance camera for this corner for months, but it has not come.'

As if to confirm my thesis, whereby the backdraught of crime-noise adds value to property, by increasing demand for CCTV systems and stimulating an anxiety-lust to secure your own private space, a letter arrives from Currell, the estate agents.

'On the corner of Middleton Road and Queensbridge Road, E8, is Middleton Court, an interesting prospect for anyone wishing to take advantage of an investment or rental opportunity. This exciting new development, close to the London Fields conservation area, comprises thirteen apartments . . . If the current development of the East London Tube link is maintained, the future accessibility of the area to the City and the West End will be assured, therefore this is an opportunity not to be missed . . . Car parking spaces are also available at £15,000.'

Before I open the front door, before the dog accompanists and preoccupied joggers hit the early streets, the first of the hustlers is at me. A middle-aged black man in a dark suit, single gold-capped tooth in winning smile. Perhaps one of the professionals from the Professional Development Centre across the road? A Hackney educational adviser with a parking problem? He says, talking very fast and avoiding my eye, that he is Carol's husband. From no. 20. She's the midwife, you know her, the one with the blue Volvo? He's locked himself out. Can he use the phone? Of course he can. But he carries on, loading the riff with too many precise and unnecessary details. There is no answer to his call. Or my guilt over *not* knowing Carol, the Volvo-owning midwife. Call aborted, he asks if he can 'warm his hands' for a few minutes on the radiator. I'm drifting back, to finish my transcript of the Kagan interview, while he thaws out – until Anna appears on the stairs, well aware that Carol is a fiction and the blue Volvo has never been parked on this stretch. The soft-access sweep of the house must be filed alongside the rest of the sob stories, specific amounts of cash solicited for taxis to accident sites, hospital runs, dying children in the Whittington Hospital.

'I am the proprietor of a successful retail business in Basildon, Essex, and I need £19 to reclaim my vehicle, after a minor accident on Queensbridge Road. The garage won't take credit cards. I'll pay you back within twelve hours. I will leave three brand-new shirts as a guarantee. In the cellophane packaging.'

They tell us far more than we want to know. Charitable instincts have long since been eroded. We have no greed left to take advantage of the paper fortunes offered by the Central Bank of Nigeria: who operate for convenience from a bedsit in Leytonstone.

'Another 419 this morning,' I report. The relevant number in the

Nigerian criminal code for internet fraud. The contract to which we have put our signatures, for the good life in Hackney, is low-level tinnitus, acoustic irritations that spoil our sleep.

The throb of engines as couriers wait to make their exchange. A man bleeds to death on Albion Square. A former council employee with a disabled parking permit is thought to have enjoyed a substantial bingo win. Two bandits force their way into his house. Rob him, beat him. He gives chase, collapses, heart attack. Major family funeral.

I wake in the night to discover a fishing-rod poking through the letter box, baited for car keys.

And now, as I turn the corner into Queensbridge Road, a Rasta is at my shoulder muttering: 'Givus 20p, man. Givus 20p.' On and on. Until I give him the money and he spins away to attach himself to a builder in a yellow tabard, who is heading in the opposite direction. 'Givus 20p, man. Givus 20p.'

The snaggle-toothed hoodie, the next in line, has a mild approach. Hands spread wide. 'I don't do this, boss. Just a quid.' He is not offended when I pat empty pockets. 'Good luck, boss. All right? Next time, OK? You take care.'

The waif in the bus shelter is after a cigarette. I can't help, but an older man, grey hair, grey tracksuit, briefcase, gets her lit. And stays to chat. The kids who dance around asking for the time are sizing up the watch I don't wear. They don't know what day it is but they know they don't care.

On a bench, outside the Belgrave Arms, where Tony Lambrianou's father took his once-a-year Christmas drink, a gaunt female in a headscarf calls out: 'I need 50p to go to the toilet.' A superfluous request, it would seem, from the evidence of the pavement.

Lately, these episodes have diminished, replaced by an hysteria of squad cars launching themselves into the air, blue lights flashing, as they fly from the hump of the Queensbridge Road Bridge. I miss the action, the Jacobean dialogue: the acknowledgement of my presence as a very minor contributor to the circus of the streets.

A raid took out the crack dealer who operated from Shoreditch Court, a block once favoured by retired local folk, builders, small tradesmen. Pat the school-keeper (and special constable) told me that he'd seen a black zip-up bag that you could hardly lift for the weight of handguns, along with an AK-47, Mace, machete, grenades. Overnight, the beggars and tollers and con artists moved on. I would have to find new fictions to lend credence to my continuing documentation of a place that didn't exist. Were Henry Mayhew's painstaking interviews with urban invisibles any more reliable than the wild exaggerations of Charles Dickens?

The last time I walked down Queensbridge Road with a tape-recorder was in 1992, for a slightly furtive assignation with Tony Lambrianou. He was out of prison, on licence, after the fifteen-year sentence for his involvement with the disposal of the body of Jack McVitie, out of the Evering Road basement. Jack had been a friend, in as much as friendship had meaning in that world of constantly shifting alliances, brotherly love and rivalry: hard masculine embraces, blood spilled, drinks bought, suits admired. Jack, with his buttoned cardigans, shitty loafers, trilby, was a social embarrassment. They called his manners 'unpredictable'. Which was nonsense. Jack was very easy to predict, he would always let you down.

Lambrianou was under the plane trees, by the bridge, waiting. A man of about my own age in thin-rimmed aviator spectacles. Broad shoulders displayed in yellow suede bomber jacket. Black polo shirt with fancy white collar. Handkerchief peeping from breast pocket. Tasselled slip-on shoes that never walked the streets. Tony kept his fists bunched. Like a resting actor, he projected: righteous gloom. The post-Parkhurst afterlife was a constant telling of the tale: for a consideration. The logistics of that fateful night when Jack went over the river, suicide by default. Lambrianou had witnessed a drama in which his earlier self was a person he barely recognized and for whose actions he took no responsibility.

Look over to my right, there's a block of flats. Look to the middle of them, ground floor: that's where I was brought up as a kid, Belford House. Looking back on it today, it seems a million miles off. My school was further down Queensbridge Road. It is still there. I can't get over it. You'd think nothing had changed.

This is the first block of flats I can remember in this part of the East End. They went up in 1948. I remember my family moving in, to live somewhere like that was a new thing. Unfortunately, coming back today, it's just not the same any more. The whole character has gone out of it. This was such a part of my upbringing, me and my brothers. You can never go back, that's the tragedy. The houses, the kids. It's not the same, it's gone. I find that tragic.

The last time we was there was when my father died, we had the funeral. I remember we all stood in the room and we said, 'That's the end of it.' We knew it was over. Now and then I come back to Hackney, me and my Wendy. To have a look round. I show her the buildings and the pubs. It brings back the memories. It's something you don't want to never let go of. It's part of me.

I'm not the same person. The kids now. It was never like that when I was young. Half of us never had shoes on our feet. At this time in the afternoon, everybody was out and about. There was no television.

When you look at Haggerston Estate, the flats look pretty modern. But, believe me, it was a rough life back then. Walking up Queensbridge Road from Hackney Road, you pass the coal and coke yards. As a kid I used to go round, and for a shilling I'd get the old people their coke and coal of a Saturday morning.

It's like another world, it never happened. And yet it did. The tragedy is: there's no record. That's tragic, absolutely tragic. A dream that never really came true.

My father spoke very poor English. He came over here in 1914. It might have been a bit earlier. All the years he was here – he fought in two world wars – he never captured the language. He used to mix it all up, even to the end of his life. My brothers have gone on to do better things. He would never move out of the flat. He said, 'That's where I'll die.' That was his attitude to life. You do what you can for your family, bang, finish. The ironic twist: my father's never been in trouble with the police. My mother the same. They were decent, clean-living people. Yet me and the boys. . . it turned out the other way. There's no single reason for that, a tough life. I look back on them days with fondness. It's not the same any more. There are only a few places left. I find that tragic, absolutely tragic.

We moved across the road, down the ramp, to the canal. Under the bridge, waves of dancing water-reflections on the curve of brick. Lambrianou, hands bunched in pockets, eyes moist, took up his position on the path, careful not to brush against the wall with his new yellow jacket. He was possessed, once again, by the location in which he found himself, events he had run over, so many times, during the years of imprisonment. *There and not there*: a personal history from which he had been banished. The past was an exclusion zone, an enclosure with no entrances or exits.

As I boy I can remember coming down here to kill rats. A lot of people used to sit by the canal, all night, fishing. I remember seeing the horses, the ponies, when the barges were coming through the bridge. They dropped the rope, so the barges could float free. If they didn't do that, sharpish, you'd see the horses dragged in. You can still see the slats, what we call slats, the ramps where the horses could come up out of the water, back on to even ground. It was a big thing to see the horses fall in.

You'd hear the clip-clop of horses coming along the towpath. Incredible! Absolutely incredible!

It was said, yes, that the weapons went into the water here, after the murder of Jack McVitie. The main witness, a man called Ronald Hart, came from a flat along Hackney Road. He says he drove up here, that night. There is a dispute about this. Hart said he turned left, directly, as soon as he came over the bridge. A few months prior to the event they put bollards across the entry. If you look, they're still there to this day. A car could never have done a left. Well, Hart stated categorically that he done it, took a left.

When they sent the diver down to search the canal, he found two pieces they thought resembled *a gun and a knife. It was never proved. It's like an armoury down there, in the mud, goes back generations.*

You're calling a witness to the witness box who says he drove to a stretch of canal which is just where we're standing now. We will never know. But this is where they found the gun and the knife used in the murder of McVitie. And it was said to be done by Ronald Hart.

I was not part of that. Yes, I admit I did remove the body from the scene, the flat in Evering Road. Hart is said to have taken the Krays, from the Regency Club, down to Hackney Road – over the bridge that is directly above us. And afterwards, Hart said, he threw the gun and the knife into this stretch of the canal. Whether this was true or not, nobody will ever know. He changed his evidence.

If I'd known what he was putting on me, at the time, I might have had a word or two to say. Fifty yards from the flat where we lived! The place where we shot rats when we was kids. My father who never had a day's trouble with the law. A total liberty. But I could see the logic of it, the canal was handy. Ironically enough, I threw the keys to McVitie's car into this part of the canal. The two-tone Ford Zephyr he had at the time. I came down the ramp, under the bridge, out of sight. Splash! They are probably there to this day. This is the actual spot where McVitie's keys went into the water.

The body, wrapped in a carpet, concealed in the boot, went on another journey: under the Thames, Blackwall Tunnel, to south-east London. It was left there. Arrangements were made with certain parties.

There have been allegations of other things happening around here, not down to us, going back to Victorian times. Murders, bodies. It's got a great history, Hackney, when you come to think about it. If you ever dredged this stretch, you'd be surprised what you'd find. Proper heritage. It's part of the mystery of it all. It's part of your tradition if you live on the canal.

Coming back with you today, it's like being in another world. Part of it I've forgotten, but I want to remember. And then again I don't want to remember. You can never walk away from the past. Occasionally I come back just to say, 'This is what it was all about. This is where it happened. This is where my career in crime grew.'

It was tough. The pubs around here were not like discos. They were hard-drinking pubs. Dockers. You settled your disputes, Saturday nights, round the corner. Down the ramp. All along the canal path. The first fights I saw were down here, between grown men. That's the way we was brought up. The local bobby was never involved. He turned a blind eye. That disciplined the lot of us. It's gone now, gone for ever. It's not coming back.

If our disputes involved something a little bit more serious, you went that step further. The razor gangs in the 1950s, we was totally different from them. Guns. We moved on.

Looking at the area today, you've got a very high crime rate. Diabolical really. That's the tragedy of it, you haven't got that community relationship among your own people. Different cultures have moved into Hackney. I'm not saying it's a bad thing. When we was kids we never done a lot of the business that goes on today. And look how we turned out. I fear for the future.

In sombre mood, we walked down to Whiston Road, the swimming pool that played such a part in the childhood of both these immigrants, Erol Kagan and Tony Lambrianou. Both men started their education in the now demolished Laburnam Street Primary School. They shared a proprietorial attitude to familiar streets, the illusion of belonging that is reaffirmed by constant reference to fixed points: the Acorn pub with its ever-open door and 'Continuous Sky', the weathervane boat on the roof of the swimming pool.

I liked that ironwork galleon very much; it offered us, as inland prisoners, a promise of the Thames, a way out into the world ocean. A wink at the mythical dockers of Lambrianou's memory: the port of Hackney. The Haggerston pool, with its curved roof and cathedral windows, was where our children learnt to swim; and where, on winter afternoons too wet for a walk, I did my laboured lengths, chlorine-burnt, white-fingered, drifting out of time in a reservoir of echoing communal voices: the tolerated residue of something that was too good to last.

I stood with Lambrianou on the balcony above the pool and then we found our way into a new gym, exercise machines that nobody knew how to use. Too many mirrors: the *Lady from Shanghai* repetitions of his yellow jacket, heavy head, narrowed eyes, made the old villain uneasy.

'I don't like the word "gangster", it wasn't like that,' he said. Recalling how he'd sawn off the barrel of a shotgun, on the kitchen table, while his father was otherwise occupied.

The litany of street names, McVitie's body carried from Evering Road, down Lower Clapton Road, Narrow Way, Mare Street, Cambridge Heath Road, was a map scorched into his consciousness: chauffeur to the dead, Cypriot Anubis. The story of the hat, the knife, the car keys, was a penance to be swallowed in the lapping waters of the pool. With all our other dreams and fantasies. Before Whiston Road was locked up, sacrificed to the tainted illusion of the Grand Project, the Clissold Leisure Centre which was commissioned to impress: by the size of its debts, the incompetence of its design, its status as yet another hyped New Labour showpiece incapable of making the transit from the computer screen to allotted position in the geography of the city.

Talk with Lambrianou had run out. Focusing on the rectangle of the deserted pool, the pattern of lights, the echoing hangar, was too sad. But there was one surprise left. I was always asking about the places in my book: Kingsland Waste Market, the German Hospital, London Fields. Tony told me that the boys had no truck with hospitals, socialist medicine: they went private. Old Swanny never let them down. Stitching up wounds. Signing prescriptions blind. Taking care of inconvenient pregnancies. He was a diamond, Swanny. But he liked a drink. The drugs that recent incomers brought into the borough were diabolical. Swanny could be relied on to see you right, uppers, downers, horse tranquillizers to keep Ron this side of a straitjacket, he never crossed the line. He only peddled gear to his own. Educated man, old school, chalkstripe, waistcoat, collar and cuffs. On a retainer, a regular bung. Stood up for Reg in court. Good as gold. And bent as a horseshoe. Retired, dead. Down on the coast. Ramsgate. Southend. Old cunt.

*

21 September 2006: no trace of Lambrianou's cold stores and coke heaps remained on Queensbridge Road. I pursued my hospital quest by asking Emily Richardson about her experiences, giving birth, at the Homerton. A major development, Adelaide Wharf, loomed over the canal like an oil tanker that had ploughed into a wood yard. 'With its 147 units (prices up to £395,000), this is a tremendous example of aspiration coming to fruition,' said Stephen Oaks, area director for English Partnerships.

Emily's mother was in attendance, and the new baby, awake, unflustered, was tolerant of my invasion. The flat was still in that magical state of novelty, reassessing itself as a suitable domain for fresh life. Even the coffee mugs seemed born again, fresh coloured, virgin bright, as Emily remembered. And talked.

I went to the Homerton, when the time came, because I wanted to stay local. At one point I thought of having him at home, but I went off that when I realized I'd have to clear up afterwards.

I'd never spent a night in a hospital. I'd never broken a bone. I'd never had any dealings with the Homerton.

I'd done antenatal classes. They were good, matter-of-fact. They tell it like it is: noisy, messy. I didn't try breathing exercises, I did yoga. The classes were packed, you wouldn't believe how many people are giving birth in Hackney. The room was absolutely jammed.

We had a midwives' group. There were no doctors. There's a birthing pool at the Homerton. I wanted to do that, the pool. But unfortunately my waters broke as we were travelling to the hospital. I was lucky. I got on well with the midwife. It's really nice to have someone you are comfortable with in attendance.

I went in on Tuesday afternoon and Augustine was born on Thursday. I had to be induced. I was induced on Tuesday. I started to have contractions during the night. But they don't class you as being in labour until you're three centimetres dilated. I went all through the night having contractions quite strongly and regularly. In the morning they were, like, 'No, you're still not in labour.' Twelve hours and I wasn't even classed as being in labour! They gave me some more of the hormone. And every-

thing ground to a halt. Later that day, it kicked in. After twenty-four hours, it started up, really quite quickly. I had an epidural at that point.

They were constantly asking me what I wanted and giving me the options. I felt like I was making the decisions.

Different midwives, doctors, were coming through. All sorts. That was good. My fear, being induced, was of being in a hospital situation where I lost contact with the midwife. I felt that I might lose control of the process completely.

We were there so long. I went for walks down the corridor. I could see other people, other scenes. The labour rooms were quite close together. Some of them were adjoining. There was a small sluice room, very bloody. There was a loo door on one side. As you go to the loo, you see the sluicing area. Blood. And the sound. The moaning. This really low moaning. Labour. Sometimes you could hear people screaming. Then you hear the baby cries! *I think I heard four or five baby cries, with all the other sounds.*

We paced the corridor, people shuffling around in dressing-gowns. Quite a strange world. I was only there for twenty-four hours after the birth. You used to be there for a week. They would teach you about baby care and breastfeeding.

There was one girl whose boyfriend was still painting the front room. She was hoping that she could stay until the next day. They told her, 'No, no, you've got to go.' 'Yeah, but my boyfriend's painting the front room. I can't take the baby home yet.' She got chucked out.

My son was born at half-two in the morning. We drove home. It was that strange feeling, like when you've been ill. You've been in bed with 'flu: after a few days, you go outside and everything is hyper-real. Colour. It was a beautiful day. Really clear autumnal light. Bright. And crisp. Everything was heightened. I felt like I'd been locked into some other place and was now coming back.

It's absolutely there, this special feeling, but only for a short time. The immediate area around the hospital is really odd. Actually, we went up St Augustine's Tower, in the churchyard, off Mare Street, and we saw what this part of Hackney was all about. How green it was. But that's not why we chose the name, Augustine. It was a name we liked. Also St Augustine is quite fab: 'Give me chastity, but not yet.'

When you go up the tower what you notice is how enormous those estates are, near the hospital. And the ones going out towards Hackney Marshes. You see the vast area they cover. Homerton, I felt, is quite lawless. And the bit that goes up to Lower Clapton, Murder Mile. But we're going to stay. We're going to stay in Hackney. It's got all that violence but, at the same time, it has a lovely spirit. Lovely.

Holly Street

Over the years, film crews of various dispensations dropped in on Albion Drive to demonstrate that special brand of discourtesy that is their stock-in-trade. Although you, the victim, might be the subject of the interview, you are also a nuisance, not part of the team, a major inconvenience. The crew talk over you and around you, as if you were a difficult and temperamental child. Furniture is rearranged. Rooms are dismissed with heartfelt sighs by cameramen in a hurry. The nominal directors give bored and exhausted technicians their head – while they make increasingly distracted cellphone calls. They should have been at the next location an hour ago. It takes most of the afternoon to light the inevitable chair, manhandled out of position, up against the bookshelf, before they remember that there are questions to be asked. It worked quite well, the set-up, when the runner sat in your place – but now the glint from your naked and rocky cranium, the reflections in your spectacles, the wires threaded in and out of an absence of buttons on the wrong shirt: hopeless. The questioner gnaws the clipboard in frustration, knowing there will not be time to ventriloquize you towards the answers you have already given in their pre-packaged script.

Way back, before the digital age, it was an invasion; documentaries required a unionized grump of electricians, who did nothing beyond borrowing your phone to call their brokers, helping themselves from the fridge (while disparaging your taste), then retreating to the bathroom with a newspaper. They talked property, even then: divorces, villas in Portugal. The early crews always featured soundmen who believed they should be cameramen and who set an impressive benchmark in paranoia. They were unlanguaged, spooked by the hideous loudness of the world: on permanent suicide watch. One of them, not content with halting the entire process for a plane circling around Stansted, insisted, like the unfortunate showgirl in the exploding convertible from that virtuoso opening of Orson Welles's *Touch of Evil*, that there was a ticking in the head. Everything was shut down: washing-machine, television set, radio, fridge, deep-freeze. No good. The culprit was my cheap watch. The deep-freeze was not reconnected at the end of the shoot. Puddles over the floor, ruined weeks of food.

Then there were the arty boys, doing something unfortunate to William Blake, hanging poems from the washing line. One of them, I remember, had the directing thing cracked. He lolled in a chair, passing languid but impatient instructions to his unpaid helpers, who scurried in and out of the garden, trying to peg out a photocopied set of *Jerusalem* laundry in a minor whirlwind. While the tormented youth groaned, head in hands, knowing what he didn't like, but unwilling to toss away the fruits of deep contemplation on these scabby ingrates.

The point being that I'd seen it all and reached a state of suspended exasperation and half-amused tolerance: what new tricks could they demonstrate? Residual vanity – that someone was sufficiently interested in what I was doing to trek out here – persuaded me to respond to the occasional invitations that leaked through my newly installed internet connection. And, in any case, crews were now one person. In and out. No lights. I understood the format, we had progressed backwards to the era of the 8mm diary films: shoot what you like, where you like, nobody is watching. The entire process is predicated on the absence of an audience.

The latest young man, a Cambridge geographer, was impressive. He'd been well tutored. He knew exactly what he wanted and how to go about it, causing the least inconvenience to my obsessive work routines. He was brisker, less anguished, but his efficiency reminded me of my first working encounter with his father, Chris Petit. Chris scouted his locations in advance, plotted the shots, and even laid down tracks for an elegant descent, under the disguise of an upturned boat, into a recovered wartime bunker. The shot was never used. But the principle was there: forethought, shape, rhythm, movement. If Rob Petit had been advised, he acted on this advice with considerable charm and proper determination.

He placed me in a parked car in Albion Square, under the lime trees, climbed into the back seat, and shot my responses in the driving mirror. Painless. Done and dusted in twenty minutes. The subject of this film was George Orwell. An academic paper delivered in a grudgingly accepted format: 1984 and surveillance technology. The only actual reading on the Cambridge course consisted of downloaded extracts, comments by critics on other critics. The trick was to factor in a light dressing of Walter Benjamin, Virilio, Barthes, Foucault, Mike Davis, Rebecca Solnit – without the drudgery of labouring through their books. You quote the footnotes everybody else quotes to make your invigilators feel comfortable: Xerox virtues. A first-class degree and a future cutting music promos.

Rob posted his little film on YouTube. A number of people reported back, they had seen me in this thing with Tony Blair. *What?* The one where I'm driving around the M25 with Blair. Shot by Chris Petit. None of them registered Orwell or 1984. The static car, Blair captured from a TV screen, the Petit name: sampled and scrambled into a new and entirely fictional form. Which might be seen as a demonstration of Rob's thesis. Whatever. George Orwell (Eric Arthur Blair) was introduced to the Hackney set. With lethal consequences. Blair, the Eton-educated colonial policeman, witness of savagery, morphs into Orwell, plongeur, roll-ups and moustache, the elective down-and-out in Paris and London. A namer of names. Broadcaster, spook. Scourge of monolithic socialist states. And then, triggered by Rob Petit's camera seance, the posthumous Orwell, sponsor of CCTV systems and mendacious New-Labour-speak, evolves into the real presence of the former Anthony Charles Lynton Blair, Fettes and Oxbridge educated, first-step-on-property-ladder Hackney incomer: the beaming Tony, our failed 'soft left' local councillor. The grin without the cat.

Orwell's name was also attached to a block of flats, down by the canal, that seemed to be under constant, pre-Olympic revision: mobs of Russians, Poles, Brazilians hanging around their stacked Portakabin favela waiting for the Man, the Irishman, the gaffer in the white van. Whenever there was an immigration fuss in the tabloids, they dispersed overnight; to reappear when the heat was off, with more cones, more discontinued rights of passage, cages of scaffolding. Some of the transient builders slept rough, in Victoria Park shrubbery, on unoccupied narrowboats, industrial squats, but most of them made their way, before work started, to the new Tesco Metro on Kingsland Road. You met them, processing along the towpath, clutching carrier bags, white with blue stripes and red lettering ('Crisis Care in Your Neighbourhood'). They were invariably polite, a nod, a token bow; generous margin offered to this eccentric English couple on their morning constitutional.

A curious thing, one of the first documentarists into the house, Mary Harron, went on to *American Psycho, I Shot Andy Warhol*, and a Hollywood career. We discussed Ballard at the kitchen table. She loved the deceptively plain style, the forensic terminology, the subversion. She was good. The other directors on *The Late Show* envied the time she was allowed for her portrait of the emerging Docklands. Paul Tickell, who managed, by carrying on cutting until a few minutes before transmission, to smuggle footage from my 8mm archive into a terse essay, pulled off a triumph of collaged impenetrability: the visual equivalent, so it was thought, of my writing. He was given two or three days to nail down the whole package, Tilbury, Gravesend, North Woolwich, Whitechapel; trains and boats and synagogues. Harron had weeks, down on the river, with Ballard as the *High-Rise* prophet-enthusiast for Canary Wharf and myself as the mad-eyed doomsayer in the shadows of the last boozer on the Isle of Dogs.

What I didn't know then was that Harron had been Tony Blair's 'date', as website biographers have it, during his time at St John's College, Oxford. I might have asked if she was still in touch, and if she could solve the mystery of where exactly Blair lived in those early Hackney years. So many people led me to different houses, most of them within the area, on the east side of Queensbridge Road, now known as 'Mapledene Village'. One claimed that he encouraged his dog, every morning, to piss on the doorstep. But the whole Blair-in-Hackney project was unresolved, subject to rumour: the launching of a calculated political career or a few years treading water, dabbling in law, hanging out, biding his time? The official account, put together after his triumphant ascent to first minister, has him gazing out on a vista of Holly Street towers and dangerous estates. Before crossing Queensbridge Road to sally forth as canvasser and message-bringer in territory where lesser mortals feared to tread.

Rob Petit returned: with a questionnaire and a thesis to develop. Like Blair, he went door-to-door through the Holly Street Estate, in an edgy time, handing out official-looking envelopes: University of Cambridge, Department of Geography. 'This is a very brief question-and-answer form about the use of SURVEILLANCE and CCTV. It is also a chance to voice any concerns you might have either about crime or the use of Closed Circuit Television (CCTV) in your borough for the purposes of an academic study.'

The boy had a charmed life, he made it, back to Albion Drive for a cup of tea and a debriefing: as evidence for my own resolutely non-academic, unreliable study. I was musing over a 'Demolition Special' from March 1996, a nostalgic reminder of the day they blew up Rowan Court by 'controlled explosion'. The aerial photograph of the estate refuted my conceit, that the low-level blocks, squeezed in between Queensbridge Road and the railway, were modelled on the infamous H-blocks of Ulster. (Mo Mowlam, early Blair associate, later non-person and former Northern Ireland Secretary, moved into Albion Drive. The landscape must have been a constant reminder of her previous life: overhead helicopters with blades set for maximum noise, screaming squad cars, endgame architecture. She was a very human presence on the street, slightly confused, smiling brightly to ward off damage in the native style, lugging armfuls of newspaper: which, unusually, she had bought, cashdown, from the Turkish minimart.) I'd got it wrong. The structure of the low-rise flats picked up on the green-and-red lizardly artwork in Haggerston Park, a stone serpent on which kids could climb. The planners called them 'snake blocks': ersatz Mayan. From above Holly Street was a giant swastika waiting to be connected.

Rob marched off, a fresh-faced officer heading for the trenches, to investigate streets he had already experienced in their virtual form through satellite mapping. Albion Square, Queensbridge Road, the Holly Street Estate: coded blots of yellow and green under a blue grid of celestial lines. You can understand how, working from such remote evidence, planners make their mistakes. The demolition squad talk of themselves, in their PR newsletters, as 'The Quiet Ones', specialists in implosions. 'Immediately after the blowdown there will be a dust cloud which rises from the block.' A cloud of hairballs, scorched pigeon feathers, newspaper screws, cat droppings, articulate pollution. 'Infestation is not a problem in the blocks as they have been empty for some time therefore depriving rats or cockroaches of the food and warmth that they require.'

The Cambridge geographer, child of the leafy North London suburbs, was not much younger than I was when I moved here; when I set out to explore. He is better informed, surveillance technology at his fingertips. And he is quite prepared to take on the inhabitants, directly, in their homes: where I was overwhelmed by the mystery of place, an illusion of personal invisibility.

'As you might expect,' Petit reported, 'I'm getting much more from talking to people and conducting interviews (recording on to tape), than I am from the survey. Had an interesting chat with Paul Turner of Albion Square (is he the High Court judge?). And Ann Jameson was very good as well. I also received some serious hate mail from the survey, addressed to a "slack arsed intellectual" and signed "anonymous – cos I don't want to end up in Guantanamo". There are serious undercurrents running through the estate, not what it looks like on the outside.'

8 January 2007: the survey was complete. Rob had succeeded, in a couple of months, by playing the Cambridge card and submitting himself to a rigorous screening process, in gaining access to Hackney's surveillance monitoring centre; a bunker about whose existence I had heard not so much as a whisper.

I found out where it was. You know the library in Stoke Newington? You go into the council section of that building and you find that CCTV monitoring has been twinned with Energy Planning. Which means that if there is ever a nuclear attack, this becomes the central control. This is the covert centre of operations in Hackney.

I met a man who was quite helpful. He spent half a day taking me through all this stuff. I had to pass through five levels of security, just to get to the room where I met him. I had to provide two different types of ID. The Hackney people were quite sensitive to the fact that terrorists might do some reconnaissance.

You go through numerous corridors into this big room. It's like a hospital, an underground hospital. They've got a monster generator, in case all the power trips out in Hackney. As you enter the room you can hear, from twenty yards away, the hum of these monitors. It's like being blasted by a wall of EM radiation.

The room is about five times the length of your kitchen, but not much wider. Banks and banks of monitors. There were five operators, doing eight-hour shifts. I don't think they get a lunch break. They were goggle-eyed. One of them fell asleep. I was sitting next to her.

There are two sub-observation rooms, much smaller. These are used by the Met Police. The main room is all council employees, CCTV operatives.

I have a map of camera points within your local territory. I showed it to my guide. He said that a lot of cameras on the estates are run by housing associations. On Holly Street there are three separate housing associations running the systems and consisting of nothing much more than a guy on the door, a couple of TV screens. They haven't got the technology to endlessly record on hard drive.

Most of the cameras are on main roads. There is only one in your immediate area, on the junction of Kingsland Road and Middleton Road. What they said is that they've put in a network point, further down Middleton Road, to wire in all the cameras on the Holly Street Estate. And the Stonebridge and Haggerston estates too. They are meant to be wired in to the central observation room. My guide said that the aim is to get as many cameras as possible linked to the control room. It's proving difficult, because the housing associations are very possessive.

The council shares its cameras with TfL, Transport for London. Most of the cameras on the main roads are shared. You can be operating your camera on Hackney business and be overridden. A little notice appears on the screen saver: 'This camera has been taken over.'

I had an interesting chat with the chairperson of the Albion Square Residents' Association. She said they'd had meetings where people were demanding cameras around the square. The request went through a lengthy process of evaluation. They decided they couldn't do it. The woman said, 'There's enough of a feeling already between "us" and "them".' And she pointed to the Holly Street Estate. She didn't want to create new antagonisms or to stress the divisions in city space. It seemed to me that the debate was more about funding. The Residents' Association has three grand in the kitty. It would cost more than that to run the cameras for a year. The notion was impractical.

The Residents' Association has good links with the council, the council is happy to deal with them. The CCTV operatives said, yes, they had heard of Albion Square and its problems. They are quite well connected, the people on the square. As a result, a camera was installed on Middleton Road.

In the Stoke Newington surveillance room they were saying, 'We'd have a camera on every street corner in Hackney.' Their view is that if it can be proved that this technology displaces crime, we must put cameras everywhere – so that there are no dark places in the city. Then the problem is solved.

It goes back to what my guide was saying about CCTV cutting into the budget of the library services. None of the money for this operation comes from central government, it all comes from Hackney council tax.

The Home Office in the 1990s put up a lot of money for council CCTV schemes. 78 per cent of the crime prevention budget goes on CCTV. They then commission a report. At the end of the 1990s, they conclude that CCTV does very little to reduce overall crime statistics. It might help a specific area. If you put CCTV on Holly Street, it will reduce crime – but in national terms it doesn't have any effect. They said, 'Our money has been completely wasted.' Government is now encouraging other people to initiate CCTV schemes, but they are not offering any financial support.

I asked the Hackney CCTV watchers how they stop criminal behaviour. All the entire operation amounts to, I discovered, is the collection of evidence for various Met operations going on at the time. Met officers are constantly swanning in and out of the Hackney control centre. They say, 'Can we get video footage of such and such a location?'

Hackney council taxpayers are essentially writing a blank cheque to provide resources for the Metropolitan Police. The other major activity in the Stoke Newington CCTV room is the storage of automatic number-plate recognition software. The boundary of Hackney is policed by a surveillance ring-fence. It's one of the only boroughs that has this auto-matic recognition facility. They bought it from Northern Ireland, Special Branch, RUC. Every car that enters Hackney has its number plate scanned. What this has achieved, the operatives told me, is to cause drug dealers and others with stolen vehicles to stay within the borough. It's a self-imposed tagging scheme. As soon as a car crosses into Islington it goes off-screen.

'We don't tell anyone we've got this facility,' they said. If they did, the criminals would stay inside or outside the surveillance net. What happens is that a big TV screen has footage of cars entering territorial waters. It operates like a congestion-charge camera, all the number plates are captured, then scanned, with the information sent to Scotland Yard. Details are logged against a data base for London: major or minor crimes, politics, terror. Within a minute of the car driving across the Hackney border, an alarm goes off in the CCTV room. Lights go red. The author-ities make one arrest a day. There is a 60 per cent chance that vehicles will be caught once the alarm sounds. A frantic chase sequence is imme-diately initiated. It makes a great movie.

They sat me down in a dark room and showed me this presentation they'd edited. It was done in the style of those American TV things about the hundred greatest chases. Completely sensationalist. A car waiting at the traffic lights. The unmarked police vehicle pulls up. The guy in the car knows exactly what's happening, so he runs. He's been picked up on number-plate recognition. He's running across this estate. He runs for ten or fifteen minutes, full pace. The whole chase is captured by surveillance cameras. The guy was vaulting over fences, doing acrobatic stuff. Eventually he is arrested, off-screen. They brought him back to the van. They showed footage of the van driving away. The van stops. They get out, the guy is convulsing. They angle the camera in. What happened, he has swallowed some heroin. Getting rid of the evidence. All on camera. It has burst inside him. Totally real. The guy was black.

I asked the people watching the screen, 'How do you decide what constitutes criminal activity?' They would never say 'racial profile'. They always said, 'body language'. Body language. But when I was sitting with this watcher we saw two black guys, hoodies with mobiles. The watcher turned to me: 'When you see people like that you zoom straight in.' I said, 'What do you mean by that?' He was, like, 'body language'.

There seems to be a level of tolerance, especially around Kingsland Waste. The watchers feel like they know the people, all the faces. They see them every day doing the same stuff. Any action is at the discretion of the Met. The police are the ones who make all the decisions. Surveillance operatives are just collecting footage to justify court cases. A few years ago there was a massive police operation on Holly Street. They arrested eighteen people. They were all prosecuted and convicted. There had been a fairly extensive surveillance operation. When I tried to go into the sub-control rooms where the police were, my guide said, 'We can't go in there. They're collecting evidence about a well-known local gang. They think it's time to move in.' When the watchers deem their subjects to have reached a critical threshold, they act.

Targets are watched, twenty-four hours a day. On that television screen they've got the average crime activity breakdown for that hour of that day for the last year. As soon as the sun goes down on Hackney the watchers say, 'This is when the pond life come out.' There is so much *going on. The watchers can't concentrate on every little petty thing. They're waiting for crimes of passion, crimes that happen instantaneously, rather than low-level drug dealing – which, in Hackney, is perpetual. They film it, it's logged. In the files. They're recording everything on hard drive.*

I said, 'When do you delete it?' They said, 'We don't.' It is way past VHS. The people downstairs, the parking officers, don't have this facility; technically speaking they're in another world. There is a big divide between traffic and crime. The parking people still record on VHS. They have an enormous room that is just racks and racks of tape, continually growing. Upstairs the watchers have very expensive servers. You go to a viewing room and you type in the date and time, you get whatever you want.

The watchers are such a mix of people. They get them from National Car Parks, NCP. I said, 'Why's that?' The manager said, 'They're easy to fire.'

Most of the time, the watchers are just staring, in a trance. There was this bit where fireworks went off, on one of the estates, they all got quite excited, turned their cameras to catch it. The telephoto zoom is extraordinary.

I didn't have to adhere to their code of practice. I could have quite a lot of fun. I was just playing around. I could explore the spaces that I knew – from a completely different perspective. For the first hour it was fascinating. But for them, the official Hackney watchers, it's highly pressured. If there is a crime, the responsibility to get a clear waist-to-head shot (which they need for evidence) is extreme. There is an awful lot of competition between operatives. There's an enormous buzz when they know they've contributed to the arrest of a criminal. Lock on, bring the bastards down.

When I was monitoring people on Kingsland Road you could tell that they were dealing. I was using that camera on the corner of Middleton Road. I filmed them with a zoomed-in lens. Every five seconds they were checking to see if they were being followed. A career criminal, a professional drug dealer working these streets, knows that you have to do your work down the alley at the back. Off-screen you are out of the story. It didn't happen.

Rob set down an aesthetically pleasing surveillance printout on the kitchen table: 110 KINGLD/MIDDLETON. 06MOV06. Night-colour. Halogen lamps smearing like dying stars over the railway bridge. The youthful geographer was in charge when the shooting incident happened in the barber shop. He had swivelled away, tracking other business, appreciating patterns of hot rear-lights and cool headlights on the main road. Visual evidence was lost. It doesn't matter how much bunting you drape around the scene, how many blue-and-yellow tin boards appeal for witnesses, this narrative is incomplete. No movie, no case to answer.

The Holly Street Estate, Rob reckoned, if you were dropped there, hooded, from the boot of a car, could be anywhere new in England. One of those off-highway Cambridge satellites, yellow-brick, uniform, arranged around recreational squares or concrete gardens that nobody seems to use. Names are aspirational, harking after a myth of the pastoral, woodland walks: Rowan, Holly, Forest, Evergreen Square. Evergreen Square, with its newly constructed mounds and ASBO warnings, bristled with surveillance technology.

I delivered one hundred questionnaires in Holly Street and got thirty back. Which is pretty good. Twenty-eight of them wanted the cameras, without question. Half of the responses came before the murder in Evergreen Square. After the murder, loads more questionnaires came flooding in. There was an immediate assumption that CCTV is the solution. They wanted money spent on CCTV systems rather than the Leisure Centre.

It was OK, delivering those questionnaires. I got one back that was really threatening. The guy thought the survey was trying to justify CCTV. He said, 'You go to Cambridge, how could you possibly understand? Take a walk in the real world. Stop handing out fancy surveys from your fucking ivory tower.' And then he said, 'I hope you get caught on CCTV being stabbed in the face with a broken bottle.'

Stevens Nyembo-Ya-Muteba, forty, father of two, was a mathematician who had been offered a place at Cambridge University. A refugee from Kinshasa in the 'war-torn' Congo, he arrived in London in 1997 and worked as a chef's assistant at the Criterion Brasserie, a restaurant owned by Marco Pierre White. He moved, with his young family, to the newly constructed Holly Street Estate, a flat with convenient access to the playground in Evergreen Square. His daughters were aged five and six. The *Evening Standard*, reporting on his murder, drew the obvious parallel, Hackney/Kinshasa: 'Mr Nyembo-Ya-Muteba had fled the capital to escape the violence in the region in which Joseph Conrad set his novel *Heart of Darkness*.'

The new technology, covering the dark places, pushed the dealers and runners indoors. After forced entry, they congregated in stairwells. Mr Nyembo-Ya-Muteba, trying to study, to get a few hours' sleep before the next day's work, confronted twelve youths, asking them to move on, to keep the noise down. He was stabbed repeatedly in the chest. A neighbour found him sprawled on the stairs: 'I knew from his injuries that he was critical.' Another neighbour, Hayri Kilicarsian, claimed that these youths regularly violated the interior spaces of the flats, the off-camera zones. 'They piss on the floor and smoke drugs. They climb on to people's balconies.'

The Albion Square Residents' Association Newsletter reported that the Revd Rose Hudson-Wilkin of All Saints Church led a solemn procession from the 'snake park' to the site where the victim died. 'TV cameras were present but discreet.' Overnight, Evergreen Square had acquired all the cameras in the world. Men standing on the roofs of vans. Concerned women in television slap, their backs to the flats, talking intimately to tight lenses.

The excitement of the original incident had faded by the time that Joseph Ekaette, nineteen, previously imprisoned for the rape of a schoolgirl, was given a second life sentence for the murder of Nyembo-Ya-Muteba. The rape of the fourteen-year-old girl was filmed by one of his confederates on a mobile phone.

St Philip's Road

Coming off Richmond Road and taking our time with St Philip's Road – there was an ongoing debate between us about the correct time to arrive for a meal – we ran into Charlie Velasco. Or rather, Anna nudged me in the ribs and said, 'Is that Charlie? Do you think Syd will be coming?' I'd been absorbed in the scale of some of these properties, the shabby or retrieved grandeur, the way Hackney keeps you off-balance by confounding your expectations, flitting so rapidly from action, buzz, collision to zones of recessive and haunting silence. Charlie was in snug football shorts and a starched dress shirt, open to the chest. He was carrying a wood-framed tennis racket. And flicking his hair like Ile Nastase.

'Looking for London Fields?' I said, assuming that there was a discreet meeting to be arranged, a new deal to be brokered. I never worked out what exactly Charlie did for a living.

'Same as you: Patrick's. We've now eaten twice in Hackney in fifteen years. That has to mean something.'

Up on his toes, he offered Anna a not entirely welcome kiss.

It was an era, the mid 1980s, of breaking bread, coping with olives, in other people's houses. Charlie adapted: tennis racket in one hand, plonk in the other; two bottles, to make up for the inferior quality. Back in the 1960s and early 1970s there were communal meals, we rarely shifted beyond the kitchen. Ginger cats, yoghurt cultures. Liberal councillors before they'd been found out. Then there were children and people moved away. I worked long and unpredictable hours, I was always on the road. For five or ten years, I suppose, we hadn't really seen anybody: immediate family, in-laws, an accident of bookdealers, motorway service stations, chips at the seaside. Midnight curries with Driffield in Glasgow.

Patrick Wright, moving into St Philip's Road with his partner,

Claire Lawton (who had her hands full, locally, as a specialist in geriatric medicine), signalled the social restlessness that would fuel the property boom of the Thatcher decade. Tony Blair and Cherie Booth were the paradigm, Mapledene Village and away along the path of the submerged Hackney Brook to Islington, in the shadows of Highbury Stadium: £615,000 their selling price in 1997. Then Connaught Square, a town house picked up for £3.56 million (before the revisions and the decorators). You arrive in a new setting, you cook food for new people. These occasions, with Patrick and Claire, opened up my sense of where we were; the incomers noticed details I had missed, they teased out fresh stories, they listened attentively to the neighbours. A new book was forming; Patrick would begin his odyssey down Dalston Lane, a few hundred yards to the bus stop (his way out): *A Journey through Ruins.*

I met Patrick in the Prince George on Parkholme Road, he was writing something about my first novel for the *London Review of Books*. It was a good session. And an astonishing thing for me, that a discredited poetic, buried as deep as the Hackney Brook, should be revealed, analysed, re-presented. The massive wardrobe of the Whitechapel hermit David Rodinsky would be splashed, in shades of grey, across the cover of a literary magazine. The pub where we drank, Patrick intimated, was part of the story, the social shift, the property hunger: he was the first writer I had met who talked money. Poets of the 1970s were grateful to be paid anything. Bookdealers treated all novelists as if they were the future dead, inconveniently hanging on, reluctant to make those signatures – captured through the tedium of a book launch or reading – worth something. Patrick, returning from Canada to Thatcher's Britain, had this awkward and unworkable belief: that authors should receive their due; the merit of a long-considered and crafted piece of work should receive a reward commensurate with its status. Insanity! For a while, his energy – the height helped, the Saxon flop of hair – carried it off: broadsheet commissions on top dollar, transatlantic jaunts (tickets covered), late-night television spots, lectures. But vultures in collarless shirts were waiting. The George was a birdcage, a trap in which to memorialize loss. The surrounding streets were filling with City migrants, commissioners of documentaries, advertising men, the putative tribes of New Labour. Patrick recalled the Hackney Literary and Philosophical Society and namechecked notables of an earlier generation, Michael Rosen, David Widgery, Sheila Rowbotham. Widgery, with his spicy mix of politics, topography, medicine and personal anecdote, was in some ways a rival.

Patrick was so articulate – Anna still smacks her lips over 'discontinued alternatives' – that you were almost persuaded to give him your trust; sentences launched with such schoolmasterly confidence must surely capture the world. The performance was, in the best sense, disinterested, fired by the excitement of discovery: knowledge as its own reward (in the promise of an adequately substantial cheque-in-the-post). Patrick's semaphored, straight-to-camera conviction could have initiated a major career, if there had not been one drawback: *he meant it.* He lacked Tony Blair's indifference to facts, morality, cultural memory. It was the stark contrast between a romantic puritan and a fellow-travelling papist, half in love with ritual and wipe-the-slate public confession. 'Blair's great skill,' said Denis Healey, 'was personal charisma – what used to be called bullshit.' The watery eye, the insane stare of the secular saint who mistakes sincerity for truth.

We discovered, before the first pint was swallowed, our mutual addiction to field notes: as the residue of, and the excuse for, random expeditions. *Move, dig, notice, report.* We could walk London. In Vancouver, Patrick had run up against the poet Charles Olson's notion of 'open-field poetics': everything goes into the stew, localized documentation, letters, bills of sale, news reports. Evidence. Until the greater vision is achieved, the cosmology of the impossible: the curvature of the universe that is love.

I found myself placed at the dinner table directly opposite the handwritten poem-poster by Louis Zukofsky. We encountered some of Patrick's colleagues and contacts. Potential friendships, challenges: the soups, the virtuoso carving, the cheeses and puddings. Men now seemed to do most of the cooking. The kitchen was close at hand. We sat out there with Raphael Samuel and Alison Light. Raphael, short and intense, with a shawl of dark hair swept across the skull, was an intimidating, adversarial presence. On his best behaviour. He disapproved, with good reason, of my gothic-tourist raids on what he regarded as his personal and tribal fiefdom, Whitechapel. Patrick's assaults on the heritage industry – which very soon became a heritage industry of their own, pirated and parroted by media drones – had been challenged by Samuel, who argued that the tone was patronizing. Raph wanted to defend the integrity of popular culture, the excursion, the day out for working people. His own Elder Street property, crammed to its weavers' attic with research files, never-to-be-written books, would, as a result of the heritage exploitation of Spitalfields, Hong Kong bankers buying blind from catalogue, be worth well over a million pounds.

Charlie, stepping into the garden for a companionable spliff, asked after Andrew Motion. Apparently the future laureate had a place in De Beauvoir Town. I don't know if he was a tennis partner of Charlie, but he didn't show, that night: some complication with the train from Norwich, double-booked.

'Tony won't go near the courts on London Fields,' Charlie told me. 'He tried a jog one morning, but never again. Feral dogs and worse humans, drinkers on every bench. Crime and the causes of crime. Something must be done.'

I had no idea who Tony was. Nobody did. There were people who claim to have seen Blair picking up the kids at the school gates, but that was much later, in Islington.

In our early Hackney days there were tennis courts marked out on the grass in London Fields, a cricket square, an open-air swimming pool that cost almost nothing, a coin dropped into a slot in the wall. Dr David Widgery, so my neighbour Harriet reported, strolled down to the Lido, after one of her lunch parties, stripped to the buff and leapt, with a revolutionary screech of triumph, into the cool, leaf-surfaced water: he was expelled. Blacklisted. Forgiven.

I played tennis on a slithery and pitted hardcourt with Jock, a retired postal-supervisor from Mount Pleasant, and his mate, Little Sammy from Stamford Hill. Jock's correct serves and wonky knees, Sam's darting, snapping patrol of the net, against my crude fore-hand thumps and all-court hustle. Then, on a broken bench, we would enjoy some chat, while Jock massaged the life back into his rheumatic joints and Sammy smoked the very thin roll-up cigarettes he carried around in a tin. He played in his trilby, took off his jacket – for which he came prepared with a hanger – but was otherwise suited. Waistcoat, shiny tie, black shoes: fit to move on to the synagogue. He was involved with a married woman in Clapton. The tennis was both a warm-up and a genuine excuse for an adul-terous morning in Hackney.

Charlie Velasco didn't get Blair on the London Fields court and he would never have contemplated introducing him to the regular football matches that Jock supervised – as player and referee – on the red dirt patch behind the mesh fence. These crude Sunday-morning affairs, featuring pick-up teams of anywhere between four and fourteen a side, were brawls in which Charlie took no interest. He had his myth to protect: how, in a charity match at White Hart Lane, a neat lay-off to Trevor Brooking (who was clattered by Boris Johnson) was acknowledged with a thumbs-up from his temporary manager, Steve Perryman. Charlie, like Martin Peters, was a thinking footballer – but he did most of his thinking posthumously: in the pub, the restaurant, on the train, flights to Finland or Macedonia, when he made contact with established journalists like Brian Glanville and Hugh McIlvanney. 'You're box to box, son,' Ron Atkinson told him, as they stood side by side, shaking off the drops, at a black-tie bash in Park Lane. 'Like Dracula with piles. Heart of oak, brains to match. It used to be a working-man's game.'

They were all there, kicking up the red dirt, the Irish boys, the

Turks, the black guys who thought they were playing basketball, backs to you, never passing, doing their tricks – and white strollers who would rather lose by eight goals than score with an ugly tap-in or a header that would mess up their latest cut. I had lumps kicked out of me by a five-foot scaffolder who compensated, in terms of weight, by making up for the absence of shirt and vest by wearing a huge pair of steel-capped boots. He was training his son to play alongside him, a precise duplicate whose boots were pristine and yellow. And whose patriotic tattoos were still raw and scabbed. John H. Stracey of Bethnal Green, who had recently defeated Jose Napoles for the world welterweight title, turned out. As did Eric, my neighbour from Albion Drive, oldest son of the senior long-term residents, the Morrises. A couple of the flashier young strikers were on the books at Orient, you could see immediately why they wouldn't make it: they could do everything except acknowledge there were other players on the park. One of them was offloaded to Dagenham and Redbridge (where he warmed the bench) and the other died, two weeks after the end of the season, from leukaemia.

A stately midfielder coming up to retirement, an Orient regular, gave me my local nickname: Ossie. Watching him, his unhurried control, the way the game flowed through him even when he seemed to be standing still, I understood that I would never master this discipline. Thanks to the period sideburns, my approximate size and the position in which I lurked on the field, the fact that I was wearing a Chelsea T-shirt (not because I supported them, the shirts were a nice blue colour and were being knocked out for 50p on the Waste), he christened me Ossie. 'Man on, Ossie. *Man on.* Give it and go, my son.' I was flattered by the connection with the King's Road wide boy, the roistering legend, Peter Osgood. But my team-mates never got it. They thought he meant 'Aussie'. Which made perfect sense, the way I spoke. The freakishness of our shabby clothes. Renchi, who also turned out, became 'the other Aussie'. Rough football on London Fields lasted until the dawn of the Thatcher era, when the spirit turned ugly: on-field fights, endless bickering, obscenities, playacting, appeals to a referee who was no longer there.

I helped Jock to pack up his effects and I drove him out to a new estate, beyond the motorway: a clean, safe, mustard-brick unit, with excellent parking space for the car he didn't own. He was twenty miles closer to Scotland. And he should, I told him in parting, console himself with that thought. Without his tribal football games, Hackney was no longer Hackney. It was like the rest of the world, up for grabs.

Patrick returned to Hackney, in May 2006, from his Cambridgeshire village: just for the day. Old niggles about royalties, editors, commissioners were now serious. Ever the financial realist, he had worked the changes so often, in terms of agents and publishers, that he would soon be back with the gang who launched his original career. 'I take oblique approaches, not out of perversity,' he wrote to the chairman of the firm dragging their heels over his latest epic (demanding the return of a sizeable advance), 'but because they enable me to cast unexpectedly revealing light on apparently familiar realities, and thereby to free my subject matter from the grip of ideological orthodoxy.'

Our approach to Dalston Lane was certainly oblique. I asked Patrick to lead me to Blair's Hackney property: 59 Mapledene Road. I had checked the electoral register. Blair (Anthony), Booth (Cherie) and Booth (Lyndsey) were all lodged, for the period 1980–86, on an upwardly mobile street – which looked west towards the undemolished towers of the Holly Street Estate and east towards London Fields (squatted swimming pool and discontinued football pitch). Cherie's sister, Lyndsey, was born in Hackney, in 1956, at a time when her father, the actor Tony Booth, was sleeping and drinking in Stoke Newington. Blair (Anthony), the man without convictions, had been asked by Neil Kinnock to see what he could find out about financial scandals in the City. The task was, as Tony Booth remarked, 'the lowest rung on the political ladder'. But Scouse family was family. He offered help, by way of old contacts, thus allowing his son-in-law to become righteously indignant about irregularities in the matter of undeclared donations to party funds. And the way peerages were dished out to crooks like Robert Maxwell. Blair learnt the actorly trick of puffing up his tail feathers like a coot on the canal, to signal that he was on the attack. He was sharing an office, very much the junior partner, with a brooding Scot called Gordon Brown. Brown networked, relentlessly. Blair came home to the family in Hackney.

'So why did they leave?' I asked.

'The usual,' Patrick said. 'After the fifth burglary we get nervous about putting our key in the lock. Cherie, who was the real politician, was doing her thing in the free legal advice centre. While she was haranguing the old bill about their treatment of one of her clients, the same guy was turning over the Mapledene gaff. A neighbour, an executive at London Weekend, had to physically restrain her. She was trying to nut the thief who was in the grip of two or three unusually prompt coppers.'

We rambled on to the George, a nostalgic reprise of the period when Patrick was working on *A Journey through Ruins*. I asked him if I could tape his memories of life in Hackney. As I pressed the record button, it flashed into my mind that Blair fitted my arbitrary pattern: he lived within 440 yards of Albion Drive.

I came back to England in '79. By '81 I was living in a flat in Clapton. I bought a flat for £21,000. I knew about Hackney. I knew the east was where to go. I already knew people who lived there. I'd met people in the Polytechnic world.

Clapton was all right. I'd met Claire, my wife. We stayed there for a year. Then we moved to Stoke Newington. I was there with Richard North. When people like Neal Ascherson started writing newspaper articles about Hackney, they came to me, or to North. Obviously people had been settling in the area for generations, some of them authentic bohemian geezers who drank too much. Stoke Newington was already East Islington. The question was whether it would ever get to the top of the hill – or whether it would keep falling back. I think when we were there it was still undecided. We stayed for four or five years. Then we needed more space and we moved here, to St Philip's Road, purely because the house was bigger and cheaper. What was good about Stoke Newington was that it was still a lower-middle-class mixed area. There were those incidents you get in these parts of the city. You're lucky if people spend time not raping and mugging each other. If you are Mr Patel, so to speak, running a corner shop, you do not get hit with iron bars.

St Philip's Road was somewhere you could afford to buy a house on a fairly insecure salary. My first mortgage came from some weird building society I found in Westminster. I got it despite the fact that I didn't have a job. Then, later, I was with Claire and it was a bit easier, she was a medical student.

When we moved here, this was known as the Mayfair of Hackney. The street where the pub is, where we're drinking now, Parkholme Road, was considered fairly grand. The corner up there, of Dalston Lane, was called Lebon's, nobody knows that now. There is a forgotten East End topography. The houses in the area were mostly redbrick, Edwardian and late Victorian. There was subsidence, so the earlier ones fell down.

When we moved in there were a lot of people who were basically hippies who had come when no money was required, when you could literally write a cheque and buy a house. We didn't buy on the main drag, on Parkholme Road, we bought on a street behind it. We had a pleasant situation and it worked well for us. We had kids growing up. I was upstairs working, so I was around. I used to go off into town by way of Dalston Lane. When I was writing, I used to write a lot about what I saw on the streets: disintegrating bus queues, forms of tolerance and intolerance.

You were free. You could make your own way. We got on well with the basically working-class Hackney dwellers who were still living here. There were fewer of them than there had been. But they were still around. I remember once looking out of the window to see this rather stern man taking a picture. I thought he was casing the joint, that he was going to rob us. I went out and said, 'What are you doing?' He turned out to be an Australian who had grown up in this house in the 1930s. He said that he couldn't believe how much the road had changed. He had the usual complaint: too many coloured faces. He explained that his father was an insurance company representative. He had a patch to work when this was a lower-middle-class, upwardly striving area.

This was a place of Jewish dispersal. The writer Emanuel Litvinoff's trajectory was from Jewish Whitechapel to a succession of flats on Mare Street and Sandringham Road. Leon Kossoff worked here. He had a studio near the railway. The elderly Jewish couple opposite us were always fussing about the state of the area. And their son, who was obviously gay, found the whole situation difficult.

This is not the East End. This is the first move out of the East End. If you look at the Mapledene area, the houses that are now so smartened up, you see a story that has happened often before, in the 1860s and 1840s. Then, because of the smoke and smog of the City, clerks and the better-paid workers head off to the next place up the line. There is a perpetual sense of settlement and displacement. The Jewish couple opposite us felt that they hadn't done the right thing in coming here.

The other oddity about St Philip's Road is that it houses two or three Montserrat families. That made it Montserrat-in-London, there are so few of them here. They went through the experience of the volcano that wiped out the place they came from and left them stranded in Hackney.

I wrote my first book, On Living in an Old Country, *in the Stoke Newington Library. It had everything I needed. The local markets were quite good. We used that market in Ridley Road all the time. The supermarkets hadn't broken into the area. I remember when Dalston Cross, the shopping centre, was constructed. Ridley Road still had sandwich shops. A quite Jewish focus. Also substantial African and West Indian stalls and businesses. The dynamics of the place were to do with waves of coming and going. That was the reality.*

I was writing occasional pieces. I was busy with other work. I couldn't sit down and construct and research a book in the conventional way. Who cares about that sort of stuff? It's too laborious. So what I would do is dance about, go to the library, follow hunches. My writing was based on a very fervent reaction against what had happened in critical/cultural circles. Everything was theory, everything was dogma. It was left wing, with endless quotes from people like Althusser. Dreadful stuff! And there was a political culture that said nobody could talk about anybody else without abusing them. That was a part of an intransigent feminism. A man couldn't write about a woman's experience. I got myself to a point where I liked picking up fragmentary stories and excavating them: slight, glancing anecdotes. It would be like pulling a piece of string and then seeing what you found when it came out. I wasn't just searching for evidence, I wanted to use the search itself as a critical/cultural device.

I was writing at the time of the fiftieth anniversary of VE Day. All this commemoration of the Blitz was going on. The Welfare State was disintegrating. The last housing estates were being built. And they were only just better than the dud ones that were being demolished. I subtitled my Dalston Lane book The Last Days of London. *There was a sense of endings, tacky endings, infecting that moment.*

So how do I string all this together? I felt: I don't need to string it together. Other people will do that for me. As for Dalston Lane . . . I've been up and down this street five times a day. I took the street as a yard-stick and measured it up. I also felt that everything you capture, you fix. I found myself even trying to fix the billboards. When the economy is booming, billboards move very fast. All this flyposting is going on. There were moments at the end of that era when the economy sank into complete inertia and nothing would move. You would find bankrupt estate agents who still had windows full of prices from twenty or fifty years previously. That's absolutely true. You could find estate agents advertising houses for a tenth or even a hundredth of their value. When you've got an area that is not economically buoyed up, it goes into entropy. Broadway Market was the absolute sump of the universe in the 1980s and early 1990s. It was beyond recovery.

It's extraordinary to watch when the waves of development roar through, they are so absolutely transforming. The logic is identical to what happened around Parkholme Road at an earlier period. It's what Stoke Newington went through in the 1980s. And now that whole stretch of the canal beyond Broadway Market is getting the treatment. Water is always the medium of revaluation. Canals made from mercury.

You always had these corridors of bohemianism and cultural avant-gardism with middle-class politeness and bookshops selling Winnie the

Pooh. *But it's still astonishing to see the process happening pretty much while you watch, in the time it takes to order a cup of coffee.*

I have a slightly puritanical take on all this, something I felt when I was writing A Journey through Ruins. *I thought this New Gothic sensibility, the lifestyle magazines getting off on squalor, was dubious. I didn't need the occult to be true or false, but as a metaphor it fitted the period. What we had to identify was the language of heritage. The deployment of heritage was part of the process of colonization. But in a way I have a great admiration for historical structures. They shouldn't be dismissed. Heritage just became a way of moving everything to the surface. Architects did it with façades, meaningless fronts propped up on invisible armatures.*

Dalston Lane

What Patrick didn't know, and what I didn't know then, was that the wood engraver Edward Calvert, William Blake's friend and disciple, had lived in Parkholme Road. *Had lived, lives.* Once there, always there: the traces. An underdescribed period in a half-forgotten artist's story, the Hackney years: new suburbia, substantial villa with studio space to the rear, land recently enclosed by speculative builders. Calvert's biographer, Raymond Lister, reports that Edwin Landseer, sculptor of monumental lions, borrowed the Parkholme Road studio while he painted an equestrian portrait. Calvert was offered the job of touching in the human figure, the rider. He refused, much to the annoyance of his wife who cried out: 'Edward, you will never do anything to make yourself famous.'

The engraver courted the geographical obscurity in which to indulge his passion for moving books from room to room. He retreated, deep into unknown territory – *because it was unknown.* The Parkholme Road house was an occupied storage facility. There was enough of a private income, now that he had retired from the sea, to summon the bookbinders. Every volume was stripped of its original paper (or cloth) covering and reshod. The noise of the original colours offended him; he demanded quiet uniformity, mute obedience. Rooms to furnish his books. Tottering stacks were shunted, apartment to apartment, in a never-ending porterage: the man was not to be easily satisfied. His library was a leathery great-coat.

And who were the porters, builders, layers of fires, bedmakers, scullery maids, cooks and housekeepers? Their names are unrecorded. Who – if anyone – modelled for the pastiche-classical female nudes the ageing Calvert produced? The late paintings that Lister called 'a sickly sentimentalizing of the ancient world'. Timid rear views shivering with repression. The delicious double-curves of a moist, full-cheeked grin. A sacrificial bowl raised in tribute to a louring Grecian sky: when all the gods, animating spirits of wood and stream, have died.

Calvert's granddaughter Elizabeth deflates this notion of the garden studio: it was a shed, a barn. The kind of tumbledown wooden structure the area has always favoured, beloved of toads and foxes. Food for hungry rats. Private space, that was what Calvert required: secret chambers hidden behind walls of dummy books, dim caves of seclusion in which to brood on his philosophy of light. Only by its absence, in velvet-draped windowless cells, was the prismatic essence to be found. The recipe. The equation.

'Light is orange!' he shrieked, while out walking with Samuel Palmer. In the Parkholme Road wilderness, so recently claimed from open fields, Calvert shaped an altar dedicated to Pan.

The question remains: *did those feet?* I have discovered no reference to a visit by William Blake to Hackney. He was gone before Calvert moved to Parkholme Road. It was the faithful wood engraver who followed the visionary London poet to his pauper's grave in Bunhill Fields on 17 August 1827. To the company of six unremembered others waiting just beyond the Hackney boundary.

The delicacy of the wood engravings – paradise visions, nymphs, travellers, sacred woods – had already been foreclosed by the time the Calverts migrated to Hackney. But the memory of the precision and clarity of that early achievement becomes a tribute to what his adopted home has given away: to foul-smelling industries, dank canals, railways, theoretical progress. Thriving orchards uprooted from the slopes above the Hackney Brook. Fields enclosed, hedged and sold to a single proprietor. Factories constructed, exploiting water power, to provide employment for displaced country folk and footsore immigrant labourers. The wood engravings, their ripe apples and honeymoon bedchambers, sheep and cider presses, are a graphic record of loss. Prophetic seizures accessible only at the moment of extinction. The solitary shepherd, staff in hand, journeys after an absence of sheep. Lamb Lane is a slaughter track. Markets require the death of everything they market. The hunger is insatiable. Paintbrushes from the pelts of bloody beasts. A glue of bones. Canvas stolen from sacks worn by skeletal beggars.

The white-bearded Calvert, a beached Mediterranean mariner, favoured pea-jackets with sharp lapels. His wife, Mary, took the burden of Hackney life, the children, the dirt, the horror of having to deal, on a daily basis, *with what is actually there.* No rest. No remission. Physical objects overload her dreams, she wakes cold, to the knowledge that it will never be managed. The structure of bricks and mortar in which she is condemned to live grinds away at the mantle of cloth, papery wraps of skin. Calvert paints a youth he no longer possesses. She contemplates the length of ground in which she will be laid

Overwhelmed, she decamps: to recover breath on the south coast, St Leonards-on-Sea, a newly unfashionable projection by the architect James Burton. A mile or so to the west of Hastings, in the county of Sussex. Calvert, done with false horizons, excess light, settled for Paris. And in this unaccustomed release from domesticity, the kindness of ill health, Mary indulged her true vocation: as a painter who didn't paint.

'I wish,' she wrote to her absent husband, 'you would particularly regard the transparency of shadows.'

But he was meditating on the notion that all paintings are constructed upon a musical basis. He invented codes and tables, angelic dialogues. He would never again pick up a paintbrush.

Sapphirine. Rubiate. Divine, sacrificial, and ending in blood.

At a safe distance, across the Channel, Calvert endured intimations of deep truth. The blessing, now that he was no longer there, of Hackney's rose-red empire. The paradise he had resigned.

'Piercing through veils, and passing things more and more precious – the links of the eternal chain are known but not seen.

The last and uppermost flights, through a vaulted depth, are voice-less and sublime.' He wrote. And burnt.

Cornering out of Parkholme Road, negotiating a complicated junc-tion that did its best to cull pedestrians reckless enough to attempt the tight mouth of Dalston Lane, Patrick picked up pace; he had left some weight behind in his former London life, the era of entertaining and media lunching, career grazing. In autumnal colours, a burnt-orange polo shirt and loose slacks, he revisited a previous self, a hungrier eye. The bounty hunter of *A Journey through Ruins* now demonstrated an ironic affection for the exhausted strip he had made into a symbol of the defeated Welfare State. He noticed insignificant details that dropped him right back into that earlier narrative.

I NEED A RIOT.
SAFETY HELMETS MUST BE WORN.
WHAT'S GOING ON?

Small shops were carbonized shells, held up by layers of fly-pitched posters and council warnings. Patrick's 1992 expedition was as distant as the pastoral visions of Calvert's pilgrims. The past, as we age, becomes so personal, at the mercy of unreliable witnesses. I asked Patrick to prompt Emanuel Litvinoff for anything he could recall about Roland Camberton. David Hirsch, Camberton's alter ego in *Rain on the Pavements*, learning chess, tries to fix the layout of the board as firmly in his head as the geography of familiar Hackney streets. He haunts Dalston Lane, this corner, on his way through to Ridley Road Market. It is an anchor for memory.

'Litvinoff was totally dismissive,' Patrick said. 'Those two Camberton books, he felt, had nothing to do with the East London he had known as a young man. They were opportunistic, banal. He preferred to remember Wolf Mankowitz, who hovered at the back of his mind as an impossibly conceited but likeable fellow, running a productive antiques and porcelain business. The man knew how to make money.'

In the slightly desperate atmosphere Patrick captures in his book, all kinds of hopeless scams surfaced in Dalston Lane. We ate in a restaurant, run by an elegant young black woman, that was spectacularly in the wrong place. You had to get your order in fast, on the understanding that the chef might decamp before the main course was served. Bailiffs doubled as waiters. Pamela's it was called. (Anna remembered it as: Paradise. A large man coming out of the kitchen, bottle of champagne under one arm, ice bucket in hand. To celebrate the only customers.) Pamela Hurley had trained in New York. She was determined to sell upmarket Barbadian cuisine to the City speculators who must surely one day arrive – when promised transport-hub services materialized. The restaurant vanished before Patrick moved to his Cambridgeshire village. The next time we ate out was in a Turkish café where they invited you into the kitchen to poke at bubbling pots: a feast for a few pounds.

The more insistent the wreckage, the more Patrick was inspired to excavate cultural counterweights. He came across Sheila Rowbotham, both of them jobbing on the academic circuit, and was interested to hear what I'd discovered about the Montague Road commune and the visit of Godard. In his turn, he had tracked down Andrew Holmes, who photographed every property on Dalston Lane, a full record, just at the time when *A Journey through Ruins* appeared.

'Sadly,' he said, 'the film was sent to Joe Kerr, who appears to have lost it.' Kerr taught at the Royal College of Art and was co-editor of a useful book: *London: From Punk to Blair*. To which Patrick had contributed.

'The street is really a clogged river of junk flowing through the city,' Patrick wrote. Sixteen shots survive from the Andrew Holmes traverse: architectural detail, close-ups. If you want colour or passion, Patrick suggested, you have to go back to Leon Kossoff.

'That painting, the big oil, *Demolition of the Old House, Dalston Junction* is truly impressive. I wanted to get it into my book. It's worth a trip to the Tate depository in South London to see it. Thick layers of paint denoting, more or less, the ghost presence of the old house, and then – barely visible – lots of scurrying figures pulling at the bricks and plaster without much assistance in the way of tools or scaffolding.'

From the studio to which Kossoff travelled, down the North London Line from Willesden Green, he looked west: the fleshing sheds of Ridley Road, the railway. A torn-out spine on a bed of yellow clay. The German Hospital directly behind him. He watches, participating by default, as men in blue overalls take down an old house, starting on the roof. Blood reds, chalky greens, a marine sky threaded with lint. Black slashes, diagonals. A kaddish for railway stations, concrete islands and retail archipelagos.

Stormy Summer Day, Dalston Lane. 1975. Unknowing, we pushed a buggy, hung with plastic bags, back from Ridley Road Market: past the building in which Kossoff worked.

A strange thing: that Edward Calvert, shifting east from Parkholme Road, took a house on the far side of Mare Street: 11 Darnley Road. Where he died on 14 July 1883. Darnley Road is where Kossoff lived as a child. And where the photographer Stephen Gill lodged when I came across his work for the first time.

I left Patrick at the bus stop. It was not so much a question of standing about in the vague hope that something would appear, but of waiting for one of a fleet of gridlocked buses to move. They were nose-to-tail, these bendy monsters, from Graham Road to the Junction: a stalled travelator. Everything behind the bus stop was hidden by a recent fence. Cancelled views. Excavations begun and abandoned.

A woman at the German Hospital event told me about a strange discovery in the cellars of 16 Dalston Lane, beneath the offices where she worked: shelves of primitive contraceptive devices, coils, diaphragms, yellowing pelvises like sculpted scrimshaw, untouched since the 1920s. A surrealist museum designed by a follower of Marie Stopes.

I crossed the road for my appointment with a solicitor at Dowse & Co. Bill Parry-Davies, who I'd met at the Boas Society, was prepared to give me an interview: the background to the demolition of the Labyrinth building and the suspicious Dalston Lane fires. Parry-Davies was an activist, a man of the community, the guiding light of OPEN Dalston, a group campaigning for the retention of historic structures. For local pride. Against mindless futurism, computer-generated fictions. The Olympic backdraught, that tsunami of dodgy capital, had united the warring factions among politicians, planners, development quangos and City Hall fixers. And the effect on the landscape was monolithic, devastating.

Buzzed through and pointed up the stairs, I met Bill, a tall man in a modest office, who led me first to a window that overlooked Dalston Lane. This was no Kossoff epiphany. We were staring down on affronted dust: the blank rectangle where the North London Colosseum and Amphitheatre once stood. The darkened hulk that had been the Four Aces and the Labyrinth. I took a few photographs of whatever was no longer there.

Then we went through to the office. Bill's window was open. It was a hot afternoon. I sunk low into my chair, which faced a large desk, on which were perched two plastic tumblers of water. In my enthusiasm, the heat of the questions, I drank them both. Bill was an eloquent and easy-paced talker. He had a tale to tell.

We moved to Hackney in 1984. I was working at that time in the Law Centre at Mare Street. I wanted to be able to walk to work. We live in Cecilia Road. It was my aversion to queues and public transport that brought us here. My approach, as a solicitor, was that I'd rather work in the community where I was living. You develop close relationships.

In the mid 1980s tenants from Holly Street came to see me with allegations of a corrupt relationship between Hackney Council officers responsible for repairing the estates and private contractors. I employed an independent architect to inspect all the work. We found that there were overpayments in 75 per cent of cases, sometimes even before the work

*was officially ordered. Bills were being paid before the work was done.
They said that two surveyors were supposed to inspect £5 million-worth
of work a year. Allegations eventually reached such a high profile that
the council had to appoint a QC to conduct an inquiry. Just before the
report was published, the chief finance officer of the council, the head of
maintenance, the head of building works, and others, all resigned. No
one was convicted or even charged, to my knowledge, but these officers
had presided over a systemic failure that had cost Hackney residents
millions. Corruption in Hackney was and is a recurring problem – you
have to keep weeding the garden.*

*Back in the 1980s, there were dreadful examples of corruption. Housing
officers were renting out council flats privately. There were serious housing-
benefit scams, payments being made to council officers' private bank
accounts. There was clearly a problem in Hackney.*

*Now, with the current development here in Dalston Lane, we've moved
into a new phase: the age of the fire. There have been eight fires. My
involvement began with that little terrace of shops. They came into council
ownership when the GLC was abolished. And Hackney did nothing about
them. They continued to collect the original rent, but they didn't renew
any of the leases. The traders lost any long-term security. When the
landlord says, 'I need these properties for redevelopment,' that provides
grounds for possession. Unless you've got a lease you are vulnerable.
Those shops have been there a very long time. The music shop is second-
generation. The Star Bakery has been there since the 1930s. They are
long-standing family businesses.*

*Hackney had this huge crisis: £70 million in the hole. The debt emerged
in 2001. They decided to put everything on the market. All the property
surrounding Broadway Market, Dalston Lane, Well Street, Morning Lane,
Kingsland Road. Government said to Hackney, 'Either you close the gap
in your finances or we'll move in.' So the chief executive of the council
said: 'Sell.' And that's what they did.*

*This is the crux of the scandal: council standing orders state that when
you have tenants in occupation, you are required to offer the property, in
the first instance, to those tenants. Before putting them on the open
market. In Dalston Lane they put the portfolio up for private tender: as*

a block, all sixteen houses. Unless you can come up with £2 million, you can't afford to buy.

Some of the traders rang the council: 'We'd like to make an offer.' 'Fine. Put your offer in.' They were ignored. The property went into auction. That was April 2002. The portfolio was bought by an offshore company called Dalston Lane Investments Limited, a company based in the Bahamas. If you've got an offshore operation nobody can find out who is behind the company name. It's almost impossible to identify what the real financial interests are. We know one name, but, generally speaking, it is very secretive. And they don't pay tax.

They bought, at auction, sixteen Georgian houses in Dalston Lane for £1.8 million. They also bought a load of properties in Broadway Market. Broadway Market Investments Hackney Limited. Different names, same people. The finance is mainly from Dubai. Al-Hilal Investments Limited. The prospectus put out by Hackney for Dalston Lane stated: 'Although these buildings are of historic interest, if they can't be refurbished, if it is not financially viable to refurbish, we will consider another scheme.' The landlords put in a proposal to demolish the lot. What they did was to divide the buildings. Dalston Lane Investments retained some, then they split the portfolio. The reason being that if you have one big development you are required to provide a certain proportion of social housing, public affordable housing. If you make the split, each separate development is smaller and there is less requirement to provide public affordable accommodation. Both of the companies involved with Dalston Lane put in planning applications to demolish the lot.

One of the applications to demolish was refused, the other was withdrawn – and, while the appeals of the tenants were still in the system, two of the houses burnt down. The appeals had been made on the basis that these buildings were of historic interest. I got the English Heritage people to come down and take a look. They said, 'These are really well-preserved Georgian houses, in rather poor nick, but quite special.' That bolstered the case for retention. But once buildings start burning down, that diminishes historic interest very effectively.

The fires have been investigated by the fire service and the police. They concluded that the cause was arson – but because the buildings collapsed on to the seat of the fire they couldn't tell how the conflagration was started or by whom. In two houses, nos. 62 and 64, there were squatters. A few days before the fire, a couple of guys came to the back door and said, 'You'd better get out. Now.' Two days later the houses burnt down.

The Star Bakery was facing court proceedings for eviction. There was a conversation with the landlord from Dubai. A few days later the building next door went up in flames. The little Indian restaurant, the house next to that, also went up in flames. That's four fires in one street. This building you can see from my window, Thames House, is a development site. That's been burnt twice. There's another site just down there, that's the seventh fire. The eighth was the council's own housing offices, at the back of the old Labyrinth Theatre site. That's an odd one, because at the time the council was preparing their demolition contract. The contract was put together in April '05. In May '05 the housing offices burnt down. Eight fires. All of them on sites that had applications for redevelopment. There hadn't, before this, been a fire on Dalston Lane within living memory.

You see a gradual decay. People lose pride in their environment and in themselves. 'I come from a slum,' they say, 'a dirty place nobody cares about.' This is what is happening to Hackney. So many people feel the same way. The developers want the old structures to fall down, so that they can build their rabbit hutches and make fortunes. They're not interested in the fabric, nor the history of the buildings. Planning only looks forward. If you are going to invest a million, you need to get it back within ten to fifteen years. There is no past. Planners and developers see no value in the past. It would cost more to refurbish a building than to knock it down and build something new.

The site down there, immediately behind our offices, has been empty for four years. There was a time when we had twenty New Age vans and trailers on that patch. The travellers would stagger out at midday, blinking into the sunshine. After they were evicted, the carrion of society crept in. They stripped out the old bricks and took them away to sell. Now it's crack dealers, desperate people, prostitutes. Eventually there will be some bleak stack of ten or fourteen storeys.

The theatre site we looked at on Dalston Lane is a quite separate issue.

It is owned by public authorities, TfL and others. It had an amazing history that building. When the roof came off, they destroyed the fabric. Way back, in 1920, promoters spent millions and millions to convert the building into a cinema. All the latest things: air-conditioning, beautiful lighting. State of the art. And the interior, so lavish! It was a great event when it opened, the grandest cinema in the British Empire.

Before it was a cinema it had been a circus. It was founded as a circus in 1886. The North London Colosseum. The major entertainment venue in North London. We had the railway too, that came in the 1880s. A prime position. The theatre attracted thousands and thousands of people.

After it closed as a cinema, in the 1960s, it became the Four Aces, an important centre for black music. And, finally, the Labyrinth. I never went to the clubs, but they meant a great deal to so many people. Lives revolved around that building. My neighbour met his wife in the Labyrinth. They have three kids now.

I think what's going to happen to that site is that they'll build 550 flats, twenty-eight of which will be for social housing. The rest is up for grabs. The policy is that there should be 50 per cent for social housing. Most of the development will be buy-to-let investments, offshore finance. Loads of Russian money. Huge amounts of Russian and Irish money. Those flats will be let to poor families in Hackney who are presently living in desperately overcrowded conditions. Now they will get a new flat, which will be paid for by housing benefits. The tenants will move in and out constantly. There will be no community at all.

They can try and let to City types, but they won't succeed. There are already too many choices in the borough, down by the canal, closer to Shoreditch. The landlords will try and get the most they can for their units, aiming at young white professionals, the new Hackney. These blocks will be built five metres apart. The standard for Hackney is twenty-one metres. The whole sorry business takes me back to the 1970s, Holly Street as it used to be.

Hackney transferred its entire sheltered-housing stock to a private housing association. On 1 January this year they put in twelve planning applications to redevelop the estates, all the sheltered blocks. That's what *is happening, privatization. And what are they doing with the money? They're spending £60 million on the Town Hall. They are spending countless millions on the Clissold Leisure Centre, which opened for a brief period before retreating into a limbo of allegations, law suits, prevarication.*

They want a new big bus station on the theatre site on a huge concrete slab over the railway cutting. That slab cost £39 million. How is the slab going to be paid for? We'll get planning permission to build a twenty-storey tower block right there. We'll get Hackney to give us half the value of the site, along with planning permission. And all this activity, this destruction, is to pay for a naked slab. So that TfL can park their buses and have a transport interchange. You have to build high to achieve a small footprint. High density, small footprint.

They say that the bus station is a strategic requirement for the Olympics, nothing must stand in its way. So you have to invent a method for getting clients from this new station to Dalston-Kingsland, further up the road. Try walking there now. You can't move. You can't breathe in the crush. What is inevitable is more demolition. The Crown and Castle pub, on the corner, they're talking about knocking that down. The finest building on the Junction.

Under this ground there is a tunnel which we know is a bit dodgy. They can't do restoration work from within the tunnel, only from above. Land which TfL already owns. The sop is, we'll declare a conservation area at the east end of Dalston Lane, the Georgian terrace. But, having sold off the terrace, they are quite incapable of having properties restored.

The council's vision is to have a newly refurbished Town Hall. They look out and they see their Ocean development and they see their new library block and they think how wonderful they are. 'See what we've achieved.' And then they come up to Dalston, they haven't spent a halfpenny here, and they feel proud. They owned it all, the circus building, the Georgian terrace. They sold it for a song. They don't recognize the value of what's gone. They don't appreciate the historic or the social significance. They are not from this community. They work in Hackney for a few years and then move on. Planning officers, they don't know where Dalston is. They're not even English, they're from New Zealand, Australia. A planning officer came to a meeting I organized in St Mark's. He referred to the area as 'Dal-stone'. Where is Dal-stone?

Seventy-five per cent of the population would like to see historic buildings preserved – and that proportion is higher in Dalston. It's not just the established white community, it's the Turkish community. Loads of Turkish people support what we're doing. They have an appreciation of the nature of this place, even though it is not part of their original heritage.

The forces are huge. This is a multimillion-pound development, a £200-million development. The Olympics have made everything much worse, because now all the forces of government are working towards the one strategic objective. They have immense powers: the GLA, TfL (a limb of the GLA), Hackney Council. They offer up a gesture of public consultation, but the consultation is a sham, a waste of time. A lot of work went into opposing their proposals, when they were always a done deal. A hard lesson to learn. Look outside, the site is flat, rubble. It's like a return to the first age of the railways, the total destruction that follows any major change in the transport infrastructure.

The council architect said, 'We're reinstating the historic urban grid. There used to be a line of houses down Roseberry Place.' And so there were: two-storey houses with front and back gardens. Now there will be twenty-storey blocks with no gardens. What do you mean, 'reinstating the grid'? That's architectural bullshit.

But I'll stay. Hackney is a unique place. It's cheek-by-jowl with the City. It's full of different cultures. It's full of creative people. Will that continue? Can it continue? I get involved in interesting areas of law. I did a case against the Ford Motor Corporation, in Dagenham. A race discrimination case. It was major. We ended up with a £500,000 settlement for two clients. Fascinating. The head of Ford Europe flew over to negotiate a settlement. It was high-powered stuff. If you work here long enough, you get a reputation. The cases come to you.

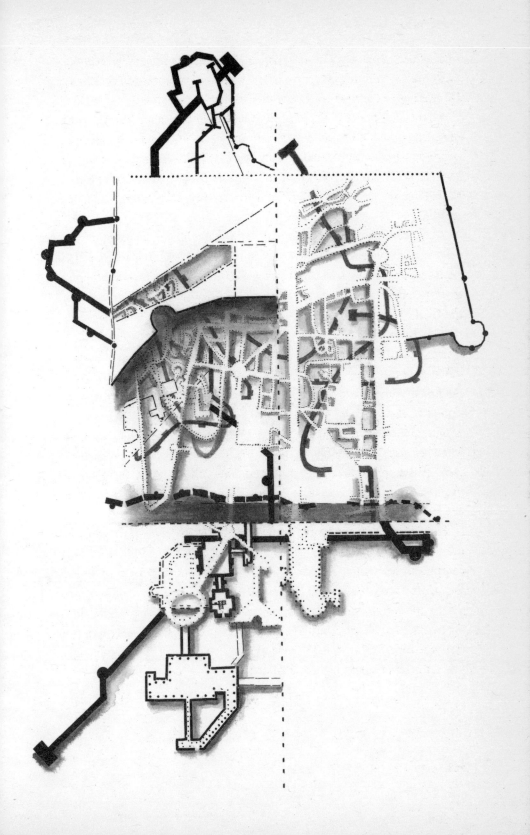

BRITISH SOUNDS

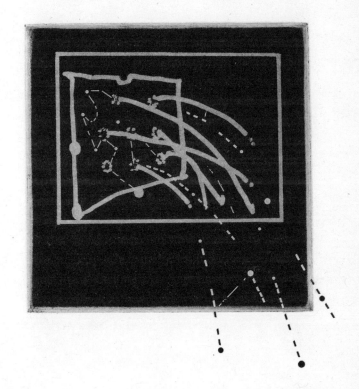

What would Hannay be doing in Hackney?

– Sebastian Bell, *Saddling Mahmoud*

Mare Street

It looked bad, the solicitor's letter. Looked bad for Mutton. This time he was going down. It wasn't great for me either, being summonsed as a character witness, precious writing hours lost to the deadly bureaucracy of the courts. And worse, much worse, the confirmation that Mutton was in town, in Hackney, on my doorstep; and likely, before the trial or after his release, to want to rehearse the manic episode at inordinate length; telling me what I had said and what I really meant, before delivering a glancing put-down. He wasn't called 'Bad News' for nothing: the invention was his own. 'I saw my arrest,' Mutton said, 'as performance art, a brand of quantum avant-gardism produced by an acausal force: the duty of appearing as a symbolic malefactor, elective bad boy, alien.'

Bad News was part-Czech, part-Jewish, adopted Brummie. A white bluesman. Autodidact. Frighteningly articulate when not gagged by a vodka bottle; then violent, obscene. A danger to himself and others. Another character altogether, as he liked to boast, a postmodern Hyde (who had drowned his Jekyll in that lovely cold-clear Russian spirit). Mutton erupted out of the barbed-wire jungle of chaos theory, over a Berlin Wall of Adorno, Derrida, Foucault: into the cruel theatre of the street. He had no purchase on reality. And this, in essence, was the case for his defence: until some sucker could be persuaded to treat him as a fiction.

Which is why I left the phone permanently switched to answer mode; the disembodied mechanical voice that comes as part of the rental package. Mutton, waiting at first light for the Bangladeshi minimart to open; hand shaking, unlit cigarette (no matches), tongue stuck to the roof of a stale mouth. Then, at the end of the working day, just as I climbed exhausted into bed – the crazies of the city have a preternatural sense of when to catch you at your lowest ebb – a stereophonic junkie pair, hammering me for their pain, screamed about the inadequacy of the portrait I had contrived, at their instigation, in my latest book. And would I please leave the usual complimentary first edition, lavishly inscribed, at some shop in Cecil Court? It's a horrible contract, mutual exploitation; the way compliant authors indulge predatory characters, take them on expeditions, buy them drinks, hoping for the worst: a new story. Without a tame scribe, the unwritten of London become desperate, pushed into excesses that propel them towards secure wards, strait-jackets, tiled cells – in the hope that somebody, anybody, will give form to the howling mania of their non-existence. And then they are sold short, misrepresented, ugly words put into their mouths. They would, it goes without saying, be writers themselves, if life only spared them the time, between scoring benefits, getting fixed, making the calls.

'You don't have to move from your desk,' said Bill Parry-Davies. 'Cases come to you.' And, to prove it, he told me about the Owl Man of Albion Drive. Action pending: Hackney versus a citizen squatter who had lived for fourteen years in a derelict property about whose existence the council had no knowledge, before this Olympic landrush. Here was no ancient hippie or German profes-sional working in a design studio and cycling by night to locate unguarded warehouses. The Owl Man needed the space, the wild garden, for rescued crows and convalescent hawks. His unofficial, self-funded sanctuary would have continued, unnoticed, if there hadn't been this unremitting pressure from above: on narrowboats, edge-land survivalists. A requirement to balance the books. Turn a profit. Pay for the new Town Hall.

The case that came to me was Bad News Mutton. By way of a letter from his legal representative, Micheline Handsworth-Beckmann.

We act on behalf of Mr Mutton who faces prosecution before the Crown Court for an offence of Racially Aggravated Assault, contrary to Section 29(1)(C) of the Crime and Disorder Act 1998.

Mr Mutton's instructions are that during this alleged assault he was merely acting out a scene in a Tesco Supermarket taken from your novel *Landor's Tower* when he made reference to a 'Paki minute mart'.

Mr Mutton has asked us to write to you in order to obtain clarification that Mr Mutton is cited as a character in your book and to ask whether or not you would consider providing a character reference for him.

We would be very grateful if you could provide any detail that you feel may be relevant with regards to Mr Mutton's character.

According to Anna, Tesco's car park, between Mare Street and Morning Lane, was the most aggressive and agitated site in Hackney. And there were plenty to choose from. A game reserve for which you had to be very game; up to speed, cranked. Combat-hardened. Ready to beat off the professional beggars, coin prospectors, thieves, peddlers of contraband DVDs, confused sad human relics, unhoused madfolk, rough sleepers, shopping-trolley chauffeurs who demanded the right to reclaim the pound you paid as security. They were lined up along the walls, under the overhang of the roof, part of the action; so that, by carrying your bags, pushing your trolley, guarding your car, they achieved status: honorary consumers. They were like medieval vagrants, barefoot pilgrims sheltering beside a great cathedral.

The supermarket had a space-platform glow. WE'RE OPEN 24 HOURS: a thorium luminescence like the lips of unfortunate women who spend their lives painting numbers on watch dials. A terminal zone for tourists who will never leave town. Malformed pigeons, feathers the colour of sodden bog paper, mobbed the spiked TESCO sign, scratching their parasites on anti-bird spikes. The canted roof was slick with droppings.

Everybody parked here, it was free and the rest of Hackney was impossible, residents only: patrolled, taxed, clamped, dragged away, crushed. Tesco tried barriers, but these were rammed, dismantled.

They tried uniformed patrols, but that only stepped up paranoia levels, the excuse for bloody rows, competitive weaponry. CCTV cameras fed mayhem into offices where security personnel dozed. The poet Ed Dorn had the right word for this hectic energy field: *aswarm*. 'Drivers bearing away their dietary burdens.'

The crunching of metal, shivering of glass. Alarms trilling at disputed parking bays. Doors slam, voices rise. Dealers swarm and scatter: the excluded. An oasis. A bright place in the Hackney night of blind walkers who decorate privet hedges with cans of Foster's and Red Bull. White plastic forks and spoons like the regurgitated bones of extinct fish. Anna carried home the blue baskets in which you piled up Tesco's goodies and she soaked them in the bath. Then she scrubbed oranges, lemons, in many-times recycled Thames water.

Mutton came to town, legitimately, in an illegitimate business: the peddling of cheap dishcloths, dusters, soaps, keyrings, pan-scrubbers, brooms. Charity. With an authentically faked laminated licence. Door to door, early evening, hitting on preoccupied rate-payers with a suitable sob story. They didn't care, some of them. They'd shove a coin or two at you, to get you off the step, into the van. The grifters would divvy up, get hammered, sleep seven to a room, or in the Transit. Down by the canal.

'I say this,' Bad News beer-breathed over a distracted Hackney-estate mother, television chiming, kids asking who it was, bathtime, mealtime, fix-time, 'without resort to algorithms. I operate in a narrow fissure between fiction and reality, ready and willing to be crushed and extinguished by unimaginable pressures from the field of treacherously shifting phenomenological pack ice. A fiver for this humble domestic implement, a lavatory brush, will release you from the burden of disbelief.'

Tesco's vodka has been arranged on the bottom shelf, at the end of a long hike from the entry doors, up against the wall. Your progress, pocket-patting, packet-squeezing, has been monitored. Noted by security with brooding Celtic resentment.

Mr Mutton (aka the defendant) was accused of a very serious offence, he was facing a prison term. Brush aside the lesser charges, aggravated common assault, actual bodily harm, burglary, blasphemy: this was racism. The conclusion of another complicated London evening. A stone bed and a bowl filled with strange puke.

'For some time,' he wrote to me while they held him, pending psychiatric reports, 'I have been feeling that I had a strange ability to conjure up coincidences that were guiding me in some oddly numinous manner. These coincidences or "synchronicities", to use the Jungian term, have grown tentacles into the world. This leads me to the conclusion that the illnesses and sufferings undergone by characters in your novels signal an occult duality in the nature of things, that sickness is a creative source, a vocation. Is it going too far to suggest that this condition can lead to special powers?'

Mare Street was forbidden to Mutton, a week hitting the pubs and offies had seen to that. Pitched out of the Marie Lloyd bar at the Hackney Empire by irate comedians, he climbed the gangplank to the Old Ship. Where almost anything goes, this side of a grating West Midlands drone, and lighting a cigarette. There was no credit to be had at Britannia Restaurant (Kebabs, Burgers), nothing to soak up the seething juices of an ulcerated stomach. The man at the counter of the European Supermarket, which offered a wide range of 'inter-continental groceries', shelves of mixed wines, a locked cold-cabinet, was a good listener. Bad News chatted, without incident, and went away, bottle in each pocket, for three nights. Until the charity-scam cash ran out and the Transit left town, to try unmapped estates, between Cambridge and Peterborough. Settlements too new for double-glazing, too remote for Mormons.

To achieve a solid purchase on the Tesco's vodka you have to go down on your hands and knees. It's a sobriety test: to see if you can make it up again, reassume the perpendicular. Unable to decide whether to save 98p on the Smirnoff (which came in at a tenner), or £2.01 on the Absolut Vodka (at £10.98), Bad News went for one of each. A snug fit inside the lining of his greasy overcoat. And a budget third, Red Square, in the basket: £8.49.

Suddenly, the aisles were too wide. Steepling shelves tottered in on Mutton. The tilted night-slippery floor had been greased with soap. Fluorescent light-tubes, buried in quilted panels, made the ceiling into a roaring motorway. He staggered, he stumbled. He tried to flap a returned cheque (with a signature that was not his own) in the cashier's face.

SHAPLA: it said on the first badge. And 'It's my job to ask' on the other. A modest blue-check blouse. Shapla didn't touch the proffered rectangle of grubby paper; she reached for the buzzer – as Mutton reached for her, grabbing at the delicate, bangled wrist. It's a nice point of law as to whether he spat, with intent, or dribbled excessively in the heat of the exchange. Uniformed security from office and car park, arriving too late to witness the action, miraculously contrived a duplicate word-portrait of the event: a detailed linear narrative of something they could have imagined only in their wildest dreams.

'Get back to your Paki minimart' was the vile phrase to which Mutton was forced to confess. There was no going around that one; the chemistry of need, the thirst-crazed cells, were no mitigation. Nor was the lengthy history he recited, shop by shop, of his prior dealings in Asian-owned-and-family-operated convenience stores. Bad News had paid, over the years, for estates to be reclaimed in Sylhet and the damp delta; his vodka binges built villages on stilts. He drained cabinets of chilled bottles for the benefit of abstemious and religious folk with whom he had always enjoyed a lively and stimulating dialogue. The alky, by his own account, was a one-man charity: pissing gold.

'I was not insulting the cashier,' Mutton said. 'I was talking to myself, a mental note to avoid ugly consumer hangars and to stick with small community businesses.'

When that line of argument collapsed, he went for a plea of diminished responsibility: he could behave only in a way that had already been predicted in his various fictional outings. The creature had standards of malevolence to maintain. Or he risked being written out, killed off. He should never have strayed from his Brummie patch, it's true. To register bad behaviour in Hackney you had to come up with premier-league lapses.

'Being of bad character is a considerable burden,' he wailed. 'And is my way of rebelling against the sterile rationalism of the world.'

Nobody had the stamina to enquire further. The card that kept him out of gaol was madness. 'I subtly planted, in the judge's mind, the connection between my obsession with synchronicity and a bipolar disorder. Nothing to be done, nowhere to go. Racism ameliorated by palpable disability.'

London's elected mayor, Ken Livingstone, purged insults offered to a Jewish journalist from that dreadful tabloid, the *Evening Standard* – for which he operated, in his fallow years, as a well-rewarded restaurant critic – by weeping public tears over the historic wound of slavery. This is never an endearing sight, politicians overwhelmed by crimes for which they could in no way be held responsible, while denying any knowledge of the horrors which can and should be laid at their door. They blub, on camera, about the brutal and corrupt colonialism which provided this country with the wealth and institutions that made us great. But present oil wars? Assassinations of the innocent? Extraordinary rendition? The price we pay for the democratic freedoms we enjoy.

The bright new buildings of Hackney were stuffed with chains and bridles, photocopies of the shipping manifests of vessels involved in that obscene trade, the export of humans. As if that was the end of it: a distant chapter fit for heritage. Compulsory viewing for crocodiles of innocent schoolchildren. 'Multiculturalism,' Ed Dorn wrote, 'is the cult par excellence of late imperialism.' A concept much abused in recent times and under whose rubric too many civic corruptions shelter.

The prosecutors were pure-blood monoculturalists, generations grown in the same villages of County Offaly, the Ganges and the Brahmaputra. Mutton, on the other hand, was a cocktail of

European sediments, settled and resettled; persecuted, expelled, intermarried, on the drift. He spoke too many languages in too few places. He was wholly English: a mess of prejudices, foul-mouthed, self-serving, an absolute pain. But always himself, absolutely that. A cultural pluralist who had spent years in public libraries, street markets, car-boot sales.

Hackney had no use for Bad News. Case thrown out on a technicality, the accused was insane. Careless in the community. Get him out of town. Now.

Anna remembers, in the days when she patronized Tesco, sitting in the café section, to recover after a hard session of supermarket sweep. An old lady took shelter at her table. She felt safer in company, she said. A lively troop, down from the closed hospital on the hill, arm-wavers, mutes, the damaged who had nowhere else to go, followed her inside. 'That's what I love about Hackney,' the old lady whispered. 'It's more of an adventure every time I go out.'

Millfields

To be waiting at a bus stop for your connection, mid-morning, work abandoned, is a rare privilege. You have to understand the pressure TfL employees are under, squeezed from above by accountants, to arrive within seconds of the stipulated time, up there in lights, above the shelter. Get ahead of yourself and you are obliged to dawdle, taking in the view, ignoring restless clients carving up seats, munching, shouting into mobiles, hefting outsize rucksacks. The white middle classes no longer use public transport, outside the early City shunt. They power-walk, pump-cycle, pile into high-wheeled Chelsea tractors or tax-avoiding electric dune buggies. If the driver of the 242, bladder bursting, is held in the Dalston Lane gridlock, he'll have to gun it past the next few stops. Cross his legs. Park up, risking everything, to acid-irrigate a convenient garden. Or ring for the wife, as happened to one prostate sufferer, to bring down a change of trousers.

To say that these men – women too – are unappreciated is to state the obvious. Like Eichmann in Jerusalem, they are prisoners in perspex cages designed to frustrate the ire of fare-dodgers, the vocationally disgruntled, new girl gangs. Rappers of counterfeit coins who block your airholes with gum. A mob who insist on riding, fifty or sixty yards, from one stop to the next. It has become a class issue: the wealthier you are, the further you walk. In order to avoid viral democracy. The yatter, the multitongued babble. Window seats are protected by large persons challenging you to get past them. *Respect*. Respect: an invisible but electric exclusion zone.

BUS STOP: that frequently ignored command. The street is so quiet I begin to think it has been closed off for one of Danny Boyle's post-apocalyptic fantasies. I can hear a man shouting: 'Give me the keys. Give me the fucking keys.' A house on the south side of Graham Road. Right next to the Turkish Cypriot Cultural Association (Education, Counselling). And then a woman, her screams. No twitch at the dirty muslin curtains.

The screaming stops, the muslin moves and a tall slim black man in a white vest glares at me. We're in a *Rear Window* scenario, the snoop and the potentially misinterpreted drama. Should I act? I'm not stupid enough to use the camera. Years ago, innocent of Hackney ways, I intervened when a child was smashing milk bottles and positioning the jagged shards beneath the wheels of the parked cars of schoolteachers. His mother, in conversation, looked on indulgently. Now it would be very different: I would stand trial for my reckless challenge, no question. I'd find myself on the register, featured in the *Gazette*. We'd have to leave London. In the 1960s, I copped a tirade of motherly abuse: wait-till-my-bloke-comes-home. Hearts of gold, those tigerish mums. That night, my first car, a distressed red Mini, was battered into a heap of scrap. A sound ecological gesture that brought me into the age of the bicycle.

The 242 draws up. The driver, who rang me to advise of his imminent arrival, is a veteran of this route. I present my orange holder with the Hackney Freedom Pass, the sole reward for survival in the borough. I hang on, trying to talk through the perforated screen, as the vehicle accelerates to recover time lost in a confrontation with a black youth who flashed a Video Library card and then jumped off, promising retribution, when challenged. This was nothing, the driver reckoned. What he can't get used to is the way some of them spit, so venomously and accurately, through the constellation of holes in the perspex.

He recalled his final night-run in a 38, that much lamented casualty of Ken Livingstone's bendy-bus fetish. As he cruised down Dalston Lane, alongside the burnt-out reefs of Georgian terrace, the abandoned family businesses, he heard a loud pop. His conductor was on the floor. Buses, in those over-financed days, still had conductors. This one, trembling slightly, said that he had dodged a random bullet. Which passed 'laterally' through the vehicle, leaving a star-shaped exit wound. A bandit salute to the 38, queen of the road, Dalston Lane to Victoria Station. Our passport to the wider world.

Roland Camberton's journey towards self-knowledge begins with bus excursions into mysterious outlying suburbs: 'Hampstead and Purley and Wandsworth and Richmond.' And then, with a schoolfriend, the extending of local boundaries as an act of initiation: 'Stamford Hill, Stoke Newington, Clapton, Homerton, Cambridge Heath, and Bethnal Green. . . Highbury, Islington, Hoxton, and Shoreditch.' The beating of bounds. The streets and trees and small parks that are lineaments of an evolving body: blood, tissue, memory. Until you are ready to break away, cell by cell, to the heat of Soho. 'So they walked along Old Compton Street, as populated and animated as three hours before, and caught a late bus to Hackney.'

Joe Kerr, who headed the Department of Critical and Historical Studies at the Royal College of Art, was happy to spend the rest of his week driving buses. Like the 242. Forced to chose between academic status and Clapton Garage, he wouldn't hesitate: goodbye Kensington Gore. If the buses paid a living wage, he would commit, full time. The life was pure romance. He saw the Routemasters, he said, as a symbol of the best of our city.

Joe was a solid, four-square, smiling man with deep-set eyes and the greying hair of a life lived to the full. He had worked, before university, as a conductor. After qualification, he came back as a driver, just in time for the last days of the Routemasters: before their banishment to ceremonial functions and the Transport Museum in Acton. They told him, the old hands, that the behaviour of passengers improved as you moved west through London. And so it proved. No bullets in Belgravia. Joe used a Routemaster, pampered and polished, for his wedding. And sometimes offered nostalgic tours from Tate Britain.

I asked, as soon as I met the man, if he would be prepared to take me on board for the Hackney portion of the 242's route. He responded, at once, by email.

'I ought to warn you that Clapton bus garage is being partly mothballed next month, and as a consequence a majority of drivers are being moved to other garages. This means that next Monday and Tuesday are my last days working there before I head to Tottenham garage. I won't be leaving Hackney altogether, but instead I'll be heading north–south across Dalston Junction on the 76s and 243s, rather than east–west on the 242s.'

'Driving,' Joe says, 'frees the mind.' He's unshaven. That easygoing independence uniformed specialists manage. He is able, at whim, to decide when to allow rain-soaked supplicants on board and when to steer those huge wheels through a puddle. Slim specs perch, pilot-fashion, in wiry hair. Joe steers and chats, as I sway with the stuttering momentum, recovering my bus legs.

'They call this the "old codgers" route,' he explains. Across the neck of Mare Street, Amhurst Road, into bandit country. Foothills of crack craziness: Clapton, Millfields. Sink estates like islands occupied by pirates. It's a Conradian voyage to bring the bus through, back to the garage. 'Africans and Poles, they don't mix.'

I move away to the deserted upper deck, to let Joe concentrate: a panoramic window on discriminations of blight. Pete Doherty would be the titular figure, holed up in a one-bedroom flat, after collecting his methadone at the Homerton. The jellyfish-white romance of urban squalor: Rimbaud on Ritalin. Pete should have stuck with the buses. Every time he slides into a car, he is pulled.

The road sign for Millfields, horribly mangled, alerts us to trouble ahead. Scratching against overhanging branches, we navigate streets that were never intended for buses. We are very close to the school where Anna taught for so many years. At the back of the old Lesney Matchbox Toys Factory. Alongside Hackney Marshes, where I had that great job, painting white lines on football pitches.

Daubeney Infants' School. When I needed that name, to my

shame, I couldn't bring it to mind. William and I had been playing football, sweaty, bedraggled in sagging tracksuits, when I realized that we were locked out of the house: the spare key left with a neighbour who was at work. We jogged across London Fields to the Central Library in Mare Street, where it was no problem, in the days of an active local-history section, to find a list of all the schools in the borough. It clicked, Daubeney. Morning Lane, Homerton High Street, down towards the Lea; we found the school, blustered into Anna's beautifully controlled classroom. The expectant faces: that we were street entertainers, keepers of exotic animals, professional storytellers, musicians. I'd been invited into Islington schools to talk about my weird and wonderful life as an itinerant bookdealer, to read from samples of the product and to gift a few duplicates to the library: but never in Hackney,

I listened, over the years, to so many of Anna's stories – poverty of means, unexpected life-altering successes – that I experienced, by proxy, the way the system collapsed. The crucial moment being the handover of control from the Inner London Education Authority to Hackney. Budgets were decimated. Bureaucracy increased by quantum leaps. Teachers didn't receive their pay cheques. And the managers were so remote they didn't even live in London. They were premature multitaskers, running businesses in Manchester and Birmingham, while advising on race and gender, accepting doctorates, hanging out on first-class trains and still finding the odd moment to invent new torments for the foot soldiers in the trenches: the wretched teachers. A change of syllabus. More tests, more evaluations. Risk assessments. Scientific demonstrations. Revisions of history. No competitive games. Withdrawal of special-needs teachers. Withdrawal of classroom assistants. Education, education, education: let's trash it. Turn rundown Victorian barracks into state-of-the-art building sites.

I listened while Anna cooked. The horrors had to be rehearsed, played over as an exorcism. Confrontations with single parents who felt themselves wronged. Ragged children who arrived hungry, denied the provision of free milk by Madame Thatcher, and lurching out of control. A boy called Leon was brought to mind: how Anna had been able to slip him an extra bottle and how much calmer he had become. The instruction from above was: let them buy biscuits. Even the ones, lacking underclothes, who wouldn't do PE. Then the reformers, the rationalists, cut library budgets and increased class sizes. For a time, Anna bought her own books and kept the children supplied. But pressure increased with every term. Incomers, such as the Chinese, even when they started without a word of English, shone. Some of the Muslim children, fiercely disciplined at the mosque, treated this liberal classroom as a chance to let rip. They didn't find it easy to accept the control of a woman.

Thirty years was a healthy span of service, it was enough. Anna's late career became a mirror-image of my own: in reverse. I'd started with hit-and-run teaching, part-time, low pay, and moved on to manual labour, parks, ullage cellars, warehouses on the river, mud yards by railway tracks. Then: street markets, scruffy book catalogues, visits from Californian millionaire dealers. And, finally, the surface respectability (in some European cultures) of being a published author. Anna, as an established teacher, was the one to put her name on official forms: mortgage, car insurance. I was a fiscal leper. In cutting loose from Hackney's patronage, my wife found herself coaching the children of aspiring families in tower blocks or teaching English to a constantly shifting group of asylum seekers in Peckham. All of this was at the edge of charity: the willing volunteer in a collapsing system that depended on the altruism of good-hearted individuals.

Search for what's on offer, given age and over-qualification, and you are soon conducting dubious surveys, door-to-door in dangerous places. Statistics to be manipulated. The fascination, Anna found, was not in the material she gathered but the glimpses of unknown lives, the way flats were decorated. The stories people told, the lonely confessions. The tea and sweet cakes they offered.

Then: books. The bane of her life. Now she was filling our house with boxes of unsold stock. The ironies multiplied. She spent her days blagging her way back into the school system to peddle children's books. Or visiting the secure nurseries of merchant banks in the City. Labouring at the broad base of a pyramid that offered a return only when you persuaded other lost souls to work for you.

The ultimate job was a complete mystery. Anna would leave, early in the morning, but she refused to tell me where she was going and I knew better than to push it. This continued for a few months. As usual, I was buried in some book, letting the activities of the real world have whatever minimal attention they required. The regular payment of council-tax bills, for example, before – being a week or two late – you were surcharged, taken to court. Kathryn Hughes, under the title of 'The Secrets Police', wrote about this in the *Guardian*: how she had responded to her Hackney summons with a 'stream of letters, emails and phone calls': none of which were answered. She locates 'moral bankruptcy' at the heart of local government and the application of 'shame' as a device to blackmail the middle classes into paying up or selling out to developers. The tax collectors and authorized bullies bleed bleeding-heart liberals to support vanity projects: inactive swimming pools, perpetual roadworks and a splendidly refurbished Town Hall.

What Anna was up to, in a backstreet by the canal, was training as a bus driver. With a supportive bunch of bandits and recidivists: on forged licences, fake passports, novel identities. Along with the victims of corrupt and dangerous regimes. Somali surgeons. Turkish economists. Hoxton robbers. Getaway-wheelmen honing their skills. The strength required to operate the lift at the back of the disability minibus was a challenge; but she managed it – giving the clients, as part of her training, a run to John Lewis in Oxford Street. She took her road test out near Epping Forest, where a dope-smoking follower of Haile Selassie banged the big coach, hedge to hedge, around tight curves, through virgin estates, on to the M25, without dropping his m.p.h.: the perfect audition for the Sandra Bullock part in *Speed*. Anna came through, she passed. And decided life was too precious for such excitement.

*

There is an official pit stop outside the Homerton Hospital. But you do not walk away from the bus. The box in which Joe should have parked is occupied by a trashed and abandoned motor, which has been ticketed by a street patrol and then left in place. 'Drive shaft's gone,' he says. Outpatients from the psychiatric department are scattered over the road like the random debris of an air crash. They can't decide whether to retreat or to get in the queue for a bus they won't take. Joe wants a nostalgic snapshot for the album, it might be his final run on this route. He leans back against the comforting bulk of the 242: Clapton, Hackney, Dalston, Shoreditch, Bank, Holborn, TOTTENHAM COURT ROAD. The bookdealers' special. One artist, I discovered, based a project around listing every tree she saw from the window of the bus on her journey into town. And there were plenty. A skinny forest ameliorating diesel insults.

Joe checks the upper deck, sweeping under the rear seats. I assume this is a cosmetic exercise, tidying away the cartons and foil trays of the mobile cafeteria. It's not: Joe is under instruction to search, meticulously, for suspect packages, bombs. A duty he has better reason than most to fulfil. His wife, Gill Hicks, was travelling to work, on the Underground, the Piccadilly Line: 7/7/05. She was lucky to survive, losing both her legs. She was brought to St Thomas's Hospital, where she received immediate and expert care. A few months later she walked down the aisle with Joe, before they had a celebratory ride in a Routemaster. She had been standing, so the *Standard* reported, 'only a few feet away from suicide bomber Jermaine Lindsay when he detonated his bomb, killing himself and 26 people and severely injuring dozens of others'.

Joe was unhappy about the response from the British authorities, who did everything in their power to pretend that such atrocities had no connection with events in Iraq. In contrast, high-ranking Australians – Hicks came originally from Australia – visited her as soon as was practicable and made proper gestures of support. She had been admitted to hospital as: 'one unknown'. By 7/7/07 Hicks was back at St Thomas's, to present them with a cheque for £13,000,

raised by the charity for which she works, Peace Direct. Too trau-
matized to use public transport, she has been presented with a
Renault Scenic, the keys handed over in a ceremony at Buckingham
Palace. It will be driven by Joe Kerr.

We went for lunch in the canteen of the Clapton Garage. The
street was the usual Stanley Spencer resurrection of yawning
vagrant drinkers, off-vertical men holding themselves upright
against St Augustine's Tower. Red buses were stacked the length
of Narroway, so that drivers could be switched. Joe points out the
tram insignia on a manhole cover. This used to be a tram depot,
now its cavernous interior finds room for one brightly polished
and restored Routemaster (for private hire) and a lesser vehicle, a
burnt shell. Which was not, in this case, one of those spontane-
ously combusting bendy buses. The driver had been pushing to
make his schedule, taking her too fast down Rosebery Avenue,
when he felt the wheels go over something soft. A soft thing was
caught beneath his vehicle. He stamped on the brakes and nothing
happened. The mattress chucked in the road, his flabby drag-
anchor, burst into flames.

Joe, as a scholar of architecture, is taken with the no-nonsense
brutalism and noble intent of this threatened structure, the bus
garage. He tells me, as we select our brimming platters of steamed
fish, that he has to complete three 'rounds' a day; starting at 6.40
a.m. and finishing at 4 p.m. The radio is a welcome companion,
warning of burst pipes, filtering national and international news.
A gang of stone-throwing kids waiting at Clapton. A white-haired
maniac in an electric wheelchair who is hogging the middle of the
road. Curtains of flowers, left for the dead, woven into wire mesh.
A man killed as he knelt down to leave his tribute. Many hit-and-
run incidents are unreported. A standard 242 bus costs £170,000. A
bendy bus costs £250,000 and returns no profit. The authorities
keep that fact quiet.

Joe enjoys his food, enjoys cooking. Like driving, he says, it
liberates your mind. There is nothing quite so satisfying, run

completed, plate licked clean, tea sipped, than watching the trains from this rounded window. We can't see into St John's churchyard, so I don't learn about the man in the walled garden until I get my copy of the *Gazette*, from the Turkish minimart, as I walk home.

> A refuse collector has told of his grisly discovery when he found a body hanging in a Hackney churchyard on his way to work.
>
> John Sylvester, 44, of Chatsworth Road, Lower Clapton, spotted the body of a man in St John at Hackney churchyard.
>
> 'I was walking through the church gardens and I thought I saw someone standing up in the walled garden area,' he said.
>
> 'At first, I didn't think it was a dead body, but as I got closer I could see a man had tied himself to a rope.'
>
> The married father-of-four was on his way to Mare Street to catch a bus to Islington for his morning shift.
>
> An inquest was opened and adjourned at Poplar coroner's court.

It was a month before I discovered that the hanged man had a name. And that name was: Kaporal. A thrice-divorced, fifty-six-year-old father-of-none. Late of Herne Hill and St-Malo. A freelance writer/producer with no known Hackney connections and no previous interest in horticulture. The self-strangled (as it appeared) Kaporal had become his own tarot. His research files were incomplete, his fee unearned. The 'final solution', promised in a recent telephone conversation (in the hope of a supplementary cash payment), would never be delivered. A pity. I wanted an excuse to check out the sleuth's favourite boozer, the Victory in Vyner Street.

Honouring my former employee's methods, should I file the cutting under 'Pest Control', 'Dumped Rubbish', 'Hackney Mortuary', or 'Whistleblower Hotline'?

Kingsland High Street

Gareth's second email, following hard on the heels of the first, reconvened our meet from 1.30 p.m. at the vegetarian Buddhist café on Globe Road, near Roman Road, to the Turkish place, Sömine, on Kingsland High Street (old Ermine Street), just up from the Rio: 1 sharp. But Gareth didn't do sharp. In the privilege of waiting for his appearance – he texted to let me know he was on the bus, from Hoxton, running ten minutes late – I could reabsorb the novelty of street energies, the chain of Turkish restaurants and walk-in canteens, the wholesalers of hair-revision products, the formerly Jewish tailors now modelling thin white suits and rip-off Americana, oversize T-shirts with branded slogans. One of the waiters from Sömine patrolled the pavement, while at the back of the restaurant women rolled out pancakes, deftly, rapidly, dividing them into squares, minute portions that were folded into sweet cakes. The recommendation from *Time Out* brought in a few Stoke Newington book-reading solitaries to swell the steady stream of local Turkish workers.

Gareth – Gareth Evans – had never carried much weight, now he seemed on the point of immediate physical dissolution: the speed at which he moved between events, open-screen discussions, the floating of festivals, in and out of Europe, late-night radio, arriving slightly after the final second, hustling down the aisle, child in tow, bounding on to the stage, flicking back Jesus-hair, launching into his introduction. On the beat, never faltering. John Berger, Chris Marker. A memorial tribute to Marc Karlin. The passionate outrush of words: in the foreknowledge that the scene was almost over, he was trading in ghosts and echoes. Emails, pouring out from one of the many office-stops he made in a complicated week – cultural listings, childcare, Hackney,

Hammersmith – concluded with a tag from one of the German poets, Heine, Celan.

The man was a memory of himself. He occupied no space at the table. If he swallowed a grain of rice it would drop straight through a digestive system too preoccupied to deal with such trivia.

On the south coast, strolling towards Hastings Old Town, I ran into Gareth, pushing his son, shocked to be on a brief holiday: staying in the house of the absent film-maker Andrew Kötting. Serene exhaustion. The muscles required to smile, how do they work? Gareth was active everywhere. Confident that the present crisis would slide over the horizon like a black ship, one of those silhouetted oil tankers. At all costs, keep the dialogue open.

'Soup and a glass of tap water,' he said.

I marvelled that he could absorb so much; even the rich air – bubbling beans, pulses and meats, honeyed tea – was too potent. He was dizzy from the concentration of our talk, the books and DVDs pulled from his satchel: Douglas Woolf ('If there were only one reader left in the world, I would write to that one as lovingly as I do now'), William Burroughs, J. G. Ballard. Interviews: drowned worlds, drought worlds, the impossible future. Gareth was facing expulsion from Hackney, a shift of operations: cheaper printers, a film festival in the Czech Republic. Reverse immigration. We get the builders, painters and decorators to sleep under the plane trees of London Fields, in the bushes of Victoria Park; they get the countercultural activists. The blind film-makers, the dumb poets. The patrons of Turkish cafés.

'Eighty per cent of the Arts Council's budget has been cut,' Gareth said, 'to make a gesture at plugging the Olympic debt. Our magazine, *Vertigo*, will have to close in September. They've withdrawn our £17,000 grant. I tried to persuade various publishers to take on an anthology: Godard, Marker, Herzog, DeLillo, Keiller, Kötting. Editors were interested, the reps turned them down flat. You can get away with best-of lists or celebrity directors with plenty of nice illustrations, otherwise it's a dog. It's hopeless.'

Gareth's film magazine had previously been run by Marc Karlin. With Chris Petit and Emma Matthews, his editor of choice, I worked on a film called *The Falconer* in Marc's cutting rooms, an office block near Goodge Street. Walking in from Hackney, no matter how early, I would find Karlin already in the smoke-stabilized basement. Mounds of back numbers of *Vertigo*, French books, unpublished typescripts, films that would never happen: a lair. For a somewhat shaggy, bearlike, interior presence. A man who had swallowed and absorbed his younger self, the guerrilla documentarist in the heroic production stills from another era. Marc prowled, he challenged, he hovered in doorways. He talked about Paris. His breathing was laboured on the stairs. It was a problem now – Marc had a film on Milton in pre-production – to secure the necessary medical insurance. Taking a transatlantic flight would be a major adventure. He had deserted Hackney years ago; news I brought, in the dust of my boots, was from a place he no longer recognized. Names he preferred to forget.

Gareth's estrangement from *Time Out*, where he had been busy for years, was symbolized by the way seventy boxes of books and impossible-to-find DVDs, rare interviews, were dumped, without warning, in skips: landfill. Much of his working library vanished before he could redistribute it – as he had furnished me with photographs by Astrid Proll, with films of Hackney tower blocks under water, a piratical resistance to the Olympic enclosures. By October, Gareth would be out of work, all the part-time employment that swallowed his waking hours would be gone. He had the lovely notion of starting his own press, on the proceeds of his share of a flat sale. He would commission the likes of DeLillo and Berger and operate out of Prague. The books would be plain, crafted, fit for the pocket; on the model of the early Divers Press publications put out by Robert Creeley on the island of Mallorca.

Douglas Woolf's first novel was published by the Divers Press. I remember the excitement when he walked into Compendium Books in Camden Town and set down a box containing copies of that fabulous rarity, the original edition of *The Hypocritic Days*. 'Get rid of these, I can't carry them round any longer.' Mike Hart jumped to the phone, the tribes descended from all quarters, single copies were swallowed up within a few hours, dealers took the rest.

'One never does quite lose hope,' Creeley says in his introduction to the Woolf book Gareth gave me.

Compendium, victim of market forces, folded in the 1990s. Nobody now would ride the Silverlink version of the North London Line, from Dalston-Kingsland to Camden Town, for pleasure. A cattle-truck of sanctioned discourtesies and electronic babble.

Woolf dies. Mike Hart gets a hungry cancer. And is gone. Along with those he did so much to promote, the faces from the Compendium readings: doors open to traffic, the burger-leather-dope-drink-diesel reek of the High Street. Ed Dorn. Kathy Acker. Derek Raymond. The living faces Marc Karlin noticed on the monitor screen in his cutting room, as Petit re-filmed them, interrogating mortality, were no longer to be encountered on London streets.

Howard Barker, whose theatre group was administered from Northwold Road in Hackney, would also be losing his funding. So Gareth informed me. 'International reputations mean nothing to them.' Barker's company, the Wrestling School, had toured new work for years. But all that was over. The Olympic enclosures were an effective cultural defoliant, an Agent Orange of edge-land jungles, marking out the flight path to dinosaur rock acts in O2, the rebranded Millennium Dome. The future is orange. The future is orange shields screwed across the blind windows of empty properties, antisocial housing.

I listened to everything Gareth said. And I watched too. The women on their dais rolling vast pancakes. Glasses of brown tea, sugar lumps on decorated saucers. My vegetable stew, today's favoured number on the laminated card, was superb. We ate: or I ate, while Gareth, barely pausing in his surge across London, ignored the tray of breads and extras. The whole deal for not much more than a fiver. In the quality of what was available, the slick way the operation was run, Hackney has gained so much from its accidental status as somewhere favourable to immigrants. I was refreshed and ready for a walk down Shacklewell Lane, where I had arranged to visit the house of a local painter, Dan Dixon-Spain. Dan was doing up a barber shop once occupied by Lew Lessen, a man who had cut the hair of Walter Sickert. This was a connection I was eager to explore.

Dixon-Spain had been making portraits of traders in Ridley Road Market and showing them on hoardings. Shacklewell Lane, right across the road from where we were sitting, was a long-established border, a footpath and a route for commercial traffic between the villages of Dalston and Hackney. Ermine Street ran north, on one side of the Lane, while the Hackney Brook remained a potent memory-trace, away to the east.

We were in the cutting room, mid-morning, when there was a commotion on the stairs. Marc Karlin had collapsed, a heart attack. They came quickly from the hospital, it was just around the corner. The ambulance men, with that smell of scorched hair, applied their pads: repeatedly. Marc was lying in an awkward position: as if attempting, for the last time, to crawl up a slippery ladder of books and proof copies. To escape his fate.

We were walking back from the Goodge Street Pret A Manger with our lunchbreak sandwiches and coffees, discussing cuts and revisions, when the news was confirmed: Marc had been declared dead in the ambulance. Tongue too heavy for his mouth.

Chris Petit, the realist, had been waiting for this. There was nothing whatsoever to be done. But guilt sticks: nothing written, no eyewitness account, can live up to the complex network of circumstances and motives that surround it. You are never quite where you think you are. Sudden death gives life a sharper edge.

Karlin's spectacles had come off in the fall, one lens had dropped out. I picked it up, held it between thumb and first finger: in the crab-claw grip of the recidivist smoker. An act of homage. I hadn't smoked for years. Then I stared through the milky optic at the mess of the bereaved basement.

Shacklewell Lane

There are mornings in the city when the light is so persuasive, the foxy smell of earth, fetid garden plots, unmanaged hedges, that you have to keep walking: you turn your back on home, walk away. Ballard speaks of a period in the early 1970s, after he'd lost his driving licence, when he was forced to walk, but never further than the immediate horizon for a man of his height. 'In effect, I was living on this planet a mile wide,' he said. 'My whole universe just *shrank*. I never fully recovered from this.'

Paolo Cash, my next-door neighbour, the former footballer (Portsmouth, Colchester, Dagenham and Redbridge), present stall-holder in Roman Road, doing the Knowledge (for years), was kitted out in zips and buckles to ride his motorbike (L-plates) to Borehamwood – 'about forty-five minutes' – for a day's work as a supporting artist on *Holby City*. We chat. He tells me how, through football, he learnt to read situation and character, fast. He's done *EastEnders*. 'Twelve million people see me leaning against that bar in the Queen Vic, Iain. This is for real. I ain't gonna mess about. When I went up for it, they told me what the part was: "leery lad". That's acting, mate. To be yourself.'

Shacklewell Lane: the wealth of history in that name. Oswald Mosley ranting his racist bile outside a synagogue (now Turkish Islam Funeral Services). A golden dome. Foundation stone set by the Hon. Charles Rothschild. Great houses where the wealthiest families in the borough turned City loot into bricks and mortar: the Herons, Rowes, Tyssens. The ones who are still remembered. Tyssen was the school on Stamford Hill where Anna finally got the measure of the job. I watched 8mm diary film of a boy called Clifford narrating the pop-eyed adventure of his recent activities. I watched Renchi shepherding the kids into Springfield Park, little girls clambering over him. Anna, in minidress, is sprinting after one who takes off down the slope: such footage, these days, could only be shown in court. The children are scattered adults in their mid forties. They recognize Anna at bus stops.

Shacklewell House, now demolished, dominated this sad scrap of green; an iron-fenced junkie refuge with a lichen-crusted war memorial. Sir Thomas More visited Shacklewell House on many occasions, his daughter Cecilia married Giles Heron – whose wardship the financially astute More had purchased. Heron, something of a wild boy, was accused of depredations of 'vert and venison' (knocking off deer in Epping Forest). He got away, thanks to contacts at court, with a royal pardon. In 1539, accused, as all who ventured into the orbit of Tudor princelings eventually were, of treason, he was executed in the Tower. The estate held, as Herons gave way to Rowes (City merchants, lord mayors) – until the last of the line, Henry, in rags and tatters, became a beggar on the parish in 1706. Hackney treated him to a new outfit, without the obligation to wear a pauper's badge; they allowed him 2s 6d a week on which to subsist.

It was at Shacklewell House, an unlucky place, that More's political downfall (and death) were assured. Unguarded remarks, at a family dinner party, about whores at court: 'Certain words touching the ladies who surrounded the king's person.' The network of informers and whisperers did their business. More's ward, Giles Heron, took his place as a juror among those who passed judgement on Anne Boleyn.

The depression peculiar to the curve of this ridge outlived its social decline: warehouses, cafés, barber shops. Poets of the Cambridge diaspora sulked and settled. I met them from time to time, distracted on Kingsland Road, shopping for fruit in Ridley Road: without bags or coins. Wondering where they were and how long they would stay; not working, part-time teaching, with mysterious sources of income, publishing invisible pamphlets.

I associated Cecilia Road with music, hymns to St Cecilia's Day.

Now I knew better: the daughter of Sir Thomas, Cecilia, was memorialized as the link between Dalston Lane and Shacklewell Lane. Contemporary musicians moved in. I heard about them from the poet Peter Riley. Who house-swapped Albion Drive with his Peak District cottage. I asked him to tell me more about the Cambridge poets and musicians, as he had experienced them, in this part of Hackney.

Dates have always been a headache for me. I know the year in which I was born, but asked how old either of my children is, I'm lost. But this is what I remember about Hackney.

The 'free-improvisation' experimentalist Derek Bailey (who by the way died last Christmas) lived at 14 Downs Road, just off Hackney Downs. The house was like . . . well there's a whole book could be written. It was like witnessing a small den from which an absolutely determined persistence emanated, not to compromise in any way the kind of music he'd created, but to doggedly carry on against all the odds, starting and running a small record label, arranging concerts, establishing global connections . . . always knowing that it had to remain small-scale or perish. I think Hackney had an urban village-like and backstreet ambience which appealed to him. He would relate rather gleefully the latest murders. There were other improvising musicians in the district or not far away and they had sessions together, usually at his place, and visiting foreign musicians would call there.

Cecilia Road was a squat occupied for a short time by a percussionist called Roy Ashbury and others. I just visited a few times and later he disappeared from the scene.

There was a strong tendency for ex-Cambridge people to settle on the Hackney side of North London. Martin Thom lived on Shacklewell Lane, in the same house as my friend Ewan Smith. I was often there and it was the only place I ever found any serious or helpful discussion about poetry and everything else – which actually made quite a difference to the course of my career as a writer (people in Cambridge generally keep their traps shut). Also, off the edge of Hackney, there was John Welch (N16). Tom

Lowenstein (ditto) and Jeremy Harding (the journalist). And others, not writers or anything like that, forming a little Hackney–Cambridge community.

What did it feel like? Mainly that this was a zone where a lot of déclassé intellectuals of a fairly unconventional and politically left kind could subsist one way or another, keeping in contact with each other and with Cambridge, among a lot of first- and second-generation immigrants, mostly black or Kurdish, with dope peddlers thick on the pavements after dark. But it wasn't a left-bank type of bohemian scene, it was much more intellectually concentrated and uninterested in outlandish lifestyles. It was getting on with stuff.

They have without exception moved out of Hackney now, though some not very far.

The characters Riley describes were themselves second generation; the earlier poets, hungrier for the city, less cushioned by their pretensions, gravitated towards Amhurst Road. Tom Raworth wrote about Hackney life – Hackney as an incidental element – in *A Serial Biography*. This book, with its terse, cynical and free-wheeling prose, was a model for both our diary films and the early publications of Albion Village Press. Another poet, the extraordinary Grace Lake, down from Essex University, was also in Amhurst Road, still operating under her original name, Anna Mendelson: an active member of the radical group made infamous as the Angry Brigade. They were at no. 359, a standard Victorian property broken into flats. Very much the setting Alexander Baron used for *The Lowlife*. Essex was always part of the equation: a bomb at the Ford Motor Company's Offices at Gant's Hill, a staging post on the road to Colchester. Communiqués from the Brigade were run off by the same crude technologies that printed small-press poetry broadsides for the Cambridge squatters.

'Live in Dalston or Hackney? Come and have your portrait drawn.' A card with a full-length, front-on impression of a man in a tie, folded arms, eyes shut, falling away to his left: *Milton*. The name of the subject is inscribed, but not the artist. Dan Dixon-Spain. Who 'aims to record and capture the local community in and around Hackney. From the butcher to the lollipop lady.' Dan's drawings take 'between 10–30 minutes' to execute. Sitters receive a free print. Dixon-Spain borrowed a stall in Ridley Road Market. The sponsors of this project wanted to blow up the portraits to life size, and beyond, for exhibition on billboards. No text, no message. The hook was that the 'project engages with ideas of communication, tolerance, identity, celebrating the cultural diversity and vibrancy of the area'. Computer-generated versions of how the billboards will look obviate the trouble and expense of actually producing them. Dan's original drawings would be exhibited in the Hackney Empire.

The portraits were finely executed, sober, lacking in weight. Characters invited to impersonate themselves float like tethered socks. Without ballast of memory and regret, they are suspended in a dream of place.

Dan's girlfriend, Anna, is leaving the house in Shacklewell Lane as I arrive. He spent the weekend at the Homerton Hospital, a problem with his nose, breathing. Anna has something to say about the difficulty of making contact with the hospital switchboard, getting information, being left alone on the ward with no advice on post-operative treatment. Nothing to staunch the bleeding. Everyone has their own Homerton horror story, it's competitive. The *Standard* reported that the A&E department had to be shut for an hour 'after a patient threatened to kill staff with a gun'.

Lightly bearded, Dan has a Tudor poet/navigator look that is in keeping with Shacklewell House in the days of Sir Thomas More. He's a plasterer as well as an artist and is lovingly restoring this property. To an alternative Provençal status. I think of my visit as a form of sketching, the equivalent of one of Dan's ten-minute sessions. He says that he's never done an interview before.

I came to Shacklewell Lane because a friend of mine was working down the road, so I started visiting here. This would have been about 1999. At the time I was looking to buy some kind of property with a studio. I found this shop in Shacklewell Lane. And ended up buying it in 2000.

There was a barber shop downstairs. It had been derelict for probably ten years. The previous owners bought it off Lew Lessen, the actual barber. And then sat on it, doing nothing. Dripping roof, no electric, no plumbing. I spent what seemed like most of my life doing it up. Four years of work.

I started drawing people around the area on a regular basis. I drew the Jamaican girls who lived and worked next door. The shop's not there now, it has changed hands. It was a Jamaican café. I photographed them for an exhibition I did, four years ago. They really enjoyed it. The customers. Those young guys of seventeen or eighteen. Their egos got the better of them at the start. Then they understood why I wanted to draw them. They were willing to stand for me, half an hour here, half an hour there. They'd come round to my place. 'Do you want to do a drawing of me?'

I met more people on the street. And then realized that I wanted to capture a large part of the community. I don't really like saying I'm an artist, you're in such a majority in Hackney. Everybody's an artist. There's a gallery called Mafuji on Shacklewell Lane. It was here when we arrived, but operating on a sporadic basis. I knew a musician and a couple of artists in a warehouse, an old pharmaceutical factory. There are more musicians in the area than artists. I've drawn a cellist and a whole family of musicians in Cecilia Road.

I tried to find people who were willing to be drawn. So I got a licence for Ridley Road Market, a stall there: £15. A lot of paperwork. I thought I'd just turn up and draw, but I needed a licence and insurance.

I did five or six days, spread over a few weeks. I approached people. I said, 'It's free. You've got ten minutes, I'll make a drawing of you. And in a few weeks' time – remember that I've got to finish the drawing – I'll give you a print. An A4 print, nothing fancy.'

Initially people were very slow to approach me. As soon as I started drawing, they were, like, 'Good. All right!' I had a great time, real banter flew around. The drawings I made were quite quick, it's a pressured situation. They were quite self-conscious. I got some good drawings out *of it. Five per cent were artworks, the others were just practice. It's important to keep your hand in. A real education. I met lots of people there. They'd come with their cousins, wanting to be drawn.*

I think the people in the market felt quite flattered that I wanted to draw them. They felt a bit threatened. After I'd done a few, and chatted to them, told them about myself, they relaxed. I got pounds of cherries given to me, bits of fruit, cups of tea. The traders are down there every day, it's not an easy job. They get stuck into each other. The abuse might be a bit racist. They call each other all sorts of names, but with humour.

I learnt a bit about the history of Ridley Road. I knew there had been riots. I found out that the train station, Dalston-Kingsland, is going to move into the front part of the market.

My personal take on the regeneration is not particularly positive. I approached Hackney Council with a proposal to show my drawings. 'Would you be able to offer support? I want to make you aware of what I'm doing with the community and community groups. Could you offer some official approval?' I wanted to demonstrate that I wasn't just some bloke off the street.

They were fine about it, they wanted to make the local community feel that they were part of the regeneration process. I wanted hoardings, billboards, to show the drawings. It soon became clear that they weren't going to help us out, financially. I got the impression that what they wanted was to make themselves look good, rather than to support the project. The Dalston that fascinates me is the Dalston that doesn't tie in with the story they are trying to spin.

The people I got to know best were the Jamaican community around Shacklewell Lane. The first ones were Jamaican, then several people from Guyana. And other Caribbean islands dotted about. Stories of coming here after the war. One guy, Clement, was in the navy. He talked about how society is now and about the younger generation. He said: 'Youngsters should do military service for three years. Get them under control. Make them realize what they've actually got.' He said, 'Television and commu-nications, digital, Sky, all that stuff makes them feel they haven't got anything.' He said, 'I sympathize with them.' He feels that the older generation have been given a bad reputation because of the colour of their skin and their origins.

There's a brothel next door to this house. They've been here since I moved in. No particular hassle. When the windows were open, one hot summer night, I heard some discipline being administered. 'You're late, you naughty boy!' Slap, slap, slap. I think the police are aware. I've told them a few times. They know the law, those people next door. They stay inside the regulations. I had a structural problem with the party wall and had to take a look from their side, to assess what we should do. I had to go into the brothel. It took me two months to get permission.

I would be interested in doing drawings in that place. There are ladies who end up working there who only operate on a phone-call basis. It's very much a knock-on-the-door-and-somebody-lets-you-in basis. As neighbours go, they're good. It saves a lot of men bouncing off the walls at home, or causing trouble in the street. People who use the service are anything from fifteen to seventy-five years of age. All creeds, races, colours. Every single kind of person, orthodox Jews to the whitest of whites. There are all kinds of working girls in there. It's generally very quiet. They work from ten in the morning to ten at night.

The ladies on the street are drug addicts. They move around, touting for business. That's what brings the road right down. I think it's because the school was knocked down, two years ago. The zone of prostitution always extends to fill any gap made by demolition. When security arrives with the new grand project, the girls are pushed towards other places. Places lose their character. What I get from my drawings is diversity. I'm white, middle class. I'd be bored if everyone in the road was like me.

I got a commission for that space on the west side of Kingsland Road, where the Jazz Vortex is, Gillett Square. A space that used to be a car park. It's one of Ken Livingstone's 100 spaces. He's put money into it. A hundred spaces he wants to be cultural centres for an area. Regeneration on a specific spot. They're opening in November. Most of the square will be a nice community space. They're talking about putting a screen all the way down one side, to hide the car park.

I drew a girl. She said, 'Can you draw me with my bike?' She works for a company that Ken Livingstone employs to promote bicycling around London. She said, 'Hackney is the number-one borough for bicycles.' She's in an office with thirty-five people who are working, full time, towards instigating more cycle paths, making people aware of the benefits of cycle use.

I went to the Labyrinth on Dalston Lane just once. I was fourteen, scared witless. This would have been the early 1990s. I was staying with my brother who was at college in Middlesex. He lived in Tottenham. I went with him and his flatmate. The girls they were going out with said, 'Let's go to the Labyrinth.'

It was dark. It was the first time I'd been in a place with black people. It was drug-fuelled. I was having a beer and thinking I was growing up. It rolled on until at least six in the morning. Then there would be the Ridley Road bagel shop. Pick up a cup of tea and a bagel – if you could manage it.

I was with people who weren't really involved with the drug scene. But afterwards somebody would have a party that would roll on until midday. It was a scene. Your weekend started at a club on Friday night and ended on Sunday morning. It was right at the start of that E culture.

Much later, in recent times, Hackney Council spoke to me about making drawings to put on the security fence around the Labyrinth, when it was a site marked for demolition. They said, 'Give us some idea of the visuals. What will your project involve?' We thought. 'Well, let's see if we can pick six drawings and put them along the fence.' We met them, discussed this, came away thinking, 'Actually, we don't know if we want to put up drawings here.'

It's such a conglomeration, Hackney. Car parks, mosques. Car washes, Afro hair shops. Turkish kebab places, brothels. Once the council have given you official sanction for your art, you represent them. You're selling something. I want people to go: 'What is it?' My work should be a tease. I want art to be seen as art and not as a corporate advert.

Understanding a little more clearly now that quiet streets above Ridley Road Market, fenced off for future development, will always conform to an imprinted identity, I wanted something more: chthonic visions. Psychosis. Dan was so right, so reasonable. His art was its own justification. Visible cafés, spicy and loud, go out of business: the action moves indoors. Ballard's classic formulation about striving to position the visible to reveal the invisible comes into play: maps of derangement. I would never know it all. There were not enough years ahead of me to penetrate Hackney's wholesale warehouses, messianic churches, people-smuggling operations.

Police raiding a three-storey house in Amhurst Road (the loop of history) uncovered a stash of 3,000 pornographic DVDs. 'The kind of material that would not even be legal to sell in licensed sex shops.' Bestiality, man-on-beast action. Dogs and women with novocaine eyes. Twenty officers broke down the door and were photographed bagging lurid magazines in evidence sachets. A connection was intimated with the Chinese gang who peddled pirated DVDs from Tesco's car park in Morning Lane. The ones rewarded with 'some of the longest ASBOs to date imposed in the borough'.

I wondered if my former colleague Driffield, who had a scholar's interest in the underside of the city, had ever visited the establishment on Shacklewell Lane. I asked if I could record the call. In his pomp, the man lived on telephones.

Sorry, no, I have never been to a brothel in England or consorted with a prostitute here. I think this has more to do with my naivety, poverty and ignorance, than reluctance.

The lady, at the house where I lived in Ritson Road, used to do voluntary work helping women who could not read. There was a very brassy blonde who came round regularly. She managed a massage parlour somewhere in Hackney. It might have been the place you were talking about. Her stories were hilarious.

What I do remember from those days is a petite young Indian lady, with hair shorter than mine and a beautifully clean jacket, offering to be a star witness in my case against Hackney Council: when I stepped off a bus from Liverpool Street and into an enormous pothole. The bag of books I was carrying toppled in after me.

She was a trainee accountant but wanted to be an engineer. Her mother wouldn't hear of it. She lived in a flat above the post office. It was around this time that I was invited to come back early on a Saturday night to be introduced to an Indian lady in Ritson Road. There was going to be a dinner party.

I arrived home at around eight o'clock, I had forgotten about the social occasion. As I came through the front door I could hear the voice of the Indian lady. It was the one from the post office, who was with her husband. Not the girl, but the woman who ran the shop. The one I had a furious row with. She accused me of being head of the National Front in Hackney. His picture was in the Gazette and he did look a bit like me. I thought it was the young lady coming to dinner, but this one had to be at least forty. I said I would have to bathe, change my outfit and I'd be right down.

I climbed out of the back window and across somebody's garden and retreated to the cinema in Kingsland Road.

This was a place never to be forgotten. Young ladies and men were going off to the toilets throughout the performance. The lady next to me tried to sell me her companion. A man brought his bike into the cinema and the manager had to persuade him it was against the rules. The audience booed every time the police came on the screen. As this was a black cop chase movie, it was impossible to even begin to ask them to shut up. Several patrons in my row were waving guns in the air.

There was an interval but I decided to stay to the death – until I knew that the Ritson Road dinner party would have broken up and the family retired to bed. During this enforced break, those strange guys you see in Ridley Road, the ones in black suits and white shirts with red bow ties, looking like Malcolm X, came around trying to sell their newspaper. As an alien, I was not allowed to acquire a copy. Now, with the lights on, I realized that I was the only white person in the audience.

I stayed there until about one o'clock. Next morning the lady of the house demanded to know why I had been so rude. I tried to explain, but she was having none of it. According to her, the manageress of the post office had brought her daughter, the accountant, the love of my life, just to meet me. I had been described as an antiquarian bookdealer in the

City. The post-office woman assumed that I would help her daughter's burgeoning career in the business world. I never saw the girl again.

I avoided the post office from then on. A fact which my customers noted with remorse. I often used to send them large parcels of books. They told me that when packages came from that particular Queensbridge Road post office the stupid buggers never franked the stamps. They would steam them off and use them again. I was saving them hundreds of pounds a year in postage. It was the only way they could afford my prices.

Sympathy for the Devil

They were dying, the film-makers from the era of my early life in London, Bergman and Antonioni, within a few hours of each other, reputations to be re-evaluated. Glib and inane provocations from media populists excusing their own inadequacies, the failure to engage with difficulty, the infantile demand for instant access. I was becoming, or had always been, a peevish malcontent, taking too much satisfaction from being wrong. Outside the mainstream.

'Don't flatter yourself.' Anna's rejoinder. She didn't need to sit through the programme. She knew them so intimately, those films. 'Silent, German?' Her code for all of it, the smug manifest of discounted seriousness.

Our dawn circuit of Victoria Park, the unspoken conversations. How we noticed the same things but felt no obligation to mention them. The woman in the white leisure outfit with the small dog. The bearded skateboarder in winter shorts who gloried in his eccentricity. The pert jogger whose T-shirt advertised her love of New York. We were stepping it out today, Anna wanted to be on the phone early. She dreaded that infuriating sub-classical muzak.

'We live in Albion Drive and we're having a problem with rats. The bins for the low-rise flats. It's their position, tight against the shelter wall. The lids won't close. They don't fit.'

The loss of the long-established caretaker and broom-man, Little Ben (as Pat Rain called him), was disastrous. He had walked away from an impossible and poorly rewarded job. Rubbish was being flung from the balconies in black bags that burst on the ground: the chutes were ignored. Scattered fast-food scraps sustained a community of rodents, feral cats. A family of foxes, wintering under our shed, turned the garden into a pungent wilderness. After some loud infanticide, the adults moved on: making way for a tribe of hungry rats, who gnawed through the legs of stored but unwanted tables and chairs. Thus removing one of Anna's recycling problems. There was only sawdust to bag.

Inside the house, that evil smell persisted. The electrical system went on the blink. One bulb popped and we were left in darkness, the computer was down.

Had Marina Warner experienced Hackney, I wondered? I was going over to Kentish Town to talk to Marina about her involvement with Jean-Luc Godard, at the period when he was shooting *Sympathy for the Devil* (*One Plus One*) in London. 1968. Geography led me back to my old obsession, the manifestation of the New Wave director in Montague Road: the serial Boyard smoker, short raincoat and tinted glasses, darting out of his cab, on the gentle slope between multicultural Ridley Road and the haunted catalepsy of Shacklewell Lane.

Thinking about it, stuck on a choked platform at Dalston-Kingsland, I realized that Marina must have made the journey east. Her son, Conrad Shawcross, the coming sculptor, had a workshop in Clapton. Where, it was rumoured, he constructed fantastic craft to launch on the Lea. I met a man alongside Old Ford Lock – now the launching point for Tony Blair's voyage around the backwaters of the Olympic Park – who had witnessed Conrad's spinning vessel, with its panoramic camera system. He was offered an original Shawcross print for a couple of hundred pounds. He declined. I suggested that he might have made a mistake he'd live to regret. Conrad's mistake was to behave as if he was still bunking down in Kentish Town. In his drowsy pitch with only subsidence to worry about.

The *Gazette* splashed a banner headline: ARTIST APPEALS FOR THE RETURN OF HIS SOULCATCHER (FEARS THAT CAR ARTWORK MAY HAVE BEEN SOLD FOR SCRAP). Conrad's missing vehicle was described as: 'a large, black Ford Capri with the letters IBLS (Investigative Bureau for the Location of the Soul) emblazoned on the sides in yellow'. It was nicked from outside the studio in Millfields Road, Lower Clapton. To make a brief excursion, in all probability, across the Lea. Hackney Wick. The nation's scrap-yard.

'"It would be devastating personally and culturally for this to disappear," said the sculptor, 29.'

Conrad has appeared on the *Richard & Judy* show. His work is collected by Charles Saatchi. The Soulcatcher was equipped with fishing rods and dream traps.

I was determined to close on Godard. I sat down with the DVD of *Sympathy for the Devil* and went straight to the extra features, which included a documentary, *Voices*, shot by Richard Mordaunt. The name rang a bell. Was he the one who rented out the house in De Beauvoir Road to Renchi – at the time this film was being shot? Probably not, but every clue had to be chased.

Sympathy for the Devil was a 16mm polemic shot on 35mm. The contradictions begin there. At £150,000, it was Godard's most expensive feature, made in a city he disliked and a language he pretended, when it suited him, not to speak. The sight of his new young wife, Anne Wiazemsky (fresh from her radiant debut, co-starring with a donkey, in Bresson's *Au Hasard, Balthazar*), wandering about South and West London, spraying slogans on corrugated fences, was profoundly depressing. The film became an inadvertent documentary about futility, ugliness, poor light; the insolent rhetoric of scrapyards, gun-waving black freedom fighters (or jobbing actors). One of whom, Frankie Dymon, Jnr., went on, with *Death May be Your Santa Claus*, to contrive his own post-Godardian drama. He called himself, with humour, 'Frankie Y, the Afro-Saxon'.

Swinging London: the psychedelic gibbet. A colour-supplement commission dressed up as a movie. Photographers shooting photographers. Antonioni's *BlowUp*, made two years before Godard hit town, predicts riverine expansionism and the future location of the Thames Barrier: Charlton to South Ken. A city of moneyed immigrants. Russians with English tailoring eating Italian food.

Godard's more troubled raid tracks around a notable English monument, the Rolling Stones. More stone than roll: even then.

Smoking defiantly, prematurely jaded musicians fiddle with a demon-summoning song, while the camera loops lethargically around them. A more unreal and therefore truer account of the psychosis of celebrity, of (simulated) Dionysiac madness, than Antonioni's guitar-wrecking performance by the Yardbirds.

The major flaw in Godard's first essay on London is that he didn't shoot it in Hackney. If ever there was a Shacklewell project, this was it: sloganeering graffiti, half-digested political theory. Black activists with designer weaponry. Porn shops. Strolls in the park. Band members, who hate each other, rehearsing in the wrong room. Making the windows rattle. Waiting for the Man.

I viewed Mordaunt's documentary, hearing about how Godard stormed out of the original screening at the National Film Theatre on 29 November 1968, waving a cheque and shouting, 'You're all fascists.' I hadn't expected, as we visit the riverside scrapyard, to encounter Marina Warner: down from Oxford, impossibly glamorous among the grunge, the car wrecks. With big brown hair, mascara, white mac and twirly scarf, she was an émigré from Antonioni. Monica Vitti in search of Alain Delon in the Milan stock exchange. Not a new magazine profiler trying, rather nervously, to catch a word with the glowering Godard in his Calvinist shades.

The interviewer in *Voices* (young, male) interrogating a fellow journalist, while she waits for her slot with the great man, is clearly smitten. Marina, without spectacles, not focusing too sharply, gives a charming toss of the hair and a little distracted attention.

'Have you spoken to Godard yet?'

'No.' She laughs. 'I thought I might try to approach him via his wife. I speak French.'

'You're doing an article for the *Observer*?'

'Mmmm . . .'

'Are you going to speak to Jean-Luc at all?'

'The first question is very important with someone like him. You have to get him, you know, in between times. I've got to think of a good first question that will make him think, "That's interesting." I respect him. I don't want to say anything that he would find stupid.'

I was now the one in search of the right question. I was no closer to finding a print of *British Sounds*: or of interviewing anyone connected with Godard's visit to the communal house in Montague Road. But Marina, symbolically, offered me what might be called the Anne Wiazemsky strategy: talk to the wife, the more civilized, approachable part of the equation.

Everything, travelling west out of Hackney, was out of alignment. The afternoon was hot. I had to stand in a crowded compartment, which hummed with a proper Godardian dissonance of sound: phones, iPods, screeching brakes. The underlying nuisance electronic hum that is London. The one that keeps us flickering on the cusp of violence. I travelled one stop beyond Kentish Town and had to walk back. Marina sent me an email, responding to my questions about her day in the scrapyard.

I think that yellow scarf was Foale & Tuffin who opened a 'boutique' in one of the alleys off Carnaby Street – a tiny booth, in an area which was practically unknown, a muddle of bombsites and derelict sidestreets just tuning in to 1960s fashion.

The fabric may have been Celia Birtwell. Certainly, Ozzie Clark's shop, also not much bigger than a wardrobe, off the King's Road, was a Mecca. Biba was crucial in terms of the look – the cut was very narrow, with tight sleeves and armholes and tying the scarf around my neck like that was no doubt an attempt to outline this Twiggy silhouette that was much desired. Kohl was beginning to be imported from Marrakech – even blue, which Chrissie Gibbs wore. Germaine Greer, when I interviewed her, smelled amazing – patchouli, which I had never come across before. She gave me a little vial of it. The smell of the times.

One of the obstacles to my becoming a real part of the movement of movements was that I was brought up loving clothes by a mother who made all her own dresses and read Vogue, turning down the corners of the pages for models to copy.

Marina's house, in its leafy cul-de-sac, was easy to locate in former times: by the lurking presence of Conrad's soulcatching car. But he had decamped to Clapton. And the car was scrap. Fortunately, Conrad's name tag was still on the door.

Upstairs there was a vast plasma-screen TV. Marina was hoping to start a movie club, showing neglected classics. The DVD of Paul Tickell's *Christy Malry's Own Double-Entry* was in evidence. After serving a cool drink, Marina put herself to recalling the events of 1968; the patronage of Kenneth Tynan, and Conrad's father, William Shawcross, then a left-wing journalist, flying back with eyewitness stories from Vietnam.

I had just come to London and was starting to do journalism. For the Observer, *the* Observer Magazine. *It was the early years of the colour supplements. It was the early years of many different things, all of which have changed. Many themes from* Sympathy for the Devil – *such as the relation between rock music and politics – were so much a part of that period.*

I suspect that I might have suggested the subject of Godard. They heard that the film was being made and wanted someone to write about it. It was done like that then. It was incredibly informal, one didn't write a synopsis and go to a committee. It was very, very casual. Even approaching film companies was casual. It was not hard to get access to a set or to see someone like Godard.

We were all involved with the world of fashion. Bruce Chatwin worked there. Francis Wyndham worked at the Sunday Times. *I was on the fringes of that world.*

Godard was very, very central to my generation. We completely idolized Breathless. A Bout de Souffle *seemed to express, to us, the meaning of life – with what now appears to be rather chic nihilism. The lives and conflicts in* Breathless *were very simply dramatized. The world divides: pigs or us. That appealed. The same themes come across through* Sympathy for the Devil. *A sense that we can be ourselves, across difficult class lines, gender lines, race lines. And just by dint of our beliefs and our ideas and our longing to cool down the old order. That optimism.*

The Sympathy for the Devil *set was by the river. A genuine disused car lot. I think the bridge you can see in the background is quite near where the South Bank later went up. It might even have been the same area, before those concrete buildings appeared. Is that possible? It might have been the other side, of course. It was a vast wreckers' yard, a breakers' yard. When I went down there – which you don't see in the documentary – there were lots of naked girls, very thin, leggy, Twiggy types, draped over the cars. It wasn't terribly warm, the weather.*

I remember being quite alarmed by the cruelty and violent sadism of these juxtapositions. It had a wasteland revolutionary look about it, all these black actors toting guns. I was just hanging around. There was this scene when one of the black actors . . . I don't know if he'd heard me talking, if that's what incensed him, or if it was just my presence there . . . but he, as it were, broke out of his role, or, in some sense, remained within it, and came striding towards me. He bawled me out for being a white motherfucker.

I conceded that it probably was the case. I was completely in love with Eldridge Cleaver and Soul on Ice. *One of the main dramas of the book was that he had this antagonistic relation with his white woman lawyer. Then he started his wonderful correspondence with her and they become very close. There was a tremendous love interest between them. A lot of poetry written by people mentioned in the book, like Leroi Jones, was constructed from sexual antagonism, pounding rhythms.*

Before visiting the wreckers' yard I went to South London. I think it was somewhere around Lavender Hill. I had absolutely no idea where that address was. I remember searching for it and feeling completely at sea. I went to the bookshop, it was very squalid. The window was covered in yellow plastic to keep the sunlight off the covers of the books. The ones on display had the kind of graphics that we now rather admire and covet, strange lurid artwork. Thrillers. Deeper inside was a lot of what you now see on the top shelf at the newsagent, but which was then not nearly so evident.

It was very small, that shop, as a set. The filming was complicated. And she, Anne Wiazemsky – Godard's wife and leading lady – was sitting on a table with a lot of books. She was reading from a pornographic book in that favoured Godard monotone. She read from Mao.

I loved the romance of the unknown actress. I loved the Jean Seberg story, this exquisite beautiful boyish girl in Breathless. And then Anne was extraordinarily young when she was found by Bresson, whose method was always to cast amateurs. There was a famous still of Anne with a donkey. She had this quiet, rather affectless, reserved personality. That photograph from the Bresson film is absolutely burned into my mind.

Of course I was quite young myself, but I looked older. I was rather made up, whereas Anne had a much more simple style. Which is what Godard goes for. He went for Anna Karina too, a very simple style. I was rather bedizened, actually. I was that type. I used to wear those huge plastic earrings and boots.

I was, although I thought of myself as very grown up and sophisticated, quite . . . uncomfortable . . . about the pornography shop. And the owner, I remember how seedy he was. I was talking to him on the pavement outside. He was thin and leathery from smoking. I sensed in him an astonishment about what had just descended out of nowhere, this European film crew. He couldn't understand what was happening.

I absolutely don't remember what Anne told me. She gave monosyllabic answers in a very quiet voice.

Godard I met in a kind of keeper's hut, rather like the ones they have in car pounds now, those horrible cabins. At the end of the day's filming. I remember that I was extremely inhibited and, though I do speak French, I wasn't speaking it very regularly. And he was a difficult man to talk to. He rather turned away from other people. Not somebody who showed any real responsiveness to one's presence. His dark glasses made him inscrutable.

I don't remember this episode as well as I remember interviewing some of the other people of the time. I interviewed Truffaut. He came later, Deux Anglaises et le Continent. *Which he wanted me to read for actually! But I never wanted to act. I didn't do it. He cast Kika Markham, she was very good.*

I tell you who I also interviewed, because of my interest in Godard – Belmondo. Jean-Paul Belmondo. That was fantastic. He'd already been in Pierrot le fou, *so this was some sort of action movie. It was in the middle of the night. I had to stay up. A location set, on a road. There were great lamps everywhere. Somewhere in the north of France, Normandy. He played the big star. Eventually I found him alone. He was extremely like himself. He was an actor of whom you didn't say, 'Gosh, he's small. Gosh, he's so ugly.' He was identical. He had exactly the charm that one anticipated. And when he smoked, he did his normal movie thing. Like* Breathless. *I asked him about Godard, that relationship. It's too awful, I can't remember what he said. I liked him. He was so vivid and full of fun. He was probably revving a bit. He'd been up for hours, his adrenalin was fizzing away. He was much more accessible than Godard.*

I think I was actually quite disappointed in Godard. What I seem to recall is that I was disappointed, not only with my own article, but with what he said. I couldn't really find out what the film was about. And also, I think, that already, although we were completely mesmerized by Godard, there was this use of women in the films – which was an area one wanted to know more about. It was terribly fascinating, Vivre sa Vie. *I was totally absorbed in it. At the same time, his obsession with prostitution, his fascination with the sexualization of women ... Ah! And in* Sympathy for the Devil *there was a lot of violence towards women. I wanted to understand it a bit more.*

And there's another aspect of the dreamed freedom of those days, in that pornography, in some people's minds, was an engine of liberation. It was an era of hypocrisy. Certainly that was one of the themes I responded to. I agreed that we were living in this stultified way. A world in which repression was the rule. But, at the same time, it was actually uncomfortable when you saw that porn shop in South London. And the guy who ran it. Somehow this didn't seem to be the way forward, the political way forward.

I never knew about Godard's subsequent London film, British Sounds, *or about Sheila Rowbotham's part in it. Of course, I'd heard about her. Her world was very attractive. I had a longing to be a more serious political person. I began reading Orwell at the time. My political views did get clearer, but I was still charmed by the more glamorous worlds of film and fashion. When* Spare Rib *was founded, I knew a lot of the people. I didn't join them. Not because I refused to join, but somehow my life had taken a different path. I wasn't a natural. People like Michelle Roberts and several of my friends, people who later became friends, belonged. They were a little bit younger, maybe that made a difference. I wasn't a student during the Vietnam War. I caught the tail end of it at university. I went on demonstrations, after university. But it was my sister's generation who really caught the big agitations.*

There is something we can take, even from Sympathy for the Devil. *Godard was very keen to use film to construct reality – as opposed to reading it or recording it. The part that is about the Rolling Stones is a documentary. The other part shows Godard forming film into life. There is a sort of push. That of course is something people don't admit now.*

When Sheila Rowbotham's book, Promise of a Dream, *with her memories of Hackney and communal life, came out, the* London Review of Books *gave it a stinking review. A close friend of mine was incensed and wrote an angry letter. I think the review was by Jenny Diski – who rather specializes in vitriol.*

I like Sheila Rowbotham as a person, her feelings. I'm heartbroken that we've been defeated, politically, culturally. I'm also sad for the next generation. The kind of hopefulness, the energy that buoyed one up in those days, is something nobody with any claim to sophistication can really entertain now. You can't believe there is something to be done that can be done by you.

Montague Road

Things started to move. Or I became aware of that movement. Slow molecules, sluggish blood. Until a random DVD pitched me forward into a documented fiction of the past. Gareth Evans, in a blur of motion, arriving before his fourth email, found me a copy of Godard's *British Sounds*. A contact in edge-land academia, one of those motorway-hugging institutions, burnt a disk from archive. And supplied me with a generous envelope of contemporary cuttings. Cultural memory, if it exists, belongs in those bunkers. All-purpose (shopping mall, eavesdropping facility) architecture, a water-feature pond, with mildly offensive statuary, contrived from a subterranean stream: conferences arranged to quantify loss. Budget dependent on high-profile absentee lecturers, air-miles professors too jet-lagged to access their standard computer presentations. Voices husky with recycled air. Engine running on hire car waiting to rush them to Heathrow.

Money, stuffing our hollow earth, is the only reliable marker of time. We age into increments of poverty, owning more without having the leisure to enjoy or exploit those holdings: books in storage, cans of acetate film stacked as a fire hazard under the stairs. Bills quantify status, mortality telegrams printed in red. The more you owe, the richer your life experience. Complexities of debt evolve with each passing year. Negative equity grows parasitical warts and fistulas. The more you lie awake, sweating through the long night, the richer you must be in claims made upon your person, your imaginary credit. No relief until the account closes, we are life-expired. The dead reckoning. The disappointed creditors.

'Don't open those envelopes. I have to get over to Kentish Town right now. Sheila Rowbotham. Two hours clear, before I've got to be in Aldgate, to walk through a poem for an online literary jukebox. Paid? Apparently. Eventually. Finish by six, to do the radio thing. The one we had trouble with last time, the fee. And tomorrow, once the Rowbotham tape is transcribed, I will deal with the post, I promise.' Brown letters with mean little windows hiding the name of the guilty party.

The council were taking me to court, reminders never delivered, not sent out, saving the borough a few pence on postage: threats, interest charges. I saw them, privatized bailiffs indistinguishable from drug collectors, kicking at a door in the flats behind us. Heaping up goods that can no longer be slung in Hackney's municipal dump: we don't have one. The eco-conscious, who prefer not to make use of the forecourts of decommissioned petrol stations, drive over to Holloway Road, the processing plant operated by Islington.

There were bills from the Whitechapel depot where I rented a tin cupboard to store my archive of papers, home movies going back to childhood, photographs, paintings. Research materials that would take a skilled researcher years to locate. There were surcharges, from a tax office I'd never previously come across, based on earlier bills I had never seen. 'Not our responsibility,' they said. When I eventually reached them: phone number on the letter invalid. The sum they required was not mentioned. It was up to me to make an informed guess. And the final insult: a stroppy invoice from my invisible accountant, the man who was supposed to sort out this mess.

Hari Simbla, give him his due, was good at invoices. They looked very professional, thick paper, nice font. Hari specialized, when he was still in Kentish Town, above the family minimart, in writers and artists. His walls were covered with unapologetic junk that he imagined would one day be worth a fortune – but which, for the moment, made his den look like an Indian restaurant of the 1970s. There was a brother, Henry. We never saw him. But his name stayed on the letterhead: Hari and Henry Simbla & Co., Granville Chambers, Kentish Town Road. The Co. turned out to be Dubliners, employed for a season, to produce a figure from thin air which they submitted to the peripatetic tax office. They made ludicrous claims for materials and services which they took to be necessary accoutrements of the writer's life (theatre tickets, magazine subscriptions, club membership) and massively underplayed the real credit-vampires (ink for the printer, books, breakfasts, walking boots, inflatable kayaks). It would even itself out in the end, Hari promised. I signed whatever they put in front of me. If a balance sheet is elegant enough you can pin it on the wall like an artwork. It's all in the presentation.

The crisis arrived, as these things always do, at the very moment when I could at last see my Hackney book finding a shape. Several of the stories I'd been worrying at were on the point of resolution. I had the *British Sounds* DVD and – thanks to Patrick Wright – an appointment with Sheila Rowbotham, the woman Godard invited to walk naked up and down the stairs.

I was summoned for examination, somewhere in Moorgate. I should have time, after the Old Street Magistrates Court and my brush with Hackney, to make it, black bag of bank statements and cash-receipt notebooks, to the tax interrogation; my seven-year retrospective, in an anonymous office block. I wanted Hari with me. Every season his address went further downmarket while his invoices climbed in compensation. Now he was perched, conveniently, around the back of Dalston Lane. The next move would be the last, for both of us.

In my excitement at securing *British Sounds*, I was prepared to see it as a solution to the problems of the post-revolutionary period: 1969. Coming to Hackney, moving east, was one small step on Godard's long march, closer to Mao. The red plastic book in the Lavender Hill porn shop. A well-chosen quote, in translation, acquires a poetry of distance. *British Sounds* supplied fragmentary glimpses of a real city: workmen, holes in the road, cows waiting for slaughter, landfill barges on a dirty river.

Agitated, in denial, Godard groped for a methodology that

would disguise the sentiment of the streets, the infallible eye on which his career had been founded. Cinema was his medium and cinema was a tool of the bourgeoisie. Even Euro-chic films had to be commissioned, budgets approved. For a brief instant, in the madness of that era when gentleman Maoists and Trotskyists infiltrated the system, trading on Oxbridge connections, commercial television channels found the perfect way to write off a substantial lump of money they didn't have: give it to an art-house director who has absolutely no intention of telling them what he would do with it. The only way you know you've achieved a major career, in serious cinema, is when you have to move to another country to avoid prosecution over unpaid taxes: Bergman, Rossellini, Joseph Losey. It's the movie version of the Nobel Prize.

I understood now why the *Orphans* script we sent to Godard was ignored: it was too long, too detailed, five pages was excessive. The synopsis offered by Godard for a sequel to *British Sounds*, sixteen years later, *Images of Britain*, got the whole thing down to:

1. *old super-eight*
2. *today VHS*
3. *still stills*
4.
5. *queen police tea*
6. *windows and gardens*

au capital de 300.000 f.

Exemplary. A description, by accident, of our own Hackney diary archive, carrying through to my present vision of a borough in which all the gardens, green spaces and public parks would be joined together in a single unblinking tracking shot. Which would, as if by magic, return us to the days of the Hackney Brook: the allotments, the hothouses of Conrad Loddiges and his exotic blooms. Leaving that fourth chapter of *Images of Britain* blank was the masterstroke: we need breathing space, somewhere nobody can find any good reason to regenerate.

British Sounds opens with a controlled drift down the assembly line of the BMC plant in Abingdon. Splashes of metallic red. Layers of cacophonous noise: grinding, screeching, submerged conversation. Workworld. With interventions, crude intertitles, a child's voice repeating details of significant episodes from radical history: dates, names. The virtuosity of Godard's aesthetic abdication is painful to watch, a riposte to the romance of British post-documentary realism: Albert Finney acting (very effectively) in the cycle factory at the opening of Karel Reisz's film version of *Saturday Night and Sunday Morning*. Sound, for Jean-Luc, is truth. Punctuated by silent flashes in which the ill-rewarded labour of the city continues and is observed. Sometimes men with picks and shovels stare right back at the camera.

And then the stairs: white walls, a naked woman (borrowed from the Electric Cinema in Notting Hill) performing a zombie-walk, out of one door, in through another. Sheila Rowbotham's voice reading from her *Black Dwarf* polemic. In her book, *Promise of a Dream*, her memoir of the 1960s, there is a photograph of Godard, up against a high wall, lighting one corn-yellow cigarette from the stub of another, standing inches behind his cameraman. The crumpled raincoat, the polished shoes: a British winter. Posters have faded to blanks. The wall could be anywhere in London.

Essex University: students sitting around penning agitprop revisions to a John Lennon song. Colin MacCabe, in his book on Godard, notes that 'some of those filmed subsequently set up the Angry Brigade, Britain's only terrorist grouping'. A voice lists the currently active cells: 'Cambridge, Essex, Bristol'. And Hackney. Always Hackney. Poets, squatters, bomb-makers: theorists.

This unseen film, commissioned (and killed off) by London Weekend Television, resulted in the sacking of Michael Peacock from the LWT board. Followed by the resignation of Tony Garnett and Kenith Trodd and other programme-makers. The board decided on a realignment, a serious grab for ratings. They brought in – sympathy for the devil – an Australian newspaper proprietor: Rupert Murdoch. Great result! As Godard may have thought: collapse of liberal consensus, the well-made drama, the illusion that television can tolerate any real form of dissenting content. Welcome to the coming age of robot celebrity, reality shows like CCTV with sequins, crash footage from motorways as entertainment, not news: the prophetic visions of J. G. Ballard made manifest. All-day TV to complement all-day British breakfasts.

After visiting Hari Simbla's office – the self-assembly desk was still quilted in bubblewrap – I turned right off Cecilia Road and found myself, camera in hand, looking up at Sheila Rowbotham's communal house: 12 Montague Road. Sheila had long since decamped for Kentish Town, where I would be interviewing her later that morning.

Hari's secretary, a stunning but minute black girl, who could have been any age between twelve and twenty, took the boredom act to new levels of refinement; not painting her nails, nor leafing through her magazine, denying any knowledge of my appointment, or the whereabouts of Mr Simbla. We had spoken on the phone, ten minutes before I left the house. She did not recall the incident. She was obliged to take calls from a whole mess of people in the course of her day, that's what she did. She may have been family, a schoolgirl taking time out. Her tiny feet, in thonged slippers, did not reach the floor. She stared out of the window at some kids who were breaking into Hari's latest Merc.

'Can I wait?'

She gestured: no chair. I stood for as long as I could bear the shame of my awkward, overburdened height, her flawless, doll-like presence: the indifference. Then I walked away, bumping into one of Hari's red-headed Dubliners, back from the Three Compasses, tearing up a betting slip, stubbing out a cigarette in the receptionist's immaculate white triangle of sandwich (which she would never, in any case, have touched). The Irishman went through to the office and got straight on the phone. I gave it up.

There was only one painting left on the wall of the inner sanctum, a pantomime horse gazing morosely at a motorway. Jock McFadyen must have fallen on hard times. Hari Simbla had secured one of my McFadyen favourites, *Horse Lamenting the Invention of the Motor Car*. From 1985. But it wasn't quite right. It was too small. Either Hari had chopped a foot off, to fit the available space, or, as sometimes happened, Jock had produced a duplicate, to fill an order. When the pinch was on he painted by numbers: like a Chinese takeaway. Hari's tuna-coloured Merc, with its personalized number plate, had been slipped in among the circling traffic flow, as Jock's private wink towards his absent patron.

I found a manifesto for the 'English Revolutionary Party' pasted to a junction box, next to a flyer (from the same source) offering cheap removals.

A NEW CONSCIOUSNESS MUST ARISE IN ENGLISH PEOPLE. A NEW IDENTITY TO CHANGE THE WHOLE NATURE OF THIS COUNTRY. A NEW MOVEMENT WHICH IS NON FASCIST AND REPRESENTS THE PEOPLE'S REAL NEEDS. THE KEY AREAS WHICH MUST BE ADDRESSED ARE: IMMIGRATION AND ASYLUM. ENGLISH NATIONAL IDENTITY. THE PROMOTION OF CHRISTIANITY. THE MONITORING OF RACIAL CRIME COMMITTED AGAINST THE WHITE COMMUNITY. THE DEFENCE OF WHITE WOMEN WHO ARE BEING SEXUALLY ABUSED AND HARASSED. THE PROMOTION OF ENGLISH CULTURE

Tall houses, once favoured by Jewish families escaping from Whitechapel, were now multiple-occupied by various communities, black, Turkish: anyone prepared to appreciate the rich plurality of sounds and smells from the Ridley Road Market, the interactions of the street.

Montague Road was a retreat, a curve leading to a synagogue that was now a gated development. I watched a Vietnamese woman raking a sharp-edged gravel bed. Sycamore and ash offered shade, dressing the broken paving slabs with green. Houses outlive their occupants, as the city outlives the houses. When Sheila Rowbotham emailed me, to arrange our meeting, she said that she had returned once, a few years after she'd left: 'and was delighted to find young people there who seemed like spiritual descendants'. Properties test out those who elect to occupy them. Many are found wanting. After ten or fifteen years, you arrive at an accommodation: inhabitants learn to serve the structures that give them shelter.

No. 12 was nicely proportioned, bricks pointed, paint fresh. Black steps to a pale blue door. Decorative plaster surround. A trellis awaiting climbing plants. The bay window was a Georgian quotation. The consoles, above the door, were clawlike abstractions, more ornamental, less dramatic, than the muscled torsos of the Hercules figurines further down the street. Historic traces, the justified pretensions of the original speculative builders, found a suitable advocate in Sheila Rowbotham. She contributed, struggled, made a life, wrote books, moved on. Godard came here, out of his car, up the steps, to argue the case for a naked appearance in a film about the impossibility of film; a strip of evidence that argued, forcefully, with the matter of London. And lost.

Sheila Rowbotham was barely a street away from Marina Warner. We sat at her kitchen table, a jug of coffee, a view into the garden beyond. Women, I felt, carried the memory-burden of their cultural heritage more effectively than the men: less ego, less noise, intimate details of ordinary life lightly held. The force of attraction in this legacy was much in evidence: the illumination behind Sheila's eyes. Her generous recollections of male absurdity held no illusions. So many men of the 1960s had creased and crumpled, waiting for the tide to turn. Incubating disaffection. Nourishing unpublished memoirs, boxes of dead photographs. Unrequired confessions.

I liked the story of how the Montague Road property was

found. Rowbotham's partner, Bob, applying occult logic – and echoing, though he didn't know it, Ford Madox Ford – set his compass blades to the map: 'an arc drawn around Liverpool Street Station and King's Cross'. He organized a series of expeditions into unknown territory. Until one particular house drew them in.

Sheila was the first person I'd interviewed who had direct experience of Tony Blair. In Hackney. A person who started where he was to finish: as self-appointed mediator in an irresolvable dispute. The flashing cuffs, the gerbil grin that doesn't synchronize with panic in fearful eyes. A wide boy used to busking it on charm, expecting to be found out. Biding his time.

I came across Tony Blair at the time of that dispute at the Market Nursery. The nursery was near London Fields. It was squatted, then it became official. Blair was visibly horrified by his first encounter with Hackney politics. More complex, more lethal than the Balkans. It was all so absurd. Bernie Grant, the union guy, was a complete pain. He was humiliating the black woman who worked at the nursery, because she didn't know all the latest terms for race analysis. She was a real Hackney community worker.

People were threatening the two lesbian women who opposed whatever was going on in the nursery at that time. They didn't think they should side with them just because they were lesbians. They believed in the nursery. They were getting threatening phone-calls for deserting the lesbian cause. They used to live in Broadway Market. It was a very popular location for lesbian communes.

There were five rooms in the Montague Road house. One of which was divided by wooden doors. That made six rooms. I can't believe how many people lived there.

Godard approached me at the time when the women's movement had just begun. I had this uneasy feeling about the film. I thought: 'I'm not quite sure.' People were going on about the objectification of women. Also, even then, I thought I was a bit floppy. I didn't know if I wanted to be shown naked coming down the stairs. Godard had this idea that he could make these rather quick films and give the money to radical causes. He was in the process of denying his role as an artist.

He still had that intensity. He sat on the sanded floor of my bedroom in Montague Road and he talked to me. I can't remember how he arrived. He wouldn't have driven. I can't remember if I'd met him before this. I can't remember the sequence of things. Mo Teitelbaum, one of the producers, knew him. I spent time in other parts of London when Godard was shooting certain sequences, I remember watching him work.

I do remember this figure sitting cross-legged on my floor and the odd feeling I experienced at the time: 'This is the famous director.' He challenged me. He said, 'You think I can't make a cunt boring?' He was so angry. I thought, 'Oh dear, here's me daring to criticize the great man.'

There were comments about the naked woman from friends who saw British Sounds at that time. Pete said, 'When that shot first appears, you think: "Wow, crumpet!" And then it just carries on and on and on. With that droning voice. You lose all interest.'

I recorded my voice-over in somebody's room. I had this thing about West London, it was so alien and strange to me. It was such a trip just to get there.

There was no filming in Hackney. Now that I think about it, I do recall: Godard arrived in a black cab. He spoke in English. I do speak French. But he spoke to me in English.

I went down to Essex University with him, in winter, trailing about, keeping my maxiskirt out of the mud. The students were unimpressed with Godard. They chucked him in a fish pond. I wasn't there at the time. My memory is very bad.

What was memorable about Godard, as I said, was the concentrated intensity in the way he worked. Marc Karlin was the same, totally obsessive. I recognize it from my own writing, you are oblivious of everything else. People at the university, in Manchester, just cannot understand.

Godard was really in there. You could feel his brain burning. I remember people groaning as they watched that film for the first time.

That famous image, the woman on the stairs of the Hackney house, was an illusion. It happened elsewhere: St John's Wood, where Irving and Mo Teitelbaum lived, or Notting Hill. Sheila couldn't remember. The walls were too white. Godard had never prowled these streets. His cones and holes and pinched citizens were far away to the west, they were the future: nobody in 1969 saw any advantage in rescuing Hackney from its dream of the Blitz. The rubble, the prefabs, the community bathhouses.

But Godard was wrong too, the prolonged close-up of the pudendum of the woman from the Electric Cinema, slightly fuzzy in degraded reproduction, is never boring: because it is not a thing, a rhetorical landscape like the beautiful Courbet painting, but evidence of a particular biography, the pale bikini line of autumn and the curving scar of a Caesarean procedure or an appendix removal. The longer the shot is held, the more of the history of skin and texture we absorb. The episode subverts the director's dogma with human awkwardness, a contrived social situation, the requirement of this woman to act – and act badly – as she echoes Rowbotham's voice-over in a telephone conversation.

The reality of Montague Road is contained in its nakedness. Sunlight polishing sanded boards. Marc Karlin settled here, seemingly by accident, but perhaps to complete the film that Godard chose, in the end, not to deliver. Rowbotham's voice, as I listened to the tape, conjured images of an interior I had never visited. The problem with this Kentish Town interview was that I talked too much; there were parallels in our lives, coincidences, crossovers from the era of Liberal Studies teaching, friends in common, shared walks. But Sheila's difficulties came from social and political engagement (individual desire set against the general good), where I was monkish and unyielding in my neurotic mapping of place. That warped and refracted autobiography.

Eventually, slurping a fresh mug of coffee, I allowed her to resume this account of Hackney in the 1960s.

I had a friend called Roberta Hunter Henderson who was at Warwick. She was very good at maths and logic, completely different from me. She did philosophy. She met Marc Karlin. She was living in my house in Montague Road. She brought Marc with her. Then Roberta moved out. I think she went to do anthropology in Oxford. Marc stayed. Was it 1969? He was working with Humphrey Trevelyan and James Scott. They raised money by doing films for a sheik. An Arab. A film about polo. They did a Martini advert too. They didn't have any money. They were going round the country doing films for Cinema Action. Marc made Nightcleaners, *it took about five years. A documentary about unionizing women who clean office buildings at night.*

It was a very chaotic period in the house. But a generally safe feeling. Neighbours were burgled a few times. One burglar stole a book of mine, Wilhelm Reich's The Function of the Orgasm.

The lorry driver who lived two doors down, he had his meter burgled. He was straight down the pub where the villains drank, checking out who had been spending money: in coins. He would go round to the guy's door, immediately. Direct action. We never went near the police. As middle-class incomers, we were sitting ducks. We didn't know what to do.

There was a woman who went into hospital to have a baby. She told me to wake her husband up, every morning. I couldn't get the guy to move. He had to go to work at five o'clock. I hit him with a pillow. 'It's really important,' the woman told me. I also had to do his washing, he couldn't cope with the launderette. He didn't know how to operate the machine.

Montague Road was an education. I should be grateful to Bob, my partner at the time, for my only shrewd capital investment. 'Rent is irrational. You should use your money and buy.' I would have just dissipated the money over the years. It seemed a vast amount then. There was also a tendency in Hackney for women to own the houses. There was a strong feeling about Hackney being a respectable borough. People moved there from East London, Whitechapel. Our neighbours included ladies who kept haberdashers and were very proper.

A lot of our life in Montague Road revolved around the Mitford pub, which featured regular drag shows. Some hairy guy singing 'Bridge over Troubled Water'. The local pubs and Ridley Road Market, that was it. I did go to Hackney Downs, but it wasn't very exciting. I liked to walk down to the river, the Lea. It seemed so far – until I moved to Clapton. I loved walking my dog on the marshes. The space! There was some ancient battle down there. I used to get these strange feelings walking across that green wilderness.

I joined the Young Socialists. I think it was my Methodist schooling. If you have views, you should do something about it. I joined the Labour Party. In Hackney the party was intensely Trotskyist. Bob Rowthorn was involved with New Left Review. We would get Robin Blackburn, someone of that stature, coming to talk to the Young Socialists. We met in Graham Road, in the Labour Party rooms. Upstairs. A very grim space with fluorescent lighting. There was a pub opposite. That's where everyone started to really talk. When we were at the meetings it was all dogma: 'The comrade at the back.' That stuff.

   Bill Fishman and Raphael Samuel were important to me. I found Bill by ringing around like a mad person, looking for work. I was doing day-release teaching, Liberal Studies. I wonder what happened to those kids? I wonder what they remember of the weird people who spouted jargon at them? Thanks to doing that teaching my pension is slightly more than I anticipated. But those forms! Those endless forms. Now, at Manchester, they make us do forms on the computer. I get into an hysterical state. The young lecturers don't understand. The new academics are completely computer literate. You are judged these days on your ability to fill in forms.

I moved into Montague Road in 1966. I'd come to Hackney in '64. The logical Bob said: 'Buy.' My friend Mary Costain, who was at university with me, moved in. We collected someone called Kathie Humby, who was in the Young Communists League. We knew her from the Dolphin pub. Young Communists used to go there. Kathie was a working-class girl.

   The people in Montague Road paid one pound, each, for the house

– and another pound for a political cause. I paid too. We collected the money, everyone paid. It collapsed when the hippie thing in the late 1960s took over. Bob and I split up. The situation was made worse by the invasion of all these people who lived through the night, getting stoned.

I used to be going upstairs, asking them to shut up. I was trying to write my thesis. Bob was getting really fed up. He was coming from Cambridge. He had a job. These hippie characters were friends of Mary and I felt very loyal to her. I felt completely torn. I had all these democratic ideas. Mary had as much right to live there as me and Bob.

I invited some guy I'd met with Bob, out in the road, to move in. There was no reason why we had more right to live in this property than anyone else. Then I did become more brutal. I ended up expelling people.

The chaos in living works as long as the people involved really like each other. To be with Marc Karlin always lifted my heart – even though he was the most chaotic person. He contributed by the meals he used to cook.

I'm not great on anything being planned by other people, I resist rotas. On the other hand, I'm quite conscientious about cleaning. I'm very untidy but a great mopper. I often felt hard-done-by, because I was doing most of the cleaning. Marc cooked one meal. Then we would take it in turns. Nigel Fountain is a great fan of systems. As soon as he moved in, systems came with him. Marc was not much good with this. We had space for people to opt out, as long as they contributed something.

People had their own rooms. There was none of the thing of having to share. We were quite traditional and Trotskyist. We didn't have much communal space, one tiny kitchen.

Dave Phillips moved in with his girlfriend, Sue. She came first, then Dave. Sue and I would go to the market with a wheelie basket, to Ridley Road. There was a system for who shopped. That's what Sue and I did. Paul – my son's father – and Dave Phillips, they were better at electrics. David Widgery was pretty good too, his father had taught him. He didn't live in Montague Road, but he was always visiting. Widgery was very keen on the Four Aces Club in Dalston Lane. We used to go there. I went a few times, it was a bit tomb-like.

We had house meetings. The house-maintenance committee used to agree that things didn't need doing. Ha! It was like reproducing the normal sexual divisions of labour. Nigel had no practical or manly skills, but he had this great flair for cooking.

I had my son, Will, in . . . I can't remember. I can't remember anything. 1977? He's thirty now, so it must have been. I lived in Montague Road when he was a baby. It provoked a bit of a crisis as soon as he began to crawl. I had a large room, but the television set was in there too. It took a long time before we had a television. People would all come to watch in my room. They wouldn't rent us a set. They said that women were unreliable. They said, 'No no, sorry. We can't do it.' We had to buy a set. Then all the people in the house would come to my room. I was trying to write. I had a baby.

By the end of the 1970s it was breaking up. The political climate was bitter. In '79 we moved to Clapton. It took time to find a house. No one, apart from myself and Paul, had any motive for moving. We wanted more space for Will. I sold Montague Road to fund the move. It fetched £17,000. It was bought for £4,000. We made some profit. The new house cost a bit more, so I had to get a mortgage. It was a difficult shape, so long and thin. Nigel moved out. There was a small room for Will.

In Clapton, I liked being near Hackney Marshes. I made friends with a Turkish woman at the cleaners. Clapton didn't have the atmosphere you would find in the area around Ridley Road. I liked the bit by the church, St Augustine's Tower. And the old churchyard, the winding medieval road.

We shift with the geography; a flit of a few streets, across the Hackney Brook, over the Downs, and our interests change, evolve. We become different characters. At the start of it, this journey into a borough too large and strange to define, we were blank pages. Nothing in ourselves, but politicized by the connection with Ridley Road, sonar-echoes of Mosley, counter-currents of necessary opposition. Drifters sucked in from Cambridge and Essex. Every Hackney ward, every warring E-number, had its disciples: the gardeners, the careerists, the ones who would move up and out. History infects us. Sheila Rowbotham, walking, exploring, recognized the long shadows in the road ahead.

Shacklewell Lane is wonderful. I loved knowing that Mary Wollstonecraft walked there. I used to lead historical tours. I followed the inspiration of Bill Fishman. We all went on Bill's Whitechapel tours. I got my information from various old books. I've still got them, photographs of places that no longer exist. Lynne Segal was very sarcastic about my Hackney tours. 'Most of your walks are to places that aren't there any more.' Ha!

The most famous one was the walk Julie Christie came on. It started to pour. I can't remember who she was living with at the time or why she decided to come. She was accompanied by a woman who wrote adventure books, a well-known person who was plotting to go off on some trip into the desert. A Turkish film star turned up, she wanted to talk to Julie. I had a Turkish film star, Julie and this famous woman whose name I have forgotten. And my mongrel dog, Scarlet. We started from my house in Clapton. We set off to look at some academy for young ladies and then a churchyard visited by Samuel Pepys.

I led the group through the very dirty streets of Hackney. We arrived somehow at Victoria Park. We went via Sutton House on Homerton High Street. It poured, absolutely poured, with rain. The heavens opened. We stood under a tree and didn't know what to do. We decided to run, to try and find a café. By the time we got to the café, we were soaking. Of course Julie still looked incredibly beautiful. She was not wearing anything fancy. Even when she wore de-glamorized things, the clothes just seemed to hang off her in this fabulous way. She had khaki trousers. She is quite practically made, but she's very interested in history. Women's history.

Poor Scarlet, my little ginger dog, was sodden. 'I'll never get her into the café.' I was tying her, rather sadly, to the railings, when Julie turned on her charm. Sure enough, she is recognized. The café owner is agog. He's got this radiant film star in his place. The dog is reprieved. That's the great power of Julie Christie's beauty.

I think Nigel was on that walk. He knew Duncan Campbell, the journalist who lived with Julie at one time, up in Stoke Newington. So he knew Julie too.

I'm not terribly good at geography, I usually get lost. My tours were always slightly anxious. I kept sneaking a look at my London A–Z. I modified my excursions accordingly. Sometimes we found ourselves doing somewhat abbreviated walks.

I was interested to discover that there had been an academy in Powerscroft Road, a dissenting academy. Which means that William Godwin and Mary Wollstonecraft must have walked up Powerscroft Road in Hackney! It felt very odd. You end up living in places through which people you have read so much about have already passed. We are treading, literally, in their footprints.

Even at the time I was in Clapton, Russian Mafia people were moving in – as criminals, not property developers. A guy called Terry, who worked at the swimming pool, told me about it. He knew, being black, all about the Yardies and the Russians. They were fighting it out in Clapton. It was getting really edgy just before I left.

I remember this scary incident. I went out with Scarlet, about seven in the evening, to post a letter. I saw this man being beaten up by a group of other men, in the road. I went back towards my house. I thought, 'This is like Enid Blyton, the Famous Five. I must remember the number of the car.' I'm hopeless at numbers. I was staring at the car when it spun round, just like in the films, and drove straight towards me. I was frozen in terror, clutching my little scrap of a dog. A guy gets out. I swear he had a purple halo of rage around his head. 'You were fucking taking our fucking number.' I thought I was going to be shot. 'No no no, I wasn't.' Ha!

He thought I was so pathetic, he gave up on me. I rang Paul. He said, 'It's your duty to see whether the victim is still alive.'

I went back. The victim had vanished. My son, Will, said, 'Mum, just stay out of it. Drug dealers. Leave well alone.' Nigel said, 'You should ring the police.' I said, 'They know where I live, Nigel. And anyway I can't remember the number of the car.' 'Forget it, Mum,' my son said. He had grown up in Hackney.

Because of coming from the north of England, I stare into people's eyes. I smile. When Will was a teenager, walking around Hackney with me, he would say: 'No no. Mum, no.' When I was in Whitby, recently, I was so much at ease. Old ladies strike up conversations with complete strangers. I carried on like that in Hackney. I do miss Hackney — but it is more restful now, over here, in Kentish Town. I don't drive. When I walked at night, home through Clapton, I was getting increasingly nervous about making it safely to my door.

Eleanor Road

There is nudity in the diary films, male as well as female, but there is no sound, just the memory of the projector grinding relentlessly on: the creased sheet, cracks in the wall. Nakedness, in theory, was democratic. Cameras did pass around between the males, women rarely got their hands on them, or showed any interest in doing so: sometimes, by use of a cable and a black bulb, a fish-eye lens, we operated a primitive form of surveillance cinema. Everybody in shot, but one person is squeezing the bulb. It was a question of recording daily life, not setting up dramas; nobody would be asked to walk naked up and down the stairs, in an attempt to render that event tedious, banal. As with any home movie, the participants were also the audience. How far would it go, this record of coffee cups, the brushing of hair, meals, baths, walks, work? The way the streets looked. People waiting for buses, buying bread. An American friend, who lived with us for some months, helping to fund Albion Village Press, sent back footage from Kabul. He also sent a copy of the Stan Brakhage film *Lovemaking*. Which, as much as anything, was about rhythms of light and breath. The intimate movements of an unknown couple, seen close, side on: flaring, burning out, as golden light pours through a naked window. The poetry of surveillance is in that quality of light. Brakhage's engagement. Our trust.

Godard challenges Sheila Rowbotham in Montague Road. Deflecting the accusations that would surely come, prurience, misogyny, by quoting at length from Rowbotham's *Black Dwarf* polemic: 'Women's Liberation and the New Politics'. Politics of the body. Scruffy rooms enlivened by the complicit presence of a naked woman. How to dress it, the question they have to ask: 'Will you get your kit off?' For art. For women's liberation. The cause.

Barry Flanagan, the sculptor, the hare-maker, friend of a friend, came to our door. His work, in the exhibition we attended on Bond Street, had progressed from provocative conceptualism, brokered by the book-destroying John Latham, to coils of rope, Habitat felt and bags of sand. Our friend Mike, a Bristol associate of Flanagan, had an early piece in his Leamington Spa flat, a cloacal-black, free-standing figure: like a compacted Elizabeth Frink rescued from the ashes of an art-store fire.

Would she, would Anna, pose naked for Barry Flanagan, a new series he was contemplating, on Hampstead Heath? The explanation became convoluted – and being there, offering coffee, I found myself eavesdropping on a parallel version of the Godard/ Rowbotham episode. The idea was: grass. The colour and texture of grass, at this time, this season, early autumn. With the naked woman an incidental but important element. At first light, one morning: soon. After-images of Antonioni's *BlowUp* were in the air. The municipal grass the art director had to spray, to achieve the required tone. Nobody, back then, was quite sure where this park was. I heard the director Michael Radford say that he was sure it was Victoria Park in Hackney. Flanagan's proposed sequence – if anyone stalking the heath photographed him in action – would recall the illicit rendezvous, the fatal assignation in Maryon Park. A live woman lying on damp ground, in place of the corpse of the distinguished older man. Silk-screen prints against white walls.

Anna declined. I said nothing. The figure of the woman in the park, the nude on the staircase, the bare-breasted cheerleader at the free concert, very soon translated into a symbol of alienation, schizophrenic breakdown. Chris Petit, launching a career as a television essayist, had a great success when he concentrated on air hostesses (fully clothed) reminiscing over the good times. Fluffy boudoir clouds and glinting silver wings: Leonard Cohen and Van Morrison on the soundtrack. But when he confronted the death of the middle classes in a film about bank managers, night-drifts in retail parks, a naked model parading through a deserted bank in Herne Hill, he took critical flak. The symbol was too stark and the nakedness too naked. Who was this person? What was her story? Was she one of Marc Karlin's *Nightcleaners* saving on her clothing allowance – or experiencing, in the solitude of the building, a moment of liberation (before the installation of CCTV systems)? Carrying a candle, she became a gothic spectre, an unclothed revenant. Kaporal, Petit's researcher, spent the entire day's shoot trying to get the model's number. His flat, he whispered, was conveniently close at hand. Vodka and cold chicken in the fridge.

David Widgery, who sits proudly in reminiscences of period and place (Hackney: 1965–92), had no problem with nudity: personal nudity. Leaping naked, as we have heard, into the London Fields Lido. The pool itself, just as naked, abandoned, squatted, reoccupied, became a privileged memory-space. Enclosed, tree-surrounded, off-limits: and therefore interesting. Announcements of its makeover, its glorious renovation, were issued at regular intervals, to deflect protests over all the other padlocked Hackney pools. Spring, summer, autumn: grand openings were advertised on posters and in leaflets dropping like dandruff on our mat.

'Construction problems have pushed the opening back until October at the earliest,' gloated the *Standard*. 'The hold-up is a severe embarrassment to Hackney Council, the Labour-run borough behind the £38 million Clissold Leisure Centre fiasco in Stoke Newington. Hackney, one of the three Olympic boroughs, has only one public swimming pool for serious swimmers.'

I found David Widgery's memorial, the drinkers acknowledged it with uplifted cans, in the little park to the south of St Anne's Limehouse, where I had worked as a gardener. And where I often ate my lunchtime sandwiches, while brooding on the mysteries of Hawksmoor's overwhelming architecture. The drinkers gave me space.

DR DAVID WIDGERY (1947–1992)
PRACTISED LOCALLY AS A GP.
AS A SOCIALIST AND WRITER

HIS LIFE AND WORK WERE AN
INSPIRATION IN THE FIGHT
AGAINST INJUSTICE.

Widgery's dynamism was intimidating. I had been sleepwalking through the same territory, struggling to read the signs but achieving nothing braver than keeping my own family more or less afloat and publishing a few booklets. The doctor part of this equation was raw: I couldn't follow my father and grandfather down that route. And while I blundered, without skill or vocation, from labouring job to labouring job (eyes open, notebook at the ready), Widgery limped and talked and drove: damp flat to hospital to committee room, to pub to party. He was engaged, hot with language. Qualified to give a clinical description of every wanderer he noticed on the street: 'The distinctive gait of the depot-medicated schizophrenic, the manneristic grimaces of the manic-depressive, the shuddering cough and luminous facies of pulmonary tuberculosis.'

While we sat in kitchens and debated, or drove out across Hackney Marshes, a smudged sun burning off the early mist, other groups were reasserting the dissenting spirit of old Hackney; or challenging it, finding new ways to make a nuisance of themselves. Quoted in memoirs, visible in documentaries, the Montague Road gang had a recoverable legend. The Angry Brigade and their associates in Amhurst Road continue to be mythologized, to inspire works such as *My Revolutions*, the novel by another Hackney dweller, Hari Kunzru. In Balls Pond Road, David Medalla and the Exploding Galaxy commune, living close to the historic site of Oswald Mosley's recruiting centre, made performance art – theatre, publications, court cases – out of a cannabis arrest. *Planted*, a report on events in 1968, featuring photographs, poems, drawings, was now a collectable artefact.

Juliet Ash, David Widgery's partner, still lived in the Eleanor Road house where he died: between the north side of London Fields and Graham Road. Juliet, who alerted me, years before, to the Limehouse memorial plaque, agreed to give an interview.

She was culling her library. Len Deighton paperbacks were boxed for disposal. The *Collected Poems* of Allen Ginsberg and *New American Poetry*, edited by Donald Allen, would be reprieved – along with a marching line of red-covered Karl Marx. Juliet had a spread of papers on the table, she was working on a book about prison costumes: backwards from Guantánamo Bay. The weird chic of high-fashion outfits inspired by orange prison fatigues.

We talked of lost Hackneys: military barracks, bottling plants, music halls, pubs. And people.

There were eight of us in a collective house in Parkholme Road, near where Michael Rosen lives, opposite the George. I wasn't with David Widgery. I was with my previous person. I moved to Eleanor Road in 1979.

There used to be a swimming pool on London Fields. We used to go there for breakfast when it was nice weather. Before taking the kids to Gayhurst. Did your kids go there?

It must have been about 1986 when the pool closed. Now it's coming back, they're revamping it after years of neglect. Because of creeping gentrification. The Olympic effect.

Whiston Road, I remember that pool. The primary-school kids used to go there for their lessons. A lovely pool. But now, since the fire in Clapton baths, there is no swimming pool in Hackney. Not a single one. They say the London Fields Lido will open again, but we're still waiting.

By the late 1980s all the money was going into the City, into Docklands. Hackney, increasingly, is becoming Islington. There is no sense of history. Which is why getting rid of Spirit and his little shop from Broadway Market, and getting rid of Tony's Café, is so appalling. The people in the surrounding flats and tower blocks use those places. They're being excluded. The only real stall left, the guy who did vegetables through the 1980s and 1990s, sells at an eighth of the price of the organic products on sale in the Saturday market. People still go to the original stall. For ordinary local vegetables.

I remember thinking, back in the 1980s, wouldn't it be nice to have a café where you could get a decent cup of coffee? Now that it has come, you realize what comes with it. You lose all the local things that were good. The council could have included the best of the old, along with the gentrification. It could have worked.

Dave Widgery was very much involved with the Socialist Workers Party. I was expelled from that in the 1970s. First I was in IS (International Socialists), which later became the SWP, but the faction I was in disagreed with the party's line on Troops Out (out of Ireland). We thought we should be involved more actively. I was always being expelled for being interested in fashion, for not taking the party line on various political actions.

Dave was as much interested in cultural politics as in the rank-and-file stuff. One of the things he felt, being a doctor in Limehouse, and being involved in the closure of Bethnal Green Hospital in the 1970s, was that unless you were part of an organization, politically, you had no power. There were different ways of operating. You operate within a party organization. You involve yourself with trade unions. There was no way you could have any clout unless you were within the party. But there was another strand, which Dave understood very well, in terms of race and music and radical politics. Even when this meant associating with people who were not involved with the party. That's why, in the 1980s, Dave Widgery worked for the Hackney Empire restoration project. He battled alongside Roland Muldoon and his partner, Claire. We knew that the Hackney Empire would go bankrupt. It wasn't like Ocean, the music venue that replaced the Central Library in Mare Street. The council poured vast amounts of money into Ocean, along with lottery funds. And still it failed, spectacularly. We won. We saved the Empire. And we did it with very little support from the council.

Dave's whole thing in Hackney in the 1980s was about how it was important to fight Thatcher in the culture, as well as through political organizations. Because he worked so much, because he wrote books and grafted away, and appeared in films, the SWP allowed him a certain amount of scope. There were areas where they didn't agree with him – on

Wilhelm Reich and his sexual theories, for example. They were uneasy when he talked about sexuality and politics.

It was Dave's sense of history. He saw the IS and the SWP operating on a trajectory back into the old Communist Party of the 1920s and 1930s. His knowledge of the history of Communism and Marxism was what kept him going in terms of party politics. The sign we have on our wall – 'Workers' Circle Friendly Society' – Dave got from a skip, at the back of the Hackney Empire. There were quite a few of these to be found in the borough at the turn of the century.

Knowing the history of the co-operative movements led to us reviving the Hackney Literary and Philosophical Society. We met in the George, upstairs. I have all the records, the minutes of our meetings. This paper is from the original Society, in 1815. A talk on 'The Natural Magic of Chemistry'. A talk on 'The Female Poets of Great Britain'. A talk on 'The Philosophy of the Earth and its Wonders: Things Not Seen'. Between 1815 and 1817, they met at the Lamb Tavern in Homerton. Then they moved to St Thomas's Square. The last meeting, in 1817, was a talk on 'The Character of the Female Heart'. 'This proved so contentious,' say the minutes, 'that the Institute did not meet again.' It was dissolved in May of that year.

Our revival ended around 1990. Clifford Turner gave a talk on Bedlam. We've got tapes of all the talks. Nigel Fountain gave one of them. 'Dr David Widgery,' according to the minutes, 'then insisted we sit in a circle and hold hands and raise the spirit of '68.' Raphael Samuel gave a talk about the history of Hackney. Bill Fishman gave one on 1888. There was a talk on Hackney and its asylums. Mike Rosen spoke about children's writing. I'm sure Sheila Rowbotham talked, but I can't find a record of that.

There was a sense in the 1980s – I don't know if it was because we were all much younger – that you could do things in Hackney. There were the Victoria Park Open Festivals with the Anti-Nazi League. That's gone. I feel that events have been taken out of our hands. History has disappeared. We can't win now.

We succeeded with the Hackney Empire because Mecca put it up for sale. Roland Muldoon bid for it and got it. That didn't happen at Labyrinth in Dalston Lane. It was already in the hands of sinister property developers. I used to go to the Four Aces, with Dave, and to Labyrinth. We went with friends and we were accepted. The place was run on a shoe-string. It doesn't happen now.

I don't remember much about Tony Blair living in Hackney. I wasn't aware of him in local politics. Patrick Wright remembers seeing him through the window, after the move to Islington, perched on the edge of a chair, watching footage of himself on Newsnight in total fascination.

We were living in Islington in 1971, we came to Hackney for a party in Sheila Rowbotham's house, off Cecilia Road. By the Norfolk Arms. Sheila and Dave were good friends. She was involved with Black Dwarf, with Tariq Ali, that lot. Have you read Promise of a Dream?

It was funny the way Dave came to the East End. He was living in Islington, a medical student, around 1967. He passed his exams. He had to be an in-house hospital doctor. He made a stab at the London A–Z and landed on Bethnal Green. He was very involved with the 1970s sit-in, the occupation of the hospital, when they closed it down. He was in the middle of making a film at the time.

Marc Karlin had this vision of independent cinema. He was very keen on Channel 4 at the beginning. He made films with Dave and Sheila. He did the famous Nightcleaners documentary. When Marc died he was in the middle of a new project.

Dave was really close to Marc, really really close. I used to go round there all the time after Dave died. Marc said that Dave was like a monkey perched on his shoulder, keeping him informed, whispering in his ear. Then, when Marc died as well, it was unbelievable. Poor Nigel, the third man, had to speak, endlessly, at his friends' funerals. And very well, movingly. He has left Hackney now. He writes a lot. He's just written a book called Lost Empires. It's about all the Empire theatres, right back to the 1890s. It was partly inspired by the Hackney Empire.

He can't make enough money to write his books. He's an obituarist now. He works, so he says, on death row.

He gets very upset about the fate of his Hackney novel, Days Like These. He knows everything about Dave and the Oz trial. Dave was very friendly with Richard Neville. I only saw Richard when he came over *here. I've got copies of the old Oz magazines. Dave would write about anything. There was an excitement of being on the edge. A sort of Surrealism. Dave saw himself as a Surrealist. He wanted to shock the bourgeoisie: drugs, sex, art, rock'n'roll. He managed this by not doing a huge amount of household chores. Ha! He loved his children enormously and put an enormous amount of energy into his relationship with them. He was always a very exciting figure. He had ideas up his sleeve. There never was a moment when he wasn't doing something. If he did childcare, it was absolutely 100 per cent.*

He took time away from medicine to write Some Lives! *And, apart from that, he'd write* British Medical Journal *columns on a Saturday evening, between four and seven. Then go out and have a good time.*

The thing about Dave, there was always a sense that time was short. He'd had polio and TB. He'd been in hospital a lot when he was young. He felt that he had to put everything into every moment of every day. He wrote a wonderful piece called 'Last Exit' for a magazine called ZG (Zeitgeist) that I edited in the early 1980s. A cross-cultural magazine. Dave's piece was about Jimi Hendrix, Jim Morrison and Janis Joplin. There is a line in there about 'you're never as good as you are when you die'.

I was reading your Limehouse book, the one where you are working as a gardener, what was it called? It so happened that Dave worked right alongside the Hawksmoor church in Gill Street. Now he has a plaque on the boundary wall of St Anne's. I go there occasionally, a magic spot. One day I found three blokes sitting by the plaque. As I went up to it, they said, 'Did you know 'im?' I said, 'Yes, he was my husband.' Tears came into their eyes. 'Do you want a drink? We knew Dave.' They were inviting me to have a drink. 'So sad,' they said, hugging me. You know how drunks go back over things, again and again, and the emotions well out of them.

St Anne's is such a pivotal place. The vicar was a nice guy. To do the plaque I had to get in touch with the LDDC. Dave was always ranting against them. Long before Canary Wharf was built. He became furious at any mention of them. He organized huge campaigns against all of them. And the irony was that I had to go to them to get that plaque on the wall: a heritage wall, a Hawksmoor wall. Eventually they allowed it. We had a little ceremony.

Dave was not very careful about his drinking. But he cared deeply about the working people he treated in Limehouse. If he was short with artists like Jock McFadyen when they came to him with worries about alcohol consumption, it wasn't because he didn't have time to waste on neurotic painters. It was the fact that he liked a drink himself. He was a terrifically controlled person – who, on the other hand, was totally abandoned to drink. When he was on call, he was absolutely responsible. But afterwards? A lot of doctors do that. They didn't have locums when Dave was around.

Michael Rosen, a near neighbour, wrote an obituary tribute to Widgery, focusing on his uncontained energy, his activism, the cropped head on the platform at the London School of Economics.

> 'We have seen through the fancy dress of modern capitalism,' Widgery pronounced, 'and found the irrational violence and the hopelessness at its core.' His enthusiasms were all-embracing: Allen Ginsberg, Breton's Surrealist manifesto, William Carlos Williams, Ian Dury. And his anathemas: Thatcher, the LDDC, closed hospitals.

He died in Eleanor Road on 26 October 1992. Rosen doesn't say how or in what circumstances.

Leaving Eleanor Road, on the morning of the interview, I walked home through London Fields. I was beginning to get a sense that Kaporal, with his conspiracy theories, his unravelling of hidden patterns, might be on to something. At our latest debriefing, in the Victory pub in Vyner Street, he was rambling about Joseph Conrad's monkey – which I now connected with Juliet Ash's description of her husband's relationship with Marc Karlin. Then there was the way that these characters arrived in Hackney, as if by accident or psychogeographical karma. Sheila Rowbotham with her partner's compass sweep of railway stations, David Widgery jabbing his finger into the *London A–Z*. Or the way I plotted that dérive out of Hampstead, walking a line from the ashes of Freud in Golders Green Crematorium, by way of the massive head of Karl Marx in Highgate, into the topographical instructions laid down in Blake's *Jerusalem*. Everything stemmed from that unthinking excursion.

SAVE OUR SCHOOL. THE MAYOR'S A FOOL.

A crocodile of schoolchildren, holding up banners and flags, beating drums, blowing whistles, protested the closure of a school, the erection of a mobile-phone mast. Stepping back to give them plenty of room, I nudged a large greyhound of benign or brain-damaged temperament. The close companion and official carer of local painter Jock McFadyen. Jock had a lock-up studio, alongside a Chinese import/export business, in a unit by the railway arches.

THE MAYOR'S A FOOL. SAVE OUR SCHOOL.

Find the dog and you find Jock. He says that he never recognizes people, even his closest friends or family, because he has been trained, by many years painting the figure, to borrow relevant body parts from the mirror. Everybody, in the end, is a version of Jock McFadyen. Or his dog. Even the women. Especially the women. Either Jock's nose, ears, the slightly quizzical uplift of the right eyebrow, the powderpuff aureole of rusty hair, the tilted grin. Or: the greyhound's aristocratic Hanoverian snout.

Jock was a compulsive wanderer, on the prowl for imagery, graphic demonstrations of blight. The exploitable glamour of urban entropy. But he was a victim of the gears of time: tick tick tick. His first question to any fresh acquaintance, especially another artist or writer, was: 'How old are you?' (Meaning: how many years, months, hours before I look as rough as that?)

'Not a day goes by,' he told me, 'when I don't think about money. It should be the first concern for any serious painter. When to shape the next move, when to trade up. I made a horrible mistake with that Roman Road development, the one with Piers Gough, but I got out of it in the end.'

Hackney suited us both. As displaced Celts, at home nowhere on this earth, we stood apart: witnessing, with cynical detachment, the mess the English had made of it, the way they allowed Edinburgh advocates and Calvinist fanatics from north of the border to destroy the established structure from within. Taking the old enemy into ruinous foreign wars, economic adventurism and social deprivation. A lingering revenge for Culloden Moor was being eaten very cold.

The greyhound seemed keen to move off in the direction of the promised Lido. I'd already had a glimpse inside. Some chemical in the suspiciously brilliant water must be attractive to dogs. A random pack, all shapes and sizes, gathered, howling, by the automatic doors. Causing the mechanism to malfunction. Heavy panels slid open and shut as the canine mob approached and retreated. Security staff massed to keep them out. A randy terrier, ducking beneath the radar, made it. I followed him in. A pool attendant, promising that the venue would open on time, for one day, gilt-card dignitaries only, let me through: in the belief that the invading dog belonged to me. By now, high on chlorine fumes and the erotic nip of blue dye, the creature had plunged, pedalling its short legs in thin air, into the virgin water. Where it circled, holding its snout aloft: a furry toy with a supercharged battery. The staff were wholly occupied with keeping the other beasts out; waving their arms, spreading their legs, as the automatic doors hissed and clumped.

Terrier secured and expelled, I was allowed to spend a few minutes in contemplation of the patterns the wind made in this expensive rectangle of Hackney water. The Lido was going to work: for dogs. And as a quiet place of meditation and melancholy, somewhere to brood on loss. I could do whatever I wanted, the man said, except take a photograph. Hackney had a total embargo on unapproved imagery. They were spending a lot of money on illusions of the absolute, computer-generated visions of sites we would never be permitted to visit. The virtual utopia we had exchanged for the pain of the past. The zone we can never control.

Empire

From somewhere illegal, on the roof of the Hackney Empire, Ron Ark tilted his camera down towards the steps of the Town Hall. Towards the dirty white block with its flags, balconies and trapped fossils. His film, in part sponsored by those he intended to mock, was called *Empire*. An ironic back reference to Andy Warhol's autistic masterwork: the steady stare that strips the Empire State Building of its flesh, dressing it in seductively grainy fug. A monolithic candle on a hazy afternoon in July 1964. Warhol's subversive crew, the poet Gerard Malanga and film-diarist Jonas Mekas, took up their watching post in the offices of the Rockefeller Foundation on the 41st floor of the Time-Life Building. Warhol barely touched the camera. 'He wanted the machine to make the art for him,' Malanga reported. This was the Factory Man's first film with sync sound. The sound of light choking: into an afterlife of non-specific celebrity. Waiting for King Kong's hairy paw.

Locked off, shooting for the length of a three-minute reel, on the hour, 6 a.m. to 6 p.m., Ark had a nice record of empty steps; of cleaners leaving, bureaucrats arriving, supplicants scurrying after death certificates and birth registers. He had smokers, casual encounters, wedding parties. He had me, limping alongside a bicycle, bumping into the visiting writer Nigel Fountain. Who, it turned out, had just resigned from the board of the revived Hackney Empire. Fountain spent too many hours staring, through a rain-beaded window, at the Soviet hulk of the Town Hall, while other business was discussed. There comes a point, he did not mention this as a factor in his decision, when the life and noise and stink of music hall becomes parodic, approved from above, patronized in the wrong sense. Conspicuous charity gigs glorying in their incompetence. Russian clowns whose virtuosity transcended cultural barriers, supposedly. Jazzed-up Shakespeare.

The original halls were grim and Sickert-unlovely; packed, ripe, dripping, overdressed. Fear-auditions. Reflex drifts of the mob, inward from the street: as if a trapdoor had opened on a candelabra-lit antechamber of hell. Now the long bar was restored, the sofas, the tables at the rear – where it was possible, even necessary, to lounge, keeping your distance from the figures on the stage, while admiring the Moorish scarlet and gold of the restored interior. A politically correct bordello of the senses.

Fountain was very taken with the state of the theatre when he first encountered it in the late 1970s, its degradation as a bingo hall. In misted panels he found engraved words alluding to the pretensions of an imperial past: 'Grand Circle', 'Upper Circle', 'Fauteuil'. *Armchair*. That was the clincher that brought him into contact with the group working to resurrect the absurdity of a Hackney Empire. A gaudy kitsch palace, won back from Mecca, to set alongside the functional austerity of the Town Hall.

Hackney: capital of schizophrenia. Circus, song, pantomime, drink, libidinous excess: the rose-red folly of the theatre. Silent corridors, watchful security, stern portraits of forgotten dignitaries: the contiguous Town Hall. And, within the belly of that municipal fortress, another theatre, a bear garden: the council's debating chamber. Where populace howls at elected representatives. Where showmen perform. Where rival managements scheme and plot and whisper, fouling their corners, like hyenas marking territory.

It was agreed that Fountain, journalist, author of a brisk Hackney novel, *Days Like These*, would give me an interview. Having heard so much about the Montague Road collective from Sheila Rowbotham and Juliet Ash, knowing Marc Karlin in his last days, in the basement beneath the Goodge Place cutting room, I felt that I also knew Nigel: as a character, a projection. The one who survived. He presented me, as we parted, with a recent book which he said had already disappeared: *Lost Empires (The Phenomenon of Theatres Past, Present & Future).* The monochrome cover was a metropolitan nocturne, an Empire seen through stuttering traffic. Rain-slicked Hitchcock cabs, papersellers, men in flat caps, street urchins.

What Ron Ark proposed was to overlay his surveillance footage of the Town Hall, even the sequences when the steps were deserted, with an absurdist monologue, describing the events and interactions of the day. He pretends that the Town Hall is a hotel (a French conceit). A magnet for plotting businessmen, property sharks, bent politicians. A hideaway for illicit lovers enjoying an extended lunch break: this works well, when Fountain and Sinclair, with intervening bicycle, worn and avuncular figures of a certain age and gravitas, are pitched as thief and punter, arguing over the price of a set of contraband wheels. The way Fountain shifts his weight, jumps back, and the way I lean so heavily on the bicycle's seat, stroke the handlebars. When a group of officials comes tumbling out at the end of the day, Ark flags it as a bomb warning: revolution by the underclass of Hackney, those who will never be able to afford a room in this opulent establishment.

In reality, I was sniffing around the fringes of a building that had no purpose beyond making me feel uncomfortable: because I would soon have to return, to deliver a talk to art honchos, civic dignitaries and the usual freeloaders, in celebration of the Chambers Bequest. Alexander Chambers, of 54 Palatine Road, a man of means, a scavenger, had willed his large and eccentric collection to 'the former Metropolitan Borough of Stoke Newington'. Which had been absorbed into Hackney.

The bequest was a nuisance, paintings of variable quality, curious objects, to be catalogued, stored, exhibited. The best that could be said of this stuff was that it gave employment to an emerging human type, the conceptual curator. Bureaucrats schooled to replace unreliable and indigent artists. Professional explainers: even when there was nothing to explain. The Chambers Collection was unfit to view, but it couldn't be sold off at auction or dumped in a car-boot sale at the Hackney Wick Stadium. There would have to be a parody of a commemorative dinner, with real councillors in robes and chains, real food and a compliant dummy, bought for a few pounds, to deliver the entertainment. I was elected: probably by default. And, eager to have an opportunity to get inside this building, without having to pay a fine or a parking ticket, I accepted.

The invitation came at the optimum moment. Having lurched from scandal to scandal – all of them logged and recorded by the late Kaporal – the borough was in financial meltdown. Central government were threatening to take over. Council-owned properties were crumbling; many, removed from the official register, were ruins, squatted by keepers of wild birds, burrowers, international anarchists without papers or identities. The builders who had taken on the Hackney Empire restoration gig filed for bankruptcy.

Alexander Henry Chambers, born in 1849 (around the time our house was being built), grew up in Aberdeen, the city of my father's family. He came to London as a fifteen-year-old and enjoyed 'regular visits to the library'. He worked as a carpenter, then a clerk in the City, made money – and, using it, established the bequest, this municipal curse. Which included 'Twenty Guineas to provide a NON-POLITICAL DINNER on the Library Premises in the month of October for the Library Committee plus the Librarian, the Town Clerk and one distinguished visitor to be selected by the Chairman of the Library Committee.'

Previous distinguished guests at the Chambers feast included Sir George Jones, Sir E. Salter Davies, Sir Alec Martin and Sir Gerald Kelly, society portraitist and president of the Royal Academy. Hackney loves to be patronized. Kelly, initially, declined to travel east: 'I am a tired old man. I have learnt that to be a guest of honour is a great burden.' Later, discovering that there were only twenty guests and that the press would be excluded, he relented. But he wouldn't speak. He munched, gnawed, sipped: mute. But for the rattle of loose teeth, the hard swallow.

After Kelly, the status of the refusees climbed: Sir Alfred Munnings (otherwise engaged), Winston Churchill (even after the bribe of fifty guineas to purchase one of his daubs). The first of the truly local figures to accept was a commoner: Arnold Wesker. Then Joan Littlewood sailed down the line from the Theatre Royal in Stratford (on the very rim of the future Olympic Park).

I investigated the collection and noted a pathological inclination towards the pastoral: *Sheep on a Common, Three Goats in a Landscape.* A student put to studying the holdings, as an exercise, remarked on a picture of 'a towering, awe-inspiring, near mountain which appears dark and mysterious, hiding many secrets of bygone ages. In the distance, a house can be observed, probably deserted, but still standing defiantly against wind and weather. Two men are shown, they could be weary travellers seeking rest in the shelter of some bushes. But one of them is pointing, perhaps to the house.'

Foxed watercolours, obscure objects in a locked room that nobody visited. Chambers, the Stoke Newington working man, maps out a hidden country beneath the bricks and terraces, the half-remembered landscapes of his journey south; the romance of Scotland before the Clearances, Hackney Downs before enclosures. Lammas land. Travellers' ponies on traffic islands: the art of Jock McFadyen, years before he was conceived. It was quite unreal, frozen clouds imagined by inhabitants of a hollow earth who had never experienced sunlight. Molemen with no use for eyes. What they imagined is what they saw.

The objects were frosted by their long imprisonment. Dubious artefacts from which a viable culture would have to be invented. Carved bust of Shakespeare. China Chelsea figure of the poet John Milton (with certificate of authenticity). Ruby-glass German goblet with inscription. Cigar box with miniature river scene. Small electro head of Julius Caesar. With annotation by Chambers: 'Made by me when a lad.' Mahogany carving: bunch of grapes. From the collection of the royal surgeon, Sir William Withey Gull.

I made notes. And I thought about Roland Camberton's tribute to the Central Library, how his friend Stanley, aged thirteen, discovered 'the unabridged and illustrated edition of Ovid'. Then, a few years later, the poems of T. S. Eliot, the works of H. G. Wells and 'a stout volume called the *Handbook of Marxism*'. Harold Pinter of Clapton, a celebrant of Hackney through his novel *The Dwarfs*, is tracked by his biographer, Michael Billington, as he moonlights in Mare Street, avoiding acting classes. The library was: 'a fountain of life'. 'He started reading voraciously on his own initiative,' Billington says, 'Dostoevsky, Rimbaud, Woolf, Lawrence, Eliot, Hemingway . . . Hackney Public Library was an intellectual treasure-house.'

A fountain of life: Nigel and his lost Empires. Pinter striding down Narroway towards Mare Street. The mysterious Roland Camberton. Traces of that subterranean stream, the Hackney Brook. Unviewed objects in a cabinet of curiosities: refracted autobiography. Alexander Chambers whispering from his grave in Abney Park: 'Remember me.'

How could I pull it all together for my talk at the Town Hall dinner? The sense of loss: it wasn't the writers, the ones who used the silence of the library as an echoing pool, it was the artisans, the hobbyists. Amateur scholars from bottling-plants, boot factories, asylums. It was Jeff Kwinter, a rag-trade millionaire, who discovered Henry Miller and then John Cowper Powys. And who opened a bookshop, to make his discoveries public, on Regent Street. Who gave employment – for a few months – to the eccentrics and vagabonds of the city. Who lost everything and was crushed, but who hung on, always, to an essential truth: that the Hackney Central Library, six steps up from the street, was a necessary portal. A door to enlightenment.

The Town Hall, in its pomp, 1934–7: Art Deco detailing, Portland stone. Lanchester and Lodge, the architects. A structure to symbolize a new emphasis on the responsibilities of local government. Three flatbed lorries belonging to H. J. Moyse, demolition contractor of Clapham Road, clear the rubble of a Victorian predecessor. And now, in 2007, £6.4 million (and rising) is being spent on extensions and improvements at the rear, a revised address for council taxes. THORP ('Town Hall Redevelopment Project') is the borough's primary strategic target: air-conditioned offices, a grand project to dwarf the hubris of the Clissold Leisure Centre fiasco.

I tried to absorb confusing information as it arrived, daily, through free sheets put out by opposing factions: *Hackney Respect* (apocalyptic gloom), *In Touch: Conservative* (crime in the streets), *Hackney Today* ('Reaping Olympic Rewards'). I brooded on how writers and artists viewed the threefold markers around which the social life and culture of Hackney had evolved: Town Hall (pinky white), Empire (terracotta, rose) and Central Library (grey as the recollection of a dead sea).

Take, by way of example, Tom Hunter: the large-format, high-definition photographer, with his posed series, *Living in Hell (and Other Stories)*. *For Better or Worse*, a print made in 2005, dresses the Town Hall steps with rioting figures. Black, funeral-plumed horses. It's either a traditional wedding-party punch-up or sozzled diners from the Chalmers Bequest being ejected by council bouncers. You don't have to know, here is a restaging of Piero di Cosimo's *The Fight between the Lapiths and the Centaurs*, to appreciate the underlying conceit. The metamorphosis: dark mound into white stone. Architecture provokes action. Buildings are scripts.

Remember Sebastian Bell and his self-published Hackney novel *Saddling Mahmoud*? Of course not. That 350pp of nicely printed, handsomely bound prose has been reviewed only in specialist publications eager to refute the Hitchcock thesis: that the Hackney Empire had its part to play in the 1935 film of John Buchan's *The 39 Steps*. It doesn't matter if Hitchcock's music hall is a set, the atmosphere is right: displacement, confusion. Conspiracy, flight. Nigel Fountain is another Buchan enthusiast. *Days Like These* anticipates Bell's fiction, by sending the protagonist away from the city, into bad weather, a highland landscape borrowed from one of the sombre oils in the Alexander Chambers collection.

'It took days for it to dawn on me,' Bell wrote. 'And the dawning hardened when I watched the film's opening again. The Music Hall in *The 39 Steps*. It's not the Hackney Empire at all . . . So it's obvious, isn't it? They filmed the interiors in the Hackney Empire and then took all their equipment down the Mile End Road where they found a suitable Music Hall exterior to use. Either that or they mocked the whole thing up in a studio and borrowed a bus to drive through the set.'

Hitchcock, with his Leytonstone birthplace, the pub stuffed with memorabilia near Wanstead Ponds, the boilerplated head in the courtyard of the Gainsborough Studios development, is a way of defining where Hackney ends. He is intimately associated with trains and borders. Voyeurism, birds massing on telegraph wires. Buchan too, his plots are about getting away, healing the psychic wound in icy streams. Killing stags and birds and fish. Handcuffed European blondes (dubbed or not) in slithering nylons. Conspirators who signal with missing fingers.

Kaporal's files were presented as spreadsheets, with phone numbers, copied emails and a pink marker for: 'They schmooze planning officers: fancy dinners, fancy charity sleb parties, keys to holiday homes in Maldives.' It was hard not to see Hackney, through the researcher's eyes, as one enormous, interconnected conspiracy. Like a pulp novel plucked from a carousel at the airport or from the receptionist's manicured hands at a Holiday Inn in Korea. Then pitched, long-distance, by Orson Welles, who is trying to borrow $20,000 from Harry Cohn at Columbia, to get costumes out of hock for a Jules Verne musical, by pimping his estranged wife, Rita Hayworth.

We read too much of this stuff, gossip. Peddled by spooks to scandal magazines funded by outreach agencies of the state. Kaporal tried to lend credence to his fictions by topping himself in a graveyard. A dire tautology. That was beginning to work.

Welles was never sure if he had in fact written the novel published under his name – no copyright line – by W. H. Allen in 1956: *Mr Arkadin*. The book of the film, which is also known as *Confidential Report*, was cobbled together by a Welles associate, Maurice Bessy. In Paris. Borrowing dialogue from the script. With minimal infusions of local colour. It was written in bars, describing bars. On the move across Europe: searching for a narrative. Like Antonioni with *The Passenger*. Enervated art-house films, played out against architectural backdrops, are quests for locations. The big decisions – where to find a camera, where to eat dinner – become the movie. A dubbed mistress, offered English lessons in exchange for the parts she won't get, is paid off with borrowed costume jewellery, stolen furs. Vienna, Budapest, Madrid: actors stranded in third-rate hotels, unable to pay their bills. No money for a flight home. No change for cigarettes and whores.

When Peter Bogdanovitch, interviewing Welles, found the writing of *Mr Arkadin* 'beautiful', the jowly, cigar-sucking director chuckled and wheezed: 'Maybe, I did write it at that.'

In those drifting, mendacious years, when Welles ran up tabs and kept his troop of actors on standby, you could expect him anywhere: but not Hackney. Not Sylvester Path, at the back of the Empire, alongside the Old Ship pub. Not dressed like a bingo caller with a shiny jacket, wide lapels and limp bow tie. Bill Haley cowlick kiss curl. I had to run the DVD over and over to convince myself that this was not a missing sequence from *F for Fake*, a body-treble, an impersonator. The actorly twinkle in the conman's eye. The weight of an alien presence, hobbled by bright shoes a size and a half too small. It was Welles all right and he was here, the heart of Hackney, in 1955. The year of *Mr Arkadin*.

I was in Broadway Market, trying to find Jayne Mansfield programmers, sounding off about films shot in the borough. Hitchcock, Carol Reed, Jean-Luc Godard. Clive Donner's version of Pinter's *The Caretaker*. The Swedish guy, just back from a festival on Bergman's island, put up Phil Collins in *Buster* and a Danny Boyle viral-catastrophe shocker. He mentioned that David

Cronenberg had dropped in that very afternoon, checking locations for a thing about Russian Mafia involvement in the borough. Cronenberg signed a poster of *The Fly*. And would I like to sample the footage Orson Welles produced on Mare Street?

Like Godard, a decade later, Welles accepted an English television commission. From Associated Rediffusion. They billed the London element: 'Chelsea Pensioners'. The person writing notes for the DVD talked up *Around the World with Orson Welles* as a seminal piece that anticipated the improvisatory realism of the French New Wave. 'Somewhere between a home movie and a cinematic essay, these short films have been described by *Cahiers du Cinéma* critics as the missing link in Welles's work.'

In Paris, we are introduced to Juliette Greco, Jean-Paul Sartre and the hardboiled American actor Eddie Constantine: who is wearing his hat in a nightclub and giving the camera a trademark unblinking stare. Then, on cue, the big wink. Welles and Constantine came together ten years before Eddie's career-defining turn in Godard's *Alphaville*. And twenty-four years before he sailed under Tower Bridge with Bob Hoskins (a proper son of Hackney) in *The Long Good Friday*. Barrie Keeffe's script required Constantine to reprise one of the Mafia figures brought over by the Krays, in anticipation of New Labour's strategic initiative: bigger casinos on more polluted brownfield sites. The political climate of Thatcherite politics is laid bare in a film made in the year of her accession to power. The way villains laundered money through Docklands developments. Corrupt relationship between planners and ambitious gangsters. Dave King, as a bent detective, makes a premature Olympic pitch: with racist remarks about black athletes doing the long jump on derelict industrial land.

Limping badly, he'd fallen off the stage the night before, Constantine effected a farewell to European art cinema in Chris Petit's 1983 film, *Flight to Berlin*. A production written and planned for Paris. The exercise was unintentionally psychogeographical: in the way that the Situationists would navigate Montparnasse with a map of Venice.

Welles drops in on a left-bank bookshop where Lettrists recite concrete poems. By shooting on the spin, avoiding scripts, letting it happen from a moving car, Orson steals a march on all the coming trends: Situationism, film-as-essay, the cult of *Moby-Dick*. That's what he was doing in the Empire, rehearsing a play from Melville's masterwork, plotting to turn it into a film. It never happened. He did deliver the Jonah sermon, as Father Mapple, in John Huston's respectful and bleached-out version of the hunting of the white whale. A single take, that was the myth. After climbing a rope-ladder to the whaler's pulpit. Welles rewrote the script, improved on Ray Bradbury: improved on Melville. Or so he said.

The actor/director emerges from the stage door at the rear of the Hackney Empire. He has invited Joan Plowright, Laurence Olivier's third wife, to play Pip (the cabin boy on the *Pequod*). He stayed with the Oliviers while he wrote the novel of *Mr Arkadin*: taking the blight off an English country weekend. There had been a brief liaison with Vivien Leigh in New York: where Welles played Lear for the youthful Peter Brook. Now Patrick McGoohan did Starbuck. And Kenneth Williams was in the cast, whinnying about the lack of professionalism, the fat American director's 'filthy tribe of sycophantic bastards'.

Taking a breather from this nest of viperous egos, Welles steps out into Hackney light. Which is to say: old stone anxious about demolition, bollocking afternoon drinkers incapable of counting their own fingers. Late history just starting to scratch and yawn.

A small flock of greying women, prepped and permed, are waiting at the entrance to the Spurstowe Alms Houses. A charitable foundation which will very soon disappear in a council-sponsored cloud of dust. The building has been in place since 1666 and time is up. This refuge for 'six poor widows of good life and conversation' was originally funded by William Spurstowe, a clergyman namechecked by Samuel Pepys for delivering a very tedious sermon. The almshouses were rebuilt in 1819.

The brief report by Orson Welles opens with a general view

of the Hackney Empire and its LADIES FOR HIRE signage: sonorously, the director invokes the music-hall tradition of Dan Leno and Marie Lloyd. 'We've been shooting a film across there. And before that we've been rehearsing a play.'

The Spurstowe spokeswoman, high bosom decorated with pearls and cameo-brooch, handles the banter effortlessly.

'I belong to the British Legion. I'm an unrepentant old Tory. And I belong to the Conservative Association. And I was Divisional Chairwoman of the Women's Section for seventeen years, now retired in disgust. We're all true Blues.'

A privet hedge divides the almshouses from the stage door, a few locals have massed on the terrace at the end of Sylvester Path. A policeman in a peaked cap keeps order. As if expecting an immediate transfer to Rillington Place.

Welles says that he has come to know and respect the ladies and 'their lovely old house'. He wants us to read the inscription above the door: 'Settled for ever certain Lands in y said Parish on several Trustees.'

For ever, under law.

The ladies admit that they cook, but not for each other. They go out to picture shows at the Empire. One of the friskier widows asks to be remembered to Jack Warner when Welles gets back to Hollywood: he's a cousin.

Cue big close-up. Orson delivers his piece, with deep and growling sincerity, straight to camera.

'All too often there's another sort of loss involved, a loss of dignity, a loss of the sense of individuality. And that's why I think British people should be so proud of institutions such as this almshouse we've been visiting with the six poor widows of Hackney, who are maintaining their individuality with a vengeance.'

To gather my thoughts for the Chambers Bequest dinner, I dropped in at the Old Ship. I ran through the elements I wanted to bring into play, the anecdotes, quotations scribbled on envelopes. It wouldn't cohere, even after a couple of brandies. The plaster

model of a ship would have to be pressed into service as a metaphorical whaler. Welles's Hackney intrusion displaced too many
ghosts.

The almshouses – Nos. 1–11 Sylvester Path – had gone, but the
fading prints remained, the Hackney Brook, the little bridge over
Mare Street: *Rural Hackney in 1738*. The kids, smoking skunk outside
the pub, wore black wool caps with the Nike tick.

SAVE SYLVESTER PATH.

Roland Camberton described an episode from the 1930s when,
as a bright Jewish history student from Hackney Downs, his character David Hirsch went up to Oxford for an interview.

'What do you think of the new Hackney Town Hall?'

The boy considers the implications of this Art Deco novelty.
'It looked all right. The stone was bright and clean, but he supposed
that before long the London smoke would turn it grey.'

Anna joined me at the bar; she had agreed, reluctantly, to take
her place at high table, alongside the mayor, the lady mayoress,
Hackney notables (notable to themselves) – and the New Labour
minister (weather and sport), who had drawn the short straw.
Bicycle people in gypsy skirts, hoop earrings, black trainers,
yellow tabards, luminescent Alice bands, wheeled their machines
up the disabled ramp, into the Grand Assembly Hall. Where they
clustered like iron filings, ignoring the suits, hammering into trays
of drinks. They ignored us too, as did the council mob, who
remained tight within their own cliques, content to mutter and
bitch. Rain had been falling steadily all afternoon – and falling
within the building. There were puddles in long corridors hung
with unsmiling portraits, as I tried to find the person with the
promised cheque. Which I hoped to post, immediately, through
another door: an instalment of overdue council tax. And an invisible carbon footprint worthy of mention in the latest
green-headlined copy of that free nuisance sheet, *Hackney
Today*.

Before my sponsor could be buttonholed, I was summoned to
high table and placed between the mayor, an orthodox Jewish man

from the northern reaches, capped and chained, and his pleasant but confused wife. What was she doing here? Where was the food? The concession, to deliver lukewarm trays of airline pap, had been granted to some meals-on-wheels outfit – who did what they could with reheated leftovers from the geriatric run. We tried to make a decent fist of carving rubber meats with white plastic cutlery: thereby protecting ourselves from the suicide option. Our thimble-tumblers were kept free from contamination with clingfilm seals. We were served in random order on a pass-it-along basis, the caterers making it very clear they were here on sufferance. And overtime. To punish us, they would hold back the wine.

Anna, who is able to get conversation from toothless mouths lost in the deepest of beards, gave up on her council statistician, and stared out at the lively time the art folk, who set up this jape, were having at their little round tables, down below. Elevated, exposed, we were the performance, an ill-assorted rack of gargoyles, unable to begin until the mayor received his tray.

A disaffected Hackney Tory told me that the empty place was being held for the minister. Who was out there, lost. And hopefully trying to prove the safety of the streets by walking his minders through Murder Mile. New Labour, so recently come to power, had no interest – beyond putting the financial bite on a clapped-out regime – in eastern parts. How that would change! It appeared that the celebrity guest was a political turncoat: and also, although I couldn't be sure of this, above the menagerie racket in the hall, a gender migrant. When the man did arrive, scarlet-necked, walnut-varnished beneath an immaculately calibrated hair decision, he made it clear his words would have to be delivered right now; he was passing through, on his way to something more important in Islington. Like a decent meal.

Kosher airline dinners take time: we waited and waited. The lady mayoress told me about her children. And grandchildren. Dry-mouthed and sober, I got to my feet to deliver my under-cooked diatribe about lost libraries, Roland Camberton and Harold Pinter, archives built by working men. None of that emerged.

'I've been thinking,' I said, 'about the Hollow Earth. Do you know about the Mole Man of Mortimer Road? Or Edmond Halley's demolished manor house? Halley stood before the Royal Society, late in the year of 1691, to read a paper proposing that our earth is hollow. Three concentric spheres lie beneath the surface, nesting within each other: the kind of symbolic topography Dante imagined. One entrance, I have discovered, is through the abandoned public baths in Whiston Road. Do you have any idea what we should do about that?'

MUNDUS SUBTERRANEUS

There were stories that the tunnels went for miles. There were monsters down there, blind reptiles and insects that had never seen the light, there were hospitals and brothels, and horrible things . . . dead babies, assassinated priests.

– Denis Johnson, *Tree of Smoke*

Victoria Park

When I switched on the computer everything blew. Clambering, old-person-unsteady, on the blackwood Jacobean chair, to flick the fuse: relief. An immediate return to the peeling hallway, the swaying walls: Old Hackney. Followed, once again, by foreclosure, darkness. The stench of rotten icing sugar and wet feathers might be explained by electricity burning up dead things; the bugs and cockroaches that give this 160-year-old property its pulse of life. How many times do you change a shirt, dripping with intensity of composition, before you admit that the fetid rot is external, part of the structure? Not your fault, not this time.

Saucers of poison were taking their toll. Consequences follow from conical powder-dumps left out for greypelt co-tenants of Albion Drive. Spiked chocolate drops. A treacherous toxicology for nocturnal tourists: mice, fleas, wintering wasps. Who pass without prejudice from property to property. Living and twitching cat snacks. Tails and pink eyes. Salty with horrible stomach-scorching additives. An exploding necrotic pregnancy when red guts hang inside out: fig jam. Cheese-coloured burger cartons to make addicts of bag-ripping feral dogs. Before the blue fence went up to remove the Olympic Park from the map, its Angel Lane boundary was identified by the stiff corpses of murdered foxes: fur ruffs picked over by maggots brave enough to carry the vitriol down an ever-extending food chain. They die our deaths, the tunnellers.

Oh! The noises in the roof cavity when we sit down after supper to bask before the grey glow of the screen: the crunching, scuttling, slithering. Floorboards creak like a venerable whaler entering the pack ice. I close the curtains to hide the zizzing head-shaped splurge on the window; stepping with care to avoid a corpse-carpet of spray-zapped flies with tiny tortured lungs. A faint scratching at the front door? It's only our neighbour, who can't, at any price, bring herself to prise the half-gnawed mouseling from her wicked tabby's salivating jaws. I keep a rusty spadehead with broken handle to remove fatalities and to bury them, my slippered feet wet with nightdew, in a mouse cemetery by the nettle patch. Where they will be dug up and recycled by ever-watchful predators.

Spike the builder, called in when we were left in darkness, in the retch of death's insulation beneath floorboards and skirting-boards, had his own complaints. His life on a new estate in the backdraught of the M25 at Waltham Abbey was not as gracious as the brochures had led him to believe. Spike's thumb trailed a dirty bandage: his girlfriend wilfully damaging his fist with her head. She had been overdoing it, socially, on the estate, while he put in all the hours. A slag, to state the case bluntly: deranged by retail parks, boarding kennels, furniture redundant before it's out of the cellophane. Spike didn't want to spend his only free day screwing glass lids on Ikea coffins. She'd been good as gold, his Nita, in Bethnal Green. Now she wanted custody of the Rottweiler.

'You was dead lucky,' Spike advised. That gas smell, it was gas: a leak from which a single spark could have ignited a major incident. 'You bin stitched up by cowboys. They've took out the old heaters and never sealed the pipes. Diabolical really.'

He was right. Spike and his dad (retired to a Portugese golf course) had done the job, twenty years earlier. Shortly after the junior partner was let out, paroled to employment supervised by a reputable craftsman: his old man. With whom he went toe to toe on slate roofs and wobbly ladders. The father cursed. The son, eyes blazing under the peak of his baseball cap, took his revenge softly. Muttering anathemas on the father's deaf side.

'They're total crap,' Anna said, back from school, three kids, disbelieving of the latest bodged repair. 'But they're reliable. They come when you need them.'

But only to make more work, I thought, insurance for the future, an effective pension plan. Like the kids who flogged Anna her Ford Escort, keeping the spare keys, to nick it back two days later. She loved that car, her first.

He wasn't racist, Spike, but he couldn't abide Poles, sleeping rough and screwing all the best jobs. In twenty minutes flat, he knocked out enough of the wall to reveal a large, barbecued rat, victim of auto-erotic excesses. It tried to lick hot wires, biting through the wrong colours: cooking itself in a microwave blast, mouth melted in ecstatic rictus as it fused the household.

I left Anna to make Spike's tea, before he headed off to take care of some other long-term incomers whose bits and pieces he had been fudging and bodging for decades. I had a date with Danny Folgate the dowser, in Victoria Park, by the Burdett-Coutts fountain. Danny had an exciting discovery to unload. It would, he was convinced, recalibrate my Hackney researches: which, from what he'd heard, were in danger of becoming bogged down in mounds of irrelevant detail; politics, art. Contradictory interviews cancelling each other out. I was forgetting the only important element: place. Energy. Lines of force. A complex mapping like the crow wires that had been knitted, unseen, around my crumbling house.

The high-frequency hum, at the threshold of actual torture, hit me as I stepped into the street. A door that wouldn't shut properly in the flats. It moaned, day and night, its whine disguised by council carts boasting of moving backwards, drills breaking up recently laid paving slabs. The road was trenched with cosmetic excavations and water was off.

'Another post strike?' I said to Harriet. Who was standing expectantly at her gate.

'How can you tell?'

I was due nine small payments for talks delivered, broadsheet hackwork, days in the Fens trying to recite the salient details of a Norwich School painting as a conceptual exercise. 'New accounting procedures, sorry. The commissioner is no longer with us.'

Promised cheques adrift in the postal system. Where they will remain. Indefinitely.

SEX CHANGE WOMAN STEALS HUMAN SKULL. BENEFIT FRAUD VOODOO MUM JAILED.

The current *Gazette* teasers on boards outside the Turkish mini-mart. Clues in a surrealist crossword?

I remembered what the Parkholme Road painter Edward Calvert said to Hannah Linnell, when he was showing her one of his works. 'These are God's fields, this is God's brook.' Folgate was right. It was time I returned to geography.

When Danny typed a letter, I could hear his voice, I could feel his breath on my neck. I could analyse the italics, the capitals, the passages highlighted in blue. Emails took more time. They were composed by an Enigma machine. Random circumflexes. An auto-da-fé procession of inquisitors in pointed hats.

I made out, with difficulty, that Danny would be 'very pleased to demonstrate the Victoria Park leyline detected by L-rods'. He did not know where it terminated but he had the instinct that it might prove to be the continuation of 'a line discovered in Poplar'.

Danny's Romford letter of 23/2/2004 was more forthcoming: 'My present main project regarding dowsing concerns Tunbridge Wells, which is a neglected Pre-historic landscape of major importance! I hope YOU have found dowsing to be a useful tool, Iain? If you like, I can show you a genuine energy line in Victoria Park, which *gives off heat!* YOU CAN ACTUALLY FEEL IT!'

As indeed I could, under Danny's instruction. Pass through the gates, into the principality of the trees, and you sense the urban burden slipping away; your stride lengthens, cleaner air. Marc Karlin, so Patrick Wright told me, when he interviewed him for radio, spoke of socialism as a 'lead raincoat' he could never shrug off. Banished to the Goodge Place bunker, Karlin was doomed to enact the role of moral conscience of documentary film-making, the scapegoat who made works designed not to be seen.

I had the same feeling about Jock McFadyen: whose studio I passed, shutters up, as I hurried towards my rendezvous with

Danny. Jock was well on the way to becoming the last painter in the world, nominating sites marked for demolition. And exhibiting them in deserted car showrooms on Cambridge Heath Road.

Jock's unit was somewhere to store his collection of Volvos, racing bikes, spare parts. With unsold canvases from the last thirty years. Unshaven, hair curled to collar, Jock looks the part, the role to which he had always aspired: motor mechanic. Painting is a nuisance hobby to pay the bills. The radio reverberated in that space as it does in all railway-arch garages. Jock spoke, when I mentioned John Minton's Mare Street dustwrapper for Roland Camberton's novel, of an earlier, 1937, version of the same scene: by an artist he respected, Lawrence Gowing.

'Gowing was born over a draper's shop in Mare Street, before going on to become Slade professor. And knight of the realm.'

1982: Gowing's mentor, William Coldstream, asked him where he lived.

'Hackney.'

'I always fall asleep on the no. 8 and wake up at Hackney Wick. Where *is* Hackney Wick? What's it for?'

The Wick was where Jock felt we might talk. He was happy to let me tape his memories – on condition that I joined him for an evening's drinking and debauch in a club he'd heard about, tickets only: squatters, Russians, travellers, lost girls. A burnt-out pub. On the Olympic frontline. Where, at the point of dissolution, anything goes.

Jock poured oil into the cannibalized Volvo. I helped him load the trailer with scrambling bikes for the trip to one of his other properties, a converted bar in a Normandy village. We gave the new paintings a cursory glance: McFadyen had taken a block of pink flats from the canal and transposed them on an estuary land-scape, where they could stand alone; tiny figures moving about the roof, wondering where London has gone.

The line of heat, picking up from the church where I found myself searching for traces of Neil Murger's Catholic heritage, ran south-east; slicing through the Jewish burial ground, brushing against, without actually violating, the gothic thrust of the Burdett-Coutts memorial fountain. This Aberdeen granite stack was presented to the people of East London by Angela Burdett-Coutts, on 30 June 1862. Ten thousand citizens turned out to witness the ceremony.

Danny was on to something: hidden springs, suppressed fountains. Water had once gushed out of the people's park, nineteenth-century maps boast of it. Let the poor and weary drink. They were drawn towards the Burdett-Coutts folly, designed by Henry Darbishire, at a cost of £6,000. Open arches reveal four plump putti riding on dolphins, mature cherubs who drip juice from uncircumcised urns. A meeting place, when the gates in the fence were still open, for young ladies in straw boaters and working gentlemen in short tight jackets, creaking boots.

It was probable, Folgate conceded, that steps led down as well as up. During the Second War, they held Italian prisoners in tunnels beneath the park, letting them out for exercise at night – when in their pale uniforms they appeared as so many phantoms flitting among the trees. Ghosts who left real infants behind them when they returned home. Ghosts who moonlighted in parkside cafés. Ghosts who opened barber shops and ice-cream parlours. Ghosts who sang operatic arias in secret gardens.

Constructing the park over Bonner's Fields, an area notorious for public meetings, meant that a dissenting spirit survived: policed by keepers, special constables, gates. Radicals, suffragettes, Mosley's blackshirt legions, competed to provoke. To rub shoulders, stamp the ground. In May 1887, the Socialist League demonstrated against the situation in Ireland. Annie Besant, William Morris and Bernard Shaw made speeches. Folgate had to absorb conflicted voices, to tremble with spent passion, arms spread wide, knees bending, heels dug deep: to earth unresolved argument. When the dead were adequately appeased, he took out his Dagenham coat-hangers, his L-rods, to demonstrate the newly discovered line of force.

'This track's a funny one, Iain. But it's definitely there. Have a go. Try it yourself. Feel it.'

A darkman, stripped to the waist, was running through his martial-arts routine on the bandstand. Harming invisibles with spiteful kicks. Rain-clouds massed.

'To search for something lost,' Folgate said, 'you hold a photograph of the object in your left hand and the pendulum in your right. Graveyards are very receptive.'

'Can you dowse for things that are no longer there?'

A cough, a laugh. The zipped green anorak with its bulging pockets gave nothing away. Danny's hands were large.

This exercise had run out of puff. We stood under gnarled London plane trees in an epic avenue and considered our tactics in the feverish light of the advancing storm. Sheila Rowbotham's story of being drenched to the skin, still firmly in mind, called down stinging rain-needles as a form of sympathetic magic.

Danny suggested adjournment to a café he favoured in Lauriston Road. The territory south of the park, he intimated, was not receptive to dowsing. 'Too many houses, too much trapped water.' The energy line, if we stayed with it, was a passage out. And there was still work to be done in town.

While Danny debated the ruinous price of Lauriston Village tea, I admired an inscribed portrait of a local icon, our version of Catherine Deneuve's Marianne, symbol of the French Republic: the restored Empress of Hackney, Julie Christie. In jungle fatigues, the actress is being tentatively embraced by the aproned proprietor, while stroking a ratty dog. Charming! I suppose my first sighting, as a schoolboy in Cheltenham, of the student Christie in a touring Brecht play, was an intimation, had I only recognized it, of future migration to Hackney. But where we had lodged forty years in one house, Julie floated like a fragrant rumour: from Stoke Newington through the foothills of Highbury to Columbia Road.

Build the market and she will come. Jane Howe, late of Notting Hill, listened to the voices in the Little Georgia Restaurant (formerly

Sir Walter Scott, a canalside pub) and knew the area was crying out for a smart bookshop.

'Banksy does well here but that's because he's local. It's so exciting. It makes me wish I was thirty years younger! The other day I saw someone in the street who was dressed very retro, very 1950s. I thought, she is really going to town in that outfit. Not unusual for Broadway Market you may say, but when she walked into the shop I realized it was Julie Christie!'

The café of Danny's choice, blessed one rainy afternoon, long ago, by the presence of Christie, was now a shrine. The two famous Christies, I thought, as Folgate's shadow fell across the table, that's the story of London: the shift to the east. John Reginald Halliday Christie of Rillington Place (now banished from the map), a figure of inward. DIY decorator, fixer of floorboards. Forever plastering the cold outhouse scullery. Amateur anaesthetist. Embodiment of Rotting Hill. Under a street lamp in belted gabardine. Behind the white stucco and the High Tory gentrification: decaying meat, maggots, coal gas. The old England of fog and noose. Now countered by this vision in khaki, walker of Hackney's parks and graveyards: Julie Christie. Patron of independent bookshops, street markets, cafés. The radiant future we have left behind.

From one of the many pockets of his combat jacket, the uniform of the deep topographer, Danny drew out photographs of excavations. A promising gambit. I knew the dowsing expedition was a front, there were darker tales to tell. Rainbeads melted on the greasy window. On afternoons like this I used to take the kids swimming in Whiston Road. The baths, opened in June 1904, cost precisely ten times as much as the Burdett-Coutts fountain. Launched to offer better hygiene and restorative exercise, the Haggerston Pool was closed in 2000, for reasons of 'health and safety'. And has remained padlocked ever since, a hazard to our moral sensibilities and a serious risk to our notions of civic shame. Danny was not a swimmer.

Tunnelling operations commenced in Victoria Park, Folgate explained, using the Second War as a cover: flying bombs on Grove

Road, factories in Bow making propellers for Spitfires. Trenches roofed with concrete slabs. A catacomb was constructed, near St Mark's Gate, with six entrances and sixty-one ventilator shafts. It could accommodate 1,386 volunteer mole-people. The Victoria Park Lido, closed after the Great Storm of 1987, was adapted as a source of water for the Fire Service. Much covert burrowing. Interlinked passageways, Danny hinted, were still active. The leyline we had just walked was a crude approximation of an unrecorded highway that lay beneath the turf, veering south-east in the direction of Beckton Alp. Beneath Danny's throaty whisper I heard the hiss of Sax Rohmer's Dr Fu-Manchu: all London's tunnels open to the river.

It's true that Danny, responsive to my mood, had plenty to say about Sutton House. How all his researches began with the discovery of a mine shaft running towards Leyton and the Marshes. He left me with a photocopy of an article from the *Hackney Gazette* of 26 September 2003: RIDDLE OF THE TUNNEL. Illustrated with a portrait of the grinning Danny, brandishing crossed L-rods.

> The enduring mystery of the secret tunnel beneath Hackney's Tudor mansion has baffled archaeologists and historians for the last century – but one man thinks he's solved it.
>
> Sutton House, built in the 16th century by Sir Ralph Sadleir, is now owned by the National Trust.
>
> So rumours that a secret tunnel ran beneath it – to help either the house's royalist owners escape the revolutionary clutches of Oliver Cromwell, or highwayman Dick Turpin evade the law – became exciting folklore.
>
> In 1990, historian and chairman of the Hackney Society, Mike Grey, discovered what he thought was the entrance to the tunnel. This was later found to be a bricked-over entrance to a well.
>
> Ten years later, however, evidence of the tunnel's existence might finally be at hand.
>
> Danny Folgate is an expert in dowsing, who claims that practitioners can also detect underground cavities.

'The brain picks up information,' he says. 'You get a reflex. My rods show you what's happening.'

Danny believes the tunnel is much deeper than originally thought. He estimates that it is 20 feet deep and says that is part of the reason why it was not discovered during previous excavations.

He says dowsing has also enabled him to calculate the width and even the age of the tunnel. He believes it is five feet wide and that it dates back to 1609.

'The width is crucial,' he says. 'It helps to distinguish between the tunnel and other underground cavities and streams along the route.'

'Tunnel building was quite fashionable in the 17th century,' says Danny, 'and Thomas Sutton, who died in 1611, had the manpower, the equipment and the money to do it.'

Danny believes the tunnel links two churches. He says it starts in Homerton at the site of the old tower of St John of Hackney church, off Mare Street – formerly St Augustine's.

From there the tunnel allegedly runs below Sutton House and along Homerton High Street, beneath Hackney Marshes and New Spitalfields Market to Leyton Parish church by the junction of Goldsmith Road and Church Road in Leyton.

The Hackney Archive Department have expressed some scepticism, the path of Danny's tunnel coincides with an old sewerage system.

Even Danny admits that, for now, his map of the Hackney tunnel is supposition. 'Unless someone digs into that land, as part of some great public project, which let's face it will never happen, we won't get an answer.'

The article, I noted, with no surprise, was credited to Julie Sinclair. This was the sort of coincidence at which Danny winked, as confirming his thesis: worlds within worlds. Fabric warmed by loving touch, human voices trapped within brickwork, allowed the sensitive dowser a glimpse of a parallel universe.

'Synchronicity,' he said, sucking at the cold tea, 'is enlightenment. Quantum mechanics can explain a lot of what common sense tells us is irrational. *Everything is connected!* Ultimately, we are all one.'

He wiped a wet mouth with a spotted handkerchief extracted from his poacher's pocket.

Now I understood where we were going. And by way of some very old friends: subterranean cities, buried rivers, the Templars of Well Street and Temple Mills. The Great London Conspiracy, a general theory of everything odd, unexplained, recurring, tapped by scholars from Peter Ackroyd and Alan Moore to Folgate, played back to a tight cast of characters: Walter Richard Sickert, William Withey Gull, John Netley. Painter, surgeon, coachman. Whitechapel: 1888. Much of the impetus for this global brand of bad karma emanated from a reliably unreliable source: Joseph 'Hobo' Sickert, the self-anointed son of Walter. Hobo was a picture restorer, gossip, street character. An associate of Francis Bacon, Dan Farson and the late Ripperologist Stephen Knight (a suborned local press journalist). Hobo was a twinkling mischief-maker, late of Kentish Town.

Danny, with his friend (and potential successor to Knight), Giscard Plantain de Wyff, had successfully cultivated Hobo's widow.

I notice a dusting of freckles on Folgate's forehead, golden-brown oil spots brought to the surface by weak sunlight. In the glass protecting the Julie Christie photograph, I watched schoolkids mob the bus stop, spill into the road. The café man is smearing red Formica, emptying metal ashtrays, one into another: a good sign. He'll turf us out before Danny can advance, with long pauses and asthmatic gasps, on the fine print of the latest Ripper narrative. The reworked yarns given out, a sentence at a time, by Joseph Sickert and his colleague, the painter Harry Jonas.

There is a colour snapshot of Hobo and Jonas, in the street, with an unidentified man. Sickert's right hand is bandaged. Jonas, in pink shirt and crumpled straw-coloured suit, has all his buttons secured. In Joseph's flat – and this is the hook – Danny has been shown a trunk of curiosities containing three great treasures. A ruby which can be verified in portraits of the Duke of Clarence. A decorative Japanese box presented to Clarence, her prodigal son, by Queen Victoria. And, best of all, a scrap of folded paper inscribed with broken letters, coded runes, alluding to the secret of the Holy Grail. Its location revealed through a painting on wood, which came into the possession of Hobo Sickert, by unknown means, from Shugborough Hall. The Grail, Danny assured me, was in England. In the keeping of surviving Knights Templar. 'The biggest mystery of all.'

Danny requests a slice of chocolate cake to carry home on the train. If Giscard Plantain de Wyff and the widow Sickert agree, I will be permitted to view the treasures and even, perhaps, to make a copy of the inscription on the paper.

Irresistible. Insane.

Reeling from hours of exposure to Danny's monologues, I found myself escaping to the second layer of the hollow earth; an alternate reality in which I was married to Julie Christie. Who, as Sheila Rowbotham informed us, participated in a legendary walk to Sutton House. The Julie Sinclair of the *Gazette* might then become part of a future in which my mundane biography would be interestingly revised. The only way out, Folgate assured me, was through a scrap of paper in a locked trunk in a flat somewhere I'd never find in North London. Enough. Give it to Julie. Let her finish the book.

Hobo's Relics

The tunnel out of Dalston, going west, courtesy of Silverlink, was becoming a regular event. The creeping, grinding halt in which to contemplate our mortality. And the idiocy of abandoning man's freedom to walk. When time was my own, I dawdled, doubled back, experimented with cafés, pissed in pubs. An hour or two, from Hackney to anywhere, in the way of duty or business. Public transport is a lottery. Easy to forget, in the arbitrary pauses and cancellations, the press of the crowd, voices, rows, your intended destination. Was this journey necessary? Mobile-phone technology hasn't advanced much from tin cans and taut string. Clients of the overground rail service are convinced that a whisper won't carry the distance: they shout. Can you hear me mother?

Danny secured permission for a viewing of the Joseph Sickert treasures, at the flat of his relict, Edna. I would reveal nothing of Folgate's Whitechapel researches: which was a blessing. Nor would I publish the mysterious paper with its coded Grail symbols. The flat, as Edna boasted, was not exactly unknown to London's rackety bohemians. Most of the convivialists brought home by Joseph from pub or market were civilized, boots wiped, caps doffed. But that Francis Bacon, she wouldn't have him in the house. Something about the man made the flesh creep. Edna washed her hands in air to exorcize the resurrected stain.

Trapped yet again in the tunnel, I thought of Emily Richardson's underworld project: car parks, abattoirs, sewers, wartime bunkers. She probed disregarded examples of civil engineering in the expectation that they would offer up a metaphor, film and sound in counterpoint, for this place where she found herself. And for the novel being she housed within the caverns of her body: her son.

Hung on three screens in high alcoves beneath Smithfield Market, grunge Hackney was translated into an image stream, with babbling disconnected narrative: black swine in the buried Fleet River, drowned mudlarks and toshers, troglodytes, blind Morlocks, albino children damaged by radiation, time-slipped wolverines and warlock cannibals out of H. G. Wells, Tim Powers, K. W. Jeter, Neil Gaiman, and Gary Sherman's 1972 film, *Death Line*.

The point, brought home to me by the chill of the slaughter-house cellars, animal fear in crafted bricks, is the profound indifference of the London you don't see. There is no requirement to absolve pain. Barbecued Protestants. Disembowelled Catholics. Mutilated Highlanders. Those who perished under the knife in St Bartholomew's Hospital. Panicked cattle. The tunnels we access, holy wells in private basements, wine vaults, are the outer rind of Edmond Halley's Hollow Earth. A poultice protecting us from the unbearable heat of a buried interior sun.

Was this, I wondered, in the oven of that sticky afternoon, trapped below the skin of Dalston-Kingsland, a verifiable thesis? Could I map the numerous caverns beneath Hackney? The grassed-over air-raid shelters. The crypts. Tiled hospital corridors rented as sets for MTV promos. We were, I calculated, directly under Kingsbury Road, the motorbike shop that took over from the jobbing printers where we laid out and produced the first Albion Village Press books. Another kind of underground entirely. An alternative to the alternative, the Notting Hill orthodoxy of the 1960s: junk conservatism, private-income hipsters dabbling in prop-erty, traders in Third World artefacts, premature sex tourists. Alex Trocchi, a terrifyingly detached and sane writer, atrophied into a spiked Gandalf: a chemical connection at the heart of a Middle-Earth labyrinth of lost souls.

After the interview, Emily kept in touch. I met her mother, out along the canal, pushing the baby: and was discourteous enough, deep in my preoccupation with Hollow Earth theories, not to recognize her. Like Jock McFadyen, I'm not really there when I'm walking. And I don't have the dog that Jock finds so useful for brokering introductions to attractive young women, the students he no longer teaches.

The underworld film project in which Emily involved me continued. In the night, there had been noises like a million mechanized locusts. Emily went out from her Queensbridge Road flat to investigate. Do you remember the Hell's Angel who was cruising down the motorway when he was shot and killed by persons unknown in a passing car? The body was brought to Dawson Street, a tributary off Hackney Road, to lie in state. Respects paid by various chapters and piratical allegiances, the party began. In the morning, corpse loaded into a hearse heaped with floral tributes from Satan's Slaves, the bikers streamed off to Mortlake.

Not many folk notice the smart and secure Hell's Angels Motorcycle Club chapter house. With its craft symbol, a machete, hanging above a steel-shuttered door. The Angels rub along, no friction, with speculators smoking outside Mecca Bingo, with new bohemians, close-cropped and tight-jeaned, in neighbourhood cafés. I searched for the building, when I heard the first rumours of an outlaw presence in the area, among the squatted and burnt-out husks a little further to the west. I was behind the times. The Angels have a solid investment portfolio. They occupy an industrial conversion in the media zone, convenient for Shoreditch and Hoxton: two minutes, tops, on the hog.

I admired Emily's courage, how she'd managed to film her Kenneth Anger tribute to the mourning bikers, while pushing a one-year-old infant in a buggy. When it was over, she adjourned to the Premises for a coffee. 'The guy who sat next to me,' she reported, 'had a completely tattooed face with 666 covering one cheek, "The Beast" scrawled across the other, and "horror show" written around his neck. When he smiled at the baby, he revealed a complete set of gold teeth, top and bottom!'

Bill Griffiths, poet, sometime Hackney resident, even in the bad times, kept a decent piano. Researchers, making his acquaintance, remarked on the blue LOVE and HATE inscriptions that decorated his thick fingers as they flew over the keyboard, ripping through the classical repertoire. Bill was found dead, up north in coastal exile, opera on the radio.

'He never lived much above the poverty line – and a good deal of his life was spent below it. Years of poor diet no doubt hastened his death,' wrote William Rowe in a *Guardian* obituary.

The Hell's Angel youth was part of the mystique: the beard, boots and jacket, stayed with him, as German guest-worker, Anglo-Saxon scholar, itinerant performer, yelping and growling through the concrete poetry repertoire. Bill spoke softly and slowly, wheezing in later years as if the supply of air in his lungs was precious and must be preserved until the next splinter-thin Borstal roll-up was achieved on the lid of his tin. The harshness of Bill's existence, his productivity, always on his own terms, made my complaints about unpaid invoices and the pinch of freelance life look peevish and silly. Apart from which, he was the real thing, that human catastrophe called poet. Whose business is difficulty, intransigence, tactical misjudgement, early death.

Unbiked by the time I met him, Bill rode with the Harrow Roadrats from the age of fifteen. Nicholas Johnson, one of Bill's numerous publishers, told me that the involuntary residency in HMP Brixton came when the poet was discovered in the grounds of a hospital in possession of a knife. He made his permitted phone call to his brother, John: asking him to read aloud from the Bible. Nick reckons that 'Bill's obsession for cataloguing, his blotting-paper mind for language, plus his sense of injustice, paranoia and highly strung vulnerability' emanated from those early prison days.

Nobody I know carried the living plant of memory quite so far under his leather jacket or held it so tenderly: Bill was a rogue classicist, Orpheus in a baseball cap. The balding skull, the silvered beard, seemed to be a way of recalling who he was, or who he had once been, against the accident of the mirror. Or the back of a bright spoon. Dalston was never more than a stopover: unique pamphlets, hand-coloured, were printed in the community work-shops of the borough. A small mistake of council funding, soon to be rectified. When Bill transferred to the liberty of a narrowboat, moored at Uxbridge, it went up in flames, along with his books and papers. Bad luck, he insisted on it; dabbling in ghost stories, reworking M. R. James. Calling the demons by their first names.

Coming east, on the train that had me suspended in the tunnel, Bill saw overground Hackney as a eruption of pigment: reds, blues, greens. The community workshop, the silk-screen process. His white pamphlets – nobody knows how many he produced in thirty-seven years of active publication, more than 150, certainly – blossomed with stencil shapes, holograph revisions. These were not little things, his freely distributed starbursts.

Biker wars. Narrowboat shanties. Edge-land rabbit hunts. Appearing, ranter-raw, with the frequency of Murdoch's tabloids, Bill's books and booklets were as sustaining to me as the notion of the Hackney Brook. That these works existed, even if I didn't see them, streaming out from printshops, from Bob Cobbing's flat in Petherton Road or Bill's John Bull printing set, his late computer, was a London benediction.

Eight Poems against the Bond and Cement of Civil Society.
War w/ Windsor.
A Note on Democracy.
Morning Lands.
A Pocket History of the Soul.
The Secret Commonwealth.

The violence of Angels, Bill asserted, chapter against chapter, was a 'valid human instinct', offering resolution – and in contradiction to the violence of the state. He died upright in his chair. There were no floral tributes from Satan's Slaves. No return to London. 'Old faces together in Sunderland for the funeral,' Tom Raworth reported. 'Flies drop all round.'

Gospel Oak: there was action on the street, but the moves were unreadable. I went into an Irish pub to wait for Danny and his colleague in paranormal and post-rational studies, Giscard de Wyff.

The violence, Bill would have recognized, was civic, tribal: in defence of territory. Afternoon drinkers, fathoms deep in cream-foamed melancholy, built Olympic rings across dark tables with the shifting of wet glasses. They inspected newspapers from which the news element had been extracted. They watched funnels of smoke slide, eel-like, into hairy nostrils and open throats: a carcinogenic communion. 'All right then?' 'Right.' 'Right you are.' 'Good man.'

Edna, Joseph's widow, patch on hand, was proud of her place, her children and grandchildren, welcoming. With tea. With offers of burger platters which handsome daughters, drop-in sons, were preparing. The young ones were hungry and deaf. Though the condition did not impinge in any way on social interaction: one of the girls featured in a television soap which went out with subtitles and a woman miming in the corner of the frame. Danny believed that the Gorman family's inherited otosclerosis was a badge of caste, the living proof that they were indeed the direct descendants of Eddy, Duke of Clarence, and of Princess Alexandra. This Gospel Oak cluster, munching companionably in the galley-kitchen, was the local equivalent of the haemophilia of the Romanovs. (The Sickert surname was down to Hobo: an elective affinity with Walter. The Camden Town Group painter, pupil of Whistler, patron of music halls, confidant of barbers. Hobo's mother, Alice Margaret Crook, married Joseph Gorman, fish-curer and sometime bare-knuckle fighter.)

The council flat, dense with evidence of Joseph's scavenging, his Camden Passage and Soho contacts, was accessorized with a large television. A watchful screen babbled softly on the room of deaf ones. Paintings jostled for space: original copies, Sickert *hommages*, family portraits. A time for roll-ups, egg rolls, brown sauce, awed inspection of the private museum. There was a magnificent oil painting by Joseph that I took to be a vision of Walter, sunk in a throne-chair, crowned with a red paper cap: Ubu or Lear. Banished from the family's Christmas party. A tribute to Walter's early days on the boards with Sir Henry Irving? No no,

Giscard corrected me, the old fellow was not Sickert; it was Joe Gorman, the grandfather.

So much paint! Turpentine, tobacco, frying onions. Out of this active domesticity, in which Danny and de Wyff were accepted familiars, tumbled conspiracies. *The Holy Blood and the Holy Grail*, by Baignent, Leigh and Lincoln, was the first book Joseph Sickert read all the way through. He was a busy man. Here was a washboard signed by the four Beatles as a memento of skiffle days with the Vipers. Hobo played alongside Tommy Steele and Jim Dale (who also made his mark on the board). One of the four palettes hung on the wall was said to have belonged to Walter, but there was no provenance.

'Joseph didn't smoke or drink,' said Folgate, handing me a photograph of Hobo at a gallery opening, pint of sherry in hand.

Natural cynicism leaves us wary of too much evidence, too well documented a lie. A small dark cloud rubbed against the low ceiling, the only naked surface in the room: there must be a book in this stuff. Money too. Stephen Knight was the first. His *Final Solution*, a runaway bestseller, stayed in print years after his death from a brain tumour. Knight had fallen out with his collaborator, the source of his revelations, Hobo Sickert. Others followed, broke the pact, and perished in all the usual ways. The unspoken invitation – *write it!* – was one I was happy to decline. Giscard de Wyff, elegant moustache and serviceable prose, could activate his own files. Cluttered rooms have a way of becoming autobiographies. And they never let you go. Rachel Lichtenstein rescued me from the detritus of a Spitalfields attic, above a decommissioned synagogue. I wouldn't make the same mistake twice.

The solution, for Danny, lay in measurement, hard miles pacing out calculations scribbled on the back of photocopies from public libraries.

'Joseph predicted Diana's so-called accident. It's a matter of establishing your baseline and your co-ordinates, the golden rhombus in a forgotten landscape painting. The princess should never have spun, widdershins, through that revolving door, duplicating her reflection, before plunging recklessly underground in a German motor.'

A memorial photograph of Hobo (22 October 1925 – 9 January 2003) was draped with the silver 'engrailed' cross that he always wore: one of his treasures. Then there was the leaf-patterned Japanese box which contained the folded parchment with its mysterious symbols. They looked like shapes cut through paper to make patterns of light on the wall: a cinema for cavemen.

We finished with the painted board that was supposed to hide, within its floating Rorschach topography, the location of the Holy Grail. A legend, recounted by de Wyff, linked Hobo's murky panel with Shugborough Hall, Scottish Rite Masonry, the Chevalier Andrew Ramsey, Nicholas Poussin, Templars and the rest.

'The panel is made up of two sections. The tapered softwood wedge that runs down the back is typical of the 14th or 15th century. The reverse bears evidence of worm damage and a red wax seal depicting a wounded panther, rampant. The panther holds a broken lance. There are droplets of blood on the chest. Layers of underpainting are clearly visible but the surface has been defaced and damaged, right down to the wood. What would merit such vandalism? And how did such a priceless object – the studio of Botticelli has been mentioned – come into the hands of Joseph Sickert, a humble picture restorer?'

I was reluctant to stare too intently at the swirling golds and browns. Memorize an image and you become its keeper. I had accepted, without bothering to read the small print, an invitation to take part in a conceptual project that I hoped would offer relief from my neurotic recording of Hackney. Lincoln was quite a step: I would have to drive, there and back, with just enough time to eat a sandwich, undertake my task, present the invoice.

A new building perched on the flanks of an old. You know the scene: budget soliciting content. Empty subterranean restaurant with food-exhibits you hesitate to rescue from their display cases. Tactful lighting in pale-grey galleries minimally dressed with digital reports on subverted water, sad creeks, military detritus. Walls that breathe a soulful muzak of sampled sound: wind in the reeds, geese shaking their feathers, whales in congress.

One modest landscape painting, from a line hooded in black velvet, was exposed. 'Take a few minutes or an hour.' I split the difference and went into a trance of intense concentration. The spindly tree. That's all they wanted. 'We walk you out into a field and you describe what you have seen, what you remember.'

I studied everything in that picture, apart from the tree: the solitary house, the upturned boat, the mudflats. Memory of memory: had I seen this place before? I would certainly know it again. *I can't forget.* I can't delete a single brushstroke by that anonymous artist. The stillness. The hour of day. The darkening sky. Human potentialities that seem to have been painted out.

Danny Folgate toyed with Hobo's ruby, his engrailed cross. He showed me portraits of Eddy, Duke of Clarence. My thoughts were of quite another Eddie, Constantine. That Easter Island face drifting through the decades: with Welles, Godard, Petit. In *Alphaville*, Eddie drove through the glistening night into the future, street lights playing across the screen of his Ford Galaxy. They say he has arrived from the 'Outerlands'. He's looking for a character from a comic strip, Henry Dickson. Who is impersonated by the baggy friend of Orson Welles, Akim Tamiroff.

Lost Kaporal was my Tamiroff. He wasn't suicided. He was hiding out, not in *Alphaville*'s Red Star Hotel, but the Victory in Vyner Street. Kaporal had evidence, so he – or a man who sounded just like him – reported in a midnight phone call: Eddie Constantine had accompanied Bob Hoskins on a big night out in Hackney, during *The Long Good Friday* shoot. They kicked off at the Four Aces on Dalston Lane. Or was it Labyrinth? With Constantine as the growling but warm-hearted minotaur. In that special darkness where poetry is the oldest and truest memory-system.

Constantine kept his coat on when he sat with a woman called Anna and listened while she improved on Paul Eluard: *Capitale de la douleur.*

Hackney Hospital

King Edward's Road was blocked by a cop car dressed in blue-and-white ribbons. Like a birthday present that had grown in the night. Some postcode affray, blood-treacle or dog piss on tarmac: another statistical Hackney incident, another excuse for a TV head-to-head between a gaudy T-shirt, new trainers, bangles, righteous indignation (the street) and a suit with a serious haircut, empathizing. Talking firmly about the need to communicate with the community, the gangs who put geography back at the top of the agenda. They were fundamentalists about borders, disputed bus stops, these negative youth affiliations.

Harry Stanley's memorial stump, the concrete omphalos, was naked of flowers. For the first time since the killing. Nobody had remembered to remember: fresh bouquets on the anniversary, plastic and cloth florets in a tartan wrap the rest of the year. All gone: a black belt on the ground with nothing to support.

The little estate where I would meet Dr Peter Bruggen belonged to the Crown and was named after the designer of Victoria Park, James Pennethorne: official architect to the Commissioners of Woods and Forests. It was going to be tricky, to find one house among so much warm-red brick, fig trees, private paths with a choice of steps or ramps: a discreet enclave hidden between canal and park. Dr Bruggen was babysitting twin grandchildren. If I did locate the right door, sheltering behind generous plantings, sensible toys and Swedish furniture in picture windows, would I recognize the man? A moment's chat at the Boas Society on the terrace of the German Hospital, an exchange of emails: was that enough? I was always confusing vice-chancellors with dentists, postmen with poets. Embracing strangers at gallery openings. Leaving spit-prints on the wrong cheek. Better to keep your head down, stay at home.

In the presence of doctors, I was comfortable and uneasy: I had grown up in a medical house with a GP father who never handed out pills if he could avoid it – and then, as often as not, used placebos. Anna did the surgery visits for both of us. I must be registered somewhere. As a workable hypothesis, I chose to avoid places where you could only have bad news confirmed. And would almost certainly pick up something unpleasant on the bus or from the sneezing suppurating mob in the overheated waiting room. Most of the ruffians from the poetry scene of the 1960s and early 1970s had become doctors of some stripe, in the forlorn hope of avoiding destitution by claiming academic tenure.

WORK STARTS IN THIS AREA FOR MONTHS: clancydocwra boasted. A fair summary. Work would start, be left off, status unresolved, for months and months and months. A tribute to the cult of interventionism. Strategic imperatives. City as maze. You can never take the same path twice. Red mesh, blue fence.

We are all Hollow Earthers. Clancydocwra have trenched, four feet down in London clay, as a hint that the surface is tired of its mourning tarmac. Cracks and narrow pits are dug, to locate rusting water-pipes, sleeping bombs, entrances to the underworld: a loud metaphor. Hardbaked mud-holes filling with autumn leaves. The compulsory chasm, shifted across the Thames, is the delight of commentators. Doris Salcedo, a conceptualist of international repute, backed by corporate sponsorship, inflicted a terrible wound on the floor of the Turbine Hall of Tate Modern. It symbolized, the explainers said, the gulf in society, haves and have-nots, the obscenely wealthy and ultimately dispossessed.

City Hall plotters (who have lost the plot) and Money Men (juggling debt) are in total agreement: when you are in a hole, keep digging. To confuse critics, your hole can go the other way and climb towards the sky, the latest cloud-reflecting insult. A city of towers is also a city of deep foundations: animal bones, sacred artefacts, plague victims, lost coins, broken clay pipes. Reasons can always be invented for the ravishment of dull and ordinary streets, the felling of trees that might, in the next storm, crash across cars or ambulances. They do not speak of the true motive: the continuing search for the portal to the world beneath, golden lands warmed by a sun that can never be extinguished.

Surgeons – Dr Swann, in particular – were the custodians of a great secret. Just as Christian churches were often built on pagan sites, so I believed our local hospitals disguised points of access to profound reservoirs of memory. Tiled corridors and basements in which lethal X-ray machines were left to brood and leak. Outdated wonder drugs mouldering in disconnected fridges. I taped Dr Bruggen, the history of his medical experiences in Hackney, in the perverse hope that his sane and reasonable narrative would lead me to the clue I was missing. And perhaps to Dr Swann.

Coffee made, comfortable on the sofa, Dr Bruggen began with a brief account of his background. A cat stalked the scene, watchful and contemptuous. Mrs Bruggen had taken the twins into the park. The doctor's voice, when I played the tape back, to check that it was working, sounded exactly like my own.

I was born in Burnley, a town in Lancashire. My mother was Scottish. My father came from Sri Lanka, he was of Dutch origin. They became general practitioners in Burnley. I went into medicine. I studied in Edinburgh. When I got my first job, I travelled some distance south. I was getting as far away as I could from my family. The job was in Orsett, Essex. House physician. A six-month job.

At the end of that period I looked in the British Medical Journal *and spotted something worthwhile in Hackney. I applied. This was July 1958. I qualified in November '57.*

The new job was in the Hackney Hospital. I thought it was in Amhurst Road, but Amhurst Road doesn't look right on the map. It's the one out there beyond the Homerton Hospital. Homerton High Street? The phone number was double 5, double 5. The building is still there, but it's not a hospital any more.

I remember there was a lovely archway you drove through to reach a courtyard. I went for an interview and got the job, houseman. I had no knowledge whatsoever of Hackney prior to this. I lived in the hospital. I was very excited to be in any London hospital – though Hackney wasn't a smart one. I was very nervous and quiet.

There was a registrar and a consultant. I remember the corridor to the right of the entrance, the operating theatre was off to the right. Upstairs there were two surgical wards, male and female. And these beautiful – relatively beautiful – medical officers' quarters.

I had a small bedroom and a sitting room. Amazing luxury! I very rarely used the sitting room. There was a doctors' mess, a dining room. It was big. And very select. A boarding-school atmosphere.

Hackney itself I barely noticed. Life was the hospital. And driving into the West End. And the station, Euston Station, when I went home to see my family.

I was very aware of the Town Hall. It was built in the 1930s. Going down Mare Street, there was a smell from the sweet factory: candyfloss. And that hospice for the terminally ill, St Joseph's. One of the first and it's still there. I looked at it and thought: 'How will anybody be made aware of this place? I'm going to write something about assisted dying.' I was certainly aware of Mare Street and Hackney Road. That was one of my ways of getting to the West End.

I went to church. I'd been confirmed in the Church of England as a medical student. Religion disappears so wonderfully! I'm a very devout atheist now. I attended a church that I'm still trying to find. My memory is of that narrow bit, by St John's Church, and then striking off, further to the left. I remember communion on Sunday morning. The church had been painted, it had a dome. I can't find it. Maybe the whole business was total fantasy. There are so many excuses to wander this area.

My Hackney Hospital experience was of local people and run-of-the-mill surgery, general surgery. Not many knife wounds then. Hackney seemed interesting. I had the socialist conviction that the working classes were good and the middle classes bad. I tended to get keen on certain patients, I would befriend them. There was a young man in for something like arthritic pyarthrosis, massive scars. He insisted it was an accident. Absolutely insisted. He was a Communist. I remember him saying that he believed what Khrushchev had said, denouncing Stalin. He mourned the millions of ordinary Russians Stalin had killed. But he just believed it must have been necessary. I was impressed by that dedication. It didn't make sense.

I was aware of young girls coming in, sometimes with severe abdominal pain. Was it appendicitis? I remember the registrar giving me a sexual leer, as he conducted a rectal examination. I felt very uncomfortable about this. But like the racism I found in my first hospital in Essex, I didn't dare to mount a challenge.

A young man came in with a head injury, but the consultant wasn't interested. Philip, the registrar, told me that head injuries bored him. So Philip pushed for the patient to be transferred to a neurological unit. The surgeon didn't want to know.

I remember Stead, the consultant, shouting at me once, but on the whole he was good. When he did shout, that was nasty. He was strong and firm and decisive. I was surprised by how difficult some surgery was. Something like appendicitis could take two hours. I was impressed by how hard the surgeons worked and by how good they were.

Surgeons had such status. I called the surgeon 'sir'. There was a patient of fifty or so, with breast cancer, and this was before the time when information was shared. He had a lump removed and he wanted to know about it. I had to say, 'Mr Stead the surgeon will see you.' I was with the consultant when he said to a man, 'Yes, you do have cancer.' The prognosis was good. The man was so relieved to be given a straight answer.

I had a sense of the landscape immediately surrounding the hospital. I drove around the area once, but I never walked it. I had a garage for my little car on Homerton High Street. A funny thing happened. The registrar was married, he'd got a house. He had a rather smart car, a tourer. The consultant got a new car, which was a Hillman – not the tourer. He was talking about his new car, as consultants did in those days, as we walked with him, in procession, to the parking place. Suddenly, he noticed the registrar's tourer: 'Whose is that?'

I went out with a girl who was a nurse. I don't even remember her name. There was also another girl you might be interested in. She was called Gill. I think she was a staff nurse. She was beautiful. A proper Hackney girl. Her mother was dead. Her father was a councillor who had once been mayor. This girl had been mayoress of Hackney. I'm talking about 1958. The mayor was Labour, very left wing.

The other interesting person in the hospital was the pharmacist. A person I never met. He slept in the pharmacy. A strange thing to do. I often had to go there. Hospital life involved a lot of drug taking. My drug taking was based around stuff to help me sleep. I took chloral hydrate, which is a liquid. I would help myself. And I would sometimes help myself to amphetamines. It was dangerous, no question. I was certainly dependent on sleeping things.

Years later, 1962 or '63, I went into psychotherapy. I was then in a psychiatric hospital, near Croydon. My course leader, who was an Indian, confronted me, in a very gentle way, about my own personality. He said, 'Look, if you're going to do this, you've got to have some therapy yourself. Your personality is getting in the way.'

I went into therapy with someone who used LSD. We used LSD in the hospital. I took LSD in therapy and it was wonderful. One of the things that evolved from that experience was that I stopped taking drugs. I was walking around with a little phial of amphetamines, a phial of codeine. Codeine in case I got diarrhoea. Amphetamines for a boost. Even if I didn't take it, it was there.

Very many nights I took chloral hydrate to help me sleep. I remember my mother being worried about this. I went into a drug trial and I noticed strange side effects. I was getting everything I needed from the pharmacy in the Hackney Hospital. I was quite obsessed with cleanliness. I washed my face before I went to bed. And I remember – I didn't wear glasses – washing my face and feeling my hands tingle.

I got in touch with the drug company and I met one of the reps. They used to come around hospitals pushing drugs on us. They were interested in what I had to say. Would I be willing to have a very small drug trial? They gave me things that looked exactly the same. I couldn't tell what they were. I knew some of them were dummies. Some were sodium amytal. One time I'd got a terrible hangover, so I recognized that. I took two of each and noted its effect. I couldn't tell the difference. That convinced me that I was into a psychological dependency rather than a physiological one. That helped me to come off.

I started with drugs as a medical student. We bought what we needed from the chemist, nobody seriously challenged us. A little bit of a pause sometimes, then: 'Oh, a medical student.'

One night in the pharmacy at Hackney, I was getting something for one of the patients and I heard a noise, snort snort. There he was, the pharmacist, lying on top of one of the benches, sound asleep. It was the only time I ever set eyes on the man. It is very strange what goes on in hospitals at night.

Doctors and drugs. Doctors and alcohol. My father drank sherry, whisky and also took drugs. For backache, severe pain. The police hushed it up, he was the police surgeon.

Hospitals ran on alcohol. Beer was given to the men, the patients. They were prescribed Guinness. When Philip the registrar collected the ration, there were always two extras. He and I would have a Guinness.

At Christmas there was a lot of alcohol on the ward. I was on duty and was offered drink. 'Would you like a glass of sherry or a beer? Or would you prefer a sniff of Dr So-and-so's breath?'

I remember a drug rep saying, 'Would you like something for your own use?' The pharmacy at the psychiatric hospital had LSD and Methedrine. LSD was very good for helping people relax. I remember Geoff, a friend of mine who was quite a bit older, getting lots of barbiturates for his mother.

In Orsett one of the consultants got a package of amphetamines every time he came in, from the sister. Another consultant was always driven to the hospital and collected by his wife. We assumed he had no licence.

None of this was news, my father was a police surgeon. I'd heard the stories. After what he'd seen as a medical student in Aberdeen, a young doctor in London, my father didn't drink. But Dr Bruggen's account confirmed my sense of those hospitals on the hill as being lit up, windows burning in the night. The agreement is, when you put yourself in the hands of surgeons or, broken in mind, are committed to a locked ward: *the world is an hallucination.* Take the curse off reality. Hospitals factor a dark poetic of abuse, institutionalization: chemical reward. Pain creeps over those high walls, through insecure gates, into the city. Down the slope towards the Matchbox Toys Factory, the River Lea and Hackney Marshes.

The territory into which old Swanny had disappeared. Drug Argonaut. Vagrant. Keeper of secrets.

'Did you ever come across a certain Dr Swann? He was at the German Hospital. And possibly the Mothers' Hospital in Clapton. He used to stitch up the Kray gang. With bulldog clips, masking tape and a shot of brandy. They called him "The Vet". The last anyone heard of Swanny was as a kind of caretaker in the bowels of the Children's Hospital in Hackney Road: after it closed down. He may be there still.'

'Swann? Sorry. The hospitals are familiar. It must have been after my time.'

In the late 1950s I went to the Mothers' Hospital in Clapton Road. It was amazing. This was my first experience of real fatigue. My job was sewing up. The deliveries were done by midwives, we were just hanging around. With Caesarean sections, an anaesthetist was brought in. Also assisting at forceps or delayed births would be the registrar.

By far the worst incident seemed at the time to be perfectly straight-forward. I was only a bystander. The baby got stuck in some way and we were called down, myself and the registrar. He was putting on forceps. We got an anaesthetist in. It was getting very fraught, we were tense. The registrar said something to the woman in a loud voice. And she said, 'Don't shout at me.' And died. We were in real shock. We didn't know how to deal with it. The patient was dead. And the baby of course. We didn't bother about the baby.

The husband was outside. The registrar got in touch with the consultant. Who was called Gladys Dobbs. A high-powered lady, very efficient, very well dressed. She came in very quickly and just took over. I saw the consultants as being the ones who grasp nettles. The terrible thing is that we never had any debriefing, no discussion. We were left in the dark.

The patients in those days knew very little, they were given a bath and an enema. Some consultants gave them an immediate injection of morphine or pethidine. Others said, 'Don't.'

Nobody went through it as natural childbirth, without drugs. Mothers were given, on arrival, even if they were too far gone for an enema, an injection.

I remember a black woman. There weren't very many black women at that time. Not as patients. This woman started to bleed and it didn't stop. We couldn't stop it. The registrar did all the right things. She died.

The worst ever thing was the dead baby. Not a stillborn baby, that's all right. It's shocking, really shocking. But this one was dead and we had to get it out. There are instruments like pruning shears, used for cutting, so that the shoulders come out. You do manage it. That was the most horrendous thing I ever experienced.

I switched to paediatrics. The interview was at the Queen Elizabeth Hospital for Children in Hackney Road. But the first job was in Shadwell. The hospital was founded by a tea-planter who had made his fortune in India and who was very concerned about the London poor. He died before it was up and running. At the age of twenty-nine.

The hospital was a lovely environment. The first time I ever had a girl in my room somebody knocked on the door. The nurses' rooms had outside stairs. All my girlfriends were from inside the medical community.

We were institutionalized. I had my laundry done. There was a maid who kissed me in the morning when she brought in the tea. There was plenty of sex. And drugs.

I met two people who had been ship's doctors. My job was coming to an end. I applied to be a ship's doctor. My Joseph Conrad period. Orsett, where I started, is right across the A13 from Stanford-le-Hope, where Conrad lived. We sailed to the Amazon. From Liverpool. Three months.

There was something very vivid about the Shadwell. When a boy died there, it was my first East End funeral. I didn't go. I saw it from one of the upper floors, a kind of procession: black horses, hearse, mounds of flowers.

Then I moved to the Queen Elizabeth, the Children's Hospital. From the very top, right above the front door, I saw the last three tower blocks as they were being built. I thought they were so beautiful.

At the Queen Elizabeth the rooms were tiny and I could actually touch both walls at the same time. But we had access to the roof. I can remember, one lovely summer, sitting in deckchairs on the roof. We had some great parties. That's where I had my first girlfriend who wasn't a nurse. I had sexual fantasies about other doctors. And I kissed, a single kiss, one of the most senior of the Shadwell doctors. Just before I left. An innocent kiss. Not even a mouth kiss really. I had a conversation with her, twenty years later, on the telephone, about a case.

In the Queen Elizabeth there was a pharmacy, up some steps. That's where one of the junior doctors was reduced to tears by this very severe consultant. The wards were so crowded. I remember the back area, lots of shelves, hidden away. Quite narrow. I remember going down this narrow passage with a nurse who was quite responsive to snuggling, to touch.

I didn't go to any of the pubs or cafés in the area, or into the little park beside the building. I was aware of other buildings along Hackney Road which were old. I remember thinking, 'They must be Georgian.' Now I can enjoy them.

When we had something to do which was difficult for a child, we would give them paraldehyde. Which has an awful smell. And is a very big injection. They would be wrapped in a blanket and held by one of the nurses, while I did the stitching or whatever. The parents were sent well away. I remember being quite scared by the amount of paraldehyde we gave. The nurse who ran casualty was a man. The injection seemed such a terrible procedure. With ECT you find that it is sometimes necessary. I would have ECT sometimes. But it's very often unnecessary. It was used punitively.

On my way here today, to my daughter's house, I wandered around a bit and found one of the side streets. Industrial buildings. I'm now interested in architecture. The style of those buildings could have been North African. I realized that, back in my Hackney Road days, if I'd been walking the area, if I'd noticed those buildings, I'd have thought they should be pulled down and replaced.

I did walk at Shadwell. The river scared me, the pubs. I walked down Cable Street, through to the end. Wonderful smells. As I approached a *derelict-looking café, I heard a noise, a scream. I was too frightened to intervene. But I'll never forget that sound.*

The space occupied by the deactivated Children's Hospital disturbed my afternoon circuits of Haggerston Park. The way it glowered across the man-made pond and the little eco wilderness. Chickens pecked in the City Farm, the donkey was too depressed to utter its plaintive yowl. Buildings of such memory-displacement won't let you pass, freely and without repercussion: I have to notice the broken panes, graffiti revisions, dirty bouquets of stone flowers.

Brian Catling, rumbling through Hackney Road towards some performance venue in Vyner Street, or new lapdancing experience, paused to interrogate the proprietor of the handbag shop where the old Nag's Head used to be. The most haunted pub in London. The horse's head, blacked up, orange eyes, still rests in an alcove: a lurid trophy. We drank here a couple of times. A floor of spongy rubber which threatened to give way, dropping you into the Sweeney Todd pit. The bag-man, Catling confirmed, was reluctant to spend time alone in the cellar. When the building was locked and everybody had gone home, he heard footsteps pacing over-head.

Public house and hospital sat on the same fault line. And were better avoided. I read somewhere that the prize-winning novelist Nicola Barker once worked in the Children's Hospital as a cook or dietician. She used to live in the borough. I liked her books very much: she knew how to walk prose across the page. With wit and consequence. One of her characters in *Reversed Forecast* is employed as a kennel maid at the Hackney track. Like Stephen Gill she notices that the area is defined by a proliferation of betting shops that allow the poor to stay poor in style. It wouldn't surprise me if the hospital helped forge Barker's quirky vision: 'Every story was one story, everything boiled down to a single narrative. Every thought, idea, commentary, fiction, was travelling towards a single meaning. She tried to find this meaning but it was hopeless. It was too big.'

There was another party on the roof. Ian Askead, who was working the fridges in the Homerton, headbutted Charlie Velasco. Something absurd about the way Charlie was looking at his wife. Two whippets slapping skin and bone. While the rest of us laughed. 'You fuck my wife, I fuck you.' A worm of snot from the wronged man's nostril. Velasco kicking out gingerly to protect his toes.

Askead pretended his steel comb was a blade. Most of his day was spent measuring corpses, entering their particulars in the register. Making tea. 'The plugging gets messy, you have to tie the legs together.' And comb the hair: his weapon of choice. Charlie escorted the drunk mortuary technician's wife home to Albion Square. As a courtesy. In the Audi. I watched the lights from above.

Anna brought our daughter, Farne, to the Children's Hospital, suffering severe abdominal pain. She was a brave and bloody-minded child. They sent her away, not for the first time, saying that it was indigestion. Farne became feverish. We got her to the hospital in Holloway Road just in time for an emergency appendectomy. Anna, overdue with a second daughter, holding off in some mysterious way until the first was through the operation, went into labour. She felt the contractions as she climbed the stairs. These dramas, hovering as we undertake our ordinary routines, arrive in clusters. William and I, in a bereft and masculine house, adventured in the overgrown section of Springfield Park. A day we both remember.

Neither can I forget the dreadful burger bar on Holloway Road. Hungry but unable to eat, we put on time while the operation took place. And the clock stood still.

Again. Coming home, after an evening up west, the cabbie began to chat as we hit Hackney Road: to establish cordial relations before the humped bridge and the potential tip.

'That park takes me right back. My life.'

He had been new to the people-transporting game. And hot. Bringing a nurse back. God's truth: the fuck of a lifetime. They broke into the City Farm. Down in the dirty hay. Absolutely amazing. True what they say about nurses: bone-shuddering. She could suck the sap out of a statue. Looking back: it never happened. Blinding. You could hear the goats cough.

   'Still there?'

   Park, yes. Hospital, no. Shame.

The Circuit of Morning

DEADLY SKUNK FLOODS CITY.

I make my October walk, solo now, towards London Fields.

CAR HID A CORPSE.

Newsprint, pulped by overnight rain, clogs the ridged soles of my Masai Barefoot Technology shoes. The water is off again while they clancydocwra barnacled pipes. So thin. So long in the ground.

Want skunk? Try this route and you will be forced to admire the dedication of self-administering chemists. By the time I've reached the Owl Man's ruin, I'm floating high from puff of youth: mid-road shoulder-rollers toking as they prowl, sharing the herbal blast. Darkened windows of untaxed silver saloons leak burnt breath. Squad cars converge on messy traces of recent crimes. And coloured screens illuminate dim basements where sleepsuit-babes wait for food.

My internet server refuses to serve. It's dubiously installed and won't stand up to investigation. There are new freelance occupations: young fixers on bicycles, barely languaged but fast-fingered, sure navigators in the virtual world. If my difficulties have to be explained in terms they understand, I'm unlanguaged too. A trip to the internet café in Kingsland Road, down skunk alley, is an education: money flies across the globe, mostly towards Nigeria. Charismatic Christian sects do photocopying, emails, faxes and keyrings: sideline sacraments. Hasids load brown packages into the Volvo as if nothing around them had changed. In thousands of years. The law is the law: even if they have to abandon war-torn Stamford Hill for Milton Keynes.

Each morning, with Anna, I walk a local circuit: before starting work. For thirty or so years, she spurned the notion. 'There's nowhere in Hackney I want to go.' Away from London, we tramped the Lake District, Wales, and even Anna's beloved Fens, but treks on home turf were a penance for my wife. To clear her head, she walked to school, beyond the Hackney Hospital, on certain summer days. And caught the best of the light.

I picked my moment. The promise of an interesting route, a bit of everything the borough offers: Albion Drive with its front gardens (compare, contrast); the informal geometry of London Fields, avenues of broad-trunked guardian trees; Bungalows, the Mare Street café where we enjoyed a full English to celebrate the anniversary of our first circuit; narrow Warneford Street with its contagious spate of loft conversions. Its colourful bins. That eccentric end-stopped terrace (like *The Ladykillers*), before the swing into Fremont Street.

The proximity of Victoria Park nudges property values, mews developments in places where there had never been stables. From one house, wedged into a tight slot like a hatchet in cake, emerged another pedestrian couple: the woman in white and her partner in trilby and all-seasons raincoat. Two small dogs. We might nod if we coincide, but we try to keep things English.

This couple, confident in belonging to the community of the park, cut through the private estate where Dr Bruggen's daughter lived. Anna did attempt a conversation, once, with the newspaper reader on his bench, when she wanted to let off steam about the way her refuge had been made into a caravan park for film crews. The man wore long shorts, a drover's brown coat and a bush hat. They were shooting some intrusive nonsense about Dylan Thomas's marriage. (A person who never came closer to Hackney than not turning up to be best man at the marriage of his friend Vernon Watkins, in St Bartholomew-the-Great, Smithfield.)

I posed against the caravan with the 'Dylan Thomas' card. Anna was too enraged by the generators, the breakfasting crew, the way the grass was dying along the stretch where they parked, to take her indicated position beside the 'Caitlin' mobile home.

While she let rip at the man on the bench, I snapped another sign: SAILOR BEATING DYLAN. The broadsheet reader growled as if ventriloquized by his shaggy dog. There was damage to his vocal cords, a hole in the throat. He spoke with a gizmo that could alarm the unprepared. Who were confronted, all at once, with their own insensitivity. Lack of observation. On some mornings there was a friend, standing close, delivering a précis of news still to be read. The dog looked forward to the chocolates he scattered on the floor.

Maaaaa-mung-na.

The dog-man pats the pockets of his drover's coat.

'I haven't got any money.'

Coming into the park through St Agnes's Gate (Protected by Armour Security) meant so much to Anna: dappled light, confirmation that the trees were still standing. She boiled at the sight of flattened grass, tyre-tracked into spirals by car thieves who torched the evidence. One morning there was a fast-food bike, tipped on its side, crows pecking at the spill. We witnessed Romanian gypsy women in long skirts breaking branches, tearing down wands of cherry blossom, carrying them off: as if the park had been their native forest.

The rising sun behind us, the towpath was a bicycle track. I counted forty-seven between Canal Gate and Broadway Market, hammering hard in stalled groups, held by a green mum with infants perched around a clumsy rickshaw, front and back. *Ting ting.* Or, failing that, a whistle before the bridge.

It was never the same, walking this circuit on my own. In Anna's company I noticed more of the surface of things. Left to myself, I brooded on work, how this book might fold together. On our last expedition, I'd been thinking about Dr Bruggen's description of the Hackney Hospital as a drug-hallucinated island. William Burroughs and J. G. Ballard both trained as doctors and carried forensic skills into their alternative careers. Hospitals of the 1950s were colonial outposts, no need to socialize with the natives. Burroughs and Ballard, detached and clinically observant, had the good manners and the mannerisms of the Raj.

Our daughter Farne was pregnant and due to give birth in the Homerton, so that building, up on the ridge, stayed in our talk. A grandchild, second-generation Hackney, was an unexpected thing.

SHOOTING INCIDENT. ON SAT 20TH AUGUST 05 AT ABOUT 9PM IN FIELDS ESTATE A FIREARM WAS DISCHARGED CAUSING DAMAGE TO RESIDENTIAL PREMISES. CAN YOU HELP US?

There is a harvest of dog hair, in thick dry curls, under the bench beside the canal. Freelance canine barbers. The pool table, slung on the path at the very moment they started construction work on the Adelaide Quay development, stayed there for nine months; acquiring a tilth of seagull crap.

We came to know the wildlife: the heron feigning indifference as it paddles the shallows of the cavern in which narrowboats used to turn, the bullying big-foot coots, the goose who sat for so many weeks on a narrow ledge, attempting to incubate an infertile egg. Every day, with every completed circuit, we peeled away something of our common history and left it behind. Our walks rehearsed an inevitable and fast-approaching disappearance: to be here, always, but not ourselves.

As we came up the ramp towards Queensbridge Road, Anna gasped with an involuntary spasm of pain. By the time she got home we had to call an ambulance. She was down on all fours. Help arrived, promptly. The examination took place in the ambulance, to the considerable interest of neighbours and folk arriving for the school. Who regretted the inconsiderate blockage of a double-parking space. Pat the keeper told me later he'd had three heart attacks so far, they went with the job. He shouldn't be doing the heavy lifting any more. Not at his age, it was affecting his golf swing.

But this was not a heart problem, they established that. Must be a stomach strain from the walking. Take a pill, carry on. To worse attacks, fever, total collapse: enough bile to ensure that something must be done.

The weekend was endured, sticky with yellow heat. On Monday morning I drove Anna to the surgery (she told me where it was). Every speedbump, and there were plenty, was an agony, a low moan. She didn't have the strength to cross the road.

Anna had done this routine many times before and she came prepared, a urine sample in a sesame-seed bottle. The doctor couldn't find the kit he needed to do the test, but he'd seen enough to call the Homerton. Where his suspicions would be confirmed: gallstones. Calculi, they call them. A shingle beach to carry around, hard pebble-like accretions that don't rattle.

Traffic that day was crazy. But normal. The orthodox Hackney hysteria of roadworks, red-fenced holes. Anger-management head-cases were bombing bus lanes, mounting kerbs, shaving nanoseconds from their criminal records: dumping cigarettes, cartons, refuse bags. Playing chicken with red lights. Hurtling out of side roads. Flying from speedbumps. Crunching into potholes. Nudging cyclists who wove, death-defying, through the stalled sections, V-signing their getaways. Bouncing on to pavements. Blind under misted visors. A fools' procession of men in helmets, acrylic-painted like hardboiled Easter eggs. They slalom though respect-soliciting, mid-road maniacs who are convinced their personal force fields repel accelerating metal. Shattered glass. Petrol pools. Human meat splattered by the amphetamine urgency of pre-emptive policing or dragged in bloody trails beneath bendy buses.

And all of this shitstorm heading, so it appears, for the high ridge, Homerton Hospital. You can't park within miles of the sick-store, although everyone tries: cabs bursting with extended families who haven't yet decided which member needs treatment, Stamford Hill Volvos of repeat pregnancies, dignified Somalis, sweating junkies and their parasitical dealers – with many more who can't resist the life–death party mood of a great hospital-supermarket where absolutely anything can happen.

I get Anna inside and run straight back out before my vehicle is clamped and crushed, or given a spin down to the Lea or Victoria Park by some freelance ecologist in a Nike skullcap. Then, jogging in a fugue of fears and imaginings from Chatsworth Road, where I left the car in the charge of a youth with a small yard and two mobile phones, I found my wife waiting, quite calmly now, though still in pain, in a kind of airport transit lounge. Which was occupied by assorted transients and sufferers, some toying with newsprint, munching apples, keeping an eye on the monitor, departure times. Others, the truly sick, are barely able to tolerate the lingering curse of occupying their own bodies. They count beads and pray aloud.

Moving through to the Nurses' Station, a good transport metaphor, we are gazumped by a large woman who announces that she's about to throw up. 'You can't be sick here,' says the young nurse, 'this is a hospital.' Handed what looks like an oversize cardboard boater, kept for the purpose, the groaning woman fills it. And overfills it with an impressive bout of projectile vomiting.

The inspection cubicle in which Anna is installed is painted with a blue-and-purple combination. It's hot. But the service is good, the nursing care excellent. That's reassuring. They do listen to what she says. Her urine, in keeping with the scheme of things, has changed from Lucozade orange to deep-grape magenta. She's clipped and wired. A tall black man, a hospital wanderer, blunders through the curtains. And apologizes very courteously. He's looking for someone who may have died months ago.

Paramedics are in soothing green. I can only sit in the corner and read my paperback of *The Drought* by J. G. Ballard. The large tap on the book's cover drips loudly in the hospital sink.

'The world-wide drought now in its fifth month was the culmination of a series of extended droughts that had taken place with increasing frequency all over the globe during the previous decade.'

I marked that passage. Ballard originally published the book in 1965. British weather had taken a few years to cotton on, but now there was no rain or it hammered down until rivers flooded their banks. A number of people, quite independently, were working on drowned Hackney films. I watched one of them when I got back from the hospital: *Polly II – Plan for a Revolution in Docklands* by Anja Kirschner. Anja produced a leaflet that went with the DVD. As well as transcripts of pirate trials, photographs of Brecht and 'Spirit' Grant (the threatened Broadway Market shopkeeper), Kirschner illustrated the enclosures of common land in the seventeenth century. Two men at a public meeting, convened by the Boas Society, protested about 'being washed out of the area' by gentrification.

I am sent home. Anna is removed to the Medical Assessment Centre and then to the Priestley Ward. An agitated dealer in the corridor is telling his client not to use the mobile number, he's in a hospital. A woman, bemoaning institutional food, accepts the takeaway curry her family bring to her bed. And is loudly, violently sick. Hungry again, she snatches the hospital tray. And repeats the process.

The initial procedure is successfully undertaken and I'm called to fetch Anna home. There will be a further, more serious operation at a later date.

Joseph Priestley, the natural philosopher who gave his name to the ward, was a Hackney man. Author of *Experiments and Observations on Different Kinds of Air* (2 vols., 1774–7). So Sheila Rowbotham told me, his house was part of her historic walk. A local mob, enraged by the scientist's notions on free will, the libertarian principles that had him nominated as a citizen of the French Republic, broke down his door and – as at John Dee's Mortlake residence so many years before – burnt his books, his precious manuscripts, his instruments. They did not appreciate, perhaps, that there is no better way to ensure transit through time than by reducing cumbersome volumes to essence. The raging pyres of fascists only confirmed the potency of the word. Inky symbols reconfigure and make their own shapes in cloying smoke. New sentences, as Danny Folgate knew and I was to discover, spread themselves across the topography of London, catching on the most unlikely fences, oversmearing walls.

'Eric Spencer!'

When Anna was back, in her own bed, the name came to her. A little white boy, reception class in Daubeney: 'all over the place'. Eric was the hospital porter pushing her gurney. He had ambitions, he said. He was going to try for a paramedic.

Chisenhale Road

A classic Hackney scam: no money spent, large boast. I sat on the bench, upwind of the unravelling ranter, the one tearing his free newspaper into smaller and smaller segments: and I laughed aloud. How do you solve the problem of vanishing gardeners? When Renchi worked in Victoria Park, and I was at King George's Fields in Mile End, we were part of a substantial team. We set out, mob-handed, to keep school fields neat, to tend graveyards and Hawksmoor churches. Now plant technicians from elsewhere arrive like hit squads, do their thing: as if they were laying carpets.

WILDLIFE AREA. THIS AREA HAS BEEN LEFT UNCUT TO ENCOURAGE BIODIVERSITY. THIS WILL ATTRACT ALL SORTS OF INSECTS, BUTTERFLIES AND NESTING BIRDS.

Brilliant! Certified walk-leaders will be able to point out the sanctioned wilderness, a substitute for edge-lands lost to Olympic bulldozers, as they show old and obese citizens how to put one foot in front of the other, according to the leaflet. The notion is a winner, we could export it, make notices to stick on dumped cars, landfill mounds, empty hospitals: WILDLIFE AREA. If you can't rent your meadow as a caravan park for a film unit, peddle it to City Hall.

Anna, sent home on the afternoon of her operation, made a complete recovery. It took months of phone calls, repeat visits, dates set and unset, to get it done. The surgeons were excellent, the nurses efficient and cheerful under the impossible stress of a collapsing system, which was organized for the benefit of bureau-crats and accountants. At one point, my wife got through the preliminaries, the pre-med, and – lying in calm resolution on the trolley, waiting to be wheeled through – was told that the operation was off: more tests needed, steroid boosts. But she made it; returned to our early-morning circuit, the old routines. Then she packed her bags and bought her airline tickets.

I was walking alone because Anna was in America, visiting our daughter. And granddaughter. I couldn't, for many reasons, break away from the problems of a book that seemed to be approaching some kind of resolution. Either that or I had lost it completely: I saw signs everywhere, paintmarks that predicted the outline of future buildings or pronounced a sentence of death. Yellow arrows, blue circles. I carried a photocopy of Hobo Sickert's Grail sheet – which I compared with spray-splatters in the doorways of condemned snooker halls. Television ghosts playing through the night in the empty bar of the Albion pub in Goldsmiths Row. Slogans on T-shirts. Or the way a bus driver's teeth were set as he reluctantly allowed me to board the 253, which passed Arthur Machen's former chambers near Gray's Inn Road.

I decided to investigate Danny Folgate's Victoria Park leyline, to carry on from the point where we left it. There might, at worst, be a path of illumination, relief from the energy-swallowing black hole of Hackney. The taped voices echoing in my sleep.

The ironwork scrolls of the Royal Gates, the crowned globes, parodied drawings on Masonic cards in Hobo's collection, his trunk of curiosities. Reflected in the dark depths of the Royal Inn on the Park, these symbols of majesty came into conflict with a wreath of thorns, a Catholic prompt. A reminder of the heritage of Lauriston Road that Neil Murger was so keen to promote in the Charlotte Street restaurant. A return to the territory of his childhood, at a period when the BBC was collapsing around him, was impossible. There was nothing left to plunder but the archive of rock'n'roll memories, the grainy romance of suicided idols. Vanished writers: Alexander Baron, Roland Camberton and the ones without names.

A greyhound exerciser exploited a gap in the fence around the

Burdett-Coutts memorial. I followed. A fifty-eight-foot needlepoint tapping into the subterranean energy stream. A dry fountain in red granite. Curling above the entrance was a Latin inscription, which I brought home for translation: 'The earth is the Lord's and all that therein is.' What was behind the locked door, inside the chamber, beneath the ground?

Cherubs, noses eaten away, mouths black, raised chubby arms in semaphore salute. Vestigial wings would never get them off the ground. Yet they were poised for flight down Danny's line, south-east towards the sewage outflow, Beckton and the river. One pudge squatted above a honey-coloured smear. There was a black hole beside his right foot, from which drowsy wasps emerged. To stagger and die. The slab bearing the obese cherub's weight was an altar, a speckled kneeling-block. Puffy cheeks were sprayed in red: CRIME IN LONDON.

As I walked towards Gun Markers' Gate, Danny's energy line bifurcated: the true path was a curving exit towards the Thames. 'The thing you're after,' as the poet Charles Olson said, 'may lie around the bend.' But this other, the ruler-straight insistence, seduced by the vulgar pyramid at the summit of the Canary Wharf Tower, was a false note. An occulted act of will to confuse innocent eyes. Danny knew when to leave well alone, opt for a cup of tea.

A miracle of light under the canal bridge revealed layers of sand and gravel, blue cans degrading into an aluminium reef. Here was where the great carp of Hackney basked, a solitary fish, last of his tribe. My walks, at the right hour of the afternoon, sought out this oracular presence: with little success. On one occasion, my way was blocked by a policewoman. Her companion was rolling out the blue-and-white tape. 'We hope it's a dog.' He pointed to a white bundle bobbing against the lock gates. The steepling fall of water.

After Three Colts Bridge, cutting back to recover alignment, I found myself in Chisenhale Road. The Spitfire propeller factory and the present gallery where Rachel Whiteread showed her frosty *Ghost*. The cast of an Archway room with the heat taken out. I climbed the front steps of a particular house, calculating the point through which the line of force would pass. I felt a shiver: unknowingly, I had entered a dead man's photograph. A negative strip recovered from Tate Britain: *Window Cleaner's Funeral*.

It was a money thing to help fund the Hackney book. I agreed to trawl the archive of the Hyman Keitman Research Centre, attempting to locate some object or image that might provoke a few thousand words for an in-house magazine.

The archive was compelling and depressing. I began wanting revelations, the glittering bones of lost or submerged worlds. Preserved street furniture of a blitzed Whitechapel. The memory-detritus of Sidney Kirsh, let us say, heaped in a warehouse: the inscrutable in quest of narrative. But the Tate archive does not advocate that kind of exuberance. Stealth, silence, walls sliding back to expose steel shelves, catacombs of labelled boxes. Buff folders in which the dead write, so tenderly, to the dead. 'God! That I were walking down the river with you now.'

All our biographies, in the end, are so much reprieved paper, sticky-stiff paintbrushes, red-letter bills, invitations to events we didn't attend. The Tate alcoves hide documents from which scholars are invited to tease out future projects: you must be interrogated, postmortem, or you will fade like an inscription in sandstone, erased by the city's indifferent weather.

I travelled to Millbank with a private agenda: did the archive hold any of Hackney's secrets? The curator showed me lists of paintings by amateurs and enthusiasts. The great Dalston Lane paintings of Leon Kossoff were on the other side of the river in secure vaults. He was fortunate that many of his works were in transit when the Momart storage facility went up in flames.

Window Cleaner's Funeral. The title caught my eye. A sequence of four stills in negative. An unrecorded English Hitchcock? Some East London fragment edited out of *The Man Who Knew Too Much*. Gondola cars. Neighbours huddled on the pavement. High-angle viewpoint. The fact that these images are in negative make this event mysterious and unstable. The chemical process, a charm against extinction, is incomplete.

'In the midst of death we are in life,' scribbled the photographer: a certain Nigel Henderson.

That was the name on the file. Night-flyer, cyclist, maker of masks. I knew something of Henderson, he featured in a remaindered book I'd picked up from a shop beneath the Old Street roundabout. *Transition: The London Art Scene in the Fifties.* Henderson (like Ballard) was a friend of Eduardo Paolozzi. He moved to 46 Chisenhale Road in 1945, where he became a compulsive explorer and recorder of East London. And a compiler, as the Tate archive revealed, of shopping lists: 'Candles, notepaper, methylated spirits, matches, cigarettes, washing powder.'

Henderson's ephemera, preserved in cardboard boxes and folders, delivered an unearned intimacy with the artist. I shared the pain when, in wartime, he was separated from his wife, a Bloomsbury person. I skimmed private letters in a flush of shame. The photographic record of pedestrian expeditions from Chisenhale Road proved one thing beyond all doubt: he was ahead of me, every step of the way. And getting it just as wrong, staying resolutely on the blindside of fashion. But shaping an archive to die for: literally. Mortality was the imprimatur of Henderson's practice – which, in life, seemed restless, neurotic, incomplete.

'I just walked and walked and kept staring at everything. And it occurred to me after a little while that I might try carrying a camera with me, but it wasn't that I decided to be a photographer,' he confessed to Judith, his social-worker wife.

He was accumulating the evidence for a book he would never write, a masterwork conceived as abandoned. Local news, for these damaged outsiders, was overwhelmingly present. But there was too much of it.

'Doreen's sharp voice is scolding away on the other side of the street. It was Mrs Horn's turn to sweep the passage mats and scrub the steps . . . There is a rattling clinking subdued rumble of a milk float being pushed along. Very few children about. Now it is wonderfully silent.'

Photographs of bicycles, bookshops, pubs, cafés, market stalls, railway lines. I re-transcribed notes Henderson made for future poems, the book that would synthesize everything he uncovered: walks, patterns, echoes of earlier artists. The fitful material of this archive was an English equivalent of Walter Benjamin's Parisian *Arcades Project*. Both men were exiles, waiting to hazard an uncrossable frontier. They knew there was no end to it, this city of the imagination: layer upon layer, story upon story, until you can crawl no further. You dump the tattered leather case hoping that it will never be found. The roof will lift away. There will be mountains. And fixed stars.

The collection, in its refusal to take shape, its records of overheard conversations, diary jottings, postcards, sketches, was the precursor of the cult of psychogeography. It was also evident that Henderson had stumbled upon Halley's theories of the Hollow Earth: the energy lines to entangle future generations of investigators. Folgate, Hobo Sickert, Stewart Home. They would be suckered into unravelling an infinite nest of conspiracies that always led back to the point from which they started: madness.

Henderson, a troubled man, used to interpreting field patterns during solitary nocturnal flights, stalked Bow, Bethnal Green, Limehouse. He noted the titles of pulp publications seen in the window of S. Lavner, the tobacconist who carried 'the biggest selection of American Comics in East London': *No Mean City (This Book Will Shock You!)*, *Crime Patrol*, *Saint*, *Flirt*, *Naturist*, *Photoplay*, *Blonde Babe*. Using a magnifying glass to pore over every detail of this print, I found just what I was looking for: the book-of-the-film of John Huston's *Moby Dick*. And the worst wig-beard-putty-nose combination in the history of cinema: Orson Welles in *Mr Arkadin* (aka *Confidential Report*).

All my interests and small discoveries had been rehearsed by Nigel Henderson. 'I keep being haunted by Arnold Circus – that monstrous bloom,' he confided to his diary. 'Here we shall have a beautiful civic centre with flowers and bandstand. Be beautiful damn you!' In prompts for poems, drawing on the experience of flying over the flat East Anglian countryside, or long bicycle expeditions, he spoke of 'the weird relics of an abandoned aerodrome, given back to agriculture ... pylons, ancient diesels and wooden mine wagons on the vast rubbish tip'. He explored the A13, the Thames Estuary: 'The mythic sweep of the liners, gantries topped by moiling clouds ... the utility structure pub ... the colour of the river ... the mud like toad skin excrement ... Spew vomit bile ... Scrambled memories of London.'

I became convinced that Henderson, with his maps and over-scribbled charts, the photographs and pictures cut from Surrealist magazines, had located Danny Folgate's leyline: the green passage. 'There is a rampart of bald grasses bonded by rushing spikes,' he wrote, 'running south-east across the roofs of Eastern London towards the Sewage Outfall Works of Barking.' He investigated, by bicycle, and discovered 'a cathedral of black bones where, through pigeon-coloured atmosphere, light percolates ... Agents of Destruction, Agents of Revelation ... Water. Fire. Air.'

Then there was the box of photographic negatives: *Window Cleaner's Funeral*. Henderson stood exactly where I am standing, the same porch, up the steps from Chisenhale Road; to record in four surviving images the funeral of a neighbour. Breaking that taboo. And preserving the evidence.

A thin crowd gathers, across from the pub which is no longer a pub. A convoy of gleaming motors with windows to make the dead man proud: his occupation was his status. Flowers on the roof of the hearse. Dustbin lids. Iron railings. At the east end of the street, a tall crane swings into view: the blitzed city rebuilding itself, anticipating the future of canalside apartments, Olympic parks.

A child, two doors down, notices the photographer, turns to face him; it's over, the illusion of invisibility. 'A vigorous movement,' Henderson noted, 'a sudden emotion and I feel as if I'm trembling on the brink of life and death.'

The positive prints, if they were made, eluded the Tate Britain archive. Leaving the integrity of the original episode unviolated.

I was putting the letters, catalogues, fetishistic mask photographs back into their folders, when I noticed a bizarre misspelling: 'collo-quay of Gulls'. Was it a mistake? Henderson was making one of his lists. 'A plaint of curlews. A scold of rooks. A scandal of star-lings.' Why was the word 'Gulls' capitalized? Still under the influence of Hobo Sickert's Masonic conspiracies, I thought of Sir William Withey Gull, a figure who haunted my first novel. One of the Gulls of Thorpe-le-Soken. William's father was a wharfinger who shipped agricultural produce to London. He navigated the back rivers. He died of cholera.

Nigel Henderson, at the finish, left Bow. Brian Catling came across him, once or twice, a civilized and reserved tutor at the Norwich School of Art. A man whose career, despite his artistic and social connections, the respect in which he was held by his peers, never quite happened.

Judith Stephen, Henderson's wife, was a relation of Virginia Woolf – and of the unfortunate J. K. Stephen, misogynistic verse-maker and Ripper suspect. A man who died in the same Northampton asylum as a far greater poet, John Clare. Judith inherited a house, at the water's edge, not far from Colchester (where her husband sometimes taught). The house was at Thorpe-le-Soken. And the reason I recognized the final photograph in the green folder was that I had taken it, or a version of it, when I was researching William Gull and his antecedents. Henderson died in the Essex village where I began my attempt at writing fiction. Or allowing books to take their shape from accidental discoveries, random images laid out, in any order, on a table.

The sequence of negatives that made up the record of the Chisenhale Road funeral led directly into the single positive print: a dark house by a muddy creek, a tipped boat, a bare tree. *The landscape I had been invited to memorize in the Lincoln gallery.* The picture I would never be able to forget.

There was also a letter in Henderson's Thorpe-le-Soken file. 'I have the good fortune to live in a house which has grown out of a barn which straddles a dyke which is part of a containing system of creeks, man-made cuttings and quays in advance decay.'

The address is Gull's address: Landermere Quay.

The place coded within Henderson's curious formulation: 'collo-quay'. The photograph, in its luminous darkness, its stately menace, could have been a frame from something by the Quay Twins. My daughter Farne worked on the production side of a television version of Purcell's opera, *Dido and Aeneas*, which had been shot in the strange mansion where the Twins set one of their films, *Institute Benjamenta*. Farne's new home, on the other side of the railway from Chisenhale Road, was in perfect alignment with the Henderson ley. And, beyond that, with a churchyard in which I recorded the names of sea captains who made enough money to set themselves up in Tredegar Square. And on again, in a fugue of disbelief, past the old snooker club where another pair of near-rhyming twins, the Krays, got their start in the compulsory life-assurance business: the profession of violence. To a grassy mound in an obscure block of council flats where, seventeen years earlier, the painter Gavin Jones excavated a wartime bunker, his secret studio and labyrinth, storehouse of snail paintings, and entrance to the underworld.

Golden Lane

Stewart Home had been beaten with a brick. Or so I'd heard from a very unreliable source, a Frenchman in transit to Los Angeles, where he had managed to parlay a casual interest in the arts, connections with literary festivals that never quite happened, into an appointment as Cultural Attaché to the Slide Area. He was still breathing, Stewart. Discharged from hospital and floating free, scurrying around town in search of a roof for the night. He could carry a few dents, his skull was strong and many miles of furious cycling, distributing Neoist leaflets, Situationist squibs, acid satires and porn-fuelled polemics, kept him fit. If marginally bow-legged. The whole episode would be recycled as fiction, within hours, if it did not already read like a paragraph he had penned many times before. Self-cannibalism, Home insisted, was the lynchpin of any career dedicated to that impossible proposition: paid publication. (With a modicum of fame, fortune and the love of numerous good women thrown in. A London perch from which to operate.)

Just when I needed him, his particular and peculiar expertise in the back story of Hackney's subterranean sects, Stewart went off radar. He had taken the decision, after the attack by a gang of street kids from the estate where he had lived with a previous partner, to shift his operations to the virtual world by way of a dozen or so websites. All dedicated to sustaining the myth of the alternative way: existence as a nest of interlinked scams and conspiracies for which he, Stewart Home, held the golden key.

Shortly before my computer gave out and its internet connection vanished, scrambled by the effort of decoding a communication from Danny Folgate, I received an email from the stewarthomesociety, detailing the assault the former skinhead had suffered.

I was beaten about the face and head with concrete and bricks and kicked a lot by a gang of about twenty teenagers who were masked up. They were trying to mug my mobile phone but they didn't get it. I kept getting up no matter how many times I was hit. I know who the gang are. I also know where they do and don't like going, so I escaped by way of Old Bethnal Green Road, then towards Charles Dickens House (where they prefer to avoid other gangs and parents). From there I went down to Bethnal Green Road, coming out by Tesco.

I'm okay. The hospital said it may take several weeks to settle down, but there are no serious problems, and the short term memory loss I've got should clear up (so hopefully when I next see you I'll be able to recognize you!).

What really annoyed me is that the assault took place right outside the Million Miles An Hour Gallery in Old Bethnal Green Road and people I know saw exactly what was going on and did nothing. There were fifty to a hundred people in the gallery, if someone had shouted and they'd come running out, I would have been hit a lot less.

The people in the gallery claim to have been too stoned to know if it was an actual attack or a performance act I had arranged. 'Brilliant, Stewart,' they said. 'So convincing, the blood and stuff. And the way you kept crawling down the road with cars skidding around. *Slow Death*, *Pure Mania* or what?' One guy said he did suspect something unpleasant might be happening but couldn't help, he was deaf.

The kids who did this are sick. They love masking up. When my son was a bit more than a year old they threw a lighted firework in his buggy. I was really sad seeing the way a lot of the adult Bengalis on the estate were afraid of them, but I was never slow about telling them to piss off when they were being a nuisance on the stairwell of my block.

Many years of wandering London, constructing energy charts of the points at which songlines, spirals, vortices, drovers' ways, pilgrim paths, lost rivers, intersect with the sacred geometry of leys, churches, markets, conical mounds, carried me to one place: the Golden Lane Estate on the edge of the Barbican. Call it the golden section of the psychogeographers, a Corbusier-influenced utopian development risen from a blitzed wasteground and snatched away from public ownership by the alchemy of freemarket capital. The property values of these slender, functional, ultimately urban flats were leaping by the month. So much so that Chris Petit, whose late career was about denial and abdication, moving house in preference to launching a new project, nominated Golden Lane as the perfect hideaway for an era of decommissioning and invisibility. Like Home he experimented with parenting, using a lively child as a good reason to re-explore the banks of the Thames, the alleys and shady squares of a deserted weekend city. Not-writing, not-filming, he asserted, was a serious vocation. The daily passage between nursery school and Waitrose brought with it a new engagement with place, with working mothers, freelance chemical entrepreneurs tugging pit bulls – and the area of London where Shakespeare lodged, John Milton was married and William Blake buried.

'Daytime television,' Petit said, 'is the final frontier. Our inland empire. There is no finer technology for discovering how the margins have disappeared and everything has collapsed into the middle.'

The breakthrough came, he explained on the phone (now his principal art practice), when he bumped into Stewart Home at the security gate. They barely recognized one another. Stewart's short-term memory was malfunctioning and Chris had never seen Home without his strobing Bacofoil suit. Stewart courteously held the door open for the Petit buggy. Both men wondered, in that frozen instant, if it were feasible for two writers to coexist on the same floor of the same block. Especially when Home's unit, owned by a new partner, an art curator, had more space, a study beneath the stairs.

The one person who rang Stewart to express sympathy, after

the gallery attack, was the writer Tom McCarthy. He'd been at the show but was in deep conversation when the bricking took place. He knew nothing about it, until it became the major talking point at the launch. Another Home triumph, was the general verdict, violence and art in equilibrium. Better than a kung fu DVD. McCarthy also lived in Golden Lane, in a different block, looking west. When Stewart was kicked out by his lover, he stayed from time to time with McCarthy. And he repaid the favour by granting McCarthy a pseudonym in his novel *Memphis Underground*. He called him 'Rob McGlynn'.

'When I broke cover, I walked from King's Cross to Rob McGlynn's flat on the Golden Lane Estate between Old Street and the Barbican. We sat on Rob's balcony looking west towards Centrepoint and the Post Office Tower. We drank beer, premium bottled lager from Belgium. McGlynn had only been living in this pad for six months, and he absolutely loved the view.'

I sat with Petit, trying to make sense of all this, the way moving flats replaced the writing of books as the preferred method for sublimating creativity and taking a stand against what the Boas Society called the 'Griffin'. Which would be: City Hall, corporate developers, Hackney Council, commissioning editors, online application forms, all politicians and professional bullshitters hiding behind Olympic quangos with fancy initials. Chris was glugging Belgian lager while languidly keying up weather images on his laptop, sampling extracts of films long deleted from the catalogue.

He gave me, in a weary but beautifully modulated voice that should have earned him a fortune doing adverts for expensive German motors, a taped interview describing his personal 'northwest passage'; a trajectory that led, flat to villa to flat to impossible mansion, to the Golden Lane Estate. Each new property was a book, film or wife. The point of Petit's autobiography in juggled mortgages was that he never lived in Hackney. The closest he came was an industrial unit with subsidence problems in Fairbridge Road,

N19, near the source, on the lower slopes of Highgate Hill, of the legendary Hackney Brook. Behind metal shutters, we cut a number of films in this minimalist bunker which bore an uncanny resemblance to the set of *Macbeth*, in an acclaimed production, supposedly taking place in a Russian field hospital or slaughter-house-kitchen.

Petit and Home: their lives and movements were mirror images, coinciding at this significant moment in the same block of flats. I would have to save the four-hour Petit tape, fascinating though it was, for another occasion: too much daylight, not enough Hackney. Hampstead, Primrose Hill, Willesden Green, Golders Green, Archway, Bloomsbury: deep cultural traces, but not the story I was after. Home, on the other hand, never really got away; he circled the borough or found himself mired in the thick of it. But how would I contact him?

Did he share Petit's vision of a covert existence, writer as spook, third-columnist, always relocating before his cover is blown? The essence of a rather noble career lay in Chris's ability to subvert the possibility of worldly success by tangling himself, yet again, in the legal and financial complexities of another compulsive flit.

'Re property,' he began, as I settled down with a large mug of coffee, 'I used it as a way of escaping numerous cul-de-sacs in my life. I worked out pretty early on that I was not hoping to get invited into the warm bath of the enfranchised. Looking back, I should have invested all my efforts in property rather than books or films. You don't have to pitch property and you don't have some arsehole reviewing it afterwards in the *Guardian*. Where I can hardly recall my Irish book, *The Psalm Killer*, I still retain very strong memories of Haverstock Hill where much of it was written. So, in their way, the itinerary of the properties becomes a record of more tangible achievement than any of the works I have published.'

When I transcribed the Petit tapes, I found another provocative argument: he saw cinema as infected topography. James Stewart, the Second War bomber pilot, brought Anthony Mann Westerns to ground in East Anglia. A rather crude mural of Audrey Hepburn invoked Chatham. London locations, once caught on celluloid, would never be so innocent again.

Julie Christie came to Hackney in the 1970s or early 1980s. She had a house in Stoke Newington. Someone I knew went round there. And Warren Beatty turned up to collect his jackets. He'd split up with Christie by then. There was this wardrobe which was full of replicas of the same jacket, a suede jacket like the one he had worn in Shampoo.

She bought property in Wales. And now has a house somewhere on the southern edge of Hackney, Bethnal Green. I was always curious about her. If you look at those English actors from the 1960s, the big stars, you wonder how she sustained it, in terms of income. She probably didn't get that much for Doctor Zhivago or Darling. Actors then were like footballers at a later period. Julie would probably have made just enough to stay ahead.

I remember when I was about to direct my first feature film, Radio On, I thought: it makes sense to try and find somewhere bigger now, while I can still technically claim an income. It was a question of scrutinizing the map. I was never any good at the inner-city thing. I was a child of the suburbs.

I worked out later that I was stuck in that northwest passage of London for about twenty years, the idea of moving inwards never occurred to me. I looked at Finsbury Park, we checked out a house there. The house wasn't in great nick. I lost my nerve. I thought, 'I've known people in Finsbury Park and I really don't like it. They're never going to get away. Finsbury Park is a black hole.'

If I had the instinct for literature and film that I have for property, I would be doing quite well. I could have borrowed against my house in Willesden Green to buy something else. It never occurred to me. I almost preferred the state of renting. You're liberated from the tyranny of taste. It never occurred to me to speculate. I figured I was pretty good at reading the market, slightly ahead of the game. I could guess the right time to sell.

Fairbridge Road, near Archway, was slightly botched. It was dangerously close to your Hackney force field. I could have crossed the border and vanished. The idea was to be able to use the property as a kind of studio, a factory, to produce a lot more work. But, in a way, I was already stuck with writing those fucking books, the thrillers. The thing I didn't realize, until I moved there, was that I'd been quite happy working that northwest passage. I knew where everything was, left and right.

Fairbridge Road didn't work. Due north you had Crouch End, at the top of the hill. Which I always hated. Finsbury Park, down at the bottom: hated. The Holloway Road was Aguirre, Wrath of God. *The ever-burning Styx. You had to do two turns across raging traffic, which I became quite efficient at.*

The other thing that dictated my move was that my son, Robert, was in school at Hampstead. I used to see that old Whitechapel writer, Emanuel Litvinoff, at the school gates. He was well into his seventies by then and had this young boy. I think I first noticed him when he'd fallen out with us, after his experience in our film, The Cardinal and the Corpse. *The notion that an author of his stature could be associated with lowlifes, street poets, gangsters like Lambrianou.*

I thought, 'What the fuck is he doing here?' He never acknowledged me. He stood there looking extremely sour. I don't know where he lived.

I worked out that my standard of living, although I was earning quite a lot, because my agent had got me on good contracts for these thrillers, was quite modest. I was doing pretty well on paper. The property port-folio didn't look too bad, but I was carrying a massive debt. My standard of living took a dive as soon as I moved east. The more money I earned, the worse it got. By the time I'd paid for Robert and the general running of things, there wasn't much left. I think I had about £8,000 a year to live off. The whole thing about debt became the legacy of the Thatcher era.

What I thought about Fairbridge Road, that it was a mental space, turned out very differently. As a physical space it was never practical. Everything for me has been conditioned by my upbringing in what Robin Cook would call 'army quarters'.

Now on the Golden Lane Estate, there is no storage, no space at all. The work has to arrange itself around the property. The days of constructing complex thrillers are over. The nature of my work will change radically, it already has. Whatever I do has to squeeze into the gap between school delivery and school pick-up, the daily excursion to Waitrose.

Property got easier as my career got harder. I realized – which had never been part of my intention – that property always fed into career. By the time we arrived at Golden Lane, fiction and documentary were absolutely intertwined. I was inhabiting out-takes from The Falconer, *our film about Peter Whitehead. I was meeting projections at every turn. Thank god the one who turned up on my doorstep was Stewart Home and not Whitehead himself.*

Stewart was pushing his bike out of the front door and he, very politely, held it open for the buggy. I thought: 'Stewart Home!' He was a bit shocked as well. You could see him saying to himself, 'Can this corridor take more than one writer?' But, like me, he's moving away from print and on to the net.

Part of coming to Golden Lane was about reducing the outgoings. The thinking was: 'How much can you owe?' Now it is more like, 'What is the least amount of money one needs to keep the game in play?'

I have thought about shifting entirely into property. We're going to have to sit here for a while. If I bought another property in this block, I could still claim this place, for something like four years, as my main residence. And so reduce capital gains.

I think Peter Whitehead's canniest move, apart from acquiring a bunker in Clerkenwell, was that he knew how to use his social connections. He always retained his film footage through those years shooting documentaries or making pop promos. He's able to present himself as the English Pennebaker. He shot Pink Floyd. It's the nostalgia card. Everyone has shot a Rolling Stones film that couldn't be released. So Charlie is my Darling puts Whitehead on a par with Robert Frank and Cocksucker Blues. Nobody has seen either of them. You are forced to assume that there is a controversial quality to the material.

Of course Whitehead had his Julie Christie moment in Tonite Let's All Make Love in London. *Did they have a thing? Must have, I suppose. Standard Whitehead practice.*

Marc Karlin wasn't that different from Whitehead, when you think about it. He can do French. Karlin's mother was French. Like Whitehead he was bilingual. Didn't Whitehead translate Alphaville? *Karlin had his Paris connections too, he was certainly close to Chris Marker.*

Marc was quite a political film-maker. At the beginning he was involved with various film co-operatives. He made things like Nightcleaners. *His work came out of the spirit of '68. I didn't really know him at that time. Strikes were always being organized. Marc had the reputation of being a political speaker and a firebrand.* Time Out, *where I was film editor, was looked on as rather commercial and suspect. It wasn't until we started cutting* The Falconer *in Marc's place, off Goodge Street, that I got to appreciate him.*

I think he founded the magazine Vertigo. *He picked up the funding to run that basement and the suite of cutting rooms. I don't think he owned the property. But, on the other hand, he – or his partner – or both together – owned a very fine house, just up from the Arsenal Football Stadium. Which is also, I'm pretty sure, where Julie Christie used to have a property. After she left Stoke Newington.*

Marc was a passionate Arsenal supporter, which didn't quite sit with the man I knew.

There was a strong, radical, puritanical tradition in English film-making. It was vociferous and influential, out of all proportion to its achievements. Some of those people ended up with considerable power in the early days of Channel 4. I remember Radio On *being regarded with suspicion, as being insufficiently political. To the point where Channel 4 had the rights to show it and never did. I'm afraid that if it was a choice between programmatic political cinema and Hammer horror, there wouldn't be any contest. Break out the fangs, bring back Fu-Manchu.*

Marc represented a passing spirit. He struggled on, heroically, beyond his time, in the face of changing values. Everything those people had worked for, people like Keith Griffiths and John Ellis, vanished before their eyes. When push came to shove, Channel 4 were pretty quick to sell out. To the point where, twenty years later, there is no independent film production.

The problem I had with Marc, and the problem with English cinema, was that if you positioned yourself, consciously, within the system, you were fucked. Every whichway. If you took a position, on the side of

Puttnam and Alan Parker, the other extreme, you were done for, finished.

I remember the whole build-up to Marc Karlin's death. He had to fly to America. Which he was very nervous about. And he had to give up smoking. The final act in the cutting room, I look back on less as something that really happened and more as a piece of fiction. Marc was obsessed with the idea of making a film about Milton. An English writer in the grand puritan tradition. I don't know if that was the reason for his trip to America. During the time he was over there, and indeed coming back safely, some Swiss airliner crashed, just off the American coast.

Marc had one heart attack already. There was talk of an operation, they weren't sure he was strong enough. I suppose, looking back, he must have been taking a special interest, as he leant in the doorway, in our footage of Whitehead in hospital, with those massive scar tracks, after his quadruple bypass. Marc battled heroically to give up smoking. I remember seeing him through the window that morning. He was looking pretty good, not bad at all. I think it was the sandwich from Goodge Street that killed him.

They did everything in the way of resurrection, kiss of life, electric-shock pads, the lot. It was pretty plain to me, Marc was dead. And he was declared dead in the ambulance. I thought, when I saw them carry him out, 'He's not coming back.'

The thing I felt sorriest about, for Marc, was that having lived a certain kind of life you get stitched up with a Hampstead Church of England funeral. It was quite hard to find a slot, but they had Marc buried in Highgate Cemetery. Big turn out. Nigel Fountain gave the funeral oration, pretty well. The vicar made a hash of it. If you're on the left in English cultural life, at least you can rely on a decent send off.

Stewart Home

Stewart Home, after the bricking, his encounter with the negative youth affiliation in Bethnal Green, went to ground. In a condition of mimicked catalepsy, writing in his sleep, parodying the mannerisms of the French nouveau roman, he produced a documentary fiction called *Memphis Underground*. Which I took to be a blatant signalling of the fact that he too was preoccupied with Hollow Earth metaphors. Home may well, in a literal sense, have gone under; hiding out, with a complimentary case of 100 Pipers whisky, in some cellar, crypt, railway tunnel. Memphis was a cult centre for the worship of Ptah, its creator-god, who was frequently represented as a mummified man. On his release from hospital, dark glasses over swathes of flapping bandage, Stewart looked more like the Invisible Man than a Hammer Films mummy. And he was just as tricky to locate.

I pored over *Memphis Underground* searching for clues. Home had certainly been influenced by the microclimate of Golden Lane, the close proximity of Chris Petit. 'Pauline had been at some arts conference and a lot of people there had been talking about how rising property prices were making it impossible for them to pursue their cultural practice in London.'

'Housing and gentrification,' he confessed, 'have been dominant themes within my fiction from the mid 1980s onwards.'

I walked over to the bookshop in Broadway Market to see if I could find anything by Home's friend Tom McCarthy. Maybe his novels would suggest another direction from which to close in on the missing prankster. The blurb for a paperback called *Remainder* said: 'The hero spends his time and money obsessively reconstructing and re-enacting vaguely remembered scenes and situations from his past.' Post-bricking amnesia? Memory loss was a popular trope. Paul Auster, Christopher Nolan with *Memento*, they were all doing it. My rose-red Empire was built around absence, holes in the narrative, faked resolution. Characters had to wear large labels so that I would recognize them when they reappeared.

Biographical notes, supplied by McCarthy, stated that he was 'General Secretary of the International Necronautical Society (INS), a semi-fictitious avant-garde network'. Such playful associa-. tions were part of the cloud of unknowing that hung over the threatened borough of Hackney. Old-time Trots, cells splintering, regrouping: the permanently excluded in quest of a new pub from which they could be honourably barred. Spot the spook. Is it the guy emptying the ashtrays? Or the girl in the beret with a hardback novel? Every drinking school contains at least one person sponsored by the security services. The Exploding Galaxy in Balls Pond Road: the bust was a publicity stunt, column inches in the *International Times* to promote a psychedelic gig. Neo-Templars. Retro-Nazis. Red Army Faction. London Psychogeographical Association. The Hackney Hardcore staking out the Groucho Club. The Mapledene Mob. The Boas Society. Conradian echoes of betrayal and conspiracy, Poles and Russians: plots hatched in massage parlours. Bomb carriers, bomb victims. Wherever a radical group met, in Stoke Newington pub or Petherton Road basement, I was else-where. But Stewart Home, if not physically present, was fully informed and writing up the minutes as a best-selling Finnish paperback. A self-published booklet.

Which was the pseudonym, McGlynn or McCarthy? Didn't McCarthy sound more like Home's invention? An obvious nod in the direction of sweaty Joe, the red-baiting senator from Wisconsin? The man who did more than any other to boost the post-war British film industry, by expelling Joseph Losey, Jules Dassin, Lionel Stander and all those other chic-left technicians, producers, actors – and making sure that, so long as they changed their names, they got jobs at Shepperton, Pinewood and Sherwood Forest.

Thinking logically, I decided that the only way to find Home was to abandon logic. In any given day, putting in my standard fifteen miles (the Dickensian measure), I would run across Stewart at least twice. As I moved slowly and steadily on foot, he serviced a much broader range of social contacts – Janet Street-Porter to acid-casualty headbangers – on his £600 bicycle. *Memphis Underground* was punk Defoe, a record of journeys through Britain undertaken by a double-man, novelist and intelligencer. Home breakfasted with vagrants, dropped in on television-production companies, blagged hospitality, delivered lectures, attempted to collect debts from a trashed squat, slept with past and future partners, attended a book launch, insulted Will Self and flew off in the general direction of Hamburg. Where all my quests dissolved into another viewing of *The American Friend*, the Wim Wenders version of a Patricia Highsmith novel: a re-recorded tape without an ending, wiped by a European Cup match forgotten by everyone except Charlie Velasco. Who was actually there. And who owned, as did Chris Petit, the striking front-of-house poster for the cult 1977 film.

Stewart Home emerged from London's south-eastern suburbs, as Petit – in childhood – occupied military quarters on the north-west rim. Home's karma was to be sucked in towards Hackney. Petit's entire career was based around strategies for avoiding this effect. If I set off down Danny Folgate's leyline, in the general direction of what Stewart referred to as 'Hither Scotland' (the mouth of the Blackwall Tunnel), I was convinced that I would encounter the vanished writer and his bicycle. I might also discover the point of access to the underworld Home had spent so many years celebrating. He would be dossing down with his friend Fabian, who was thought by many to be not only the instigator of the psychogeographic coup, but the poorly paid scribe who actually composed many of Stewart's books and pamphlets.

I reach the towpath to discover that a thirty-yard section of the fence has been knitted with alternating sections of red and blue ribbon. Criss-cross columns that remind me of the runes on Hobo

Sickert's Grail paper. Of late, unreadable messages have been sprouting all over Hackney: woven into black mesh, sprayed over flyers for garage bands whose energies were expended in deciding on a meaningless name.

There is a young Japanese woman at work. Or perhaps Chinese, Cambodian, Vietnamese. She's happy for me to photograph the work in progress, she bows.

'Are they words?'

'You can read. Yes.'

'From which side?'

'As you choose.'

The project, she explained, involved weaving a new section each day, east from Mare Street, past the bus stop, as far as Broadway Market. The ribbons, the pattern of red-and-blue crosses, spelt out words, sentences, if not a message.

I climbed on to the road, to study the effect from her side. I couldn't crack the code. If anything it seemed to say: GO HOME.

On the far bank, alongside the gas-holders, a naked woman draped in furs is posing for a fashion shoot.

Coming up the slope into Victoria Park at Canal Gate, I intended to orientate myself by the smashed dog statues on their twin brick plinths, but something caught my eye. A sequence of black crosses painted in Japanese calligraphy, like the woody cover of a book of poems by Gary Snyder, down the flaking bark of a slender silver birch. Haiku, eco-warning or map reference, I was too ignorant or slow-witted to discover. But the figure emerging from a neat pup tent in the shrubbery I did recognize: Stewart Home.

He had become a sort of honorary Pole, kipping with the migrant labourers in their covert camp. Award-winning local parks, cropped, planted and improved, also hosted the sleeping-bags of rough sleepers. Home, as ever, was ahead of the trend: everything he needed in a rucksack, a slim laptop in place of a cumbersome library of rare paperbacks, dull blocks of German philosophy.

The café by the lake was shut. We adjourned to Lauriston Road

– where, for the price of a full English with regular coffee refills, Stewart recorded the story of his relationship with Hackney. There was a new Julie Christie photograph beside the mirror. I barely recognized her. Which was appropriate. The film in question, long after my time, cast her as a woman triumphing over Alzheimer's disease: the country from which nobody comes back. Her undoubted beauty looked as if it belonged to somebody else. She was two years older than I was. And she was still in the game.

The first time I remember coming to Hackney would have been late 1970s, to see punk rock concerts. Mainly Rock Against Racism. There was a big thing in Victoria Park. I went on the march. There was one band I used to see called Crisis. I remember seeing them at Hackney Town Hall. I didn't agree with their politics, one of them was in the Socialist Workers Party. He subsequently joined the National Front.

The oddest people used to turn up at the Town Hall. Rocking Pete the Teddy Boy for some reason came to the punk gig. He said, 'I've just got my card, man, I've joined.' In the meantime, you've got Tony, the bass player – illiterate and in the SWP – being taught to read and write at the age of eighteen by some middle-class member who was a schoolteacher.

The other Hackney thing was pubs. Places like the Rochester Castle – which kept changing its name. I considered moving up to Stoke Newington in about 1980. Then I thought, 'God, I don't want to live here.' It looked pretty rough. I ended up moving in the mid 1980s. I wasn't there that long.

There was a whole squat scene, like the squats around the east side of Victoria Park, Cadogan Terrace. They'd been squatted in the 1970s. You had the Hackney Co-operative coming out of the squats. I ended up getting Hackney Co-operative and Hackney October Community Housing. Just to find somewhere cheap to live. It was about £4.50 a week. If you were signing on, as I was, you got £2 back. So long as you did a certain number of hours' work with the co-op. It was pretty good. This was Manor Road, Stoke Newington.

What you saw happening, from the late 1970s, the squats were being licensed and were becoming, in effect, co-ops. The council could control the properties. When they had anarchist squatters, they had to get a court order. It was a definite long-term strategy to license squats, to break up elements of the movement, destroy it. Get people used to the idea that they require a licence for six months or two years. And then, when the licence ends, it might be renewed. Or they might be moved on. That was how the really strong squatting movement of the 1970s got wiped out.

I was spending as much time in Hackney as anywhere else. I was seeing people in squats and housing co-ops. It was often hard to tell which was which, they looked pretty rough. I was in the October Community Housing in Stoke Newington. There was a financial crisis. I said, 'What's going on?' They said, 'We're having trouble. There's not enough money coming in.' I said, 'Let me have a look at the books.' I said, 'This is a list of people who haven't paid their rent for more than three years. Why haven't they paid? Isn't it odd that every one of these people is a junkie? And you believe them when they say their housing benefit hasn't been paid?' They go, 'Well, you can't suggest they're lying?' Schoolteacher types! I say, 'Of course they're lying. They're bound to be lying, they're junkies.'

I said: 'I'm going to phone up the council to ask what they think. We need to know whether these people are receiving their benefits.' The council told me that the benefits had all been paid. That got me a bad reputation in the co-op, my fascist attitude.

I was there less than a year. I couldn't be bothered with the arguments. I thought this was nonsense. We're going to lose our houses. They are going bankrupt because no one can run them. Nobody can make these characters do their two hours' work to get their two quid back. My attitude was: 'Go and squat.' I moved to another co-op. Having typing skills I could always do one day a week to earn my keep. I realized I was never going to get a council place in Hackney, which was my long-term aim. The list was too long. The only place you stood a chance, as a single individual, was Tower Hamlets.

The politics were mainly SWP, a lot of middle-class types who were not in the real world. In Stoke Newington you had, at the same time, the core of the anarchist faction of the early Class War group and elements who were into more ultra-left positions than Class War. Ian Bone was up there a few times. We all used to drink in the Rochester Castle. You had a lot of punk bands playing up there in the late 1970s. The anarchists and the Trots would nod to each other. To get away from all of them, I would go up to the Birdcage.

That was one side of Hackney, the politics. The other side was the Hackney Hell Crew, a notorious punk rock band. They had a massive property in Victoria Park Road. There was a guy who lived there called Andy Martin who had this band, the Apostles, with constantly changing line-up. I sold him a 1970 Fender Precision I'd acquired at one point. It took years to get the money. I used to go round every week to collect five quid, two quid, whatever. Which meant I had the misfortune of meeting the Hackney Hell Crew. They were the most out-of-it, drugged-up bunch of all the punks in Hackney in the 1980s. You'd knock on the door and eventually get someone to answer it. There would be some character playing the electric guitar, rather badly, to a record. His eyes out on plates. People literally pissing out of the windows. The toilets didn't work in that house, bunged up with laundry, shit, needles, takeaways.

'I have to see Andy.'

You'd walk past mounds of dogshit, junkies glued out of their minds. People sleeping in hallways and on landings. The guy at the top of the house, Andy Martin, lived an absurdly austere life. He'd been in a mental institution. He'd been involved with fascism. Maybe not as a member, but on some kind of kick. One of their early songs was called 'Fucking Queer'. 'In 1976 we were out on Clapham Common and beat up the queers. They are all fucking queers, they are all fucking queers.' It goes on: 'And then one day I met a strange lad and fell in love with him. I am a fucking queer, I am a fucking queer.' Ha!

The band was pretty schizophrenic. Andy never quite fitted that anarcho scene. He was working class. Coming out of this far-right homophobic background. Then discovering he was gay!

After that period he was living in a co-op in Brougham Road, by Broadway Market. I was still trying to get the money he owed me for the Fender Precision bass. I got it off some prog rock band a few years earlier.

Having to deal with the Hackney Hell Crew, going to Brougham Road, I was meeting the most bizarre people. Andy was in the house with another guy from the Apostles. I met this character, the Revd Roy Divine. I called him 'The Racist Vicar of Bethnal Green'. It turned out he had the church on the corner where I was living, Grove Road. He was the brother of George Divine, the Scottish country and western singer. He's absolutely huge in Scotland and nowhere else. This mad racist, the Revd Divine, was webbed up with the punk band, the Apostles.

I don't know where they met him. Andy Martin is now really into Chinese culture. The Revd Divine was with some woman who was obviously having immense problems. She was a cashier at a supermarket in Whitechapel. Ha!

Broadway Market, back in 1985, was unrecognizable from what it is now. Did you know that it's got one of the best video stores in London? The whole of Hackney is unrecognizable. After every shift in the property market you get new arrivals. The Angry Brigade were in Amhurst Road. I know one of them, John Barker. He still lives in Hackney, a really nice guy. I met him at a May Day party in 1985. In Bow. He thought I was a member of Class War – which I wasn't. He was rather rude to me. When he discovered I wasn't a member, he was less rude. He's been around a long time. He doesn't want to talk about the Angry Brigade. He's never talked to me about that. They have an agreement. He admires his younger self for doing what he did, but at the same time he recognizes that it was a political mistake. Which would be my feeling. A different era. You could see why they got to the point where they did the bombings. They were targeting property, not people. John is just a nice guy. I think he has a book coming out from a French publisher.

The London Psychogeographical Association had its mailing address at Centerprise Bookshop in Kingsland Road, but it was much more based on the Isle of Dogs. We all had multiple identities, which we shared around, numerous aliases. Fabian, who was also known as Richard Essex, ran it. He had worked in a bookshop in Islington. He moved down to the Isle of Dogs. I met him around '79. He's been there ever since – apart from a short period in the New North Road.

Richard Essex, as a matter of convenience, used Centerprise. When I was in the October Housing Co-op we had our meetings there, this weird community bookshop. Richard could have got an address from the Freedom Bookshop in Whitechapel but he wanted to steer clear of the anarchist association. You might get purged if you weren't a pure Kropotkinist anarchist. Centerprise was a little less sectarian.

The London Psychogeographical Association Newsletter was distributed to my mailing list, about 2,000 copies. It was easy to get rid of stuff then. Compendium Bookshop was still going in Camden Town. Centerprise was tied in to a whole network. A network that involved news of housing, flats, squats. Which brings me to the Beck Road thing and Genesis P-Orridge.

Genesis was very insecure. I made it clear I thought what he did wasn't fantastic. He was more of a conduit for ideas than anything else. A whole series of people lived in 50 Beck Road. When Genesis and Cosey Fanni Tutti moved in, some of the others got an advance from a record company and moved out. Genesis set up the Templar Psychic Youth. He moved some of his followers into Beck Road and provided free lodging if they spent eighty hours a week working in his mail-order business. Genesis would get mad because I put up a Church of Sub-Genius poster. He'd rip it down because the acolytes were not supposed to be into anyone but him. He's now had a sex-change operation.

A guy called Nick Abrahams moved in. Nick is notorious. He's a really great video-maker. He's done a lot of camera-work and editing for Jeremy Deller. Nick moved to 50 Beck Road with this guy, Barry Smith. They opened the cupboard under the stairs and pulled out a hand grenade. They thought, 'Oh yeah, whatever.' And threw all these carrier bags on top of it. They said, 'It's just a replica.'

Years later, the couple who ran the Chef's House, art dealers down in Shoreditch, bought the house. They found the hand grenade. It had been there since Genesis. They called the bomb squad. The grenade turned out to be live. It was detonated in a controlled explosion. There was a dentist's chair. Stacks of records in the basement, waiting to be shipped out. 'The Death Factory' was what they called it. Another weird side of Hackney.

*

I don't know how people live in London any more. When I was in the October Co-op, living in Manor Road, it was a massive house. I was waiting to join the co-op, so I said I'd go into this house that a girl who was schizophrenic was living in. She'd set fire to part of the house. I was desperate to find somewhere, anywhere. She did paintings that were just dots. She flipped out on an LSD trip. She didn't understand about electricity. You'd explain to her about power stations and power lines and she'd go, like, 'Wow, that's amazing!'

She flipped out and vanished before I moved in. So I was living in this house that she had wrecked. The toilets weren't working. There wasn't any water. This was when you still had public toilets in front of the graveyard, Abney Park. It goes nuts up there at Hallowe'en: Satanists, gays, cottaging. You'd see cops waiting at the gates.

For the first two months I lived in that house if I wanted a shit I literally had to walk down to the graveyard toilets. Now you couldn't do that, the toilets are not there. You'd have to shit in the street or in the bushes, taking your chances with the gays.

There had been other people in the house, but when this girl freaked out they all left. Later they drifted back. For a time I had this huge house to myself. For months. One of the drifters, this guy Brian, wanted to save money. There was no bill on the gas, although the electricity was metered. Nobody had done anything about the utilities, they would just be on. People wouldn't be paying for them. Brian was going nuts if we boiled the kettle. He was trying to save up money to pay the deposit he needed. His whole life was based around getting a mortgage on a house in Brockley. We all thought this was pretty hilarious. Who wants to go to Brockley? Brian would go absolutely bonkers if he saw us using the electric kettle, we could use gas for free. He was right. That's the saddest thing. We should all have been sticking to gas.

I used to go to those funny local shops, like Jewish delicatessens. I'd be looking at stuff and thinking, 'What on earth is that?' I don't even know what I'm looking at. It costs 30p, I wonder what it is?

Gentrification was already coming in, 1985, although Stoke Newington was still very rough. You could see the health-food freaks, the twee book-

shops, the retro-clothes boutiques establishing a presence on Church Street. The feta-cheese footprint. Ha!

When the monologue was suspended, Home in mid-rant, by the café man sweeping away our plates and mugs, dusting the Christie portraits, I posed the same questions I put to all the interviewees.

Stewart knew nothing about Roland Camberton. No paperback version of *Rain on the Pavements* had found its way to Hackney Wick. But he would mention the title to his mate John King, author of *The Football Factory*, a man who was performing a useful service by reissuing classic London fiction in well-made editions. First they would have to locate Camberton's heirs or executors.

The Four Aces Club in Dalston Lane was before Stewart's time and he had avoided its successor, Labyrinth. I spoke about rumours of secular shamanism, ecstatic drumming, initiates led through candlelit tunnels into the second level of the Hollow Earth. He shook his head, sadly, but scribbled a note on the back of a menu. My 'Mundus Subterraneus' material, I felt sure, would be surfacing in a stapled Stewart Home booklet before I made it back to Albion Drive.

Swanny, miraculously, did ring a bell.

'I was on terms with a girl who worked as a nurse in the Homerton Hospital. She was living with a couple of ex-medical students on Chatsworth Road. Their windows were broken constantly. She moved down to one of those estates by the Lea. You couldn't get a taxi driver to take you up there. I was always walking across Millfields Recreation Ground at three in the morning. She rutted like a monkey, but talked too much. I refused to stay the night. She bit. Pointed ivory teeth. Probably a vampire.'

The nurse mentioned Swanny. He wasn't kicked out for drugs, that was a given, the surgeons were cranked up most of the time. It was something quite innocent and unfortunate, sex. With a dead body. She couldn't recall the details. Now he was a vagrant ministering to vagrants, in return for booze.

In fact, going down to Beck Road yesterday, after dropping off some new titles in Broadway Market, Home thought he saw Swanny, who had been pointed out to him several times by the nurse, drinking at the table, bottom end of London Fields. He collected glasses, so it was reported, in the Victory on Vyner Street.

Best of all was the Mole Man connection. Stewart offered me the email address of Mark Pawson, a graphic artist who, as a student, had lived in William Lyttle's house in Mortimer Road. Stewart visited him there, frequently.

'Oh yes, I met the Mole Man. What happened was, the wife and daughter disappeared. But he was always friendly to me. I'd ring on the door and he'd let me in. He started digging shortly after his wife went missing. I think he told Mark to leave.'

Chris Petit once said that Julie Christie did the thing that annoyed him most about actresses from the 1960s: she flicked her eyes as she gazed into the face of the person on the other side of the camera. The one standing in for Alan Bates or Omar Sharif. Rapid movement to pantomime intensity, it pissed him off. He advocated doing nothing, with intent. German women understood the principle. Hands in coat pockets. Lips buttoned. 'Stare out of the car window,' he would instruct. 'And think of Hamburg.'

The frozen-blue irises of Julie Christie, spirit of Hackney, followed us to the door of the steamy café.

The Mole Man

How much would it cost? Cashmoney.

Over the weeks, as the chasm outside my door widened – I moved the car down into Albion Square, and moved it again to make room for the film crew shooting *Ashes to Ashes* – I established friendly, mug-of-tea relations with the odd man out, the native member of the clancydocwra mob, the one from Sligo. He tipped me the wink when the water was going to be cut off. But could he be persuaded to moonlight with his drill, to open up the buried vault, the arched chamber beneath our kitchen? For a bribe, a small wad, I wanted to undo my earlier mistake: to recover the thing that was no longer there. Research suggested that a Hackney underclass, like the troglodytes of Edinburgh's Old Town, burrowed into abandoned cellars, squatted swimming pools, hid out in sewage pipes, nuclear bunkers and mine shafts. Many of the daylight-spurning invisibles, up in Scotland, were Irish labourers.

Anna was safely out of it in America. While she was in the Charing Cross Hospital, after Farne's birth, I took the opportunity to film a beggars' banquet (out of Buñuel's *Viridiana*), in exactly this kitchen space. Which was then a corridor and a potential child's bedroom. Brian Catling was involved: making-up and dressing the assorted freaks and outpatients, cooking with maggots. The orgy went on for hours, it was the most extravagant scene I ever shot. And the probable conclusion to the cycle of diary films. Unfortunately, in my excitement at eventually bringing the entire cast together in one place, poets, dowsers, junkies, nurses, accountants, I left the camera on auto-exposure instead of making an f-stop adjustment for the shadowy and subtle lighting I'd worked so long to achieve. The resulting footage was so dark that it was unreadable, black within black. A triumph: we were free to remember the ritual as it should have been, recall untainted by the cruel evidence of actual viewings.

The walls, painted by Catling, were covered with occult symbols, Enochian tables and quotations from H. P. Lovecraft's imagined grimoire, the *Necronomicon*. Swine creatures crawled from the pit of William Hope Hodgson's *The House on the Borderland*: at the point where our own secret cellar had been enclosed. All of this in screaming fire-hydrant scarlet gloss. Which came through, despite many layers of calming eggshell white, year after year, until the old bathroom wall was knocked down by the Irish cowboys making a crisis out of a minor drama.

The whole episode was reported to Anna, as soon as she was safely back with the baby, by the old folk on the balcony of the flats, the ones who watched every move I made. But now visible traces of excavation could be explained away as safety tests in advance of a serious kitchen rethink. A generous gesture, on my part, to welcome her home from Washington.

It could wait. Clancydocwra would be there for months, carving into rubbled clay, the compliant skin of Hackney. Mark Pawson, Stewart Home's friend, was cycling over to Hoxton, the shop with artists' books, to deliver a consignment of badges. He said that we could meet in the café next door.

My son William and his mates declared an interest in the Mole Man. From the earliest period when his activities were made public, they took photographs of placards with Mole Man references. They collected newspaper reports and rumours, constructing a mythology around the burrower's fictive status. I was sensitive to the fact that, in recording an interview, I might spoil their fun: by disinterring some sorry human fact like the pauper's death of David Rodinsky, revealed by Rachel Lichtenstein's remorseless detective work.

One of these youths, Rowland, lived in Beck Road. He appeared in that dynamic mural in Dalston Lane, the Mexican Day of the Dead procession of Hackney's vanquished utopians. His father, who died before the project could be completed, was the artist responsible. Rowland, I believe, helped touch in the final details of what now stood as a memorial to the spirit of the demolished Labyrinth on the other side of the road.

Anna rang from New York. For most of our time together, she dreamt of America, of being on a certain street near Grand Central Station; the smell, the noise, it was tangible. The closest she came, bags packed to accompany me on a reading tour, was 9/11: our flight was booked for the following morning. Evil news found her in the hairdresser's chair. I was in the City, looking for Marmite and Frank Cooper's Original Oxford Marmalade to carry to Texas, when I saw them pouring out of banks and offices. But now Anna was actually there, the dreams changed; every night the same thing. She stood on her remembered spot, breathing a sigh of content-ment, but terrified that she could never come back. Her suitcase was filled with bricks, it was much too heavy to lift.

A bike like Stewart Home's. Pawson reminded me of the book-runner Driffield. He was cycle-fit and a little red in the face. He offered me a choice of enamelled badge. He did HOMES FOR ALL. And aerial views: CAN YOU SEE YOUR HOUSE? Pretty neat. I settled for DIS-INFO-TAINMENT. Which seemed to be the territory we were covering. Mark recalled his days with the Mole Man as an initiation into the quiddity of London.

I came to university in 1982, the City University. The first year I stayed at the hall of residence, very near Moorgate Station, Bunhill Row. The second year I lived in Dalston, Mortimer Road. William Lyttle, the so-called Mole Man, was my landlord.

It was the first time I'd ever had to look for rented accommodation. I had no idea what to expect. I didn't know what rented houses were like. Mortimer Road didn't seem that odd to me.

I was sharing with a friend from my home town, Lymm in Cheshire. She was a music student. The house actually had a piano in it. That was the selling point.

We went round to see the room. The landlord had been doing it up. It was wallpapered with newspaper. Unpainted newspaper. Which was a bit strange. Obviously, the whole scheme was bodged, home-done. William said, 'I'll paint it over if you like.' So it was painted, but you could still see the newspaper.

My room was a big, regular, rectangular space. Looking out on Mortimer Road. There were three floors and then the basement. The floors were let out in various combinations. At the back was a little private area. William had done it all himself.

I got the feeling that he'd been there for ages. He wasn't very talkative. But when you met him for the first time, he used to introduce himself as 'Mr William'. On the phone he used that version of his name, 'Mr William'. But, very quickly, he slid back to 'Bill'. There had been a wife and a daughter at some point. I know that because there used to be a fair amount of mail for them. I assume, from the names, it was a wife and daughter. We speculated about their fate. Especially when William started digging.

I used to get a lot of mail, I was involved with mail art. I would be down at the door first thing in the morning. I would rush down and there would always be a stack of post. I'd lay out William's mail on the steps, all the letters for his wife and daughter.

We were on the first floor. There were some guys in another flat. There was a spare room and occasionally Bill would have people to stay. He advertised rooms to let even when the house was full.

The guys next door were at the LSE, London School of Economics. The girls upstairs were at King's College. He wanted someone in the spare room, so that they could share our kitchen. We went: 'No!' It was tiny, that room. Where the bed was positioned, the wall overlapped it. There was a dark hole into which you were supposed to put your feet.

I think the rent was £25 a week. Quite cheap at the time. We paid cash. William would appear in the room. He had his own key and he would just walk in. He often did that when he knew I was out. And my friend was at home. She had her room at the back. William would open the door and shout. He knew I wasn't there. We stayed a year. Towards the end William had this digger, a mechanical digger.

He built this – how can I describe it? – structure. It was half-dug out of the earth, a bit of a concrete dome over the top. The digger was right there in the garden. The garden was accessible from the Mortimer Road side. The house was like the prow of a boat, at the point where two roads meet. William would occasionally move the digger. There was just enough space to contain it in his concrete igloo. He would fire the machine up. Everyone called him Catweazle, because he looked like Catweazle, the television character. He hadn't achieved Mole Man status, not then.

He was Irish. But age was difficult, he was such a wiry thing. He had short fuzzy hair, it was always grey. We never knew if it was dust or if he actually had grey hair. It could have been either, he was always tinkering, building, digging holes.

I went home for the summer. But, because I got such a quantity of mail art, I called at Mortimer Road as soon as I returned to London in September. To ask if there was any post for me. Bill might have saved it. He just about recognized me. He came out of the front door. 'I think there were a few things this morning.' And he opened the dustbin and pulled out sacks of letters. The bin was packed solid. He gave me a couple of pieces of mail, but as they had already been binned I didn't bother.

After that I used to see him at the Vallance Road boot fair, the one where the car auction used to be. It was a site that was developed for Sainsbury's, a little car park. He never acknowledged me. I nodded but he never looked in my direction. He had a tiny, light blue Triumph pushbike. He pushed it all the way round the boot sale. He was looking for tools, secondhand nails.

I don't recall seeing William down Kingsland Waste. There were plenty of tools to be found on the Waste at that time. It was my Saturday-morning routine. I would do the market, take everything back to Mortimer Road, then go to Ridley Road. I was looking for junky toys, collage stuff, stamps, stickers, weird books, bits of clothes. I was going for cheap stuff rather than anything specialized or collectable. There was a guy who had lots of cheap Trojan records, compilations, all the ska stuff. He always had the brand-new ones, he obviously had a connection. The Waste was very, very local, it wasn't one of those places you felt had been picked over by collectors.

Hackney Wick too, I lived up there. When I was living in Dalston I *would have been nineteen. I collected more and more stuff off the streets, out of markets. I wasn't much of an explorer.*

Dalston was my introduction to the East End. We did a few things in the area. The bagel shop, a couple of pubs, the Sussex, the Mortimer. A real spit-and-sawdust place, very wide open. A little stage, a piano player. Old guy. He had two stacks of music. And he would play all night, pick up the next sheet, play it, put it down on the other pile. He never turned round. He drank Guinness. Someone would buy him a pint of Guinness and put it on the spot, the wet ring on top of the piano. No acknowledgement, he never looked up. That was the routine. Occasionally people sang.

Our launderette was in the Englefield Road baths. You could still take a bath there. The launderette was at the back, you had to walk through all the wooden cubicles. I remember there was a price for the bath and then you had to pay for extra minutes. They still had 'Hackney Council' woven into the towels.

Stewart Home used to come down to Mortimer Road to stay. He must have been getting around, seeing people like Pete Horobin. And Fabian. Distributing copies of Smile *magazine. He was someone that I'd been in touch with in the past. Quite a few people would pop around to the house.*

It got pretty crappy, Hackney Wick. I still used to go up there, but less and less. I can't remember when the greyhound stadium went bust. It must have happened twice. They had that really big, glass-fronted observatory thing. The oval of the stadium, the purity of it, was wonderful. I loved the way they used the space. There were gypsies there for a while. There were raves in the Wick. There was always overlap: people coming out of a club, piles and piles of nightclub flyers blowing about, gypsies moving up and down, little bits of business. On the scavenge.

I didn't go to Labyrinth. I do remember the Four Aces before that. Labyrinth wasn't really my scene. The Four Aces was pretty . . . black. The Club of Mankind, as well, on London Fields. I remember going home from a party and there was a coach, the driver was a Brummie. A coach full of African blokes and girls, down from Birmingham. The driver didn't know where the club was. I had to show him. I had to show him where this African club was. I was quite proud of myself.

I haven't followed the Mole Man story. I've seen a few bits in newspapers and heard Robert Elms mention him on the radio.

William Lyttle had a skip on Mortimer Road. There was a toilet seat in there, we could see it from the window. Some local characters picked it up. William shouted at them, told them to put it back. He was giving them an earful for taking an object that was obviously waste.

If you went through the Mortimer Road door, there was a single room with a couple in it. A young Spanish girl. Bill had this idea that she would cook for him. I don't think he ever managed to persuade her to do it. Bill was down to the left, that was the room we knew he had. I never went into his room.

There was also a little V-shaped garden at the back, he had a patio door into his room from there. If you went down to see him, he would come to the door. You would never get inside. He used to cook outrageously stinky meat stew that you could smell upstairs. It really did smell like dog food. Foul. I hate to think what was in it.

I used to lock my bicycle in the little garden shed. There was a tiny lawn. And the concrete igloo in which he did his digging. One time, when my bike was there, I had the front wheel stolen. I'm fairly certain Bill saw someone do it. Probably kids.

He dressed in work boots. He always wore a grey jacket from a suit. Never clean. He could put up a bit of a façade, like the business about being called 'Mr William'. He did once have some relatives to stay, when the tenants were away. A middle-aged Irish couple, very straight. Like someone's aunty and uncle. They stayed for a weekend. They were definitely from the south. I should know where Bill came from, he might have mentioned it. It was very weird when he produced these relatives.

When I lived in Mortimer Road we never used the words 'De Beauvoir'. It was too poncey. Now I'm proud to tell people that I used to have a place in De Beauvoir Town. Islington, even then, was creeping eastwards.

The street markets are pretty much dead, Brick Lane has been captured and colonized. The age of the boot sale has gone. Hackney Wick was the end of an era. One of my flatmates used to collect your secondhand book catalogues. The very last one sticks in my mind. You said, 'The prices are valid until such-and-such a date, after which time the survivors will be relocated to Dalston Oxfam.' Ha! It was dear that you were winding things up.

A few days after my encounter with Mark Pawson, I found myself in the Stoke Newington Library, ostensibly for an event celebrating the rich diversity of Hackney literature, but actually to see if I could follow up Rob Petit's account of the surveillance-screen bunker. I decided, after a number of false starts, corridors going nowhere, that Rob had confused the library with the municipal offices, just down the road. A block big enough to service outstanding council-tax demands. If local officials had explained to me, years ago, that I was supporting the art practice of Stewart Home and Mark Pawson, and not some flimflam about refuse, schools and hospitals, I would have paid up with a good grace.

Michael Rosen, who was chairing this event, had recently been appointed Children's Laureate for the Nation and, more significantly, the Laureate of Hackney. The titles we were invited to discuss ranged from Pinter to Xiaolu Guo, by way of Alexander Baron and Stewart Home. I said a few words in recommendation of Patrick Wright's *A Journey through Ruins* and revisited Pinter's memory-fiction, *The Dwarfs*. I floated *Rain on the Pavements* but drew a blank, nobody in that engaged and opinionated Stoke Newington audience had heard of Camberton.

Among the group who approached me afterwards, with allotment petitions, demolition promos, anti-Griffin propaganda, was an older man, with better shoes than the rest: Anton Spur. Who told me that he lived in Albion Drive and had filmed an interview with the Mole Man for Channel 4. A researcher had noticed a *Guardian* article – 'After 40 years' burrowing, Mole Man of Hackney is ordered to stop' – by Paul Lewis. And had contacted Spur. The original piece pointed out that this property, 121 Mortimer Road, was now valued at over a million pounds. Ultrasound scanners, brought in by council surveyors, revealed 'a network of burrows' underneath seventy-five-year-old William Lyttle's house. 'Half a century of nibbling dirt with a shovel and home-made pulley has hollowed out a web of tunnels and caverns, some 8m (26ft) deep.'

'Was the researcher's name, by any chance, Kaporal?'

'Well, yes, actually, it was.'

Spur tapped social funds set aside by the council, the evicted William Lyttle was invited to put his side of the story. Amazingly, the reclusive but aggrieved Mr William agreed to talk. By this time, Channel 4 was in crisis: premium-rate telephone scandals, faked documentaries, racism on *Big Brother*. The whole commissioning process could be summarized as: creative dis-enabling. Commissioners have now, themselves, to be commissioned. The structure is labyrinthine. Proposals pass through more levels and hierarchies than there are ladders in a Piranesi prison. The idea is that there will be no idea: nothing that can be articulated. Boil content until it turns to steam. The age of the meeting as an end in itself – weak coffee at a round table – has been discontinued.

Anton Spur shot an hour of William Lyttle, his rants and his silences, before the plug was pulled. The news in the *Guardian* was old news, Kaporal's short-term contract was not renewed. The Channel 4 commissioner transferred to the Roundhouse in Camden Town, a railway shed dedicated to the erasure of its own cultural memory. Office wits said that the Antony Gormley jumper on the roof was a portrait of this suicidal careerist.

I was promised a glimpse of the Lyttle tapes, if they could be found: they couldn't. Spur was preoccupied with an alternative proposal on the life and times of the Hackney Owl Man – who, it was felt, would tick the eco box. A house of wild birds played better than a mad old Celt digging his way to Ireland.

There was however one major revelation. Spur mentioned that

William Lyttle was back. He had slipped through a gap in the corrugated fencing and reoccupied the tunnels.

I wrote to Mr Lyttle in the refuge to which he had been sent by the council. I supplied a stamped return postcard with a nice picture of a plastic parrot, but received no answer. I visited the house and, failing to make any impression on security, was sent packing.

DANGEROUS STRUCTURE, KEEP OUT! BY ORDER OF THE DISTRICT SURVEYOR. High fence with mesh barrier outside it. This triangle – Mortimer Road, Stamford Road, Englefield Road – was an exclusion zone. While much of Hackney was being expensively split open by clancydocwra, this Irishman, Mr William Lyttle, was unhoused, for the crime of digging his own cellar.

The tall house, additions spreading like wildfire cancers, was forbidding. They said that Lyttle had filled the deserted rooms, one by one, with London clay. Neighbours complained about their power lines being cut, no water in the taps, but that was a given in an Olympic fringe borough. They were terrified, in the pub, that the cellar would collapse into one of the Mole Man's tunnels.

I photographed his property from all sides, dirty cream emulsion over grey stone, brown trim for the bay windows. Remedial work by council teams, trying to get to the heart of the mystery, uncovered a dying swan, a mural drooping with sexual symbolism. Painted lemurs peeping from a buddleia and convolvulus jungle. As Marina Warner pointed out, when she discussed the devil as an ape of god: 'monkeys (*singes*) are also the masters of signs (*signes*)'.

I watched for ten nights before I spotted William Lyttle, flapping trenchcoat, trim beard and frosted shock of hair. Economical with the truth, I introduced myself as a colleague of Anton Spur. Could I follow up that interview? I might be able to make the story part of a book about Hackney, its politics, its corruptions.

'Are you an Englishman then?'

'Certainly not.'

'Book writer, is it? A Taffy?'

Into the igloo. Over rubble, a blocked passageway. Tin door draped in sacking: he barges it open. Fit for his age, Mr Lyttle. Sharp, sudden. Then still. Waiting. Catacomb walls with alcoves in which candles have been set. Chalky dry. Quiet as a bell jar with the air sucked out. The clockwork of a beating heart.

'I thought I'd try for a bit of a wine cellar,' Lyttle said. 'And found a taste for the thing.'

He unwrapped a hunk of pungent meat, trapped in a wedge of white loaf. Perched on a broken chair, the Mole Man was happy to yarn about boreholes he'd uncovered along the towpath of the Regent's Canal, about bunkers beneath municipal buildings and how they linked up with the crypt of the old church in Abney Park.

He scuttled into the dark, bent over, stooping, although the space above his head was generous. Passages divided, branched out, but he never hesitated. The glow from his lantern played on dripping walls, where snail shells glittered. It was like choosing to crawl inside the hollow trunk of a drowned tree.

Remarks thrown back over William's shoulder were of a racist tinge. I felt no shame in letting them pass, there have been no prosecutions, as yet, for those who are rude about the Welsh. Our nation has become a comedy stereotype: stupid, drunk, fat and probably gay. The valleys of South Wales – line-dancing, fast-food binging – stand in, as far as the metropolitan media are concerned, for America. Much safer to mock the disenfranchised tribes of the near-west than the global bully.

'You can call me a natural philosopher,' Bill said. 'Curiosity is my curse. If I make a start, I must know where it ends.'

In alcoves carved into the sides of tunnels were votive offerings, saucers of secondhand nails, nosegays of rusty spanners, mud madonnas. And, amazingly, books. Pawson had got it wrong: William Lyttle, Little Bill, trawled the boot fairs to confirm his thesis. The only highway to freedom is under our feet. Out of sight.

The Mole Man had built up a useful Hollow Earth bibliography. *The Narrative of Arthur Gordon Pym*, credited to Edgar Allan Poe and Jules Verne, in a Panther paperback. Michael Mooorcock's *Lord of the Spiders*. *At the Earth's Core*, a Tarzan adventure by Edgar Rice Burroughs. *Moby-Dick* in abridged pictorial form, Classics Illustrated. William Hope Hodgson's *The House on the Borderland*, a battered Grafton reprint, with red-ink annotations.

The inference was clear: where Hodgson's Wellsian fable placed English incomers in a ruined house in the far west of Ireland, somewhere as otherworldly as the folded limestone pavements of the Burren, Lyttle was taking his revenge by digging a pit beneath Hackney. He was the architect of a fairytale subterrane where former navvies from Galway, Connemara and Sligo made their fortunes hiring out plant and excavating London with the blessing of their oppressors, the British State, and all its grisly instruments.

Lyttle had moved ahead, into the dripping darkness, when I heard a noise too loud for rats, more like the rush of water: as if our tunnel had breached the canal. I pressed hard back against the wall, sound became light. A single glowing eye, purple-red at core, hot-orange at rim, raced towards us, unstable in its nuclear heat.

A train.

One tributary of Lyttle's civil-engineering project led straight into the Dalston Lane tunnel. Into the world of strategic-planning targets, demolished theatres, 20-storey glass towers. I was the sole witness of the moment when incompatible systems met. I wish I could pretend that I had the presence of mind to take a snapshot, to put alongside historic images of transcontinental railway tracks, slaved over by Chinese work gangs, coming together in the American wilderness. William Lyttle, the Mole Man of Mortimer Road, had something of the dignity, the inner conviction, of pioneer photographer Eadweard Muybridge's Shoshone Indians: lifting redundant weapons while they crouch beside their iron nemesis, the Central Pacific Railroad.

When the train carried Natches and his Apache remnant into exile, in the Florida swamps, warrior dogs followed the cattle-cars for forty miles. 'Before they fell away in exhaustion.' Nobody ever forgot the sound those dogs made.

Vyner Street

After that uncomfortable incident in the tunnel, I limited myself to terrestrial tracts of Hackney. I returned to old habits – street markets, afternoon pubs, cemeteries – and always with the intention of bringing my confidential report to a conclusion: *unfinished*. If I wrote a harmless sentence such as 'everything was zeroing in on the Victory in Vyner Street', I struck it out, as over-freighted, lazy and altogether false in its suggestion that my fractured narrative of manipulated facts, poorly recorded and inaccurately transcribed interviews, could achieve resolution. I had been invited to Vyner Street for a wake, the literary baggage that went with that was accidental and should, if anything, be played down: the life of a dead man celebrated by other dead men on parole. Postmortem memory-parties in which trembling and ruined participants drank themselves into blackout and amnesia were the only social events I now attended.

Patrick Wright talked about an unnoticed film by Marc Karlin in which 'he imagines a repository for all the tears shed for the late-departed Lady Di'. We were becoming a nation of grief technicians, neutralizing horror by trapping it in cycles of digital repetition. We dressed street furniture with wreaths and smiling photographs. The grimmest estates and the emptiest suburbs were carpets of sweating cellophane-sealed flowers.

Norman Palmer, on Kingsland Waste, was having one of his better days, a nudging mob of eight or ten irregulars tipping out the boxes. Modernist poetry, experimental fiction, bundles of art catalogues, these were not Norman's stock-in-trade. But in clearing houses, working with Essex solicitors, he took what he could get, flogged the gems and dumped the rest. After I'd picked up an uncommon William Burroughs first edition and found the crabbed presentation inscription, my interest quickened and I went home with a bulging bag. Annotated film scripts, poetry by Basil Bunting, Ed Dorn and Allen Ginsberg, artists' books by Gilbert and George, Jake and Dinos Chapman, Banksy, Jock McFadyen: all affectionately signed and doodled to one man. In gratitude, with respect. It was Jock who rang me with an invitation to the wake in the Victory, our accountant had claimed his last hire-car expenses. Hari Simbla, financial fixer to the counter-culture, had submitted the final return.

I think it was Jock who said that Hari had been discovered in a Russian massage parlour in Camden with a briefcase of punishment-porn DVDs, each one wrapped in a copy of the *Financial Times*. Total fiction and probably based on the flakes of green paint I'd pointed out in Broadway Market, where David Cronenberg dressed a respectable barber shop as a Moscow mafia club for his Hackney shocker, *Eastern Promises*. Stewart Home laid the blame on Hari's involvement with Alex Trocchi, laundering illegitimate income, dabbling in property, sorting out contracts that would never be fulfilled with defunct publishers. As usual it was Chris Petit, a meticulous researcher, who came up with the true version, as revealed in a *Guardian* obituary: prostate cancer. Basildon. Painful and distressing treatment. A rapid wasting away in the suburbs, the semi-detached home to which none of us had ever been invited. A second wife of thirty years, four children. Framed graduation photographs. No books, no art. An unused piano.

Petit, always sharp where money issues were concerned, left Hari early, well before the substantial thriller advances. 'As soon as he moved into that place on Regent's Park, I knew I'd have to jump ship. It was going far too well, the Richard Hamiltons, the Jim Dines, the soft Oldenburg typewriter. Who was paying for the collection? You don't live shoulder-to-shoulder with the Pinters without some form of retribution. I like my accountants above a betting shop in the Uxbridge Road.'

Barry Miles, official archivist of the era, filed the obit. It appeared that Hari was the person responsible for keeping the whole flaky 1960s scene afloat, he was the ultimate enabler. Peel away the bullshit, the Be-ins, Technicolor Dreams, perfumed gardens and psychedelic rabbit holes, and you come down to Peter Rachman's multi-occupied Notting Hill warrens and Hari Simbla's creativity with a balance sheet. Hari was the true visionary of the period: unpapered chaos finessed into a valid tax return. He scrambled reality with magical sleights of hand, smokescreens, dummy companies, plural identities. He claimed for lunches that were never eaten, charitable events that should have taken place but never actually did: even though we remember them in intimate detail, those parties in Panna Grady's mansion to which we were not invited. Baton wounds received in Grosvenor Square were inflicted by an overdose of newsreel footage. And the compensation cheques for months away from jobs we didn't have.

Hari helped R. D. Laing and the anti-psychiatrists by locating properties in Hackney as outstations for voyages through madness. Charlie Velasco was his fixer, he had an in with the council and an unlimited supply of the raw material, acid-casualty crazies. Many of the early communards made the seamless transition from sitting around smoking dope to sitting around acting out psychodramas for future medical papers and plays by David Mercer. My old colleague, Tom Baker, hammered by the stress of cinema, became the caretaker and general handyman of a Laingian house in De Beauvoir Square. Thus, very neatly, making a connection with the Hogarthian asylum run on the same turf by Warburton.

The Barry Miles obituary revealed the fact that Hari had been with the Inland Revenue, a Tax Inspector. He learnt his trade from the inside. 'Things did not always go smoothly. Hari's unorthodox approach sometimes caused mayhem. Many clients left, horrified at unexpected tax bills. Others had problems getting their papers back – there seemed to be a black hole into which his files vanished.'

That black hole, for today, was the Victory in Vyner Street. To walk there, across London Fields, picking up Jock at his studio, was like clumping through the trenches. Local topography resembled nothing so much as the barranca or ravine in Malcolm Lowry's *Under the Volcano*: a ditch for dead dogs. With the guns, knives, populist murals, bands, firecrackers, barrios, Dalston was Mexico City: without the justification of a successful revolution. Simbla, I discovered, got his start with Margerie Bonner Lowry, Malcolm's widow; a woman who wrestled with trunks of feverishly composed Lowry fragments, while necking as much booze as her tragic partner. The posthumous works belong as much to Margerie as to her addled castaway husband.

Chris Petit, the first man at the bar – he would have to get away sharpish for the school run – was not drinking. Straight tomato juice: to the evident disgust of a dwarfish barman. An unlit small cigar was sniffed and returned to its flat yellow tin with an erotic gesture of renunciation. 'This is the finish,' Chris said, tapping an item in his paper. 'Michael Winner promoting a diet book at the London Review Bookshop. That's it, the last gasp of the culture.' In many ways he was right, any pretence at finding a successor to independent bookshops like Indica and Compendium was ridiculous. A matter of geography. Bloomsbury was for American academics, thesis trufflers, tourists. Camden, always ugly, had now achieved a critical state of colonization by sponsorship and mindless development. Post-junk architecture soliciting unexplained fires.

For years Petit had been convinced that the two English careers worth investigating were Jimmy Savile and Michael Winner. He was determined to live long enough to see the pair out, with his magnum opus beyond the reach of libel laws. The files, provided by Kaporal, were extensive.

'Winner's no fool. Looking back, he's been very canny with his investments. Made the right moves at the right time. He knew how to operate a franchise. Just enough controversy to keep his name in the tabloids. And cult credibility by importing Brando and Mitchum. I used to see him, cigar in mouth, parking the Roller as close as he could get to one of the alternative cinema clubs. He knew his Fassbinder. And paid for the dinner by dictating a few choice insults to a secretary. Admirable.'

With the arrival of Jock's friend Paul Burwell, riverboat pilot and percussionist, the wake livened up. And Petit slid towards the door. Then Catling in loud pinstripe and Hawaiian shirt occupied a corner table with a group of acolytes, students or children. Hari was honoured in readings, songs, anecdotes. We were soon wet-eyed, garrulously fond and forgiving, remembering the parts of ourselves we had lost. Most of the company were of an age to regret the National Insurance contributions they had volunteered to ignore.

Stooping to recover brown change from the bar, I met the snake-eye of the potman. Leering, he sucked smoke while he waited for recognition to dawn: it was the taste of hot nicotine flakes filtered through a scrub of demi-beard that did it. The way he twisted a length of white cord around his little finger, doing it and undoing it. Chewed lips in a salve of Guinness froth: Ian Askead. The feisty Glaswegian I met in 1968 when I took Renchi into the Metropolitan Hospital with his grumbling appendix. Askead played a part in our lives for maybe four years, then stepped aside, never to be seen, or thought of, until today.

He'd moved in on us, with wife and infant, occupying any vacant spare room. They shared a mattress on the floor, the three of them. Along with assorted lovers and co-conspirators. Askead's baby-minding techniques were borderline criminal, a pint of Guinness to put the two-year-old to sleep, then off to the pub, the anarchist meeting in a cramped basement. I can't forgive my own complicity in this or forget the diary film sequence in which the half-naked babe pisses through the bars of the cot, in the grand house Ian was minding. The child, so I heard, turned out well: sleek-suited adviser to the Treasury or some such.

Through Askead we were roped in to document squats in Ellingfort Road, by London Fields, and out in Redbridge. An interview, sound only, with Ron Bailey. Assignations with fringe Angry Brigade cadres in Stamford Hill. Without him, I would not have experienced these manifestations before they decayed into late fictions. Never imprisoned, never named in books or newspaper articles, I assumed that Askead was a paid informer. That was how he could afford the drink, the cabs he insisted on taking, between dole office and bomb factory. The permanent ciggie, the speed.

The hospital job provided a place where he could hang out at night. And where, as reward for introducing us to activists, dangerous madmen, we agreed to film the corpses. I persuaded myself this was a Stan Brakhage routine. The virgin dead in their white plastic wraps were a valid part of any record of the city. Lovemaking, childbirth, death: the proper content for a diary. Along with mountains climbed, trees chopped and meals taken. But Askead had another agenda, he was peddling autopsy footage, mortuary frolics, to unrevealed contacts within the hospital, for cash. Or drugs. Which would be traded for weapons. Immunity from prosecution. A complicated equation into which we had bumbled. And put from our minds as soon as Askead was gone.

Two women approached. They were not family or intimates but they seemed to require a friendly mime, a raised hand, if not the full embrace. Standard Hackney types? Intelligent, focused, aggrieved: belted and booted, conforming in nonconformity. One favoured red, the other black. Kaporal followed, trying to slip an arm around their shoulders, hoping to sacrifice the pair as a buffer to my wrath. 'You know Alice and Anya from the German Hospital?'

I do. Now. The Conrad prompt: *Victory.* Part Three, Chapter 3: 'We lodged in the north of London, off Kingsland Road. It wasn't a bad time.' Or so the fatal woman says, the travelling musician in the novel. And you believe her story, because she is following in the author's wake. 6 Dynevor Road, Stoke Newington: 1880. Just where Kingsland High Street becomes Stoke Newington High Street. Joseph Conrad rented a room from William Ward – WW

– as if in tribute to Edgar Allan Poe's doppelgänger, William Wilson, from the tale set in a Stoke Newington private school. Roads bifurcate, lives too. I explored this ground when I tried to trace the meanderings of the lost Hackney Brook.

The Victory, with its classic L-shaped bar, was a working canalside dive that sustained a downbeat air of welcoming its own and offering savage indifference to the rest. Kaporal fitted in: like a dying fern in a chipped chamber pot. He wouldn't give back any part of his research fee, when I exposed his lies (creative re-imaginings), but hinted instead at further revelations, not included in the original contract. Available for the price of a drink. And, in due course, a percentage of the royalties.

What Kaporal had not grasped is that I would investigate, on foot, every inch of his documented research. Including poor Harry Stanley's final dérive, from the pub to his encounter with the state-authorized shooters.

'I walked the last stage,' Kaporal had written, 'from the Alexandra pub on Victoria Park Road (no. 162) towards Mare Street – and saw the spot on the corner of Fremont Street where Harry died. Beside a fading wreath of plastic flowers around a bollard, there are some holes in a low brick wall which some have said were made by the bullets.'

Kaporal expanded on stories he had heard while drinking in the Alexandra, how the police managed to insert into one of the inquests the fact that Mr Stanley had 'a bit of previous, a marginal role in armed robberies, back in the 1960s'. Two days before the fatal shooting, he had been given the all-clear in his battle with colon cancer.

I strolled out, one afternoon, to see if I could track down Kaporal's informants. There was no Alexandra. The pub had changed its name to the Lauriston; rebranded to appeal to a new clientele, wealthy incomers. Kaporal's tale was manufactured, quite accurately, from the internet and phone calls to bent detectives.

The ashes, when the time is right, will be scattered over Culloden field, a sorry place for Jacobite clansmen and highlanders, but visited by Harry and his loving wife, Irene. When the man from Lanarkshire was gunned down, a hundred yards from home, a dish of traditional Scottish 'stovies' was waiting in the microwave.

Most of what Kaporal now offered, after major sessions in the Dove, the Cat and Mutton and the Dolphin, was off the record.

'Too late and too little,' I said. 'I've got another month before funds run out. I'd rather have fifty quid on the bar than yet another uncorroborated Hackney conspiracy. When you're writing fiction, ethical standards are higher.'

'Bushmeat? Trade in body parts?'

'Seen the film. It stank.'

'A Clapton newsagent married to a Jamaican, she'll give you the works on the battle between the Yardies and the Turks for the heroin trade.'

'Flog it to *The Bill*.'

'Did you know the top enforcer on Murder Mile is an orthodox Jew? Women love the guy and he scares the shit out of the lowlife. They call him Kosher Ken, the people's mayor. The adjudicator. Wears leathers and a skullcap (with skull and crossbones). Roars around Stamford Hill on a hog, chewing a cigar and breaking legs to order.'

'Please.'

Anya came to Kaporal's rescue. Her latest architectural project, conceptualizing a structure that would never be built but which would resonate in the memory, was Labyrinth. She saw the benefit in starting from a flattened meadow of rubble and aggregate. She liked my Hollow Earth stories.

'I'm going to record the accounts of everyone I can find who visited Labyrinth, the Four Aces, the old cinema, then bury sound-boxes in tunnels that connect with the railway system.'

She showed me a lovely sequence of Labyrinth photographs – posing celebrities, bluesmen – she had rescued from oblivion. Bob Hoskins with Eddie Constantine, fedora tipped over the eyes. She had Orson Welles with a bloated young man, who looked like Dan Farson, striking a pose alongside Francis Bacon in a slippery, high-zipped blouson. Surrounded by clubbers in zoot suits and co-respondent shoes, Orson might have been auditioning for another Harlem *Macbeth*. Dark voodoo in a dark place.

'The clincher,' Kaporal said, 'is the film. You know Welles did that interview at the back of the Hackney Empire with the old biddies? Right. But nobody has ever viewed the *Moby Dick* footage, the scenes with Welles and McGoohan which Chuck Berg compares with the Kane/Leland exchanges in *Citizen Kane*. Wolf Mankowitz put up the readies for a trial reel, to see if he could raise proper finance. They shot for three days, before Welles took off on a monumental Hackney bender. A collector, living out in Ware, responding to my internet enquiry, said that he bought four cans at the Wick boot fair. The label said: *Moby Dick – Rehearsal*. I have those cans out in the car. And they'll only cost you another grand.'

Ian Askead tucked something into Kaporal's breast pocket. White string. In the shape of a noose. Pure theatre. The researcher's story deserved a bottle of fizz. I signalled the bar. The old boy who cleared the glasses brought the bucket over, moving very slowly, weaving through the drunken mob. Askead shouted: 'Come on, Swanny, for fuck's sake. You're not in the morgue now.'

There was a startling poster on the wall, advertising a show at the Alma Gallery, down the road. An eye on fire. A stark black globe veined with blazing rivers. Athanasius Kircher. 1665. *Mundus Subterraneus*. With a Marina Warner quote: 'Part *Illuminati* poetics, part dazzling scientific analysis, part alchemical and zodiac magic, part cabinet of curiosities ... all-encompassing airy space.'

Swanny

A game of swans: that, apparently, is the collective noun. A pair of birds who had migrated to Hackney, west from the Lea or east from Islington, squatted on the ramp of a stinky cave beneath the Mare Street Bridge. An enclosure fetid with pigeon droppings and hardened crusts of green-white slime. Then we noticed a solitary cob swan patrolling the area, soliciting sodden, oil-dunked bread; his mate was not seen again. On some mornings, when we paused in our walk to look at the first colonists of a many-windowed block, as breakfast preparations became a theatre for curious pedestrians and flash-past cyclists, the basin by the lock-keeper's cottage was a ruffled carpet of crusts, sliced white, tipped from sacks by Broadway Market cafés.

For alchemists the swan is the symbol for mercury. Quicksilver imaginings. Transmutations. A notion laboured over with considerable energy, and buckets of paint, by the guerrilla muralist known as Sweet Toof (or the Dentist) and his associate, Cyclops. These men track development along the inland waterways and into the Olympic Park: wherever a pseudo-wharf is laid out, a salmon-curing shed demolished, Sweet Toof will spray a graphic tribute in the form of a giant pink mouth loaded with monster molars. His serpent forms, Mayan in ferocity, devour glitz and offer blight the kiss of life. Near the meadow of electric-green scum that chokes the Lea Navigation at Old Ford Lock, a swan with a Philip Guston bite has been painted in loud acrylic along the entire length of a doomed warehouse. It resembles a feathered eel whose every twist and wriggle maps the bends and creeks of the threatened river. Sweet Toof, a white boy, lives somewhere in the edge-lands: where he was arrested, and held until first light next morning, for work that was not his own. As Jock McFadyen remarked, 'The sodding graffiti on the shutters of my studio is worth twenty grand more than anything I've got stored inside.'

Stephen Gill, who cycled this area on a daily basis, travelling between his home near the filter-beds and his studio in Bethnal Green, produced two books that recorded major losses: the dog-track boot fair and land captured by the Olympic Park. The first book, *Hackney Wick*, opened with a single swan, a white signature on dark water, drifting under the louring concrete mass of a road bridge. In its successor, *Archaeology in Reverse*, an anticipation of future stadia and opportunist cities, the swan is dead: a mess of feathers, spirit evaporated, on a lifeless green canal that is neither land nor water. Pylons have not yet been hidden under the ground and the melancholy of the scrublands is not disguised by a tall blue fence.

The swan is the messenger. And the swan's head has been cut off. Nasty anagram: *sawn swan*.

At Hari Simbla's wake I met an old friend, the musician and book-dealer Martin Stone. Who was strategically suited, fit, twinkling with good humour beneath beetling brows that made him seem like an erudite grasshopper. Living in Paris and trading out of Nice and Cannes, he no longer required the beret. He had adopted in its place a squashy pork-pie jazzman's hat: like Hackney's own Pete Doherty. After three months on a health farm.

Not only was Martin keeping his fingers supple with the occasional gig, but he'd been booked to appear in a big-budget Euro extravaganza in Zurich. A German rock'n'roll opera featuring an armada of hundreds of swan-pedalos on a Swiss lake. The pitch, Martin thought, was based on the myth of a young boy who has his cock bitten off by an angry swan. The scary Leda in this multimedia spectacular would be Tina Turner. Martin, outfitted in a skintight suit of feathers, stood in for the dead Ike. Coincidences were commonplace, as Bad News Mutton (who used to busk the Paris Metro, another labyrinth, with Martin) reminded me in daily phone calls. 'Morphic resonance or what, man?'

When Leda was ravished by Zeus in the guise of a swan, she gave birth, from two shining eggs, to sets of twins. 'The swan,' wrote J. C. Cooper in *An Illustrated Encyclopaedia of Traditional Symbols*, 'combines the two elements of air and water, the swan is the bird of life. It also signifies solitude and retreat and is the bird of the poet; its dying song is the poet's song.'

As I pursued old Swanny, my dumb muse, keeper of secrets, I logged swans that marked Hackney's borders: from Swan Wharf, where the subterranean Hackney Brook still gushes into the Lea, to the plastic swan in a canalside garden that confirms Danny Folgate's Victoria Park ley, to the flame-feathered swan on the pediment of a white building on Bethnal Green Road.

And soon, I hoped, Swanny himself would arrive for his breakfast appointment at Eddie's Café on the corner of Mare Street and Andrew's Road: within spitting distance of the murky swan cave. He would put in a courtesy appearance at his club, the blue-bag drinkers' table on London Fields; then shuffle along, folded *Telegraph* in pocket, for a full English and a debriefing. No bribe was necessary, Swanny had been waiting for this moment: he couldn't recall Dr Bruggen, but he knew Widgery (as a writer) and claimed to have tried my own *Lud Heat*. The history of Limehouse fascinated him but it was too painful now to tramp down to the Thames. Suburban Hackney was a sorry substitute, but the company was excellent. London Fields at dawn, afternoons on a reserved bench by the canal. You would be amazed how many medical men from how many diverse cultures found themselves with time on their hands. Along with a cigarette and a blue can.

Tinned tomatoes, a boiled egg. Mug of hot sweet tea. Eyelids drooped, the Adam's apple bobbed. Swanny was tall and brittle. I was frightened when I shook his hand that it might come off. He had a dry cough that he countered with long sucks at the surface of the pale brown tea, which was never quite cool enough to swallow. He steepled his fingers and, keeping a watchful eye on the pocket-recorder, began by confirming Dr Bruggen's impression of the local hospitals as colonial outposts operated through military or public-school hierarchies. The drug part of it, a minor perk, kept you going: the horrors were real. Coming down from Scotland or the provinces, you were shocked, at first, by the brutality of London life. And the matter-of-fact bravery of the underclass. The pantomimed sentiment, the forelock tugging. Extraordinary. The same cap-doffing characters who would rob you blind. There was true scholarship among the basest working men, library Marxists, natural philosophers. It was the lack of inhibition that Swanny never learnt to handle, the rutting, casual adulteries undertaken between shifts and meaning no more to the participants than blowing their noses on their sleeves. Sex, Swanny admitted, had been his undoing. He was criminal in one thing only: his innocence. His shame. That never-extinguished torch burning a hole in bulging, semen-stained corduroys.

I found myself, after leaving the German Hospital under something of a cloud, appointed to the Salvationists' place on Clapton Road, the maternity wing. It was like being banished to Asia Minor from Rome. The religious aspect should have put me on my guard, the naked passion that goes into that grip on a tambourine. It was a cottage-hospital operation overwhelmed by local fecundity, although many women preferred to get the parturition business done at home, and back to the toy factory or the cleaning job by the following afternoon.

I knew nothing about women, nothing at all. I came from the better part of Edinburgh. And had been in private schooling since the age of seven. They put me in a little room on the top floor. A nice room with a gas fire. It was terribly cold that year, the pond in Clapton was frozen. When it thawed, I remember, a body was discovered beneath the ice, dead for three weeks. I arranged my books and kept as close as I could to the fire.

The next morning, I was wandering through the wards, feeling rather rough, a cold coming on. The staff nurse on the ward said, 'You need your chest rubbing.' I said, 'Yes of course I do. When will you come?' And after supper she did. I was technically a virgin, or something close to it. The episode at the German Hospital was never properly investigated and seemed in retrospect more like a fantasy or late-adolescent projection of something I'd read in a magazine. Penetrative intercourse with a living breathing woman was unknown to me. I was really quite scared. After this first brief and exhilarating encounter, we went out together. Cinemas and concerts. Church too.

Once, when I was sewing up a newly delivered mother, this nurse stood close behind me. She put her arms around my waist, took out my penis. Discussing the matter with other medical men, at the table in London Fields, I discover that such incidents are not uncommon. In Aberdeen, for example, the venerable figure who retired as senior lecturer in anatomy told one of my colleagues that he picked up men, rough trade, on a regular basis, through the venereal clinic or in public toilets. He regarded it as academic research. He would have no dealings with women. And was reluctant to accept them even as students. He showed my friend lengthy accounts he kept in bound journals, medical students talking about their sex lives. One entry described how a nurse, when she encountered a young doctor on a stairwell, leant over the banisters and lifted up her skirt, pulled down her knickers and invited the man to enter her, there and then, from the rear.

I was brought off, without preliminaries, as I undertook surgical procedures: blood and sperm, the life juices. Eros and Thanatos. Astonishing! The risks we took excited some of the nurses, the shamanic stature of the surgeon. A very powerful aphrodisiac. That was when I started using pharmaceuticals on a regular basis, to maintain concentration, oxprenolol or propranolol for the tremble in the wrist.

The hospital secretary was a colonel. Nearly all the staff, permanent staff, were Salvationists. The ward sisters were certainly Salvationists. The nurse I spoke of, her parents were Salvationists, serious figures in the hierarchy. She took me to one of their meetings, a hall. It might have been part of that round chapel. We sat on the stairs afterwards, fondling each other. There was a discipline about the Salvationists that was impressive.

In the end one develops an unhealthy obsession with danger. I couldn't dress a wound without picturing a throbbing vulva. Sleep was out of the *question. I would volunteer to stay on the wards all night, hoping for an excuse to go into theatre, praying that this particular nurse would be on duty. It had to end badly – and of course it did. Horrible really, the scenes with her parents, the church people. The hospital administrators were much more understanding. I transferred again, out of maternity, away from living things into forensic medicine. Corpses. A custodian of refrigerated meat. An impossible labour without the relief of drugs and alcohol. But very much part, as I know you'll appreciate, of a great London tradition. Resurrectionism. Salvage. Recycling.*

Before Swanny could describe the incident, in the cellars beneath the Children's Hospital in Hackney Road after one of their drunken Christmas parties, Anya Gris arrived to collect him.

'Come on, Gramps, I'll walk you home.'

This was no casual endearment, she meant it. Swanny had a blood relative to keep an eye on his welfare. Anya covered his expenses at the sheltered accommodation on the edge of London Fields. The refuge was threatened and would probably close, but for now old Swanny was fed, housed, cherished within the borough where he had worked for so many years. And where, to the death, he would remain.

Anya warned me, as I accompanied her back to Fassett Square, that I shouldn't take Swanny's tales too literally; much of his material was apocryphal, borrowed from other quacks, adapted from medical journals or the Paris-published pornography of his repressed and circumscribed youth. *He* was the one with the Quaker upbringing, a man unhinged by premature exposure to the fecund energies of the metropolis. The bishop at the orgy.

And the Mole Man too. I should treat that interview with extreme caution. There was a very good reason why the Channel 4 documentary was pulled. Anya was a friend of the writer Stephen Smith who did a nice book on *Underground London (Travels beneath City Streets)*. Hearing of my Hackney researches, Smith wanted to pass on a word of warning. He looked after the culture slot for a late-night BBC news magazine. He met William Lyttle with a view to shooting a filler item. 'If I might presume, a wee word of caution about Mr William,' Smith said. 'He pestered the life out of me to intercede on his behalf with the authorities (Hackney Social Services). But buried in the back story, we discovered, was a serious allegation. I won't go into who or what it involved, but we felt we should leave well alone.'

'Use what Swanny told you this morning, but forget the rumours about the mortuary film,' Anya said. 'Treat him with discretion, please. He's been stitched up too many times by people who can't differentiate between truth and fiction. Fools who think cobbled-together interview transcripts make a proper book.'

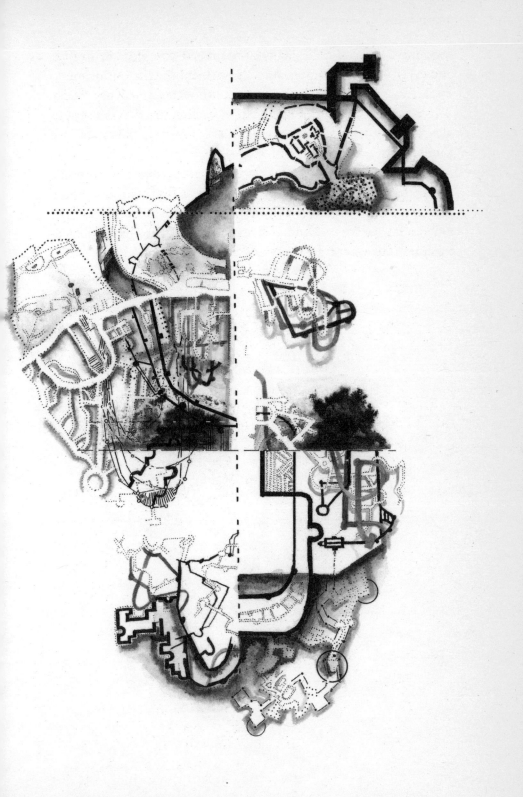

SCRIBES AND WITNESSES

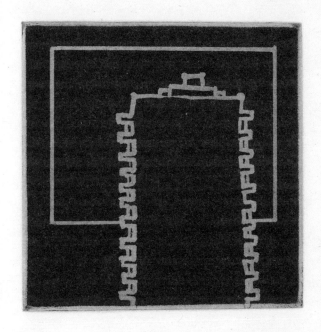

whatever happened to the old men of Hackney
who sat around a wireless, weeping tears of pride
at weather forecasts from Radio Moscow?

– Bernard Kops

Will Self

Hackney once again topped the list: it's official, according to this morning's radio statisticians, we are the worst borough in London for car crime. Licence dodging. Petty theft. Taking without the owner's consent. Which is pretty encouraging, I felt. The more cars taken the better our chances of surviving another day. Best practice: remove and destroy.

Coming from elsewhere and crossing the Hackney border, shock-waves knock you back. The whiteknuckle, choke-smoking panic of stopped pod people. Who never, *ever*, climb out of their vehicles: they hoot for colleagues, wives, ex-wives, elbows on horns, lighting up, using cellphones as smoke extractors. Spare hand dangling, miming self-love. Venom, vitriol: give them just half a chance to headbutt cruel fate. *Please, please.* Make their day.

They mount kerbs, hurtle into dead-end tributaries, scrape through on the inside, outside, over the top: screaming, hammering the wheel, hot to kill. Multitasking private chauffeurs of businessmen and media casuals, hopelessly lost, jump lanes, beat lights, investigate improbable short cuts. White vans hunt cocksure cyclists. There are stand-offs, hideous collisions. *Kill me then. Try it.*

Kids leap from behind parked juggernauts. Thief-scooters and fast-food scramblers dispute the pavement, using speedbumps as ramps to set them up for virtuoso wheelie demos. There is one spot, part of the afternoon school run (that epic of aggrandizing status war), between a hard left into Middleton Road and a lane-swerve, picking up speed after the camera, which traps the unwary. Shattered glass, crunched metal, blood, bored police: on a daily basis. They have widened the pavements to make room for insurance-claim photographers.

Will Self had it covered in *How the Dead Live*: Dalston (his

Dulston) as an enclave of the living dead. Sub-immortals cursed to hang around in our memories, like bats in a foul cave. It doesn't matter that Derek Raymond used the title fourteen years earlier. In Raymond's London, a posthumous dream, *everybody is dead*. Crematorium ash in the omelette, dog fur on the tongue. You stir sand into black coffee, feel the clinker in a scalp wound that is never going to heal. Your wife's memory is wiped, her babysitter is a television set in a suburban hospital that will soon be a gated community with an upbeat heritage title. Raymond worked his own Hollow Earth system; within the dream of the book, its hallucinated language, were further nightmares. Worse imaginings. And within those nightmares? Hammer horrors to shock us back to consciousness. The romance, Derek Raymond acknowledged, came from his experiences as a night-shift minicab driver: knife to the throat, lines of Shelley and Keats floating on a loop.

Will Self's cabbies are more human. You've met them. They absorb and distort the unofficial history of the city; which becomes, in their accidental and obsessive journeying across it, a physical body. You can map Self's mythologized topography, where Raymond's space is entirely propositional, argumentative, absent. Like an outdated Ordnance Survey of the wrong town. In my eccentric bibliography of the borough, *How the Dead Live* had a firm place on the shelf (where it nudged against Pinter's *The Homecoming* and Stewart Home's *Blow Job*). Home, in his interview for this book, talked of a Notting Hill meeting with Self. They didn't get along, prejudices on both sides. It was visceral, like Brown and Blair. With no requirement, on either side, to fake an alliance. Or Brown and Cameron: seething Scot and Oxbridge toff.

Self was tall and lean. Sardonic, saturnine. He was married, had children, visited theatres. He appeared on television. And was enough of a figure in the culture to remain in London. Much of his journalistic material came from cycling – epiphanies such as a whale swimming up the Thames – and collisions, rucks with SUV pilots. 'Who d'jew fink I am, some fucking punk?' he has the mannerless motor-fiend shout before he lashes out. And Self is decked.

Home, shorter in the neck, lower to the ground, was also a convinced cyclist – now a walker – getting from place to place, rather than striding off along the South Downs. A reluctant economic migrant, Stewart was continually sneaking back to town with a new scam, new partner: London was his life, but it refused to support him. These writerly squabbles were nothing: we were, all of us, energy vampires. Predators, in good heart, hoping for the worst.

Boots on, rucksack prepared, I waited at the kitchen table, fiddling with chopped-up sections of map. I sensed a reluctance on Will Self's part to involve himself with this one-day circumambulation of Hackney, a yomp of around fifteen miles. The distance was nothing. But would it fit the book? His book, my book. My concept was too rigidly schematic. Will's walks carried him back to the village from which his father's family had emerged. His expeditions pushed out from Stockwell like the spokes of a wheel. He relished zones that offered maximum resistance, air terminal to city centre. Poor old Hackney was hag-ridden, airless. Dulston could be fictionalized but not documented. Had we doomed ourselves to lurch between polemic journalism and undercooked literature? My perverse contention: if it can be commissioned, forget it.

There was a radio item that morning about a woman whose sight had been restored by a blow to the head. On a 243 bus, as it crept towards Shoreditch. The white assailant, known to the police, was going down for two years: despite this accidental miracle. Meanwhile, in Croydon, a black man blinding a pensioner in a random assault, on another bus, received a reprimand, but no custodial sentence. To the outrage of tabloid commentators.

River successfully forded, Will arrived on time. And away we went. To beat the bounds. As we eased into it, I recognized that I felt protective of place; the expedition should demonstrate quirks and hidden charms, but it was also a renunciation. To construct a Hackney book, after all these years, was to say goodbye. I thought the walk might teach me how warring postal districts could fit together in a healing arc. Nothing connects with nothing until you spread a little mud from your footprints.

Will, as he later reported, saw the Hackney peregrination as: 'a framing device for an anti-Olympics rant'. That shadow, the imposition of future memory, laid a dark cloud across our solar circuit. The borough, as I pointed out when we checked my collaged map, was made in the shape of England. With Homerton as the London of London, the city's City. We would roam the south coast of the Regent's Canal and the white cliffs of Shoreditch, before attempting a bucolic drift through the West Country of De Beauvoir, with its Mole Man. Then the Bristol slave-port of Dalston, the Lake District of Clissold Park. Gritstone uplands of Finsbury Park and Stamford Hill. The Wash of Springfield Park Marina.

I tried it first with Renchi. He was ill, pale, clammy beneath his Inca flaps: we misremembered or reinvented the separate pasts we shared, thirty years ago. We tracked a red line someone had painted through Hoxton, while Renchi recalled how he marked out chalk arrows to guide visitors from Hampstead through this unknown land. We found, beside the New River, a memorial to George Bunting, a local sculptor and fellow stallholder at Camden Passage. I hadn't seen George, a child emigrant to Australia, in years. Now I knew why. He pushed a pram of legal documents, battered London books, from Southgate Road to Islington, by way of the canal. He gave the start to my research collection, providing ex-library copies of Walter Besant, Lawrence Hutton's *Literary Landmarks of London*, Gordon Home, William Kent, *London's Lost Theatres of the Nineteenth Century* by Erroll Sherson. Hackney pamphlets. Recollections of the Elephant Man. All for a few pence. With the gift of a property map of the Springfield Park Estate printed on canvas.

What struck me on that vernal equinox walk with Will was how the Hackney border was defined by everything of interest being outside, beyond its patronage. Hitchcock in Leytonstone. The mad poet Christopher Smart in his Bethnal Green asylum. William Blake and John Bunyan in Bunhill Fields. And Will himself, the height, the flattened cap, was an exotic outsider: miasma of Arthur Machen's *London Adventure*, pipe and pouch, the deep growl. He marked our progress by pissing at relevant points: behind Blake's grave, in Shepherdess Walk, Seven Sisters, Springfield Marina, Hackney Marshes, the Royal Inn on the Park: a glittering uric ley. Hackney has this diuretic effect on tourists. Samuel Pepys reported, in July 1664: 'And so we rode home round by Kingsland, Hackney and Mile End, till we were quite weary – and my water working at least seven or eight times upon the road, which pleased me well.'

There was a boyhood game, a Stamford Hill friend once told me, called 'Spot the Yock'. Jewish lads hung out in Springfield Park trying to identify trespassing Gentiles, rarer than radium in those days. Stamford Hill would prove the most disturbing passage for Will.

But first the super-urban traces: Broadway Market, where squatters have been expelled from a captured café to make way for a fortified box. Which stays empty, bristling with wire, surveillance, dogs, as a memorial to its own lack of content.

Hackney Road. And the challenging hulk of the Children's Hospital, sealed for so many years, and now accessed by film crews attracted by the caravan-friendly spaces of Haggerston Park.

We encounter a Staffordshire bull terrier attached by a blue string to a (body-)builder whose tracksuit bottoms are punningly customized with bulldog clips. 'Name?' Will demands. 'Buster.' Man or dog, I'm not sure. Released from Oxford, Self took a job as labourer/driver with a firm of builders near Clissold Park. He began by filling up the truck with diesel instead of petrol and thereby taking another hazardous vehicle off the Hackney roads. Further disasters followed, wrecked machines, lost tools. Trading on charm, he lasted six months.

The Shoreditch/City nub of the borough is provisional, uneasy in its new status. In Worship Street I ponder the obvious question: 'Worship what?' BRITISH LAND (Bovis Lend Lease) are throwing up a stick-in-your-throat tower. The foundations look like a submarine pen. This sun-splintering thirty-six-storey monster has been 'meticulously designed by the Chicago office of architects Skidmore, Owings and Merrill, to meet the needs of both financial and professional occupiers. This development will provide major new public space and galleria, with shops, bars and cafés.' A sundial-finger to count down the dissolution of breweries, fruit-and-veg markets, rough trade. Freelance pedestrianism.

Will tells me that he lunched here yesterday with his brother and two of the American princes involved with the project: £600 on the plastic, plus VAT and a stonking tip. These promoters and projectors, with their Nehru-collar international architects, see nothing beyond the space they intend to carve out and occupy. Nothing coheres. The tower has been presented, praised in its virtual form: building the thing is a chore. Wherever that long shadow falls, across Spitalfields, the railway, Bishopsgate, the Griffin rules. Human dots moving through the chasms of this computer-generated landscape are the pinpricks Harry Lime gestures towards from his Viennese Ferris wheel: how many share options would you sacrifice to save one soul?

Bill Parry-Davies was fearful of the way Hackney would trouser its windfall from the developers and squander it on vanity projects. 'The forces of darkness are indeed enveloping us,' he told me. 'The City Corporation and Hammerton, the major developers, are seeking to redefine the northern boundary of Mammon. They have planned a tsunami of demolitions and tower blocks. The shadows will extend as far as the Regent's Canal. Hackney's Planning Department have not made public their study into sunlight deprivation. This, of course, has nothing to do with the fact that the council own the land on which the first fifty-one-storey tower will be built. Hackney stands to receive around £10 million in "planning gain" money. The sale proceeds won't be reinvested to benefit Shoreditch, they are already earmarked for the council's £45-million Town Hall extension.'

Will's spindly roll-ups give way to a pipe when we breakfast in Shepherdess Walk. The fantastic topography of a Self novel is honourably researched and grows from a foundation of books, reports from edge-land legmen, conversations with connected cabbies. And a London life, from childhood, criss-crossing the Thames, roaming the Hampstead heights: interrogating horror. Scratching the membrane that conceals the pit. He sniffs. He blows his nose, paper napkin crumpled in tin ashtray. Mephitic boils bubble under placid Formica, bacon sandwiches bite back. Delving into nineteenth-century science fiction, speculative literature, the romance of English downland pastoralism, is Self's chosen method for admonishing the willed stupidity of the contemporary scene. How he continues to push through his highly wrought fictional constructs, while operating, with considerable vim, in the disposable media world, is a mystery into which I should not enquire. None of my business, obviously. But the question lingers, unresolved.

In Old Street Will's mobile tweets for the first time, against the cacophony of the roundabout: 'I'm walking in the City.' But outside its walls, in the zone of Bedlams and archery grounds, rancid pubs, rotten vegetables, dead cinemas. The *Standard*, for whom he is on a retainer, want a piece, like now, for tonight. Their attitude is: undecided. Don't go too hard at the Olympics. Not yet. See how the deal pans out. A steady drip-feed of niggles, toxic-waste discoveries, soaring budgets, lost allotments, financial advantage to Lord Coe: nothing major, nothing that plays against support for disadvantaged London youth.

The *Statesman* calls next: a promise from Will to do a thousand words when he gets home. Acoustic twitterings are absorbed into the general Old Street microclimate of madhouse memories, power-hikers ranting to themselves, blank-eyed office drones wired to electronic pacemakers. A cakewalk of catatonics using broad pavements like escalators; eating, chatting, applying lip salve as they move. Picking noses, fingering hot buttons.

Passing at last through Dalston Junction, Will's ghetto of the inconvenient dead, he remembers visiting the Four Aces Club in the squatting era. But that was another country and its traces are gone. He undertook long, five-day hikes with his father through the West Country, Taunton to Lyme Regis. All of that is vivid still. The father's loose flannels, his thin belt. The knapsack known as a sacheverell.

Stoke Newington Green (with its nonconformist heritage). Clissold Park. Blackstock Road junkshops with war toys Will isn't going to buy for his son (not at £8 for an aircraft carrier): we push forward at a brisk pace, the story is out ahead, shifting and revising as the horizon retreats. I can't resist a strange little book by H. Kaner, plucked from the glass-fronted cupboard: *People of the Twilight.* Self-published in Llandudno, 1946. And what a weird tale that proves to be, transportation to an interior molecular world, germ wars, flying ships, interspecies romance.

Describing his fellow excursionist Antony Gormley, as he hurled himself at a perimeter fence around a firing range near Foulness, Will says: 'There are no barriers for him between inside and outside.'

Finsbury Park is a green wall confronted by anonymous small hotels. At Stamford Hill, Self bristles and fumes; he is violently agitated by the Hasidic community, long black coats in cramped shops. He is writing about London as a drowned ship. A thought that carries us down to the Marshes, the Lea, the endgame of Hackney Wick: travellers, wrecking yards, studios under sentence of death. Under such wide skies, standing on the bridge over the rushing A115, we reach agreement: we will walk again.

Will's piece appears before we fix a date to track Danny Folgate's leyline down towards the river.

> In a way, this beating the bounds of a single borough was a highly contrived exercise. At ground level Hackney exhibits no coherence, or unity. But looked at another way, our circuit represented a synecdoche: taking a part of the great conurbation for its whole. Moving through time as well as space, we espied William Blake's decaying tomb as well as the

diamond mullions of Thirties suburbia; the 21st-century 'wharf' developments beside the Regent's Canal – each with its tacky accretion of eco-planking – together with aspirational, 19th-century ironwork in Victoria Park.

However, it wasn't until we stood on the grey-green football pitches of Hackney Marsh and looked south to where the brutalist skyline of Canary Wharf thumped the low cloud cover that I realized we were looking at the future. For here, in among rusty oil bowsers and light industrial huggermugger, is where Tony, Gordon, Tessa, Seb, Ken and all their yea-saying, log-rolling confrères, are intent on building the New Jerusalem of the 2012 London Olympics.

Another walk, towards the Thames, allows us to stretch in pastoral delirium, to chase the benediction of Danny's invisible line. Will is sensibly equipped with floppy hat, blue T-shirt, long shorts. When he stops to buy plastic water, I snap him against today's headlines: ARMED DRUG ADDICT JAILED. SHORTS BAN IN HEATWAVE. After a twelve-year gap, Self tells me that he has interviewed J. G. Ballard for the second time. About the compulsive journalism, Ballard is upbeat and dismissive of cant: 'Do *more*, Will. Do as much as you can.' In this sticky urban summer, Self sleeps on a Thatcher schedule, four hours a night. Twice as long as the now manic Gordon Brown. Who has been driven mad, stuttering, jaw-thrusting, air-gargling, by having to live in a world with no past, no viable future, and an infinitely fixable back story.

In the excellent café of the hangar-sized Woolworths, alongside Beckton Alp, I take out my pocket-recorder.

The whole Olympic Park, the regeneration of this part of London, is doomed. It seems to me to have no more forward logic than the original development of the city itself. So when we stand on top of Beckton Alp and we see a slice, a gnomon of retail parks flung down at the base of it, we also notice a queered sports field. This is an idea of America imposed on human topography that is so much older and more ancient, confused and anarchic. It has the air of imposture. I don't think the Jim Ballard territory of the M4/M3/M25 corridor can be imported across London. The lines of force, as revealed by your dowser friend, are negated. The shit-river we walked along, the arsenic mountain: the whole atmosphere is toxic. It's distempered. And, frankly, I don't buy it.

This is a quintessentially English vision. It isn't postmodernism. The English never really got to Modernism. It happened too early, it's been forgotten. This is a hinterland of a hinterland. People are being drawn out of the city towards it. It's about legibility.

This landscape reminds me very much of developments in upstate New York. But it's very nice here in Woolworths, the coffee place has a solidity. It's an antique. You can feel yourself travelling back to the Woolworths of the 1950s. There is a lovely smiling couple over your shoulder. They're so happy. And well-upholstered. Comfortable with themselves.

This is a happy mart. A clearance outlet. So it's already being run down. My grandfather's job, in the States, in the Depression, was to shut stores down. He was an asset-stripper in the 1920s, after the Wall Street Crash. That's what he did. In a sense he was far in advance of conceptual artists like Michael Landy. He was doing it for real. That is what is now happening here.

The atmosphere outside, in this heat, is toxic as hell. Kenyan distance runners are going to be falling by the wayside as they attempt to breathe the foul air. This is the colon of London, really.

After that circumnavigation of Hackney, I felt as if we had been traversing a widening gyre. Having completed the circuit, I realized that it had been a very interesting exercise. The route imposes a centripetal force, pulling you out still further. In other words, Hackney was defined as an absence. And the London beyond it was therefore a more graspable presence. And in defining this presence, as it were, within the walls of Hackney, Hackney itself becomes apprehensible. So our walk did work.

I was surprised by that, actually. I was very sceptical initially. It is something you could only achieve in an ambulatory context. It needed to be genuinely periphrastic in that way.

I suppose the major line that interested me, the one I was picking up, *was the Jewish community. I don't like frummers. I don't like any people who try and arrest time in the name of the supernatural.*

And again the thing about the Jews leaving Stamford Hill, the move-ment out, the proposed evacuation to Milton Keynes: there is something odd going on. The Hasids don't care about place – because of course they're in an endlessly imminent millenarian city. They don't care where they are, so long as they've got their Volvo.

For me, it's trans-generational, Jewish anti-Semitism. My mother was not comfortable with her Jewishness. It was something she was in flight from. I suppose I've inherited that. When I was a kid in Hampstead Garden Suburb, there was an old Polish woman on the corner who never cut her privet hedge. This interwar redbrick detached home was completely overgrown. My mother used to say, 'It's because she was in the camps. She thinks if she doesn't cut her hedge the Nazis won't come and get her.' And this was a completely double-edged fable. It said such a lot. For a start, it was my mother distancing herself from the mad Jew on the corner. Secondly, she wanted to appropriate that paranoia for herself. It was a really uncomfortable position to be in. She was intensely ambivalent about her Jewishness.

And lied about it! *She didn't lie about her Jewishness, but she under-stated it in so many ways. I've inherited this to a greater degree. I have a 'white nigger' thing. People love to flaunt their Jewishness. I've been guilty of doing that. The truth of the matter is, I'm not circumcised. I'm not bar-mitvah'd. I never went to shul. I'm kind of not Jewish. I'm really not Jewish. People say, 'You're Jewish, aren't you?' I say, 'I'm half-Jewish.' They say, 'Who's Jewish, your mother or your father?' 'My mother.' They say, 'Well, you're Jewish then.' And I say, 'No no, that's something Jews think.'*

In the Hackney context, there is a lot going on: the idea of Jewishness and Hackney. On the one hand you have the Jew who has moved through the borough, as a conduit. And moved on. To sub-dormitories of Jewishness, Golders Green and Hendon. But the next generation, the ones whose grandparents had come in through the docks, they stick. The grandparents were people of the Pale in Eastern Europe who never made it to the United States. The third generation of acultural Jews have now married out completely. They are barely Jewish any more. Marrying out was easily 50 per cent, twenty years ago.

The other thing that struck me as we were walking, you spoke about the submerged Hackney Brook and how you would once have found villas, like Marble Hill or Strawberry Hill, along the banks. And one knows, from reading Pepys or Evelyn, that this was indeed the case. But in fact I have to walk with you to see, vividly, that what happened in the nineteenth century, what happened to the dialectic of London, was the final and irrevocable imposition of an east/west divide. In a sense it was a kind of class- and ethnic-cleansing operation, an expulsion of the bourgeoisie from the east.

I didn't read the book, because I worried that it would influence me too much, but After London by Richard Jefferies made me think very hard about these topics. One of the ideas in After London is that the lake that has overwhelmed the city is toxic. And this has been so for hundreds of years.

I was cycling over Vauxhall Bridge and saw all these people standing by the parapet. I got off the bike and walked over. 'What are you looking at?' This woman said, 'That whale.' I looked down and felt two things. It is a whale. And, secondly, it's dead. It's moribund.

One thinks of the opening shot of A Touch of Evil. When Orson Welles, as the grotesque sheriff, hauls himself out of the car, he is about forty years old and he looks like his own future: unshaven death. An astonishing performance. The longest opening tracking shot in any film. About two and a half minutes. I digress.

Hackney Town Hall is as moribund as that whale. They are using it for weddings. You can get married in the council chamber. They'll get Richard Rogers or Norman Foster to build them a new glass bivalve. That's Hackney, that's progress.

Ken Worpole and Alexander Baron

Whatever else it achieved the Hackney circumnavigation with Will Self focused my attention on a sense of the borough as an organic entity, even when the border outline was created by political surgery and gerrymandering. The completed circuit, with its spurts and stalls, canal path, marshland, reservoir, high street, suburban narcolepsy, oddities such as the Mason with folded regalia leaving a small hotel on the heights of Stamford Hill, activated dormant energies. Opened up fresh fields of enquiry.

I noticed, without having time to carry out a proper survey, the enclave of 1930s modernist flats on the north side of Clissold Park, tucked away in a bask of well-kept box hedges, ruled lawns and considered plantings; fruit trees, hawthorns, shrubs that avoided the dead hand of municipal uniformity. Here was a garden city oasis, a fragment of some benevolent planner's dream: Abercrombie's green London escaped from the drawing board.

If I had any hope of recovering the untold story of Roland Camberton, it would be through the recorded memories of another Hackney writer of the period, someone like Alexander Baron. But Baron was dead. I had visited his home in Golders Green and spoken to him about his long career, from the novels of wartime to the realist Hackney books, the years in television drama, classic serials. 'All gone,' he said. 'I still work, but I don't know anybody in publishing these days. They have no idea who I am.'

The Lowlife, a tale embedded in the Jewish northwest passage, was reprinted as a paperback. I wrote the introduction. Now I returned to my taped interviews from 1992. Had I missed any references to Camberton?

My parents escaped to Hackney. My mother came from Spitalfields, Hare Marsh. A year after they married, they took one room in Dalston. Dalston is now considered part of the deep East End, but they felt that they'd taken a step up in the world. I was born in Dalston and we continued to live there, very happily, in one room. Until I was six years old.

When I came back from the war, I had no home. I'd been knocked about a bit and was quite unwell. My imagination was seized by the Hackney area in a way that it hadn't been when I lived there.

It was then that the seeds of The Lowlife *were planted. I walked about the area a great deal. I would write mostly at night. During the day I spent my time walking the streets. And continued, even after I'd left Hackney, to become a kind of ghost haunting the whole borough. Then gradually there took shape in my mind the idea of a novel, refracting some of the life I had witnessed in my wanderings. I began to see through the eyes of a character who was very much on my mind, who attracted me. And who, like me, had been formed by this place, while remaining something of an outsider.*

In the wider social sense one minor theme in The Lowlife *is the way in which the diligent, ordinary Jewish community continued to move on. Having graduated from Whitechapel to Hackney, almost all of them carried on to the north-west suburbs. The respectable, ordered life they led is one against which my central character, Harryboy Boas, rebels. He would rather remain free – and live in the more turbulent life of post-war Hackney.*

I was lucky, so far as the East End novel was concerned, that I'd already established myself by writing about other things. When The Lowlife *was written, publishers saw my material as droll and rather colourful. The novel was optioned as a movie. At that time* Steptoe and Son *was a great success on television. Film producers saw Harry H. Corbett as the ideal actor to play Harryboy Boas in a movie version of Hackney. Nothing came of it. I think Corbett died.*

The tapes were interesting, but inconclusive, part of a television commissioning process that was already losing its nerve. The Marc Karlin era at Channel 4 was long over, utopians and Marxists replaced by premature New Labour careerists and neurotics in black shirts whose only strategy was to have no strategy, like ex-Stasi function-aries reinventing themselves after the Wall came down.

And no mention of Camberton. Baron, exposed to the once familiar streets, the corrugated fences, fires, feral kids, was a man in shock. Hands in raincoat pockets, collar up against the wind from the east, he blinked behind stern spectacles as he drifted into reverie, letting the ghosts, of which he was now one, return.

I had been thinking about Ken Worpole when I got the letter. Ken was very much our local scholar in the literature of the lost and a pioneer of oral history. Working lives recorded and turned into booklets. Might Ken have taped Camberton? Or, at worst, made a more substantial transcript with Alexander Baron? The exhibition at the South Bank Centre curated by Worpole and Nick Kimberley in 1986 launched a cult of literary gravedigging: *20,000 Streets under the Sky. The London Novel, 1896–1985.* Alexander Baron's *The Lowlife* was included: 'a wonderfully evocative account of Stoke Newington and Stamford Hill in the late '50s'. As was Nigel Fountain's *Days Like These* with its punchy strapline: 'Fascist Terror – Cynical Hack Investigates.' Nick Kimberley wrote the summary: 'Revives the figure of the lone individual searching for truth . . . and places him at the heart of radical politics in London. Meetings in pubs, violent confrontation with neo-fascists, bookshop browsing, all sardonically observed, are linked together by the key bus-routes on Fountain's London map, the 38 and the 253.'

But no R. C. Hutchinson, no *Elephant and Castle.* No Camberton. The rain had dried from the pavements.

Taking a break from transcribing Will Self's Beckton Alp inter-view, I opened the letter from Ken Worpole.

I understand from several sources – including a recent conversation with Will Self – that you are once again engaged in writing about Hackney. You will not be surprised to hear that this interests me greatly.

453

There are several things I'd be happy to pass on to you, or which I feel are important aspects of post-war Hackney life which have been under-recorded. Firstly, many years ago I did a long interview with Alexander Baron for a feature for *City Limits*. I still have the tapes somewhere, which you are welcome to listen to. They are fascinating about his early political involvement on the left.

There was a time when I considered writing a book about Hackney Council corruption – a long-standing tradition – truly terrible financial, political and moral corruption, and began to collect material. In the end I hadn't the legal knowledge or the energy to do it.

Maybe we can meet?

Ken's flat, a couple of floors up, was in the 1930s block that I had admired on our Hackney circumnavigation. In such a place, with its sanded-wood floors, its wide Crittall windows looking down on the masts of the trees, I appreciated how clean, simple architecture enhanced lives. The civic possibilities of these connected but independent units made the notion of community viable. I had seen nothing like it in Hackney since I visited the German Hospital.

A plate of fruit on a pale blue table, so highly polished that it reflected the window grid and the pattern of the trees beyond. Its surface floated like a horizontal marine painting, drawing the eye towards the pebbles on the window ledge. I was reminded of the title of one of Ken's books, *Staying Close to the River*. The good life in a good place: shelves of books, racks of CDs and silver-haired Ken Worpole in blue shirt to complement the table. He had been out in the weather, on his boat, his bicycle. His relaxed posture reflected journeys made, a city experienced.

It felt rather strange, and impertinent, to be recording a man who had spent so many years building up an archive of Hackney voices.

We came here in 1968. I'd just trained to be a teacher in Brighton College of Education. My first job was in Hackney Downs. The school where writers like Harold Pinter and Alexander Baron got their education. Pinter's English teacher, Joe Brearley, was still there. It was a very interesting school, very Jewish. Fifty per cent Jewish. Lots of the teachers had been pupils there. Very strong, the loyalty. Blair's friend and fixer Lord Levy, the honours broker, he was there. Tony's favoured tennis partner. He got his start in Hackney Downs.

Alan Sugar and Arnold Wesker didn't go there. They went to the other school, the one near the Homerton Hospital.

There was a fire at Hackney Downs. A lot of building work was going on. The school went comprehensive. It couldn't cope with the transition. A very significant number of Afro-Caribbean pupils arrived. A complete shift out of the Jewish identity. I was there for only four years, it wasn't my fault that the school collapsed.

I set up Centerprise with a key operator who was black, American: Glenn Thompson. A great hustler. He had been illiterate, got politicized, went into Black Power politics, learnt to read. Then he became a draft resister. He went to Hoxton as a youth worker. Astonishing, really, for a black American to get a job with the Inner London Education Authority in Hoxton. Hoxton was rough, very rough. Glenn befriended two or three lively local lads who had form. The ILEA put money into setting up new approaches to youth work.

Centerprise, on Dalston Lane, was funded as a youth project. There was also a bookshop. And a café behind the bookshop. We did outreach youth work. My role was publishing, oral history. I did that for five years. I left because I felt that I shouldn't stay too long.

The first book I wrote, Dockers and Detectives, was intended as a recovery of a certain twentieth-century literary tradition. Which included, obviously, the London-Jewish novel. Alexander Baron was part of that. The interesting thing is how quickly he was forgotten. In Michael Billington's biography of Pinter, he can't work out why Pinter's stage name was 'David Baron'. Pinter must have been living three streets away from Alexander Baron. They went to the same school. He must have known Baron's work. I can't believe anything other than that he borrowed the name of a successful local writer.

With the whole Centerprise thing, I was very influenced by Raph Samuel: the tradition of oral history and the reconnection with a variant past. Books and authors do vanish. Take Simon Blumenfeld and Jew Boy. It turns out he wasn't even Jewish. He's quite open about it. In an obituary tribute there is a revelation that his parents were originally Polish, Spanish. There really is some question about whether they were actually Jewish. Blumenfeld didn't die until two or three years ago. He was about ninety-four. His world was dance bands. There were very consciously Jewish dance bands.

We had quite a good library at Centerprise. I collected books, I picked up books from the market in Kingsland Waste. I haven't been back for years. I also bought stuff from you, lots of it, in Camden Passage. I worked on that exhibition on the South Bank with Nick Kimberley. He lives here now, over the road, the next street.

Nigel Fountain was featured in our catalogue. He was connected with David Widgery, people like that. Didn't they resurrect the Hackney Literary and Philosophical Society?

When Centerprise moved to Kingsland High Street it was only a block away from the pub which was the meeting place of the Hackney Left in the 1970s and 1980s. In the summer, when the hospitals emptied out, all the crazies and outpatients descended on Centerprise.

Widgery, Fountain, they were there all the time. Doing the crossword. The shop was a meeting place. The pub was occupied by the Socialist Workers Party. Doctrinal disputes. It was the place for about five years. Friendships were forged, ideas exchanged.

I never joined a political party. Well, I was in the Labour Party, but that doesn't count. Hackney was very important to the Communist Party. There were numerous CP activists in Kynaston Road. New politics were being tried out. Peter Fuller lived in Graham Road. We had every left group: SWP, IS, Militant Tendency. Centerprise ran poetry readings and book launches in the SWP pub. No charge. I think that era is over now.

In the early days, before all this communal activity, I cycled to school. We lived in Stoke Newington. Then I walked, every day. The kids in Hackney Downs thought cycling was a joke. Both our children were born in the Mothers' Hospital in Lower Clapton Road. I would walk across

Hackney Downs in the snow. To the Homerton Hospital where my father was sectioned. One's life is made from these Hackney walks.

We had a boat on the River Lea. I thought Springfield Marina was a most interesting place. Particularly after the poll tax was introduced. It was an outlaw community. People who refused to pay the poll tax bought themselves any kind of hulk. The Marina had a little bar. It was pure anarchy. Very few of those boats ever went anywhere. They never went out on the river.

There is something mysterious and intangible about Hackney streets. In high summer or deepest winter, there is a tendency to overpower you. Especially when you've been living here for forty years. It is a transitional place.

What we have noticed is the reverse of the traditional pattern of urban migration. We bought a house in a little street, Oldfield Road. The street was probably 30 or 40 per cent owned, owned, or in the process of being bought, by West Indians. Who were working for London Transport and so on. They were struggling to buy – and so were we. But their children could never afford to follow them. You have a disrupted story of the onward progress of the immigrant. The children of those very hard-working people were unable to remain in the place where they had been born and brought up.

I took Ken's Alexander Baron tapes home with me and spent a couple of days transcribing them. The story would fit neatly into this book – childhood, Hackney Downs, street football, leftist politics, war – but time was running out and I had no ambition to produce a definitive account. I chased down personal obsessions, the way certain buildings, certain people, suggested the rough outline of a fiction that blended history, unreliable memoir and faded cultural traces. I underlined passages in the transcript where Baron appeared to be anticipating my quest or scripting a fresh approach.

I joined the Labour Party. I soon became prominent in Labour politics. I was in the Labour League of Youth. The adjacent branch was run by Ted

Willis, the future Lord Willis, and we soon teamed up. We formed a kind of militant tendency – small m, small t. Very soon we were running the journal of the local League of Youth. The circulation was boosted from 2,000 to 30,000, or 50,000 in a good month. We were writing most of the material ourselves, under different names. We'd spend all night, sitting in this little office we'd acquired, writing articles. The most important ones in our own names and the rest under names we made up. I don't know to this day if journalism is corrupting if you want to be a serious writer. Or if it gives you a fluency of thought and word.

At that time we met this crowd of radicals on the Daily Mirror. In the pubs around Fetter Lane. They told us how you load the whole story into the first paragraph. You've got to keep the reader's attention all the way through. Flair and technique in a writer may be inborn, a talent like my dad's talent for cutting furs. Perhaps the gift for writing can also be developed by journalism, I really don't know.

Baron in this passage seemed to answer the questions I didn't put to Will Self on our hike around the Hackney borders. Baron's journalism, like Self's, had a political or social agenda: survival was the best training. Everything Michael Moorcock developed, in the way of style and technique, came from his years writing and editing Tarzan and Kit Carson comics. He also adopted Fetter Lane, Holborn, Brooke Street, Bleeding Heart Yard as the labyrinth at the centre of his 'multiverse'. A zone of space-time anomalies where mortality is negotiable and death never strikes a good character from the story.

My pulse quickened, once again, when Worpole directed Baron towards territory in which Roland Camberton might at last make an appearance.

'You obviously weren't going to write the London-Jewish novel, were you?' Worpole challenges. 'Were you aware of a school of Jewish East End writers?'

I was a generation younger than them. I was post-war. The people you speak of belonged to the 1930s. They were all discoveries of John Lehmann, a part of his attempt to find a proletarian literature. This had its conde-scending side. The Jewish school had a condescending side too. There is, from Lehmann and his ilk, a homosexual attitude to the working class. It was a valuable enterprise in its time. Lehmann gave these writers a chance to express themselves. The only one I knew was Ashley Smith. He got in touch with me, because he was very lonely and had drifted away from the world of writers.

I lived on my own then in Marylebone. I asked Smith to come up and have a drink or some tea. We became quite friendly in a very occasional way. I took him to lunch with the editors of a new series of books which sent writers back to their original environments. Ashley wrote, I thought, a very good book. He went to live in Bethnal Green, near the brewery.

I knew both the Litvinoff brothers well. Manny had a great success with his trilogy about the Russian Revolution. I haven't seen him to ask if it was the kind of success one could live on. He used to be married to a woman with a thriving model agency in the West End. They lived in some state outside London, mainly on what she earned. They split up. I don't know where he is now or what he does. Except that he continues writing.

Oh yes, there was one other. I'd almost forgotten him. Roland Camberton. He died quite young. I saw him once at a party. He wrote specifically about Hackney. I think he was another one who went to Hackney Downs. I have an idea he wrote a book of short pieces about a comic opera staged by the school head. I don't know.

I don't even remember when I met him. It must have been fairly early on in my career. I can't remember whose party it was, except that it was somewhere in St John's Wood. I didn't venture very often into these exotic territories. I had this little uneasy talk with Camberton. A strange man. That's it. That's all.

Oona Grimes, Dr John Dee and Moby-Dick

Impossible to tell if Kaporal was dead, the man with a rope around his neck, trouser cuffs wet with dew, in the churchyard of St John's, or if this was another instance of the shady researcher's ability to plant false information in the local press (where he had excellent contacts), before absorbing a new identity in a more obscure corner of London. He might even have fled to the south coast, somewhere like Pevensey Bay, Bexhill-on-Sea. Kaporal, on the final night in the Victory, said that he had 'cracked the Conrad code' – and was reading *Nostromo* with an eye to simplifying the obtuse prose, changing the names of the characters and shifting the location to East Sussex. 'Publishers give unsolicited submissions to work-experience kids. I might cop an advance, hide out in Brittany for a couple of months in Jock's place. Finish my film. The one about Orson Welles and the Hackney *Moby-Dick*.'

With Kaporal beyond my reach, except by seance and planchette board, there was no hope of a refund against the inadequacies of the research file: the way this devious character had inserted fictional asides into genuine documentation, the transcripts of interviews downloaded from the net. There was still a chance that if I went through the box of unconnected papers he supplied me with, for a grand I could ill afford, I might find a clue to the location of one of his lock-ups or secret studios. The man had more boltholes than Walter Sickert. And nothing to hide.

A morning was wasted in relishing Kaporal's footnotes and asides: 'Another interesting Hackney character I came across last night in the Ol' Sam Pepys was Micky Zipp – a potbellied Scouse waster of fifty or so. His schtick is to say he can do anything you can do, but better. Micky claims to have been a runner for Welles when he was a kid. He also dealt speed for Dr Swan. But mostly it was cab runs up west, Chinatown, for Orson's between-meals snacks. He wouldn't touch the local all-day breakfast.'

'It's official,' Kaporal wrote, 'Hackney is more dangerous than Soweto. Figures from the main trauma centres in each area show that while Homerton Hospital in Hackney treats fifty-five knife wounds each month, the Chris Hani Baragwanath Hospital in Soweto – which has ten times as many people in its catchment area – sees only six times as many such cases.'

The trade in body parts, my researcher reckoned, had replaced the more traditional vehicle-stripping operations in the caves beneath the railway arches and lock-ups around Ridley Road. 'During my preliminary investigations, I was shown pictures of bodies plundered for organs, eyes or complete heads. In one example, a woman lies on a slab, her body cut open from the chest downwards, her reproductive organs removed. In another, a child sits bolt upright in rigor mortis, his head removed and placed on an altar, three feet above his ragged neck.'

At the end of an article Kaporal downloaded on 'The Clapton Messiah', Henry James Prince, who claimed that the Holy Ghost had taken up residence in his body, the researcher made his one mistake: he scribbled the address of the studio to which a suborned library assistant should send items stolen from Hackney Council's private archive. Before I set out to find this place, Scarborough Road, Finsbury Park, I couldn't resist reading about Prince, his successor John Smyth-Pigott and the Agapemonites. Smyth-Pigott was a compulsive womanizer who managed to convert (and seduce) numerous Salvationists, nurses from the Mothers' Hospital. To avoid retribution from the inevitable Hackney mob, he attempted to prove his divine status by walking across the murky waters of Clapton Pond. With farcical consequences. The lettering above the arched stone lintel of the Church of the Ark of the Covenant read: LOVE IN JUDGEMENT AND JUDGEMENT IN VICTORY.

Judgement in Victory!

Start where you will, open any book, explore whichever direction takes your fancy, and you must arrive in Vyner Street. The

461

backstreet pub where the dead drink until dawn. And the living, staring into their empty glasses, watch enviously. While texts unravel and words escape to decorate undemolished walls.

Finsbury Park was the next step in my recapitulation of the Will Self walk. Kaporal's files had a cutting from the *Standard* nominating Scarborough Road as the 'fifth spookiest street in Britain'. Spectral children at twilight playing forgotten games. Kaporal combed cyberspace and found a solitary girl, a faery presence glimpsed among the silver birches and long grass at the edge of the railway. There were reports of such sightings, from dog walkers and train passengers, that went back over forty years. In 1953, a local historian made the association with Madimi, the provocative sprite who appeared to the Elizabethan geographer and magus Dr John Dee.

I took part in a cricket match on the over-springy turf of Finsbury Park. An encounter from which half the players were taken to casualty wards with broken bones. Our team was captained by an Ahab with a tin leg. Mesmerized by the sidling crane-dance of his three-step approach, I was bowled by a gentle looper from the artist and Charles Manson lookalike, Ian Breakwell. A Stoke Newington librarian called Richard Boon published an article in which he argued that Breakwell and I were linked: 'Born a month apart, Breakwell and Sinclair comprise a psychic doubling, similar both in name and pursuit – notebooks, diaries, film and, above all, walking and its observation inform both their practices.'

The coincidences ran deeper than that: Ian lived in Albion Road where I was mired in Albion Drive. When Anna went into labour with William, our second child, the midwife rushed to the wrong address, Albion Road in Stoke Newington.

Breakwell's diary films were now part of the art-school canon. His genius lay in a trick I never mastered, knowing what to leave out. The film he made about tea-dancing at the De La Warr Pavilion, Bexhill-on-Sea, was a poignant and delightful elegy. He died and we gathered, yet again, to celebrate the passing of a good man. In the bar of the Cochrane Theatre, Brian Catling, nursing a whisky which he produced from a pocket inside his heavy leather coat, told me about his latest enthusiasm, a video-installation artist. 'Straight out of a Hitchcock film, this iced blonde with immaculate tailoring walked towards me across Tower Bridge. Hat, gloves, heels. *Marnie* or *North by Northwest*. We enjoyed a four-hour lunch while she described her *Moby-Dick* performance piece.'

London bridges and white whales. As preparation for my expedition in search of Kaporal's studio and the missing Welles film, I looked again at Orson's virtuoso turn, the sermon delivered from the ship's-prow pulpit in John Huston's film. Colour had been vampirized to invoke old whaling prints. The cast were English and Irish grotesques. Ray Bradbury wrote the script. One of the model whales drifted out to sea. Cetacean appearances in unlikely places suggested the imminent arrival of a drowned world. Catling called his first son Jack, Jack Ishmael.

The haunted building stood between the railway and an overgrown green path that led towards Alexandra Palace. Pulling myself up on a low wall, I was able to peer inside the reprieved development opportunity. Herman Melville in Ishmael's opening monologue from *Moby-Dick* speaks of 'pausing before coffin warehouses'. This dark-windowed hulk off Scarborough Road was one of those. How does Melville continue? 'Circumambulate the city . . . What do you see?—Posted like silent sentinels all around the town, stand thousands upon thousands of mortal men fixed in ocean reveries.'

One studio dimly lit, a figure dressed entirely in black hunched over a table, hair on fire. It was a woman, slender as a child, rapt in such furious concentration that my waxed-moon face at the window didn't break the spell. If she noticed the unmannerly intrusion, it could be incorporated, effortlessly, into the work in progress. Thick black shadows flattened in an etching press.

I knuckled the dirty pane. I gestured. Caught her attention. She pointed towards a metal door. I was let in.

Oona Grimes was the etcher's splendid name. The huge sheets

pinned to the wall, the fiercely delicate topographical drawings on the desk, were part of a John Dee working, Enochian cartoons made in response to long study of the Mortlake scholar.

The black Oona favours is eloquent and hard won. She seems to be processing the graphic novel of a city that exists outside time and beyond place. A narrative of fragments and fractures constructed from old postcards, torn maps, cells of film recovered from Wardour Street bins. We have to imagine the angelic argument between Grimes and Dr John Dee. Which conjurer summons which spirit? Does the contemporary artist pitch herself back to haunt the precocious nightmares of the Elizabethan geographer? She walks in his sleep (as a forgotten pulp novel was once titled). An outline with no fixed core. A sketch come to life: Madimi dressed as Minnie Mouse.

The man of Mortlake was a true London presence, but any previous attempt to approach him ended in failure or farce. A sequence featuring Dee and his scryer, Edward Kelly, was aborted from my novel *Radon Daughters*. Misplaced. The saxophonist and composer John Harle conceived a Dee opera for which I was asked to write libretto and book. We lunched Elvis Costello, who agreed, so it appeared, to take the magician's part. Before he actually read the synopsis and remembered, with relief, an orthodox Catholic past. A television-production company had the hare-brained scheme – even by their own fantastic standards – of walking myself and Alan Moore to Prague: as an Oxfam Dee and Kelly. I'm not sure who got which part. Several hours of recorded interview vanished into the same black hole from which Oona Grimes extracts the eye-tar to factor the nigredo for her etchings. The midnight black.

'She seemed to play up and down, child-like, and seemed to go in and out behind my books.' Dee recorded a sighting of Madimi in his *Diaries*. He whispered: 'Whose maiden are you?'

To which there can be only the riddling reply: 'Whose man are you?' A circular exchange without resolution.

*

Grimes was a scavenger as much as an etcher, cranking her heavy press, attacking a white scroll. She brought in, from the street, schools of those little plastic fish that contain soy sauce. And she nailed them to her wall, alongside cards, toy wheels, ice-lolly sticks. Her icons and equations, derived from Dr Dee, became storyboards prophesying future horrors: the fate of London. This woman, I realized, might prove the salvation of my Hackney project. She could convert the inchoate mess into a formal system. If she could devise symbols for each section of the book, like the intertitles of a silent film, readers would have something on which to rely. Trust the picture, not the word. And, more importantly, she might be able to crack the code of the ribbons tied to the canalside fence, my catalogue of tin notices and shifting graffiti, the mad runes of Hobo Sickert. Amassed evidence, I tried to convince myself, was moving towards a mathematical system I would never interpret. But Oona, staying in one place, taking her time, evaluating the Jiffy bags of material with which I would keep her supplied, just might.

We talked: unconnected anecdotes, gossip. We had friends in common. Oona, as a mature student, knew Catling from Norwich. Where she had also come across the mysterious mask-maker Nigel Henderson. Much of Oona's work, it was obvious, derived from cinema: as memory and inherited technique. Her father, Stephen Grimes, began as a storyboard artist. It was in her blood, this ability to break narrative down into sequences of stopped movement, fixed sets: each image affecting its successor.

Stephen Grimes was taken up by John Huston. He was officially the assistant art director to Ralph Brinton on Huston's *Moby Dick*. He was responsible for the model of the white whale, the one that floated away in search of its own northwest passage. Oona spent much of her childhood on film sets, and even appeared in the background of several major films she prefers to forget. One of her sisters, she thinks, was born in Fishguard, at the time of the *Moby Dick* shoot. Another sister, Sarah, invited to recall a visit to the studio, drew up a short list of memories: 'The pulpit where the preaching happens. A full-size model head of the whale with guys aiming water sprays at it. Steve's little model boats in a water tank. His super sketches.'

Oona agreed to look at my Hackney documentation. When I returned the following afternoon to Finsbury Park, slender trees along the railway were whipping in the wind. The etcher responded at once to Edmond Halley's Hollow Earth theories. She pored over maps of subterranean continents, Symmes's holes, patterns of interior fire. She was charmed by snapshots of coloured fences, dog fur under broken benches, plaster swans. She asked if she could hold on to the drawings I'd made of the letters woven, in red and blue, into the railings by the canal.

ON TUESDAY, 3RD FEBRUARY 2004 AT 8.00AM, EXACTLY ONE YEAR AFTER MARGARET MULLER WAS MURDERED, A MEMORIAL SERVICE TO COMMEMORATE HER LIFE WILL BE HELD IN VICTORIA PARK. A TREE WILL ALSO BE PLANTED. WERE YOU IN VICTORIA PARK AND HAVE NOT YET COME FORWARD?

A head-shot, smiling, of the murdered woman. Who, it seems, was a good friend of Oona from the Slade. They took tea together, often. They talked. Every photograph I produce, every name I mention, Grimes is already there. She is the missing link in my incomplete tales. Snapshots from forgotten walks become an identity parade.

'Oh, Anna,' she said. With a smile. 'Anna, yes.'

'That's not Anna, that's one of the Red Army Faction when she was on the run, somewhere in East London.'

'I don't mean your wife. I mean Astrid. Astrid Proll. She was with my sister, they were close. Astrid lived with us in the country. She called herself Anna. That's how I knew her.'

This German woman was everywhere. I must be the only person left in Hackney who didn't meet Proll, argue with Jean-Luc Godard, deliver fast food to Orson Welles, drink with the Angry Brigade, take walks in the rain with Julie Christie. All those dim years, in the slow dream of a vanishing city, rolling kegs across the yard of Truman's Brewery, painting white lines on Hackney Marshes: what did I think I was doing? Jock McFadyen said he was quite surprised when he saw the family babysitter on the *Six O'Clock News*: Proll. Anna. Her Hackney identity. They say she lived somewhere around London Fields.

It struck me: why did Oona let me in? This wool-capped figure at the window on a dark afternoon.

'I thought you were the fellow with the next studio.'

'Which reminds me – do you know a man called Kaporal?'

She shook her head. My researcher was unique. The only Hackney character with whom Oona was not involved in some way. She was quite alone in the building, working long hours, painting black dots, practising mirror-writing, experimenting with Letraset.

I was convinced that Kaporal had the next unit, the Finsbury Park cold store was his kind of place. When I peered in through the cobwebby window I could make out cans of film stacked on a table, tottering columns of box files. A Kaporal bolthole.

'The guy next door said "Hi" in the corridor once. Offered me a drink from his flask. He slept here, but he didn't do any work. I was quite sure, that first afternoon, that you were him, come back.'

'Does your key open his door?'

'We could try.'

There's a passage from *Moby-Dick* in which the steersman claims to be sailing 'east-sou'-east' (the direction of Folgate's ley) when Ahab snarls, 'Thou liest!' And smites him 'with his clenched fist'. They are, in fact, being carried in the opposite direction. Thunder in the night has 'turned' the compass: 'The magnetic energy, as developed in the mariner's needle, is, as all know, essentially one with the electricity beheld in heaven; hence it is not to be much marvelled at, that such things should be . . . The needle never again, of itself, recovers the original virtue thus marred or lost.'

Kaporal's metal tins, his film archive, had that effect. For the nameplate on his studio door, he used a card of a rucksacked figure tramping down a country road. There was a name: SINCLAIR. And a phone number. Mine.

'It's uncanny,' Oona said. 'Kaporal has *exactly* your look. The drooping shoulders, the weight of the world. Managed despair. Even the Masai Barefoot Technology trainers. In the wrong size.'

Nigel Fountain and Marc Karlin

I sat on the train, going through the tunnel towards Kentish Town, the Hackney Diaspora, with the dead poet Ed Dorn. Or rather: I stood, sweated, swayed, struggled for air – which my fellow travellers, electronically preoccupied, paper-pampered, were reluctant to cede. We fought hard, elbows, bags, for a wrap of our own space: buried standing. Dorn floated free, around the curved lid of the mortuary torpedo. At full length along the floor. Across moraines of lap. Inside and outside scratched obscenities on the windows. He was happy to share my experience of the Marc Karlin tape and seemed to approve the tone and tenor of an argument in defence of a Miltonic republic of letters (spurned, disregarded). Dorn, who pitched himself as a Protestant, always moving west towards 'maybe Las Vegas', admitted that of late, postmortem, he'd flirted with the Eastern Orthodox Church and was thinking seriously about relocating for a season to the environs of Constantinople. But then he thought seriously about everything, with a cynical whip of the tail, acceptance of responsibility for what language can do. Or undo.

The slim book-shaped thing that brought the poet back was called *Ed Dorn Live*. In defiance of obituaries published around the end of the millennium. Which he saw no good reason to contradict. His abhorrences, spearing public clowns and civic cant, had never been more pertinent. How could he share American ground with Reagan and the Bush boys, the oil pirates and their feeble opponents, the neo-lib breastbeaters who derided the forces of darkness into a significance they didn't deserve?

It was not a popular position to maintain against lachrymose confessions of historic guilt (and avoidance of present action). The 20-zeros, greeted with the worst architecture since the retreat of the glaciers, achieved new and improved levels of double-speak. Notices around the latest field of rubble boasted of IMPROVING THE IMAGE OF CONSTRUCTION. The thing itself no longer mattered, and barely existed, but the image got sharper and sharper. High definition, finally, absolves content. Any municipal scandal or act of pillage can be countered with the green card: more bicycles, less road. Recycling, as Dorn pointed out, has itself become a major polluting industry. 'Nobody wants to live downwind from a poly-urethane recycling plant.' There isn't time to unscrew the lid on the jar, to scrape the food-substitute out, before the object becomes the problem. Huge fuel-burning trucks rumble around the borough collecting skeins of plastic bag.

After Highbury, I managed to capture a seat, the space in which to listen to the Marc Karlin interview that Patrick Wright sent me. Wright had delivered a series of portraits of cultural 'outriders', who operated on or beyond the fringes of the known world. The irony being that Wright himself was very soon removed from the equation, nudged aside from his late-night radio slot, while his long-mediated, hard-travelled epic on the Iron Curtain was decom-missioned for the crime of being too much itself.

I had, at last, run Nigel Fountain to ground. His novel, *Days Like These*, was out of print and pretty much forgotten. The mix of John Buchan, Hitchcock, fascist conspiracy and grunge topography was a secret history I wanted to revisit. Fountain, one of the Montague Road musketeers with Karlin and David Widgery, was stuck with an impossible role: he was still alive. The pain of memory. What should he do with it? How should he behave in a culture determined to stitch his eyelids shut, to block his ears? The Third Man, with his posthumous tapes, transcripts, photo albums, spiked articles, remaindered books, was hiding out, very comfort-ably, on verdant slopes above the Kentish Town Underground station.

Pressure of time (money) had folded in on me. I couldn't recog-nize any person or object outside the field of the present book; taking a short Silverlink commute was also a Karlin tutorial, an opportunity to listen again to the living voice of Fountain's dead friend. Wright launched his free-flowing introduction half a dozen times before it satisfied his producer. He had come to Karlin's lair, the Fitzrovia bearpit beneath the editing suite where I was, at that moment, working with Chris Petit.

The quality of sound, the clarity of this tape, made listening painful: two men fought for breath in a basement, stacked with paper, from which most of the oxygen had been sucked out and replaced with blue smoke. Patrick, an articulate language pro, was operating on one lung; he'd lost the other in Paris. He took an ambitious flight across areas of common interest, before surfacing, when Karlin was least expecting it, with a loud question mark. Marc responded with a weighty pause, he wasn't glib and he wanted to mean what he said. Then he gasped, coughed, steadied himself with a cigarette. Dry clicks of the plastic lighter were registered. Wright mentioned the convenience of the Middlesex Hospital, around the corner, where their conversation might have to transfer.

The unedited tape was more poignant than the cropped version that went out on air, or the printed summary published in Marc's old magazine, *Vertigo*. It was good to hear the three attempts at every question. The film-maker spoke with much heart and humour, no regret, with becoming modesty and a sense, perhaps, of having made difficulty for himself by working on the wrong side of the Channel. His films were about 'distances', the impossibility of speaking for another person, representing alien lives. He resisted Wright's thesis about the loss of cultural memory, willed amnesia and talked of the situation in terms of 'glide'.

Patrick laboured to keep the tone upbeat. 'You're still alive,' he said. 'You've stayed in work.' It didn't register. Karlin spoke of London insomnia, pacing the house at night. The hour of the wolf: anxiety, phantoms from other worlds. 'We're so good at burials,' he said. 'Burials make me very angry. I don't belong to the memory department.'

He brought back so vividly the last time I'd worked in film, the long hours running and re-running our own footage and that of the 1960s counter-cultural archivist Peter Whitehead – whose life, as he wanted to remember it, was on celluloid. Marc was the lurker in the doorway. The morning chat in the smoky cellar: the certainty that time was running out. I felt that we were tolerated, in our digital technology, by a generous figure from another, purer tradition. And, now, I was moved to hear, in this final Karlin interview, that he had appreciated what we were attempting to do.

'The Avid gives the creative person an enormous possibility of making the film in the editing,' Marc said, 'and, if it's used creatively, it's incredible. I mean, an example of that was Chris Petit's and Iain Sinclair's film, *The Falconer*. You can really work on the image, on the text of the image, on the quality of it, on the feeling of it, and it really is like a painter's tool, and, if it's done with a sensibility, as opposed to a trickery, it's an incredible piece of equipment.'

Karlin made it sound as if film was still a potentiality. It's like what Dorn said about poetry, when he gloried in the triumph of obsolescence. 'It's obsolete, yeah. But so what? There are lots of great things that are obsolete. Kerosene lamps are obsolete, but there's no light like it in a cabin in northern Wisconsin . . . Think of the best things in the world, actually, and they're all obsolete. Sure. But that's because a world that grows more and more venal and greedy and opportunistic makes things obsolete at a great rate . . . So poetry is real obsolete . . . It makes me feel great. It makes me feel like I'm working with something that's good enough to be obsolete.'

Nigel Fountain, in his Kentish Town kitchen, with coffee bubbling, foreground music, spice jars, cookery books, spare morning time, was wholly obsolete. And knew it. And gloried in it. And managed the emotional hurt of hanging on, in memory, to the sepia newsreels of a highly selective past. He was slightly shocked, traumatized even, to be in a comfortable house with friends and food and library.

Lucifer-like, he led me up through the house, to a flat roof, warmed by nights of love, to show off the vision of London. I imagined that he would be the final witness, the end of the Hackney story. Leftist utopianism, bohemian collectives, detective novels coding political critiques: he had experienced them all. What more could I expect to learn? This was the place I had already visited, to interview Sheila Rowbotham. They were in the same witness-protection programme. Keep schtum, stay alive.

Fountain's study, where we settled ourselves to make the recording, came out of a Stephen Poliakoff play. One of those high-end dramas that splash budget on empty Belgravia mansions, lush soundtracks and Michael Gambon's baggy integrity. Fountain gave good Gambon. The passionate irrelevance. The anecdotes that meandered around the risk of revelation, without ever quite getting there. Old loves, lost lives. Hotels by lakes. Children in forests. Without the horror behind glamorous drapes, the Holocaust surrealism. Just friends whose foibles Fountain was condemned to repeat to predatory interviewers, waiting on small mistakes.

I complimented Nigel on the bookshelves carved into the door and he threw back an immediate Gambon riff: the previous owner of the house was the actor Denholm Elliott. The carpentry was all his work. Remember him in *Bad Timing*? Nicolas Roeg's Vienna, failing flesh: 'a labyrinthine enquiry on memory and guilt'. Elliott did all that stuff with consummate ease: corruption, compromise, decay. He enjoyed himself too much, Fountain told me, in Thailand. On location for *Bangkok Hilton*. And he came home, here, to die. Quietly, without fuss. No serialized memoirs, no confessions. No scores to settle.

Nigel suffered with his back; he struggled to find a tolerable position in which to sit. He wore a pink shirt and my spectacles. He said that Marc Karlin had a fetishistic love for pre-war English movie actresses. In his opinion, Denholm Elliott's best performance was in *The Cruel Sea*. With Jack Hawkins and Donald Sinden. I switched on the recorder and Fountain launched unprompted into an account of the gestation of his novel, *Days Like These*.

Writing became more and more of an obsessive activity. I was working in a Latin-American news agency in Farringdon for half the week. My novel, apparently set in the 1980s, is really about the 1970s. My chronology is simple. 1970: move into 12 Montague Road. 1980: leave 12 Montague Road. That house, looking back, was a phenomenally creative place to live. It has to be said that 70 per cent of the creativity was being produced by Sheila Rowbotham. She was hammering away. She wrote in the middle of chaos, but she also made her own chaos.

She was a more glamorous figure than the rest of us. Although she is one of the most magnificently down-to-earth and unpretentious of people, she mixed in elevated circles. That Godard episode was in the late 1960s, just before I met her.

When I moved to Montague Road I was a dedicated member of the International Socialists. I worked for a paper called Idiot International, *non-sectarian with revolutionary leanings. It had a circulation of about eight. In fact it didn't have a circulation at all. After it collapsed, we realized that the villainous Ratner, who was the guy distributing the paper, had simply stuck all the copies in a warehouse in Shoreditch.*

After that I got a job with the Socialist Worker. I was the first person to resign from that paper. Everybody before me was pushed off a cliff. Then I worked for the Street Life, which also collapsed. After that I was motorcycling correspondent for the Sunday Times. Which was rather curious because I couldn't ride a bike and didn't own one.

Much of my political life was organized around pubs. Especially in Hackney. My friend David Widgery was very fond of a drink, but drink was not always fond of him. Some of my happiest memories of the International Socialists came from a pub called the Rose and Crown in Albion Road. We moved to the Stoke Newington International Socialists from the Islington IS – which was dominated by a core membership of myself, Widgery, David Phillips and a guy called Ross Pritchard. Marc Karlin was never a member of the organization. That's Marc's photo, up there on the wall. With the hair. He looked like Jesus back then.

I miss Marc tremendously, even to this day. I'm fed up with the bloody situation, people dying. The thing about Marc and Widgery is that they had an incredibly tempestuous relationship. Half the time they were not talking. I was the intermediary, saying, 'For Christ's sake, let it go.' Marc's demons stemmed from the fact that he'd had a very traumatic childhood. He would mutter about his father who was French-Jewish-Swiss-Latvian. A mysterious background in the Russian Revolution. Marc and I lived in the double room, on the ground floor, in Montague Road. If you ever went into Marc's room, when he was asleep, he looked incredibly tense.

We got on pretty well from the first time we met. Marc's politics were anarcho-Marxist. When I moved to Montague Road, Sheila saw me as a symbol of stability. When I arrived the place was pretty much drugged out, bombed out.

Sheila, who generally speaking is of a sweet disposition, could erupt. You see her cheeks go pink, it's time to run away. She hurled a loaf at me on one occasion. I instituted a more and more Draconian and Stalinist eating regime. I would be chasing Marc down the road, demanding to know whether he would be in or out for dinner on the following Thursday. This would produce the situation where Marc would send home a side of beef in a taxi.

I bow to no one in my admiration of Sheila's honesty, but it is a flagrant and utter untruth for her to claim that she did all the shopping. I was always in Ridley Road with a loaded trolley.

David Widgery was in and out. He kept one foot in Islington, at 2 Chapel Market. I arrived in Montague Road being pursued by a former landlord. There was a constantly shifting cast list. The core was Sheila. Widgery was around. I lived there. Marc lived there. Other interesting people passed through.

I was lurching from one failed publication to the next. I wanted to get into fiction and I kept trying to get back to my abortive novel. Days Like These *was worrying at me. I was inspired by the milieu I was living in, by having rows with Sheila, interchanges at three in the morning. Sheila has very little concept of the difference between the living and the dead. Or those who are awake in a house and those who are asleep. You can have a conversation with Sheila and realize halfway through that you are talking about people who have been dead since 1880.*

★

I was part of that famous Julie Christie walk across Hackney. I've got the photographs. There was a Turkish academic. There was Julie. There was a woman who was then very big in EastEnders. She played a Further Education teacher. I knew Julie. She lives in Columbia Road now. With the film-director Sally Potter. I know Julie in the sense that every five years or so I would see her and she'd say, 'Hello!' And I'd say, 'Hello.' That was about it. She's an extremely nice woman, but we don't go out drinking together.

What was hilarious about that walk was that as we wandered haplessly about, Sheila would be announcing, 'This is where Joseph Priestley lived,' pointing to some wine bar around the back of Clapton. Then we'd be staggering along talking about some battle the Romans fought. It was pissing with rain. Nobody who saw us paid a blind bit of attention to Julie Christie. They were all gaping at the EastEnders woman.

When I was working, shortly after this, at City Limits, *I got a call from some strange character in Limehouse, name of Folgate. About* Days Like These. *He said, 'Nigel, you've got that community wrong.' I said, 'What do you mean?' He said, 'It's not where you said it was.' I said, 'This is a work of sodding fiction. I made it up.' He said, 'It's still in the wrong place.'*

All the exchanges between Marc, myself, Sheila and David Widgery went into the novel. I was reading a lot of John Buchan. He is a really great writer. I find his politics fascinating, that brand of mystical Toryism. I come from a Tory family myself, a petit bourgeois Tory family. In the 1960s, I wrote the first article on the National Front. I wrote articles on the National Front and the Monday Club. I'm a child of the British Empire, I grew up in that kind of Tory imperialist fantasy world. I could understand the Monday Club quite well.

This is before Thatcher. My novel should have been set during the period of the three-day week, a time when the left seemed to be making some progress. The two groups who took politics seriously were the far left and the far right (including the far right within the Tory Party). There was an MI5 agent within our group at IS. Looking back, she was rather nice. A lot better than all sorts of authentic members of the organization.

That was the atmosphere of Days Like These: *Montague Road, my study of British fascism, coupled with a social life that involved long hours spent in the Norfolk Arms. Which at that time was a 1970s modern pub with fluorescent plastic.*

Sheila had been a member of IS and had quit in fury at being bossed around by a bunch of deadbeats. SWP hated those characters with an Angry Brigade tendency. That awful blend of self-dramatization and dangerous naivety. My last hurrah for IS was in 1976, the Walsall by-election – after the postmaster general, John Stonehouse, that crook, staged his suicide by leaving his clothes on a beach. The IS candidate, a wonderful guy, was the inspiration for the Scottish character in my novel.

The other great excitement of the time was watching Barlow and Watt Investigate *on television. TV detectives look into the Ripper murders, using documentary and forensic evidence: another marriage of fact and fiction. I became utterly fascinated with the series. I wrote an article for* Socialist Worker *about the programme and its conspiracy thesis. I went along at once to interview old Hobo Sickert. I became obsessed, for about a fortnight, with the royal surgeon, Sir William Gull. As I was poring over the photograph of the final victim, I began to have doubts: 'Is this really a good idea?'*

Sheila said to me, 'My friend Bill Fishman is leading a tour of Whitechapel, why don't you go along?' I went on Bill's walk. Within five minutes of Bill opening his mouth, my interest in Jack the Ripper began to fade. But my interest in East End radicals grew and grew. Bill got to Frying Pan Alley and said, 'Everyone assumes that when such-and-such a character was sent to Siberia, he died. I know better. I know that man came here to this alley.'

Wow! It was the key point in the genesis of Days Like These. *I became utterly gripped by the East End.*

Hobo Sickert just repeated his story of the woman dying in the madhouse in Fulham in 1921. He didn't show me his treasure box, the painting or the parchment with the Grail message. It was a very good yarn. It was seeing Hobo on television with Barlow and Watt that led me to Bill Fishman and the real East End.

I spent a lot of time hanging around tatty bookshops. The funny thing about the bookshop in my novel, the place where my character acquires that photograph, is that I made it up. And then I found it! Walden Books, Harmood Street, Chalk Farm. I found Walden Books after I'd written the bloody place into existence. After that, every time I went past, I thought: 'That's my shop.'

Chandler and John Buchan were my main influences. I was otherwise reading Marx and Marx-related material. David Widgery went to the States in the mid 1960s. When I assembled my counter-cultural memoir, Underground, I interviewed David. I have a very large collection of interviews. David absorbed all the American Beat stuff, directly.

The funny thing about David limping around was that I never realized how badly polio had affected him. It was one of the reasons why he was so staggeringly rude. It didn't bother me. The only way to deal with him was to say 'fuck off'. You had to be faster than he was. If you weren't, he would destroy you. I've seen people whose jaws literally dropped. He would say, 'Your acne doesn't seem to be quite as bad as it was.'

He could charm the birds from the trees. He was wonderful company. Marc and David were intellectually stimulating in conversation. I miss that. Sheila and I both miss it. David's death was dreadful, a horror story. I don't want to go into it. He choked to death on his own vomit.

He had quite a hard time with his father. His mother, who loved him dearly, was a dedicated Christian. David went through an awful lot of pain in his childhood, from TB and polio. Two years of absolute agony. He was enraged by that. His mother's Christianity amounted to nothing very much in the face of his suffering. When I first met him, 1965, he looked perfect for the decade. He looked like Mick Jagger. The beret came later. The mid 1960s was the blue suede jacket and those huge eyes.

By the 1980s, I moved across town. I was living in Endymion Road. There was a very nice woman there, an anthropologist, who was married to a man called Charlie Velasco. They'd been together for years. He was a total football freak. He was always arguing with Marc. Velasco was Tottenham and Karlin was Arsenal. The Calvinist rigour of George Graham and his New Model Army suited Marc perfectly. Velasco had front, the gift of the gab, but there was something wrong: he knew Tony Blair. They used to go around together. Not to football. Don't know where really, rock concerts? Long discussions in that yellow kitchen. Blair didn't do pubs.

The bloody Labour Party was a million miles from where we were. Checking the files, I found that I'd written an article in 1970 in which I referred to this guy from the Labour Party in a white suit and flares. I managed a tone of total contempt. His name was Ken Livingstone. Who was talking his usual reformist twaddle. The Labour Party, as far as we were concerned, didn't exist.

Nobody wanted to infiltrate Hackney Council, that would have been heretical. IS had been expelled from the Labour Party in the mid 1960s. We were briefly involved in local grass-roots activity with a tenants' association. Two things came out of it. David Phillips said he'd met a woman who was Charlie Watts's aunt. And then someone thanked him for stopping people putting dogs in the spin-dryer. I said, 'That's our revolutionary triumph, mate.'

We lived next door to Tex and his wife. They were great. A West Indian couple. I loved that life, summer in Hackney. I loved the market. I loved the Norfolk Arms. It was a small world bounded by Dalston Lane, Colvestone Crescent and Ridley Road. I did not go to the eel and pie shop more than once. I didn't like it. I used to eat at the Indian in Kingsland Road with Marc Karlin. I remember dragging him to see ABBA The Movie. Marc sat in the cinema shouting, 'Sync! Sync!' The audience were muttering, 'What the fuck is he on about?' After forty-five minutes we had to leave.

Kingsland Road was like a game reserve, but it was better than the Holloway Road any day of the week. I didn't get around a great deal. Victoria Park, I didn't go there. We hardly moved at all. Montague Road had been a Jewish area, we had those little things above the door. I said to Sheila, 'What is this?' She said, 'It's a scroll.' A girl who had once lived in the house committed suicide because she couldn't marry the man she wanted, a Gentile.

When I look back on the move from Montague Road to Clapton, I feel guilty about it. Montague Road wasn't big enough after the arrival of Sheila's son, Will. I should have said, 'I'm going to leave.' If I'd left sooner, Sheila could have stayed on. We moved to Clapton and, after a year, I packed up. I'd known Will from the time of his birth to the age of five. I remember the day I left. I've never had any children. Will, aged five, said, 'You're not going?' I was absolutely pole-axed. I drove off with tears streaming down my face.

When I moved here, to Kentish Town, I said to Sheila, 'Do you fancy having the basement?' What goes around comes around. Sheila is the Charley Varrick of contemporary culture. She's a lot prettier than Walter Matthau, but you know what I mean. The way she operates, whatever happens, to stay in the game. If she has to go to Manchester, to teach in the university, she does. If she sits down to write a note, it turns into a twelve-page letter. If she sits down to write a letter, it turns into a pamphlet. If she sits down to write a pamphlet, it turns into a book. She never bloody stops. She is one of the purest scholars I've ever met.

Now I work at the Guardian, three days a week. Death Row. Obits. I leave it to Sheila to trash my name. Have you read her memoir, Promise of a Dream? I get one mention. When I suggest that pornography be introduced into Black Dwarf. Great! And she got it wrong. I stole the idea from Ulrike Meinhof of the Red Army Faction.

An old friend of mine, a rock writer, was sitting on a train reading the Sunday Times, when he noticed a headline: POLICE RAID NORTH LONDON HOUSE. TERRORIST HELD. At this point he realized that the nice quiet German girl who had the room upstairs was in fact Astrid Proll, a member of the Baader-Meinhof gang. Poor Gary, he had something hapless about him: he would never have made a connection with Astrid's past. There were plenty of direct links between the German political underground and Hackney. Rudi Dutschke used to stay with Tony Cliff in Allerton Road. Proll was everywhere, in communes, with poets.

Sheila was fearless. She got into a fight on Victoria Station with a group of fascists. And you know about her lunatic dog? One night in Clapton they were woken by the dog barking. They rushed down to find a burglar standing there. Sheila pushed him out of the front door. She patted the dog and gave him an extra bowl of food. The following night they were woken again by this mad beast. The dog was standing, barking away, at the bottom of the stairs. Sheila realized it was only making a noise because it expected to be fed an extra meal.

So much of my time now is taken up with the dead. You have to be over seventy to get into the Guardian crypt. After that you might qualify for an entry in the obit files. Some people make a good living bounty hunting, chasing hearses, hanging around terminal wards. We have slots waiting for totally obscure B-movie actors, bottom-of-the-bill music-hall turns, concrete poets who have sunk into the ocean depths. Footballers with centre partings and long shorts. I work on the theory that Brian Glanville takes Charlie Velasco out for a lunch he can't afford and has to knock off an obit on Ron Clogg who played for Huddersfield Town in 1934. Brian still writes on a typewriter, faxes his copy in.

I should have packed this game in years ago. It's gone on far too long. I need the money. Days Like These will never come back into print.

Now comes that Poliakoff moment, when we stop the tape and send the camera tracking, quite independently, across the wall of photographs: the record of a life, friends, lovers, and children who seem older, calmer, wiser, than the parents who have gone. Bearded Marc Karlin, eyes shut, on a bed: like Guevara laid out for the Bolivian military photographer. A youthful leather-jacketed Widgery supports the bleeding Fountain in an iconic scene from the 1968 Vietnam demo in Grosvenor Square.

'I tripped on the kerb and bashed my head. We spent the rest of the afternoon sitting under a tree while David tended my wounds. We didn't have anything to do with battling police horses. But that photo has gone into several books.'

A damp Sheila Rowbotham, clutching a dog, shelters with Julie Christie under a London plane, one of the trees that would be lost in the Great Storm of October 1987.

I picked out, against the fence of somewhere that looked like the wood yard, up the River Lea, near Millfields, a woman who just might have been Astrid Proll, dark hair hanging over one stern eye. Heavy brows, jaw set. Unhappy to be witnessed in this place.

'Who's that?'

Nigel moved closer.

'Did you know him? Strange cove with a crazy name. Kaporal? Worked part time in the BNP bookshop in Tulse Hill. He gave me shedloads of inside dirt for *Days Like These*. I had to bloody pay for it, fifty quid. Two weeks' wages! Not sure who the woman with him is. Some Hackney artist? From the lesbian squatter community around Shrubland Road, Broadway Market? Kaporal hung out with those types. Drank in the Britannia, before it became the Samuel Pepys. He booked to go on the Christie walk, I do remember that. Never showed. Probably dead.'

Douglas Lyne and Henry Cohen

I'd taken it as far as I could, my confidential report. No Arkadin, no master manipulator, stands revealed; nothing but dead white skin when Orson Welles unhooks his horsehair beard. Hackney excavated was as mysterious as ever. And as perverse. I acknowledged the potency of certain archaeological sites, future ruins: Labyrinth in Dalston Lane, the German Hospital, the Mole Man's tunnels. And that restored pink music hall, the Empire. A cavernous stage on which to project the phantoms of figures who lived here once or passed through. Jean-Luc Godard, dark glasses and corn-yellow cigarette, mimes a silent comedy: soubrette wives kick up shapely legs in front of a burning screen. Welles, mopping his brow, saws the Lady from Shanghai in half, in quarters. The trick being that there is no trick: Rita Hayworth folded away among squashed furs in a cabin trunk. To gasps and wild applause, he produces the severed head of Jayne Mansfield from the mouth of a plastic whale. Walter Sickert, lounging at the bar, fills his pad with loose notations. He is treating his barber to a pint of whelks. Leon Kossoff, up in the gods, sees it whole, the pulsing energy field: like a swimming pool, a gene pool of all the coming races. Edward Calvert, crossing from Darnley Road, pictures Marie Lloyd as a draped nymph beside the recovered Hackney Brook. Swanny is present with his drinking school: Samuel Richardson, Joseph Priestley, Edmond Halley, Daniel Defoe, Arthur Machen, Alexander Baron, Harold Pinter, Patrick Wright and Stewart Home. Hollow Earthers relishing a funny night out.

No Roland Camberton, our everyman: the missing narrator. Realism has no part in the story. Depicting Hackney, through manipulated autobiography, the author is airbrushed from his own script. Through slashing rain, the jaundiced tonal values of John

Minton's cover design for the lost Camberton novel, the proud dome of the Hackney Empire is barely visible. Minton is looking south. Everything is fudged, in the wrong place.

The high-angle viewpoint took me back to Hitchcock and Buchan, *The 39 Steps*. Nigel Fountain and Sebastian Bell, in their very different novels, drew on the notion that a section of map, properly interpreted, would point the way to revelation. The maps were not of London. They fell from a dying hand: the Scottish Highlands, remote cottages in Wales where fictions might be contrived and love affairs broken by the challenge of intimacy.

I wanted Hitchcock, excited by what he had learnt in Germany, to open with a track across light bulbs spelling out: E-M-P-I-R-E. But, in reality, when I view the DVD, it's MUSIC HALL. His theatre has been constructed in a studio, but is otherwise accurate: a bar at the back, curtain of tobacco fug, urgent faces. A gunshot. Ribs crushed, women and old folk trampled in the stampede: 'Fire!' A device Hitchcock reprised, in one form or another, right through the catalogue to *North by Northwest* and *Torn Curtain*.

Out of animal heat, and damp night, a woman with a fur collar confronts Richard Hannay: 'May I come home with you?' 'It's your grave.' A real bus on a contrived set that has none of the grandeur, or pretension, of the actual Hackney Empire. Destination? Holborn, Bank, Aldgate, Bow, Stratford. Joe Kerr, driver and transport scholar, reckoned it would be a 25, the predecessor to the Routemaster. The route was west–east and not, as would be required for the Empire, north–south. Hitchcock's music hall is located in Nowhere-Whitechapel.

'You may call me Annabella.'

That's a given: when slender creatures offer up their naked backs to bread knives. Or announce themselves as secret agents. Or eat haddock at midnight from the kitchen table. Sexual favours are on sale to the highest bidder. With optional extras. Silent stars voiceless in an age of sound. Look out for the man with the missing finger joint.

The Annas protest: we won't die in the first reel. And we don't belong in the East London swamps.

To firm up memories of the period immediately before our move to Hackney, I read the transcripts of my interviews from 1967 with Allen Ginsberg, R. D. Laing and other counter-cultural luminaries. I flicked through books dealing with that period. One of them, *Walking the London Scene: Five Walks in the Footsteps of the Beat Generation* by Sydney R. Davies, had been passed on by Gareth Evans. Gareth's interventions often anticipated my needs.

A person called Douglas Lyne, described as 'archivist and Chelsea habitué', came across William Burroughs in the Lillie Langtry pub. Lyne had picked up a copy of *Naked Lunch* in Paris. It interested him enough to phone Arthur Boyars, Burroughs's editor, to see if an introduction could be fixed.

He is given a number: the Empress Hotel. He phones and leaves a message. A meeting is arranged for 7.40 p.m. Precisely. In the cab, Lyne's wife, Monica, panics: what should she wear to socialize with a notorious junkie?

'Would you like a drink, Mr Burroughs?'

'That's what we're here for. Brandy.'

'Double?'

'I could do a triple.'

He knocks back five of them before the money runs out. They agree on another session in Lyne's Chelsea local, the Surprise. It goes well: Burroughs taps Lyne for a pound and leaves, almost immediately, for Tangier. From where he sends a card with a hand-painted desert scene. And also a copy of Jeff Nuttall's *My Own Mag*, inscribed 'cordially William Burroughs'.

The next time the two men meet is back at the Surprise. Burroughs, spectral as ever, walks into the pub and hands Lyne his pound. He accepts a round or five, before returning to Lyne's flat to record, on a reel-to-reel machine, an interview for the archive. A drinking friend of Lyne, some Soho associate, is persuaded to

take part. He doesn't like Burroughs: unwholesome. A lemur dripping poisoned fruit. The fellow has the knack of lisping your
thoughts back, before you can get them out. Or putting obscene
words in your mouth: dead flies wrapped in sandpaper.

They are, all three, quite drunk. Brandies have been fired back
all evening. The man from the pub, the one working the machine,
was a writer himself. Years ago. That might have been the source
of his irritation. His books were classically constructed, widely
reviewed and completely forgotten. He was out of the loop, off
his turf: a Hackney man. Name of Cohen. Henry Cohen. In his
pomp, to keep the shame of this literary habit from his orthodox family, Henry sailed under a flag of convenience: Roland
Camberton.

It was a relatively simple matter to track Burroughs into Hackney,
the drug and rent-boy underworld of the Kray era, the connections
with Swanny and Genesis P-Orridge. There was a full-blown *Arena*
compilation by Neil Murger, shortly after the great man died, which
included Burroughs and Patti Smith doing a drunken turn in a
Smithfield cellar. She asks if he's going on to Hoxton. He yawns.

There were snippets of film: Burroughs hiding his face with his
hat on London Fields, recordings from bunker performances in
Vyner Street. What I couldn't get across, as I made the calls, knocked
on doors, was the fact that it wasn't Burroughs who interested me.
Not this time. It was his Chelsea collaborator, Henry Cohen (aka
Roland Camberton). *Who?*

I tried to reach Sydney R. Davies, who was published by a small
press in Glasgow, and eventually, by email, contact was established.
Mr Davies was protective of Douglas Lyne, who lived in active
retirement, with his massive archive and, potentially, the Burroughs–
Camberton tape, somewhere south of the river. The former
Chelsea habitué, I calculated, must be well into his eighties.

We fenced around the thing I really wanted: the story of
Camberton's lost years. Was it possible to make a second life outside
Hackney? Davies fed me fascinating sidebars.

'Douglas showed me a copy of a book called *New Writing & Daylight*, published by John Lehmann in 1946. There was an article, "The World of Alfred Hitchcock", by Julian Maclaren-Ross. Douglas knew Maclaren-Ross and Dylan Thomas. As did Henry Cohen.'

The tape archive, stored in many cardboard boxes, would take months to sort through. Lyne was however prepared to grant me an interview, if I understood that he wouldn't approach the subject of Camberton directly: I would be responsible for making a record of post-war life in Soho and Chelsea. The pubs, the films.

'I saw Douglas last night,' Davies emailed. 'He has managed to dig out various papers relating to characters he knew from his old Chelsea days, many of whom used to drink in the Surprise. And there is one particular box of reel-to-reel tapes, not labelled, from that era. I would have to assess if they are still playable on his old machine. He saw you on TV the other night in a programme about J. G. Ballard and has agreed to meet you – if you can come to his house next Sunday afternoon.'

It was a long way from Chelsea, through the hell of late-weekend traffic, in cold November rain. A large villa in one of those streets you can never find again, deep in Kaporal territory: Tulse Hill, Herne Hill, the slopes above Brixton. A cemetery of private lives in houses from which furtive men appear with dogs who piss in hedges. And, always, beyond the local darkness, blue television screens muted by net curtains. A demented high road where the real action goes down, speeding aliens chasing reluctant contacts. Trying, unsuccessfully, to buy single cigarettes on tick.

Mr Lyne lived deep in historic time; military anecdotes were intertwined with genealogies of the Welsh Marches and musings on his blood relationship to Father Ignatius, the charismatic priest who raised a girl from the dead in Wellclose Square.

The man was a charming and persuasive talker, the years in pubs and clubs had not been wasted, but he wouldn't be deflected from the slow unravelling of an invisible thread. An allusion to Camberton would be parenthesized for an aside on the Napoleonic

Wars. In his own good time, Douglas would return to my topic. There were mugs of slow tea and chocolate biscuits. Tape followed tape. Mr Lyne, with his swept-back silver hair, trim moustache and milky eye, was like a benevolent Pinochet. Military bearing, liver-spotted hands. Clean white shirt. Dark waistcoat. Lightweight suit.

He started by speaking of his childhood in Monmouthshire. A family of land agents and German Jews, railway builders and importers of Portuguese wine. But everything, I understood, led to the war. Douglas expressed his enthusiasm for the accuracy of Alexander Baron's early books, the private soldier's tale.

In all the slit trenches and foxholes, in Italy or Africa, there were books. I started at Alamein and ended up at the Alps two years later. One's constant companion was Penguin New Writing, *anything published by John Lehmann.*

As I was a private I had plenty of leisure time in which to read. And my mother, who didn't really resent my not going into the Guards, kept sending me books. Huge parcels every week. I read Connolly, Horizon *and so on. I've got them all in there. I have a large library, mainly books from my father and mother. They had such different tastes. She had a passion for the classics of her day, Vera Brittain, Virginia Woolf, E. M. Forster, Bloomsbury.*

I took to the life of an artillery man because it's not really dangerous. One has to go to the front about one week in four. That leaves three weeks a month without a great deal to do: reading, talking, drinking, social-izing. I learnt Italian. As I had so little to occupy me – I was no. 6 on the gun – they sent me off to get provisions. Sorrento, those nice places. The thing in the army is to keep in with storemen and cooks. They always had plenty of extras, which we used for trading, down in the destitute cities. The cooks always had sardines. It was a gentleman's life really. A marvellous preparation for the post-war years.

Before all this, I was sent to Oxford. I went to Trinity College. Our library had been taken over by Graham Greene – who didn't want his collection of books to be bombed. His wife was living down there, a very charming lady. They weren't together, but they knew of one another's movements.

The president of the college asked one to breakfast, once a term. I was seated next to a lady who didn't have much to say. She asked, 'What are you interested in?' I mentioned Frank Harris. She said, 'Oh, that's good. Have you seen the first editions?' She said, 'You ought to try my husband's collection. It's in Trinity Library.'

I trotted round there and found Greene's books, a huge collection of erotica. Amazing pornography.

There was a strange thing called the Army Bureau of Current Affairs, ABCA. Very dangerous people. All sergeant majors. They'd been set up, actually, by a chap who was a cousin of mine. A German speaker who had been advising Beaverbrook on black propaganda. He said that what we were going to do was make sure we win the post-war election. The ABCA were left-wing Oxbridge intellectuals. They were given jeeps. To go wherever they liked, to talk to anybody they could find about the course of the war. They indoctrinated the men. Anthony Burgess was involved. William Empson and so on. Totally left. They directed us towards Sartre. They were all communists.

As soon as the war ended, May 1945, they set up a class system, officers' mess, sergeants' mess: a replay of the pre-war world. I tried for a vacancy in the Intelligence Corps and was posted to Austria. Vienna, in many ways, became the centre of Europe. Austria was totally and absolutely The Third Man. The Third Man was all about the Intelligence Corps, Trevor Howard and all that. The atmosphere: Carol Reed knew his stuff.

Meanwhile, Henry Cohen – which was Roland Camberton's real name – joined the Air Force. I think he was my age. I would be very surprised if Henry was more than two years either side of me. I think he was probably born in 1921. His attitude, now I come to think of it, was similar to my own. There were people born before '21 who had some kind of civvy life. Monica, my wife, was born in 1918. She was quite a different kind of person. She had a civilian attitude.

Henry had gone straight into the RAF at eighteen. We came out around the same time, 1946. I took one look at the family home, Woodlands, and decided that nothing had changed. I'd made a few contacts in the film world. The 1930s was a great period: Eisenstein, Hitchcock, John Ford. Documentary was a huge thing: Paul Rotha, Basil Wright, Cavalcanti. Lots of people gravitated to Ealing Studios and Korda. I'd been able to help, while I was at Oxford, with Crown Films, Strand Films. They came down to make something called Oxford at War.

Dylan Thomas was at Strand Films. I met him there. A most vain and cultivated man, strange man.

It was a time of jobs for the boys. The Cambridge people had one set-up and the Oxford people another. Burgess and Maclean, Philby and so on. Humphrey Jennings was slightly younger.

Film had been my thing. I did my own Bell and Howell home movies before the war. In colour. Family. And, later, evacuees. It was a natural progression to join a documentary film company. There was plenty of money about, the government was socialist. The industry was dominated by communists.

Julian Maclaren-Ross was a very great friend. It might have been through Henry Cohen. Henry knew Maclaren-Ross. They drank together.

Worldwide Pictures, where I worked, was based in Soho Square. Elizabeth House. For five years this was the centre of my life. A spectacular melting pot, Soho. Fitzrovia. Rathbone Place. The Wheatsheaf. Every pub had its own clientele.

For some reason, perhaps because of my curious background, I never got too thick with any coterie. I moved from one to another. I had a share of my mother's flat in Sloane Street, a penthouse. I would buy a carnation for my buttonhole every morning, before going to join my communist friends in Elizabeth House. I moved in two worlds. My friends would come back to Sloane Street.

Henry was with me. This was the atmosphere in which I got to know him. He was no doubt pursuing a course of his own. When peace came, film and arts people all got together. Johnny Minton, as a painter and a drinker, was one of us. He did the covers, the dustwrappers for Henry's books.

I met Monica in 1949. We had a short time together in Sloane Street:

before it became intolerable. My mother kept bombing in. There was a hair salon below. It was all very awkward. One of my people, who worked for Rotha, found what he called a 'studio flatlet' in Oakley Street. They say of Oakley Street that you go there twice: once on the way up, once on the way down.

I suppose I was on the way up. There was a very weird landlord, a man called Hector Freeman. He'd been a sort of car salesman in Mexico. He was a flamboyant Freemason and he chose his tenants rather carefully. Friends of mine recommended me as a possible lodger. I went with Hector to the pub, the Pier. It's turned into the Warehouse now.

You saw Peter Ustinov. The Sitwells. Lady Colefax. Dame Sybil Thorndike. The Pier was frequented by the old intelligentsia of Chelsea.

I met Orson Welles once – with Monica, in Rome. I was overwhelmed. We spotted him looking at jewellery in a window. Whilst I was asking Monica what I should say to him, I turned back and he was gone. Like Harry Lime. I'd seen Moby Dick in the theatre. One of the most amazing productions ever. A small stage but Welles suggested the scope of the thing much better than John Huston in his film. I remember one marvellous line: 'They're making hay under the Andes, Mr Starbuck.' Welles was mesmerizing.

Citizen Kane was our 9/11 moment. I remember the premiere, it had a qualitative change on my thinking. Welles became a sort of god figure, unfortunately. He was a one-off. He is no template of how to do things. He ended up extremely badly. He was always sitting around with that man who made terrible films. What was his name, Johnny Depp? No, that's right: Ed Wood. They met when Welles was just sitting in cafés writing scripts, trying to raise money.

I was disenchanted with Soho when I met Henry. In the Pier Hotel. All the Chelsea mandarins were lolling about – with the great Henry. Dregs and real dregs. I had the studio flat in Oakley Street. Hector Freeman said, 'Let's go to the Pier.' And here is Henry. An extremely distinguished-looking Jewish man. Like a great composer, a huge brow. Hector introduced me to Henry. 'What'll you have?' I said. We drank and we chatted away. 'Another?' Then we bought – it must have been me, Henry never had any money – a bottle of wine. I really couldn't tell you if Monica was there.

We went back to Henry's room. I think he had already published his first book, Scamp. He never really made a living. But he was writing still. I said, 'What are you doing?' He said, 'I've just won a prize. Somerset Maugham has given me £500.' It was for Scamp. Henry said, 'Soho people don't like it.' He meant Maclaren-Ross. But Somerset Maugham liked it. He much preferred it to Kingsley Amis, actually. Lucky Jim, he hated that book. He didn't care for Amis at all. Maugham thought Henry was a good storyteller – which he was. And he could do colourful characters. He had great warmth. Henry was warm. He loved listening to what you had to say. He was very approachable, but he didn't like wasting his time on doing practical things.

We talked about his experiences, which were much like mine. He came from an extremely orthodox Jewish family in Hackney. He seemed to be part, not only of a family, but of a community. Almost like Amishes. They didn't go outside. Hackney, one small part of Hackney, was their cosmos.

Henry like myself had been groomed for stardom – and he had broken away. He'd gone into the Air Force, where he was respected. He'd done a lot of literary courses. The people there said, 'Don't waste your time in the forces, have a go at writing.' Someone told him that the best way to learn to write was by being a clerk. You had to compose reports, stick to the facts. Henry said, 'I followed the advice. When I had a spare moment in the office, I would write bits and pieces and read them out at lunchtime and see who laughed at which passage.' He said, 'I was quite surprised. They liked my stuff. They found it interesting, episodes I thought nothing of. The bits I liked they found highfalutin and boring.'

He said, 'I saw an article in the paper by John Lehmann, who was very highbrow but who remarked that such ideas had nothing to do with the sort of work he wanted to publish.' He wanted to build up a popular following. 'I'm looking for the picaresque,' he said. 'John Wain. Or Saul Bellow. I'm looking for something that's on the edge, a little bit sexy. Topical.'

Henry had got his gratuity from the Air Force. 'I was spending all my time in Soho,' he said. 'Living it up as far as I could. Drinking. Courting the girls. I'd come from this very stuffy orthodox Jewish background. I found Soho life fascinating and I thought other people would want to hear about it. So that's what I wrote. And I remembered John Lehmann.'

William Plomer was the reader at Cape. Ian Fleming owed his existence to Plomer. Everybody thought Bond was bloody awful rubbish, but Plomer said, 'Yes, but that's what we're looking for.' I think Henry met Plomer and, by way of that, Lehmann. Lehmann was just starting. Henry was one of his first authors: along with Gore Vidal, Paul Bowles, Dos Passos, Raymond Queneau, George Barker. Not a bad list.

Then Willie Maugham started this prize thing. The money had to be spent outside England. He thought the country was going to the dogs. So parochial.

Maugham didn't have much to do with the actual choice. He wasn't even on the election committee. I remember Henry saying, 'I've got to go and see the old boy in a couple of days, he's got a suite at the Ritz.' I said to Henry that I'd like him to sign my own copy of Scamp. So he came round and I asked, 'How did you get on with Maugham?' He said, 'Oh, marvellous. He asked if I wanted tea or whisky. I said whisky.' Maugham said, 'That's right, good show! I'm going to have both.'

We warmed to one another. We chatted. Henry said, 'Let's go up to Soho, old chap.' I introduced him to all those people. The documentary people I'd been living with for five years. We came out of the pub. 'We don't want to spend much time with people like that,' he said. 'They only talk about one thing, this bloody film business.' He took me into another pub, I think it was the Wheatsheaf. There was another crowd, William Sansom and so on. Hogarth Press. Very literary – but modern, up to date. It was around the time of the Festival of Britain, everybody was into the arts. A lot of BBC people too.

Henry got some money, momentarily. Everybody thought he was the chap to know. He was quite well reviewed with his first book. There was talk of a film. That never happened.

Henry got caught up with a man called Adrian Seligman, a buccaneer, quite extraordinary. He was part of the banking family, they were island *hoppers. Adrian knew people like Patrick Leigh Fermor, Crete and so on. SOE stuff. We were all unemployable. But Adrian managed to get a job in public relations, assistant to the governor of Cyprus, Lord Harding. The actual PR officer was Lawrence Durrell. Island people, beach people. Henry Miller. Adrian set up a firm called Engineering in Britain. They issued a magazine. Henry wrote an article for them. This would be a decade after Scamp, around 1964.*

You couldn't say that's what Henry was doing, freelance journalism. You couldn't ask. He wasn't a man who did things. He just ran out of ideas. He used to talk about it. I should have learnt more from him, I didn't take him seriously. I think he had an interior purpose. He hated to be known, he was a very secretive man.

He took a non-Jewish pseudonym for his book. I remember, in my studio flat, this very sort of Hatton Garden chap came around. He had a set of sacrificial knives, which he used for circumcision or cutting animals' throats. A butcher. I was there with Henry, chatting away, when he jumped up. He said, 'This is my brother.' The brother said, 'I've come to get him to go home to Hackney.' Henry said, 'We have this every week. He comes to see me to persuade me to go home. It's useless.' The brother said, 'Your father is getting quite old and ill. I think you should come and talk to him.'

The family thought Henry was in Sodom and Gomorrah. They wanted him back to do his job. He was the eldest son. But he didn't want to know. They didn't leave him alone. The brother came every week.

Henry said, 'What can I do?' I think he kept on the move. I got married in '52. We moved into a small house in Christchurch Street, still in Chelsea. I don't recall Henry ever coming there, but I think he must have done. You change your house, you change your pub. Henry didn't like the Surprise. Which was what you might call our watering hole.

The Surprise was where I saw William Burroughs. Henry was there too. That's the most fascinating thing, those two meeting. What put Henry against Burroughs – he was pro-Burroughs at the time – was that Bill was short of cash and borrowed a pound.

Henry was also there, a couple of years later, when Burroughs came back. They were not so very different. They were both renegades. Myself also. I think Henry was surprised at the honour of the thing, the punc-

tiliousness of Burroughs in returning the loan. I was anxious to get Bill on tape. Very engaging fellow, no doubt about it. Patrician, old style: Emerson. Monica adored him. He had this extreme capacity for alcohol which I found very impressive.

I asked Burroughs if he'd be taped. 'Oh yes,' he said, because he liked making recordings very much. He liked those old machines. He came round that evening. Henry had been in the pub. He was actually quite drunk, which was unusual. He wasn't a particularly heavy drinker. He didn't mind drunks, but he found them rather boring. As soon as he was bored, he would go. But that night he was blotto and Burroughs was fidgeting around with the tape-recorder.

Henry said, 'We'll both say something about ourselves on tape.' Burroughs said, 'Mr Lyne wants me to talk.' I said, 'That's right. I can hear you any time, Henry.' Henry said, 'My friends are always telling me about Burroughs. So I'd like him to know what I think.' And Burroughs said, 'I'd like very much to know what Mr Cohen thinks.'

I was in a complete state of nerves, I could sense the mounting needle beneath what they were saying. I knew Burroughs as a personality, but I wanted to hear him talk: that voice, the delivery. I knew Henry too. The groundswell of tension was building up. I got a tremendous coughing fit. They were talking at each other, sniping backwards and forwards, with great politeness and froideur. Henry said, 'What friends of mine do you know and where do you meet them?' Henry was telling Burroughs that I went occasionally to Pruniers in St James's Street. They talked a lot about Madame Prunier. Henry liked Madame Prunier.

And Monica said, 'For god's sake, I can't stand any more of this. I want to go drinking with Bill. He likes drinking, don't you, Bill?' And Burroughs said, 'I do.' Henry said, 'I'm off.'

Whenever I saw Henry after this, he would say, 'How's your chum Burroughs getting on?' In a very scathing way. I didn't thereafter socialize with Henry very much. He dropped in one day to the offices of EIBIS (Engineering in Britain Information Services), which were located above the Jack Swift betting shop in Swallow Street, just behind the Piccadilly Hotel.

Did you ever come across Peggy Guggenheim? She had a spectacular sister, Hazel. Their mother was a Seligman. They linked the two great families of New York, the Seligmans and the Guggenheims. Peggy and Hazel considered themselves to be poor, their old man was between fortunes. He only had a couple of million. The sisters rubbed along, but they had to work. Hazel became an artist. That's a portrait of me by Hazel on the wall. Adrian Seligman was very fond of Hazel.

And look at this too: it's a photograph of Graham Cutts in a boat. We made films together. After the Expressionist cinema of the 1920s, Cutts was a big name and Hitchcock was his first AD, his assistant director. The most eminent of the silent directors of the time, Cutts was with Michael Balcon. He made a film called Woman to Woman in 1923. It was written by Hitchcock. It's disappeared. A masterpiece. It's mentioned in Truffaut on Hitchcock, look it up. Cutts always had trouble, films had to be made around the availability of his mistresses.

Seligman would only employ first-rate authors. His office was on the edge of Soho. I used to go to my old watering holes occasionally. One of those days, it must have been around 1965, I met Henry. He was with a very attractive woman. I think he'd been knocking about with her for quite a long time. She was very Gentile, very county. Enormously devoted to him, in a distant kind of way. She didn't like being associated with Soho or drink. Or the people who were around.

I said, 'How are you going?' Henry said, 'Rather well. She's got a lot of money. She wants to get married. She's got a house, with hunting and that kind of thing. I go down there. My family have cut me off, they don't want to see me again.'

He said, 'I can't go on. I really don't have anything to do.' I said, 'Look, are you still writing?' And he produced this article. I said, 'That's exactly the stuff we want. Why don't you come round to the office and talk to Adrian?' Henry said, 'I don't know. I can't go into an office.'

Adrian had an open-plan design, ahead of its time. He was very laid back, but he was a great stickler for prose style. And for delivery to deadlines.

We went round. Monica was there. Hazel was there. It all developed into a party atmosphere. We decided to carry on to the Studio Club, which was just opposite.

I said, 'I think Henry would be a good writer.' And Adrian said, 'What has he written?' I said, 'A picaresque novel and a book about Hackney.' Adrian said, 'Good god! I can find twenty people to write picaresque novels about Hackney. I want someone who writes dull-as-ditchwater technical material.' Henry said, 'I'll give it a go.'

He turned up for about a month, I suppose. He changed. He became incredibly absorbed in getting it right. He was always asking, 'What do you want and how do you want it?'

At the end of the month, Adrian said, 'We ought to have a party.' I said, 'What are we celebrating?' He said, 'Henry's departure. He's a marvellous writer, but it's taken him months to write two short pieces. It's not his fault. This is not his cup of tea.' That was about the last I heard of Henry.

This takes me back to the period in Oakley Street when I was thinking about writing novels myself. Henry said, 'You'll have to learn how to do it the same way that I did. You know about films. I know nothing about films but I do work for Metro-Goldwyn-Mayer.' He said, 'I'm a reader for MGM books. They like to keep a blanket coverage of all novels published in Britain.' They had an office in Golden Square. There was a woman called Mrs Vaughan who swam around, a PR lady, Korda era, she was in charge.

The pay was minimal, but it was regular. You had to read two or three novels a week. And comment on them in detail. It did teach you to do that sort of thing quickly. Monica would type the reports for me. I was able to do them with the minimum of engagement. Peter Watling, Mrs Vaughan's assistant – who was homosexual before the days when people were gay – was very fretful with me. He said, 'You're not really trying, Douglas.' He knew me quite well. He'd been a preparatory schoolmaster. He said, 'You despise this job, don't you? It's your business to find merit, not demerit. Unless you give me something, it's no go.'

I said, 'You could give me something worthy of being liked.' He said, 'Here's one. But I won't tell you which of the bunch it is.' There was a novel by a man called Ernst Jünger. He was greatly admired, a military figure. Clean, you might say, he wasn't a Nazi. He has come back into *fashion now. He writes absolutely superbly. He wrote one around the Second War called* The Fort.

Watling put this Jünger in my bundle and he also gave me I Was Monty's Double *– which seemed to me a grotesque concoction. I read the Jünger with enormous attention. I put my back into it. And I said the other had absolutely no hope at all.*

The next day Watling called me in. He said, 'You're at it again, Douglas. You're just trying to annoy me, aren't you? There is nothing in your choice, it's impossible. And in my view Monty's Double *would be absolutely perfect.'*

It was that kind of job. I used to go up once a week to collect the books. Sometimes I'd see Henry. And he'd say, 'It's a terrible choice, this life.' I think he hit the bottle a bit. We used to go to a club called the Caves de France. It was quite close to the Colony Club. And the Mandrake. And the Gargoyle. It was quite a nice pub crawl. It was pretty obvious that Henry was in a downward spiral. He wasn't pissed, but he was pretty worn. He hadn't a lot of cash and he found the situation difficult. His friend Elizabeth insisted on being with him at all times. I don't think she drank. They were unhappy occasions.

The man who knows everything about Henry's final years is his accountant. But he's dead now. When I first met Henry, he said to me, 'The one thing you must have, old boy, is a good accountant. Come along with me and meet Leslie Periton.' The story is rather odd. Periton was one of the most charming men I ever met, but he was lowly – in class origin. Unlovely Slough. He didn't get an education worthy of his talents. But he got apprenticed very early to an established firm. He was extremely clever. In those days it was very difficult to break through the class barrier.

The accountancy firm, A. T. Shenhalls, specialized in top-flight artists: Terence Rattigan, Benjamin Britten. Those kind of people. Periton was handling big and important accounts and being paid an articled clerk's wages. He was also given the job of taking on authors who might be successful. Who weren't anything at the time. That, ultimately, was Henry.

A. T. Shenhalls had a jealous working relationship with the rather bloated Winston Churchill. He was always being mistaken for Churchill. One of his clients was Leslie Howard, the actor. Gone with the Wind, all that. Howard was a great promoter of British cinema. He had a date with some film-makers in Portugal, Lisbon. They were going to do a big deal, there was money knocking about. He decided to take Shenhalls along with him. And for some reason which has never been explained the plane was shot down. Howard was killed and so was Shenhalls. The theory was that Shenhalls had been mistaken for Churchill.

Shenhalls ran all these accounts, Rattigan, Britten, Howard. Nobody else in the office knew anything about it – except Periton. And Periton, sensibly, saw a serious opportunity and said, 'Right, I want to be a partner.' So they made him a partner on his own terms. He was now an important and likeable man. Rather unusual, that, in an accountant.

One of his clients was John Lehmann. Lehmann had multifarious interests, lots of pies in the oven. His income must have been quite large. He never made a real success of publishing. He persuaded Periton to take on Henry Cohen. They absolutely hit it off. Henry was exactly the type Periton wanted: a man who didn't have any interest in making money. Henry always needed to write. He wasn't having a great deal of success at the time – then Scamp came along. Periton enabled him to get very good publicity. He asked Henry what he would do next. The Hackney book was the big mistake, careers have been destroyed by writing about Hackney. Kiss of death. Henry said something about trying short stories. Periton probably got him the job at MGM, to keep him going. Nobody knows if Henry ever wrote anything else of substance. I don't know if there was anything under another name. My view is, at the times I ran into him, he was a declining person. He had huge genetic problems with his Jewish orthodox family. He had problems with his inamorata. He was terribly fond of Elizabeth.

He told me to get out of documentaries, to go in for a novel. He said, 'Go and see Periton, old boy. See Leslie.' I had money at that time, nothing to do with the world of literature, trust estates – which Periton was incredibly good at. He became my accountant. And from him I would hear quite a lot about Henry's life as a sort of scholar gypsy. We would have lunch, Periton and I, once a year. He said Henry had this woman to support him. She was finding it difficult, Henry wouldn't take anything from her – but, at the same time, he wouldn't do anything. They seemed to be at an impasse.

Every year I'd say to Periton, 'How's Henry?'

Then one day, it was probably mid 1960s, Leslie said, 'Henry's not so good. In fact, he's dead.' But before we come to that I must tell you about another weirdo who entered the picture. My most intimate friend from the Winchester and Oxford years. He was rather like that fellow in Brideshead, the Charles Ryder thing. Granville Byrd was a phenomenon, an obsessive figure in my life.

It started at prep school and it carried on right through public school and university, Granville was always the best of the rest, the head of the list who didn't get the scholarship. In Oxford, he began to develop severe problems. He had a very unhappy war in South Africa. He added drugs to alcohol. He got a job in Ealing Studios, when I was still in films. He was good at it. In the film industry there are lots of adventuresses about, very attractive women. One of the problems with Wykehamists is that they are inept with ladies. They are desirous, lustful as a raft of monkeys, but have no idea how to gratify that desire. This can lead to misunderstandings.

When Granville, who was getting into very sticky water, inherited, never having been given a sou by his mother, he started a publishing house. If they were strapped for cash, they would advertise for a new director – who needed no knowledge of publishing, but who should have five or ten thousand pounds to invest.

I began my novel. It was based partly on my war background, partly on my country family. Granville had a lot of Welsh in him. His great-grandmother came from America, the time of the War of Independence. The family sided with the British. They went over the Alleghenies and were captured by Red Indians. The whole lot were slaughtered, apart from her, the great-grandmother. She joined the tribe, eventually she married the chief.

The whites sent a punitive expedition to liberate the girl. A young officer, Lieutenant Byrd, was put in charge. He killed all the Indians and liberated her. Which she was extremely displeased about. Byrd took a *fancy to this girl and married her. She came back to Wales with him.*

I said to Granville, 'This is quite a story.' He had a pair of moccasins from the old lady, which he kept in a box. He had pictures of his ancestors, leaning on long guns. They owned most of Chicago at the time.

I said, 'This is a bloody good idea for a book.' Granville said, 'I need a research operator.' On one of my trips to Periton, I said, 'Do you know anything about Henry?' He said, 'He's not doing much.' I said, 'Would he like to do a bit of research?' Leslie said, 'I'll talk to him.'

Henry said, 'Oh, you're up to your old tricks. Can't you understand? I don't want to do anything.' I said, 'Can you afford that?' And he said, 'I can't, but Elizabeth can.' I said, 'I've got a friend called Granville Byrd. He needs somebody to do research.' Henry said, 'Will I be paid?' I said, 'Of course you'll be paid.'

So he did go round, he worked with Granville for about six months. He kept ringing up. 'I can't stand it with this friend of yours. He's completely mad. He's trying to sell some spurs to me, a family heirloom. What does any of this stuff matter? A ridiculous man.'

Henry wasn't interested in families and family histories. That was what he was trying to get away from, Hackney orthodoxy. He said, 'Your friend thinks we've got a good novel. He's trying to get me to collaborate on it.' I said, 'Isn't that a good idea?' Henry said, 'Not at all.'

The news I was getting of Henry was all through Leslie Periton. One day Periton said, 'It's all up.' I said, 'What's happened to Henry?' He said, 'It's a great tragedy.' I can't remember the details, aorta, aneurism. I should think around '65. Henry would be about the age I was then, forty-five.

Granville Byrd died in '77. In extraordinary circumstances. He'd become obsessed by conspiracy theories. It was the time of Watergate. Granville was fanatically on Nixon's side. His contacts led him to Nixon's doctor. Nixon was alleged to be ill at the time, he couldn't answer the charges brought against him. He wasn't fit to be impeached. Granville got hold of Nixon's doctor and collected all the real stories on tape. His solicitor, when he died, wanted to pass them on to me.

Granville had what you might call a 'superior daily' who looked after him. She went round there at about half-past nine in the morning. She rang me: 'We've had a terrible disaster.'

I went straight round, down into the basement in Thurloe Square. Grey flagstones. Granville was completely naked. He had fallen on his face into the basement. All the services in his flat had been turned off, water, gas, electricity.

I rang the police. They said, 'Are there any signs of foul play?' I said, 'That's for you to determine.' They said, 'Well, actually, we're working to rule at the moment. We've got a pay claim in. Unless you establish foul play, or attempted suicide, we won't bother. Ring the hospital.'

Granville was unconscious for five weeks, then he died. He'd broken all his ribs.

I've no idea whether the Red Indian novel Henry was researching was ever finished. I do know that all Granville's papers were taken over by his solicitor. Granville said, 'The contents of my papers must never be divulged – but the papers must never be destroyed.' The sort of instruction that solicitors absolutely hate.

We had a memorial service. The solicitor came sidling over to me: 'Do you want the tapes? You know Granville was tapping phones, recording everything: Nixon's doctor, Watergate, China, Vietnam. I don't want these things in the office.'

There were a number of significant moments when our paths crossed, Henry and I. We were birds of a feather. We emerged from unusual backgrounds where assumptions were made about us, the kind of people we should aim to become, the paths we would pursue, the people we would marry. If we had followed those paths, we would have had no problems at all.

I had no particular reason to listen to gossip about what Henry was doing – but I have, as accumulated memories work their way to the surface, a pretty good notion that he and his lady did get married. They had a child. I think so. It could be a whole new chapter in Henry's story.

Granville was rather the same. Granville Byrd, Henry Cohen and myself: there wasn't any reason why any of us should have lived the kind

of life we did. My father thought all this was rather amusing. He was
particularly amused by my decision to go into the artillery instead of the
Guards. I said to him, 'What do you think about it?' And he said, 'All I
can tell you is that your mother's relatives went into the Coldstream
Guards. They are all now either dead or mutilated.' I went into the artil-
lery and I'm still here to tell the tale.

Douglas passed me his yellowed copy of *Scamp*, pointing out Henry
Cohen's inscription. The Minton dustwrapper was gone, removed,
as was the fashion in those days: no bald man stalking cobbled
streets, hand in pocket, bundle of papers crooked under his arm.
The box of Lyne's unsorted tapes took up most of the table. We
replenished our mugs of tea.

I faced days of work transcribing the interview. I would need
to cut much of it, while trying to preserve the essence of Lyne's
discursive style; the way one story always folded into another. If
I had closed one quest, I'd opened plenty more. Could we find the
Burroughs tape? The Hackney short stories? The Red Indian novel,
which sounded like an anticipation of John Ford's *The Searchers*?

Douglas led me upstairs, past dark family portraits, paintings by
Hazel Guggenheim and others from the bohemian years. He had
an attic room with a set of tables, along which a mappa mundi
had been spread: a chart of Lyne's life, his contacts, influences,
experiences. It was a script, a history, a mystic instrument from
which to conjure the dead. He showed me how Henry Cohen
aligned with William Burroughs, how Father Ignatius (Joseph
Leycester Lyne) could be referenced with Graham Cutts and Alfred
Hitchcock. Where possible, Douglas invited the figures in this
enormous scroll to sign their entries and to make a short
comment.

Now I was being added, in my role as author of an obscure
novel of the Welsh borders, *Landor's Tower*, to take up a red pen
and join the company. Douglas looped a secondary path to William
Burroughs, whom I visited in Lawrence, Kansas. As I left, I saw
him recalibrating the lines, predicting future walks. And I remem-

bered Burroughs's left hand as it reached out for the first drink of the evening: the joint of his little finger was missing. He had taken it off, years before, with poultry shears.

'Child Roland to the dark tower came.' Shakespeare. Was it *Lear*? 'His word was still, – Fie, foh, and fum.' Edgar: Act III, Scene IV. Roland Camberton's alter ego, the bright Jewish boy David Hirsch in *Rain on the Pavements*, would have known his *Lear*, mugged it up for the Balliol interview. He might have a passing acquaintance with Robert Browning and that questing poem in which Roland negotiates the landscape of nightmare to arrive at the point where a more traditional narrative would begin.

Returning from Douglas Lyne's memento-strewn tower, I thought the job was done. The sorcerer left me with enough of the story to put me off the scent. But two questions nagged. The first I could resolve with some degree of conviction. The name, Roland Camberton, where did it come from? Schoolboy scholarship provided the Roland part: Shakespeare, Browning or medieval French romance. And Camberton? The pseudonym was resolutely Aryan. Henry Cohen cast himself as a matinée idol rescued from a forgotten Hollywood programmer witnessed at the Clarence Cinema in Lower Clapton. Ronald Colman, Madeleine Carroll and Roland Camberton in *The Prisoner of Zenda*: such was the fantasy of a bookish adolescent.

It was the second question that really troubled me, the other kind of child, the one Lyne alluded to in such an off-hand way. 'They had a child. I think so. It could be a whole new chapter in Henry's story.' There was no way of forgetting this phantom. If there was a living child, wasn't it my duty to find him or her?

From time to time, I tried to interest publishers in bringing Camberton back into print. I was an admirer of the series of London Books Classics being put out by John King and his partners. In considering *Rain on the Pavements* they made the usual attempts to find the person who held the copyright and they came up with a name: Claire Camberton. I was given Claire's details, a meeting was arranged.

A woman with bright eyes, an animate but tentative presence, arrived on my doorstep, dragging a large red case on wheels. She was, so she told me, no stranger to Hackney. She brought reams of documentation, photocopies of letters, snapshots, books: the fruits of twenty years' research. She was astonished to meet another Camberton enthusiast and we were instantly exchanging snippets of information, trying to fit the jigsaw together. Claire was indeed the daughter of Henry Cohen, but not the child of the late marriage. Her story was unexpected and poignant.

'I was born in December 1954. My mother's name was Lilian Joyce Brown. She was from Andover in Hampshire. She lived in London during the war, working as a silver-service waitress at the Savoy. She was three years younger than my father. She died twenty years ago at the age of sixty-four. She was a bit reclusive towards the end of her life and fairly secretive too.'

Lilian Brown met Henry Cohen when she attended one of the evening classes he gave, in short-story writing, at the City Literary Institute in Covent Garden. Lilian, her daughter recalls, was a pretty woman frustrated by her lack of formal education. She had a sharp eye for antiques and secondhand books and she haunted street markets. Very soon an affair was under way: 'Mum liked Jewish men, it was a bit rebellious at the time. My father pursued her and chatted her up. Mum told me, in her rather prim way, that he was very virile.'

They came to an arrangement: Lilian Brown would carry Henry Cohen's child and, after giving birth, hand her over. Cohen's mistress of the moment, a Jewish woman, couldn't have children. Claire's mother moved to London, Thornton Street on the Stockwell–Brixton border, and she received an allowance of £26 a month from Cohen's solicitors. She changed her name by deed poll to Camberton. Life in those ground-floor flats, as Claire remembers it, consisted of 'plastic knives and forks and making do'. The pseudonym had a simple explanation. 'My father made the name up by combining Camberwell and Brixton. He hated them both. He hated coming south of the river. He was very proud of the fact that he lived in Chelsea.'

Lilian decided to keep the baby. A terrible scene ensued, the last time the infant Claire saw her father. 'It was all Hollywood then. Everything was a story, a romance. When mum decided to call herself Camberton, my father slid away. He ended the association.' The estranged couple met on Clapham Common in 1956. 'My father produced a huge stack of legal papers and presented them to my mother. Isn't that dramatic? I was in the pram. That was their final parting, the end of the relationship. There was no further point of contact.' It was like a replay of an image from Graham Greene's Clapham Common novel of secrets and betrayal, *The End of the Affair*.

As Claire pointed out, the character Margaret in *Scamp* seems to be a guilty memory of her father's relationship with Lilian Brown; even though *Scamp* was published before her parents met. 'It's a melodramatic plot line,' Claire said. 'She's three months pregnant and she kills herself. The whole theme is right there: a woman who is not of his class, not in his league, and having a child. That's probably why he didn't want my mother to read it.'

Scamp presents an anti-hero, Ivan Ginsberg, who courts failure, relishes obscurity, and has an eye for a waitress. 'Ginsberg was very much aware of her desirable presence by his side; so delightful were her little moues and winks that he . . . felt like . . . whispering into her ear an invitation.' And there was always another woman in reserve. 'Until Lolita became his mistress, Ginsberg was delighted with the novelty of this courtship. But afterwards there was nothing to sustain their relations except recrudescent desire . . . Ginsberg was also still ashamed of Lolita's background, which, though it might supply colour for an adventure, an anecdote, made a long-term affair impossible. At the same time he was ashamed of being ashamed . . .'

Among Claire's papers was a photocopy of 'Truant Muse', an article by June Rose published in *The Jewish Chronicle* in 1965, just before Camberton died. Rose wanted to discover why certain writers 'whose names were once well known . . . sped into obscurity'. Henry Cohen, she decided, was 'the kind of individual who finds it pleasant to vegetate'. He retreated to a bungalow beside the sea. 'London history is his special subject and he writes with erudition and clarity in small reviews.' The article is accompanied by a photograph of a balding, melancholy man: like a cinema organist after the coming of sound. Here, without question, is the figure drawn by John Minton for the cover of *Scamp*. That image is taken from life. A stalking solitary. A crow in the rain.

And there is one more surprise: a 'major work', never published, *Tango*. The journal of a hitch-hiking odyssey around Britain, an English *On the Road*. 'The writing is at times Orwellian,' Rose enthuses. Camberton laid out his plans in a letter to *The Jewish Chronicle*. 'My intention is to make two journeys: one, partly on foot, through Europe . . . and the second to North America.' *Tango* was rejected by his publisher and has not resurfaced.

'Roland Camberton is essentially an isolated figure,' Rose concludes. 'A man in a mackintosh, dignified, anonymous, alone. He is isolated from other writers, from the Jewish community . . . and his essential anonymity implies almost an element of choice.'

A firm of Wimbledon solicitors informed Claire's mother that Henry Cohen had changed his name a second time, shortly before his marriage. The new name was never to be revealed. The allowance would stop. The site of the grave would remain a secret.

I had been chasing the wrong story. Dying at the age of forty-four, Roland Camberton left behind books that are worth searching out, as well as the manuscript of a journey on foot across Europe. I had missed vital clues in *Rain on the Pavements*, material about random and reckless expeditions around England; the begging of water in Surrey, hitched rides that deposited him in Bedford instead of Cambridge. 'The bleak, unlit, and half-made roads of an industrial estate.' Slough. 'Long, low factory sheds . . . private railway lines . . . an immense hangar-like structure.' I totally failed to grasp Hirsch's drift out to the edge-lands in search of a more inspiring poetic of entropy. At the age when Henry Cohen was buried, I had scarcely begun: a Jewish bookseller in Uppingham was considering taking a punt on my first eccentric novel. I had lived in Hackney for twenty years without becoming part of its dream or its meaning. And I never succeeded in getting away. Where did Cohen keep his seaside bungalow?

WICK AND FLAME

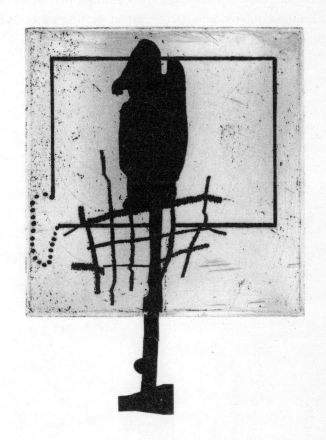

Since when did divine thunderbolts go falling on Hackney?

– Paula Rego

The Lord Napier

Jock was quite disturbed that the old bill had not been around to see him. About the murder. The fatal stabbing of the jogger, Margaret Muller, in Victoria Park. Especially with his house so close to the police station. Not that he had any fresh evidence to offer, no sightings during his afternoon walks, his bicycle excursions down the canal path. The only park assassin within Jock's immediate circle was his dog, the ex-Hackney Wick greyhound. This beast, so preternaturally calm in the studio, his rug in the corner, reverted to type when confronted with squirrels. Jock's hound was the only way of keeping the bushy-tailed vermin population within limits. The snapping of spines, the tossing of Nutkin in powerful jaws, was not a popular spectacle with card-carrying greens and homeward munching infants.

'I was her tutor for fuck's sake,' Jock said. 'A Vicky Park regular. If they don't interview me, who are they questioning?'

It was Bosun, a dog from Grove Road, who found the body. 'Forty stab wounds. Margaret died in my neighbour's arms.'

We met in Jock's industrial unit, among the stripped-down bikes, the stacked canvases, the totemic hare that toast-rack-ribbed hounds chased around the Wick stadium: the famous electric rabbit that no greyhound ever caught. Jock acquired it from among the sea of rubbish photographed by Stephen Gill during the last days of the boot fair, before the Olympic shutdown. Either there or from eBay: Jock scavenged compulsively, as he worked, ate, listened to the radio.

WE BUY GOLD. WE SELL BOXES.

Among the threatening shadows hanging over Hackney Wick, its storage facilities, cafés, communes, junk yards, tyre mountains, messianic warehouse chapels, were capitalized notices, wired to chainlink fences between compulsory-purchase orders: the alchemy of ruin. We buy gold from the teeth of the dead. We sell cardboard boxes for cremations. *But who are we?*

Jock was about to fulfil his fantasy, a night out at the Lord Napier. We had heard about these sessions from Timothy Soar, the architectural photographer. Tim would be in the old pub, undoubtedly; he would want to pay his respects to another discontinued artist, Stevie Dola. I felt that I was trespassing on Nigel Fountain's *Guardian* turf: every chapter an obituary, for people and places, loved by their own, meaningless to the world at large. Brian Catling composed the tribute to Dola for the *Independent* and made a good job of it. The astonishing details of those last years, when we had drifted out of touch, could now be pieced together from the variant accounts of Catling and McFadyen.

Dola and Soar: you could not imagine a more ill-matched pair in habits or art practice. They came together through a love of this doomed landscape, the magical island of Hackney Wick. Soar has a white cube, close to the railway, a controlled space cleaner than any hospital. He lodges comfortably, behind a secure gate, in the company of the dying industries with their dazzling sparks, their eternal grinding: white vans, hoists, fork-lifts. Dola was an invisible: post-squat, pre-oblivion. Soar ground his own coffee, worked with assistants, filed his prints in steel cabinets. Dola's Scottish breakfast came in bottles from the Russian supermarket: whisky and milk chocolate, cold potatoes and peanut butter. The conjunction of such lives was possible only in the limbo before demolition, security fences, insurance fires. Newts and allotment holders to be offered alternative accommodation.

The small irony here was that Tim Soar got his living from making the new buildings of Stratford City, the only active element in the Olympic smokescreen, look good. A cool eye on hot money. Within the Lionworks studio, frozen architectural prints were presented, lit from above, like a choir of icons. Tim told Jock about the sessions in the Lord Napier, a squatted pub spray-painted by Sweet Toof, Cyclops and their associates. Lock-ins for Wick irregulars: waifs and strays, Poles, Russians, anybody outside the system. Thirsty young women with no food in their bellies. Men rarely exposed to daylight.

Catling's obituary for Dola spoke of his early involvement with a 'multimedia urban-junk-and-pyrotechnics percussion trio'. The final retreat to Hackney Wick was a sort of homecoming, the artist moving out of the gallery and into the source material of his performance pieces. Boundaries dissolved. Whenever he had cash-money, Stevie took to the water. He was a skilled pilot. I have seen him, so drunk he had to be strapped to the wheel, easing his battered craft, a Lowestoft tugboat, through the narrowest and most deceptive channels between sandbanks. He dredged for maritime detritus and sounded it, teasing rhythms from murky water, the pluck of sediment; barely perceptible vibrations of tarry ropes, echoes within anchored barges, decommissioned lighters. He staged lethal firework displays, crawling up chimneys with cans of petrol on his back, a potential holocaust. It was inevitable therefore that when fire-raising became a valued craft in the edge-lands, a tool of the economy, Dola was hired by shady developers and impatient strategic planners. Remember the headlines? INFERNO. RAZING OF AN OLYMPIC TORCH. 'Fire engulfs an empty warehouse on site of Olympic Park as giant cloud of smoke is seen from across the capital.'

Flush with dirty money, Dola recognized himself as being in the same business as Tim Soar: making the best of the worst of it. From Springfield Park Marina, south along the banks of the Lea, rough sleepers took to bushes and scrub woods, tumbledown sheds, allotments, cold concrete bunkers. They had been moving out of Hackney, to narrowboats and engineless cruisers, from the poll-tax days. Now impossible rents, empty apartment blocks, increased mooring fees, social clearances, drove them deeper into the undergrowth. Into derelict Hackney Wick pubs like the Napier.

The story of Dola's last years was horrible. He found an abandoned boathouse, a rowing club that had been closed down while the site was tactfully redeveloped for Olympic kayak racing: a proposition discreetly shelved when the toxicity of the water was discovered. Bill Parry-Davies, who came along to the wake in the Napier, with several other members of the Boas Society, told me what had been happening behind the security fences.

There is documentary evidence of radioactive material, used in the manu-facture of luminous watch dials, at two burials on the Olympic Park. The Clays Lane Estate was owned by the Lea Valley Park Authority, they had a cycle track there. A 1980s estate, with student accommodation. There was concern when the contractors started boring deep holes on the site. This was done, we believe, to detect what was actually under there.

I applied for legal aid and was refused, twice. The first application was turned down on the basis that so many people could be affected, the dispersal of radioactivity was so widespread. Even though my client lived right alongside the boreholes, the fact that he could suffer serious injury was not deemed sufficient.

I adopted other tactics. I got a letter back saying that because the Olympic Park was a national project of strategic significance, it was unlikely that the court would grant an injunction.

The nature of radioactive material is that it only becomes dangerous once it's been disturbed. Once you release it into the air, as dust, it becomes a major problem. And that is what they were doing: on a daily basis. They decided to ring-fence the entire site. Then, at the end of last year, they undertook tests on the run-off into the River Lea. They found levels of thorium in the water.

W. S. Atkins, the engineering company, considered that it was possible that the thorium had dispersed along the water table, south-south-west – which is where the Clays Lane Estate is. And the cycle track. Thorium is ductile and malleable, it's used as a source of nuclear energy. You get a coating of it on sunlamps or on vacuum-tube filament coatings. When they found the run-off in the Lea, not at dangerous levels, it was enough to confirm the engineers' prediction of what could happen. The effect being that the entire Olympic Park is contaminated with thorium at water-table level.

This is quite a major consideration, when you don't know the concen-trations or the amounts in the ground. And when the mayor, Ken Livingstone, is saying: 'We're going to get all the money back, because we're going to sell the land.' Which they will not be able to do, unless they clear the whole thing: a huge undertaking. There are strong parallels with the Millennium Dome fiasco. But, politically, this is on a much grander scale.

There wasn't any control over the burial of radioactive substances until 1963. They gave the dirty industries a two-year window to dispose of the stuff. The Environment Agency report says that it's likely there is radio-active material buried in several places on the Olympic site. We can detect it. It was fortuitous that whoever buried the stuff lost it in the cesspits of the old houses. Nobody is going to go near that, are they?

The reason why they've gone ahead with the digging on the Clays Lane Estate, despite the risk to tenants, is that there is such political pressure to finalize the budget for the Olympics. They sent the bulldozers right in.

Tenants are gradually being dispersed and rehoused. People are being evicted from other places in order to make room for those who have been evicted from Clays Lane. It's musical chairs. One of the residents told me that to get into the estate, to reach his own property, he had to go through a security barrier and produce ID. It is a police state. Those unfortunates who still live there are woken at five in the morning to find a police and army exercise going on, counter-terrorist war games, bombs and guns and helicopters, smoke everywhere. Nobody told them this was going to happen.

In such a climate, when, as Bill says, nobody is going to go near the forbidden zone, Stevie Dola took up voluntary residence. It was a penance for his part in the arson wars. And a retreat, now that his scavenging art was impossible, his boat in dry dock, his wives scattered, into the place he loved more than any other: the urban wilderness.

He was not alone. Warring tribes were all around him: fixed travellers facing eviction to less desirable sites, roving tinkers in a camp under the motorway bridge, *Mad Max* biker gangs, latter-day saints and sinners, ranters, levellers, prophets in bulletproof Mercedes limousines preaching apocalypse and ritual immersion in the algae-clogged shallows of the Lea and its rust-red tributaries.

Dola retreated to his boathouse, his books. At night, he drove without lights across the marshes, the squared-off football pitches, unmapped dirt roads at the rim of the Olympic Park, super highways that ran out on high bridges that didn't connect with anything. Drinking, tapes pumping out heartbeat rhythms, he looked at the fuzzy lights through his bird-streaked windscreen. Distant Canary Wharf winked red. Circling aircraft waited for clearance above Silvertown. The traffic snake, in and out of Essex, never stopped. Convoys rumbled into the Olympic Park, reshaping pyramids of yellow clay.

Stevie did a bit on the water with the Irish kids, but he was not always in the mood for it. Some days he couldn't crawl from his bed: even when they smashed his windows and burnt his library. Ugly drunk and sick with the world, weeping, he ran at the mob, out on the marshes – and got one of them, breaking a few bones. Nothing serious enough to justify the reprisal attack, the beating with a metal pole from which he never properly recovered.

With winter coming on, Stevie Dola, coated and booted, went into hibernation. One of the traveller kids agreed to fetch his whisky from the Russian supermarket: there was still plenty of cash stuffing the pillow. 'Keep the change, son.' It might have worked if the boy's brother hadn't thought of a way to improve the profit margin: by judicious decanting, cutting the cheap booze with antifreeze. Dola's punished but resilient system stood up to the insult for a few months. He was partly paralysed, it's true, sucked into a cocoon of hopeless craving, memory-flashes, marine replays, vegetative sexuality. 'The tide re-seeds the barren shore,' he whispered. To the screeching gulls, the bottom-feeders.

They found him, stiff as a board, one January morning, on the snow-powdered diamond-hard ground where the Hackney Stadium had once been. A dog licking his bare, black feet.

Jock McFadyen

As we struck east across Victoria Park in the direction of Hackney Wick, Jock told me how he had recovered his memorable edge-lands painting *Horse Lamenting the Invention of the Motor Car*. An old girlfriend kept it for years, it went with the minimalist style of the time: a contradiction, a window of bad taste. When she got a better offer and moved on, closer to the river, she left the painting behind. The film-director Paul Tickell's daughter took over the lease. Paul helped with transport. With his restless and sharp-focused eye, he immediately recognized Jock's missing masterwork.

'It was one of those great moments, London moments,' McFadyen said. 'Twelve million people and a random connection. Paul did a piece on me for *The Late Show*, back in the days when I was getting commissions from the Royal Opera House.'

'He did us all,' I said. 'I hear he's got one-day-a-week teaching now. Some of the kids are bright. None have heard of *Performance*. And *BlowUp* is as remote as Homer. He tried to interest Neil Murger in a Hackney night for BBC4: forgotten punk bands, Genesis P-Orridge, Burroughs in Vyner Street, Orson Welles, the Angry Brigade, Astrid Proll.'

We both laughed.

I asked Jock's opinion on an offer I'd received, indirectly, from one of Ken Livingstone's apparatchiks: to give a talk on the River Lea to a pre-Olympic seminar in Stratford. The whole business was dubious: if you are paid to oppose, you are paid. Period. You are part of the machinery of neutralized dissent, hired to perform as a sanctioned critic. You are recorded, revised. In the brochure. On tape. In cyberspace. Subject to editorial control.

'You refused?'

'Initially.'

Until Charlie Velasco came in with an offer of lunch in the new pub, by the German Hospital, the Pequod. A set like a Nantucket whaler serviced by dockside barmaids who didn't have to fake their unfamiliarity with the English language. You perched in tilted cabins, crow's-nest eyries and chain lockers: low-ceilinged, close-confined, hot but private.

Anna hated those booths. She was prepared to come along, to hear what was happening with Syd and the children; she often remarked that Charlie and Syd were the only ones from the early days of the communal house, the 8mm diary films, who were still together. Despite their ups and downs. Syd's intense and demanding work schedule. Charlie's increasing visibility in places where New Labour interfaced with the arts (celebrity bands in Downing Street, attendance at big football matches England were fated to lose). Being so far ahead of the game, as a world-travelling footie fan, gave Charlie a major advantage over latecoming Mellor-types who followed the money. And were never short of a crass tabloid opinion. Uninformed sports punditry was a good career for the politically disgraced, the equivalent of the US lecture circuit for dumped prime ministers. The alternative to post-prison theology.

But Anna was not invited. That was made clear. Boys only, work. Charlie brought along a media fixer from City Hall, one of Ken's seamless and invertebrate salesmen. This character had been trained in Atlanta, back in the Jimmy Carter days. His opening gambit was: 'I live in Islington with my black boyfriend.' Why should I care? Somebody has to live in the place. It was Charlie, the Tottenham fanatic, who winced.

Velasco was as lean and hawkish as he had been thirty years before, with the same enthusiastic grin, the relish for ideas, debate. His companion was more watchful, deputed to road-test my attitude: would I go too far? He didn't drink, sitting back, flicking imaginary motes from his sleeve, as we broached the third bottle. He gossiped, within safe limits, about Ken and Lord Coe, the City Hall power-broker Len Duvall, but no word on Blair.

'Will you do it?' he said, picking up the bill.

'No way, sorry. I'm preoccupied with a Hackney book.'

'Twenty minutes. Off the cuff. Piece of piss.'

'Paid?'

'Car. Good lunch. Honorarium.'

I hated that word.

'How much?'

He glanced at a smirking Charlie who was signing the menu for the barmaid who'd seen him, only that morning, on breakfast TV, playing keepie-uppies with the Archbishop of York.

'Two grand? Not a lot, I know. Things are tight just now. With the election coming up, the shits are on to everything.'

'I'll be there.'

Passing Sidney Kirsh's shaded flat, where it all began, I held my pocket-recorder close to Jock's chin. It was habitual now, this dredging of memory: houses, work, movement. A city obscured by revelation. The greyhound loped alongside, jaws slack, alert for squirrels. Jock was the mouthpiece for the dog's more considered soliloquy. His dreams of a saliva-sodden furry rabbit.

Victoria Park was my first experience of living in Hackney. Brookfield Road. A very grand house in its own grounds, large garden at the back. You could hear the speedway bikes at the Hackney Stadium, off in the distance. I only went to the stadium for the dog races.

It was a terrible time, actually. A one-way street, Victoria Park Road, on your doorstep. You are psychologically someone who gets passed by. It's like living in the middle of a roundabout. Nobody came to visit me, they couldn't find it. I was only thirty and fantastically cut off. I'd just split up with my girlfriend. I was a bit down. Stuck in the basement of this gloomy place which I'd bought for fifteen grand. No, make that fifteen and a half.

I dropped off the property ladder. I couldn't afford the flat, I sold it. The mortgage was £100 a month. I'd made some money from painting for the first time. I had a good deposit. Then I had a financial crash, early 1980s, when I changed my style of working. I stopped doing schematic pictures and tried realism. The horse painting was transitional. My human figures were all based on people I had seen. I started doing pictures about place.

I sold the Victoria Park flat for twenty-two grand. I made seven grand on it in a very short space of time. I got an Acme house for the next eight years. The paintings were changing.

I tried the pubs around the park. I'd sit there, not knowing anyone, feeling totally pissed off. Drinking slow pints and thinking: 'What the fuck am I doing here?' Feeling fucking miserable. I was young. I used to drink and drive in those days. I used to get in my yellow car and drive down to the pubs I knew in Bow, in the days when I was happy. I went to the Five Bells & Blade Bone, by Limehouse Church – which I started! I started the artists going in there. Before me it was just Czech car thieves and tarts, a real dive.

I'd go every night, the Blade Bone. I got to know the landlord. A Scottish family ran the pub. I told all my friends to stop going to the pub on Flamborough Street, off Salmon Lane. A nice Young's house. I wanted to frequent the Blade Bone, I liked the shape of the bar. I would go there at eleven o'clock at night. I wouldn't bother to sit through an entire evening. I'd do the art openings, up west, practically every night. I was single and looking for romance.

Sometimes I'd be sitting in the Caprice with patrons, famous names, the movers. Then I'd rush back to the Five Bells in Limehouse, tap on the window, and drink until three in the morning. Get up late, start work. Like living in Berlin, I suppose.

I was still in Hackney, but my studio was in Turner's Road, a short walk from the Blade Bone. Around 1986 I started making proper money. I was earning fifty grand a year. I had a gallery in Cork Street. But I was living in a dump. I had sixty grand in the Abbey National and I didn't own any property. I didn't know what to do with the money. I didn't have a clue about investments.

In 1989 I bought a flat in Edinburgh. A year later, I bought a little house in Grove Road, Bethnal Green. That year I met Susie Honeyman, who moved in with me. We got married. Much later, in another recession,

I got into the Roman Road development with Piers Gough. The recession of '93 was really bad. Everybody was facing repossession. When my daughter, Annie, was born, we were totally skint. Susie was doing teaching. I wasn't selling anything, I didn't have a studio. The market came back in '95. I learnt about using property to survive. It's just another form of banking. I bought a bigger flat in Edinburgh.

I'd never, up to that point, drawn money against any of my properties. Well, I did sell the place I developed with Piers Gough. We didn't make any profit on that, we got ripped off. We made a paper profit of fifty grand. Capital gains took 40 per cent. We made a small loss. A negative project, but a steep learning curve. A fucking scary moment, actually. We faced selling the house.

I was with Agnew's in Bond Street. Agnew's were the first dealers to show Bacon. That's where I had the show of my new realist paintings. One show. Lots of reviews, a little money.

I cut the tape when we passed the pathway where Margaret Muller was attacked, between the rose garden and the children's adventure playground. It was clear, when you walked it, that this was the direct route into Victoria Park from Hackney Wick – where Muller, like so many other students and artists, lived. There was only one exit from the island, the impacted community tucked against the back rivers and the A102, the Blackwall Tunnel Approach.

When we stood on the bridge, logging the KILL MATTHEW BARNEY sticker, Jock pointed out the embankment where his pantomime horse lamented the invention of the motor car. 'I'm not a libidinous shooter,' he said. 'I'd rather save my bullets. If I do decide to do a Matthew Barney painting, I'll need one of your snaps.'

'Strange thing,' I muttered, pointing to the Top o' the Morning pub. The plaque for the first Railway Murder. 'The man arrested for the lethal assault on Thomas Briggs was called Müller. Franz Müller.'

Limehouse, on the southern horizon, was the favoured destination for Jock's nocturnal drives. This was the ramp where he skidded, half-cut, out of Hackney, back towards the grotesques who haunted his early paintings: bow-legged strippers, porcupine junkies, rutting dogs.

'How well did you know David Widgery?'

Widgery was my doctor. I went to the Gill Street Health Centre, where he was in practice with four others. He called out my name and I went in. He said, 'Oh, it's Jock McFadyen. I'll have you. I like to have all the artists.' I was quite flattered that a doctor would know what I did. I had been painting these pictures of Hawksmoor churches and the general neighbourhood. Widgery was alive to things. When Susie came on the scene, he was made up. He was a big Mekons fan. He loved punk. He was a rock'n'roll person. And a mad socialist. From a posh background.

A posh leftie, basically. There's a lot of that about. Susie was charmed by him. And he was very taken with her. He said, 'I remember going to see the Mekons when they were being supported by the Clash.' The Mekons were now obscure and the Clash part of rock history. Widgery liked to champion the underdogs. Whether it was single-parent Asian claimants or forgotten punk groups.

I read his book, which I thought was so clunky: Some Lives! It started well, down Mare Street, on top of a bus. He hears a conversation with a black girl. I thought: 'He's got the images going.' Then it descends into sixth-form socialism, maundering on about injustice and how rickets has been eradicated. I got so bored with it. Eye-wateringly dull.

Painters work in private. You wouldn't get beyond the first couple of hours if you thought like Widgery. You're sitting there with a cup of tea and Radio 4, day after day. You hope for rain, because you don't want to be stuck inside if it's not raining. A shitty life, really. Being a professional painter.

One night in the Five Bells, Frank McLaughlin – who is ten years younger than me – said that he'd got a letter from the Gill Street Health Centre. It said: 'Now that you are thirty, we advise you to come in and have a full test for liver function, cholesterol.' Frank said, 'Fuck it, I've got to go round for these tests.' He was from Northern Ireland. I was saying, 'Let me see that. I'm with fucking Gill Street and I'm thirty-eight. Why haven't I got one?'

I went round to see Widgery. 'Why can't you check me out, doc?'

He said, 'You must have slipped through the net. Is there anything in particular you're worried about?'

I said, 'Well, there's my drinking.'

I must have reeled off what was, for him, a modest amount: five or six pints a night, with a couple of Scotches to get me ready for bed.

He made notes about units. He said, 'You could piss in this bottle if you want to.' He went through the motions. Then, when I met Nick Fox, another doctor, the Labour Party candidate, I got the full story on Widgery. Fox was a young guy in his forties, he used to campaign for Peter Shore. He was shafted, they wanted Oona King in there, a babe.

I was chatting to Nick, shortly after Widgery died, about the drinking thing. He laughed. Widgery was a complete alcoholic. He'd also had polio. He was a friend of Ian Dury. Widgery said to Dury, 'You're a spastic and I'm a spastic. Let's form a club. Club foot, ha!' To be empowered. They wrote this song together, a sort of anthem for spastics.

He had a posh voice, Widgery. He was my doctor, an authority figure. The previous quack, the one before Widgery, died of AIDS. I can't remember when that was. I think I'd already moved into the London Fields studio, by the railway. There is only one other artist around, John Davies. The Chinese are taking over, the noodle people, they've got three units now.

My place used to be a garage. They did gearboxes. They were smuggling drugs, cocaine. They would take all the gears out. All the cogs. They filled the shells with cocaine. You'd get hundreds of thousands of pounds of powder in each gearbox. They were caught because the customs officers realized that the gearboxes were too light.

When I arrived here, arrest warrants were all over the floor, a carpet of paper. There were bars across the toilet windows, excellent locks. A steel door. I thought, 'We're fine for security.' There was a false wall with holes punched in it, plasterboard cavities.

I bought the place, cash down. I can store anything, art, bikes, cars.

Storage and recycling is the name of the game. I'm going to vote fucking Green Party next time. I'm becoming phobic about anything that has to be thrown away.

My new paintings, the A13 and the Olympic Park, are faction. What I liked about Kojak, Telly Savalas, he'd be running along with a gun, diving through a door: and it really would be the Bronx. Not a studio. That car with the wheels off – it's true! They haven't invented the car. They may have kicked the panels in, roughed it up a little. But it's an actual Lincoln, a Cadillac, a Buick.

That fusion of the observed and the non-observed, the accidental, is what I strive for. I wouldn't dream of taking a landscape straight. My graffiti is real but it doesn't come from here. I'll borrow it from another section of the towpath and patch the world together in an original configuration. To bring you closer to the truth.

You had to buy a ticket to get inside the Napier. Then you braved the set of monster teeth and walked through a pink mouth. Drink was served in chipped mugs. Jock looked disappointed, nothing lurid was going down; no sex traffickers, no truck girls, nobody who looked as if they'd escaped from one of his early paintings. Conversation was muted, lighting low: Stevie Dola's wake would have astonished the man, it was more like a gallery opening from the old days. Or yet another 'ongoing, interdisciplinary, interventionist protest' about the Olympic enclosures. Folk from Clays Lane, the Manor Garden Allotments, the Boas Society, the Lammas Land Defence Committee and the Hackney Marsh User Group calibrated loss with computer presentations, schematic maps, field reports.

Dola's ashes sat on the bar in a snowstorm globe, like the one seen in Orson Welles's expressionist close-up: the 'Rosebud' fall from the dying grasp of Citizen Kane. Stephen Gill's photographs of the Lower Lea, in its interim period of yellow paint markings and surveyors' dinghies, played on the wall. A shot of David Cameron and Lord Coe, blue-suited on a dirt road, raised a derisive cheer. There was a shaggy horse in a field of pylons that seemed to have strayed out of Jock's painting.

A young man from Buenos Aires was reading from Hubert Waley's book about his brother Arthur, the Chinese scholar. 'More enterprising expeditions took us in an easterly direction, particularly to Lea bridge, where we hired a boat and plied our oars energetically, looking neither to right nor left, so as to avoid seeing the dead cats and dogs which floated near the banks. A puzzled friend once asked Arthur what attracted him about the River Lea, to which he replied that he admired the abrupt way in which London ended there instead of tailing off into suburbs.'

We joined some women I recognized at a corner table. They were listening to the travel yarns of Dan Dixon-Spain, the Shacklewell portraitist, who had recently returned to England. I gestured with the recorder. It felt right to get down as much as I could of this event, surely the last of its kind.

I had a studio in the Wick, in Queen's Yard, right next to the train station. I took the whole top floor. I did large posters, fifty feet by eight feet. There was one good pub. The Wick felt like a place where big lorries thundered through.

I remember going to the studio one Sunday morning, to start work. A rave was going on in the warehouse. When I left to go home, ten hours later, people were still sitting in the street. The rave continued for thirty-six hours.

I went to the pub when it opened, usually at half-ten, to get something to eat. All the postmen used to be in there, drinking beer. Along with secondhand car dealers and scrapmetal traders. I bought a van door for my Transit. I worked with a character called Banksy. Did you ever hear of Banksy?

He commissioned an art sculptor to help with one of his pieces. I met him a few times, but I didn't know it was him. He was a shrewd guy. I didn't like that piece at all.

At first, I found him quite obnoxious, but when I got to know him better, I liked him. He had to maintain the mystique of anonymity. He didn't want to let anyone know who he was. He was doing a piece called The Rodin Thinker. *A copy of Rodin's figure with a traffic cone on its head, cast in bronze, to be stuck in some square in Soho. Two fingers to the art world.*

He didn't know who Rodin was or when the original was done. He just picked on this as a famous sculpture. Which I thought was a bit trite. In general, I liked his work. An interesting guy. Two policemen kissing. Banksy was in the Wick, on and off, for a few months. He has a number of people he works with, studios in different places. Generally, I stay away from artists. I like to fill my life with normal people, people who are not self-obsessed.

Sarah Wise, the London historian, who had been giving a talk on Arthur Morrison to the Boas Society, was showing a set of drawings to Emily Richardson and Susanna Edwards, the graphic designer. I was astonished to see late-Victorian steel engravings of Hackney Marshes. We could have walked through these scenes on our way to the Napier. Tents of tattered cloth, greasy bivouacs, buckets heating on improvised brick ovens. 'You probably know,' Sarah said, 'Romanys and didicai gypsies began to come off the road and settle in Hackney, Dalston, Walthamstow and other north-eastern suburbs from the 1880s onwards.'

Thanks to Sarah's researches, I understood how important the threatened water-margin of Hackney had always been; an unpoliced, unloved strip where dirty industries could cohabit with travellers, aliens, the electively destitute. A few miles upstream, the peasant-poet John Clare met his gypsy troop in the forest and decided to risk everything on a long march north: to bring his first love, the inspiration for his poetry, back from the dead.

The caption to one of the engravings took my eye: 'Knife-Grinder, Hackney Wick'. A service industry tolerated in a place the mercantile bourgeoisie refused to colonize. Nature nudging at brick. Scrub wood for small fires. Rivers cleaned out for profit. A rogue ecology to be celebrated: because it required no approval, no funding. No double-tongued rhetoric.

Tapes of Stevie Dola's underwater Thames recordings were

played, creaking anchor chains, hammered keels resounding like whale music. Anya Gris questioned Jock about Margaret Muller. Several of the women were very concerned about the failure of the police to bring their investigations into the Victoria Park assault to a conclusion. There had been a number of failed attempts to assign Muller's murder to accused killers in other parks and contiguous areas of East London.

> Drug addict Christopher Duncan, 21, was convicted yesterday of bludgeoning 28-year-old Jagdip Najran with a baseball bat at his flat in Bethnal Green. Duncan, who was obsessed with rap star Eminem, stuffed 5ft 2in Miss Najran into a suitcase where she bled to death last year. He will now be formally questioned by detectives about the frenzied stabbing of Miss Muller, an artist who was murdered as she jogged through Victoria Park in Hackney.

It was shameful, a stain on place and people, on investigators and citizens, that the culprit could not be located. The wrong men were brought in: from Clissold Park or territories far beyond the reach of this mindless assassin. There had been further attacks, less frenzied, in the poorly lit and now deserted streets around the Hackney Wick station. But the thrust of security and surveillance was to do with keeping trespassers out, on the 'safe' side of the Olympic fence. Repulsing photographers, nuisances.

A painful story for Jock to recall.

Margaret Muller was a student of mine at the Slade. She was essentially a life painter, no dreadful pun intended. She painted the figure. She was about twenty-eight. She wasn't mature, as a person, although she was six or seven years older than the other students. A postgraduate. She came from Virginia, I think.

Margaret arrived in London because of the painter Euan Uglow. The man who did the famous nude of Cherie Blair. She worked in the life room on what they call 'perceptual' painting. It's to do with measuring, retinal truth. You paint from the model. This practice grew out of the Euston Road School.

Some of the students subscribe absolutely to these rules. Margaret wasn't one of them. The others were like devout, fundamentalist Muslims. They didn't look at Sickert. He said he painted in the English style for the French market.

Institutions are about one personality within them being too powerful. Uglow's life room was like a school within a school. Closed doors. Margaret was there for Euan. She was not conspicuously talented. Who's that black man, the Olympic sprinter who failed the drug test? Linford Christie. She painted Linford Christie. Margaret was a non-fundamentalist member of the life room.

Then Euan died. That left the room to me. I only did one day a week. For the last year of her time at the Slade, I was teaching Margaret Muller. She left. And then she got a studio at Hackney Wick. There are lots of studios out there, industrial buildings. The Wick is where you find the artists.

A couple of weeks before Margaret died, I was in the Slade. As I was leaving she called me over. I hadn't recognized her, she was wearing a woolly hat. And she was wearing two coats. She'd come into the college for some forms. I sat down and had a chat with her. I thought maybe she was one of those rich Americans. She'll go off to New York and get a studio. But actually she was toughing it in London. She'd done what all the students do. They go to the East End and get a studio that is terminally freezing. They live in that studio, they can't afford to rent a room as well.

Here was Margaret in the Slade, so overdressed, wearing all these layers of stuff. Two weeks later, I was in Scotland. When I came back, Susie said, 'Something terrible has happened. This woman has been murdered in Victoria Park. You'd better sit down. It must be someone you know.'

And, of course, it was. Dreadful. It left me depressed for about a year. I don't know if you're like that, because you're round and about, all over the place. I'm in two worlds. In Bethnal Green, I live in the ghetto: Mrs Patel, the corner shop. The tube. Woolworths on Bethnal Green Road. A *bonny little town. It could be anywhere. It needn't even be in London. And then there's the West End. There is no relation between the two places, my two lives. Quite disturbing.*

Margaret visited my London Fields studio. She might have been out to the Roman Road factory with Piers Gough. But she was in my studio, definitely. There are so many artists in Hackney now, and the art parasites, the middlemen and operators; so many galleries and merchandisers. I know some of the Young Turks. If you can't beat them, join them. I had my last gig in a car showroom on Cambridge Heath Road.

We lived next door to the police station. All the television people were out there. Susie said, 'That's because Margaret Muller's father has been to Bethnal Green police station.' It was then that I felt as if the carpet had been pulled out from under me. My two worlds had been ripped apart. It was later that year that I left the Slade. Now I hardly go to the West End. I feel as if I've been cut loose by Margaret's death.

I went around to the Slade afterwards, open-mouthed with shock. The Slade was getting on with its life. They don't live over here, in Hackney. The professor of the Slade lives in Crouch End. Most of the teaching staff would hardly have known Margaret.

There was another student, she got run over and killed, on her bicycle, around the same time. In this area, the Old Street roundabout. She had a studio in Cremer Street. By Hackney Road.

There are so many young women out there, jogging in the park, cycling. It worries me. I'm not sure about anything any more. Property is the only security. You can live off borrowed money. Painting is a precarious career. Last year I went eight months without selling a thing. When you get to my age, you've got something in all those public collections and institutions: the Ashmolean, the Tate, the V&A, the British Museum, even the National Gallery. I've got something in the bloody Imperial War Museum. And the provincial ones: Glasgow, Manchester, Birmingham. Now they wouldn't buy the skin off my shit. I'm not fashionable. I'm fifty-five years old. It's like trying to be a geriatric pop singer. When Lucian Freud was fifty-five, he was quite obscure.

Some Hackney painters – Leon Kossoff, for example – are top-flight. Kossoff is up there with the powerful galleries. You get known when you're quite young and you manage to survive pop art, conceptualism, Schnabel. Kossoff gets a one-man show at the National Gallery, drawings of Spitalfields.

I muddle through. I haven't got an international reputation. Cracking America is impossible. If Midwest museums feel they have to have your work in the collection, that's great; you're in a different category to some little cunt like me, who fiddles away with observations on the tatty fringes of a great city.

You learn to live with fear. 'Fucking hell, I'd better make sure this shit is properly documented before it's taken away, bulldozed, burnt to the ground.' I feel that acutely and I always have. Remember the ginger hare in my studio, the one from Hackney Wick? I've not only got the dog, I've got the fucking rabbit as well.

Old Ford

'Is crazy, Mr Sinclair,' Mimi said, 'is completely crazy.'

I met the Sicilian photographer, a Wick resident, at the Napier, knowing the work he had done on Mafia families, back home, but unaware, until he showed me around his studio the next day, of the project based on Italian cucumber growers in the Lea Valley. A well-established enclave who imported the old ways into Enfield, Broxbourne, Ware: Wednesday-afternoon meals at long tables, then dancing; religious processions carrying their saints down to the river; established dons of the green-vegetable business, unlanguaged newcomers in caravans. Feasts for Sicilian pensioners organized by priests and nuns.

'Like *The Sopranos*. On the edge of reality: superstition, poverty, gold under the bed. They have their own words. Like "capita": cup of tea. "Coroom": fridge, cool room. Is crazy, Mr Sinclair.'

Mimi Mollica was a welcome infiltrator of this territory. He shared the first-floor room in a warehouse on a street of Russian clubs and supermarkets. On his shelves were books by Plato and Adorno. His large black-and-white prints could be viewed from outside, an exhibition of marginal lives and occupied faces: the urban poor of Brazil or Brixton. 'Rough boys,' Mimi said. In Africa he argued with Don McCullin who confessed that he paid his subjects to be photographed. Mimi will teach his rough boys how to use a camera. His windows are dressed with permanent cobweb cracks.

We decide to walk down to the southern boundary of the Wick. To Fish Island. Once it was a place with respect for a tradition that went all the way back to the marsh people, who got their subsistence living from a lake beneath the high ground where the Olympic Park was being constructed. Among rubbled ruins, scavengers

trawled for wire. Conceptual artists furtively captured their incur-
sions or logged signs and peeling flyers. Gold was solicited and empty
boxes offered, a poor exchange. Fish Island, like Hackney Wick, was
now a destination for buses travelling to a terminal that no longer
existed. The Wick was the second most popular endstop in London.
Second to OUTER SERVICE, the place confused newcomers always
enquire about. 'Please, where is Outer Service?' The more often a
bus boasts of going somewhere, the greater your risk of stepping
into an unmapped nothing. Into whiteout, erasure. A blue fence.

Mimi spoke of his life in this part of London.

*I moved, six years ago, to Hackney Wick. Felstead Street. One of the old
warehouses. The landlords were a group of orthodox Jews. They made a
good deal because I was a photographer. They wanted artists to come.*

*There was water everywhere, Mr Sinclair. It flooded whenever it was
raining. It was wild west. Every day the window was broken from kids
throwing bottles. Or Russians. Drunk. Below my building was a Russian
cash and carry called Katyusha. They threw Russian bottles of beer. I
thought, 'That is interesting, multicultural.'*

*Every week, at least once, a car exploding. Cars stolen for joyriding.
Russians, gypsies. Black kids, white kids. I called the police I don't know
how many times. They never came. Always cars, explosions. It became
famous. While I was having parties, dinner parties, the people eating:
Blam! Bloor! Like Beirut. Good thing to talk about, very exciting.*

*From four-thirty until five-thirty, in the early morning, there was illegal
rubbish dumping, vans. They were coming and dumping mountains of
waste. Not one: six, eight. You know when a car has to slow down for a
police check? This is Hackney Wick, exactly. A war zone. It was scary
but beautiful. I felt privileged to be in the front line.*

*An island, Mr Sinclair. Like Sicily. Hackney Wick is the door to London.
It is visible and invisible. There was a café just behind my building. A
low café, sausage and egg, old working food. Probably good. All the lorry
drivers are stopping there. I thought that in ancient times there were
coaches with horses stopping at a pub in Highgate. Here is exactly the
same. Lorry drivers arrive from every part of Britain. Incredible.*

And then the market, the Hackney Stadium Market. The idea of a Sunday fair. You had everyone selling everything. Desperate people selling to desperate people. The poor trying to make some money. It worked perfectly, everybody needs something.

It is sad to think that Hackney Wick will change, without any grounds for change. There is no reason, Mr Sinclair. So many social problems in Hackney. You cannot tackle them by imposing new rich people, City people, new things from above. I've talked to people in Hackney Wick, very local people. They have an immediate response: 'Ah yes, it will change for the better.'

In a few years the same person will tell me, 'It's not better.' Somebody else will live where they are now, in their houses. They will be gone, lost in Essex.

I made my own bed. I had to buy the wood from the small hardware shop down the road. I produced the catalogue of my exhibition here. I went to the local printer, Mr Schwarz. I use all of these things. I saw the Turkish shop downstairs go from an empty place to a little business, then a bigger market, like Costcutter. I had a fantastical pub, the Queen Victoria, now gone. Is sad.

The Lord Napier, when it first started, I had an exhibition there. But the people changed. It became a squat. Another pub was the Lea Tavern, really beautiful. With a painting on the signboard, of the countryside: beautiful. I used to go there, very old people coming back from Hackney Wick Market on a Sunday. A bus stop full of people with blue bags.

I did a project on the 30 bus. I was taking pictures of the route, five days after the bombing. I was away when it happened. My sisters, my friends, everybody was here. I was very upset. I decided to take pictures along the route of the 30 – of people waiting for the bus. It was really moving, because for the first time I had positive responses when I was taking pictures. Very unusual in London. I learnt to look deeper and deeper into who was living in Hackney, who was taking the no. 30 bus. I started in Hackney Wick and finished in Marble Arch.

The bus. That was the talismanic photograph, in colour, in the newspapers. Not Mimi Mollica. Before Mimi began his project of restitution and recovery. The crumpled wreckage of the bombed bus with its visible destination window: HACKNEY WICK. Which stood, not just for the destruction of an everyday vessel for trans-porting preoccupied Londoners, but for the sentence of death passed on a redundant strip of land. Those two days in July 2005 connected the two events, indissolubly: the hysterical celebrations of the great Olympic deal and the response of disenfranchised fundamentalism. Dancing in the studios, weeping in the streets. Laurel wreaths for the victors. Carpets of cellophane flowers. Portraits of the missing pasted to fences around building-site stations.

A time of fugues and forgetfulness: post-traumatic wanderings from the epicentre of the blast. The driver of the bus, so it was rumoured, walked through the rest of the day, out to the western suburbs; before he recovered himself. In Hackney, a couple of years later, the skeleton of a woman called Shirley Slade was found in a ditch near the motorway: Temple Mills Lane, Hackney Wick. She had been with her husband, going for breakfast to a café on Kingsland Road, when she disappeared. He was a little ahead of her on the broad and busy pavement. He turned around, she was gone. The coroner's verdict was that she had succumbed to hypo-thermia: 'becoming more and more confused and disorientated as a result of the cold'. Mrs Slade grew up in Dalston. It was not clear how or why she had walked three or four miles across the borough, to the edge-lands ditch where her remains were discov-ered. Stripped of flesh. White bones in mud exposed by surveyors of the development site.

A passenger, known as 'M', on the bus ahead of the fated 30, said that he lost all sense of time, place, identity. He tramped, 'in a daze', to Shepherd's Bush. 'I think the 30 bus should have been renumbered,' he said, 'without anyone knowing. Every time I notice one of those buses, it is a painful reminder. I wish I had been physically injured that day because at least people would be able to see that something was wrong.'

*

Without discussing it, the destination of our walk becomes clear: Old Ford Lock. Strolling with Mimi, the war-zone photographer, through the contradictions of Fish Island, it is obvious we have reached a parting of the ways. Arriving from everywhere, constantly on the move, Mimi belongs here. My forty-year Hackney residency disqualifies me from this virtual playground. Ambling through shadowy chasms between warehouses, we are schizophrenic: post-traumatic tourists in a pre-traumatic landscape. Bad things are coming over the horizon very fast. To devour a stubborn rump of holdouts who are slightly deaf and rubbing sore eyes. Mimi is concerned about the way evangelical missions are colonizing the ruins. Sunday-morning fleets of shiny black cars. Rapping mission-aries in white suits. Mimi saw how they operated in Brazil. Now an organization called American Truce has arrived in Hackney with a determined homophobic agenda. Their website asserts that 'being homosexual is as much a handicap as being hooked on junk'. The Truce people were invited here as 'a strategy to tackle gang activity'. They were funded by a £20,000 grant from our Safer Communities group.

At Old Ford, the former media zone, you can see the lock-keeper's cottage that became the television set for *The Big Breakfast Show*. You can find red markings in wild orchards that confirm the extension of the Olympic Park. You can watch a dredger scraping off a green carpet of scum. You can identify the point where the buried Hackney Brook gushes into the Lea.

We have just passed Percy Dalton's historic peanut factory, with its powdery-hot stink, when a scrawny white youth with a rucksack bouncing on his back runs towards the lock. He is overtaken by another youth, wobbling on an unfamiliar bicycle. They are pursued by a black guy in the overalls of a Percy Dalton labourer. We were reluctant to take a photograph at the works gate: sunshafts through dust, yellow sacks being humped into a blue van by black men wearing bright orange. Cameras are put aside. The man's bicycle, his only means of transport, has been stolen by the two white boys.

Mimi offers to call the police on his mobile. I chase after them, as far as the lock, but they're gone. A choice of directions: to the Marshes, Three Mills, the Sewage Outfall. The Dalton labourer does not want to get involved. No police, no phone. A woman with a small child tells us that she witnessed the entire episode. It's astonishing. All these interested parties, so suddenly, in a deserted street. Between a working peanut factory and the other part of the building, which now features the Bridget Riley studios.

The bereaved black worker is wearing a red hairnet. He wants to be sure that I haven't made a record of the crime or the workers – who carry on loading their truck. Peanut shells crackle underfoot. I promise the man that I'm no photographer. A storyteller. Nobody believes a word that I say. Without evidence, this never happened.

After the 7/7 bombings, carrying a camera was seen as a provocative act; mobile phones impregnated by the smoke of Underground tunnels, passengers shuffling towards daylight. The writer and academic Bas Groes reported that his wife had been prevented, by unusual circumstances, from taking the Piccadilly Line train that was blown up. Two of her colleagues were aboard, but survived. Bas was arrested, later that day, filming near a police station.

'After handing over the tape, I met a person claiming to be a Professor of Languages at King's College. He said that he was on his way to the British Library for a meeting on the Future of Languages and Mankind. He bought me a pint and talked for an hour. About Gerald Kersh's novel, *Fowlers End*. And about how he had lost his sister during the Blitz. He was convinced that Tony Blair had organized the attacks. Subsequently, I tried to track this man down, but have been unable to find any trace of him. I still don't know whether he exists or not.'

I sat down with Mimi in a new bar called Lighthouse that had appeared out of nowhere in Wick Lane. It was air-conditioned and empty. The barman gazed at a silent golf course, with palm trees and blue water, on a giant plasma screen. Mimi recalled another drinking spot, on the edge of the Wick, close to where the road sweeps you away towards the Blackwall Tunnel.

Another element in my life out here was Geneva, the black Jamaican club under the motorway bridge. Coming back to Hackney from Brixton, I was always stopping to have a beer in Geneva. I was the only white man. They looked at me with suspicion. They think I look like a cop, but when I open my mouth they know I could not be anyone like that. I like the music so much. The club was another source of shootings and stabbings and violence. The area was crazy, dangerous but exciting. Really beautiful. I asked one of these guys to give me a lift to the other black club, in Clapton, by the roundabout. When I stepped outside, they jumped on him, my driver, and beat him with a metal post.

And the religions. Unbelievable! All black, African. Incredible. It's very sad, this evangelical reality. Mr Sinclair, it's a power religion. Is crazy, crazy, but very beautiful.

The Russians came to Hackney Wick because it is the edge of London. It's cheap to live, to buy stuff. You can make whatever you want to make. Black jobs, disappearances. Nobody asks any questions.

Revolution? The ground for revolution should become a bit bigger. In Hackney Wick the invisible will become visible.

The first time I am here I ask a bunch of people waiting for a bus, a ghost bus that never comes, 'Excuse me, where is Hackney Wick?' They looked at each other and then they look at me. 'You're in Hackney Wick!' This was very strange. Being in a place and not knowing where I am.

The trains, the buses, until last year, all were free. The platform at Hackney Wick was deserted. Nobody buys a ticket. All travel free. I travel east. I wanted to see the area. People go to Stratford for different reasons. I walk down what is left of Carpenter's Road, where all the garages used to be. This is the first thing that disappears, the garages.

Old Ford, out of Fish Island, was a numinous locale in London's deep-topography: the crossing place on the River Lea – which was a major obstacle, a much broader stream. Here was a border between cultures, between Vikings and Saxons, pagans and Christians, travellers and fixed citizens, the living and the dead.

The critic John Adlard, back in 1973, had the interesting idea that William Blake confused Old Ford with old Stratford. Blake's south-eastern sweep, from Plate 31, Chapter 2 of *Jerusalem*, directed my reading of London, anticipating every move I made.

> *He came down from Highgate thro' Hackney & Holloway towards London*
> *Till he came to old Stratford, & thence to Stepney & the Isle*
> *Of Leutha's Dogs, thence thro' the narrows of the River's side,*
> *And saw every minute particular: the jewels of Albion running down*
> *The kennels of the streets & lanes as if they were abhorr'd . . .*

'Highgate thro' Hackney' was the journey of our lost river, the Hackney Brook, trickling down from the foothills to flow into the Lea at Old Ford. With Mimi I searched out the point where the stream bubbled into the sluggish river. There were two possibilities. One, right alongside the lock bridge, was the more fierce. But a closer examination of nineteenth-century charts inclined me towards a mean dribble, a little further downstream, where the pipes carrying London's sewage cross to the east bank, the Olympic Park. A new development, dark glass, balconies, has infilled the space behind us. A folded set of wings. A luxury prison.

Adlard, in his short essay, speaks of Blake walking, in a single day, 'up to forty miles in the environs of London'. But *Jerusalem* is not the record of a gruelling hike, it is the heartbeat of a 'mental traveller'. Los, Blake's solar daemon, blazes like a comet. He maps energies, not in the robotic voice of a Sat Nav system, but with rhythms of blood; pulsing, hammering, driven onwards.

'Approaching Stepney from the direction of Hackney,' Adlard wrote, 'Los with his globe would have walked down Globe Street and Globe Lane, past Globe Place, Globe House and an inn called the Globe. The route today is known as Globe Road.' And the inn, the New Globe, is just one of a number in this area with a Hollow Earth design on its signboard. Jock McFadyen's realist painting of the pub was used on the cover of Ed Glinert's *East End Chronicles: Three Hundred Years of Mystery and Mayhem.*

What Adlard struggles with is a topography that detours east to Stratford, before heading down to the Isle of Dogs. It strikes me that Los is not following the money but predicting its swinish rush on unexploited brownfield sites: Docklands and the future Stratford City, with its Olympic rings and satellite parks. 'All the tendernesses of the soul cast forth as filth & mire.' Towers of hungry capital 'builded in Jerusalem's eastern gate'. To dominate and divide.

Of stones and rocks, he took his way, for human form was none;
And thus he spoke, looking on Albion's City with many tears . . .

Stratford was no accidental station on this Silverlink itinerary.

But Adlard is puzzled; finding no mention of 'Old Stratford' on any map of the period, he delves into the *London and Provincial New Commercial Directory for 1827–8*, issued by Poe and Co. In which Old Ford is described as 'a small village pleasantly situated on the banks of the River Lea'. The directory also mentions 'an immense artificial mound or hill', another Silbury or Beckton Alp, from the summit of which, Adlard glosses, 'Los might have viewed to advantage the London he was combing'.

A vision without boundaries. Outside time. And not, certainly not, the limited prospect of pre-Olympic mud offered to the privileged few, from Holden Point, the twenty-one-storey Stratford tower block: where a fit and vulpine Lord Coe throws back the silken linings of his deep-blue jacket, like a fallen angel, to offer this virtual world, its mounds and stadia, to investors prepared to mortgage a city's future on the demolition and ransacking of a mythical past.

Hackney Brook

The story was contracting around itself. It was futile to try to stay ahead of the enclosures. There was nothing to do but invite as many witnesses as possible to accompany me on pedestrian circuits of the Olympic site. They came with their own baggage: Andrew Kötting's projected swan voyage, Robert Macfarlane's passion for climbing trees, Stephen Gill's kayak and bicycle odysseys. Cycling in Hackney, so heavily promoted, had reached the critical stage in its inevitable progress towards being as much of an urban pestilence as the motor car. I don't mean hooded pavement jackals cruising for unguarded shoulder bags. Or lights-jumping speedsters ploughing through bus queues to shave a couple of seconds from their run to the City. Or even that twilight hour on the canal, when drug casuals coincide with power-pumping Dockland drones returning to their new waterside hutches.

ASSAULT. ON WED 7TH MARCH A MALE CYCLIST WAS ASSAULTED AND PUSHED INTO THE CANAL. CAN YOU HELP US?

I mean the incident I witnessed on London Fields. A Broadway Market mother, gypsyish in Bolivian poncho, with the right number of children, apple-fed, unpolluted by E-numbers, crossed an invisible cycle path, twenty yards ahead of a helmeted artist who must have been hitting 30mph as he swerved through dog walkers and potential clients of the play park.

Cuntwankeryoublindstupidbitchdickhead . . .

An hysterical exchange with no physical outlet. Shocked kids. Half-dismounted cyclist, fists pumping. Woman swearing and stamping as he decides to take off. Road rage has trickled down to the recycling classes. There will be knife fights in the street over blue bins with the wrong category of potato peel.

I agreed to walk down the canal, to the condemned allotments and on to old Stratford, with a group of students. The hook being that one of them was a direct descendant of Thomas De Quincey. They loped along, chatting quietly among themselves, never picking up a sketchbook or making a note. Once in a while, if there was a quaint alignment of pylons, the view of a poisoned creek that suggested the headwaters of the Orinoco, they might indulge in a digital transfer.

A young woman, long hair almost controlled by a complex arrangement of clips, held up a notice for me to photograph: KEEP OUT JAPANESE KNOTWEED. A racial prejudice supported by severe fencing and the Portakabins of security hirelings in the pay of the various construction companies. Ancient woodland had been rearranged as a ribbon of naked logs. Like a very amateur railway.

It was Ms De Quincey who understood, precisely, what was required. The unreality of the occasion. The ludicrous amounts of money squandered on this unwanted sports day. No more evidence, please, of the machinery of destruction. No approved edge-lands surrealism. No rhetoric of protest to confirm our impotence. This person, dressed in a shapeless grey waterproof smock, reached into her purple shoulder-pouch, and produced a slim booklet on friable yellowing card. Her dark hair and smooth oval features supplied the necessary gravitas. In my photograph her eyes are closed and her faint smile is stern. The rectangular pamphlet was issued by the Collège de Pataphysique and appeared to date from the mysterious year 86. It was credited to Marie Louise Aulard. The document was entitled: *Rapport au Tr. Corps des Satrapes sur la Géographie du Néant*. An expedition to a place that never existed. A confidential report, at last, from the centre of the Hollow Earth. A real river with an invented pedigree. Future memories disclosed in a theoretical past.

Ms De Quincey, as we stood beside the security fence, overlooking the costive stream with its banks of illegitimate knotweed, offered a timely reminder that certain life-sustaining characteristics pass down the DNA spiral through the generations. At Oxford, Professor Catling invited me to look at the work of a group of postgraduate students. One of them, who revealed the inhabitants of a barely visible world, by arranging tableaux of angels and insects, was the great-granddaughter of Arthur Machen. She brought inscribed first editions of some of the books with her, to further agitate me. Handling the pataphysical guide with care, I realized that it was time to walk away from the weight of all this, to follow the Hackney Brook: to discover, by way of De Quincey and Machen, if the projected curvature of their northwest passage had any relevance to the geography of Hackney.

Renchi came up from Glastonbury with the restored *Pierrot le fou* triptych. Inviting him to put himself back into the ecstatic and troubled mindset of the period when he produced these paintings, the mid 1960s, was a large demand, to which he responded: with frowns, smiles, attack. He started spit-washing the dirt, stroking silver snail-trails of household gloss. The triptych became the autobiography of an earlier self, a time of visions and elective poverty, confusion and elation. By way of such artefacts, paintings rescued from oblivion, we travel through parallel worlds in which the original acts of creation remain suspended in a perpetual present. I was taking Renchi away from his latest enthusiasm, reworking Blake's versions of Bunyan's *The Pilgrim's Progress* as a set of etchings. A physically demanding process that required the learning of new skills, such as writing in mirror-script, along with a double reading: of Blake and of Gerda Norvig's book on this beautiful sequence of twenty-eight watercolour drawings.

A walk to honour the subterranean Hackney Brook was also an opportunity to discuss previous expeditions and perhaps a future collaboration down the northwest passage. Renchi's daughter, Annie, had a friend who was out of town, a flat in which he could stay. Alice Oller at the German Hospital. I went around there, the evening before we set out, bringing old maps on which to plot the river's course.

As we sat on the roof terrace, it was disconcerting to hear the introductory thumps of the *EastEnders* theme drifting up from converted nurses' quarters – while looking down into the real Fassett Square, through which no cabs moved, and nobody reeled, covered in blood, from a non-existent pub. In pre-Olympic Hackney, those territorial markers, the public houses beloved of Socialist Workers, were vanishing; being converted into investment opportunities, revamped as gastro-lounges, or left alone as blank spaces while the price of land climbed.

When, on the following morning, we walked through Broadway Market to the canal, I remembered the photograph Anna took, outside the Cat and Mutton, the model for Albert Square's Queen Vic. I am standing next to my son, William, who is taller, leaner, acceptably unshaven, before he went off to the northern suburbs for a television directors' course. With the market stalls set out, this urban revival does indeed aspire to the condition of the infamous soap opera: a fake, a fraud, an imposition. The wall of Ada Street, around the corner from the bookshop, is a constantly evolving work of public art. A backdrop for Sweet Toof with his pink gums and grids of teeth, his Russian unorthodox domes, his feathered serpents and bleeding hearts. Today's message is stark: OUR TIME WILL COME. Thick wrist with clock face and strap: 12.15. A wad of £50 notes in a knuckled Philip Guston fist.

It's astonishing how a narrow towpath yields so much meaning to so many people. Voices from countless earlier expeditions. Andrew Kötting grabbed my camera, holding it at arm's length for a double portrait. Which I followed, immediately, by snapping a poster in which a shirtsleeved Tony Blair takes a self-portrait on his mobile, in front of a wall of apocalyptic oil fires. FALLUJAH LONDON. BOMBS = BOMBS. When we arrived at the courtyard of the Gainsborough Studios, the powerful Kötting, in white vest, leant on the rusted support structure, to stare respectfully at the hieratic head of Alfred Hitchcock. Andrew, close-cropped, blunt of feature, perfectly reprised the Soviet propaganda look of the revolutionary years. The bald Hitch, through this confrontation, became the Lenin of our defeated inland empire.

Brought to the point where the Hackney Brook bubbles out into the sluggish river, Kötting was also forced to contemplate the Olympic enclosures on the opposite bank. 'I believe there is a way of walking and moving through these landscapes,' he said. 'The paths are called "desire lines". It's where the people win out. And they will win out. They'll beat a path through. That's where morphic resonance comes in. The sense of paths being created in bygone times. That is what I find most reassuring. It'll be interesting to see whether some of those desire lines are moving in parallel with leylines. This will show whether the planners have got things wrong.'

Noticing Sweet Toof's mural, at the Old Ford Lock, a swan that becomes a plan of the river, a direct confrontation of security fences and high walls, Kötting announced that this was 'the great unexpected moment'. 'It is almost as if,' he said, 'somebody had painted that swan as a little welcoming map, a welcome to our journey. This is where the Hackney Brook joins the Lea, it's the beginning of the story.'

The more youthful Robert Macfarlane, purposeful shorts and boots, glinting spectacles, pounced on the Hitchcock effigy and tried to climb inside the giant nose. Like Cary Grant in *North by Northwest*. The aspect of most interest to Robert was the vegetation; slender silver birches, poking through slats in the mount, formed a sacred grove around the boilerplated Buddha. Macfarlane offered the best example of what Walter Benjamin called 'botanizing the asphalt'.

I saw the symbolic head as a memory-device, an oracular receptacle for myths and legends. Graham Cutts, the silent-movie director whose assistants ranged from Hitchcock to Douglas Lyne, was the leading light of Gainsborough Pictures. In 1922 he introduced fears of downriver Chinese villainy into London, with his melodrama *Cocaine*. Matthew Sweet, in *Shepperton Babylon*, reminds us that Cutts 'had a reputation for promiscuity as well as tyranny (Islington gossips were particularly fond of recounting the story of how he took two sisters into his dressing room in the course of one lunch break)'. The old studio complex, now a depressed courtyard with an underused gym and listless water features, once specialized in sadomasochistic costume romps and invented jobs for Hungarian exiles. Isidore, one of the five Ostrer brothers who owned the company, paid the rent by working as a dominoes hustler on the train between London and Southend, where he lived with an obliging dance teacher.

Macfarlane, the age of my son, ripped into this marginal landscape with pen, notebook and sample bags. Through him, I noticed the pathside weeds (soon to be hacked away in a cosmetic makeover). Nests of coots. Patterns in the bark of trees. Coming across a weeping beech, Robert was straight up it, exclaiming loudly over the initials of generations of Hackney lovers carved deep into the trunk and out along the most precarious branches. But the most memorable of Macfarlane's discoveries came on the path beside the rose garden, as we made for Hackney Wick. He parted a curtain of willow to disclose a white life mask of the murdered Margaret Muller. Staring, through thick foliage, at the fatal spot.

Back at Old Ford Lock, with Renchi, I watched the white foam of the buried Hackney Brook gush into the darkness of the Lea, like a spill of light travelling across millennia, the afterburn of an extinguished galaxy. Then, invoking Danny Folgate, we set out to retrace the path of the lost stream: which I identified with the suppressed life-force of the borough. What else were clancydocwra digging for?

Renchi speaks of his time working as a gardener in Victoria Park, of the paintings he made. It was an era of fractured consciousness, heavy consumption of cannabis-enriched chocolate cake. Planting and painting were complementary activities. Renchi weeded, dug over, set the semicircular bed, beyond Gore Gate. He took out his sketchbook. A Tibetan monk appeared from the curtain of shrubs, the skirts of Macfarlane's weeping beech, to mimic Renchi's gestures. The futility of making a picture of a picture. And then he vanished.

There were other park memories: a young woman gardener forced to quit the job she loved by remorseless tabloid chauvinism. Stories of war, tunnels, bunkers, bombed terraces. The culling of the small herd of fallow deer.

The subterranean pressure of the brook was clearly felt as we followed a natural curve, past the Thames Water plant, around Cadogan Terrace, into Wick Road. We are part of the geography, simply that. The villages of Hackney, Dalston, Stoke Newington took shape from the way this bright stream carved through the valley, beneath the heights of Homerton. Mansions, orchards, formal gardens. Industries grew up to exploit a natural feature and, in doing so, they made its defilement and disappearance inevitable.

Noticing two Hasidic gentlemen, black suits and skullcaps, one blind, white-sticked, leaning on the arm of the other, Renchi decided to follow them into the cream-coloured block building with the green windows and prayer scrolls. The rigour of the formal design is contradicted by the bureaucratic insensitivity of the working interior: a social-security office. Ticket machines for appropriate windows. Racks of forms. That suffocating air of institutionalized inertia, barriers between clients and salaried officials: those who are paid to know as much as, and not a syllable more than, the book requires of them. The maimed, mutilated, ancient, incapacitated, unlanguaged sit on firm chairs or queue to ask the wrong questions. There is no cruelty in the officials, a terrible world-weariness from having to attend to so many hardluck stories, knowing there is nothing to be done, watching the loud hands of the official clock.

Renchi persists. They know the type, but are thrown – and finally intrigued – by the nature of his question. 'Was this once the Berger's paint factory?' *It was, it was.* Enquiries in the backroom confirm it. While we wait I read council leaflets that explain how to walk around the park and how to apply for repatriation. Berger had the reputation of being a benevolent employer. The poet Bill Griffiths, in his Hackney years, worked in a paint factory. The old Hackney Brook flowed through the industrial estate. The business of manufacturing colour, later paint (the strident hues of Renchi's *Pierrot*), was brought to this site from Shadwell in 1780, by Lewis Berger (formerly Steigenberger). A farmhouse was rented in Shepherd's Lane with fields that ran down to the brook – which was diverted to pass through the factory grounds. By 1890 the old Hackney Brook was covered over and lost; represented by an ornamental water feature which gave a pastoral glint to promotional postcards and posters. The Homerton workers were noted for their long service, although the inevitable sickness consequent on the manufacture of paint, the inhalation of lead fumes, brought a serious strike in 1911. The model employer was denounced for operating 'sheds of death'. Berger severed the connection with Homerton in 1960, when the operation merged with Jensen & Nicholson and became a public company.

A linear connection between the industrial firm and the borough was re-established when John Berger, critic, novelist and painter, paid a visit to his enthusiastic supporter Menzies Tanner in Graham Road. Berger would, in the new millennium, be the subject of a series of celebratory events, films, readings, conversations, curated by Hackney's dynamic one-man arts council, Gareth Evans.

Dowsing the brook along Morning Lane (formerly Money Lane), street people become flotsam carried by the force of the stream they can't see, the memory of water and the actuality of clay and gravel, the terraces of Homerton. We detour to Sutton House, achieving a sense of what it must have been like to look back down on the unblemished river.

Right at the mouth of this ancient road, where it snakes behind the decommissioned library (now offering a beer festival), is a Hollow Earth pub, the Globe in Morning Lane. A signboard with northwest-passage emblems: the navigator Frobisher brandishing Newton's compasses, a vessel wedged in Arctic ice, a blind search for new oceans. The fleet of solitary ships, unknown to each other, sails on; before running aground above the buried Hackney Brook. The Old Ship on Mare Street is the next craft in this phantom armada of painted Mary Celestes. With Orson Welles as its Ahab.

After the agitated microclimate of Tesco's car park, its beggars and buskers, we pause for breakfast in the Bohemia Café, alongside Joe Kerr's bus garage.

'Very weak tea, please,' says Renchi.

'Milk?'

'Hot water with just the shadow of a tea bag.'

I fortify myself with an omelette woven from jute, like a spongy bathmat studded with small greenish mushrooms.

The point where the brook crossed Mare Street is well represented in views of Hackney as a village in the 1730s: the tower of St Augustine, the Eight Bells pub, the footbridge over the river. Then the Pembury Tavern, the riverside gardens, pictorial impressions of early balloon ascents. The selective slideshow of the past throws up a melancholy youth in a wide collar and a black cap leaning on a wooden bridge as the brook slithers unseen down the western perimeter of Hackney Downs. To reach this green table, we negotiate a set of garages tucked under railway arches: drench of paint droplets from respray shops, aerosol obscenities, miracle-promising messianic franchises, guardian dogs.

They tried to fence off Hackney Downs at the time of enclosures, but the natives were having none of it. Crops were stripped. The privatized abundance of hay and corn was promiscuously harvested. An excuse for riot. Sticks, staves, stones. Wounds staunched in the fouled and polluted river, the coming sewer.

Templar lands granted by William of Hastings. Church land. Land bestowed on courtiers and City magnates. By the seventeenth century, Hackney Downs offered the only arable farming left in the district: Lammas lands. There were rights of pasturage on the Downs, on London Fields, Well Street Common, North and South

Millfields. And the Hackney Marsh: much of which was *humbra*, or sodden meadow, rather than *quabba* or bog. Free grazing was seasonal, Lammas Day to Lady Day. Asses and mules could be impounded and the tolls paid into a fund for the upkeep of these important wetlands.

Now invisible, but felt and known, the brook was a mischievous actuality as it continued to flood Stoke Newington cellars. The nature of the stream changed as it pulled west in a meander around the edge of the Abney Park Cemetery. This was convenient, because I wanted to show Renchi the place where Edward Calvert was buried. On an expedition with Susanna Edwards, whose flat in Jenner Road was right above the path of the brook, we found Calvert's green-stained gravestone. The engraver, who died at the age of eighty-three, is buried with his wife, Mary. Reading a memoir by Alan Wilson, who grew up, before the Second War, at 12 Darnley Road (Calvert lived in number 11), I was interested to find him recalling his immediate neighbour and childhood friend: a boy called Kossoff. With whom he indulged in 'primitive theological arguments'. Wilson went on to discuss a doctor who practised in Lower Clapton Road. This man's gloomy chambers were 'more like a funeral parlour, or a place for seances, than a surgery'. He looked like Neville Chamberlain, kept his medical instruments in his pockets, and was rumoured to carry out illegal operations. 'Mother doubted whether he was ever a qualified doctor. He disappeared during the war without leaving a trace.'

Hacking into tangled undergrowth, as clinging, dense and light-devouring as my book had become, bumping against obscured gravestones and the sharp wings of ivy-cloaked angels, I remembered what Poe and Arthur Machen had drawn from this area: confusion, doubled identities, a shift in the electromagnetic field. There was a long tradition, beginning with De Quincey, of searching for a northwest passage out of London, away from restrictive conventions of time and space. The route these men hinted at seemed to have an intimate relationship with the course of the submerged Hackney Brook: Abney Park, Clissold Park, pubs named after Robinson Crusoe, the slopes of Highgate Hill.

Machen called this part of London a 'Terra Incognita': 'obscure alleyways with discreet, mysterious postern doors . . . a region beyond Ultima Thule'. There is always a Machen theme, an excuse to draw the unwary in. A search for Edgar Allan Poe's school: the one he actually attended or the more engrossing fiction from his 'William Wilson' tale. Autobiography mulches down to let richer weeds break surface. Those who embark on a London quest begin in a pub. They yarn, they misquote, improvise. They walk out, eventually, through a one-off topography they are obliged to shape into a serviceable narrative. Language creaks. 'The dreamy village, the misty trees, the old rambling redbrick houses, standing in their gardens, with high walls about them.'

There is a magic place, close to Abney Park, which nobody can find twice. Believing this consoling fable, I suppose, makes Stoke Newington possible: the self-confident, self-contained inhabitants, their nice shops, their historic library and surveillance monitors. Living here allows you to peruse the dangerously vulgar streets of Lesser Hackney and to congratulate yourself on your good fortune. Villas of successful Nonconformist tradesmen survive. Defoe plaques and pubs. We enter the library and ask to be pointed in the direction of the local-history shelves.

'There is no local history any more,' says the woman at the desk. 'It's out of date.'

All that's left has been relegated to a cardboard box kept under the counter. I buy a booklet on Clissold Park that characteristically boasts of a connection with William Wilberforce and the Stoke Newington abolitionists, while turning a blind eye to fortunes built on the dark trade, sugar and slavery. There is a smudged photograph of a policeman feeding swans.

After Clissold Park and the crossing of Green Lanes, the infant brook is teasing and difficult to trace. It passes under the building site that is the old Highbury Stadium and then bifurcates. One branch starts as a hidden spring beside the Holloway Road and the other must be taken on trust, a few hundred yards to the north of the new Emirates space station where Arsène Wenger's Arsenal thrill their thousands with intricate pattern-making displays. Renchi crouches in the shrubs of a small park near Tollington Road, pressing his frozen ear to the ground. Long shadows stripe a carpet of fallen leaves. Men with dogs give us a wide berth. That's it, done. Time for Renchi to head for the station. We've touched on a number of themes and resolved nothing. The sun is dropping but I decide to carry on, northwest, in the spirit of Machen's woozy pilgrims. There may never be a better opportunity to track a passage out of a forty-year fix: my obsession with a Hackney that never was.

Letting my feet carry me back over Highgate Hill where I struggled, months ago, with a painful ankle, thinking my hiking days were over, I advanced into that half-light where an orange industrial glow merges with the green rays of the disappearing sun. I like to start early and return for the evening meal. Striding on at this hour, into the night, allowed me to conjure up Machen's 'parterre or miniature park'. Somewhere between Finchley and Totteridge – I'm sure I explored the area with Renchi in the period of our *London Orbital* wanderings – I stumbled on an enclosure that failed, but not by much, to live up to Machen's copywriting. 'Before me, in place of the familiar structures, there was disclosed a panorama of unearthly, of astounding beauty. In deep dells, bowered by overhanging trees, there bloomed flowers such as only dreams can show . . . I saw well-shaded walks that went down to green hollows bordered with thyme . . . A sense of beatitude pervaded my whole being . . .'

And then, like a hand closing around the throat: 'revulsion of terror'. Flight. The weary, footsore progression of suburban streets at the wrong season. Trim hedges. Winter jasmine. Violas. Pyracantha. Dahlias. The sort of spiky patches I weeded and scraped as a jobbing gardener. We were always let go in November, in time to sign up for the Christmas post.

It was late when I elected to find somewhere to sleep for the night, a pub or bed-and-breakfast place. I was still inside a nominal London, the collar of the orbital motorway, close to old Ermine Street, tramping downhill towards Borehamwood, when I was stopped by a helmeted and goggled man on a motorbike. It is assumed that pedestrians know where they are. And especially pedestrians of a certain age. Why else would they be let out? The worst of it being that even on home turf I find it impossible to give a simple answer. I forget the names of streets. I feel an obligation to send the enquirer on an interesting journey, on the 'I wouldn't start from here' principle. I disregard recent closures, demolitions, compulsory detours. Often, I end up chasing after the lost person with supplementary advice: more, much more than they want to know.

'Iain?'

The biker knew me. He took off his helmet. Stretched out a hand. We had our conversations on the doorstep in Albion Drive, not here, at night. In different places we are different people.

'Paolo?'

'Honest, Iain, this is totally amazing, mate. Borehamwood? I thought, fuck it, no . . . All down to William, god's truth. Doing a lovely job. Think the world of him. Actors, producers, crew. Asked for me special, William. Tell him thanks. Bottle of wine, that's a promise. Kids kicking a ball against the garage, Iain. Now this. Amazing. And your mate, Charlie. Lovely feller, diamond. What he don't know. Fantastic. We've come a long way from London Fields, right?'

Paolo pushed the bike alongside me as we turned in at the gate of what appeared to be an industrial estate.

'I'll give him a bell. Getting set up for tomorrow. He'll be made up. A proper worker, William.'

The stories Paolo told were dramatic recitations that compensated for his silence as a supporting artist. He carried his uniform handsomely as copper or security guard. He drove limousines or walked through the soft-focus margins of a scene looking as if he meant it; as if the repeated transit between fixed positions was an everyday event, anaerobic exercise. Today there had been some business in a bar, near acting, loutishness, a slap from the pop-eyed alcoholic who ran the place. Paolo knew that it was too much. And he wouldn't be sorry to have it cut: become too visible and you're out of work.

It seems that Charlie Velasco, coming around to pick me up for the lunch with Ken's man at the Pequod, met Paolo loading the van for his stall on Roman Road.

'Penalty shout. Colchester–Southend third-round replay. Paolo Cash? Dodgy knee, medial ligament.' Charlie knew it all. 'Brought off the bench, ten minutes to go. Wrong club at the wrong time. Never appreciated what they had, the class. Shocking the way Eddie Bailey treated you at West Ham, Paolo. I thought your old man was going to nut him. Right there in the car park.'

The tribute didn't surprise Paolo, it used to happen all the time, football was conversation. But this bloke, Charlie, was an encyclopaedia. Portsmouth, Colchester. The time young Paolo almost signed for the Dutch mob, over in Amsterdam eating a pizza, glass of wine with his agent, after checking out the complimentary motor, when the news comes through that the manager who fancied him was moving to Spain. 'I tell you, Charlie,' Paolo said. 'That's was the best fucking pizza I ever tasted. Honest to god, it turned to ashes in my mouth.'

Velasco patted Paolo on the shoulder, said he'd bring around a few of his programmes for a signature next time.

'Top woman with him, Scandinavian bird,' Paolo recalled. 'I tried a couple of months in Finland. Lovely people, Iain, but you can't play in those temperatures.'

'Dark? Well built. Five eight or nine? His age?'

'Tall blonde. Nicely spoken. Twenty-two.'

Must have been a PR person from City Hall. Too smart to stick around for the Pequod lunch.

The troubling thing was my sense of London being turned inside out, of having trudged all day to arrive back at an open-ended conversation, with my neighbour, at the front gate.

Then William, grinning, appeared at the security barrier. And Paolo went home. I hadn't realized that this was where my son was directing his soap opera. The actors and crew had departed for the night, William was blocking out the moves. They churned this material out with multicamera set-ups and a producer whispering in your ear. Most of the work involved soothing the troubled egos of actors who, in several cases, came through the same schools as my son. He was of the territory, born and bred, in a fashion to which I could never aspire.

There were two hangars. In the first they kept the operating theatres and corridors of *Holby City*; a series to which, catching one episode by chance, Anna had become mysteriously addicted. The Queen Vic, in truth a rancid hole, was assembled in the other block; with grease caff, nail parlour, allotment shed. *EastEnders*, in its topographic reality, was an enclosure on the northwest fringe of London, a suburban fake. Closer to Metroland than to Mile End.

Maybe I could kip for the night in Arthur Fowler's shed? Or down by the war memorial that commemorated people who had never lived? The cast of *EastEnders* were always vanishing into prison (cosmetic surgery, rehab, tabloid-scandal suspension) and decanting, like cab drivers, to the Costa Brava. A euphemism for *The Bill*. Never to be glimpsed again, apart from Christmas specials. Or reappearances with a different face.

Paolo's walk-on announced the arrival of new blood, mad sisters, blonde harpies from a beach bar. With no sense of history, or perhaps too much, they decide to open a club called the Double R (for Ronnie and Roxy): in hideous parody of the infamous gangland haunt of the 1960s. Ron and Reg reborn, to their shame and delight, as a pair of feisty, hard-talking, hair-pulling females. True drama queens, at last, hosting this never-ending party in hell. The diva of the Mitchell clan is played by Barbara Windsor, once an intimate of the Bethnal Green twins. The premiere of her Joan Littlewood film, *Sparrows Can't Sing*, was held in the Krays' club.

Much of my London – Fassett Square, Kingsland Waste, the Cat and Mutton, the video shop, Indian restaurant, Manor Garden allotments – has been compressed into this site, a retail park trapped between the M25 and the M1. It is very disconcerting to travel so far and to finish in an architectural crash, a six-lane pile-up: chunks of Hackney gravity-sucked into a dense ball. With no breathing space between square and pub, pub and playground, car dealer and tube. The houses on Albert Square were inches deep, façades that admitted no interior life. Cultural memory, if it existed, belonged to the actors. Ray Brooks, Phil Daniels. The woman who played Mo Slater was Gary Oldman's sister. Brooks of *Cathy Come Home*, a social-realist drama from 1966, found himself performing a part based on a real man who died as guru to the squatters of the M11 extension protest in Leyton. They gave him a boat burial, a Viking send-off. Ray couldn't abide his fictional wife.

Rats sprung from tables of fruit left out in the rain, the market never closed. Maud's bookstall featured real books: Heine, Conrad, Jackie and Wilkie Collins, a biography of Brian Clough. All stuck together in the damp air. The allotment, regularly serviced by gardeners, thrives. Giant sunflowers, runner beans. The swing in the playpark, unused by children, was available to any suicidal adult with a sub-Ibsen monologue. *EastEnders* has two modes, shouting or sullen. Giving away the plot on a mobile phone or gobbing a lifetime of grievances into a sibling's rigid face.

William had a job to do. My northwest passage was over. It had twisted back on itself, into a temporal cul-de-sac unimagined by Arthur Machen. With my rucksack of grey fug, a London Peculiar, I was the ghost: a lost father wandering aimlessly around the perimeter fence. Soothed by distant motorway hymns.

'Is that so you remember who you are?' William said.

I was wearing a sweatshirt from an American university with the word SINCLAIR in dark blue relief across the chest.

A fly-pitched poster on the corner of Albert Square advertised a show at the Tate with one of Fuseli's crouching, red-eyed demons. I had no more stories to tell. Everything I tried to express was better done elsewhere. This mad fugue, between traumas, was nothing more than a feeble echo of Conrad's *The Secret Agent*: when human relationships have broken down and Comrade Ossipon the anarchist, the betrayer of women, walks away from history.

'His robust form was seen that night in distant parts of the enormous town slumbering monstrously on a carpet of mud under a veil of raw mist. It was seen crossing the streets without life and sound, or diminishing in the interminable straight perspectives of shadowy houses bordering empty roadways lined by strings of gas lamps . . . He walked. And suddenly turning into a strip of a front garden with a mangy grass plot, he let himself into a small grimy house with a latch-key he took out of his pocket.'

The Blue Fence

Contact with this woman was made by way of Stephen Gill, emails were exchanged. I was vetted, checked out; a meeting was arranged at the café by Springfield Park. However it went, this would be the final interview. A covert story that shadowed my time in Hackney, but one of which I was wholly ignorant. Paranoia, spookery, involuntary exile. Factory work, gardening. Bomb plots, bank robberies. Lost photo archives. All of this activity – politics and terror, global publicity, flight – earthed in or around Hackney Marshes. And now enclosed or repulsed by the Olympic Park's security fence. Our new model army of insecurity guards.

Then the phone rings, lesser duties are set aside, and we are, willingly, joyfully, on a bus, the 236. Heading down Queensbridge Road, Pownall Road, London Fields, Mare Street: towards the Homerton Hospital. In that lull before kids are let out of school, Anna beside me, I can enjoy the experience of sponsored transport, the active streets, veiled women, husbands with awkward packages for wives who will soon be returned to them. Nobody lingers in the Homerton Hospital. But this birth, our first grandchild, a girl, is a special thing. The heart does flutter as the news comes through. By this gift we are changed and do not know ourselves. For a day or so, we are our children's children. We're not in charge any more. If called on, we can offer tentative advice, but we are also free, liberated, released from one kind of biological responsibility. Hackney, more itself than ever, is an entirely new place.

Anna carries food, a teddy bear, champagne. The stairs at the Homerton are out of action, we use the steel-box lift. Templar Ward. Sabina Brown lingered, she was ten days overdue. Now she is very calm and resolute in her hamster tray, sleeping with so many overlapping memories, exhausted after a long tight swim.

The curtained corner, beside the window, becomes an occupied tent in which an unprepared London stretches itself to accommodate this new and demanding soul.

We walk home with Anna leading the way, demonstrating the route she took from her Millfields school, the old Hackney of Sutton Place, the garden of St John's church where Kaporal was found, and St Augustine's Tower. I make the call to confirm my appointment with Astrid Proll.

Stephen Gill met the former Red Army Faction chauffeur at an exhibition of his work in Arles. He keeps a good library in his Bethnal Green studio and he lent me a copy of Proll's *Baader Meinhof, Pictures on the Run 67–77*. Which proved to be a cannily edited photo-novel of a troubled period in German history; a documented fiction of the aesthetics of terror, action and counter-teraction. Gerhard Richter's expropriation of the images of the prison dead 'freed' Proll to return, after a long period, to snatched newspaper truths that decay into art. Her introductory essay was brief and intelligent.

'We were afraid of photographs,' she wrote. 'Nobody was supposed to know what we looked like, so we became invisible and more like ghosts. The RAF possessed neither a film camera, nor picture archives . . . Only later, during the kidnapping of Hanns-Martin Schleyer in autumn 1977, did our successors make Polaroid pictures and video recordings.'

Returned to the London of 2007, Proll asked Stephen Gill's advice about marketing a set of limited-edition prints of the photographs taken when members of the group were on the run in Paris. They borrowed a tastefully furnished apartment, belonging to the journalist Régis Debray, on the Ile de la Cité. Debray was then in a prison cell in Bolivia. Proll's café shots, playful, casually framed, capture hip and arrogant young tourists who know how to smoke for the camera. Proll also appears: an alien hand spooning tears of laughter from her eyelid. Thus proving that photo shoots were a communal activity. The camera passed around.

In a 1968 retrieval from *Pictures on the Run*, a close-cropped, leather-jacketed Proll is seen from above, splayed across the frame, intertwined with Ingrid Schulbert. The photograph features, quite distinctly, a period toy: a Polaroid camera.

Proll speaks of her band of hunted activists as 'self-timers cut off from reality'. They never left the autobahn, radio on, in stolen cars. Andreas Baader was bourgeois-proud of his white Mercedes. They had a taste for *Viva Maria*, Louis Malle's revolutionary Mexican romp, with Brigitte Bardot and Jeanne Moreau. 'We lived a kind of armed existentialism ... The women did the major part of organizing and thinking. The women did bank raids, too, but more carefully and reluctantly.' Cameras were self-timed, so that the whole group could get into frame: as were bombs. Think of *The Secret Agent*, of poor Stevie, the idiot boy from Soho, who is blown to pieces when he trips over a root in Greenwich Park. And who has to be scraped up on a spade: with rags and bones and bark.

Setting off down the canal for my meeting with Proll, I was overtaken by Jock McFadyen on his bicycle, the hound in loping pursuit. I shouted, Jock climbed down. The dog, as short-sighted as its master, sniffed the weeds for fantasy rabbits.

'How was the show?'

'Plenty of punters, no sales,' Jock said. 'I'm not expensive enough for serious collectors and too steep for Shoreditch riff-raff. Thirty grand a pop is an awkward price. I'm too old to start spraying walls and there are major extensions to pay for. So it's a fucking book. I'm working on a scandalous memoir of my drinking days in East London. I'm calling it: *The Confessions of Jimmy Seed*. From when I came south to the night you wrote about a blow job in a Travelodge on the A13.'

I had to push on, Astrid Proll wouldn't appreciate being kept waiting. 'I am a bit tired of memory-work,' she warned, 'please send me your thoughts in advance. And also a list of your published books. I have talked too much in recent times.'

'Proll?' Jock said. 'She used to live in a squat in Gospel Oak, next door to my ex-wife and infant son – who is now thirty-five and managing a repro-furniture shop in Hackney Road. She was a very diligent babysitter, by all accounts. Got on well with the wife. Who was fucking amazed when Astrid's cover was blown. I think she was calling herself Anna back then.'

Walking out here with Stephen Gill, earlier in the week, I asked him about Proll. They had a few dealings through Stephen's time with the Magnum Agency. She visited his studio when she was in town. Gill saw the best in everyone he met. Even as the Hackney Wick edge-lands were enclosed, he continued to roam, carrying the cheap camera from the boot sale, chatting to scavengers and wild naturalists. Like all the haunters of the margin he was shocked by the sudden appearance of a great blue fence. And like so many photographers and keepers of documentary records, he was challenged by security, held for several hours (without authority), warned off. Overgrown paths and ancient rights of way were blocked with boards and fences.

I asked him what it had been like in former times.

I used to wander the Wick, completely on my own, exploring and taking photographs. Now there are lots of people in yellow coats, boots and hard hats, saying, 'Sorry, mate, you can't come in here.' I tell them, 'I've been coming for years.' 'Not any more you're not.' Suddenly there are places where you can't walk. It's upsetting. They are obsessed with health and safety. They deny access. They say, 'Can't let you in, you're not insured. Health and safety.'

This area has given me so much. It's not just obsessive recording, it's a kind of escapism. There's no denying that as soon as I arrive, I go 'Ahhhhh!' It's wonderful. It gives me a lot of energy. I don't always take photographs. Often I go at five or six in the morning. I think: 'What the hell am I doing here?' So I go straight back home again. I cycle. I really enjoy that.

The camera is just part of me. I need it with me at all times, for whatever might inspire me to take a picture.

These days I do some writing. Things I've seen or overheard. Odd snippets in passing. I might take a picture as well. I like the idea that the picture has nothing to do with what I've just heard. I'm doing something about the removal of words from notices. A project about deleting words, seeing them covered over. The making of new words.

I've been trying to allow the area to work on my pictures, a collaboration. I've been finding objects, other people's discarded images, and intertwining them with my own. I've also been taking my prints back to the wilderness of Hackney Wick, burying them, and allowing the processes of nature to begin. Then digging them up again. They are covered in soil. The element of chance. I'm burying them in places where I think people won't find them. The excavated prints are in an in-between state. I use the prints as a base on which to create. I lay flowers over them and re-photograph them.

I keep my eye on the weather. Buried photographs can bleach completely in a very short time. I usually allow a week to three weeks, not long at all.

Somebody did see me burying one of the prints. 'What are you doing?' I was so embarrassed. I said I was looking for newts.

Did you know that Astrid worked out here? You'll be bringing her right back to her old stamping ground. She had a job at Lesney's Matchbox Toy Factory, making toys cars, in the machine shop. I collect any ephemera to do with Matchbox Toys. I think they closed in 1982.

I'm in good time and I wait at an outside table, reading over my notes, preparing myself, and keeping an eye open for Proll – who is walking over from a borrowed house near Finsbury Park. This area, the Lea, the Marina, Springfield Park, is a favourite of mine. At a difficult period, when Farne had been rushed to hospital for an appendix operation and Anna was in another hospital with Madeleine, our new daughter, William and I made the best of it by coming here for expeditions through the undergrowth, raids on the playpark, cups of hot chocolate in this café.

As described in her email, Astrid Proll is wearing a bright red jacket. Her face is not as 'collapsed' as she suggests. It still easy to recognize her from the *Pictures on the Run* impressions of a slim, handcuffed young woman in a trouser suit, flopping fringe of hair, strong jawline, being escorted into a Frankfurt court by two men in uniform. Who scratch and blink and stare with vegetative disbelief at the news cameras.

Beneath the bangles on Proll's forearm, angry scar tissue is evident. She has a forceful style. I try to express my admiration for the editing job she achieved with her book, the adept use of archive, the economy of the text. 'Yeah yeah yeah.' She has no time for food and drink; after a prolonged interrogation of the cold cabinet, she settles for a bottle of mineral water.

She can't understand how I, a writer, came to work with Chris Petit, a film-maker. Which is another category entirely. *Radio On* she has heard about, but never seen. The graffiti under the Westway: FREE ASTRID PROLL. The connection with Wenders, Hamburg, Bruno Ganz, *The American Friend*. Yeah yeah yeah.

Was Patricia Highsmith of interest? It was easy to imagine common ground.

'I have no room for romances.'

She smokes Spirit cigarettes. Before she came to Hackney Proll had never met a member of the working class. She loved having an English car, a Morris Traveller with wood trim. Hackney was good for pubs, pub life, English beer. Yeah yeah. Great nights.

'We don't know your writing in Germany. I check on the internet. Tell me, please, what is "Gritty Brits"? Are you dirty realist?'

Proll didn't realize, before she came to London, the other meaning of RAF. That there had actually been an outfit in operation a few years before the Red Army Faction. Defending Thames Estuary skies from squadrons of night raiders.

The archive was everything. 'Image is property,' Proll said. 'Pictures are sold through an agency. Selection is all about victims and – what's the word? – aggressors. My book is different. I get accused of doing Prada-Meinhof. Silly journalism. I made the book to explain that film itself was the enemy. I had to throw my camera away.'

Before I was allowed to start the tape, I faced a series of challenges. 'So tell me, what is the form of your Hackney book? Do you find stories? Do you find me, for example? Why is my story surprising in the context of Hackney? Yeah yeah yeah. There are all sorts of memories, all sorts of archives. What do you want to hear? Is it only for your book that you took so much trouble to find me?'

I don't have to say anything. Proll is limbering up. My instinct is that, like Tony Blair, she will be a shadow in the borough; present and absent, arriving from elsewhere with her own agenda, taking what we have and moving on. Unlike Blair, she worked here, lived, drank, formed lasting attachments. And felt the urge, every few years, to return. To visit old friends.

I put the pocket-recorder on the table. She didn't care. She was more concerned about getting her cigarette lighter to fire.

Can I smoke? I want people to stop me smoking. I will stop this year. You say you lived in Hackney from '68? I was here in '74. I only had a few contacts, I ended up with a women's movement group. I didn't know people like Sheila Rowbotham. Not then, not really. I only knew two people. Knew of two people I could trust. One of them was Marc Karlin, the film-maker. We argued about Nicaragua.

I was on the run. Some things I did were hard. Lots of things I did were hard. But it turned out to be good. That's why I'm sitting here with you now. I had to leave Germany. I didn't know anything about England. I'd never been here. I thought I was hundreds of thousands of miles from the country where I was known.

England saved me from prison. It also saved me from the RAF. I said goodbye to the RAF. In that sense, coming to England saved my life. I have terrible gratitude to this place. That's why I come back, whatever my personal relationships are, however good or bad. That's my main reason.

I got very attached to England. It's a great achievement if you know another country quite well. I can't afford to come back and live here. When I came first, I only thought: 'Is it safe for me?' I met people and they lived in this part of London. They helped me. I married. I had to have papers. I was so German. We Germans are fixated on papers. I couldn't understand that you didn't need papers. Now you do. Then you didn't.

When I got settled, I realized that, healthwise, I was in a pretty bad situation. I run and run, I break down. Like a young kid. I was still pretty traumatized.

I made very close friendships, as you do. They cuddle you, they look after you. That helps. I was also very cautious, I only met certain people that I didn't know. In Germany it was only Germans, only white middle-class Germans. Only the RAF, the police. It was the most narrow experience until I came to England. Here, all of a sudden, I met the whole world. It was a huge experience for me. I was twenty-six when I came to London. I'd been four years in prison. I was in prison very young. I had been to America a bit, because my mother lived there. I wasn't completely enclosed. The RAF was such a movie.

England was not a liberation at once. I could never have said goodbye to the RAF if I had stayed in Germany. The people I knew were talking about actions, about other comrades. Here was a different life. In England people used words like 'pleasure'. 'This gives me pleasure.' I used to shout and say, 'What are you talking about? Pleasure? What is that?' Life was struggle. Pleasure for me was a soft word. Most of the first people I met were from a middle-class background and education.

Then, once I was a bit settled, I looked for work. I knew people connected to this organization, Big Flame. Their headquarters were down in East London, Tredegar Square. I had friends in Hackney who were part of that group. People I don't want to mention now. They had connections with Italy. Italy was very strong in the revolutionary struggle.

I hung around with illegal people, it was my crowd. They did all sorts of things: general politics, psychology, Wilhelm Reich, communal work, housing work. They did strikes. I saw factories. I saw gated communities next to factories. Architecture. My father was an architect. I have a feel for architecture. Here were factories next door to a community where workers live. I was romantic about the working class. That's why I went into the factory. I needed a job, I wanted to earn money. I wanted to integrate myself. Women did very low jobs. I was young. I could run around in a boiler-suit all day. I was like a young guy. I was a fitter. Macho. It was all women's liberation stuff.

At the Matchbox Toy Factory, I went to the assembly line, with the women, but only for one week. I became a fitter's mate – which meant that I carried his tools. I thought I was a skilled woman! That was the romance. It brought me into a strange world. I thought that the stranger the world, the less chance I would be recognized. It was a big mistake. You go into a world which is so far outside your experience, you don't know the codes. I met all this anti-German racist stuff – which I didn't know at all. It schooled me, it educated me.

I was fascinated by the tools, doing something with my hands. I was a year at the Lesney's Toy Factory. Later I worked for this drug-rehab programme, helping young people, black people, to become car mechanics. Hackney Council paid for my training. Normal women, at that time, did not run around like that. I was so security conscious. I didn't live anywhere. The news from Germany was bad. Things happened, the situation got more and more brutal. The atmosphere was affected here too.

I remember at one point there was a new WANTED poster for me on Bethnal Green police station. I couldn't believe it. It was like Germany was coming here. But everything was so different. Different language, different architecture. I felt I was in a really strange place, but I felt quite secure. Also I could speak the language. If you go to other European countries, you are a person from the north. Here there is such a mix. Freedom. If you go, let's say, to Italy, Spain, a woman has to be a role model: beautiful clothes, make-up. It was easier here. It opened up my mind. How young people lived and survived.

The European Union had just started. That's why I married. You had to leave the country every six months. There were many people here from America, they started marrying. I thought marriage would give me status.

I never went abroad in those years. I had enough to see in England. We went here and there – Wells-by-the-Sea, Bridport, Liverpool – but I was always very careful. The people I would completely avoid were Germans. I met one German woman, she became one of my best friends. Certain people arrived to see certain people.

When I heard about the death of Ulrike Meinhof in Stammheim Prison, I lived in a street that no longer exists, Lamb Lane. Beside London Fields. I lived around Broadway Market a lot. There was a huge women's movement thing, a whole scene. I was living with women. People came from all backgrounds where they wanted only to do projects. Projects projects projects. Political. Women. This friend of mine became a midwife.

Before I left London in 2002, I rented a room in a road just the other side of London Fields. You know where the swimming pool is? Between there and Dalston. In earlier times, I used to swim in the lido. It was always empty in the 1970s.

I did semi-skilled work, mechanic's work. I went to get a job with Hackney Council. I was a park-keeper. Ha! In Clissold Park, my favourite park. At that time parks in Hackney still had keepers. Clissold Park was some sort of centre, with offices, men with bowler hats. I was working with an Irish guy, raking, mowing. They threw us both out, him and me. After six months. They had either to take you on or let you go.

I had Clissold Park. I had London Fields. I had a little park which was in Shoreditch. It was around a church, a little garden. I had to go out in the morning and open it. I was always scared to go there. It wasn't my patch. It wasn't where I was running around. I had this blue minivan. I would drive up, open the gate, jump back in the car. Very fast, but not because I was scared.

The day I told you about, when I was driving my car down the wrong side of the road, after hearing about the death of my comrades in prison, was near the Lesney's Factory. A big road across Hackney Wick. I was completely calm, the car gave me security. I thought I could just keep going, drive away. I could escape. It was a stupid idea. The car gave me confidence in terms of my body. I had physical breakdowns. I felt completely exhausted. I used to go and sleep in the park. I began to build myself up again. I had endured some shocking experiences.

When I was let out of prison, in Germany, to go to hospital, I was sick. I didn't want to escape but I knew that I must do it. Otherwise they would put me back in prison. The public memory is all about Ulrike Meinhof, because she is so famous. She was in prison, in Cologne, after me. *The treatment we received is still criticized. Every other part of our period of imprisonment, so they say, was champagne and strawberries. All shit, bad propaganda. About Ossendorf Prison in Cologne, where I broke down completely, they still say: 'I hope the authorities keep this up.'*

I was in the silent wing. A new building, a new prison. The wing wasn't yet used. I was the only one, nobody would walk through there. I was there for four months, Meinhof was there for seven months. I was twenty-three years old, I couldn't believe what was happening.

The deaths of all those Red Army Faction people in prison are a mix of everything. I think they killed themselves. Not Meinhof, the other ones. They say it was a plot. They made it look like they were killed. The whole thing is incredible. The story goes on, it sells. The state is only interested in keeping power. Left and right are coming together. Like here. Both your parties are conservative. The people are nice but England is completely conservative. Everything is property, everything. Terrifying.

I didn't have anything, directly, to do with the Angry Brigade – not when I was in London Fields. I heard there was one guy around Broadway Market, a communicator. He had a child with a woman there. John Barker was in prison at that time. I never met those guys. I knew the people around them, the Hackney people.

I took no photographs during my period in London. No, wait. That's not true. There were some pictures – because my girlfriend of that time was with me, walking in Greenwich Park. We made some photographs. I always did make photographs. I had a camera, yeah. Probably I did have a camera. I had one when I felt secure enough. I lived, for the last months before I was arrested, in Bow. A friend of mine was a photographer called Carlos. I won't tell you his other name. He took some stuff. We went out in East London to make photographs – but only of cars, Fords. Ha! I think Carlos had a dark room, an improvised dark room. It would be nice to have those pictures.

I have the photographs I made in Paris. Photography and picture editing were important to me. I came back much later, after they'd sent me back to prison, to work in Canary Wharf. For the Independent. *That was 2000. When I was finished with prison, I went to Hamburg and studied*

film. With a German film-maker, Heke Sander. I worked with new maga-
zines. I worked a lot with Magnum. These magazines wanted English
style, American style. I made lots of connections in England. I understood
why English photography is so interesting: it is in the imperialist tradi-
tion. The Germans are very narrow-minded, yeah? I worked for nine
years and then the Wall came down. The magazine in Berlin folded. You
had to be young to work in Germany. And I was getting to be fifty.

I had ex-partners here in London. I came back to London to look for
somebody I had known in the 1970s. That's how I ended up at the
Independent. Then, a week later, they heard who I was. The shitty press,
down in the bottom there, tried to make a splash of it. The English are
very clever. They bash you, but they're also proud to have you. I gave only
one interview. To the Independent. *Out of loyalty. It was such a fantastic*
paper, a fantastic experience. I was only there for half a year. They said,
'Do mention that you worked for us.' Ha! In Germany they would go
hundreds of miles to stay away from you.

People now are more aware of an archive. An archive has a value. It's
a thing about history. History is a business. In England you have heritage.
You have so much media. Most people take their history from commercial
outlets. Others take their work more seriously, they try to gather up all
the evidence you find, in objects, in images and recordings.

Isn't age important here? Don't the ones who give commissions say,
'Please, we only want young people. Innocents who are not tainted by
history or memory. Save them from books and the old lies of unreliable
witnesses.'

A good day to walk south down the Lea path, with Astrid Proll,
in the footsteps of the Will Self circumambulation. She was
prepared to revisit the Matchbox Toy Factory, which still survived:
a block building on Homerton Road, overseeing access to Hackney
Marshes. In our earlier lives we were all here, all out of place:
Proll, in dungarees, a boy-girl on the assembly line, producing
miniature blue-grey Mercedes 450 SEL models of the cars she used
in her freebooting autobahn days; Anna taking her Millfields infant
class out on the Marshes; and myself, under those epic skies,

painting grids of white lines like a demented Nahuatl. The Lesney operation began further upstream, in Edmonton, as an industrial die-casting company based in the Rifleman pub, an adjunct to the BSA weapons facility. In 1947 they were invited to make parts for toy guns, but the real breakthrough came in 1953 with their matchbox-sized replica of the Coronation coach.

Proll was a giant in this weird Lilliputian world of tiny ordnance, death-kit replicas for tots, royal ephemera, German luxury motors and fleets of trucks, cranes, petrol tankers to anticipate the future devastation of Hackney Wick and the creation of the Olympic Park. A cement mixer, a tractor, a bulldozer: these were the first precision models built to reflect a post-war landscape of rubble and reconstruction. But on my birthday, 11 June, a good few years after that event, in 1992, Lesney was declared bankrupt. Brand names were sold off and distribution switched from the East End to the Far East, Macau. I could, if I had the right temperament, read the span of my life in terms of Matchbox Toys. We both adapted to events in the same place over the same period of time.

I wanted a photograph of Astrid in front of the factory. She agreed, reluctantly, making minor adjustments to a girlish fringe of hair. I assured her that this snapshot would not appear in my book. I told her about other unlikely personalities filmed in the borough. Jayne Mansfield. Julie Christie. Orson Welles by the Hackney Empire. She said that *Moby-Dick* was the only work of fiction read by members of the Red Army Faction. 'We had no use for novels, but Ulrike Meinhof appreciated this book.' It provided, as a battered copy passed between the prisoners in Stuttgart-Stammheim, a source of coded references and alternative identities: Ahab, Starbuck, Queequeg. And Ishmael: who must be Proll herself, the survivor, the teller of the tale. 'Go and gaze upon the iron emblematic harpoons.'

As we advanced, deeper into unresolved and unreadable blight, tyre mountains, oil creeks, burnt-out factories and churches, Astrid perked up. 'Where is Hackney Wick?' Over and over. 'Where is

Hackney Wick? I do not understand.' The map meant nothing. The Wick had no *where*. The question was redundant. Hackney Wick was a sign on a bombed bus. A loaf of hard mud where a dog track once existed – if we accept the romance of Stephen Gill's photographs of the vanished market.

I tried to explain how the violence of the Olympic assault unpicked identity, made everything into a kind of fictional bouilla-baisse: heritage myths, untrustworthy documentation, computer-generated visions. Political wisdom insists that we believe what we are told to believe.

I was walking down the canal one afternoon, beside Victoria Park, at the point where the Hertford Union branch cuts away to the east. I saw a young woman, pushing a new baby buggy, coming towards me, and I had one of those seizures when the laws of the physical universe by which we navigate fall apart. It was Anna, aged about thirty, in the glow of her moment, slightly tired, heavy-footed, airing our first child, a daughter. We would meet in the park. I cycled from my gardening job in Limehouse. But if that transitory, unphotographed incident, fondly misremembered, could be revived: where was I? *Now*. Are memories absorbed – and released – by place?

Except, of course, that this was Farne. With her own new fierce daughter. Shaping an afternoon circuit that duplicated, as I explained to her, Danny Folgate's leyline. A turn around the lake, the south-east path alongside the dry Burdett-Coutts fountain. The Gun Makers' Gate exit. The baby is floating-dreaming as she forms and is formed by her original imprint of grey London skies.

An allotment in Berlin was a very expensive proposition, Astrid said. Across the little bridge, on the private island of Manor Garden, Proll took photographs of the sheds, plantings, crops that would never be harvested. A melancholy business. We looked through the fence, beyond huts assembled from driftwood and the panels of abandoned cars, at coloured ribbons marking out future stadia, media concessions. Small groups wandered the half-abandoned plots, hacking through green tangles that would soon be dug up and flattened to become part of a perimeter fence. There was talk of a harbour for craft ferrying tourists into the Olympic Park. Venice by Old Ford. A Venice crying out for its furious Ben Jonson.

When we were approached by a young German woman, Astrid feared that she had been recognized. 'This is very unusual. The kids know nothing of our movement. Prada-Meinhof. Cars, uniforms, music: that is all they understand.'

There followed a brief, intense conversation. A Proll interrogation. Gesche Wuerfel, the visiting artist, had no notion that she was talking to the notorious Astrid Proll. She had attended the talk I gave for Ken Livingstone's Lower Lea seminar and wanted to keep me up to date with recent work. She handed me her card, a shot of the ruined Cosy Café where I had just snapped Astrid. 'I am interested in how, over time, the urban fabric changes. In *Go for Gold* I critically investigate how the Olympic Games 2012 will impact the landscape of the Lower Lea Valley, London.'

On the sorry mound of the Clays Lane Estate, flags and duvets were draped from upper floors, while ground-floor windows were sealed with metal shutters. There was a palpable sense of abandonment. The travellers at the foot of the mound faced expulsion. They lurked behind a mesh fence, dogs primed for fools with cameras. The estate, a minor utopia, a community of solitaries, students and young couples achieving a foothold on London, had been disbanded. Many of the flats were already empty. Unwanted white goods were stacked on streets dressed with saplings that would never grow.

A slow-cruising car turned in beside one of the shuttered properties. Disembarking, a lean dark-suited man rummaged for a door key that didn't fit. His companion, a tall polished blonde in a fur-trim coat looked around at the panorama of earthworks, fences, pylons. With my overdeveloped sense of drama, I read the situation as: lunch-hour quickie, a liaison between a council official or

Olympic Development Agency manager and some television producer from Sweden, checking out the facilities, discussing a promotional documentary. Over American cigarettes and a bottle of Scotch. Bare mattress on a borrowed bed. Ribbed condoms floating in a bowl that didn't flush. No water, no electricity. Self-generated heat. Dying geraniums in a cracked pot.

'That guy,' Astrid said. 'I know him from the old days, '74 or '75. He hasn't changed at all, a comrade. With the council? An architect, maybe? He helped my friends in Broadway Market. Houses with mad people, you know? Where they could live together instead of hospitals. Charlie, yeah. Charlie Velasco.'

I'm sure that's what she said. But when I asked her to repeat the name, she refused. 'No. There must be no names before I see and approve your text. There were so many others in those times, like this guy. Like Charlie. He was not so special.'

On my next walk to Hackney Wick, I ran up against the blue fence. An exclusion zone had been declared. The only way in, now, was by water. Meeting Stephen Gill at Old Ford Lock, we made a slow circuit in an inflatable kayak, witnessing the pylon forests being dismantled, warehouses and small businesses reduced to rubble. Paddling through tunnels of intertwined and overhanging vegetation, we were noticed but unchallenged by work gangs. We understood very well that even this privilege would soon be suspended.

The walk to the corner shop for an evening paper gets harder every day. The street was deep-trenched by clancydocwra, the jagged wound protected by red sheep hurdles. Pile-drivers, under the patronage of Quinn, assaulted the foundations of the school. 'It won't take more than eighteen months to two years,' Pat Rain assured me. 'I'm buggering off to Ramsgate.' Shrapnel. Bomb fragments. Mounds of 'big old bones'. As we stood there, shouting to make ourselves heard, the extended arm of a large digger pushed the top off the birch tree that had stood on this corner for all of our Hackney life.

The *Standard* ran a piece about swans being slaughtered on the Olympic site. 'Piles of carcasses, thought to have been stripped for food, were found at a camp used by Eastern European immigrants. One of the birds was discovered with its wings snapped off, with its bones and feathers next to a tent beside the River Lea.'

The gossip column was led by an item, timed to coincide with the Princess Diana inquest, claiming that she had held a series of private meetings with Blair and Alastair Campbell in Hackney. They were brokered by someone who was a friend of both parties, Charlie Velasco. A gym acquaintance of the princess from the Harbour Club. 'They can take a lot away from you,' Diana is quoted as saying. 'But they can't take away your pictures.'

Proll came back to Albion Drive for a cup of tea. The two Annas, as if this had all been a Brecht play, met. Proll, the false Anna of years on the run, was coming home. She told us that she too had lived for a time on this street. 'Albion Drive? Yeah yeah.' The other Anna, my wife, was rebuked for the treasonable act of carrying a tray out into the garden. 'Why do you do this? You must have a career of your own.'

When I brought the cups back inside, Anna whispered that she'd had a call from Syd. Who was upset, enraged. In shock. Something about Charlie. All those years. The betrayal. The football trips: a convenient cover. Some woman in Hamburg. The story of their life together a lie.

Proll had a way of tilting her head to stare at you. Anna, distracted, sat with us for a moment. We watched thieving squirrels bounce along the old wall, headbutting the last petals from yellow roses. We heard the scream of the door that can't be shut.

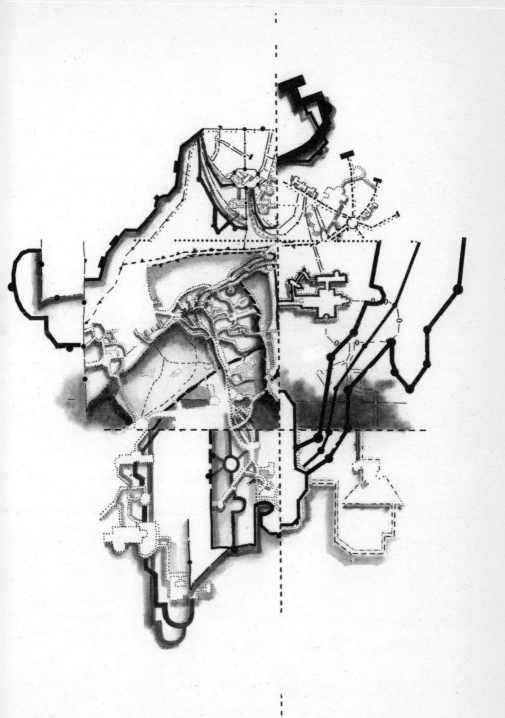

Acknowledgements

Hackney, That Rose-Red Empire is a documentary fiction; where it needs to be true, it is. The fiction of place is dictated by many voices, physical structures without number, the visible and the invisible. I acknowledge them all, even when, especially when, I am unaware of their existence. This is a story of fallible memory, inaccurate or inventive transcriptions, hard-earned prejudices, false starts and accidental epiphanies. 'I live underneath/ the light of day,' said the poet Charles Olson. 'And the rosy red is gone.'

The Hackney bibliography is large and I have trawled it recklessly, but I must credit, in particular, the books that became characters in my book: *The Lowlife* by Alexander Baron (London, 1963); *Saddling Mahmoud* by Sebastian Bell (Ware, Herts., 2005); *Rain on the Pavements* by Roland Camberton (London, 1951); *Glimpses of Ancient Hackney and Stoke Newington* by Benjamin Clarke (London, 1894); *Days Like These* by Nigel Fountain (London, 1985); *Hackney Wick* by Stephen Gill (London, 2005); *Memphis Underground* by Stewart Home (London, 2007); *Tales of Horror and the Supernatural* by Arthur Machen (London, 1975); *The Dwarfs* by Harold Pinter (London, 1990); *Promise of a Dream: Remembering the Sixties* by Sheila Rowbotham (London, 2001); *How the Dead Live* by Will Self (London, 2000); *Hollow Earth: The Long and Curious History of Imagining Strange Lands* ... by David Standish (Cambridge, MA, 2006); *Mr Arkadin* by Orson Welles (London, 1956); *Some Lives!: A GP's East End* by David Widgery (London, 1991); *A Journey through Ruins: The Last Days of London* by Patrick Wright (London, 1991).

For permission to quote from copyright material, I would like to thank: Juliet Ash for *Some Lives!*; J. G. Ballard for *The Drought* (London, 1965); Mrs Alexander Baron (and the Harvill Press) for

The Lowlife; Claire Camberton for *Rain on the Pavements*; Jennifer Dorn; Stewart Home for *Memphis Underground*; Astrid Proll for *Baader Meinhof: Pictures on the Run 67–77* (Zurich, 1998); Alasdair Reid for *Saddling Mahmoud*; Michael Rosen; Will Self; Matthew Sweet; Patrick Wright for *A Journey through Ruins*. And the *Hackney Gazette*, that fountain of inspiration.

Thanks for their time to all those who submitted themselves to recorded interviews: Juliet Ash, Alexander Baron, Dr Peter Bruggen, Claire Camberton, Dan Dixon-Spain, Driffield, Nigel Fountain, Stephen Gill, Darwood Grace, Anya Gris, Stewart Home, Ann Jameson, Erol Kagan, Sidney Kirsh, Andrew Kötting, Tony Lambrianou, Rachel Lichtenstein, Douglas Lyne, Jock McFadyen, Mimi Mollica, Norman Palmer, Bill Parry-Davies, Mark Pawson, Chris Petit, Rob Petit, Astrid Proll, Emily Richardson, Peter Riley, Sheila Rowbotham, Will Self, Timothy Soar, 'Swanny' (Dr Swann), Marina Warner, Ken Worpole, Patrick Wright. With special thanks to the late Mr Kirsh, my guide to the memory-grounds of old Hackney. And thanks to the others whose tapes, for strategic reasons of geography or narrative construction, could not be fitted into this project.

Anna Sinclair was a valued prompt, co-walker, researcher. Farne, William and Madeleine Sinclair, co-opted at various points into this adventure, suffered the experience with a good grace. Stephen Gill was a reservoir of images and a fellow traveller of edge-lands. The drawings and etchings of Oona Grimes were a moral map by which I navigated. Others who were generous in so many ways and who deserve better than the inadequate accounting of this tale include: Tom Baker, Renchi Bicknell, Darryl Biggs, Brian Catling, Sydney R. Davies, Judith Earnshaw, Susanna Edwards, Gareth Evans, Edna Gorman (Sickert), Alan Hayday, Timothy Hyman, Nicholas Johnson, Joe Kerr, John King, Robert Macfarlane, John Matheson, Emma Matthews, Charlie Mitten, Clare O'Driscoll, Ivan Pawle, John Sergeant, Paul Smith, Susan Stenger, Paul Tickell, Anthony Wall, Adrian Whittaker, Sarah Wise, Michael Witt.

And thanks to my agent, John Richard Parker, and all those at

Hamish Hamilton who lived with the length and complexity of this book: Simon Prosser, my editor, and Juliette Mitchell, Anna Kelly, Sarah Coward and the designer of the mythological map-cover, Nathan Burton.